D1522364

And Wait
for the Night

Other Books by John William Corrington

Poetry
Where We Are
Mr. Clean and Other Poems
The Anatomy of Love
Line to the South
Collected Poems

Fiction
The Upper Hand
The Lonesome Traveler and Other Stories
The Bombardier
The Actes and Monuments
The Southern Reporter
Shad Sentell
All My Trials
The Collected Stories of John William Corrington

With Joyce H. Corrington
So Small a Carnival
A Project Named Desire
A Civil Death
The White Zone

Edited with Miller Williams
Southern Writing in the Sixties: Fiction
Southern Writing in the Sixties: Poetry

And Wait for the Night

A NOVEL BY

John William Corrington

Published by Joyce H. Corrington
New Orleans

And Wait for the Night
© 1963, 1964 by John William Corrington
All rights reserved.

Published in 2013 by Joyce H. Corrington

Requests for permission should be addressed to:

Joyce H. Corrington
JoyceCorrington@hotmail.com

Cover and book design by Robert Corrington

Printed in the United States of America
1st Printing, 1965, G. P. Putnam's Sons
2nd Printing, 2013, Joyce H. Corrington

ISBN-13: 978-1484163221
ISBN-10: 1484163222

A. M. D. G.

And for John Wesley Corrington —
my father and my son

NOTE

This is not a historical novel. Beyond those obviously real figures, who played some part in the War, others are fictional and bear no resemblance to persons living or deal. Moreover, no attempt has been made to follow with exactitude the closing days of the Vicksburg resistance or the early days of Shreveport's military occupation. The author vouches only for the accuracy of feelings ascribed to the Southerners. *Le plus ça change*, and so forth.

PROLOGUE

SHREVEPORT, LA: 6 JUNE 1865 — It was raining and it was going to rain. Sentell stood with the rest of them under the shelter of the long gallery that shadowed Cleburne's porch. He was watching a line of men and horses, caissons and wagons threading its way through the porridge of dark mud, lashed by the spring rain, an uncertain serpent stopping and coiling upon itself, starting forward again only to be brought up short by another pothole, another slippery untraversable rut.

The men on the porch with him stared, unmoving and silent, as the column lurched down Texas Street, as under the rain's flail blue-coated men in rubberized ponchos and bright neckerchiefs cursed without heart and mechanically whipped their horses forward. Finally part of the column halted while half a dozen men tried to push free a single fieldpiece sunk almost to its axles in a deep slough opposite Cleburne's store.

As the six worked and stumbled in the mud, wagons and other artillery began bunching up behind the stalled piece, and the struggling troopers, sick and shivering – more used to spurring then pushing – looked enviously at the porch as the men behind them collected in little groups around the canvas-topped wagons.

A young officer splashed through the open space alongside the column, his mount's hoofs sending long arcs of cold water into the huddling groups near the wagons. The men on the porch could hear him speak:

"All right, Sergeant, this isn't a bivouac. Move these men out of here."

And the bearded sergeant, stepping away from the six still grappling with the gun, respectful but unawed:

"I can move the men, sir, but horses and ordnance don't take orders very good."

The two of them talked on, the lieutenant leaning out of his saddle, looming over the sergeant as he pointed down the street toward the front of the column, the serpent's forward coil, as it slid sullenly away from its own rear. The sergeant hunched under his poncho, listening patiently to the lieutenant's tired petulant voice while those near the wagon smoked clay pipes with their bowls turned down away from the storm and watched the discussion indifferently, without concern, since they knew that whatever should be decided would inevitably fall to them to do.

And finally, after a minute or so of it, as the sergeant still shook his head doggedly, gesturing toward the spent horses leaning together under the rain's punishment, the lieutenant jerked his mount's reins sharply and moved closer to the porch.

The men there watched him come. No face changed its expression. No one moved. They watched apart, discrete, and yet somehow in group as if they had been chiseled from living stone or stamped motionless, impacted forever in the anonymous compounds of a photographic plate.

"I'll give a dollar to any man who'll help get that piece free," the lieutenant said briskly. "It only needs a few good backs and shoulders."

The lieutenant waited.

"Come now," he called patronizingly to the graven figures on the porch. "I know you men aren't afraid of a little rain. I'll pay a dollar and a quarter."

"I don't believe it's any use, sir," the sergeant was saying to him softly. "Don't you see their clothes?"

And the lieutenant, angry now, astride a winded pony with an unco-operative noncom telling him what he should notice, and left with his dollar-and-a-quarter offer hanging unacknowledged in the sodden air, seeking some object to spend his anger on, some inferior to be ordered that could be counted on to obey, looked at the porch again.

Each of the men there, except for one tall beardless one dressed in black with a wide-brimmed white hat, was wearing a motley of gray and blue and butternut. One wore a buckskin shirt cinched at the waist with a broad leather belt. Below the belt, a pair of tight cavalry britches, dirty and worn to incredible thinness, but clearly gray with a wide stripe of gold down each outside seam. Another of the statues, stooped and warped, minus a hand, was dressed in a shapeless homespun shirt and a pair of light blue Federal trousers patched and re-patched from crotch to ankle. On his head, that one wore a small forage cap, gray, with double whorls of gold wound across the flat crown, tiny crossed sabers in front, and an even smaller brass plaque above the sabers: 5/TEXAS, it said. Among the rest were Federal overcoats and Federal shirts mixed with butternut pants and jackets cut clumsily from tenting. Only the man in black wore no portion of a uniform – and only he had a pair of decent boots.

The lieutenant looked at the tall man's boots carefully. They were Union officers' booths, cavalry boots – of a quality that only a field-grade officer would wear.

"So every damned one of them was a practicing rebel except that one in black," the young officer snarled, "and he's a boot-thief."

"Well," the sergeant said, his voice slow and precise with weariness, "I don't think you're ready to budge any of 'em. They had their fill of mud and rain doing this for their own people."

The lieutenant's eyes narrowed. "By God, if they hauled cannon for Jeff Davis, they'll damn well haul cannon for the United States."

And then aloud:

"I have the authority to order any or all of you off that porch. I'll make it two dollars for the first three men. If you don't come over her under your own power, I'll have you dragged."

On the porch, a single figure moved. He was small, and, even in the flat unrelieved shadow of the gallery, he squinted as if gazing perpetually into the round of a bright sun beyond the others' seeing. He rose from a hogshead near the store's entrance.

"You sit down, Murray," the man in the buckskin shirt said in a conversational tone, but not too low for the lieutenant to hear. "You sit on down or I'll cut your damned throat."

And the porch was a tableau again, silent and unmoving, the small squinting man back on his hogshead, his face showing no resentment, and the other faces still turned incurious and emotionless toward the young lieutenant whose horse's legs were beginning to tremble now from standing still in the deep cold mud.

"Two dollars," the squinting man was saying softly, as if the amount were a prayer. "Two dollars."

"You can't spend it in hell, Murray," someone else said just as softly, just as prayerfully.

11

No one laughed, and the lieutenant, chilled to his Indiana marrow by now, and thinking almost desperately of the long sodden impatient line of troopers and wagons stacked up behind, waiting for the street to be cleared so they could move out of the endless downpour and into the commandeered stables at the end of the street, leaned down to the sergeant again. With his head turned toward the porch, he spoke loudly without even trying to disguise the fact that he was speaking to its occupants as much as to the sergeant.

"Take five men and prod those loafers out here, Sergeant. And arrest anyone who resists."

"Sir," the sergeant began, his mouth working and the rain draining steadily downward through his beard, "sir, our men are rested now. We can handle . . ."

"Don't make me say it again, Sergeant," the lieutenant snapped.

And the sergeant, turning slowly toward the nearest huddle of blue-coated soldiers who had been watching it all, motioned them to him, and in his turn watched them lift their carbine muzzles from boot-toes and swing the length of each weapon from under the tent-halves and ponchos that had been covering carbines as well as men. They had expected something like this from the moment the young officer had come pelting by, spewing water and mud into their faces. There would be controversy, that was certain. And whatever was to be done would fall to them.

But they moved slowly to join the sergeant, whose expression, like their own, was grim.

"Youall see that dandy on the horse," a voice from the gallery's shadow interrupted suddenly, lazily. "I want youall to watch his right eye when the first one of them blue bellied bastards sets foot on this porch."

"Reckon I'll do for that sergeant," another voice added.

"I'll take that little blond mincin' one afraid to get his shoes dirty," a third voice said kindly, without rancor. "Maybe I'll get his shoes."

"Boys," the sergeant said unhappily, "don't make us do nothing. The trouble's over."

"Don't jaw with them," the lieutenant said, his voice a shade less positive than before. "Get on with it."

The sergeant and his covey of soaked troopers, carbines held at port, began picking their way across the ruts, through the slippery skim of muddy water toward the porch. They stepped slowly, deliberately, as if attenuation, deliberation, might bring a change of orders, or at least bring the men on the porch to realize that one more fight could not possibly be worth what it would cost. As they neared the porch, the man in buckskin stepped toward the edge of the planking to meet them. He did not look at them or even at the lieutenant, but rather seemed to look beyond them out into the misty screen of gray rain. He put his hand inside his shirt as if to scratch, and when he drew it out, he was holding a short Colt cavalry pistol.

"I can't get but a couple of you," he said to the rain, "but the first one dead is going to be that loudmouthed sonofabitch doing all the ordering."

"Wait a minute," the man in black said, breaking his silence, moving for the first time.

In the street, the sergeant, his handful of men drawn up close around him, paused and looked toward the man in black as if he had issued a countermanding order, the order all of them had been hoping to hear.

"I'll help you," he said, shucking off the dark coat, dropping his tie beside it, setting his white hat on top. He stepped into the street, passing between the man in buckskin and the soldiers, stepped past the lieutenant, who had forgotten to authorize the sergeant's pause or even order him on, and strode through the thick mud that rose above his ankles. He stopped beside the mired piece.

"Well, I'll be damned," the man in buckskin whispered. And behind him there was an almost imperceptible settling among the others. Hands moved back into sight, tiny lines of tension melted from their faces to be replaced with surprise – or possibly disgust.

And even as the tautness, the unspoken unit of purpose in violence began to ease among the men on the porch, the sergeant felt the receding flow of blood spiced with anxiety within him, felt the invisible filaments of doggedness that bound him even to the most absurd of orders, relax and fade. One towheaded boy, his pale hair standing out from the confines of his kepi, almost lost control of his legs, almost sat down in the mud when he saw the danger was past. Without even looking at the lieutenant, the sergeant waved his men toward the nearest wagon.

"Stack them arms under a piece of tarp and get over to that damned piece," the sergeant barked, more loudly than he had intended.

And Sentell, coatless, his face white against the indifferent gray of sky and street, turned to face the lieutenant who, now that the impasse was broken, was beginning to realize how close it had been, how nearly his first command had been his last.

"You can call it off now, Lieutenant," Sentell called to him though the rain. "You've got a rebel down in the mud with you."

And the lieutenant, oblivious to the rain now, unconscious of his horse's tottering, mutely waved the sergeant and his men toward the stalled piece. Then, along with the men on the porch, he watched Sentell bend to the dripping hulk of the cannon, watched his hands clutch and slip along the mud-slick gun carriage, his shoulder lower to its weight, seeking a hold, a point of leverage, a way to free it from the rut.

BOOK ONE

... This Fite Will Do ...

Cant you come up and take a hand this fite will do to
hand down to your childrens children ...
—Gen. Nathan Bedford Forrest
to D. C. Trader, 23 May 1862

I

VICKSBURG, MISSISSIPPI: 23 JUNE 1863 — By the middle of June, they knew what the Unions were up to. At night, when the usual bustle and movement of the lines had stilled, if you placed your ear against the base of the works closest to their lines, you could hear the digging. You could hear the picks biting into the earth, the dirt being dragged laboriously backward down their tunnel.

Masterson and Sentell squatted listening one night.

"You hear that? They're within fifty yards of where we're sitting. But something went wrong. They're higher than they think. Maybe the ground-water kept 'em high. They'll load this end with blasting powder and blow this works higher than hell."

"They're likely to get a surprise," Sentell said.

"It's no good," Masterson said glumly. "They'll only feint at us with a couple of regiments. Grant's not fool enough to risk everything, even with Pemberton in command. Why should he make a major effort with the risk it always carries when he's got us sealed in here like tobacco in a pouch?"

"Maybe we ought to see the general anyhow."

Masterson pushed his dark red hair back from his face. He scowled and dusted his hands against each other as he stood up. "Don't waste your time. Whatever fight he had got knocked all to hell at Champion's Hill."

"I've seen it worse," Sentell said.

"Sure you've seen it worse. I've seen it worse. At Buena Vista. I seen it worse than this up the country when we came out winning. But Pemberton ain't Zachary Taylor or Forrest. I don't think we're gonna get out."

"What about the tunnel? What if they blow a hole through us before we starve?"

"Don't worry, I already started a second line of earthworks that'll make a nice half-moon right around where they mean to blow us up. They'll blast and attack right into a crescent of new works and massed fire. Bouvier's fixing to pull the guns out from up and down the line, one or two at a time, and put logs in place of 'em. So every night we pull back a few pieces and stick those tarred logs up there and, as far as the Unions can see, it's all the same and we don't know a thing."

"What if they blast without warning?"

"They can't," Masterson grinned viciously. "They're still digging, and when they stop digging, they'll make more noise stacking kegs. And when that stops, we'll be listening for the silence. Then's when we'll pull back. They're about under our lines, but they got to start broadening the diggings if they want a hole fit to attack through."

Masterson picked up something from beside two soldiers who lay outstretched on the ground at the base of the works, below the raised rifle-pits and cannonades. "Look what I made the other day."

It was a cone of heavy paper rolled and glued, with one end broad, and the other narrowed almost to a point.

"How's it working, Johnny Dee?" Masterson asked one of the soldiers.

"It's fine, Major. I kin damn near hear 'em breathin' down there," he grinned.

"You put one finger in the off ear and stick this little end in the other one. You can hear 'em digging real plain. It keeps out the noise and concentrates the sound underground. I wonder could I get a patent for it?"

"Sure you could," Sentell told him. "Just send a working model up to Washington to the patent office."

"You reckon they'd deal with me?" he asked in mock seriousness.

Sentell handed back the cone of paper. "You can count on it. Take this gadget of yours and listen to that digging down there. They mean to deal with you just as soon as they can."

"And I ain't even written 'em yet," Masterson said quizzically, notching his copper hair with a dark crusty finger.

By then some of the Confederate garrison were eating rats. Not the sleek fast rats that flashed in and out of the bushes between the lines, that burrowed and gnawed in the abandoned trenches forward where both Union and Confederate men were buried. There was no way to get those, and no one had a taste for them, anyhow. It was the thin long-nosed gray rats of the city's alleys and cellars and shops that they snared. Rats that had eaten little better than the soldiers for the past two months, and that crept slowly between houses, fell listlessly into traps. Lean and gray like the men who ate them. Between riflemen and rats only a quantitative distinction remained.

"If a lean gray creature is large enough," Masterson said, "you should free him from the snare, apologize, and conscript him. Because if you don't," he finished, "he's a sure thing to creep out at night and go get him a blue coat and some fine rations. He'd surely feel at home over there."

The women and children suffered badly. But complaints were few, and no man said within another's hearing that it was time to surrender. They all believed that if they could hold out long enough, perhaps the Virginia army or Johnson's would hit the Federals somewhere else, hit them hard enough and long enough to force them to release Vicksburg and use Grant's army in the campaign for that somewhere else. But June was passing, and the cool pleasant days of spring were behind. Heat joined with hunger, and the pitiful little vegetable gardens some had planted in their yards, in the esplanades, in the parks – anywhere a bit of soil was exposed – began to droop.

The shelling went on. By day and night, the Union mortar barges lofted projectiles into the town. Union gunboats, careful to stay beyond range of the river batteries, shelled home and churches and business establishments indiscriminately. Occasionally, as if by accident, a shell or two would fall into a military area. But by then the daily bombardment had become almost comic, because the Union cannoneers, both on the river and in Grant's lines behind the town, either through laziness or stupidity, had begun to fire round after round into the same places each day. Whole blocks of houses had been perforated or blasted to pieces, while half a block away, not a single building had been touched.

That evening, Sentell, Masterson and Bouvier wiped the crust of early dew from their saddles and started riding toward the southern end of the lines. Above them the sky was clear and luminous with the last attenuated and almost indiscernible traces of summer twilight fading from ashen dusk into black. Stretched out overhead was a parcel of dim stars, broken here and there by the branches of oak and sweet gum under which they passed. In the east, long streaks of crimson throbbed over the top of the earthworks as if a city were afire just beyond sight. It was the reflected glow from a crescent of Union campfires.

Bouvier's horse lurched and almost lost its footing.

"This damned brute picks up every stone in the road," he said. "He malingers."

Masterson reined in until Bouvier's horse began plodding forward again. "He's just hungry, goddamnit. He ain't made out of railroad iron."

Bouvier shrugged. "I guess you're right. This poor broken-down heap of infirmity is going to be on the mess table in a week."

Masterson grunted. His own horse was still sleek and spirited. Each week he bought a few precious quarts of grain from river-runners down on the levee who risked the Union gunboats at night to bring tiny handfuls of tobacco and whiskey into the town. Masterson had a standing order for oats. They cost him five dollars a week in gold.

"I wouldn't let the mess have my horse," Sentell said. "It's a long walk from the lines to town."

"Don't let that give you pause," Masterson told them. "I got me a solution for that."

"You think they can bring a few horses over from Louisiana?" Sentell asked him.

"Naw," Masterson laughed. "But when we run short, we'll just declare us an emergency and saddle up the general staff. Half a horse is better than none."

It had been a long day and hot, and there had been another Union assault that they had withstood. Bouvier and Sentell laughed because they wanted to laugh. Almost everything was funny now, because not much was left that mattered.

They had met at Vicksburg, and, barring a war none of them had brought into being, they would have spent the reminder of their lives within four hundred miles of each other without ever having met.

Masterson was from Texas. From that flat tree-covered and grass-choked stretch of land below the village of Houston and a little east and north of Texas' biggest city, Galveston. He had red hair and a beard he claimed was four inches longer than Jeb Stuart's. His father had fought at San Jacinto, and Masterson had learned to ride, to shoot, to handle himself and to love his country under the enormous shadow cast by a tiny shot-battered mission church half a mile outside the town of San Antonio de Bexar.

They rode into Sentell's regimental area. Masterson's orderly met them, another Texan, sullen and undernourished – getting as much food on the cut rations of the besieged town as he had ever managed to claw out of his own land in the northeast Texas hills.

"What'd they have to say, Major?" he asked. "What did them generals allow? What did youall do?"

"Well," Masterson told him, licking his fingers and writing each item in his other palm, "they had these girls from Natchez, and there was a couple of fiddlers, and we all swore to safeguard whatever part of Southern womanhood we didn't corrupt ourselves, and toward the end General Pemberton give us a few recollections of Pennsylvania and said if the grub runs low we could take to eatin' the niggers. What else you want to know, Cully?"

"I ain't eatin' no niggers," Cully grumbled. "What I'll do is eat that damned stallion of yours."

"Hey, you . . . ," Masterson bawled after him as the boy dragged the horses toward a makeshift corral.

They passed from the torchlight around Sentell's tent and walked up the sloping ground toward the rifle-pits that faced over the tortured earth between the Confederate lines and Grant's army. They climbed an unmanned artillery platform three or four hundred yards from the Jackson Road and, making sure that no campfire or torchlight behind would outline them for a Union sharpshooter, they leaned against the wooden reinforcement of the dirty parapet and looked at the thousands of winking fires scattered to the east like the reflections of stars in clear water. As far as they could see, the campfires stretched. To the south, they thinned in numbers, but there the irregular terrain dipped and rose so that many were hidden.

"Jesus," Masterson said softly. "They must of cut down every tree from Memphis to Jackson."

"It must have looked like this from inside Troy," Sentell said. "With Hector telling Priam that it was all right and even then feeling the death in his bones and knowing that nothing would be all right again."

"I remember him," Masterson said.

Bouvier laughed without humor. "I knew you were too damned old for this war. I didn't know you were old enough to have been in that one."

20

"I mean I remember how good that Hector went down. He stood up good, right up to the end. At the end he broke some."

"He should have bushwhacked Achilles. Caught him with his armor off," Bouvier mused.

"That Greek stuff ain't gonna get us out of here," Masterson said. "I don't see anything but cutting our way out in little bunches, or trying to swim that godawful big river behind us."

"That's the hard way," Bouvier said. "Why not let the generals surrender the place, sign our paroles, and then ride north and join Forrest?"

"Would you lie to them Yankees?" Masterson asked in surprise. "I thought you gentlemen didn't hold with lying."

"Would you lie to a mule?"

"You can't lie to no dumb brute. I mean they don't know a lie from the truth."

"All right. I'd lie to a Yankee," Bouvier replied, still gazing out toward the enemy lines.

"I reckon you learn something new about them gentlemen every day," Masterson grunted. "Next time I hear 'em tell about the immutable principles of Southern gentlemen, I'm gonna kick one of them gentlemen in his unalterable ass."

"Pemberton is a fool," Bouvier said, thinking aloud.

"You don't want to talk about the garrison commander that way," Masterson mocked. "I mean, he give up his Yankee home and his Yankee friends to fight for dear old Dixie. You can't ask more than that."

"He could have made the ultimate sacrifice," Sentell said, "and stayed in Pennsylvania."

"He came South with his Southern wife, dreaming of setting himself up as a gentleman in the only section of the country where tradesmen and mechanics and bootblacks don't rule the roost," Bouvier said. "But he brought the tradesman with him in his heart. He has the shabby inflexibility of a wheelwright. Right now he thinks all Southern eyes are on him, expecting him to pull some low Yankee trick, to show by his conduct that you can't make a gentleman out of a peddler. The old fool actually thinks there is a difference in men and that it would be more to our taste for him to surrender us like gentlemen than to fight it out like animals."

"He gets his orders and his attitudes from Jeff Davis," Sentell said.

"And Davis in only one generation from pulling his own plow with his wife guiding it. The illusion has hold of him, too. Neither one of them realizes why gentry arise, how they hold their places. We'll have to lose this war for them to understand anything."

"It ain't lost yet," Masterson said. "I ain't ready to hand it over to 'em just yet. When all the gents finish with your part of the dance, I'm gonna find me some open ground and kill some more Federals."

"The only way you'll get out of Vicksburg is to sign a Yankee paper," Bouvier said.

"When it gets to lookin' that grim, I'm gonna saddle up old Santa Anna, kick Cully's knife and fork out of his hand, and ride right on into the Mississippi. Then I'm gonna keep moving till I come to old Mexico. I might could be a *jefe* or a *presidente* down there."

"You better change that horse's name before you cross the border," Sentell said.

"No need. Only half of him is named Santa Anna. I call the front half Jeff Davis. If I have to go down younder, I'll just swap names and ends."

Then the Union artillery began again. Masterson craned his neck to see if he could locate the battery. The shell whistled overhead and landed back in the town with a muffled sound not much like an explosion.

"They use cheap powder," Bouvier said. "It fires slowly. It doesn't go all at once."

"Sounds like somebody dropping a suitcase," Masterson said.

They watched the streaks of red and dark yellow for a few minutes.

"They never seem to fire at the works," Sentell said. "They don't even hit the regimental areas."

"Once in a while you get a bad round," Bouvier said. "I hear they killed a man in a Missouri regiment last week. It was such a shock his friends gave him a full military funeral."

"I've had enough," Sentell said finally. "They may finish the mine tomorrow. I wouldn't want to fall asleep with company on the way."

They half walked, half slid down the steep slope of the earthworks. "Considering the handicaps they're fighting to get here, I reckon they got a right to some old-fashioned hospitality," Masterson said.

"I can guarantee them some fireworks," Bouvier said. "Have you gotten your men replaced in the rifle-pits?" he asked Sentell.

"Some of the Kentucky men are coming up. They've been playing provost guard ever since we took them off their horses. It's a shame to waste good riflemen back in town."

"Anyhow, some of 'em could get hurt back there," Masterson said.

Bouvier had originally been quartered back in town. It had been his job to inspect the river batteries each day. But when Grant's army had moved in, he had been released for artillery duty on the land side. He had set up his own tent in the area of the 26th Louisiana Regiment, Sentell's command since its lieutenant colonel and senior colonel had been killed at Champion's Hill in May.

Masterson had no command. He had lost a battalion of Texas cavalry between the battle of Jackson and the last fight at Big Black River just before Vicksburg was invested by the Union Army. What was left of his men had been scattered among Missouri and Kentucky infantry regiments. Now Masterson was a soldier-at-large. When there was a Federal assault, he looked for action. When there was none, he rode the length of the lines, able to find a meal in any regiment, no matter how little food there might be.

As they reached Sentell's tent, small groups of sentries, off their posts, smoking and talking together, parted before them. The Federal artillery was still firing. They could hear the thin hollow sound of field guns and the deeper thunder of naval ordnance. The shells, many of them short-fused, burst high over the town to the west, spiraled across the dark sky in brilliant red and yellow billows, hiding the pale stars behind. In the city, bits of metal were clattering across tenantless roofs, stuttering through the fresh leaves of the trees, hissing as they fell into dew-damp grass. As they watched, there was an explosion almost overhead.

"Goddamn," Masterson shouted, "did you see that thing?"

"Mortar-shell," Bouvier said. "They hardly ever get them this far. The Yankee navy must be using up some of its courage tonight. They have to be within range of the river batteries to get them here. I wish I were down on the river. I want . . . "

As he talked there was a faint growl in the air above them. It was mixed with a sound like that of glass breaking and falling a long way off, and the growl became a shriek and the distant tinkling of glass breaking mounted and changed pitch until it became almost a pressure rather than a sound. And then the stuttering thunder of many locomotives and a multitude of wagons all filled with terrified madmen and maimed animals erupted just over their heads. And even before Bouvier's last word, before the impact arrived, the pine-knot torch fastened with wire to a tree next to Sentell's tent shook as if an enormous wind were rising, and their shadows on the hard dusty ground twisted and leaped like lunatic dancers, bizarre shapeless things bowing and scuttling along the glassless earth.

And then it hit. The torch, the tent, the tree and the very earth itself dissolved like smoke freed from a bottle. Sentell felt something, a blanket neither of sound nor pressure pressing him down and into the earth – the earth which itself was not still, but was teetering and bucking as he fell into it. And the force that brought him down did not stop when he was sprawled face down, but went on pressing and sounding beyond feeling or hearing, and he felt loose dirt rising and bubbling into his mouth and nose as if it were water, and then there was no more pressure or sound, only darkness and a feeling of casual falling, and finally nothing at all.

"Ed," someone was shouting to Sentell. "Goddamnit, Edward. You're all right. You ain't dead. Come on and get up."

Sentell felt hands turning him over. He tried to spit out the dirt, but he could not get his breath. The hands were feeling his scalp, moving his arms as if they were a puppet's wooden limbs.

"How about his back? He was facing away from it."

Sentell felt himself turned over like a potato-cake.

"Shit yes," he heard. "Look. Blood and rags. If they've killed . . . "

"Move over. No. It's not much. Cuts. Slivers and scratches. It was all going up, and he caught edges of it."

For a moment there was silence. "I think it must be past his bedtime," Bouvier said. "I think he's asleep."

Sentell managed to get his elbows under him. His back stung as if someone had used a lash on him. "Are youall all right?" he asked, still coughing and trying to choke out the grit.

"They skinned my knee bone," Masterson said. "Something caught my knee and took me down like a mule run over me. I thought they'd shot my leg off."

Bouvier helped Sentell to a campstool – almost the only piece of furniture that had survived. Behind them, the shattered tent smoldered, and here and there tiny winks of flame flared and went out.

"You'll need something on your back," Bouvier told him. "They're only scratches, but if they went bad, if they didn't heal . . . "

"I know. Even if they do heal, in this heat . . . "

Masterson was poking in the rubble of Sentell's tent. "I can't get used to it," he said. "I just can't get ready for it."

Bouvier turn to him. "What are you mumbling about?"

"Those Yankees firing on military personnel. The Yankee navy firing at us. They ain't never done it before."

Sentell rested his elbows on his knees and put his head in his hands. He felt he might vomit. "Maybe they thought there were civilians out here. Maybe it was a mistake."

Masterson had found another pine-knot and lit it. As Bouvier walked beyond the circle of its feeble light, he called out. "If they ain't got any clean cloth for bandages, you might bring them spirits back anyhow. I could spray it on Sentell's back through my teeth."

Then Sentell was sick. He did not manage to control his heaves until a few minutes before Bouvier returned. By then, he was almost asleep, and he hardly moved as the fragments of wood and iron were picked out of his back by a nervous apothecary originally from New Jersey, whose residence in Vicksburg before the war and whose Southern sympathies were not quite enough to reconcile him to a menu of rat, and who, that same night, crossed into Union lines shouting the name of his town to the Federal pickets, who, hearing him well enough, stuck to their orders and cut him down thirty or forty yards from their cook-tent.

II

24 JUNE 1863 — All through that night the sprinkling of tiny wounds itched and festered in the unbroken heat. Sentell could not sleep, and the combination of fatigue, itching, hunger and heat had him close to internal surrender. He sat on the edge of a cot in the doorway of Masterson's tent. He was trying to remember what he had learned fifteen years before in Mexico. But those campaigns were blurred and ran together with the early minor actions of the present war in his mind. He could not remember how he had held off inner collapse in those long gritty burning days of 1846 and 1847.

Maybe I was just too young to suffer, he thought. Or at least too young to realize how much I was suffering, too young to think about it. Anyhow we were winning, we couldn't lose. And we were all coming home to a greater country. That was my first and last mistake about war and America. If I had known how the Northerners would use that conquest over Mexico, I guess I would have deserted. If I had understood what we were doing to Mexico, I might have gone over to the Mexican army.

The Union artillery had slacked off, but in the silence following, he could hear the screams of a man in the hospital tent. He tried to sleep again, but every ten minutes or so he would jerk awake as if he were a puppet tied to the end of that scream.

Sentell sat up again. His hands were trembling, and the perspiration was running down his neck into the cluster of wounds in his bandaged back.

Tomorrow I'll hand it over to Grubbs. Tomorrow, if the Unions are still digging, if things look steady, I'll take the day off.

Before dawn, Masterson and Bouvier were at it again, out on the new works, planning and re-planning, calculating fields of fire, moving each piece, trying to determine where each caliber should be placed for maximum effectiveness. By that time their work had reached a point of diminishing returns, but neither of them admitted it, and even the hungry enlisted men did not seem to mind the work, the hard digging and pulling. All of them enjoyed junking one set of emplacements in favor of another as if they were a committee of bored housewives with an impossibly large parlorful of furniture to be shifted and arranged endlessly for lack of anything better to do.

Sentell watched for an hour, and then called his executive officer, a Mississippi captain whose commission stated baldly that he was twenty-six, but which made no effort to explain why he had no sign of a beard.

"Grubbs, I want to ride into town. I want you to check the posts and keep the men in them."

Grubbs' shoulders sagged. "Sir," he said, "I been wanting to talk to you about that. About the men staying on the works. I got sixty men who say they're gonna die in front of youall's tents if you don't send 'em to the hospital."

"Can any of them show blood or broken bones?"

"No, sir, but they said they could show you . . . "

"Dysentery?"

"Sir?"

"The drizzles," Sentell said.

26

Grubbs though for a moment. "Yes, sir, that's what most of 'em have, and one or two's got risings in their skin, and there's one feller from Corinth with a blue tongue. I don't like that blue tongue."

Sentell shook his head. "Tell the ones with boils to poultice them with tobacco. Tell the others to drizzle where they stand. Tell them I wish I could lay them off for a few days, but it can't be done. Then you tell that one with the blue tongue to stop sucking indigo root or I'll put a collar around his neck that will turn his tongue black."

He took Masterson's horse and rode slowly toward the town. The Jackson Road – what had once been a road – was now a twenty or thirty feet wide track of dusty crevices, and only a rough and irregular beard of dying grass at the far edges showed its limits.

He could not see the town until he was in it. Vicksburg itself was built in a nest of hills and bluffs, each road and street slanting up and down from one slope to the next, and the steeper ones cobbled with large rough stones to give heavily loaded mules and wagons some purchase as they hauled upward.

There were no women on the streets. No children playing in the yards. Even where Sentell could see no shell damage, the houses seemed deserted. Here and there Negroes sat on porches or under shade trees staring out into the road. One Negro woman sang as she pinned sheets and pillowcases to a line tied between two saplings. Next door, the remains of a shelled and burned house still smoldered. Bricks and planking lay scattered on lawns, and men, black and white, were digging shelters and piling the dirt and brick and wood over the tops.

A provost guard stopped Sentell. "Have you got orders for town?" he asked.

Sentell stared at him. "I'm a field officer. I write my own orders."

The guard smiled and shrugged. "All right. I ask people in officers' uniforms that. If they don't get riled, I take 'em in."

As he neared the river, Sentell could feel a sweep of cool breeze. On the river itself, the air was never still and the stands of pine and sweet gum and cottonwood swayed and turned their leaves under the brazen sun. Between two batteries of artillery aimed toward the northwest where Union gunboats lay just out of range, he found a tiny park.

The grass there was still green – not yet the ugly devastated tan that July and August would bring. Only a few shells had landed there, and those few holes had filled with water in the spring rains.

There was still green in the park because the City Council had decreed that this one place should be left alone for "the pleasure of the citizens." It was too small to make any difference in the food situation, and people found empty bellies and shattered nerves easier to take sitting under thick-branched oaks and magnolias and thinking that blades of grass did not really look like bayonets at all. Private soldiers came there in the afternoon and early evening, bringing whatever food they might have been issued or managed to forage on their own, and if they cooked, they brought small charcoal braziers with them and were careful not to ruin the grass or leave any rubbish behind. In the late afternoon, when most of the women had herded their children homeward, when the soldiers had moved back to their posts, local girls and officers, a few enlisted men with tradesmen's daughters would walk among the trees and pretend to look at the flowers or stop beside the shell craters that shone like dwarf lagoons in early evening. They would talk softly and the men might slip their arms around the girls' waists. Sentell wondered what they talked about. He wondered if it was the same kind of love talk he had known in Shreveport before the war, at the cotillions when that same kind of gentle summer evening flared long beautiful dresses with spits of tempered breeze, when young Ed Norton Junior or Amos Stephen's boy whirled the Vivian twins at the military balls that had become so popular. He wondered if love within the shadow of death and defeat speaks itself the same. He decided probably not; that likely these men who walked under the summer moon, these girls who leaned on the arms of men scheduled to die or be defeated before autumn, enjoyed a special kind of love, and that the tense pace of ordinary love and courtship must be accelerated, pushed to even greater intensity so that they could distill into the days left them by war all the tenderness and feeling that their fathers and mothers had payed out over half a century.

Sentell came back from the park in early evening. Masterson was sprawled on a campstool in front of his tent. He had a small shabby metal tray with glasses of different sizes and a half-empty bottle standing on it.

"So you've been holding out on us," Sentell said, falling onto the other canvas-seated stool.

"Naw," Masterson said. "It ain't a holdout. I found it in Pemberton's adjutant's saddlebag. I was looking for a knife."

"I guess you wanted to cut bait."

28

"Naw," he said again, looking solemn and innocent. "It was Barley Jim Finch from the Missouri regiment. He had this great big plug of chewing tobacco, and he said he'd split it if I could find something to cut with."

"So you went for the adjutant's saddlebag. Did you find a knife?"

Masterson was pouring the bourbon into two of the glasses. He added some branch water out of another glass. "No," he said, running his tongue along his narrow lips. "No, I didn't find a thing except maps and this here old half-empty bottle. But it turned out all right. Barley Jim's tobacco turned out to be twist. I reckon he forgot. So I gave him a little out of this old bottle and got us three twists. So the bottle got me the tobacco, and that's what I wanted the knife for, so I figured taking the bottle was like borrowing a knife – if I'd of found one."

They drank and waited for Bouvier, who was finishing the last repositioning of artillery. In the twilight, they could hear his voice sounding out over the rattle of caissons and the midget thunder of cannonballs being rolled across the log serving-platforms next to the guns.

"They stopped digging around six o'clock," Masterson said lightly. "We heard 'em rolling the powder down about thirty minutes ago. Damn near caught us right in the middle of rearranging the living room, too. You ought to of heard the noise. It didn't even take any patent-pending gadget to hear 'em."

"Maybe they'll blow it tonight."

"Naw," Masterson said, stretching and yawning. "They don't know what they're going to find over here, and they figure the surprise will be enough advantage. Darkness works both ways. 'Specially for the man who's dodging."

"So early in the morning then?"

"I reckon. But I've been wondering about something."

"You don't wan to shift those guns again?"

Masterson laughed loudly and leaned back against the taut canvas of his tent. His eyes shone in the light of the single pine torch they kept lit at the tent entrance to draw the insects from it. Sentell thought what a fine good-natured animal he was, and how any army, any group of men, was lucky to have him with them. He realized how much of his own control and apparent nervelessness was on loan from Masterson.

"Oh no," he choked out, still laughing. "It's just that I've been pondering Grant."

He turned serious then, and leaned across toward Sentell.

"I guess we've all been pondering him," Sentell said.

"No, I mean I've been wondering why he'd waste time and powder and men on this sapping when all he has to do is wait for the rats to give out."

"I guess Washington is in a hurry. Maybe they think he should have reduced us sooner."

"Well, I think you're half right. I think that stubble-chinned sonofabitch has got Washington on his mind, all right. But I don't reckon he even hopes to push a hole through us tomorrow."

"He's spending a lot of effort on nothing then."

"Wait a minute. Think about it like you was him. First off, he's doing the same thing Bouvier and I have been doing for two weeks. He's keeping 'em working and keeping the word out that something big is up. Good for morale and keeps the junior officers with their prat in the saddle. Then he thinks there's always an off-chance that we're worse off than it seems. Maybe he could plow us under after he sets off his mine. But even if we wallop him, even if we hack a regiment or two to pieces, he can wire Washington that things are moving, that stubborn resistance is being met with, but he's chopping away anyhow."

"If I were reading the dispatches, I don't think I'd let a little chopping away impress me much. I'd want logs, not chips."

"But you're not a damned politician. Every one of them Yankee sonsofbitches is a politician. Grant wants more than a victory. If he could of walked in here the day after he took the hill, the day after he got Grand Gulf secured, he never would of done it unless he couldn't of helped it. If this town is going to make anything out of him, he's got to slug us, he's got to milk a little drama out of Vicksburg. 'Cause if he don't, they're going to thank him, pin a medal on his butt, and tell him he's taking orders from Meade or Hooker or whoever they put in the field next."

"So cutting the Confederacy in half makes him a king."

"It does that," Masterson said. "And if he blows a hole in the works and storms and gets flung back, and charges again – terrible losses all the time – and finally extorts an unconditional surrender out of us, he's made something for himself. The way he sees this fight, it ain't worth a thing if it don't look hard from the White House window. If he just walked in, they'd say, 'Why, a damned corporal and ten half-breeds with hatchets could of taken that town. It wasn't nothing but a shell when Johnston's plans fell through.' But if he sends a nice fat casualty list up home, if he grits his good Union teeth around that stub of a cigar and wires every evening how it's in doubt. No, we're pushing 'em back. No, they've turned. Now they're breaking out. No, we've got 'em cornered – O Jesus, what a fight . . . "

"Only a god could win it, huh?"

"Nothing less," Masterson said somberly. "It may not make any difference, but a lot of decent men are going to die in the morning trying to do what can't be done so that barrel-gutted maniac can get him another star and a chance at Uncle Robert."

"Maybe that's the best thing that could happen," Sentell said. "Maybe the best medicine in the world for him would be a little dance with General Lee."

They talked on. They talked about the Texas Gulf coast where Masterson had been raised. Anahuac, Texas. A green point drifting to sand, then suddenly falling away into the billowing waters of the Gulf. Cattle and rice, and farther north, cotton.

"Most of the people been there since the thirties. Not many of 'em are big landholders, and most of the slave-owners are west toward Galveston. My old man fought the Mexes at Anahuac back before independence. He gave me a Texas flag when I went with the army into Mexico. Wanted it on a flagstaff over Mexico City. I put it there, too. It flew three days over the Customs House before Scott saw it and told one of his bootjacks to drag it down. It cost me five dollars to get it back, but the old man had him a Texas flag with Mexico City dust on it. I remember the old-timers used to come around to the house and look at that flag, and the old man would roust me out of the barn or send a nigger out in the brush after me, and I'd have to go on back and tell all them old bastards how many Mexes I killed and whether I seen any decent grazing or planting land on the way down, and what sort of fellow Taylor was. It got downright silly, and it got to where the old man's nigger couldn't hardly face me when he got sent to bring me in. It was all right, though. I sure love that old man. Here, give me that whiskey."

Sentell picked up the bottle and set it under his stool.

"You know, Ed, I kind of wish I'd got married."

Sentell looked up surprised. He had never heard Masterson mention women before. "Well," he told him, "you can take care of that when you go back."

"The old man wanted a grandson," Masterson said as if he had not heard.

"You can take care of that later, too."

"Not in this world," he said gloomily.

"Why not?"

"Because we'll be fighting as long as we're alive. If you don't have a woman already, you ain't gonna find the time or the heart for one. If you don't already have a child, you wouldn't be mean enough to get one in the kind of world we'll have."

"This war isn't going to stop people living," Sentell said. He thought of the park, of the young lovers standing in the track of shells under the Union's red sky. "Nothing keeps them apart," he said. "They say 'until tomorrow' even when they know there won't be a tomorrow."

"No," Masterson whispered. "It won't end life, but it's already crimped it a good deal, and as far as we're concerned it's stopped it altogether."

Before Sentell could ask him what he meant, Bouvier stepped into the torchlight. He was smiling, and his thumbs were tucked into his belt. He wore no tunic, only a white full-sleeved shirt without a collar, and gray trousers tucked into low boots. He had a Navy Colt strapped to his right hip.

"They're finished loading," he said almost breathlessly. "They've planted their pumpkin, and nobody can say when it's going to turn into a battering ram."

"Have a drink," Sentell said, reaching under his stool and lifting the bourbon bottle into sight.

"Have a drink?" Bouvier said unbelievingly. "Is that the pressings of some raisins you fellows found? Or is it boiled chicory and potato mash?"

"Well," Sentell told him, "it's Tennessee bourbon, but if you don't trust us . . ."

Bouvier had the bottle and the remaining glass in his hands before Sentell could finish. Masterson had not turned around. His eyes were narrow and calculating, and Sentell wondered if he was thinking of a wife and child and his father's pleasure, or about the mine and what would follow its explosion.

Masterson turned and walked back to his stool. His face was set, and his eyes, gray and wide-set, were as hard as the thin geometric edge of his mouth.

32

"I don't want to surrender this damned place," he said absently. "I'd rather die right here than give this place over to 'em."

Bouvier held his glass up to the torchlight and turned it slowly. "You keep thinking of the Alamo," he said. "But fighting to the last man here won't do any good. The death of fifteen thousand of us here would only mean that fifteen thousand rebels were dead. Travis and Bowie and the rest of them saved Texas. We'd be robbing the Confederacy."

"My people never walked out of a fight yet," Masterson said suddenly.

"In a few weeks, we'll be out of here," Bouvier said. "We'll be fighting with Johnston or Lee. This is just another battle, not the war."

Masterson rose and touched Sentell's shoulder as he walked toward his tent. "I'll see you in a little while," he said.

After he had gone, Bouvier drained his whiskey and hooked his feet on the rungs of the campstool. It was late now, and he put his hands under him and hunched his shoulders against the chill. He grinned and nodded in the direction Masterson had done.

"Absolutely a dying species," he said gently, respectfully. "Practically impossible to find over here, and absolutely extinct on the Union side."

The pine-knot torch was beginning to flicker, and the whiskey was bitter in Sentell's mouth. Out on the works he could hear a sentry whistling an old tune. "When the Mastersons are gone, what happens then? What do we use for a heart?"

Bouvier was staring in the direction of the faint whistling out beyond the circle of light thrown by the torch. "I expect we'll be heartless," he said archly. Then he turned to face Sentell. "We'll fight without hearts," he said. "We'll fight with whatever's left."

III

25 JUNE 1863 — Sentell was already sitting up on his cot when he came awake again, and a boy, a corporal from Bouvier's batteries, was shaking his arm gingerly. But even before the boy touched him, he was shaking off sleep and beginning to compose himself. The tent flap was tied back, Sentell could see the dense shadow of trees outside, and the brightening dawn above them. The corporal was trying to talk to him.

"Sir, Major Bouvier said I should . . . "

"That's fine, boy," Sentell said. "I'll be right along."

"The major asked me to bring you this," the corporal went on with the same breath. He reached outside the tent and pulled a short rifle in. It was a Yankee repeater, one of the new carbines they had begun issuing to their cavalry.

"Are they fixing to blow it?" Sentell asked the boy.

"Sir, Major Masterson – pardon me, sir – is capering like a snake in a nest of frogs, and Major Bouvier has got some kind of spyglass he points over toward the Yanks, and when he puts it down he goes to laughing and running around with Major Masterson. I don't know what's going on up there. But they want you, sir."

So Sentell picked up the carbine and sent the corporal ahead to rouse Captain Grubbs. The infantrymen were already stirring, and by the time he reached the new works, they were parching corn and braising mule steaks and drinking the herb brew that was not very much like coffee but even more to some of their tastes since the coffee they had been drinking all their lives had been cut half-and-half with chicory anyhow.

They were spread four and five companies deep all along the crescent of the new works. The riflemen were packed so densely between the artillery that only about two or three men out of every five available could stand at the firing line. The rest passed up coffee and bits of food to the men in firing position and loaded their muskets so that they could pass them up too and keep the firing continuous when it started.

Sentell found Bouvier and Masterson about the same time his captain found him. Bouvier was sitting on a campstool with his battery officers. Masterson was prowling back and forth, listening to Bouvier and the others and making gestures of impatience.

"You know about those ramps down at the end of the semicircle? All right, then. I want light pieces – the ones we put at the flanks of the new works – ready to move at discretion. When the blue bellies see what they're into, all they're going to think about is getting out of this salient they've cut for themselves. They're going to break all to pieces and start turning back on their own support. The big guns can sweep the inside of the circle, but I want you ready to move out of the firing order and get those light pieces up on the old walls. Then you'll start firing at the outside of the breach. You'll be firing at the support to begin with, but before it's over you'll be shooting at a mob. When you see the ranks inside really break apart, run those pieces up the ramp and start raking the edges of the breach."

"Major," one of the battery officers raised his hand. "Major, why don't you just put us up there to start with? We're going to lose time making that change."

Bouvier motioned him into silence. "Because if you're up there before the blast, you're going to get blown off the works. If you're up there too soon afterward, they'll know something's wrong. This plan is going to work, Captain. Jeff Davis hasn't had his hand in it."

They all laughed, and the battery officers moved out. Grubbs touched Sentell's sleeve. "Sir," he said, "there's not a damned thing for me to do. The men are set and I can't even jack up their spirits. If they were any higher, they'd give us away. What should I do till the counterattack?"

Bouvier turned quickly and pointed at the captain. "There isn't going to be a counterattack, Grubbs," he said. "You keep those men behind the works and let the artillery take care of the Unions who get out of this cul-de-sac."

Sentell finished for Bouvier. "A counterattack would ruin it. We're going to cut them to ribbons in here, but if we follow them home, they'll do the same to us out there in the open. The only way to hurt them bad is to tear their point to pieces and not give them a chance to even things up. That wears at them. That sticks in their throats and batters their morale into pudding. They'll lose a thousand and we'll lose ten or fifteen."

Grubbs was satisfied. He went back toward his men and Bouvier followed him with his eyes. "Nobody thinks," he said wryly. "Nobody thinks. They use their nerve ends to make decisions. Does that boy think we could pierce Grant's lines?"

"I don't think so," Sentell said. "I guess he's a Mastersonian."

"The Yanks would love him and his prototype if they knew," Bouvier said. "There'd be one great bloodletting and they'd lose thirty or forty thousand men and we'd be finished. The Alamo with nothing after it."

"It's only because we're short of Mastersons," Sentell said shortly. "If we had five hundred thousand, we'd go out and push them all into Lake Erie."

Bouvier smiled and rubbed his unshaven chin. "I guess you're right at that. Maybe he's not an anachronism after all. Maybe he's just in short supply."

Masterson came up then. His face was clouded. "Any time," Masterson said nervously. "Any time at all. They got their infantry massed right across from us, and you can hear some firing down to the left where the cavalry's making like an attack. When they start the barrage, you better grab dirt and hold on for the blast."

"You think they'll get mortar fire from the river?"

"I don't know," Masterson said. "If they do, it'll either land in a hospital or blow their own troops to pieces. All we have to worry about is the mine."

"What makes you worry?" Sentell asked him.

Bouvier sat down on his campstool again and poked Masterson in the leg. "He wants to know whether we figured the size right. He thinks it might blow up the new works right along with the old. He thinks maybe we ought to have told Pemberton all about it."

"No," Sentell said. "You don't want to tell Pemberton anything. If he heard there was going to be trouble, he might surrender the whole town and accept a brigadier's commission under Grant."

"Even if he didn't," Bouvier grinned, "I don't want to see him cry."

"Besides, if they blow us wide open, nothing would stop them anyhow. Maybe you'll get your Alamo."

And then it blew.

The ground beneath them shuddered at first the way they say the first tremor of an earthquake comes. It shook, and below ear's threshold something loomed and became larger in proportion to the shuddering, which grew from the smallest of vibrations to the consistency of a freight train running on the underside of the earth where they stood. And as the ground twitched under their feet, the whole world seemed to be pushed into the gray dawn sky as if a huge hand underneath had made a fist and then struck from an immeasurable distance, driving earth and trees and flimsy works skyward before it.

Sentell was sprawled across Masterson, and somewhere to his left Bouvier was cursing and trying to untangle his legs from the campstool. He felt something wet on his face, and he touched it. His nose was bleeding and it felt as if it were broken. Then something hit Sentell between the shoulder blades and he thought for an instant that the Yankee infantry had already broken through, that their inner works had been taken and that a rifle butt was about to strike once more and end it for him.

But he turned over and saw clods of earth falling and the air choked with dust and falling debris. The last rumblings of the blast were dying away, but beyond that there was nothing to hear. Sentell looked in the direction of the inner crescent, but it was as obscured with dust as if a ground fog still hovered waiting for the sun to burn it away.

Bouvier was up again and pulling Sentell to his feet. "I think you're jinxed," he shouted. His voice was louder than it need be. "Every time something blows up, you're under it."

"Save the jokes," Sentell yelled back. "Did the new line hold?"

But Bouvier was pulling Masterson from under a pile of canvas tenting that had fallen on him. "Goddamn the quartermaster!" Masterson was sputtering. "Goddamn all this . . ."

"I can see the outline of the new works," Sentell called over to them. "They're still there."

The rumbling had stopped, and except for a cry here and there, a shouted order, Sentell could hear nothing. Then he realized that he had been hearing something more, but that it had been so muted, so distant, that at first it seemed only a part of the blast itself.

"Listen, they're coming," Sentell said. "But no one is firing."

"Goddamnit," Masterson choked, climbing to his feet and trying to dust off his uniform. "Goddamnit to hell, of course, they're not firing. I'll kill the first sonofabitch that touches a match until the salient is full of Yankees."

"Don't worry," Bouvier smiled. He sniffed the air like a fine hound tracing the scent of a fugitive. "They're coming now. They're about fifty or sixty yards from the gap. I just hope to God the dust and smoke doesn't settle until they're inside."

"That won't make a goddamn bit difference," Masterson said. "If they're at the gap when it clears, those captains and lieutenants ain't going to turn around and go back. So long as we don't fire, so long as we don't give 'em an ironclad excuse, that scrub-bearded bastard will expect 'em to keep going."

They were walking through the pall of smoke and dust now, walking fast and talking breathlessly as they moved. "Anyhow," Sentell said, "they'll think the crescent is just a secondary works – until they're inside and see the closed ends."

"And it won't make a good goddamn then," Masterson crooned.

A young officer, his face white, without a uniform jacket, ran up to them. "The general wants a report, sir," he said to them. "He wants to know how long you can hold them. He's got the regiments along the west side of town thinning out. He says to hold and fall back and prepare to make a stand near the old freedman's school east of the park."

Bouvier nudged Sentell and he tried to keep a straight face. Masterson used no restraint at all. "Aw, horseshit," he bellowed. "You tell the old fool we'll run 'em into the Georgia swamps if he'll just leave us alone."

The young officer looked as if he had been slapped. "Well, sir," he choked, trying to keep pace with them, "you'll have reinforcements soon, and I hope you have the best of luck."

"Don't worry," Bouvier called to him as he fell behind. "We've got something better than luck."

"Sir?" the young officer asked.

"Cannon, you half-witted puppy," Masterson roared. "Cannon."

As they reached the works, Bouvier's junior officers were moving stealthily about, stooping as they ran so that the oncoming Unions would see no movement behind the new line. One of them waved, and held up his hand with the thumb and first finger joined to make a circle.

Masterson turned and asked, "What's that supposed to be? A bung-hole?"

Bouvier smiled as they climbed up onto a firing ramp.

"It means the soup is good," he grinned. "It means we're having guests for dinner."

Sentell rose up slowly to watch the guests arrive.

They were packed elbow to elbow and there was no way of counting the ranks that pressed forward, much less the number of men. They were still coming up from the Yankee trenches three or four hundred yards away, and as they rose in dribbles and bits, they would look to either side to find another company to join, to guide on. Ahead, their junior officers rode, shouting the old slogans and occasionally riding back to lay their sabers across the backs of stragglers. There were color-bearers in front of every company and as the units joined into regiments and brigades midway between their lines and the Confederate earthworks, as the fragments pressed together into one immeasurable surge, Sentell could hear their bugles and the shouts of the soldiers in front. He saw one huge bull-chested noncommissioned officer shaking his rifle above his head, and he could hear him yell:

"For the old flag, boys. Take them works for the flag."

38

There was a young officer mounted on a bay mare racing back and forth in the vanguard of the blue tide. He waved his saber and pointed it toward the breach, toward the works that looked useless and deserted through the haze that still drifted across the crater where the mine had exploded.

"They're on the run, boys," the young officer cried. "We've got 'em running. Don't let 'em breathe, boys. Run 'em into the river,"

He forced his horse down the slippery incline and into the loose damp earth at the bottom. The mare foundered, and the more it thrashed, the more deeply its legs sank into the slough beneath it. Masterson nudged Sentell.

"That eager fella down there is going to get trampled by his own men."

"They'll steer around him," Sentell said, not taking his eyes from the crater.

"Not going back they won't," Masterson said.

"I wonder if it's genteel to enjoy killing," Bouvier said mildly.

"I don't know about that," Masterson whispered loudly, "but if we didn't come here to kill, I don't know what we did come for. And a man does better if he gets to liking his work."

The Unions had begun slogging their way through the pit. The young officer was still urging them on as he sat absurdly upright in the saddle. His mare was sinking still, and she was already mired almost to her belly. The infantrymen moved past the officer and began scrabbling up the side nearest the Southerners. But the crush of troops behind made it like some desperate game of king-on-the-mountain with the troops behind catching the legs or clothing of those in front, and more often than not pulling half a dozen men down into the bottom of the pit again.

Some of them were trying to negotiate the ledges of more or less solid earth on either side of the crater, and a few were even climbing the outer walls of the old works.

"Get a few sharpshooters to working the tops of that wall," Sentell called back softly to Grubbs. "And have one or two pick off the first one out of that pit. It's no good if a handful reach us and find out what's up."

Grubbs ran off along the crescent and Sentell cocked his carbine.

"You may make them turn," Bouvier said dubiously.

"Naw," Masterson cut in. "He's right. We got to make sure the ones in front don't find us out. They'll expect a little rearguard action. If I was running that hole in the ground, I'd sure get my tail up if it was as quiet as this. It wasn't that big a blow."

"I guess you're the infantry tactician," Bouvier grinned at Sentell. "I just hope you don't rob my guns."

Sentell raised his head again and looked down the outside of the crescent. The outer wall, dirt about twelve or fifteen feet high, was littered with old branches and rubble in a random pattern. There were some broken cannon placed there before the blast, but they looked from a distance as if they had been blown there. There were papers and some tents, some tree trunks and roots tossed up and down the uneven sides of the works.

A few Federals had managed to climb out of the crater. They stood looking down at their comrades still clawing and cursing below, and some of them lowered the stocks of their muskets to help other men scramble up and out of it.

"There," Masterson said. "That's sweet. I didn't know those bastards believed in helping one another. If they keep that up, we won't have to open up until . . . "

But others had made the top of the old walls, and Sentell saw Grubbs, lying flat thirty or forty yards away on top of the crescent, signal some of his men to take care of them. A half-dozen rifles cracked, and every Union soldier who had made the climb fell either forward into the salient or backward onto his climbing friends. As the riflemen fired, Sentell saw one of the Unions, who had leaned backward and begun shouting to someone below him, fall.

"That one like to have tipped it," Masterson said, following Sentell's eyes. "You think anybody could make out what he was yelling?"

"Don't worry," Bouvier said. "Look at them."

There was no sign of alarm below. The Unions had managed to get a company, possibly two companies, out of the crater, and the young officer had left his mare to root out or drown in the muck. He was standing in front of the men who had filtered into the salient and was forming them to storm the crescent.

The rifle fire from the Confederate works, perhaps a dozen shots since the Unions had begun moving into the breach, had begun to mount a little. More Unions were gaining the outer walls, and it was only a matter of time before one of them got a look, at least a quick glimpse, of the activity behind the crescent. So far as Sentell could tell, a Union soldier fell for every Confederate shot. Even the young officer in front of them had begun to notice the firing, and one of his sergeants was pointing up to the top of the works, then down to the closed ends of the crescent.

"Goddamnit," Masterson bawled, leveling his rifle. "That worthless three-striper's been around too long."

He fired, and the sergeant, a tall thin man whose boots looked ten sizes too big for him with the thick red earth packed about them, fell sprawling sideways against a blasted tree stump in the flat between the crater and the crescent.

Then Bouvier's hand was raised, his saber whirled in long slow circles above his head.

"We can't wait any longer," he shouted full voice. "We have to take what we've got."

And the saber fell.

The first salvo sounded as if the floor of heaven had given way at last. As if God and his angels and his saints, sick and angry at the stench of blood and wasted life below, had loosed the supports of the earth's vaulted ceiling and let it crumble upon itself.

What they saw was an almost solid sheet of flame and black smoke spurt jaggedly across the packed Union troops. From the crescent, it looked at first as if the artillery had been aimed high, as if the shot and scrap in the guns had been pointed over the old works toward the swarm of Federals massing and funneling through the thirty-yard breach.

But the cannon had not been wrongly aimed. When the dark smoke began lifting, they could see what had happened below.

"Jesus," Bouvier breathed. He crossed himself and lowered his eyes.

Sentell glanced sideways at Masterson. He was looking down on the flat before them, into the crater beyond. The line of his jaw was tight, his hands were pressed against the earth, and Sentell saw his fingers knot and curl, dredging loose dirt into his palms.

The Yankee company had vanished. Not only were there no ranks, no men . . . there were no bodies and only a scattering of clothing and rifles and supplies; only a wide strip of earth plowed fresh again without a footprint or the mark of a groping hand upon it. Beyond, at the crater's edge, Sentell began to see bodies, parts of bodies. The Federals lay on top of one another like cornstalks fallen under the scythe, like grass cut and bundled carelessly, left to rot by the mower's hand.

In the crater itself the Unions had begun to scramble, to turn upon themselves, but the press of men still running or falling into the pit was too great, and some of the front ranks, which were no longer ranks at all or even individual soldiers but simply desperate trapped men, were beginning to realize that their great assault, their run-over victory against the rebels, had become something else.

The crumbling wall of the crater, the far side of it, had been raked clean by the salvo, and yet beyond, the Unions still came. Behind other ranks kept pushing, and the officers at the rear or far enough back to stem the tide could not make out what was happening. So when one company or a single squad tried to turn, to escape the next fusillade, the officers would strike at them with their sabers, and order the men in the rear to press the cowards toward the crater, toward the broken rebel line.

The side of the pit nearest to Sentell and the others was the only place where a few Federals had survived the first blast of the cannon. On the extreme edges of the crescent, Southern marksmen were beginning to fire toward the wall, toward the broken cowering men who could neither charge nor retreat nor surrender. And the two light field pieces hauled to the edges of the crescent were beginning to fire out beyond the collapsed side of the old works. Sentell was accustomed to death, and yet there was a difference between swift charges across an open field, the dying and the wounded falling under a gray driving rain or wilting gently into tall dry grass with a clear southern sun above – a difference between that and the casual slaughter here. He put his carbine down and lowered his head to rest it on his arms. But he thought: Don't turn away. Don't act as if you had nothing to do with any of this. If you didn't start it, you came willingly enough, and this belongs to you as much as to any of them. So do what you came to do.

He picked up his carbine, and as Bouvier dropped his saber again to signal continuous fire, he heard his own piece crack, felt is recoil, and saw a towheaded Union private, hatless, eyes wide with terror, who had made it over the rim of the pit and begun crawling toward them, stand erect for an instant, holding his belly tight with both hands as the rolling smoke and burgeoning flame of another salvo flowed down the incline and shrouded him in darkness.

It had started a little after six o'clock that morning, and as the sun rose, the intensity of the Federal attack seemed to mount. The crater was packed over and over, only to be swept clean by the artillery and rifle fire each time it began overflowing. Five, perhaps ten Union soldiers began climbing the other wall of the crescent before a sharpshooter spotted them and ended their advance. The rest died by the squad, by the company, below and beyond the wall where Bouvier had set the light pieces loaded with grape and canister. Somehow the Federals seemed to think that the roar they heard, the crackle of small-arms volleys, was only sharp rearguard resistance; that, pressed hard enough, it would collapse and free the Jackson Road that led directly into Vicksburg.

"If they still think this is delaying tactic," Masterson bawled at Sentell, "we must have been giving 'em a worse time than we thought at Champion's Hill and downriver. If they still think this is rear guard, what the hell do they think our whole concentration could do?"

Once, after the main strength of the Federals had begun to break, when it was obvious that they had chewed up and spit the better part of four or five regiments out of the salient, Masterson rose, waved his musket, and took one step forward as if he would run down the outer side of the crescent and finish off the pathetic remnants of Union opposition still cowering in the protected near side of the crater with a bayonet charge, and a battering hand-to-hand finale.

Bouvier and Sentell reached for him at the same time. But even as they pulled him back down, they could see others rising along the top of the works ready to join him, ready to run down into that wallow of blood and blasted bodies and mud and wipe out the rest of the enemy in a personal way. When they dragged Masterson off his feet, the rest, seeing him fall, began to drop back and start firing again from the protection of the rifle-pits along the top of the crescent.

"Why don't you bastards leave me alone?" Masterson yelled. "Don't you see one charge would run 'em into the Atlantic?"

He went on struggling, trying to break their grip on him while Bouvier talked soothingly.

"We can finish it from here, Sam. We don't need the heroics, and we can't stand any losses we don't have to take. Anyway . . . "

Just then, the artillery blasted once more, and the last few Federals who had been hopping from clod to clod, trying to get out of the breach in the old works, melted away. Bouvier frowned and raised his sword – still holding on to Masterson.

"That's enough," he shouted, waving his sword. "Hold your fire, damnit. You're shooting dead men and plowing corpses under."

By then they had Masterson under control. He brushed off his tunic and sat up, still frowning, still unhappy.

"Goddamn tin soldiers," Masterson muttered red-faced. "All you want to do is fight them bastards from back of a wall. What if there wasn't no wall here? What if you couldn't build a goddamned wall?"

"Then we'd fight them without a wall," Sentell told him. "We'd go down there just like Bowie or Crockett and give it to them with bayonets or sabers or pistols."

"But there *is* a wall," Bouvier finished. "And for every one of us there are at least five of them. Now why don't you just lean over and kiss this wall while you're down so close to it?"

But now no more Federals were swarming around the outer wall. Sentell and the others could hear an occasional musket shot, they could hear the solid undertone of moan and sigh punctuated now and then by a shriek. They could hear that, and a single raucous officious voice bawling Masterson's name over and over. With one last withering glance at Sentell and Bouvier, he climbed to his feet.

"Who the hell's yelling at me?" he bawled.

"It's Maxell, Major. We got something for you to see. Youall want to come on down here?"

Masterson shrugged his shoulders and hitched up his pistol belt. "If you walk me all the way down there," he yelled, "you better have a brigadier general by the balls or a thirty-foot wooliebugger blown out of its nest by that mine. You hear me, Maxwell?"

Maxwell's voice was clear, but there was still smoke and dust mingled into an impenetrable cloud down between the crescent and the crater. All they could see were vague edgeless forms flitting back and forth through the gloom. Even the bright sun, touched once in a while by thick-piled Gulf clouds, did not illuminate the haze.

"Well," Maxwell shouted back, his voice edged with sarcasm, "we ain't got no brigadier for you, Major, but we got what looks like twenty or thirty wooliebuggers sure enough. You better come one down and see this, 'cause you ain't gonna believe it if I tell you back in headquarters."

44

So Masterson led the way, and they stepped down the easy slope of the crescent's outer wall. The rubbish, the tent-halves, the old crates and pieces of uniform had mostly been blown away. The incline was bare except for hundreds of tiny bits of cotton scattered up and down like coveys of tiny butterflies.

"Wadding," Bouvier grunted. "We sure shot up the ammunition on this one."

"Don't feel bad," Masterson said over his shoulder as he moved to the bottom of the slope and almost disappeared into the murky air. "It's that much you won't have to surrender."

They followed him into the choking gloom. The smell of powder, of raw earth, the sweet smell of blood, struck them before they reached the bottom of the slope.

"You coming', Major?" Maxwell yelled through the drifting smoke.

"Yeah," Masterson coughed. "Just as soon as we can get through this murk."

Then they hit the relatively level space between the crater and the inner works. Masterson stopped for a moment, his face red, his hands stuck first into his belt and then hanging loose and awkward at his sides. When the others came even with him, they saw why he had stopped. There was no way to get to Maxwell except to walk on bodies.

They were sprawled in every attitude and posture that imagination could discover for them. Some lay with both hands almost buried in the soft loam, fingers twisted into the soil as if one last terrible squeeze, one last pressure upon the earth, might hold off its power over them. Some lay with their broken faces, empty and expressionless, tilted toward the pastel shimmer of the sun above the haze of smoke and dust. There were arms and legs, whole bodies stripped of clothes, corpses without heads, heads resting disembodied on chests or bellies that did not belong to them. At the edge of the crater, caught in a heap of dead, one man still stood erect, his legs caught between two corpses, his bayoneted rifle pointed toward the slope of the inner works, his eyes squinted and his shoulders hunched as if he were struggling against a great wind. When they stepped into the tiny crevices between corpses and came closer to him, Sentell saw that a solid shot had passed through his chest.

"How in the goddamned hell could a solid ball go through a man and not knock him down?" Masterson asked softly.

"What I'm wondering," Bouvier said with a trace of anger in his voice, "is who the hell was firing solid shot when I ordered canister?"

Then they found Sergeant Maxwell. He was a tall boneless Missouri man whose body seemed held together with nuts and bolts, with pegs, possibly even strung together by the quantities of coarse red hair that covered his head and face and curled in tight clumps at the collar of his homespun shirt, and that grew almost as luxuriantly on his wrists and forearms as on his head. His eyes were red, too, from the acrid stinging powder smoke, and his shoulders were jerking as if he was somehow holding back tears or on the verge of uncontrollable laughter. Beyond him, almost at the breach in the outer works, stood a half-dozen men of his squad. All of them were staring into the crater.

"All right, goddamnit," Masterson said. "Speak your piece."

"Piece hell," Maxwell snorted. "Look down there."

Then Sentell was close enough to see that it was neither sorrow nor laughter that had set Maxwell's shoulders to twitching. It was anger, the kind of absolute anger that renders a man almost helpless in its grip until finally it shakes him into violence beyond sense, into unconsidered retaliation far in excess of what his mind tells him is required. Maxwell's mouth was twitching under the red beard.

"Well, I'll be damned," he heard Masterson whisper wonderingly.

"See what I tole you, Major? You see what I meant?" Maxwell almost shrieked. "I tole you you wouldn't believe it if'n I was to come up afterwards. And I want to tell you right now I saw that big gray sonofabitch right over there near the dead roan throw down on Bobby Lee Quinton and put a minie right through his head."

Then the dam broke, and through the weird sun-tinted haze they could see tears begin to run down Maxwell's face. His eyes closed and the tears ran faster, and Sentell could imagine his mouth twisting like a painful old scar under the red mat covering it. Sentell and the others looked away, down into the crater.

Beside the monotonous heaps of dead, the shattered rifles and the thick tatter of flesh and clothing, there was something else. It was a small group of survivors cowering together near the outer wall of the pit. One had wrapped a handkerchief around the stump of his right arm and another was holding him erect. A few more stood straight and defiant and stared up at them as if the difference between death and imprisonment was really no difference at all, and that however the

46

Southerners might decide it, there would be no begging, no more bowing and smirking, no more deference at all.

"Niggers," Masterson said. "Niggers."

"You bet your goddamned soul they're niggers," a rifleman farther down the breach yelled almost hysterically.

Then Maxwell got hold of himself, gave one final swallow, and spoke quietly to Masterson. "You want us to take these bastards back up to town and let the folks see what they've got fighting 'em, or you just want to shoot 'em here?"

Masterson shrugged. "It just couldn't make me any less difference," he said. "Anyhow, that's Sentell's business. I'm just a cavalryman without nothing to ride."

"What do you say, Major?" Maxwell said, turning to Sentell.

It was easy to see that he expected one answer, that possibly the only alternatives Sentell had were to let him shoot them under orders or force him to break orders by doing it anyhow. Maxwell might be able and even willing to get them back to Vicksburg, but even if he tried, the rest of the men might start shooting no matter what orders they were given. They had suffered too much. They had seen their country invaded, their people reduced to scavengers, their friends killed. They had fought an army three times as large as their own, and they had been pushed all over Mississippi until finally their last protection was a shell-shattered town on the bluffs of the river where they could either fight or surrender. And now the Federals were using former slaves against them.

"You know this is hard, Major," Maxwell was saying. "It's damned hard to have to fight like this. I don't mind the mule meat and the double duty, and I don't reckon I mind us getting whipped a little if we can get back at 'em like today. But I wasn't raised up to fight a nigger like he was a white man."

"I know," Sentell said. "I know what you mean. You better get them out of that hole anyway. I want to know what regiment they belong to. Maybe we can find out what the strength is over there."

"Bullshit," a soldier muttered down the line. "That's the nigger brigade of Grant's chicken-snatchers, and they're as strong as a little white Yankee pussy can make 'em."

"You hold that down," Masterson bellowed. "I'll shoot the next son-ofabitch that bad-mouths me. I may want one of them black toadeaters for target practice. Hey, you niggers," he yelled. "Get your butts up out of that hole or I'll come down and help you out with a saber."

The Negroes began limping and stumbling toward the near side of the pit. One was gut-shot, and as the rest moved away, he began to moan, to beg for someone to help him. The rest continued to climb across the bodies and tangled harness and scattered rubble as if they could not hear him.

"God Almighty," one of the privates whistled. "I want you to look at that. Them no-good apes won't even help out their own fellows."

"I seen a major who owned thirty slaves walk into the open at Shiloh to haul in his body-servant," another one said.

Then one tall Negro with a bandaged head stopped. As he turned back toward the injured man, Sentell could see the sergeant's stripes on his sleeve. "A couple of you men go pick him up," he ordered without raising his voice.

As first no one turned. Then the Negro sergeant looked up the hill at Maxwell.

"Johnny Rebel," he said in a conversational tone, "I'd take it kindly if you'd put a ball through the first man who steps out of this hole until we get that private soldier over there taken care of."

For an instant Sentell thought Maxwell would shoot him down. He raised his carbine, and his eyes narrowed. He had probably never been called by his first name – or addressed in a familiar way – by a Negro in his life. Then Sentell heard the low sputter of voices on down the line. Masterson was grinning and looking at Maxwell, and down in the pit the Negroes had stopped moving, were looking up the side of the crater almost expectantly.

Maxwell reddened, and his carbine moved to cover the edge of the pit. "All right, Sarge," he said finally without inflection. "I'll just do that fer you. Now a couple of you niggers get over there and do like yer officer tole you to. You ain't out of the army yet."

Masterson grinned at Sentell, and made as if to wipe sweat from his forehead. "Some nigger," he said softly.

It was still morning when they moved down the Jackson Road and turned their prisoners over to the provost guard. They were drained of strength and of courage and almost emptied of humanity. It was not that they had seen anything new; it was simply that there had been too much too quickly, and that, for all the killing from Buena Vista to

Champion's Hill, neither Masterson nor Sentell had ever witnessed a massacre.

The sun was high then, and in Masterson's tent the air was still and hot as the inside of a kiln. Sentell lay supine on his cot, trying to keep the sweat from pouring into his bandages. There was no chance of sleep, he thought. The heat, the battle at the crater and what had come after – and the shadow of surrender, all of them flowed and eddied in his mind.

For Sentell, the United States and its flag had ceased to represent anything worth fighting for. For him they had slowly changed from the instrument and symbol of liberty into the bludgeon and rag of tyranny. When he had accepted the Louisiana militia commission, there had been no anger in him: only the certainty that every Southerner would have to fight in order to stay free. There was no drama in his decision and when it had been made, when he had sent his acceptance to the Governor, there was no pleasure in it either. He had been a captain then, and he had taken his company of Caddo Rifles and headed for a rendezvous with the other Louisiana companies at Corinth, Mississippi. Sentell had waved no flags new or old and was unavailable for speeches in front of Shreveport's City Hall, where enlistments were taken, or down at the Gaiety Theatre, where young planters and the sons of local merchants and businessmen were trying to bribe or cajole or shame men into their own volunteer units for direct and immediate service with the Confederate States instead of waiting for the slow process of entering state forces and waiting to be transferred to the Confederacy.

Sentell had known enough about war, had remembered enough from Mexico, to wish that there were some decent way simply to refuse service. He thought at first that he might leave the city and volunteer in Mississippi as a hostler or a stretcher-bearer or a courier. But the more he thought, the more he realized that this would not be the kind of war that Mexico had been, not the kind in which tender feelings could be saved, high impulses humored and indulged.

He had taken his commission and held his peace, still silent when he boarded a train headed east in 1861. By leaving the fire-eating speeches for his neighbors to make, he had failed to satisfy them; by taking the commission when he was not sure he wanted to serve in combat, he failed to satisfy himself. But on the train, riding through the dusty crossroads towns and townless parish depots on the way to Monroe, he realized why he had not wanted the commission and why he had taken it anyhow. He came to understand why he could not produce a rousing patriotic speech for his new country, and why, finally, he would fight as well as he could anyhow.

Because, no matter who won or lost, neither the South nor the North would ever be what they had been before. Either there would be two nations (and possibly a dozen since there was already talk of Louisiana's secession from the Confederacy when the danger from the North was put down), each struggling, plotting, threatening the other over expansion into the western lands, over commercial matters, over boundaries, over all the trivia of government which means so much to clerks and so little to the people who must pay for the quarrels and the clerking. Either that, or there would be a single monolithic giant of a nation with its heart in New York, its brain in Washington, and its cells, the states themselves, only ciphers, only shadow governments to pass edicts from the central rulers to the people ruled.

Outside the tent, a Union shell whistled overhead and exploded weakly somewhere toward town. Sentell sat up. He had almost slept, but now he was thirsty, and the bandages on his back itched terribly. He pushed the tent flap aside and walked outside. Masterson was sprawled on one of the campstools, stripped to the waist, his chest bright with moisture. He was rubbing a whetstone along the edge of a bowie knife.

"Sooner or later," Sentell said, "you've got to use that thing. You won't rest until you do."

Masterson paid no attention. "They're talking again. They say Pemberton means to give us up before the Fourth of July."

"I heard Joe Johnston and most of the Confederate army was on its way to help us. None of the talk means anything."

Masterson put down the knife and whetstone. He spread his hands wide, almost in supplication. "Ed, I just don't want to give up."

"Maybe Bouvier has your number," Sentell said quietly.

"What're you talking about?"

"He calls it your obsession."

"Talk like a white man," Masterson spat out.

"He thinks you want to die here. He thinks you want to be Travis and Bowie and Crockett all rolled into one. I suppose he thinks you'd rather be a legend than a man."

Masterson sat down again. The anger and excitement were gone from his face. For a long minute he looked at Sentell almost with pity.

"Sentell," he said finally, "the trouble with you is you've forgotten too much. Let me ask you something. Is this an honest fight? Are we right or wrong?"

"It's an honest fight," Sentell said. "We were invaded."

"Was Mexico an honest fight?"

Sentell did not answer. He remembered the long tortured negotiations that summer before the war with Mexico, the equally tortured logic of the administration, the coarse gleeful representatives in the Louisiana legislature who wanted a war that would net not only Texas to the Rio Grande, but the whole of the subcontinent down to Central America if the Mexicans gave trouble. He remembered the ugly selfish talk, the cheap self-assurance of the slave dealers who saw in their mind's eye a whole new country opened up with the fall of Mexico to the United States. And he remembered the pathetic Mexican government, caught between turmoil at home and armed blackmailers to the north, and later the Mexican people, dark and enduring, as the gringos marched through their land, shattering every attempt of their young men to stop them. He remembered the deep personal shame of fighting campaigns they could not lose for a cause they should not win. Finally Sentell looked across at Masterson again.

"No," he said. "It was a low stinking fight. Isn't that what you want me to say?"

Masterson shrugged, but the shadow of a smile touched his bearded mouth. "I want you to say what you think. But you've said it. Mexico was a rotten fight, and you were right on top of the heap. You fought 'em from the border to the City of Mexico itself. You saw Scott ride in, and you were part of what went on before he made that ride. I bet you remember Chapultepec."

Yes, Sentell remembered Chapultepec. He would never forget the hot glare of a sun that stood forever at high noon and throbbed like a brass gong, and the stench of powder and the sweet terrible smell of broken flesh ripening in the sun. He could still hear the cries of the wounded, and the low countermelody of the Mexican women mourning their dead.

And he remembered that afternoon as Worth and Pillow sent their men pounding up the steep incline from the huddle of buildings at Molino del Rey toward the fortified ruins of the palace on Chapultepec

Hill. A rain of musketry and grape had slashed across them; trench after trench of the Mexicans had fought to the last. Sentell had commanded a company of the campaign that numbered ninety-seven as they began the final attack on Chapultepec, that would number fifty-three when they rode at last into the City of Mexico.

"I was down below," Masterson said. "They used my cavalry as provost guard after we got among those rocks and lakes. I was standing next to the gibbet with twelve men on it. You remember the deserters who went over to the Mexicans after Cerro Gordo? They put me in charge of the execution. Colonel Morris of the Ninth Regiment came up to me and said 'Lieutenant, I want you to keep your eyes on that castle up there. When the stars and stripes breaks out above it, I want those traitors to swing.' So there I was with my sword raised, looking up through the smoke and haze waiting for the flag – and the twelve of 'em knowing that the ensign of their own country was going to be the signal for 'em to die. I won't forget that ever."

As he talked, Sentell was in Mexico again, climbing over rock and broken roots, lying in the dust and then running forward until he reached one of the fortress' gates with half his command sprawled dead or wounded behind. They chopped at it with spades and bayonets, and finally broke through. On the other side, the Mexicans were waiting for them, scores of Mexican soldiers standing and kneeling in the open courtyard. They fired a volley and killed the first five or six Americans through the gate – except for Sentell and one other who had dived through and sprawled headlong on the stone. Then the Mexicans had begun moving back into the passages on either side of the courtyard, moving into the cloisters and behind crates and sandbags. Sentell and his men had had to fight in the open until sheer numbers pressed the Mexicans back inside the main building. Down corridors, around corners, up and down stairways the Americans had fought, with the endless thunder and echo of their own musketry and the enemy's making it impossible to issue orders or to hear them. It was every man's own fight, and a lonely one. Until at last Sentell's company had pushed them back into a chamber at the top of the building. It was a huge tower room and they fought across it, tripping, firing, using pistols and bayonets. They were stopped and forced back into the outer passage. They counterattacked, and the Mexicans broke and formed behind a last forlorn barricade in the far corner of the room. It was an old unused altar of heavy wood with a bright brass tabernacle and a large discolored crucifix that slanted drunkenly above the candle shelves. The Americans fired a quick volley, and the rest was close work with bayonet and bowie knife.

At the last, a final Mexican, bleeding and helpless, had pulled in the fortress flag through an open port that faced toward the city. Staggering and alone, armed only with a saber twice too large for him, holding the banner against his breast, he had chopped and slashed two more of Sentell's men before Sentell dived beneath the swinging blade and buried his knife in the Mexican's belly.

Then it was over. Then a color sergeant, slowly and with exaggerated precision, had hooked the American flag to the long lanyard rope, and let it flutter outward so that its width obscured the City of Mexico beyond. For a moment there had been silence. Only the hard breathing of the men inside the room, the muted sobs and moans from the corridors outside. Then the air was filled with a low rising cheer as if a thousand – ten thousand – charging men were shouting victory and moving nearer with every cry. Soon they could hear drumming footsteps below, and the concerted roar of the whole American army that was watching from the foot of the citadel.

Masterson was speaking again.

"Yeah, and so I waited with my arm raised and the sword heavy in my hand, feeling like I was a statue of some old-fashioned hero waiting for the judgment blast. What could I see? Nothing. Not a thing but waves of blue-coated ants swarming up that steep incline, and the puffs of smoke from the toy guns above. Haze and the sun scalding me blind, and the ropes and coils of white and gray smoke wove around that fortress like a shroud. And the artillery fire began to fade so you could hear the muskets, and then even the rifle fire slacked off so you could hear the yelling. And when it was mostly yelling with only a shot now and then, a gust of wind broke up the smoke and haze, and that damned killer sun caught the stars and stripes bellying on that flagpole, catching the breeze and fluttering as if it had been there all the time."

He paused for a moment and settled his eyes on the ground. He swallowed and went on.

"And my arm dropped. But even as it began to fall, even as the rest of the provost men each aimed a foot at a wooden crate to kick their traitor countrymen to hell, I heard it. I heard a cheer that muffled the final shots up on that hill of yours, a cheer that drowned the army's yelling. It was them – it was the turncoats. As the boxes spurted from beneath their feet, as the nooses were closing on their throats, they were cheering the flag they had betrayed, the flag that was killing 'em. And even as I turned to see where the shouting was coming from, it stopped, was cut off as if a bandmaster had slashed his instruments into silence at the end of a piece.

"And you could hear the army again, a musket shot here and there, the wagons rolling up from the lake. You could hear the whole clutter of disconnected noises – and you could see twelve men swinging, a few of them still kicking, with the taint of their treason black on their faces and the dregs of that last yell still caught in their throats.

"And I looked at my sword hand as if it didn't belong to me, as if somebody had grafted a marble arm to my shoulder. I turned cold. Because it struck me how much that sword looked like a baton, and how I had been the bandmaster without knowing it. I don't know why – I never figured why – but all the fight was gone out of me in an instant. I had come to Mexico to kill as many of 'em as I could shoot, stab, or ride down. For Travis and Bowie and Bonham. I came to burn or devastate, it didn't matter who or how. But there I was with a clean sword in my hand and twelve of my own men turning in the hot wind, and the words of politicians and land-grabbers elbowing each other in my memory. Then I saw how rotten it all was: how from the start to the finish of it there wasn't a good thing or a good minute to it, and how even the revenge tasted like crabweed because my hand had killed more of my own people than of theirs – and because anyhow there probably hadn't been ten men in the Mexican army we were facing who had fought at the Alamo or murdered at Goliad. I was cold and then I was hot. And then I walked away from the gallows real quiet, out of sight of the enlisted men, and threw up my guts. I spewed for five minutes, and I guess because of the heat and the fatigue and the heaves I found myself with tears in my eyes and a promise writing its way into my brain: that I'd never lay hands on a gun or a sword again except to protect myself or my own people. Never another Mexico."

Masterson stopped talking. A light breeze rustled the tent flap, and outside a Negro messman sounded supper call on a wrought-iron triangle. He cried in a high woman's voice:

"O Loozianaaaaaa, come git yo' grits and grass. Looooozianaaaa, come git it fo' it goes to seed."

It was twilight then, and the men were slowly moving out of the trees, out of the rear positions, coming from sentry duty at the powder magazines nearby – all walking slowly to their company areas to eat whatever their officers had been able to cadge or buy or steal for them.

"Looooozianaaaaa, don' hol' back, come befo' it crawl away."

But Masterson and Sentell were still beneath the Latin sun a thousand miles and twenty years away. They were still junior officers in an army which had since been broken in two. And Sentell remembered the rest of that afternoon in Mexico.

He had been sitting on the raised edge of that broken, riddled altar high in the fortress. He was dog-tired and wiping his knife blade aimlessly against his breeches, watching the flag whip and eddy in the sudden wind-rise. One of the sergeants and a pair of enlisted men were going over the Mexican dead, looking for money or trophies, for anything of value. The sergeant walked over to the wide window and picked up the bloodstained Mexican banner from beside its dead defender.

"Lieutenant," the sergeant said softly, "maybe you ought to take a look over here."

The Mexican was barely five feet tall, dark and soft featured. He had no beard, and his eyes, wide and beginning to lose the sheen of living eyes, seemed to be fixed on them in a mixture of anger and utter disbelief. One of the enlisted men squatted beside him, turned him slightly, read laboriously the inscription on his belt buckle: COLLEGIO MILITAR DE MEXICO.

"It warn't no soldier at all," one of the enlisted men said without inflection. "That ain't nothing but a goddamned caydet. He warn't but a kid . . . a little boy."

He was right. And afterward, as the Americans marched into the city, a captured Mexican captain told them the rest. Told them how, in the closing days, the commandant of the military academy had given leave to the boys, had tried to scatter them to their homes before the retreating army fell back on the city and the fortress.

But it had failed, the captain told them. Before the commandant had even joined the advance guard of the army to take part in the hopeless bloody defense he had tried to spare the boys, they had met and reorganized into a battalion and had been told to fortify Chapultepec. And there, high above the City of Mexico, protecting their capital, they had stayed.

"*Los niños heroicos,*" the captain whispered, making the sign of the cross. "*Muchachos, estaban siempre en mi corazón.*"

Masterson brought Sentell back to Mississippi with a word:

"The kids," he said. "You're remembering the kids."

"Yes," Sentell told him. "I'm remembering the kids."

"That's where I was taking you. Back to those kids we slaughtered for less reason than a man would kill a cur. Back to the men who were traitors because war pushed 'em too far and they didn't have the sand for it. If we'd stayed home, them kids would be men today – and them traitors, not meeting a situation they couldn't face, would have farmed or kept store or loafed their lives away instead of lying in unmarked graves with a length of army hemp around their necks. It was rotten all the way, and yet you and me stayed and did what we like to call – still twenty years later *have* to call – our duty."

He paused a moment, his hand on the tent flap, his eyes dark and determined. "Now tell me," he said without irony. "Tell me what to do with these troops – not a traitor in five thousand of 'em – who've fought this far. Will you do it for Pemberton? Will you get up and say, 'We're sorry, awful sorry, and you've been a good bunch, but it's gone too far now. Now they mean it. Now they want to starve us or hang us or shoot us up; anything to rid themselves of us. So better a rotten Union than a slack belly with a hole in it . . . you boys understand, don't you . . . .?'"

Outside, men were moving from sentry duty to their tents, from sparse flavorless meals to unquiet sleep.

"We've reached the end of the line," Sentell told him without conviction. "There's no place left to go."

Masterson shrugged. "There's always hell," he said. And a quick way to make the trip."

The rest of June passed like a hallucination. More sun, a lack of even mule meat – the bowels of an army slowly degenerating. Day after day, the Yankee sharpshooters taking a small but certain toll of the men still able to stand in the rifle-pits. No drugs to ease the pain of amputation or even the last agony. And each day saw fewer men able to stand muster. Of Sentell's regiments of infantry, there were less than seventy men still on their feet, and of the seventy no more than thirty who could have withstood a hand-to-hand battle. Thirty men responsible for eighty yards of front before an enemy which could easily throw thirty men at every yard of the works.

"It's like reaching past a cottonmouth for a drink of water," Grubbs said, one day after delivering a sick list longer than his effective muster.

"What's like that?" Sentell asked without looking up from the handful of papers.

"Us sittin' here with a few hundred scarecrows and lookin' out there just like we was tough and ready and able to give 'em what we give 'em back in May."

Grubbs paused for a moment, then went on, his voice dark with sincerity. "Major, if they was to really want in here now, we couldn't keep 'em out. I don't know how it is to the south or on the river side, but we couldn't hold off a pack of tumblebugs if they was out to get in here, no matter what."

Sentell looked up at him. Grubbs' brows were knitted together over a thin sunburned face. He looked ten years older than he had when he was assigned to Sentell's regiment at Black Rock. "Grubbs, you look peaked. I think you need a vacation. How about a summer camp up in Indiana?"

Grubbs look back at Sentell with mild patient eyes. "No, sir," he said pleasantly. "No, sir, I just want to get killed or go home."

As June ended, even the fiercest patriots, the dead-end fighters, were either beginning to say the same thing or at least, failing to say it, to think it without the stab of remorse they would have felt a month or so earlier. Because by the end of that steaming June, the reality of the war outside their lines, the meaning of it, had begun to fade, to simmer away under the ubiquitous sun. The lines, the camps, the town itself, had become a vast prison with nearly forty thousand inmates.

In town there were murders. Not simply predictable and inevitable cuttings and shootings that grace the docks and underside of every city and town, but pointless killings for neither profit nor revenge nor even anger. Killings that seemed somehow to smack of the berserk – as if killer and victim had plotted together to break out of Vicksburg in the only possible way. Sentell heard about the hanging of an elderly clockmaker who, having done for his wife, quietly turned himself in to the Provost Marshal, and asked that he be hanged by the military, and that, if it were not too much trouble, the death march should be played and he permitted to ride to the gallows seated on his coffin.

"They do it with notorious stranglers and abolitionists," the old man had pleaded, smiling idiotically. "You could clip off my buttons, too, if you've a mind to."

The hospitals were packed with men whose bodies, weak and useless, bore no scars, and the daily rate of death from disease had surpassed the number dying of gunshot wounds by the middle of June. Discipline remained because it was habit by then, and because no one had the strength or initiative left to stir up mutiny even if he cared enough to consider it. But beneath the shuffling obedience there was little spirit left. By the first day of July, no one, not even Masterson, could claim that the garrison was ready to hold out till fall. It was not that individual soldiers or units were ready to quit: it was just that neither units nor men cared very much what happened next.

And there were the rumors. It was said, and the saying had begun at staff headquarters, that Kirby Smith, a faded hero of Manassas, was pushing toward them from Shreveport along the railroad that cut across north Louisiana from the Texas border to within a few miles of Vicksburg. It was said that, below Millikin's Bend, he would punch a hole through the light holding parties Grant had left there, bring gunboats up from the confluence of the Mississippi and the Red, or simply use rifled guns to hold the Union ironclads at bay while the Vicksburg garrison crossed in rowboats and barges, and that Joe Johnston would hit Grant from behind.

But after Pemberton called in his senior commanders on the evening of July second, the rumor of impending surrender gained almost the currency of fact. It was said that Kirby Smith's expedition had been stopped at Delhi, Louisiana – stopped, shaken loose from its supply train, and sent reeling back along the railroad away from the Mississippi. To the north, there was no word of Johnston – not even rumor.

IV

3 JULY 1863 — The third of July dawned livid and mercilessly hot. The sun rose quickly, burned away the river haze and scalded dew from leaves and grass and late-blooming flowers. By nine o'clock the temperature was above ninety and climbing rapidly.

Sentell's regiments were scattered along a section of forward works south of the Jackson Road and, standing on a rise of ground a few hundred yards to the rear, he could see the sharpshooters leaning close to their narrow embrasures, straining to catch any sign of movement across the scorched and broken field between the lines. Walking down to the works, he saw a rifleman from Shreveport who had come to Vicksburg a nineteen-year-old boy full of riding and shooting, parties and military school at Alexandria. Now he was lean to the point of emaciation, dark as one of his father's mixed-blood servants. If he was spared, he would go home a man older than his father by every reckoning except chronology. Sentell climbed the ramp of banked timbers, taking care not to show himself above the parapet.

"Ed Norton," he called softly.

The boy was hunched forward, his eyes slitted and his mouth closed tightly with a tiny swatch of tongue pressed between narrow lips. He did not move when Sentell spoke. "Ed," he said again.

Ed Norton turned quickly, his eyes still locked in a marksman's frown. Then he recognized Sentell.

"Aw, Major," he grinned. "Sorry. I get so sunk in watchin' for one of them buzzards to show an elbow, I don't hear a thing goin' on. If they was to break in behind while I'm lookin', they could eat up the town 'fore I roused. How you doin', Major?"

"Pretty well, Ed. No indigestion."

He laughed, showing startling white teeth out of his dark face. "Yeah," he said. "Everybody's got 'em a sad song, but nobody's cryin' that one. How does this fight look from upstairs?"

Sentell hesitated a moment. Then he shrugged. There was no secret to be kept. In a few hours, the surrender talk would be common knowledge.

"It looks like quits upstairs," Sentell told him.

He was squinting back through his gun slit. His expression did not change. "Heard that," he said softly. "Heard the big shots was losin' their taste for it. What do you think, Major?"

"What I think doesn't make any difference," Sentell said. "What I think won't feed a squad or stiffen a general's spine."

"That's okay," Ed said. "What do you think anyhow?"

"I think . . . no, I feel we should fight until we're whipped."

"Ummm," the boy said. Then, sudden as a striking cottonmouth, he brought the heavy rifle to his shoulder, steadied the telescope sight by wrenching his arm outward against the leather strap wound around his left arm and squeezed a shot toward the Federal trenches. The report was flat and lifeless as it rolled across the field before them, and the boy moved a few inches backward across the dusty platform on the seat of his pants.

"Sonofabitch kicks like Katie's mule," Ed Norton grinned. "But it don't hardly ever miss."

"Score," somebody down the line a few yards called out.

"Score?"

"You bet," the voice said evenly. "Knocked the head off somethin' with gold on its shoulders."

"'Nother damn bottom looie," a second voice remarked from one of the embrasures.

"Too fat for a looie," Ed said flatly. "Had to be a captain. I don't hardly waste a ball on no looies nowadays."

"You know what tickles me, Major?" he asked, turning back to Sentell. "What just gets inside and purely busts me up is they don't never learn. I've killed goin' on twenty of 'em in the last six weeks, and I can still be sure of getting' me at least one shot a day. Seems like even Yankees could figure it out."

"I guess that cuts both ways," Sentell said. "We lose a man every day or so."

Ed shrugged and squinted at a paper cartridge he had picked up from the dust-covered shelf at the edge of his slit. "Well," he said, "we do lose a few. But the last three we lost in this regiment was only niggers. The niggers just don't believe all this. They think it's somethin' we all of us got cooked up for sport. I asked 'em, I begged 'em – I even told one of 'em I'd shoot him myself if he didn't keep his damn head down. You know what? He laughed and grinned and handed me a tray of soup and a piece of cornbread he stole off an officer 'cause he liked me. And soon as he saw I was busy eatin', he took off runnin' down the walkway and caught a minie in the ear 'fore he'd made ten yards. I was so goddamned mad I started to put another one in him till I saw he was past hurtin'. Then I was so damned mad I got to cryin' like a little kid. You know what I mean, Major?"

"I know," Sentell said.

"About that surrender business," Ed began, looking through his slit carefully, then glancing back at Sentell. "You reckon the big shots'll go through with it?"

"They'll go through with it if Grant gives them any terms short of hanging the whole army."

"That's so," Ed said slowly. "I guess we never had much chance. What with them gunned and manned ten to one on us, them with gunboats for the rivers and torches for folks' homes. And us with one of 'em for a general. You think Pemberton's been square with us?"

"I expect so. He's not a traitor, just a boiled shirtfront with a West Point textbook where most of us have brains."

Ed smiled wryly. "I seen them West Point textbooks when I was down to school in Alexandria," he said. "I don't recollect a chapter on how to surrender your army without a fight."

"He thinks we've fought."

"That's so," Ed said, his eyebrows lifting. "That's true enough. But we ain't fought very good 'cause we ain't been led very good – and we sure as hell ain't fought long enough. Why don't he ask Grant to let us send the women and children and old folks out? Even that bluebelly would have to go along. And once we was shut of worryin' about them, we could make do for a couple of months. The way this war is goin', a couple of months could spell independence."

They talked on, and Ed shook the last few drops of water in the canteen onto a pair of dirty shapeless handkerchiefs. "Got to cover up now," he said. "You stick this kerchief under your hat till the sun starts fallin'. Nigger'll be along with some more water in a little while – if he makes it this far."

"How good are the Unions at sharpshooting?" Sentell asked.

Ed Norton Junior drew the ramrod from his rifle. "They wasn't worth a tub of horse turds when we settled down to this," he said casually, raising the ramrod above the edge of the parapet. "But shootin's like anything else. The more you do it, the better you get. There just ain't nobody can't learn to shoot if he fires up a couple hundred cartridges a day."

Before he finished, a fusillade of gunfire came from across the lines. Shot after shot blended into a solid chain of riflery. Ed's ramrod bent and whipped back and forth, from side to side like a willow twig lashed by a hurricane wind. After it had been hit two or three times, he drew it in. "See?" he grinned with pride. "We done made marksmen out of them clerks and dock-wallopers. Hittin' a quarter-inch rod at a hundred and fifty yards is all right, ain't it?"

Sentell nodded glumly. "I guess it might do," he said.

"Don't look so whipped-out, Major," Ed said. "If they was to lift one, it'd get hit twice as many times. Them boys is good, but they still got plenty to learn. We got one boy over in Milby's company who comes down the line once a day. He's got this Austrian rifle with a scope as big as your arm, and it fires brass-case ammunition around caliber .50. Major, he hits the Yanks through them four-inch peek-holes of theirs."

61

"If you can hit a ramrod, you ought to be able to do that," Sentell said.

"Naw," Ed said. "Them holes are a good eight inches deep. You got to shoot awful straight to hit a man at the back end of eight inches of dirt. You aim off a little and you sink your slug in the sand. You ought to stay around to see him work."

But as Sentell rose to begin checking the rest of the line, there was a stutter of hoof beats to their left rear, and Pemberton and two staff members rode up to the works that spanned the Jackson Road.

"There's your white flag wavers," Ed said casually.

Along the line, a staff officer rode on a broken-down artillery nag. "Cease firing until further orders. Flag of truce is out. No firing until ordered . . ."

"Well," Ed breathed slowly. "That is that."

He propped his rifle against the parapet, letting its muzzle show above the rim. "You know," he said with sudden intensity, "I may never fire that piece again."

Pemberton and an aide, accompanied by another officer in full-dress uniform, urged his horse, remarkably healthy and even prancing and fighting the bit, over the steep incline atop the outer works. Across the field Sentell and Ed Norton could see three Federals riding slowly toward their lines.

"You don't reckon they'd risk old whiskey-breath, do you?" Ed Norton mused. "Look at that one in the middle. Looks like a lump of lard painted blue and tied to the saddle."

It was Grant. Sentell had seen his picture in a copy of some Chicago illustrated newspaper after the fall of Fort Donelson. He was small and built solidly with a fringe of beard covering his chin. Despite Ed's remark, he sat his horse as if he were part of it.

Ed reached for his rifle, stood up slowly and pointed it toward the oncoming Union horsemen, leaning forward to sight them through his scope. Sentell moved by reflex, knocking the rifle out of Ed's hands.

"You try that," he said, "and you'll damn well get the whole garrison strung up."

Ed frowned at him irritably. "Aw, goddamnit, Major, I wasn't aimin' to shoot that old fool. I was just tryin' to get a better look at him through my telescope."

"Looks more like they're standin' for their portraits than anything else," Ed mused. "Call it 'Judas at it again.'"

The conference lasted no more than five or ten minutes. Then the officers mounted up and rode back to their lines, leaving a plume of white dust curling behind like the path of a snake crawling in two directions at once.

Ed picked up his rifle and held it toward Sentell.

"Care for a shot at Pemberton, Major?" he asked.

Sentell shook his head. "Would you have a rope in your knapsack?"

"I got an antique haler my great-grandpap picked up in Palestine," a voice bawled behind them.

"Where the devil have you been hanging out?" Sentell asked Masterson.

He shook his large burnished head slowly. "I been busy in Missouri and Kentucky," he said. "Looks like us Westerners didn't carry secession far enough."

"I reckon you got something there, Major," Ed Norton said. "Only maybe the horsemen ought to secede from the doggies. I got in this damned foot 'n' shoot-it outfit when my horse died up near Corinth. I fought 'em mounted at Pittsburg Landing."

Masterson looked the boy over carefully. "You look kinda skinny for hard riding," he said at last.

Ed shrugged, his smile unwavering. "Makes it nice for the horse."

"Anyway," Masterson said gruffly, "I got one of two dozen live horses left in this hole. If you didn't bring one in, you ain't likely to be taking one out."

"Horses ain't the only critters a man can ride," Ed said, staring in admiration at Masterson's pair of huge Walter Colts with stag grips.

Masterson did not smile. "I don't want no pig-fuckers riding with me. It's bad for morale."

Ed stretched out and leaned his head and shoulders back against the parapet. "How about mules?"

"Mules," Masterson spat disgustedly. "Mules. A mule's got to be outside a man before you can saddle him. You done eaten all the mule you likely to get."

Ed squinted at him like a horse trader. "I can lay hands on seventeen mules 'fore you can draw one of them irons," he said. "And there ain't a bite missing' out of 'em either."

Masterson's eyebrows lifted. "Boy, if you're foolin' with me, you better desert or hope that surrender goes through in a hurry."

63

"I ain't foolin'," Ed shot back. "If you want seventeen good mounts, all you got to do is come up with fifty dollars gold apiece and promise one of 'em to me."

Masterson scratched his beard. "These mules," he began warily, "four legs apiece and all able to bear two hundred pounds?"

"Major," Ed said exasperatedly, "I ain't tryin' to air your pockets. These mules'll take us out of here, and that's what you want, ain't it?"

Masterson glanced at Sentell. "That's what I want," he said.

Ed Norton's relief sentry showed up, and the three of them backed down from the embrasure, still careful to keep the earthworks between them and the Federal sharpshooters.

As they reached the bottom of the works, Sentell turned to Masterson. "All right, Sam, what do you mean to do?"

Masterson smiled innocently. "I mean to buy them mules . . . if your little buddy ain't just dreamed 'em up."

"Them mules was across the river two nights ago," Ed put in.

"They've been bringing mules across the river?" Sentell asked him.

Ed shrugged. "Been bringin' stuff over ever since the Unions enveloped this place. You can buy sausage, cornmeal, shoes – you can buy apples. George Peavey bought the mules near Jena, drove 'em north, kept 'em out of sight of the Federals, and swam the whole drove across the river night before last. He's been doing it, Major. I thought youall knew about it. That's where the meat's been comin' from. We used up the commissary mules a couple weeks ago. All that plow collar mutton you been eatin' comes from over the river."

Masterson cleared his throat. "Sonny, we ain't been eating no kind of mutton. I ain't had meat since the fifteenth of last month – except a rabbit Cully, my orderly, run down by accident with my horse."

Ed's eyes widened. "I guess maybe the staff's been eatin' up them critters."

"I guess they have," Sentell said disgustedly. Because Sentell had not seen any staff officers in almost two weeks except for the brief appearance of Pemberton and Bowen and their flunkies at the truce talk a while before. Because, moreover, the men in the works had not seen meat in nearly a month except for the sporadic inclusion of rabbit or squirrel or pigeons. The men who had been doing the dying had not even been given that last prerogative of the condemned: a decent meal; and some had died with their bowels so raddled that the final agony

64

had brought with it the final indignity too. Riflemen, sick and gaunt, had died squirming in their own filth.

"Well," Masterson said, "there's always some sonofabitch standing downwind when a norther hits the merchant and farmer's bank. What I want to know is how come we can get those eatin' mules so cheap?"

Ed shrugged again. "Them plowbirds was worth a hundred dollars gold yesterday," he said. "But now word's out that Pemberton means to quit. When the flag comes down and the Unions march in, they're gonna hand out grub and confiscate the mules anyhow. Peavey figures fifty gold dollars beats a receipt from a bluebelly."

"Major," Masterson asked Sentell, "is this boy off duty?"

"He is."

"All right, boy. Pack up that long arm of yours and let's go see if we can strike some gold in Missouri and Kentucky."

"I heard all the yellow's out Californy way," Ed told him.

"Gold," Masterson said with ponderous good-humor, "is where you find it."

"So is lead," Sentell told him.

"The trouble with you, Sentell," he said, mounting and giving Ed a hand up behind him, "is that you got this deep secret wish to outlive yourself. You think about afterwards. I got good information from my old man back in Anahuac. He told me, 'Son, tomorrow is a whore's dream. Sign a quitclaim on the future for a witnessed deed on today any time you got the option.' You can't talk down an old man like that."

Sentell didn't try. He watched Masterson gallop through the dust toward the seething miserable town, young Ed Norton hanging onto his tunic with one hand and holding his sniper's rifle tightly in the other.

That evening Bouvier brought Sentell a folded order written on stationery from the Moultrie Hotel.

"Official communication," he smiled wryly.

"Should I read it?"

"No," he said. "You know what to expect. Terms of surrender having been reached – in order to forestall the useless effusion of blood – troops of the United States will occupy this place tomorrow at nine o'clock. Truce will be continuous until that hour. Regimental officers will receive details of organization for surrender and parole after the regiments have been formed up . . . Do you want to hear the rest?"

"No," Sentell said. "I think that will do nicely."

"In a few hours we'll officially be turncoats," Bouvier said broodingly. "We should have assassinated those spineless fools three months ago after Champion's Hill. We should have put Stephen Lee in command."

"We're only soldiers, not professional revolutionaries."

"And we'll lose the war as soldiers," Bouvier shot back. "Lose it as soldiers and be treated as rebels. You're too old and too smart to believe any different."

Sentell looked up at him sharply. In the firelight Bouvier's face seemed boyish, but the fierce concentration of his eyes, fixed on the crumbling fire near the tent, gave him an unhuman appearance. Not inhuman, simply not human at all. More like some mythical slaughtering device. Achilles or Ajax – not bound to the plodding and profitless conventions of another century that held most men, even in battle, within certain limits of action.

This was Bouvier's first agony, his first experience of coming to grips with something that could not be shrugged off or ignored or challenged to a duel. Without realizing it, he was calling for the cup to be passed from him, or at least asking mutely for strength to bear the inescapable which neither violence nor good blood could solve. He was beginning to sense himself part of a starved and defeated host, and the alternatives that remained were self-destruction or acceptance – and he had been trained for neither.

"Forget it," Sentell told him.

Bouvier raised his head slowly. "Forget?"

"Forget tomorrow morning. It will come and pass, and afterward you'll still have both hands and possibly even a stomachful of decent food. Then you can plan."

"I'm already planning," he said.

Beyond the tent they heard the unexpected clatter of hoofs and the jingle of canteens and spurs. As the first rider reined in, they could hear more behind him.

Bouvier and Sentell stepped outside. Masterson was swinging down from his saddle. With him, young Ed Norton and a score or so of others milled and cursed their mounts into temporary submission.

"The Mounted Muleteers," Ed laughed. "Did youall ever see anything as pretty in all your life?"

66

Masterson still had his horse. But the rest, mostly unsmiling and sweating profusely, rode ugly buff and gray wagon-mules.

"I just come by to give youall one more chance to join up with a fine mixed company," Masterson said smiling. "How about it?"

"It looks to me like you're already filled," Bouvier told him. "I don't see any empty mules."

"Shit," Masterson boomed, "if youall want to give it a try, I'll empty a pair of mules before you can get another breath."

Sentell looked up at him through the darkness. "You know I can't go. I relieved Grubbs, but who is there to relieve me? The next grade above me in command of these regiments is a major general."

"Send him a note, Major," Ed Norton said.

"I fought these men from Shiloh to Black River to here. When they walk out and throw their guns on the pile, I'll be walking with them. Leaving is nothing to you, Ed; it's nothing to Major Masterson. You're a private and he's a horse soldier without a command to take care of. If he had two regiments and I had none, he'd be down here and I'd be up there. Am I right, Sam?"

Masterson was trying to free a jammed revolver one of his men handed him. He frowned and thumbed his hammer as far back as it would go.

"Major Masterson," Bouvier said. "Major Sentell asked you a question."

Masterson glanced at them in feigned irritation. "All right," he said. "I might be down there and I might not. I'm glad now I don't have no command to worry over."

He paused and the rest of them said nothing. "All right," he went on. "Whichever thing I did, I'd know I should stay with my command. I ain't making light of you, Sentell."

Bouvier stepped over to Masterson's horse. "I'll be staying, too, Sam."

Masterson frowned again. "What's your reason, Frenchie?"

Bouvier smiled easily. "I mean to find out all I can before they turn us loose. Then, if you get to Forrest, I'll be seeing you there."

Ed Norton whistled. "Major Bouvier," he said, "breakin' parole ain't no lark. If they get hold of you again and find out you been paroled and not exchanged, they'll just shoot you right there without a trial or nothin'."

"I could get killed as easily falling off a mule," Bouvier said slyly. "Besides, they won't be capturing me again. Just this once. I want to see what these people are like at close range."

"Well," Masterson said restlessly, "we're ready to give it a try."

"How are you going out?" Sentell asked.

"There's a trail that passes through the works about two miles south and east of town," Masterson said. "It cuts between Lauman and Ord, goes right through the hills and bluffs toward the Natchez main line. If there's a way out, that's it. We can't fight, but we can sure as hell run."

"I hope these mules understand that," Ed Norton said dubiously.

Masterson turned to Bouvier and Sentell again. "So once we get beyond 'em, we'll cut north and skirt Jackson, keep at it past Corinth and pick us up some Confederates in lower Tennessee."

For a moment, neither of them spoke.

"Well," Bouvier said slowly, "Forrest broke out of Donelson with over a thousand men. I guess it *can* be done."

"He didn't have the best part of five hundred miles to ride before he was safe," Sentell put in.

Masterson leaned out of his saddle. "Miles is just like hours," he said. "Ten miles is too much for a coward like ten minutes is too much for him on the firing line. This time we ain't got no conscripts or skulkers. You can bank on this. If we *don't* make it, it can't be made."

The talk stopped and Sentell and Bouvier mounted behind Grubbs and Ed Norton to ride as far as the dirt road with them. The night was utterly quiet and the day's heat seemed to have been embalmed in it. Only the sounds of hoofs and harness, an occasional birdcall, the soft tiny thunder of insects, broke the stillness. There was no talk as they passed a few pickets, a scattered campfire or two, a broken caisson or a huddle of graves cut out of the uneven earth. Then they all reached the outer works.

"Well," Masterson said as Sentell dismounted, "I'll see you next time in a free Confederacy or in hell. Charlie, get off that mule so we can ride."

Bouvier shook his head. "I'll ride out to the beginning of the bogs with you," he said.

Masterson shrugged. "All right, but you're going to have a mighty heavy pair of boots when you get back. That stuff sticks terrible."

"Don't you worry about my boots, you lard-assed Texican."

Grubbs and Ed Norton waved to Sentell as they guided their mules down the slope of the works and threaded their way through the broken maze of abates on the far side. Masterson grinned and leaned back out of his saddle. "Don't you let Mexico chew on you no more," he said softly. "That was over the river a long long time ago. This here is another war, and all the kids dying are ours. The only thing in God's world I hate worse than leaving youall is being whipped. I got to ride out."

Sentell held onto his hand a moment longer. "If I was plus a horse and minus a command, I'd be with you," Sentell told him. "Sooner or later I'll be exchanged and then I'll be with you anyhow."

"Right," Masterson said. "One way or another, we'll all be together again."

Masterson straightened in the saddle and clambered down the easy slope after his boys. Sentell watched them ride toward the edge of some second-growth trees that became an almost impenetrable morass of vine and sapling and soft marshy ground within a dozen yards. If they missed the one or two vague paths that finally ran into the Natchez road, they might ride an hour or a hundred years without finding another way. Sentell was hoping one of them knew the trails.

Sentell had walked back almost to the first picket fire when he heard musketry rattling faintly out of the woods into which the men had ridden. A thin boy in denim and a Federal jacket challenged him:

"Who the hell are you, mister? You better call out."

"Sentell, 26th Louisiana Regiment."

"Come on over here and get recognized," the boy called falteringly.

Sentell stepped into the light of the fire, but he was still listening to the flat clatter of rifle fire and the deeper sound of something heavier back across the works.

"All right, sir," the boy said with relief. "I didn't mean to scare you none."

He had lowered his rifle and was watching Sentell curiously. "Sir . . . ," he said.

"Wait a minute, boy."

"Sir?"

"Shut up. I'm listening."

The firing had almost stopped, and through the spasmodic scattering of single shots, Sentell could hear voices high and thin sifting through the dense mass of woods beyond the point where Masterson and his people had disappeared into them.

"Hey," the boy whispered loudly, nudging Sentell with his elbow. "I can see some kinda something' movin' out there."

Sentell squinted and stared. Nothing but darkness and the soaring bulk of cypress and a few sweet gum and slash pine on the higher ground near them.

"There," the boy pointed. "Near that mess of bush and saplin'."

Sentell could see movement, but it might have been a mule or a bear for all he could tell.

The boy cocked his rifle.

"Put that down," Sentell told him. "If it's our people, they don't need a salute, and if it's the Federals, we can't stop them."

Then he heard a voice from the shaking bush. "Help . . . I need help."

"Frienderfoe?" the boy called in a quavering voice.

"Friend, you sonofabitch," Sentell heard Bouvier shout back angrily.

Sentell and the boy were running, tripping down the slope of the mound before Bouvier had finished. "Have you got a light?" Sentell asked the boy.

"I got two sulfur matches," he said. "But I need 'em."

"You won't need them if you have a pair of broken arms," Sentell told him without breaking stride.

"You're the boss," he called back, breathing heavily.

As they reached the bottom of the slope, Sentell's foot caught in a root and he fell rolling forward into the heavy thicket. He twisted onto his knees and, without pausing, crawled toward the sound of Bouvier's voice, still cursing in the darkness.

Sentell came to a break in the bushes and weeds, and pulled up short with Bouvier's pistol in his face.

"You," Bouvier gasped. "It had to be. Nobody else in the world."

Bouvier lowered his pistol and gestured behind him with a turn of his head. "I got him back his far. You're going to have to take him back inside the lines. I seem to have a bad arm. The damn briers out here."

His jacket was torn in a dozen places, and even in the darkness Sentell could see the glimmer of blood dripping down his arm from near his shoulder.

"Who?"

"Who," he spat. "The goddamned Yankees, who do you think? I'm no Jackson, and no one picketing down at this end could hit himself in the jaw with his own rifle butt. They hit us before we'd . . . "

"Who did you bring in?"

The boy had found them, and was striking one of his precious matches into a pile of broken twigs and brush.

"You watch that fire, boy, or you'll burn us up in here. This grass is dry as a mummy wrapping," Bouvier said.

Sentell reached for his arm as the little fire flared. "Who?"

"Who do you think?" he answered woodenly. "Masterson."

Sentell climbed pass him and pulled the unmoving body into the circle of light. Masterson's eyes were closed, and above the fringe of auburn beard his face was pale and expressionless. His breathing was shallow, and neither his lips nor his chest moved.

Bouvier was still talking. "We followed this hairline of a trail until it joined a cowpath about six hundred yards out. Then we came to some kind of clearing. We started across with Grubbs and Masterson at the point. They hadn't passed the edge of the woods before the whole swamp came to life. They even had a little popgun on a wooden platform that raked the cleared ground from a clump of trees on the far side."

"You mean they had a whole detachment waiting and ready for you?"

"I don't know who they were waiting for," Bouvier growled, "but they took up a good deal of their time with us. There had to be a company out in those woods."

"Do you think they were warned?"

Bouvier frowned questioningly. "Warned? By whom? What are you getting at?"

"Nothing," Sentell shrugged. "It was probably a bad idea. We've got to get Masterson back to the tents. Boy, put out that fire and lend a hand here."

It took all three of them to get Masterson to the picket fire. His dead weight and dangling limbs made the trip back more difficult that the going had been. Back at the boy's post, they lowered Masterson onto a dirty raveled blanket and began working his blood-soaked tunic off his shoulders.

"Shoulder and chest," Bouvier grimaced. "Look at that."

"His wrist and forearm, too. These aren't musket balls."

71

Bouvier used his knife to cut away the shirt. "Canister," he said. "The popgun. The same shot killed Grubbs and a boy from the 12th Arkansas and scattered the rest. I was talking to your friend from Shreveport – what's his name?"

"Ed Norton?"

"That's him. We were riding just behind Masterson and Grubbs, and when Grubbs called back to us that the main trail to the Natchez road was ahead. I slipped up to tell Sam good-bye. I was almost abreast of him when we suddenly came out into this clearing. I never got to tell him."

Bouvier had finished cutting. Now he probed gently, trying to find the heavy leaden balls and fragments in the flesh of Masterson's arm and shoulder. He gestured to the gawking boy picket who, leaning on his rifle, watched the makeshift surgery without comment or expression.

"Boy, do you have a canteen and a mess cup?"

"Sure," the picket said. "My daddy give me his canteen and things from when he soldiered in Mexico."

"All right" Bouvier broke in. "You pour what's in the canteen into the cup and boil it up. And I'll need your shirt, Ed," he said turning to Sentell. "And you better get me a piece of wood."

Sentell began taking off his shirt. But the picket did not move. He continued to stare at Masterson's pale unmoving face, at the ugly wounds running from his collarbone down past his elbow.

"Boy," Bouvier barked at him.

"I don't know," the boy said hesitantly. "I don't know."

"Goddamnit, what don't you know?"

I never heard nobody boiling decent whiskey."

"Keep your whiskey. I need your water."

"What's in my canteen is whiskey," the boy answered placidly.

Bouvier raised himself from a crouch. "Boy, have you got water?"

The boy shrugged and touched a large jug with his toe. "Water," he said.

"Boil it quick," Bouvier said, subsiding. "Or I'll give you to the Union navy."

Sentell tore his shirt into long strips and found a thick piece of branch, stripped it of bark, poured a little whiskey over it, and handed the wood and strips of shirt to Bouvier. He took the canteen full of whiskey and lifted Masterson gently with his left arm.

"Here, fossil," he said softly. "This will do for blood."

Masterson stirred as the whiskey played across his mouth and ran down his beard. He opened his eyes and turned to look past Bouvier at Sentell.

"Shit," he said weakly.

"Shut up," Bouvier whispered. "You can't talk and drink."

The picket brought the water and took up his vigil again. He grinned down into Masterson's blinking eyes. "Hurt much?" he asked.

"Naw," Masterson choked. "It don't hurt enough to mention. How'd you like your throat cut, you little bastard?"

The boy stepped back from the fire's circle and nudged Sentell.

"Mean feller youall got there. How'd he cut anybody's throat with his arm all chewed up like that?"

"If he wants your throat cut, he'll tell one of us."

"You, boy," Bouvier snapped. "Get down the line to the head-quarters of Forney's division. Tell Colonel Russell to send Bouvier a stretcher and some people – unless he's kept a mule and ambulance. You get over there and bring some people back with you. You hear?"

The boy nodded and broke into a run, disappearing into the darkness.

"That boy might just keep right on running," Sentell said.

"Not if he knows what's good for him."

Masterson tried to push himself up on his good arm.

"All right," Bouvier snapped, "get on your back, Texican. You'll bleed all over us. Lie still."

But Masterson still squirmed and motioned Sentell over to his side.

"I'm sorry," he mumbled weakly. "Afraid I lost your boy Grubbs."

"You didn't twist his arm," Sentell said. "He knew they might get on to youall."

Masterson shook his head. "No, he didn't know it. He couldn't have known it because I didn't believe it myself. The Federals haven't had nothing but a picket force and a couple of courier-stops in those woods since they invested the town."

Bouvier looked at Sentell expressionlessly. "He's right," he said. "I know they had no artillery down here. Some of the Arkansas people rode these woods in late June hunting wild hogs. They killed one picket, and the captain told me they ran into him a good two and a half miles north of here and beyond the woods."

"They was up for us," Masterson gritted. "They knew we was coming through tonight, and I bet you a chicken dinner there's a gun over-looking every footpath in those woods. I wish to God I could find out who set us up."

Sentell pushed Masterson back against the bedroll behind him. "Maybe the Arkansan's dead picket ruffled them," he said. "No one has been through the woods since the hog-hunting."

"You're wrong," Masterson whispered. "I had four of the Missouri boys go nosing through there yesterday, Ed. They took mules and eased on up the paths to where they could see the Union flank and outposts and the Natchez road. There wasn't a thing along the paths. They didn't even see a picket."

Masterson drifted in and out of consciousness while they waited for help. Bouvier and Sentell divided what was left of the picket's whiskey, and Sentell poured his part over the deep scratches on Bouvier's upper arm.

"It's all right," he protested. "Don't waste the liquor."

"Shut up," Sentell told him. "You've been falling around in the swamp water, and those cuts needs cleaning out."

Bouvier shrugged and smiled for a moment. "That picket is going to wish he'd never seen any of us."

"He won't need the whiskey now. Now all he needs is patience. The whiskey was important last week and last month."

At last Forney's people came with a stretcher, and they tied Master-son to it, lashing his legs and middle to the poles. They slogged the mile or so to their area, stopping often to change bearers.

Finally they reached the regimental area. There were extra fires burning near Masterson's tent and a group of silent soldier-scarecrows, men from the Kentucky and Missouri cavalry regiments, milled around talking and gesturing. As they moved into the firelight, some of the soldiers approached them, and one, dirty, the monotonous color of the land over which he had fought, stopped Sentell.

"Ain't that Major Masterson?" he asked harshly.

His face was a wilderness of untrimmed whiskers which followed the sunken contours of his face and stood like underbrush on the high banks of his dark cheekbones. His eyes were red and a maze of tiny lines ran from their corners into the rubble of his beard. He was hold-ing a pistol at his side.

"Ain't that Major Masterson?" he asked again.

74

"That's right," Sentell told him. "What can I do for you?"

The man's sun-tortured eyes narrowed, and Sentell thought for an instant that the pistol was for him.

"What you kin do fer all of us is say how he got hit."

"They were waiting for him. They ambushed the whole bunch."

The scarecrow turned to his friends. "You hear that, boys?"

"They was sold out," one of the Kentuckians shouted.

"We don't know anything," Sentell said. "All we know is that the major and his men were ambushed out there. I guess the rest either got through or were captured."

"Well, by God," a voice from the rear called out. "I was picketin' right square across from Ord's people tonight, and one of my pards snuck through their lines, bought him some food, and come on back without bein' challenged once. They're all drunk or sleepin' over there. They think it's over, and there wasn't to be no picketin' the swamps unless somethin' special come up. That's what one of 'em tole my pard."

Sentell shrugged. "If that's so, we're no closer to knowing the why of it. Or the who. There's no way to find out."

"Maybe not tonight," the red-eyed whiskered man spat. "But them Yanks are comin' in tomorrow, and if there's talk, I'm gonna hear it. And when we *do* hear, there's gonna be a lynchin' sure as hell has a iron floor."

The rest yelled agreement, and Bouvier, frowning worriedly, came out to quiet them down. "Major Masterson needs sleep," he said. "He said to thank you all, and that he'll be up and ready to ride west with you in a week."

"You tell the major Kaintuck and Missouri and Arkansas'll be waitin' fer him," someone bawled. "We'll all ride outta this rat's nest together."

"You tell him," another yelled.

The group dissolved slowly, and soon Bouvier and Sentell were left standing in the guttering light of a single torch at the entrance to the tent. Bouvier scuffed the dust with his boot. Sentell noticed for the first tine how shabby his tunic had become, how the neck of his collarless shirt was caked with damp filth and perspiration. His hair lay in thick curls over his ears and down his neck, and there were new lines and deeper furrows in his cheeks and around his eyes.

"Charlie," Sentell said, "you look as if you'd campaigned for a dozen years."

Bouvier smiled. "One good campaign can put the marks on you, I guess."

"Is there something extra troubling you?" Sentell asked.

He shook his head slowly. "It's not the surrender," he said. "I've stopped thinking about that. The metaphysics of giving up had me in knots. Now it doesn't matter. I'm going to fight these goddamned butchers behind walls or in fields, in my town or theirs, in uniform or not, by rules of war or with no holds barred. That's settled, and I'm glad to get the thinking behind me. Now all I have to do is react: no decisions, no questions. If they want to meet me with pistols, I'll oblige. If not, I'll shoot them in the back or shoot their children out of their arms. Only the killing matters."

He had said all this without raising his voice, and the expression on his face was as gentle and forbearing as that of a father speaking to his child. Sentell thought, So this is what hate looks like when it is not alloyed with greed, or lust, or any one of the softer virtues.

"They've killed Masterson," Bouvier said matter-of-factly.

Sentell turned toward him quickly. "He was alive ten minutes ago."

Bouvier turned his hands upward in a gesture of pointlessness. "He's still breathing," he said. "But when that week he promised the Kentucky and Arkansas boys is past, he'll be underground – not riding on it."

"I didn't know you were a surgeon."

Bouvier shrugged. "My father is a surgeon . . . among other things. Anyhow, it wouldn't take a medical man to see that."

"Has he lost too much blood?"

"He lost plenty. But it was the fall off his horse that will finish him. No, not the fall: what he fell into. The swamp, the filth. It may be typhoid, it may be his blood is poisoned. But his fever goes up and his strength goes down, and I haven't got so much as a drink of cold water or a glass of herb tea to give him."

"Tomorrow," Sentell said hopefully, "tomorrow the Union doctors will be coming in. They'll have drugs and equipment."

"That's true," Bouvier said. "The Federals will have everything."

He turned to Sentell, speaking earnestly. "Ride north with me. Ride to Forrest with me. We can still make a fight of it, and whatever happens – win or lose – there'll be no questions, no laughter. At least we won't be able to hear it."

Sentell shook his head. At last, frowning, Bouvier stopped arguing.

"All right," he said defensively. "What's their damned parole worth? Half the Union army has signed paroles since Manassas. All they do is shift the parole-jumpers from one front to another. If they get captured in Virginia, they ship them to Tennessee. Should I stand on my word when my people are dying?"

Sentell returned his frown. "You're doing the talking," he said.

"All right," Bouvier went on, hardly addressing Sentell any longer, more nearly involved in monologue with himself. "All right, I can't stand the idea of going back to New Orleans and living under a Union garrison. I can't stand the idea of some of my true-blue Unionist neighbors throwing my own words back in my face. 'Say, Charles, I thought you'd be in Washington City by now. Trip too long for you?' I can't stand the idea of my own father looking at me and wondering why I'm neither victorious nor dead. I can read his mind before he begins to think: *The Old Guard . . . a hundred days of glory worth a thousand deaths. Our blood steeping the soil at Austerlitz and Ulm and Waterloo. My father's father dead by his own hand in the Rue de Constantinople, a tricolor cockade in his hat, a golden N sewn on his epaulets. And this boy home with no wound, no amputation . . . our cause still in the balance. This boy home and keeping to the house like no aristocrat, no merchant, no peddler, no beggar ever spawned by France.* All right, I can't face any of that."

"All right," Sentell said as he subsided, "you measure yourself against one standard; I measure myself against another. Just remember you stand nearer to Masterson than I do. You laughed at his Alamo and can't get from under your own grand gesture. I wish you luck and health for ninety-seven of your hundred days – and wisdom or something like the Alamo for your last three. You can start counting anytime now."

It was dawn, and the tents and dugouts nearby began to empty their occupants into the early sunlight. The men walked stiffly from one fire to the next, talking with their comrades in low portentous voices. Some of the older Negro servants sat in front of their tents and cuffed one another as if they were co-conspirators in some fabulous joke. Most of the officers had put on the best uniforms they had: a number still possessed fine gray coats with gold epaulets and bright flashing on the sleeves. A few managed to dig out an unworn pair of gray flannel trousers. But many of the resplendent coats were matched with homespun britches, or dark blue pants off Union dead, and there were field-grade officers, swords swinging from their waists, who were preparing to march their regiments out to the surrender dressed in plaid cotton shirts and butternut trousers, or in gilt-buttoned Union jackets dyed an execrable dingy gray after having been stripped from Sherman's poor sheep the day after Chickasaw Bluff.

"Well, Major Sentell," Bouvier said with false humor, "you'll be joining your division. What sort of mustering-out pay do you expect?"

Sentell was tucking what was left of his last white shirt into the dirty remains of some cotton britches he had brought from Shreveport. He had no belt. It was tied through the broken spokes of an artillery piece on the far side of the Black River. His hat looked as if an overseer had thrown it away, a field hand picked it up, and then done the same – leaving it for whoever might need a hat that badly.

"Keep him wrapped up," he told Bouvier, "and I'll bring back one of their doctors when the burlesque is done."

V

4 JULY 1863 — Grant's army was drawn up across the Confederate front in brigades. Its officers sat silent, mounted on well-fed horses that pranced and paced in boxlike patterns. Behind them, the infantry ranks, row after row, column on column, stood at attention. The Southerners marched out by divisions because there was not enough left of regimental organization to warrant unit separation. Instead of being executive officer to a regimental commander, Sentell marched ahead of the remnants of seven regiments, the total number of which barely added up to a full-strength regiment and a half.

The Confederates halted, forming a division front opposite the Unions, and one by one, their regimental colors were taken forward and deposited on a ragged corner of tent cloth between the two lines. Then the infantry men stacked their rifles in dozens of nine-piece pyramids and, weaponless, most of them for the first time in three years, fell back into place.

There was no sound but the faraway hollow shout of a regimental commander's order – forward, stack arms, fall in – and the endless undertone of metal against metal, half-shod and bare feet shuffling in obedience, and the occasional snort of a Union officer's horse.

As the last division stumbled back into formation, Pemberton and Grant rode from the ranks, met in the center of the field, and exchanged stiff salutes. Grant, stooped and slovenly, sitting his horse as if he were a tumorous outgrowth of it, gestured up and down the ranks, pointed back at the town, and seemed to invite Pemberton to ride back into his lines with him. The Pennsylvanian shook his head primly and cantered down the Jackson Road toward Vicksburg.

As he left, as Grant turned to look at the Confederates, the Federal troops began cheering. At first, only a single harsh voice – perhaps two – started it, but like a grass fire, unit after unit picked it up and increased the volume of it. Behind him, Sentell's men stirred restlessly. Down the line, a few Confederates were shaking their fists at the Federals. Then, as quickly as it had started, it was over. Grant had cut them off with a single chopping motion of his arms. As he took up the slack in his reins preparing to move off, he lifted his hat to the Southerners, inclined his head slightly, and shouted something to the Union troops behind him.

"Hip hip . . . 'ray . . . hip hip . . . 'ray . . . "

" . . . defenders of Vicksburg," Sentell heard a shrill voice call to them from across the stacked rifles and drooping battle flags. "'Ray the men of Vicksburg."

And before he could grasp what the Federals were doing, Grant had disappeared, and the far end of the Southern line had begun to march back into the empty works around a fallen city.

Union wagons had started to press through the gap in the abandoned works that issued on the Confederate portion of the Jackson Road. The muleskinners, cursing and sweating in the fry of morning sun, seemed each one to be determined to push ahead of the rest. A few troopers, blouses open, neckerchiefs soaked and wrapped around their foreheads, rode up and down the lines trying to keep order, but the attempt was useless.

Sentell stopped one of the troopers, a fleshless hard-eyed man with bad teeth and his yellow neckerchief almost brown with seat and dirt. "No ride, reb. I got to keep these dumb bastards moving."

"I don't want a ride," Sentell called back. "I need a doctor."

The trooper looked him over quizzically. "You're the best lookin' reb I seen since Belle Isle. What do you want with a sawbones?"

"A friend . . ."

"All righty. You go on back down this Jackson Road toward the town. The medical wagons for Ord's people are all past here. They'll be set up somewhere along the road. Look for a red flag at a big house or barn, and for a lot of no-good stragglers standin' around waitin' for a pill."

"I thank you" Sentell said, and began to move away.

The trooper pranced a step or two closer to him. "That's a nice pistol you got there."

"Thanks again."

"I reckon I better confiscate that thing. You ain't supposed to have no side arms. It'd just get you in trouble."

He leaned out of his saddle and extended his hand.

"I'm an officer," Sentell told him.

"Shit," he said, "that don't cut no tobacco. You better just hand it over."

Sentell pulled his pistol and cocked it. "Did you ever disarm a Confederate officer?" he asked the trooper.

"No," he said. "Not a live one."

"Nothing's changed," Sentell said. "If you want the pistol, it'll cost you the usual."

"Yeah," the trooper shot back in good humor. "It'll cost me a hole where I can't use no hole, huh?"

"You've been there, solider."

He saluted and pulled his mount around. "I hope you find that doc," he called, riding headlong at a stalled wagon whose driver had stepped down to urinate against its dusty wheel.

It was a four-mile walk to the nearest medical station. As the trooper had predicted, it was located in a half-burned barn on the outskirts of the town. For every Union solider standing in the yard, there were four or five Confederates, and more lay on makeshift stretchers or were being held erect by pole-thin friends so desiccated that it was impossible to tell the ill from the sound. At the door of the barn, a Union sentry stood at ease, his bayoneted rifle pointed vaguely in the direction of a clump of Southerners gathered near a low stone well.

"I need one of your doctors," Sentell told the sentry.

He looked at Sentell without interest. "Getcha a place an' wait yer turn," he snapped in a Northern accent.

"I can't wait," Sentell said. "A man is dying for want of drugs and treatment."

The sentry smirked and scratched himself. "Jeezus," he groaned, "they been dying without so much as a preacher's whisper for three years. What's different about yers?"

"Are you going to take me to a doctor?" Sentell asked evenly.

The Union sentry turned his rifle, its muzzle pointed a little to one side, the bayonet cutting uneven ovals through the hot morning air. "Naw, he blustered. "Naw. The onliest place I'm likely to take ye is to the provost. Who the hell told you you could march aroun' here like a free man? Yer a stinkin' whipped reb dog, an' if a couple hunnert of you die without no morphia, that'll suit me fine. Now get . . . "

Sentell caught the muzzle of the rifle and jerked the piece from the Federal's hands before he stopped talking. He turned the bayonet toward the Northerner and rested the blade lightly against his throat. The Federal swallowed hard and stared at the injured and sick Union soldiers scattered around the barnyard as if he expected help from that.

"Don't cut his throat, Southron. It ain't worth no prison time," Sentell heard a heavy New England voice say behind him.

"Do cut his throat," another put in. "That greasy-thumbed sonofabitch been keepin' me out here since ever they set up shop. My goddamn leg's black all the way up to the knee. Go ahead, reb. I'll serve half your time or cut the hangin' rope 'fore they swing you."

None of them moved, and only a handful even seemed interested in what was going on. "Turn around," Sentell said, "and march me into a doctor. Pick out the best one."

The sentry turned slowly, trying hard to appear unconcerned. As he opened the door, he said, "I'll get you a damned horse-doctor and see you in hell for this."

Sentell let him have a quarter inch of bayonet in his buttocks. He squealed like a girl, and hopped into the barn, a wave of weak laughter sweeping past them from the yard.

Inside there was a constant hum as if the place were full of mosquitoes or blowflies. The floor, deep in straw, was covered with sick and wounded. Some lay staring at the dark rafters; a few, leaning on elbows, played a desultory game of cards. One man, eyes shining feverishly in the gloom, told his rosary beads in a cracked dramatic voice. A few orderlies in shirtsleeves were stepping carefully from one huddle of rags to another with dripping canteens and bundles of bright bandage.

At the rear of the barn, where the planks had been burned away and the rafters collapsed, the early sun cut tracks through the gloom and reflected off a crude table covered with surgery instruments. A pair of doctors, in Union trousers with butcher's aprons tied around them, was working on an unmoving heap of rags and boots stretched on a long troughlike table. As Sentell watched, one of the boots and the leg wearing it were lifted away from the table and handed to a Negro orderly, who took it gingerly through the broken rear wall.

Beyond the surgeons, among the fallen rafters and planks from the blasted wall, some officers in shirtsleeves sat on campstools around a folding desk and drank from a coffeepot on a tiny fire or from an unlabeled bottle of whiskey. Sentell nudged the sentry and stepped past the mounds of wounded men and the busy surgeons.

"Who commands?" Sentell asked the sentry.

"Colonel Lodge will have yer tail dryin' from one of them rafters," he sneered, glancing around quickly to see if Sentell meant to use the bayonet again.

Stepping up beside the Union, Sentell handed the rifle over. "If you point it at me again, you'd better use it," he said. "Which one is Lodge?"

"The one in the tunic."

Colonel Jonathan Lodge sat with two or three other officers. One of them, collar off and sporting three days' of beard, was thumbing cards into complicated solitaire patterns. The others talked in low voices, not looking at one another, staring out the back of the blasted barn. Lodge paid no attention to them. He was a heavy man, overflowing his uniform and straining its bright buttons. His face, fleshy and meticulously shaved, seemed almost transparent, and visible below the skin was a network of crimson blood vessels and larger bluish veins that gave his cheeks and forehead the appearance of a military map in full color. His eyes were cold grayish-yellow agates, eyes of a lynx, that contrasted almost comically with the quartermaster's insignia on this collar. His lips were thin: they formed a straight unpleasant line the color of his eyes. He was sitting, arms folded in the manner of a baroque painting of royalty, and staring fixedly at the bottle of whiskey in the middle of the table.

"Colonel Lodge, I believe?"

He did not look up when Sentell spoke, although his companions turned at the sound.

82

"I am Major Edward Sentell of the Twenty-Sixth Louisiana Regiment," Sentell went on. Lodge continued to stare at the dusty bottle.

"Major," one of the other officers said with courtesy, "can I help you?"

"Thank you, sir. I came here looking for a doctor. One of my fellow officers was wounded last night, and he needs attention badly."

The man with the cards looked up, his eyebrows raised.

"Last night? Did we shoot him last night?"

Sentell hesitated for an instant. "I can't say it was Federal fire," he finished lamely.

"We're trying to take care of as many of your people as we can here, Major. Could you have your friend brought over?"

Sentell shook his head. "His arm and shoulder are torn, and he fell into some swamp water after he was shot. I'm afraid the movement might finish what the shell began."

Lodge glared up at him suddenly. "Shell? There was no shelling last night . . . except in the woods to the south. The only shellfire last night was directed at some rebels trying to break the truce terms by coming through our lines."

The officer who had spoken first waited until Lodge had finished. Then, mouth tight, he dropped his handful of cards on the table.

"Major," he said, "could you wait a little while? I think it might be possible to send someone with you after we get the first rush of people taken care of."

The officer speaking, Sentell noticed finally, had the insignia of a contract surgeon on the folded tunic which lay near him across a battered sawhorse. Sentell shook his head slowly as the officer finished.

"I don't know," he said. "The man was feverish last night, and he seems worse this morning. Between the pain and the fever, I don't know how long he can hold out."

A scream tore the darkness behind Sentell, and he turned toward the sound, his pistol half drawn. The medical officer laughed without humor. "One of our men just woke up to find he was parted from his leg, I guess."

A moment later, one of the apron-clad surgeons walked out of the shadows toward them. "I swear to God," he said exhaustedly, "one more day like this, and they'll have me on the table."

The surgeon stepped past Sentell and began dipping his bloody hands in a bucket of water already colored a deep scarlet. He scrubbed

83

compulsively and blinked his myopic eyes like an albino exposed to sudden sunlight.

"You tear 'em to pieces and then bring what's left to me," he tossed over his shoulder. "You blast and cut and rip and then bring 'em here like this whole goddamned pestilential circus was for fun and the last thing you ever guessed was that somebody would be torn apart or killed in it."

As he turned from the bucket, his hands continued to rub one another as if they were operating independent of his will. The morning light shattered against his heavy spectacles and made his weak eyes dissolve into edgeless patches of space and color behind.

He walked around the table and sat on the narrow beam of the saw-horse near his companion's folded tunic. He was blond and balding, and his face, like his restless scrubbed hands, was pale and endlessly in motion. "Clarkson, when you finish saving your Union," he said more quietly, "do you think there'll be anyone left to be unified? Or will we have the largest and most varied collection of cripples and hopeless lunatics this side of Tyburn and Bedlam?"

Clarkson, a dark-jawed cavalry officer, stood up. "I've told you to shut your mouth a dozen times on a dozen fields, Robertson. If you open it again against the war, I'll shut it for you myself."

Robertson's pale face went stiff. "Try that," he said. "Try that. If you raise a finger and point it toward me, I'll have you court-martialed before you can bayonet another prisoner."

Clarkson leaned across the table, his hand drawn back to slap the other across the face, but before his hand started forward, another voice froze him in mid-act.

"Gentlemen," Lodge spat, "take your seats again. Your quarrels and feelings make no difference to me, but keep them to yourselves before the enemy."

Robertson began taking off the bloodstained apron carefully, trying not to get his freshly washed hands smeared again. "'But rather the multitudinous seas incarnadine,'" he quoted hollowly.

Lodge was still watching him. Clarkson had irritably lapsed back to the bottle.

Robertson turned to Sentell. "I'll go with you, Major. Give me a minute to gather some things."

As he stuffed vials and instruments and strips of tenting into a leather case, Lodge continued to stare at him.

"Surgeon," Lodge finally said, "are those your instruments?"

Robertson turned from his hurried packing. "What do you mean, Colonel?"

Lodge's cold eyes caught his and held them. "I asked if the equipment you are gathering is your property."

"Of course not," Robertson shot back. "It belongs to the government."

"Then its issue falls under the control of the commissariat."

"All right," Robertson said frowning. "So?"

"So leave the government equipment here," the colonel said. "I prefer it remain here."

Robertson glanced at Sentell, and then walked over to Lodge. "You are forbidding me to go with this man?"

Lodge stared out the shattered rear of the barn as if he could not hear the moans of the wounded or the endless passage of wagons and marching men outside in the Jackson Road. "I am not your superior," he said. "You can go where you please unless ordered otherwise. I am only concerned with government property."

My God, Sentell thought. This is your future. This is the end result of losing a war. They'll make this man President if he manages to escape our bayonets and the bullets of his own men.

"I'll be responsible for the property, Colonel," Sentell said finally.

Lodge looked up suddenly as if he were seeing Sentell for the first time. His eyes, gray mixed with a strain of yellow, gave him the appearance of a peculiar and dangerous animal.

"You? I am supposed to trust you?"

Sentell said nothing.

"You stand there in traitor's rags, weapons about you drenched in loyal blood, and you ask that I trust United States property to you?" His face twisted with hate.

"I would not trust you," he gritted through his teeth, "with the fate of an Indiana fly. I would not trust you with straw or with a dead horse. I would not trust you with a length of rope if you swore on God's testament that you meant to hang yourself with it."

Sentell flushed, and his expression matched that of Lodge. "I withdraw the suggestion," he said shortly. "I thought I was addressing a gentleman."

"Gentleman?" he laughed curtly. "Gentleman? How could I be a gentleman? I have never owned a slave, never bought or sold another human being, never beaten a fellow creature to death with a trace-chain."

"I wonder," Sentell choked, trying to hold himself in check, "I wonder if you might be gentleman enough to satisfy me for those remarks outside."

Lodge's face did not change, but through his thin lips something like contemptuous laughter escaped. "Satisfy you? I hope to God I have a chance to satisfy you with a bayonet on another field."

Before he could think, before he could even consider, Sentell's gloved fist had tumbled Lodge from his chair. Sentell was shouting something, demanding that Lodge arm and meet him outside the barn either now or in the morning, with pistols or sabers or knives or clubs – whatever they used in his damned hogwallow of a home. And then Robertson and Clarkson had hold of Sentell, pulling him away.

Lodge rose and righted his chair with no more show of anger or hatred than before. "Gentlemen," he said, licking away a trace of blood at the corner of his mouth. "I believe this rebel scum has broken the conditions of parole. I think you had better take him to the provost marshal."

Sentell stood almost limp in the hands of the two Federals. He was past anger now, past fear or even hatred, and only Masterson's feverish face and torn shoulder stuck and twisted in his mind.

Clarkson, dark and smelling of cheap whiskey, cleared his throat. He looked toward the others who had said nothing, who had taken no part in any of it. "I didn't see him break no parole," he said as if each word were especially tasty in his mouth.

"I never saw a thing," Robertson said flatly.

Lodge looked at all the others who had been watching. "You saw," he almost shrieked. But both shook their heads slowly and turned their eyes from him.

"You saw," he cried again.

"What I saw," Robertson said, "was a United States officer insult a conquered foe. Then what I saw was that same officer refuse a direct challenge delivered properly. What I saw made me sicker than all those corpses," he finished.

"That's what they'd say where I come from," one of the officers at the table drawled. "'Course Kentucky ain't Massachusetts," he said, grinning outright.

Lodge sat down at the table again, his face purged of emotion. "I can wait," he said. "There are plenty of days, plenty of other times."

Clarkson let go of Sentell's arm and slouched back toward his chair. "I got no love for rebels," he said tartly, "but a brave man's a brave man. And a skunk's a skunk."

"Come on," Robertson whispered to Sentell. "Let's go."

He and Sentell started toward the front of the barn, but Lodge's voice brought them up short.

"Surgeon," he called mildly, "leave that government satchel."

Robertson looked at Sentell. "He could get me two years if I carry this bag out of here."

Sentell shrugged. "I think he would if he could."

Robertson walked back and set the bag on the table in front of Lodge. "I hope I have a chance to render you service one day," he said. It was nearly two o'clock when they reached the tent. Bouvier was seated on one of the campstools, and a handful of butternut scarecrows hovered among the dusty trees in little groups, looking toward the tent as if important orders were about to issue from it.

"Here's a doctor," Sentell said.

Bouvier, who had been looking straight ahead, his eyes lusterless and empty, glanced at Robertson. "Is he any good?" he asked in a monotone. "Because he's going to have to be good."

Sentell felt a quick chill stutter along his pine. "Is he . . . .?"

"Not yet, but the crows can smell him. His shoulder is going dark, and we've been packing him in wet rags since eight o'clock this morning. His head is on fire."

Robertson stepped past them and pushed the tent flap aside. Sentell sat down next to Bouvier, and noticed for the first time that the buttons from his tunic were gone, and that in their place were tiny nubs of freshly clipped thread. He saw Sentell's eyes on him.

"A squad of Yankees came by, handed out paroles for unattached officers to sign, and finished up with a button-twisting ceremony. Regulations, a nigger sergeant told me."

"So . . . "

"So I saw that they were going to make it easy or hard depending on whether I gave them any trouble. I saw that they would as soon go in and stand Masterson up and try to make him sign one of their papers and then claim, since he couldn't sign, they'd have to take him along. So I let the nigger get his buttons, and gave my pistol to some walleyed bastard from Boston who couldn't keep his spittle in his mouth when he said 'rebel.'"

"You did better than I did," Sentell told him.

"How do you get that? You're back with a doctor and you've still got your buttons."

Sentell told him about the run-in with Lodge, about Robertson's having no instruments.

"It may be," Bouvier said slowly, his eyes on the powdery dust at his feet, "it may be that he won't need instruments. I don't think Sam will come out of this."

Sentell felt the chill again. "He's tough. You might not make it. I'm sure I'd go under. But he's tough as an ax handle."

Bouvier looked up, his face drawn and filled with sudden age. "Ed, while you were gone I found another hole in him."

"Another piece of shell?"

Bouvier shook his head. "This one is worse. He doesn't give a damn whether he comes out of that tent or not. His guts are intact, but he's run out of reasons to bite back."

Before Sentell could answer, Robertson stepped out of the tent. His eyebrows made a single troubled line across his forehead. "Your man is in bad shape," he said. "If I had my bag . . . "

Bouvier's eyes narrowed. "You mean the stuff that colonel made you leave in the barn?"

Robertson pre-empted Bouvier's stool. "That's right," he said. "At last I could probe and take out the biggest fragments. I could patch and stich a little. I could clean it up."

"Would it make the difference?" Bouvier asked him.

He shook his head. "I don't know, Major. I honest-to-God don't know. I need anesthetic. I need clean swabbing."

Bouvier turned to Sentell. "I want to see that colonel," he said with exaggerated calm.

"I've got one thing," Robertson went on.

"What's that?"

Robertson held up a small glass vial. "I put this in my pocket while you were bracing Lodge. I couldn't get any instruments out and hide them quickly enough, so I thought . . . "

"What is it?" Bouvier asked him again.

"Nitric acid . . . "

Bouvier looked at Sentell. "What's it for? What good is it?"

"You cauterize wounds with it. You burn them clean." Sentell answered.

"I don't suppose you'd have any ether at all?" Robertson asked apologetically.

Bouvier looked as if he had just noticed the color of Robertson's coat. "No," he said coldly, "I don't suppose we would."

"Can you use it without?" Sentell asked.

Robertson shivered. "I can use it," he said. "But Jesus . . . "

"If it's the pain that bothers you," Bouvier told him, "you can forget it. He's past worrying about the pain."

Robertson, apologetic until then, faced Bouvier squarely. "He's not past the kind of pain nitric acid produces," he said angrily. "Nobody alive is past that kind of pain."

Sentell took hold of Robertson's arm. "If you burn away the bad flesh, will it save him?"

Robertson shook his head. "I don't know. I don't think so. He's burning up. I think his blood has gone bad. But I know we have to clean up the shoulder or he hasn't got any chance at all. The wound has gone bad, and it's pumping poison into his blood. Do you see?"

"We see," Bouvier said. "All right, what do you need that we might have?"

Robertson's eyes went flat again. "I'll need both of you," he said. "You'll have to hold him down when I start swabbing. And if any of the fragments are near the surface, I'll want to take them out, too. You'll have to sit on him. Between the probing and the swabbing, he's going to come apart."

Sentell caught Bouvier's eye. He turned to Robertson, saying not so much to Robertson as to his blue coat, "Do you want to bet on that?" It was a bad hour, and Masterson, sick and haggard and near the end of his endurance even before they started, came very near fulfilling Robertson's prediction. But when it was done, the most the knife or the nitric acid had drawn from him was a moan that he smothered in one shoulder as they cut and tortured the other.

At the end of it, with his shoulder wrapped in clean, freshly boiled linen contributed by the enlisted men, who still came by to stand near the tent and talk in muted tones, he lay somewhere between sleep and waking, his hot body seeming oddly small and delicate on the narrow cot. When they left him in the tent with Cully, his orderly, Masterson was back in Mexico. He lay delirious on the uncomfortable cot, squinting upward into an invisible sun obscured by smoke and cloud, up toward the grim squat fortress where hard-eyed frontiersmen were pounding out the guidelines of a new and unimaginable destiny in the courtyards and dim halls of Chapultepec.

Some of Sentell's men set up a tent for them next to the one in which Masterson lay. Robertson, who had sent a passing Union medical orderly for some clothing, took some of the blankets and made himself a pallet.

"Never leave a patient who needs you," he smiled as he sat down next to the fire. "First rule of medicine."

Bouvier turned a long thin cigar over and over between his fingers. The food and the absence of command pressure had relaxed him a little.

"He's a good man, Doctor. It might be better for your Union if he stays here forever."

Robertson flushed. "I expect the Union can always find use for a good man."

"It's been a hard day," Sentell put in before Bouvier could answer. "I think a little walk might make us feel better. Who wants to walk?"

Bouvier shook his head, and as the sun touched the horizon behind the lines, fell into the earth on the other side of the great river, Robertson and Sentell walked along the works that had held the Union army away from the city for so long.

"Sometimes," Robertson said, "it seemed that we might be here as long as the Greeks were at Troy. Sometimes at night I would stand with a few enlisted men at one of the observation posts and watch our lines for a long while. I would wonder what kind of men were behind those long mounds of earth, those endless hills. I would wonder what we had done to drive you there, and then wonder what you had done to bring us down the length of a continent to force you out of there. I would think of the conventions, the election, the riots in Baltimore – the endless haggling over that heap of rock in Charleston harbor. Negroes, cotton, tariffs, insults, political regionalism. I would take all the words and phrases, all the acts and claims, all the omissions and counterclaims, and add them up. Sometimes I would think for just a moment that I could see your side clearly, that perhaps I was part of a damned conspiracy to oppress a whole land. Another time, I could see our part of it: I could see the ugliness of slavery, the senselessness of gentry.

I could see the tragedy of a single great nation mangled and broken into two endlessly disputing portions.

"Then, filled with the rightness of your side or my side, having added up all the interminable odds and ends that had to be fitted into it, I would get back to the surgeon's tent and they would bring me a boy with his arm off, or an ounce of leaden ball nestling in his broken belly. And I would cut and patch and possibly lose him, feel his life slipping away from me even as I tried to keep it within him. Then, when I finished, when they took him away for the burial detail – or sometimes even if I had managed to close his stump or sew up his belly well enough to keep him breathing – I would go out again and all my political arithmetic, all my certainty would come up along with the hard biscuit and bully-beef and the rest of the swill I'd been feeding on."

Robertson talked on. None of it was surprising, and most of it was no more than a recapitulation of what Sentell had thought since the day he had left Shreveport. Sentell thought how much more difficult Robertson's predicament must be than his own: he was sworn to defend his people, his state; Robertson was sworn to preserve life.

By the time they got back to the regimental area, the darkness was complete. Sentell took a last look toward the old Union lines, thinking how something seemed abnormal, strange. Then he grasped the oddity: there was no red glare in the sky. The darkness eastward was solid and unbroken, and as the pulsing redness was gone, so an immense and overwhelming silence had come over them. There was no rifle fire, no distant artillery, no shouts up and down the line – not even the call of sentries marking every hour. As they moved like two tardy moths toward the campfire, Sentell was thinking that now there were no enemies crouched near Vicksburg. No carefully organized human machines that would tomorrow clash again and grind away a little of the living material that was their substance. There were only groups of tired men sprawled around spotty campfires, eating the same food from the same wagons and perhaps, Northerner and Southerner, exchanging grim remembrance and the careful explanation of soldiers who have seen too much, done too much, experienced too much to really hate their enemies once they have done to them what had to be done. Sentell walked with a Union surgeon as anxious as he to save a man who only hours before probably would have ridden this surgeon down in his desperation to escape the press of Union all around him.

Now what Bouvier had thought of Masterson from the first was at last a reality. Now he was an anachronism, a broken feverish reminder of a battle decided, lost and won.

Bouvier came out of Masterson's tent as they stepped into the firelight.

"He's weak. He can't lift either arm off the cover."

"How about the fever?" Robertson asked him.

"I think it's down."

Robertson frowned. "It has no business being down. The poison is still in his blood."

They went inside. Cully, the orderly, had stopped soaking rags in water and packing them around Masterson.

"Major Sentell, he wants to see you and Major Bouvier. He says he's got to talk to you right off."

Bouvier and Sentell knelt down beside the cot. Masterson's face was pinched with the agony so recently past, and his usual ruddy complexion seemed to have gone crimson as the gusts of high fever swept through his body. His hands, void of color and somehow delicate despite their size, lay crossed on his stomach. The bandaged shoulder looked like a pillow next to his head. He was conscious and his eyes, bright as bullets dropped fresh from the mold, skipped back and forth from Bouvier's face to Sentell's.

"It's over, ain't it?" he said in a diminutive voice that did not belong to him.

"They took our surrender this morning," Bouvier said.

"Fourth'a July?"

Bouvier's dark face flushed even darker. "Yes, Sam," he gritted. "Independence Day."

Robertson's open, unimpressive face was clouded. He dropped Masterson's hand and touched the bandages impotently. Sentell saw him shake his head as the corporal looked at him expectantly. Bouvier's back was to them, and he went on talking to Masterson in a low voice, almost as if he were talking to a beloved woman.

"It doesn't matter, Sam. They hand you a paper and you sign your name to it – or possibly you sign another name to it – and then they turn you loose."

"And then you ride North and find another army of your own persuasion and you break your word," Sentell said.

"Shut your mouth, Ed," Bouvier blazed at him. "Can't you see . . ."

"I can't see so well," Masterson said, as if he had heard nothing but Bouvier's last words. "I can see the tent post and I can see youall's ugly faces, and that little sonofabitch Cully waiting for me to step breaking so he can make off with my horse."

"Major . . . ," the orderly began in a pained voice.

"Anyhow, you don't have to eat him," Masterson said, his voice fading. "Don't eat him."

Bouvier turned to face Robertson. The Union doctor shook his head again. "Maybe an hour," he whispered, almost without sound. "Maybe till morning."

The orderly's shoulders heaved, and he sluggishly moved past Robertson out of the tent.

"I want . . . ," Masterson started. He tried to point toward the brass-bound leather trunk at the foot of his cot. "I want . . . ," he stammered weakly again.

Bouvier moved to the end of the cot and began holding up objects he found in the chest.

Masterson shook his head. "Boots. Them cavalry boots I got . . . in Shiloh from . . . Yankee captain. Jesus, he bled. His shirt and pants wasn't no good. Even . . . in the boots."

Bouvier found the boots under Masterson's clothing, folded and lying in a corner of the tent. "Sentell," Masterson was whispering. "You take 'em. The boots. You go on and wear 'em out. They still got some wear in 'em."

"I'll hold on to them for you," Sentell managed to say. "Until you're ready to go again."

Masterson shook his head. "Don't shit me," he said. "I done seen too much of this. I'll be . . . out of here in an hour."

Then he raised his arm, pointing at the foot of the cot again. "Star," he whispered, his voice choked and dry. Robertson took a cup of water and held his head while he drank. "Star," Masterson said again, his voice stronger. "The star."

"The flag," Sentell told Bouvier. "He wants that flag."

Bouvier rooted in the trunk and lifted the carefully folded Texas banner. He let its folds fall loosely across Masterson's unmoving legs. "Is this it, Sam?"

"Sure," Masterson said, rousing a little. "I ain't too smart. I can't keep all them ideas in my head when I fight. I need something I can see. I need . . . "

93

His vice faded again, and his eyes closed. Robertson dropped to his knees and searched for a pulse, lifted one of Masterson's eyelids.

"He's going to lose this one," he said, looking at them quietly. "Maybe he'll come around again. But the pain . . . "

"The pain," Masterson repeated. "And the knowing about the pain, and the sorrow for what they'd done, and then the flag and the cheering and pain. Sure you could see through the mist and smoke. You could see because you had to see. You could see it catch the breeze and wave over the top of the world and make the blood and the pain right. You . . . "

Masterson rose on the cot, his eyes wide and fiery, his head moving from side to side as he tried to find a familiar face. He stared past Robertson and Sentell without recognition, and turned to Bouvier.

"Charlie," he said clearly, strongly. "You take it. You know what to do."

His hand groped for the flag. You take it," he almost shouted. "You goddamned well know what to do. Draw yourself a line in the dirt, you know."

"I hear, Sam."

"Tell 'em you need 'em. Show 'em this. You show 'em this. Remember," he rasped. "You hear me? Remember . . . "

Masterson's eyes flared and his voice stopped. He fell backward, his body's sudden movement guttering the single candle near the cot as Robertson caught him in his arms and Masterson's fumbling hands caught spasmodically in the surgeon's rumpled tunic.

Bouvier stood up as Robertson touched Masterson's eyelids gently. The candle shook again as he moved, and cast long distorted shadows across the sunken canvas wall of the tent. Bouvier pulled his buttonless tunic together mechanically and turned to Sentell.

"Do you want me to get some men?"

For a moment he did not trust himself to answer. Then, clearing his throat, Sentell shook his head. "No. Just a couple of spades and tent-half, if someone wants to give it to you."

Robertson looked up from the cot, his eyes glistening in the wavering candlelight. "I can get a pine . . . "

"No," Bouvier said with precise courtesy. "No, you've done enough."

VI

5 JULY 1863 — Then the ground mist was beginning to fall away, skipping between tree trunks, nuzzling depressions and juts of weed and bush. Without cloud, without more than the least gust of morning wind from the river and the mute stammer of drying leaves above, the horizon eastward began to break into dawn. In the regimental area, tents were coming down. Dugouts carved into hillsides or flatland and covered with scraps of timber and heaped dirt were beginning to empty of anonymous identical men, unshaven, unsmiling, ragged and bent with loss and hunger and fatigue. A growing line of them had begun shuffling down the Jackson Road toward town, and on either side of the road, near campfires banked with coffeepots and skillets full of bacon, in curious unsneering groups, the Union infantrymen watched the line pitch forward and halt, lurch a dozen yards more, and pause again.

Then, under a spread of ash and cypress a few yards from the regimental area, they were burying him. A half-dozen Missouri and Kentucky troopers armed with Union spades were digging him a grave in the soft earth while beyond the trees their fellows marched from mist into dust, stumbled endlessly toward the west.

Without a coffin, wrapped in a square of borrowed canvas (and even that borrowed finally from a Yankee sutler whose business had so expanded in the chaos of victory and defeat that he could not resist an openhearted show of kindness toward those rebels who had, albeit unwittingly, filled his cup to overflowing), they laid him in the dark root-choked earth, and as they lowered him a handful of troopers who had yet to make their pilgrimage to town slouched past the open grave, each one saluting and crumbling a handful of moist soil into the raw narrow pit. A burial deferred, Bouvier might have said. A burial twenty – no, thirty years late, and on the wrong side of the wrong river after all.

When they had finished, it occurred to Sentell that Bouvier had not appeared at all – that he had not seen him from the moment the Union surgeon had closed Masterson's eyes the night before. But there was no mystery in it, and his absence meant nothing. He would have risen early, ridden into town on Masterson's stallion with Cully by his side and his saddlebags packed with a Texas flag and whatever supplies he could manage – more supplies than he could possibly require for the trip by steamer down to New Orleans – would have smiled blandly and signed his parole, bantering, perhaps, about the fortunes of war and how peace at any price whatever has its compensations and attractions. And then, with the mechanics of deception behind him, he would have ridden carelessly, openly toward the north, confiding in some sentry how long and difficult the road to Memphis, his home, would be, and possibly even getting more supplies for his graciousness.

Behind him, Sentell could hear the Kentucky and Missouri troopers pounding a cross of nailed stakes into the loose mound with the blade of a shovel. Now it was done, and there was no more reason to avoid the road, to watch the long dismal column instead of joining it. So he shouldered a pair of saddlebags filled with the trivia collected in two years of service and started toward Vicksburg, where clean-shaven, neatly dressed young lieutenants sat stiff and upright in their new importance, issuing paroles to defeated rebels like high-toned spinsters dishing soup to derelicts in a New York river ward, each cardboard soldier proud of the weight of his epaulets, conscious of the burgeoning of their powerful ruthless new nation, and of the long terrible dying of the old.

The homecoming was worse than the battle or the losing of it. All the way across Louisiana those early July days in 1863, Sentell had to face people who had placed their lives, their futures, their honor in the Confederate army's hands. A captain from Minden, half his face swathed in clean Union bandages, rode beside Sentell on a mule he had purchased from a corrupt Federal quartermaster. The same quartermaster from whom Dr. Robertson had bought Sentell's horse.

"It's like being drummed out of the service," the captain said. "All but the button-clipping."

"The Federals did some of that when they first came in," Sentell told him.

"Button-clipping?"

"They clipped some, and confiscated all the personal property they could lay hands on."

"But the worst part," the captain went on, "the worst part is the people along the way. Instead of turning their backs on us, instead of accusing us, they . . . "

Instead of anything else, as they passed through little towns, and towns only large enough to dream of being cities, through nameless unmarked crossroads huddles of raw houses and unpainted cabins, the people would gather beside the road in silent unblaming groups. An old man would wave his cane, a small boy would hold a Confederate battle flag as high as his short arms would permit. Women, wives of men in other regiments on other fields – or under them – would stand quietly, hands wrapped in tattered aprons, lips bitten against their anguish, and watch as they passed. Sometimes Sentell could hear their voices, soft and almost blending with the hot summer breeze.

"Did all you could, men."

"God bless your families. God bless you. God bless . . . "

"Did well, Johnny Rebel. Give all you could . . . "

"Be another day, Johnny."

And near Delhi, an old woman, with the help of a Negress as old as herself, had brought a table down to the edge of the road. She sat watching the men riding or walking footsore and broken, and on her table were great crystal pitchers full of cold spring water, and a dozen or so unmatched glasses. Near the water were a diminishing plate of corn pone and a half-empty jar of Loganberry jam. She said nothing unless a soldier, pausing for a drink, should thank her while the old Negress poured. Then she would smile shyly.

"I had buttermilk this morning, son. I wish I had some more."

"Ma'am, the water is best. Good fresh water is best."

Men with full canteens and five hundred miles of Louisiana and Texas left to cross stopped and passed the time of day, took water, and gently refused to reduce that tiny heap of cornbread by so much as another piece.

"My son," she told the captain and Sentell, "my only son is imprisoned in the North. He was too old to go, too old to run fast or march long. Do you think some lady there will . . . ?"

"I'm sure of it, ma'am," the captain told her as he set his empty glass down. "Our respects, ma'am. Our thanks."

At the end of the second day, they came to Minden. After a night in the captain's home with his wife and family torn between happiness at his return and gloom at the surrender, Sentell began the last thirty miles alone. There were others riding or walking, but each one seemed unconscious of his fellow travelers. Each one was locked into his own thoughts and miseries and forebodings, and they continued westward under the looming sun like pilgrims on their way to a terrible shrine . . . not out of love but from necessity.

It was almost twilight when he reached the Red River ferry. Beyond the narrow sluice of dark brown water that summer had left in the channel, a blood-red sun had slid underground, leaving Shreveport bathed in a sickly afterglow, making the town look somehow as if it were encircled by a dark fire that burned without consuming. There were only a few of them for the trip over, and without a word passing among them, they sprawled on the flat barge deck while the ferryman, a wizen Negro freeman, tended fishing lines that he kept hanging over the sides. They waited for the crimson glow to subside, waited for night. They would ride into Shreveport after dark.

BOOK TWO

... The Arms of the South ...

*So the king of the north shall come, and cast up a
mount, and take the most fenced cities; and the arms of
the south shall not withstand.*

—DANIEL 11:15

I

SHREVEPORT, LA: 6 JUNE 1865 — Colonel Jonathan Lodge shivered slightly in the chill spring downpour, and squinted along the line of troops and wagons ahead. The column had unaccountably slowed down, and the rain, which had followed them for two days, still fell. It would lessen in intensity, drizzle softly for an hour or so, and then mount again into a torrent. Even in the intervals between heavy gusts, the rain fell heavily enough to obscure the head of the column where it entered the town's main street.

Vicksburg was a year and ten months behind the colonel, and even the chill rain could not diminish his pleasure in the new infantry insignia on his collar or in the prospect of being military commander of a garrison that would pacify and order the last principal Southern city over which the Confederate flag had flown.

Even if his new post had not been assigned him as a recognition of merit (the truth was, and Lodge knew it, that with the fighting ended and the army shrinking like ice in springtime, the War Department could not pick and choose among the few officers of rank who remained to command garrisons all over the conquered South), there would be pleasure in it. There would be a great deal to do, and the doing of it would be in his hands. General Philip Sheridan would command the district from New Orleans, but Sheridan was no molly-coddle: his leisurely incendiary trip through the Shenandoah Valley had shown that. Sheridan would leave things with his local com-manders, and at least one of his local commanders would deliver with a vengeance.

Shreveport had held out too long. Even after the arch-rebel Lee had surrendered, after Johnston and Richard Taylor – even after Nathan Bedford Forrest had given way – the town and its commander had held on. For almost two months these people had kept the rebel flag flying. Now it was down, and Colonel Jonathan Lodge would make them wish it had never been raised. He would make rebellion terrible to them. He would fasten the guilt of chattel-slavery around their necks so that the memory, the shame of it, would not diminish for a hundred years.

There are all kinds of monuments, the colonel thought. There are bronze and granite monuments, and there is the kind I will erect here.

A passing wagon driver cursed his mules and cracked his whip over their streaming backs. The wagon and caissons lurched and slid and stalled in the thick mud. The mules, worn down by too many miles in too short a time, their hoofs clotted with mud, no longer paced but simply slid forward through the stew of the road. Every few miles the column had lumbered to an unscheduled stop as some of the animals lowered their heads and bore the lash and the rain, refusing to more on.

The line of soaked and footsore men had stopped completely now, and Lodge began spurring his own tired mare along the narrow width of grassy shoulder between the road and a deep ditch. Men watched him ride past without raising their heads. They squatted in the road, their buttocks almost in the mud, their hands pulled beneath water-proof capes, and watched Lodge's mare negotiate the slippery edge of the road until he reached a point midway up the line, well into town, where buildings closed in on either side, and Lodge's horse began to slide in the deep treacherous ruts of the street.

One of his officers, a young lieutenant only weeks from West Point, rode up beside him. His face was pale in the gray morning light, and even under the brim of his campaign hat, Lodge could see moisture on his forehead.

"They'll be moving again in a minute, sir," Lieutenant Raisor said. "One of the guns . . . "

"If you need more people, get some of those loafers," Lodge said, pointing at the porch of Cleburne's store where four or five men still sat watching the Unions in the street. Another man on the edge of the sidewalk was pulling on a black broadcloth coat and kicking mud from his high cavalry boots.

"I got what help we need, Colonel," Lieutenant Raisor said quickly. "We'll be moving now. The stables are up there, at the head of Texas Street."

"I know where they are," Lodge cut him off. "I want you to get these men there. Tell Sergeant Packard to see the animals are cared for before any of these people lie down to rest. Tell him to post sentries up and down the street. And tell him to organize patrols."

"Yes, sir," Raisor said and, as he wheeled his mount to join the column, it began to move again, to lurch forward slowly, uncertainly through the liquid street.

The two men ate an early lunch and dressed in their least shabby coats while the rain fell outside. Then they had pulled wicker chairs back from the edge of the porch and placed a bottle of brandy and four glasses on a weathered unsteady table between them.

One of them was white. There were not many like him. In less time than anyone could guess, there would not be any more like him at all. A leonine edifice of a man just past fifty who had lost his left arm almost two decades before, in another country: Amos Aurelius Stevens' face was burned the color of mahogany paneling by a lifetime under the sun. Not only his six feet three inches and deep color, but the sharp lines of his nose and chin made his oldest friends wonder if an earlier Stevens back in Virginia had not had more than casual conversation with an Indian maiden. (One had: lost in time and name except for an approximation of birth, that Stevens had lost his English wife in the dank fever land along the Chickahominy where it runs into the James River, and had taken to wife an Indian girl whose beauty and strength had more than made up for the resultant loss of position he had suffered in the eyes of other colonists. Six generations had passed, but the Indian maiden lingered.) Amos Stevens' eyes, recessed between overhanging brows and high Asiatic cheekbones, had given him an appearance of incisive wisdom long before that wisdom arrived. There was even a faint slant to his eyes and some of those same friends noted that he resembled nothing so much as John C. Calhoun gotten on some Tartar princess by a Shawnee brave.

The other man on the porch was black. Rye Crowninshield was almost as tall as Amos Stevens, but with a stringy build that seemed to distribute height and weight so as to minimize both. His hair was curly gray and cropped close to his head. Time had been kind to him, and the planes and curves of his face were firm and unlined except for a labyrinth of tiny thread-thin wrinkles around his eyes. He was dressed like Amos Stevens, in a black frock coat with shiny sleeves and a blinding white boiled shirt, frayed and thin as paper from long wear.

They had said so much to each other for so many years. Now the silence was good. Rye Crowninshield let his eyes close as he folded his arms across his chest without touching the shirtfront. The rain had tapered to a gentle shower, and spring sun had begun to show through the broken clouds. The sun was warm on his face. It made him remember the long hilarious summers on the island, summers of calico and fish, rice Sundays and bells on a passing cart full of men in knee britches and white wigs, ladies weighted down under voluminous skirts and piled hair, protected from the overwhelming sun by gauzy parasols. He could remember the wharfs cluttered with British and Dutch ships, the long impossibly white and perfect Jamaican beaches covered with jewel-like shells and delicate branches of seaweed, the water rolling inward toward him like a blue blanket pulled up the length of a bed by invisible hands.

Even with the clouds beginning to break up, there was a chill in the air, and Rye hunched his shoulders against it.

"Cool," he said. "Pleasant an' cool."

"I know it's cool," Amos muttered. "Cool and yet to be cold."

"He be home in good time."

Amos Stevens gripped the arms of his chair until the gray flesh of his hands went pale. "Good time," he repeated abstractedly. Then he turned to Rye. "When will we see a good time again? Even if they both get home. When will we see a good time again?"

Rye stared into the wide unkempt weed-filled yard. The oaks and gum trees were fully leafed now, and the rain had darkened their trunks above the whitewash that circled each one from root-level to the height of a man's shoulder. There were still rosebushes, thick bright-leaved gardenia bushes, and beds of similar flowers, but none of them had been pruned, and only the vegetable garden behind the house had received any care since winter.

He knew Amos was thinking of his son: Linus Morrison Stevens, who was somewhere in Virginia, so far as either of them knew. Possibly walking across the burned and violated Virginia earth. Or possibly below it. They had last heard from him in the beginning of April – the briefest of letters from a town south of Richmond called Petersburg, where the Army of Northern Virginia had been entrenched for nine months.

They both had sons, Rye was thinking, and Amos had been lucky in his. Whether Morrison came home or not, he had lived honorably, had gone to the defense of his people. Then there was Phillipe. Who, living or dead, was no long his father's son.

"Anyhow, yo' boy be home," Rye said evenly. "God spare de just."

Amos squinted across at him. "What about your boy? What about Phillipe?"

Rye's expression stiffened. "I dunno. Maybe God spare even traitors, too."

Amos shrugged and reached for the brandy stopper. "I give up on you. You owe your son love whether he did right or not. Every man owes his son love."

Rye pushed his glass across the uneven table top. "Mahn owe what he think he owe. I keeps my own books. You got a son who fought fo' his people. I got one who went over to de Yankee. I owe him somethin' fo' de shame. If he get home, I see if I can pay him for dat."

Amos shook his head slowly and sniffed his brandy. "I give up on you," he said again. "I should have given up on you twenty years ago in Mexico."

Rye lifted his own glass and shivered as the fierce liquor sluiced down his throat. "We ain't goin' around on dat another time. I done heard all I mean to hear on dat. It didn't signified nothin' then, and it don't signify now."

But as Amos leaned back sipping his brandy, Rye was thinking of that day, of how much it had signified. We come to one another that day, he thought. We had loved and fought and worked and wed together. From the time we was old enough to know what a friend was, we was all the friend the other needed. But that day we come to one another, and that day was worth all the other days put end to end.

That day worth all the rest had been the 13th of September, 1847. They had been with a Louisiana volunteer regiment outside the fortress of Chapultepec. It was a long way from New Orleans, from their wives and children, from the plantation their joint efforts had begun to hack out of the swampy wilderness east of the city. Neither of them had much use for the war with Mexico, but there was duty – not enforced by draft or conscription, but implanted from childhood. And duty had to be discharged.

Between them and the fortress was a Mexican company dug in across the road and firing whether there were targets or not. Above, the sun burned relentlessly, and some of the men, still tired from long marches and frequent battles, were beginning to fall out of ranks.

"If dey wants dat 'trenchment reduced, dey better get on with it," Rye said.

Amos and Rye were squatting behind a pile of quarried stone with some other privates. American artillery had pounded at the Mexican earthworks from a distance, but there had been no results, and the Mexicans still held fast.

"They're just stirrin' the dust," someone said.

"Makin' the Mexes mad, too. Them greasies is goin' to be layin' for us when we got to foot it down the road," another said.

Amos examined his pistols and glanced over his shoulder where their captain was hunched behind a tree talking to another officer. The rock Amos was leaning against was hot, but he had not noticed it. Too much excitement, too much tension. A Mexican ball sang off the top of the rock, and somehow Amos kept from flinching at the sound. Rye crouched a little lower and tried to move his shotgun to a more comfortable position. They hadn't given him a musket: the army didn't supply slaves – didn't, in fact, recognize them as combatants. So Rye took to the field with a fowling piece Amos had brought along hoping for a shot or two at the kind of Latin bird with tail feathers bright enough to grace a lady's hat. It was a good shotgun, but there was no reach to it, and anything hit by it farther than thirty yards away was simply unlucky. Now Rye had it between his knees, and the hammers were pressing into his thigh. He tried again to stand up just a little – far enough to free the gun.

"Drop, goddamnit," one of the soldiers yelled from behind him. "If'n they cain't shoot, they ain't blind. You want 'em to dust us with a shell or two?"

"Can't see a feller lettin' his nigger come up here anyways," another complained.

"Got to have their darkie," a thin buck-toothed soldier with a Northern accent put in. "Got to have their uniforms brushed before they charge."

Amos turned in the dust, setting his back against the hot stone. He faced the rest of the platoon while Rye slipped the shotgun from under his leg.

"I don't need any smart noise out of youall," Amos rasped. "When we finish these Mexicans, I just may get my uniform dusted off and put a bullet in a couple of you."

"Let it go," Rye whispered, embarrassed.

"Might touchy about that nigger," one of the soldiers grinned unpleasantly.

"Touchy your ass," Amos shot back. "I don't want any of you trash making comments about me – not good comments or bad – and none about my man. We pull our weight."

The Yankee snickered. "Southern gennelman's saying he don't want anything to do with us. He'd rather had intercourse with his nigger there."

"Intercourse," another one laughed outright.

Amos went for him as Rye dived for Amos, and a volley of shots came from the Mexican trenches. Everybody fell flat till the firing died away.

"Don't get in front of me when we go up against them Mexes," the Northerner spat across the dust at Amos. "I might decide to put you and your nigger both out of business."

"Mahn get killed a dozen different ways out here," Rye said easily. "Even suicidin' by his own mouth, I reckon."

The captain broke it up without even realizing it. He crawled over from the ratty little grove of trees and began talking without noticing the tension in the hollow space behind the rocks.

"If they don't give way, we're going on in," he said excitedly. He was young for a captain in that army that had been so long at peace, and the only combat he had seen before Vera Cruz had been against a parcel of demoralized Indians in the Florida swamps. "There'll be a section of artillery coming up, and more infantry. The artillery will try to pin them down until we can get in amongst them."

"Awright," someone said. "I'd as soon get shot as roast to death. Another hour in this sun . . . "

It was a scarf tied to the end of a cannon swab. A young Mexican officer stood atop the earthen parapet waving it back and forth vigorously.

"They want a parley," the Northerner said.

"Reckon it's hot over there, too."

"Hope he go away," Rye whispered to Amos.

"Who?"

"Cap'n. Dem Spanishes got tricks enough fo' a medicine show. What if dey jus' want to draw us out, see what we got?"

"No sense in it," Amos said while the captain paused to drink from his canteen.

"No sense in holdin' out, far as dat go," Rye said. "Dey bound to know it all up. Might be dey jus' wants a few more of us 'fore dey give it up."

"Suicide," Amos said. "We'd kill every one of them if they fired on a white flag."

"Well," Rye said dubiously. "Well . . . "

"You've just gotten chary of your hide," Amos smiled.

"Yo' hide," Rye smiled back just as warmly. "You owns it. Like de man say."

Amos flushed under his sweat. "Not that again. Not even joking – and not here funning or serious."

"Sorry," Rye answered with something like contrition. "Forgets my place."

Amos grabbed his arm. "Stop it. Stop it or start back to the camp. I've got Mexicans and maybe even a couple of Yankee white men to worry about. I'm not going to add you to it."

Rye looked at his dust-streaked earnest face. This time the sorrow was real, and there was some of it for all of them: the Mexicans, the whites, Amos, himself. "I'm sorry. It was de talk. Like I was some roasted meat, or somebody's clown."

Amos shook his head and turned toward the captain, who was gargling a last mouthful of water and spitting it in a thin jet onto the light colorless dust.

"All right, Stevens," the captain was saying, "you and I . . . and Frank Worley, you come too. Leave your weapons here and let's see what they have to say."

"Shouldn't we ask . . . ?" Amos began.

"Oh what's the matter?" Worley, the Northerner, asked mildly. "Haven't you had a chance to get your boots licked by your nigger?"

"Let's go," the captain cut in.

They rose from behind the rocks and started across the flat pebble-strewn ground toward the Mexican officer, who stood in the road now with a black and white shako on his head, and the white flag limp and motionless at the end of the swab. The Mexican officer was young, and his dark eyes moved from one to another of the Americans. Sweat was pouring down his beardless cheeks and into his unbuttoned collar. He licked his lips and glanced over his shoulder at his own lines where no heads were visible.

Worley squinted in the direct rays of the sun. "I don't give a damn for that fella's looks."

"I don't reckon he likes yours any better," Amos said in a hoarse whisper. "He looks decent."

"Shut up," the captain said. "We don't want to seem shifty."

They reached the Mexican officer. He wanted terms. He was, he said, not prepared to surrender. In fact it might be the gringos who would have to surrender ultimately. But he would consider terms, he told them in broken English.

The captain told the Mexican officer that he was not empowered to discuss terms. He could accept only unconditional and immediate surrender.

"Or the general commanding proposes to move on your works at once. There will be a great deal of bloodshed," the captain told him. "But nothing will be changed. At the end of it, you will lose and we will win. We are on three sides of the fortress. When it falls, we will be behind you."

The young Mexican shook his head vigorously. Chapultepec would not fall, he said. There could be a discussion of peace terms, but not simple surrender. There was honor . . .

"You have fought with honor," the captain told him. "You have fought with much honor."

But to surrender in the field, the Mexican said. To surrender in the field with ammunition in one's weapon. Possibly an armistice.

"Let's get on with it, goddamnit," Worley whispered loudly. "Between the sun and those Mexican guns I feel pointed at me, and this sonofabitch's gabbling, I'm wrung out."

"Shut up," the captain said without turning around. As the young Mexican began talking again, Amos noticed a large brown stain on the tunic just above the belt. As he looked at it, it seemed the dark patch was spreading slowly. Then, while the captain's voice went on patiently, quietly explaining the situation again, Amos saw that the young Mexican was crying. The tears blended with sweat as it poured down his face, but two thick rills of tears ran down either side of his nose, and his smooth unshaven face was like that of a child faced for the first time with a tragedy.

"That sonofabitch is sniveling," Worley said, noticing the same thing. "There's your raising for you."

Amos held himself in check. "You ignorant bastard," he said in low measured tones, "It's his country he's holding in his hands. If he quits, we can walk into the City of Mexico. You don't hand over your country like a sack of potatoes.

There was the sound of horses behind them, and the rattle of something being pulled by the horses, but Amos was too taken up with watching the Mexican to turn and look.

"And a piss pour country it is, too," Worley was saying. "A sack of potatoes would be better than a fair trade for . . . "

But Amos saw the young officer's expression change suddenly from shocked pleading to alarm, and then to anger. "*Pérfido*," he shouted, turning toward his own lines and barking out commands in an impossible Spanish staccato that no English-speaking tongue could match. Amos turned toward the sound behind in time to see horses cut loose from gun carriages, and the swift efficient American gunners passing powder and shot from caissons, ramming it home in the brass pieces and turning the guns toward the Mexican lines – where, on order, the enemy infantry had begun to flood out of its trenches to counterattack before the fresh American artillery could finish them off.

"No!" Amos shouted. "No!"

But even as he called out, the Mexicans began firing, and the young officer had closed with Amos' captain. Worley, unarmed and terrified, turned and began running back for the rocks, screaming out in his high voice, "Let 'em have it. Cover me, goddamnit. Let 'em have . . . "

Worley had almost reached the rocks when a pair of Mexican riflemen, kneeling quickly and firing their long, antique flintlocks, brought him down.

"No!" Amos called out again, and began running toward the artillery section which had loaded half its pieces with solid shot for use on the enemy lines, but which was hurriedly finishing its preparations with canister to hold off the charging infantry.

"No!" Amos shouted, running, his arms waving above his head. "No, it's a flag of truce. They think we . . . "

And the men of a New Hampshire volunteer battery were treated to the unbelievable spectacle of an American in a dirty private's uniform running toward them at the head of a wave of Mexican infantry.

"What the hell is that?" one of the gunners called across the glittering barrel of his piece, but the voice of the lieutenant cut his question off. "Fire," the lieutenant bellowed, and the artillerist's sight of the

109

ground in front dissolved into a billowing tide of smoke and dust, and the sound of his own voice was drowned in the assertion of his guns.

Rye was on his feet and running, the shotgun's butt striking the rocky earth at every other bound, its barrel alternately pointing at the blue cloudless sky above and at his lower jaw. The dust rolled on every side of him, and when he ran clear of the dust, coils of thick blue smoke twisted and curled around him. Running through the smoke and dust on his left were Mexican soldiers in their white or tan *comisas* and baggy trousers, and one or two officers in lacquered hats and gray uniforms with scarlet trim. They glanced at him in surprise, never breaking their stride, and ran on past wondering possibly if he were a courier from some other regiment, or an imbecile farmer lost in the midst of his ravaged land.

The artillery had not stopped. It was all canister now, and the farther Rye ran, the clearer he could hear the vicious depthless drone of the central projectile as it disintegrated, spewing its hoard of lead balls in a lethal pattern yards wide. He discovered himself slowing down, and once, as a ball actually plucked at his coat, he felt his body quiver, and the strength pour out of his legs like water from a sprung keg.

Then he burst out of the smoke to find himself behind the Mexicans. They had gotten in among the artillery in a brave suicidal dash, but more American infantry was pressing up to cover the gunners' defense, and now the little patch of riflemen in the dry leafless trees and scattered rocks from which Rye had run were able to see the Mexicans' right flank and fire directly into it. Some of the fresh American infantry had smashed past the trees and rocks on the far side and were beginning to overrun the handful of Mexicans left in the trench across the road. Now there was no place to fall back. They began to break, and to move down the road in the direction from which they had come. They could not tell yet that they were being fired upon from their own works.

When Rye found Amos he had somehow managed to rise to his knees. His face and upper body were covered with blood and dust, but his lips were moving, and as Rye bent to him, he could hear the croaking shadow of Amos' voice saying over and over, "No, it was a flag of . . . they thought our guns . . . O for Christ's sake don't . . . no . . . "

And he would not be still even when Rye had managed to lower him to the ground again, and while Rye pulled the ramrod from his fowling piece and ripped loose the tail of his shirt to make a tourniquet, Amos kept on waving his right arm and the broken stump of his left as if to call back all the shells fired and bring to life by his delirious gesture the Mexicans whose corpses littered the ground on every side of him. Even when his fever began to break and Amos' delirium gave way to what approached rationality, the Mexican nuns could not get Rye out of the tiny windowless stone cell (which was all the hospital had left for private soldiers, what with American and Mexican officers and gentlemen having taken over the suites and airy rooms above). Once an army doctor gave Rye a direct order to vacate the pair of filthy blankets and the disintegrating knapsack he had piled on the floor at the foot of Amos' narrow cot.

"You can't order me in," Rye told the surgeon with direct eyes. "You can't order me out. On top of dat, you can't send fo' no soldiery to do de job. I belongs to dis mahn. You want to mess wid a sick soldier's property? Why don't you go to pickin' his pockets?"

The doctor shrugged, and went out to tell the good sisters that it would probably be as well to let the mad Negro alone.

"You get that kind sometimes," the surgeon told the mother superior.

"May God spare him, the poor black," a young nun with wide dark beautiful eyes said in horror. "The *norteamericano* must be a monster beyond description."

Within a few days Amos was well enough to sit up – and to take an instant dislike to the cell. "It looks like an undertaker's workroom," he told Rye weakly. "Let's get out of here."

"You ain't got no strength," Rye told him. "You can't go nowhere yet."

"If I stay here, I'll get some pneumonia and not ever leave."

Rye shrugged and kicked the blankets and knapsack beneath the cot. "All right," he said. "We can give it a try."

They walked out with no nun, young or old, to challenge them. Amos wondered if he should go back to the regiment.

"Dat stump ought to serve fo' a discharge," Rye said, "wid honor."

"I reckon," Amos said. "I've had enough of this soldiering anyhow. We've whipped them and I've got me a remembrance of the war. I reckon we can go home."

"Most folks take something away from a place to remember it by," Rye grinned sadly.

"Well, we're leaving a few things," Amos said as they walked slowly toward the center of the city.

"I see what yo' leaving'," Rye said. "What yo' gonna have me put behind?"

Amos grinned with no sadness at all, and handed Rye a folded piece of paper.

"It was in my duffle along with that letter from Kathy. They would have come across it if you'd ever let them come close enough to me to find anything at all."

Rye opened it. It was dated the day of their landing at Vera Cruz:

I, Amos Aurelius Stevens, do hereby declare that the man Rye Crowninshield, late of the Indies and Virginia, my lawful bound servant, be manumitted and made free altogether along with his wife Saranne and his son Phillipe Crowninshield, and all subsequent issue. I also ask that, in the event of death and in return for his loyal service, my heirs do hand over to him either title to one fifth of my estate near New Orleans, or a sum of money equal in value at such earliest time as this be possible. I ask this be done by my survivors that the man I best loved in life should not be made a free beggar by my death, for I would not remove him from one kind of slavery only that he fall victim to another.

Done by me this 9th day of March, 1847
Amos Aurelius Stevens

Witness:
J. A. Porterfield, Capt. USV
Charley Pomeroy, Pvt. USV

Rye held the paper as if it were brittle glass, or a piece of the most delicate china. He remembered later that at first he had felt nothing at all, and then when he could feel again, when at least the first solid meaning of the words had touched him, he had felt not joy or elation but only a surge of love and oneness with Amos Stevens that had battered his self-control into pudding and sent his hands to shaking like trapped sparrows. It's too late, he remembered thinking. Or too soon. Or maybe I'm the wrong man. Maybe some men are born for bondage and lust for freedom until it comes, and then shrink back like women faced with a snake. I never really thought about it, and now it don't mean anything.

"Of course, I'm not dead yet," Amos went on. "So only the freedom part counts. If you want the land, you'll have to work for it. Or I can lend you some money if you want to try your wings up north in Pennsylvania or New York."

It's like a man born with a stone on his back, Rye remembered thinking. Born with a stone on his back, grown up with it there. Used to it like it was part of him. And then somebody takes away the stone and the man falls for the lack of its weight, and he's afraid to stand up and feel how it will be without the stone. Afraid to stand up for the giddiness. Lord God, and he's got to stand up because they done thrown the stone away, and anyhow what kind of man asks for a worthless burden back? What kind of man can't live without an affliction?

"Seems you might say something," Amos broke into his thoughts. "You've been poking around about freedom for twenty years off and on, one way or the other. Now you've got it, and you haven't even got a set speech ready telling your old master to go to hell?"

Rye heard only the last part clearly, and when it shook itself out in his mind, the final reserve of control gave way completely. He started to cry. In the middle of a plaza in the center of the City of Mexico, he stood bent like an old man, and the tears flooded his eyes and kept coming and kept coming even after Amos had steered him to a bench and begun talking to him as if he were a child who had suffered some enormous and unaccountable loss.

"It's all right," Amos said. "Listen, it's all right." He paused and looked embarrassedly around at the Mexicans, who had paused to see the tall one-armed white man and the tall sobbing Negro on a bench in the middle of their city.

Then Amos thought of this same scene transplanted to New Orleans – with his factor, his tailor, his merchant acquaintances and possibly his father-in-law in the watching crowd.

"O Lord," he groaned. "In New Orleans. O Lord, think of it in New Orleans."

Somewhere behind the tears and the confusion, a part of Rye's mind was unaffected enough to hear and make sense of that. Like Amos he saw himself in front of the Custom House or in the street before St. Louis Cathedral. And the tears began to change into laughter. At first, the sobs and the laughter were of a piece, but the more he imagined his old fisherman friends stopping in the street to watch his performance, the more his laughter grew. It caught hold of Amos, and rising as if on signal, the two of them walked on past the U.S. military headquarters, roaring through the narrow streets of Mexico, leaving a wake of startled peddlers and uncomprehending workmen behind.

Amos' father-in-law came to the door with a lamp in his hand. They could see the old man long before he reached it, through the French windows that graced that side of his New Orleans house. His legs were thin as sticks, and his white hair was ruffled, almost standing on end.

Amos watched him impatiently. "I hope he finds the latch before he falls down. It looks like he drinks more now than when Kathy was at home. You catch him if he looks like he's going to pitch on out into the street when he opens it."

Rye touched the door lightly, tried the handle. "I thought in he cups he might have left off de latch."

"What's that stuff on the door under the knocker?" Amos asked him.

"Dunno," Rye shrugged. "Leaves. Look like leaves all twisted up."

They heard the old man fumbling on the other side of the door.

"If he passes out, or forgets why he came down and starts back up, I'm going to break his damned French window and sleep in the parlor."

Amos stepped closer to the window to see the old man's progress. "Looks like he found the latch," he called back to Rye. Then the door opened and the old man stood blinking in the combined light of his own lamp and Rye's lantern.

"Mistah O'Brien," Rye began.

"Rye? Rye Crowninshield," the old man squinted, trying to focus his eyes.

"Yes, sar."

"Jesus, it would be this night," the old man croaked. Something in his voice kept Amos from moving into the light. Later, when he recalled that moment, he remembered best how tiny shards of mist had risen from the garden behind him, how they had seemed to gather around Rye's legs as if they were trying to get past him into the house.

"Sar," Rye was saying apologetically, "we only wish a place till the mornin'. Den we rides fo' . . . "

114

"No," the old man almost shouted. "You're too late. It's too god-damned late."

"Sar," Rye began again, "we only asks . . . "

The old man's grip on the lamp loosened, and Rye reached out to steady his arm. "You can't see her," O'Brien went on almost petulantly. "You're too late to see her. We wrote . . . "

"She her, sar?" Rye asked. "See who?"

Amos stepped back toward the door, and as Rye raised the lantern and held it closer to the old man's face they could see the bright rill of tears moving regularly down his cheeks as if they were fed by an inexhaustible spring. "They put her away this evening. They had to put her away this evening."

Rye frowned and glanced at Amos. "Sar, you mean Saranne?"

"Dead," the old man sobbed. This time his grip went altogether, and the lamp fell to the steps, flickered and went out. "Dead and buried before sundown because they had to, because the law . . . "

"Saranne?" Rye said unbelievingly.

Amos reached for O'Brien's arm as the old man slid strengthless against the doorway.

"You," he snuffled, seeing Amos for the first time. "You too. What good is it? It's too late. You're no better than your nigger, boy. It's too late. The police made . . . "

"You say Saranne is dead," Amos shook his. "How did . . . ?"

"Fever," O'Brien coughed. "Yellow jack. And nothing you can do . . . "

Rye lowered the lantern slowly and leaned against the wall. His face was pressed against his coat sleeve, and even in the shadow, Amos could see his shoulders rocking.

"Kathy," Amos yelled, shaking the old man again. "You didn't say . . . "

"Kathy," O'Brien said dreamily. "No man ever had a daughter so lovely, so . . . "

"Old man," Amos thundered, "where is she?"

O'Brien smiled gently as Amos turned him loose. He wilted like a wax statuette exposed to a burst of sudden heat, and slumped almost gracefully into a sitting position in the doorway. Rye's lantern, still held at knee-level in his nerveless hands, illuminated the old man's face.

"Why where would she be?" he said kindly, whimsically. "She's out there," he said, pointing vaguely. "Out there with Saranne."

The rain had stopped, and the clouds were beginning to fall apart. A shaft of diluted sunlight lay across the bottom of the porch steps. Rye found himself watching the sun's pale stain, thinking not of Saranne or even of Phillipe, but of a long-dead captain sprawled in a ditch with a saber angling out of his chest in the shadow of the City of Mexico.

Amos Stevens shifted his weight carefully. The chair beneath him squeaked in protest, and he stared at the bulk of his belly, almost unable to relate it to himself.

"Sentell said he would . . . ," Amos broke the stillness with a voice more gravelly than he remembered it to be.

"He be late," Rye said without taking his eyes from the steps. "Miz Sentell say he got to conduct business in town. She say he come in time fo' a toddy."

"It's been hard for Sentell."

Rye nodded. "Too hard fo' a good mahn. But it always hard fo' de best."

"He could be one of my father's boys."

"He could dat. De old gentlemahn would of puffed up like a toad to see him stand on dat parole."

"He had no choice. He had it to do."

"I'd say so. Wisht to God all our people thought to hold so close to honor."

Amos frowned. "Don't start on him again. We'll hear that boy's side when he comes. There's nothing wrong with him. Phillipe never went over there for a cheap motive."

"He went," Rye grated. "He went. What you gone say about dat? Jus' de simple fact he went over dere. You can paint it or gild it, you can blow it up or cut it down. An' it stay de same. He lef' Morrison and went over."

"Maybe he had reasons," Amos muttered.

"You think maybe Morrison shame him? You think Morrison whup him?"

"No," Amos said slowly. "No, I don't think that."

"No matter what happen, he could of run away. He could of come home. He could of work fo' another mahn."

Amos shook his head irritably. "Why don't you let go of it? Why don't you do what the most ignorant man ever to serve on a backwoods jury has learned to do? Hold up your judgment till the evidence is in.

What do you think the old man would say if he heard you convicting that boy before he's even had a word to say for himself?

"They *can't* be no reason fo' selling' you' own people out," Rye spat savagely. "He's my blood an' I say they ain't no out fo' him."

"You mean you can't *think* of any such reason. I can't either. But we're both old men, and what was reason and unreason to us doesn't look the same to these boys. Remember Mexico."

"Reckon I ought," Rye murmured, glancing at Amos' neatly tucked empty sleeve.

"It was a rotten cause."

"All right."

"But for our country, we went and did what there was to do."

"Sho."

"And twenty years later the general government of that country of ours turned and smote us hip and thigh. Now we're whipped and hurt worse than Mexico was."

"Well . . . "

"Should we have fought for a government that would turn on us, kill our people, destroy our cities, ruin our land?"

"We didn't know . . . "

"Could it be a judgment on us, I wonder. We put aside principles to fight in a bad cause. Now men of the North have returned the favor. Now we know how that Mexican boy felt just outside the city. Remember?"

"What do all dat have to do with Phillipe?"

"I was only thinking of how simple the right and the wrong seemed to us twenty years ago. I was thinking maybe our boys have found that nothing is simple. Maybe Phillipe found principles in . . . "

"If he principles carried him over to de Yankees, dey mus' be fine principles."

"You just got to judge that boy, don't you?" Amos barked.

Rye would have answered, but then at the end of the drive that ran between rows of tall oaks, both of them saw a group of horsemen reining in.

Amos leaned forward squinting as the men turned up the drive toward the house. "Can you make them out?" he asked Rye.

Rye stood up slowly and watched the blue-coated riders as they came closer. "Yankees," he spat. "Maybe they bringin' dat black son-ofabitch I fathered back to where he come from."

Amos stood up trembling. "Rye, don't say that again. I won't have it on this place, and most of all I won't have it said in front of these people. Hold your tongue or go inside."

Rye turned toward him slowly. "I didn't mean to get you riled," he said. "I don't know what's got hold of me. I just think . . . "

"Never mind," Amos said. "Here they are."

Colonel Jonathan Lodge drew his stallion up sharply and sat for a moment looking at the two old men on the porch. He was growing weary of that flat noncommittal stare. He had seen it in every face since he had reached the town. It was an expression without shame or fear or newfound expensive wisdom in it. It seemed to be made half of pride and half of ignorance. Pride in the knowledge of how much the trip south had cost the Yankees, and ignorance of what defeat in war actually means. It was in the faces of the sullen ragged young men on the porch of the general store. He saw a hard-eyed girl wrapped in a flimsy shawl on the gallery in front of the hotel. She had followed the passing Union column with her cold indifferent eyes, her mouth twisted downward, her nose wrinkled as if she had discovered an evil smell. There had been other women and children standing along their line of march down Texas Street. None had smiled, none had paid even curious heed to the Union flag – the United States flag – as it passed. None of the women had herded their children off the streets. None of the old men had made way for Union troopers' horses. One carriage had been stalled in the mire, its horses cut loose, and Union men had had to drag it free by themselves, since the only townsman who had lent them a hand earlier moving a fieldpiece had disappeared before they came upon the carriage.

So it had been an unsuccessful entry into what might prove a difficult town. Not that Lodge had expected flowers and cheers. He wanted no false tokens of loyalty from the last Southern town to lower its rebel flag. But he had expected fear. Not hysterical desperate fear, but at least the kind of grudging respect given any victorious army by a foe completely at its mercy.

Now at the end of the ride, stopped in front of a rebel legislator's home (which would be his residence and his headquarters as soon as he handed Stevens the notice commandeering it for an indefinite period), he was face to face with the same expression, that same passive implacable resistance not only mirrored in the face of the one-armed frowzy-bearded old fool who owned the house, and could be expected

118

neither to possess shame nor intelligent fears, but even on the face of the skinny gray-haired Negro beside him, who looked at least wise enough to recognize good fortune when it clattered, booted and spurred, up to the doorway of his servitude.

"I am Colonel Jonathan Lodge, Army of the United States. Your name is Stevens."

The old man did not move. His eyes, deep-set and inscrutable as an Indian's, never moved from Lodge's.

"Late representative of the so-called Louisiana legislature in this town?"

"So-called," Amos Stevens bowed with light irony.

"This house is designated headquarters for the garrison comman-dant until further notice. Have your people clear out the front rooms for office space, and the three largest bedchambers for myself and my staff. Then you may sign a parole and go about your business until I send for you."

"Why dat . . . ," Rye began.

"You heard the colonel," Amos cut him off. "Do it. Get Elgin and Josie to work on it."

"We'll need food at once," Lodge went on as he dismounted. "And someone to care for these horses."

"The groom will be around shortly. There's food in the kitchen."

"Have it served," Lodge answered shortly.

"It will be on the table when you get there," Stevens said easily. Rye had stepped inside to give orders. Now he came back.

"Is there a colored man?" Lieutenant Raisor began. "A colored man here called Rye Crowninshield?"

"What he want wif me?"

"How should I know?" Amos smiled. "Maybe someone nominated you for governor."

"I have a letter for you. From your son. It came from Washington City."

"What he doin' in Washington City?"

"He'll be home before long. You should be very proud of him," the lieutenant said, almost without patronage.

Rye mouth twitched. "Yeah," he said, "damn if I ain't proud of him."

"By the way," Lodge said, removing his gloves and mounting the steps, "in case your master has neglected to tell you, you are a free man. As free as any one of us."

Rye looked at the colonel without expression as he reached the porch. Then he turned, still expressionless, toward Amos. "Thanks," he said softly. "Sho' thank youall a lot . . . boss."

II

6 JUNE 1865 — By moving his head a quarter-turn to the right, Colonel Jonathan Lodge could see beyond the wide windows of Amos Stevens' study a lawn so deep that the fields beyond seemed more like painted stage properties than real terrain. On each side of the house, and growing in casual disarray across the lawn, were oak, sweet gun, magnolia, and down near the road into Shreveport a thick huddle of pines with no branches to speak of lower than thirty feet above the ground, The trunks of the oaks were whitewashed – had been whitewashed long before – and the traces of that antique painting still lightened the bark. Under one twisted sprawling oak, with branches extending nearly as far outward as the tree was tall, dainty ironwork benches, once painted white too, now big with rust and bird residue, stood tenantless and dripping from the recent rain.

Lodge could see too how the white paint on outer window frames was beginning to crack and peel. He found it symbolic of the slave-power that all the trappings of gentry, the house, the lawn – the entire establishment – were beginning to decay. The whitened sepulcher begins to peel and crumble, he thought. Lodge wondered how such a society had survived even before the war, how a society in which human sweat was the cheapest and most readily available commodity could have survived the first onslaught of Union arms. It should have cracked like a rotten egg, he mused. Cracked and spewed its putrescence into the light of civilized opinion. How did the serpent live on? He set himself that question, and meant to have it answered before he returned to Massachusetts.

But before he could arrange his papers, stationery and supplies in Amos Stevens' quickly emptied desk, the scavengers began to arrive.

The first of them was Pony Mueller, late of Columbus, Ohio, and fresh from a week's ride north out of New Orleans. Pony Mueller had a number of things to show the colonel. He had a Treasury Department warrant to search for and seize any cotton, mules, food or other supplies that could be proven Confederate States property. He had also a

War Department permit to purchase and transport such property once confiscated with the approval and assistance of whatever United States forces he should encounter. Finally, as a kind of clincher, he showed the colonel a frayed letter from the Honorable Ben Wade, Senator from Ohio (and a South-hater of such dimensions as to call into question Thaddeus Stevens' preeminence in that category), that said, in words or substance, how much the senator would appreciate any service rendered his constituent, Pony Mueller, whose unswerving loyalty to the Union cause made him both a proper instrument of federal justice and a worthy recipient of whatever profits the stern administration of that justice might coincidentally yield.

"The sonofabitch is a walking monopoly," one Union orderly, his ear pressed to the library door, whispered to another clerk. "What he don't get away with, you can pack in a thimble. You better keep your extra shirt tied to your belt."

"What he don't manage to steal," the other yawned, "he'll probably shit on. We seen 'em in Virginia and the Carolinas. I seen one stripping shoes off dead Michigan volunteers before the captain had them bucked and slung."

"Naw," the first one whispered loudly. "He weren't stealing. He was taking them shoes on back to the next of kin."

But Pony Mueller, sweating and anxious to get on with his dispensation of justice, knew that he was not alone. There had been half a dozen other agents on the road with him – any one of whom might have beaten him to Shreveport had they not stopped in Alexandria two days before to break the journey over a whiskey or two. Mueller had ridden that whole night through, had rested only an hour or so in Natchitoches, and then had covered the seventy-odd miles into Shreveport with only stops for water and to pull the foamy saddle off one of his nags and cinch it to the shivering back of the other.

His legs trembled from exhaustion, but it would be worth the lost sleep and the sore ride if he could have a day to work ahead of the others, if he could contact a few pliable locals who would show him where the cotton was, where the mules and goods were hidden. That one day, if he could exploit it, would put him so far ahead of the others that they would be reduced to bracing old ladies for gold lockets and claiming that pillowcases and kitchen pots were contraband. All Pony was asking for the long ride through cold rain was a little luck. He had to have a little luck.

Lodge finished with the papers. He stared at Pony Mueller for a long uncomfortable moment.

"So you are empowered to seize rebel goods, set a price on then, sell them to yourself, and then ship them wherever you please."

Pony's heavy face, white from fatigue under a week's beard, tried for a smile. "Well . . . ," he began.

"And in this interesting commercial venture, Senator Wade asks the United States Army to assist you."

"Well," Pony started again, "only if I was to have trouble. I wouldn't want the army . . . "

"Watching you," Lodge offered.

"Now look here, Colonel . . . "

"Shut up," Lodge snapped. "You've identified yourself and notified me of your presence. Now get out. If you require assistance, see Lieutenant Raisor."

"How come you're so snotty?" Pony complained, trying to counterfeit something between dignity and injured pride. "Don't you want to see traitors sweat?"

Lodge's face flushed the familiar shade of purple his clerks had seen so often the past weeks. His eyes, chips of emotionless granite, glittered as if they contained quartz instead of moisture. "*I* want to see traitors hang," he rasped. "The proper penalty for a traitor is death – not to have his pockets picked."

The colonel's complexion did not appreciably lighten for the rest of the day. Before one of the orderlies had started unpacking Lodge's kit again after showing Mueller to the door, three more disheveled agents of the federal government, inches deep in mud and smelling of whiskey, were cornering Lieutenant Raisor on the front porch of Amos Stevens' house.

"Come on, Lootenant," one of them pleaded, wiping his nose on his coat sleeve. "We *got* to see him right now before that slabheaded Dutch sonofabitch picks the whole northwest end of the state clean as a bone. We got a right."

As representatives of the government, Lieutenant Raisor finally decided, they had a right. All three of them did, and so would the dozens of others who would be along in the next few weeks.

Even after he had worn the afternoon thin with ubiquitous Treasury agents hungry for cotton and mules, Lodge was not done. There were more functionaries of the Republican party and the federal government up from New Orleans to see the last rebel stronghold: a flock of clerks and petty appointees sent from Memphis and elsewhere to set up a new and loyal government for the town and for Caddo Parish. Some of them came ready to begin registering eligible voters that same day.

"No field grade officer who served a day in rank with the rebel army," Andrew Tocsin, until recently a federal clerk in Memphis – before that a substantial Union men who had shown his loyalty to the United States by spending three years of the war in a federal prison for forgery – was explaining to Colonel Lodge. "No man who ever held office, place, or sinecure under the rebel government. No man who ever lent aid or comfort, material or otherwise, to the late rebellion, loaned out niggers or supplied units of rebel army with necessaries. No man who, by sworn affidavit of two loyal witnesses, ever voiced sentiments favorable to the rebellion, its purposes or conduct. None of 'em can vote without a pardon," Tocsin finished breathlessly. "Not a one of 'em."

Lodge pressed the tips of his fingers together and stared at a portrait of Thomas Jefferson above Amos Stevens' fireplace. "It seems you have taken care of all the whites in the parish," he said at last.

"Yeah," Tocsin leered. "Ain't it the damndest thing you ever heard in your life?"

"So you'll begin registering the Negroes and what few whites can pass your muster?"

Tocsin nodded cheerfully. "We already got set up in City Hall down from where your lieutenant's got an office for you. We got the niggers comin' in, an' all the safe white men."

"Safe white men?"

"Aw, you know. Loyal."

Lodge's eyes narrowed. "How can you determine the loyal men from the disloyal?"

Tocsin grinned. "We got us a machine. We got us a gadget for surefire testin' before we was in town twenty minutes."

So Andrew Tocsin was marshal. He was also, considering the vacuum of loyal men, mayor, registrar, commissioner of works and police, sheriff, and sole authority in charge of reestablishing judicial, legislative and executive functions in Shreveport and the parish outside. In short, he could do anything. So long as Lodge was satisfied.

"Make sure your machine functions," Lodge told him. "When machines fail, they are discarded. And the operators replaced."

Lieutenant Raisor was back from the office of the *Shreveport News* where he had gotten Lodge's proclamation of eligible voters printed – along with a public announcement of the arrival and impending business of Pony Mueller and the rest of the Treasury agents.

"The people have to know about the agents," Raisor had said, "because if a man went into your barn and started taking the mules out, or began pileing your corn or cotton into a wagon, why you'd think he was . . . "

"A thief," Lodge finished.

"Well," Raisor said flushing, "wouldn't you?"

Lodge pursed his lips. "how will your announcement assist in this matter?"

"Sir?"

"How, for example, can a man tell when he sees his mules being led away, whether the man at the other end of the rope is a government agent or a thief?"

"The papers. Our people have papers."

"Fine. Although papers can be forged. Especially with Andrew Tocsin in town. But considering that the papers are valid, and the man taking your mules a bona-fide Treasury agent: what difference will it make to the rebel civilians whether his mules are being confiscated or stolen?"

"If thieves took the mules, I'd call the marshal and . . . "

"But the mules," Lodge cut him off, "*all* the mules in this parish have the Confederate States brand. Because all of them were at least temporarily commandeered by the rebels. So all of them are subject to confiscation."

Raisor's eyes widened. "So if somebody came into my barnyard tonight and began taking the mules out and hitching them, I . . . "

Lodge shrugged. "You would simply turn over and go back to sleep." When Raisor left his parcel of printed bills on the desk and closed the study door behind him, the colonel turned once more to face the full-length double windows that opened on Amos Stevens' lawn. Twilight was ending by then, and the moon had risen behind the clump of pines at the yard's far end. Colonel Lodge poured himself a glass of brandy and tried to relax the parade-stiffness of his shoulders and neck.

In a sense, he had been on parade all his life. Born of a minor branch in an accomplished New England family, Lodge had been bred for exhibition, for place. He had never had what most men would consider a private life. There had been private schools enough: a private Latin academy in Boston; a private preparatory school in England; a private university of the firmest repute back in Boston again. But there his privacy began and ended.

"A gentleman," his father had intoned (not only for his benefit, but for that of his younger brother Paul as well), "a gentleman *has* no personal life. His every thought, his every act is calculated in such a way as to reflect honor upon his family. A gentleman, be he merchant or scholar, banker, prelate or statesman, is before all things a public man."

"But Poppa," Jonathan Lodge's brother Paul had complained, "there are *some* things in life a man must keep secret in order to be a gentleman at all."

His father, as pale of face as his eldest son, and burdened with the same embarrassingly veined nose, cut him short with a wave of the hand. "Sir," he boomed, "I would expect you to conduct yourself in the privacy of your wife's bedchamber as if you were on the Commons at high noon."

Allowing only a little for hyperbole, Jonathan Lodge had fulfilled his father's bidding. Rather than attempt a compromise between the ideal and the expedient insofar as boudoir conventions were concerned, he had negated the problem by stepping stiffly past it. At fifty-seven, he was still, determinedly, a bachelor.

Bedchambers aside, there had been few problems of conduct for Jonathan Lodge. From the starched rectitude of the family, through the unsullied rondo of the schools, to the rich proprieties of his father's bank, young Lodge had stepped without a hitch. There was one city: Boston. One church: Episcopal. One state superior in all ways: Massachusetts. One law: gentlemanly conduct and smart business practice. One political party: Whig. And one view of life not sicklied o'er with the film of degeneracy and indecency: his kind of life.

It was possible for a man to be born, to live, and to die within this regiment. It had been done. His father had done it. But as the century moved forward into the middle 1840s, that pattern began to crack and shred along the edges. Vast new territories were being consumed into the Union (already swollen beyond decent bounds by the damnable and possibly treasonous Louisiana Purchase – which yet might prove the seed of ultimate disunion), and almost all of this territory was either in the hands of slave-state representatives, or well on the way to falling into their grasp.

Not that Lodge, in 1845, was an abolitionist. Hardly that. Abolitionists were seedy radicals at least as distasteful as the slave-owning, pseudo-aristocratic barbarians themselves. A conservative man would have as little truck as possible with the latter and no conversation with the former at all. Still, the slave-power burgeoned and thrived: in Virginia, Nat Turner had revolted, slaughtered, been captured, and executed, and still the threat of another Santo Domingo, another slave-rising under a L'Ouverture yet to make himself known, seemed to hover over the states south of Washington City. Even a conservative like Jonathan Lodge could say this much:

"The system is basically unstable. You cannot have an enduring republic when millions of blackamoors are endlessly seething and brewing toward inevitable revolt."

"Lovejoy said . . . ," a friend might try to interject.

"Damn Lovejoy and all the rest of the abolitionist scum. Do you think I care a clipped shilling for the niggers? I say again that slave-holding endangers the republic. If I am offered a toadstool at luncheon, I refuse it. Do I refuse because I wish to do the toadstool no harm?"

"But human beings are not . . . "

"Precisely," Lodge would cut his friend off (in the manner of his father). "Just so. Men are not toadstools. They are infinitely more deadly, and rarely as easy to keep in their place. Thus, the blacks, out of place on this continent to begin with, serve to endanger our establishment more considerably than the most virulent toadstool might threaten our health."

And so it went through the days of the great compromise. Banker Lodge cared less than nothing for the debate over chattel-slavery that continued to bubble out of the political caldron. But brother Paul, failing to establish himself in the import business, had turned to literature of a political nature, and his first pamphlet, "The Shame of Negro Bondage," only seemed to harden his elder brother against the increasingly fashionable outcry over slavery.

"If you persist in this," Jonathan Lodge told his brother, "you will find yourself reduced to living within your personal means. I do not intend to have doors slammed in my face because my younger brother, having botched his chances as an importer, compounds his idiocy by exporting revolution to the South. Let the slavers go about their business," he added. "When they fall of their own bloated weight, there may be something for you in land speculation down there."

For a few months, brother Paul held his peace. But spring came on, outside the bank at least, and with it into Boston came a fugitive slave by the name of Anthony Burns.

According to law, Anthony was taken in charge by the United States marshal and held until transport back to Virginia could be arranged. The humanitarians with whom Paul spent his time would not have it so. On the 26th of May (it was 1854 then, and the years were somehow closing in on them all; on the Jonathans and Pauls, the Anthonys and the marshals – even on that anonymous slave-owner in Virginia, who had the bad luck to let this particular Negro with a yen for Boston slip his halter). Paul and his friends hired Fanenuil Hall for a protest meeting. Chancing his brother's wrath, Paul had read from his pamphlet, scoring the demonic Southern barbarians who dared traffic in human flesh. It was spring and youth's hot blood, mingled with the spirits of a righteous cause, went to his head: he overreached himself.

"Could slavery go on? Could the people, the *free* people of the Commonwealth of Massachusetts, permit within their very sight a suffering fellow creature to be dragged through the historic streets of Boston (the cradle of liberty, the citadel of freedom, where every paving stone could tell its tale of the courage and patriotic sacrifice of those who had run to the cause of independence and bled for it on those same stones)? No! A thousand times no! It could not and would not be borne; the glory of the past, the honor of the present, the safety of the future all militated against it. So fellow citizens . . . "

So what had begun as a meeting of protest within the reasonable confines of a sort of unscheduled town meeting from which, at most, a withering petition to the authorities might have been expected to issue, turned from meeting to patriotic orgy to Jacobin bacchanal, and before Paul and his friends had time to reflect or consider, the entire mob, howling and chanting, was pouring through the streets toward the jail – pushing Paul ahead of them.

Even then it could have been contained. Jacobins require unfailing leadership lest they question and discover their cause borders on the altruistic and there is no foreseeable personal profit in it. Bur for the first time in his life, Paul did not question. And, in a matter of speaking, he did not fail.

They stormed the jail. The front door, designed with reasonable citizens of the town-meeting sort in mind, gave way before them like paper. Even the cells were easy enough to open. But the marshals were made of better stuff and managed to crack a head here, break an arm there, and push the mob, still howling for freedom and Anthony Burns, back into the street. As they massed for another try, one marshal, his stomach full of feathers as a result of the shock at seeing a mob in the streets of Boston, fired, possibly by accident, a single shot. It was enough. It was more than enough. Because the mob ceased to be interested much in Anthony Burns at the instant it heard the report and smelled the black powder, and dissolved into a dwindling collection of sheepish men who suddenly remembered sundry tasks that had nothing to do with fugitive slaves at all – except for the few who stood around the door under the marshal's gun and looked with mingled interest and clinical sadness at the riot's only serious casualty: Paul Lodge, who lay stretched across the shattered threshold with a single bullet hole squarely between his eyes.

When the news was brought to Jonathan Lodge, he sat without expression behind the enormous desk that had served his father and his grandfather before him.

"It is no surprise," he said, the least trace of annoyance in his voice. "But it *is* an imposition. The boy (Paul had been forty-one) was bound to make his mark one way or the other. He was an ass, but there is no reason he should have been killed."

At the inquest that followed, it became abundantly clear (to the federal judge, at least) that there was a good deal of reason to Paul's being killed. The marshal's testimony suggested that Paul had been the ringleader of a bloodthirsty pack of goons bent on felony.

"When they come," the marshal told the judge, "we didn't know what they was up to. I said to Abner, 'They're after that poor nigger.' And Abner says, 'That's so, but are they out to hang him or set him loose?' Well, it didn't make any difference to us because . . . because he was *bound over* to us, and this bunch coming wasn't no flock of Virginians up to take him home. Then they come at us, and we pushed 'em back the first time. But they got set up to come at us again. And Abner had a bloody nose, and his scalp was all torn loose up over his ear, and he said to me, 'Goddamn this, Humphrey. If they keep it up, we're going to get hurt.' Then his pistol went off, and inside of five minutes it was quiet as a . . . as a . . . grave."

Jonathan Lodge heard the verdict of justifiable homicide with as little expression as he had received the news of his brother's death. But below his phlegmatic surface, things were beginning to happen. The chemistry of change was in motion, and Jonathan Lodge was on his way toward finding what more emotional and less sensible men called, in those days, a "cause."

Not that his brother's death had roused the vengeful spirit in him. Vengeance was, if anyone's the Lord's. Besides there was little to avenge. Not that Jonathan Lodge had come to see, through the shock of such near violence, the real evil of chattel-slavery. He cared no more for the condition of Negroes in the South than he cared for that of immigrants in Boston or New York, but there was another element to be considered.

His brother, rightly or wrongly, had committed himself to the cause of destroying slavery, and had, with characteristic maladroitness, managed to get himself killed in a minor skirmish before the main battle had even shaped up. There seemed to be a question of family honor in this. A Lodge had been, as it were, executed for stupidity. But if the antislavery cause were to be advanced, if, regardless of its merits, it should become a national issue and end with total or even partial manumission of slaves, then the character of his brother could easily be altered from that of buffoon to that of martyr. Not that martyrdom was essentially superior to buffoonery (in truth, Jonathan Lodge himself saw little distinction between them), but in the public mind a victim of oppression was more to be honored than a clown who had miscalculated himself to death.

At first, then, abolitionism was something more than a casual interest, something less than an obsession. He began by giving small sums to *The Liberator*, attending a lecture by William Lloyd Garrison, a series of illustrative talks on the morality of Southern slave-owners by Frederick Douglas. After the latter speeches, one of his senior clerks, a heartfelt enemy of slavery and slavers (abolition was clambering up the social staircase in those days: from laborers who hated the idea of cheap competition in the form of slavery, to petty industrialist who despised the Southerners for their eternal war against high tariffs, to merchant princeling and banker whose scions, decaying in the dull and samely air of New England, found it a heady and edifying fad), asked him what he thought of Douglas.

"An educated nigger," Lodge had growled, "a phenomenon, sir. Like a dog in a silk hat and gaiters, or a silent woman. But I wonder where it will end. This equalitarianism could go on and on until we find Irishmen leering at us over luncheon at the club."

But even though the basic premises underlying abolitionism were repulsive to him, he kept at it. When some flap-brained talkative woman would bore him into near insensibility with her talk about Mrs. Stowe's oh-so-terribly-*true* novel, he would smile and cough and retreat into himself to gaze at a fine bronze statue on its wide granite base. SACRED TO THE MEMORY OF PAUL LUCIUS LODGE, it said on a bronze plate, WHOSE SELFLESS SACRIFICE IN THE NAME OF HUMAN FREEDOM KINDLED AN UNDYING FLAME IN THE BOSOM OF THE COMMONWEALTH, AND STAMPED FOREVER THE PRINT OF HIS NOBILITY UPON HIS NATIVE STATE. Sometimes the wording was altered a little. Sometimes it read, AND STAMPED FOREVER THE NAME OF LODGE UPON HIS NATIVE STATE, but the statue was always the same: Paul standing next to a lectern, quill in hand to commemorate his single contribution to American polemic, and a half-naked Negro recumbent at his feet, having what looked to be about two or three hundred pounds of chains struck off by a typical New England Irish laborer. Paul's expression would be one of firm but sympathetic determination, his sculptured eyes staring southward across the Common toward that faraway land of darkness. The Negro's expression, Lodge considered, would be one of almost hysterical (but respectful) exultation, and his hand would be raised toward Paul as if in tribute (or, Lodge thought, as if asking for his first handout as a free man). The worker's expression would be that of a man paid for his labor in advance: sullen and contemptuous of both the others.

So it went at the beginning: a few dollars, an occasional appearance – even a few monosyllabic remarks at a public meeting of Fusion Party stalwarts, Free Soilers, and Conscience Wigs. Nothing so spectacular as leading a mob, but any number of small things that, added together, raised the Massachusetts temperature a degree or two, and prepared the ground for vaster undertakings in due time.

Slowly, Lodge found himself becoming not only a public figure in the modest sense of that term as understood by a Boston banker, but in the largest possible sense: in a word, he had begun to collect notoriety. At first the realization sickened him. There was a whole universe of difference between being a public man and a public property; between standing as a figure of solidity and substance in the Union's prime city and becoming a watchword passed from mouth to mouth among the rabble. But he recalled his purpose and applied good banker's sense to the situation: in order to achieve a desired end, one had to pay a certain price. Energy had to be expended to move an object; money had to be used to make money – and it followed that he would have to contribute something to the furtherance of the plan if he hoped to rehabilitate his brother.

From that conclusion, it was only a step downward, so to speak, into politics. Jonathan Lodge, banker, man of incontrovertible substance and unsullied good taste, stood for election to the Congress of the United States.

Long afterward, there were those who claimed that the campaign was no campaign at all, and that the result of it was not so much an expression of popular will (as Jefferson would have had it) as a complete vindication of Hamilton's most violent opinions regarding what he (and Jonathan Lodge) fondly called "the great beast." Not, God forbid, that Lodge showed himself a demagogue in banker's clothing: far from it. Rather that his method of soliciting votes was of a sort to make seasoned politicians wonder whether he was trying to gain a seat in Congress or to meet an end similar to his brother's – at the hands of the voters.

At one public meeting, Lodge was called upon to give the crowd an idea of his stand on certain issues. After perhaps five minutes of grudging monosyllable generalities in which he would at first state a moderate position and then qualify that moderate position into a kind of intellectual limbo, the chairman of the meeting asked for questions:

"How do you stand on slavery?" someone bawled in a thick brogue.

"I own no slaves," Lodge ground out.

"But will you fight it?" a tall woman in gold-rimmed spectacles cried out.

"Madam," Lodge returned, "you jeopardize your good reputation. Kindly be seated."

There was a question on tariffs. "You may rely on my discretion," Lodge assured the questioner, who sat down at once without being told.

Finally someone asked if he would vote for the repeal of the Fugitive Slave Laws.

"I have not yet satisfied myself on that point," Lodge answered in measured accent. "But you may be sure that when I reach a decision, it will be the proper one."

When the meeting adjourned, there were no cheers for the candidate. Not that the crowd seemed offended by Lodge's noncommittal attitude. On the contrary, they seemed too dazed to be either resentful or enthusiastic. They had come to be fed the loaf of bombast; he had given them good New England stone. They had expected exorbitant promises, fulminations against slavocracy, praise of their own worthiness and at least implied slander of the comparative morals and mentality of every other constituency in the Union. What they had gotten, even they could not be sure. Was the candidate an untutored madman or a keystone of rectitude so adamantine and immovable that he feared to air his opinions lest someone take them to be less than the deepest and holiest outpourings of his meditation?

The manager of his campaign, a long-time board member of the most respected gun manufacturing company in the country, could not contain his gloom.

"This is not a campaign," he told his wife. "Lodge is not running. He is simply exhibiting his person to assembled gatherings and offering them a close look at CHARACTER. It may edify a few of them, I guess, but I don't think even the enlightened will vote for him. I'm not sure I will."

But he did – as a matter of plain decency and so that Jonathan Lodge would get at least two ballots in his favor. That, his campaign manager thought later, explains two of the votes. But it was not possible to explain the other tens of thousands that put Lodge beyond sight of his nearest red-hot abolitionist rival for the seat. When the canvass was complete, Lodge was on his way south with the largest plurality ever polled in the district, and leaving behind him a gaggle of politicians whose consternation was as nearly sincere as anything to do with politicians can ever be.

He went to Washington, not only with a voters' mandate the size of an elephant gun, but with *carte blanche* to load and fire it how and when he saw fit. He was committed to nothing. For all he had told the voters, he could have voted to dissolve the State of Massachusetts and pass out the fragments to Connecticut and New Hampshire. If the Congress ever contained a free agent, Jonathan Lodge, the public man, was it.

But not for long. He had run for office because Congress was the place (if any such place there were) where he could begin refurbishing the image of his luckless brother. He had not run on a strong platform of antislavery because such a position would have committed him not only to abolition (which he had to embrace, however gingerly, in any case to accomplish his object) but to a certain rough method of attaining the destruction of slavery. This was not admissible. If simple reason and compromise could begin the dismantling of slave-power, that was good enough. In fact, it would be better. Paul's name would shine the brighter if there were no more violent deaths on account of slavery. If the question produced too many martyrs, the best Jonathan Lodge could do would be to make Paul come out posthumously even; if there were only a handful – and those scattered in rare and honored graves all across the country – Paul's antic departure could be the foundation stone of the family's fame and honor for a hundred years to come.

Thus Lodge entered Washington City planning a course of action counter to that of his fellow delegates from New England: not force and moral shrieks – which were enough to set any man's teeth on edge whether hot-blooded cavalier or cold-blooded Yankee. Rather, an approach understood, admired by all right-thinking man: a straight business proposition. Value given for value received. What man could gainsay that kind of settlement?

He discovered exactly what kind of man could gainsay it, and the sort of language in which he would choose to do so on his third day in Washington City. He was introduced to the Honorable Robert Toombes of Georgia at Willard's Hotel.

"What I do not understand," Lodge replied stiffly "is your failure to invoke logic. If the South is adequately, no, even liberally, compensated for these blacks – who would then be sent at government expense back to their homes – then we can all be satisfied. The Union . . . "

"Wait a minute," Toombes cut in. "You'd pay *liberally*?"

"For myself, no possible sum could be too much to end this controversy."

Toombes chewed his lower lip. He sat back in his chair and rubbed his paunch reflectively. "Liberal compensation," he repeated to himself. "Any possible sum." Then he sat up again, eyes twinkling.

"Suppose . . . ," Toombes began slowly.

"Yes," Lodge urged him on.

"Suppose we were to hash this out? Suppose we decided to take your proposition up?"

"Yes," Lodge almost whispered, feeling the weight of all American history pressing upon him, the silent thankful gaze of generations yet unborn playing on his expressionless countenance.

"Would you let us take the money and buy us some Yankee white men for the chores?"

Listeners from the bar, porters and servants had gathered nearby as he and Toombes spoke. When Toombes finished, the sitting room exploded with laughter. Peal after peal of it echoed down the murky corridors and out into the street where Negro flunkies held their masters' reins or sat sketching circles with their bare toes in the dust of the walk. Toombes was laughing with the rest, and as the merriment spread, as the story passed from mouth to mouth, room to room, Toombes rose, still laughing, and walked away from Lodge toward the bar.

It would be neither accurate nor even a tutored guess to say that Bob Toombes unwittingly had severed the last thin cord holding back the steeds of war that afternoon. But it is certain he had done himself, and what was at that moment his country, no favor; that the price of his heavy humor would not begin to be paid that afternoon or even that year, but that before Lodge exacted what a Southern gentleman would have called "satisfaction," the old Union both men claimed to love would be as dead and beyond reclaim as the sound of Hannibal's elephants trumpeting through the Alps, or the thick smell of careless blossoms at Versailles on an evening in July just hours before the Bastille gates gave way and turned a new ravening age loose in Paris streets.

Because the affront Toombes had offered Lodge was beyond any hope of mere personal reprisal; even if the New Englander had believed in the *code duello*, nothing in the way of justice provided by it could have wiped out the sound of Negroes and prostitutes, barflies and common loafers laughing, laughing at him, and pointing wildly at his back as he walked rapidly through the lobby of Willard's Hotel with no more emotion visible on his pale face than when he come in.

So that now what had begun as a kind of eccentric desire to ameliorate the family honor as it had suffered in the person of his brother became, almost in the space of that single afternoon, a personal vendetta, an icy stiletto pointed not merely at Southern slavery in the person of Robert Toombes, but rather at the whole South herself. A Southerner of wide renown, certainly a representative of that land below Washington City, had made him the butt and foil of his humor before the trash of the whole district; had compromised his position both in Congress and society at large by playing him for a fool. Now the abstract cause of family honor paled, and a new and personal reason surged to the front of his mind. There would still be a statue of Paul in Boston Common, but then there might be ten thousand statues – because a peaceful solution to the problem was out of the question now. Paul's singular glory might have to be shared by many, because Negro emancipation was no longer the object. Now Lodge's purpose was annihilation of the South.

As his new purpose hardened into shape, Lodge discovered strange things about himself. He found that he loved to envision destruction. In the evening, after a day of insignificant committee work or tedious House debate, after an early and abstemious supper, he would sit in the darkness of his suite with a snifter of Napoleon in his hand and picture explosion and holocaust. He could see long lines of men storming rocky places, and bright flags flapping at the head of an assaulting regiment. He could imagine whole cities given to the torch, populations handed over to the sword: it was a dream of cleansing and purgation to equal the Last Judgment, except that the god of this judgment would be named Lodge.

Then he would sit stiffly for hours. Only when the lights of the city would wink out long past midnight and the shards of Potomac fog obscured and diffused the few streetlights, did he put down the snifter of brandy (frequently untouched) and prepare for bed. Then, lying outstretched as stiffly as he sat, he would go on thinking, studying the war his imagination had created until some simulacrum of sleep claimed him, and the imaginings shifted into dreams.

Now the problem in abstract seemed simple enough: how could he catapult two disenchanted, feuding portions of the nation into an open and irreparable break? How could he force into actuality the enormous, long stored potential of violence held barely in check by the leaders of each region?

It seemed easy: in a roomful of gunpowder, only a match is needed. But human events are not to be equated with anything so simply elemental as a powder magazine. Certainly the explosive was there, but it was a more mysterious kind of energy, and it would take a primer more subtle, more certain, than a mere speech or an unfavorable vote on the Fugitive Slave question to set it off. It would require an incident, a calculated and prepared incident that would somehow touch the deepest emotional fibers in the men of both sections. It would have to be an incident not only inflammatory but symbolic of the whole raw and pestilential paradox of human merchandise in a republic dedicated to human freedom. What it would require, in short, could not be planned in an hour and executed the next day. And so Jonathan Lodge waited, and improved the time until it turned at last to his service.

It was the winter of 1858, and the delicate balance of the nation was reaching the point at which balance collapses, at which unendurable attenuation snaps like a tortured rope, and all the components of the balance rush together – or apart – into chaos from which none can possibly emerge unchanged. Step by step, move by move, speech by speech, the sections of the country were rushing apart, and even in the mounting certainty of separation, it was somehow implicit that they would rush together again as quickly as they parted: not into reunion but into war. It required now only the final turn of the screw, some fatal event that could be so clearly interpreted as an act of surpassing bad faith that both sections would rather march into slaughter than suffer it.

And during that winter, a Congressman from Ohio came to Lodge's suite to describe a plan for freeing the slaves of northern Virginia. Not a legislative plan: the time for that was past. Not even a campaign of political harassment and agitation. Rather a scheme of clear-cut violence and sedition that, if it worked, might even move across the line into treason. Lodge listened and considered.

It all had to do with a man from Kansas, a jawhawker whose reputation had already preceded him eastward, and whose part in the border war was almost legend. The man and his sons would go into Virginia with arms and rouse the slaves to fight for their freedom. The insurrection would sweep not only the state but the whole South. It would dwarf Nat Turner's rebellion, and it would succeed. Then, faced with a *fait accompli*, what could the slavers do? What, indeed, could the United States government do?

" . . . for the best," the Ohio Congressman was saying. "Take their Negroes from them. There are plenty of people who will never fight to bring an end to slavery but who would fight to see that it not be reinstated once ended . . . by whatever means."

Lodge did not smile because he was not used to smiling – and because irony as such meant nothing to him. But behind the pale and increasingly sullen mask of his face, something like a terrible humor rose and moved. Because Lodge was, even caught up in a frenzy of hatred and justification, a logical man. He knew – knew for certain that the planned insurrection had as much chance of success as would a man shot at the moon out of a cannon. He knew, or at least suspected, that no man who attempted to lead such an uprising would come back out of Virginia alive, and that the Negroes themselves, so long schooled in endurance and the cautious scrutiny of reality, would sense the comic-opera proportions of the expedition and stay clear of any connection with it. Beyond this, he knew something more.

"Yes," he said slowly, pressing the ends of his thin fingers together. "It is a good plan – a Christian enterprise – and I will support it. You may draft upon my account at the Merchant's Bank in Boston. I shall require receipts for monies used, but so long as they are used in such a cause, I will not stint."

And then, as the Congressman from Ohio rose to leave, full of thanks and the religion of their common goal, the smile inside Lodge very nearly surfaced.

The end of it was as Lodge had guessed. There was slaughter at Harper's Ferry (and the first to die, almost as if he were a symbol of Lodge's own feelings, was a free Negro named Hayward Shepard: a hard-working man, respected and liked in the town. It took Shepard twelve hours to die, but by the end of that time, if he was capable of thinking at all, possibly he had divined the sort of release a black man could expect from the North) and the rank breath of hysteria and hatred swept the whole South. It had been Nat Turner's bloody revolt all over again except that, instead of a crazed Negro preacher, the leader this time was a walleyed Yankee, a white man whose record of assassination and mutilation in the Kansas border wars would have earned him the title "mad-dog butcher" in any civilized state (so a Georgia weekly newspaper said). And worse: there were Northern business men who counted it a matter of pride that their money and reputation had helped him on his way to Harper's Ferry.

It was just as Lodge had supposed. The slow alienation of the sections picked up velocity: Southern fire-eaters whose rabid regionalism had been suspect for thirty years suddenly gained a host of listeners, a wealth of new respect. The Union must be destroyed, they shouted, because it is a corrupt union, a worthless union – no, worse than that: a union positively injurious to the South. If the South alone adheres to the moderate principles of the Constitution, she will be reduced to peonage at the hands of Northern men who claim no personal honor, who care nothing for the Constitution, and whose only principle is the kind that draws interest in a Yankee bank.

Sleep on, the fire-eaters warned, and you will awake to find that a host of John Browns has swept over you, and those who live when the bloodletting is over will discover that master and slave have changed places. And the South, if it had been sleeping, growled itself awake. The states of the new South (Louisiana, Mississippi, Arkansas, Texas, Florida, Alabama), so long at odds with the old South (Virginia, the Carolinas, Georgia, Tennessee) as to method and attitude toward the North, found one of the original states ready and able to lead. South Carolina, the home of Calhoun and Rhett, became the center for a renewal of secession sentiment dormant since 1832 and the nullification brawl with Andrew Jackson.

And Lodge was satisfied. There was no war yet, but even as Hayward Shepard lay on a railroad platform bleeding to death, even as, a few weeks later, the rope gave way under cockeyed John Brown, Lodge knew that the solution of Union was becoming supersaturated with mutual hatred and distrust; that an irreversible reaction had started, that Seward's "irrepressible conflict" was crystallizing in villages and hamlets, cities and towns, up and down the length of the continent. Poor whites in the South, who had either cared nothing for slavery or who had actively hated the institution that kept them forever surplus hands whose labor could not compete with that of a slave, began to identify themselves with the plantation owners, who at least had no desire to set at liberty thousands of Negroes and thus wipe out the single fragile margin of superiority that even the poorest free white could claim over the most prosperous Negro in bondage. In the North, small farmers and laborers and businessmen saw in the raid and death of John Brown a new crusade. Their indifference or casual sympathy toward slavery fell away, and overnight the abolitionists gained new followers and fresh funds for their underground railroad. More important: the drama of Brown's raid and the angry Southern reply to it opened ears that had been deaf before to abolitionist cries.

But now Lodge was silent. He made no acknowledgment of his part in financing the raid. Not because he feared the result, but because the ferment caused by it remained unpredictable still. There could be division; there would most likely be war. But now his plan was to have no plan. He served the time one more – until the time was ripe to serve him fully.

It was only a little less than a year after Brown's execution that Lodge sat in his dark suite again with a snifter of brandy in his hands. It was the thirteenth day of November, 1860, and the election of a Republican President was assured. The President-elect was no prize, to be sure: grotesquely tall, blatantly ugly – given to rough jokes and speech, so one of Lodge's acquaintances had noted, and very possibly something of a boobie. But he was a Republican. He was opposed, he said, to the "spread" of slavery. Not strong enough. But twice again as strong as Douglas or Bell, and at the least, no matter how foolish and awkward, a block to the hopes of the South personified in Breckenridge.

On the ninth day of November, a bare three days after the election, South Carolina had given her answer to a Republican victory: her governor had called a convention. The convention's sole business would be to consider an ordinance of secession to remove South Carolina from the federal union. Word had it in Willard's bar that Mississippi was considering the same tack, and that the whole cluster of states bordering the Gulf of Mexico were certain to follow.

If they secede, Lodge thought over his brandy, there will be collision. And if there is collision, Lincoln will not be able to rein in his own horses. There will be war, and no end of it until slavery is ended – and the South a wasteland.

Lately Lodge had started a new practice. When he finished his evening brandy (he drank it now: even his nerves had begun to fray under the mounting tension that strummed like a damaged heart beneath the skin of the whole nation), he would light a lamp and take down a group of volumes from his shelf. There was Napier's *Napoleon, The Principles of Military Etiquette,* a book on infantry tactics by an obscure major named Hardee, the *Maxims* of Napoleon, and a few treatises in French and German, including one by a Prussian staff officer dead not of wounds but of fever half a century before. It was called *On War.* Alongside the military volumes was one other: *The Prince,* heavily marked and underscored (five years later, he would be sitting in another dimly lighted room inside the house of a man dead less than an hour. He would pick up his Machiavelli again, and unmarked, not underscored, he would find these lines: " . . . in republics there is a stronger vitality, a

fiercer hatred, a keener thirst for revenge. The memory of their freedom will not let them rest . . . "). A public man, awaiting the time of his
usefulness, prepares.

Soon enough the time began to serve. There was disunion, there was a
Southern Confederacy. There was Sumter, and Lincoln's demand for
75,000 troops "to put down combinations too powerful" to be handled
in the ordinary way. There was Lodge, who had resigned his seat in
Congress to claim a brigadier general's commission in the militia of
Massachusetts. And there was war.

Only one portion of his plan miscarried. When the Massachusetts
troops were called into federal service, his general's commission was
not recognized. Lacking military experience, and without a friend close
to the administration, he could salvage only a colonel's commission in
the United States volunteers. And even that commission, based upon
his apparent qualification, was in the commissariat. He stayed in the
commissary for four years.

Resignation was impossible. He needed to be where the fighting was.
What had begun as a matter of family pride, what had become a matter
of personal vengeance, was moving toward the nature of obsession. It
could not be worked out at a desk or in a backwater camp. Whatever
name he chose to give it (sometimes he called it honor; sometimes duty
– on occasion when the brandy drove his father's stark shadow far into
the recesses of his mind – where Paul forever preached and chided and
gazed with warmth and pity upon The Poor Negro, bronzely grateful at
his feet – Lodge called it vengeance, and repeated the word with the
same relish as now he drank the brandy), it pushed him and mauled
him and carried him from one fruitless campaign to the next.

At First Manassas (he called it Bull Run when he was forced to mention it), he lost an entire wagon train and came within inches of being
dragged from his horse by rough-bearded cavalrymen who wore no
uniforms and carried no rifles, but who managed nonetheless to cut his
guards and drivers to pieces with huge outdated sabers that had last
been so used at Molino del Rey or Cerro Gordo. In the peninsula,
Lodge lost still more wagons along the single tortuous road through
White Oak Swamp. At Second Manassas (another Bull Run, and no
luckier than the first), he salvaged his wagons and some portion of his
supplies – only to be ordered to burn the supplies and carry wounded
away from the field in the empty wagons. There was no vengeance, no
pleasure in any of it, and a man less committed to his own views than

Jonathan Lodge might have given it up. But Lodge, now a public man for certain, and somehow insulated against the agony and loss of it, simply held to routine, kept his inventories – if not in order, at least in some wholehearted counterfeit of order – and awaited a better time.

For a few hours on the seventeenth day of September, 1862, he thought the good time had come. He stood with field glasses in hand looking down on a little Maryland village called Sharpsburg set near to a shallow creek called Antietam.

On the right, across the center, finally on his left, he saw the Union divisions smash themselves into rubble. At the Dunker Church, Hood's Texans served their guns and filled the road and yard there so full of smoke and steel that even Reynolds' Federals faltered and broke. In the center, a sunken road filled and overflowed with dead and wounded from both sides, and those who managed to find their way back from the nightmare of it would remember for as long as they lived the snake-rail fence, the low shrubs burned away by musketry – and how the dirt turned into scarlet mud in Bloody Lane.

From where Lodge stood, there was nothing to see but long lines of men moving into rolling patches of smoke, nothing to hear but a continual ragged din as if the sky were collapsing above them. Some-one told Lodge that Robert Toombes was commanding a Confederate brigade on the left across Antietam Creek, beyond a stone bridge. Leaving the wagons in charge of his executive, Lodge picked up a musket and joined a New York regiment of Burnside's command as, in midafternoon, they stormed the little bridge.

It came to nothing. There was slaughter, and after so much of it, the Union artillery pushed the Confederates back through the ravines and across the brow of a low hill. They crossed the bridge and moved up the high ground. Lodge saw small bunches of Southern infantry scuttling back out of range, running, it seemed, in complete disorder toward the rear.

Waving his bayoneted rifle above his head, Lodge shouted to the soldiers around him, who were moving forward with measured, careful strikes: "They've broken! The rebels have collapsed! Charge them, push them into the Potomac!"

"Shut up, old man," a hatless bald-headed infantryman near him growled. "If you think them rebs is through, you never fought 'em before."

"They're just regroupin'," another man said. "About the time we reach them trees, you'll see how Lee's boys collapse – right on top of us, like a frog fallin' on a Junie-bug."

So on down the slope toward the last thin line of Toombes' Confederates.

Later – so much later that even Lodge cared nothing for the knowledge – it was shown that the New York volunteers had been wrong. It was the first time they had been wrong, and there was no way for them to know how near a thing those last minutes on the Union left had been for the Army of Northern Virginia. Another headlong try – one more hell-for-leather assault, and Bloody Lane might not have been reenacted before a low stone wall at Fredericksburg or against a failing sun at Chancellorsville. It could have ended there, and Jonathan Lodge, absent from his commissary without permission, might have returned to Massachusetts to find a statue of himself in the place reserved for Paul – instead of returning to his wagons covered with dust and a little blood (not his own) to find a preemptory note from the corps' chief of staff commanding him to report to headquarters armed with good and sufficient reason for absence from his post of duty before the enemy.

But there was no last effort. When the Unions paused, that last mile was possibly the shortest one in the whole war, and there was not enough Confederate strength to bother scouting. By the time their wind was up, the mile might as well have reached the Gulf of Mexico, and the Confederate strength required no scouting at all. It was more than obvious.

Because in those crucial moments, while Lodge tried to bully and wheedle the men around him into a final attack, and while they coolly ignored this colonel with quartermaster's insignia and an annoying Boston accent, something portentous and unforgettable took place a few hundred yards farther on where Bob Toombes was prevailing on his two thousand men to stand fast and die in their places.

Confederate General A. P. Hill came up. Came from Harper's Ferry so rapidly, so careless of good order and proper marching procedure, that he left a good half of his Light Division broken with fatigue along that dust-fogged road (no, not the good half: that part arrived ready for anything and cut off Toombes' rhetorical marathon mid-course) and Hill brought with him besides his red flannel shirt, his awesome beard, and his razor-edged disposition, a new life for the Army of Northern

Virginia and the Southern cause – and almost two and a half years more of bloody war.

Even as Hill's men began filling the gaps in Toombes' frail line and passing beyond to try the Federals, Lodge's casual companions made ready to do what he had been trying to make them do for fifteen minutes. The skirmishers moved out, and double lines of infantry came behind. Then, suddenly, what had started as something between a battle and a mopping-up operation turned within moments into a rout – and again the Unions were its victims.

Because directly in front, marching in double line toward the New Yorkers (and some Pennsylvanians, who had come across the bridge with them) was a dense crowd of riflemen – all dressed in Union blue.

The bald-headed New Yorker near Lodge dropped his rifle butt near his foot and stared. He scratched his head and narrowed his eyes.

"I'll be goddamned if I can make it out," he muttered.

Lodge could make it out. "You waited. All of you waited, and now the job is done. Now they've finished it, and there's no glory left."

"Fuck the glory," someone else said. "I can pass that up, but I'd like to know what regiment come over the bridge after us, made that ravine and high ground, flanked them rebs and marched through 'em without a fight."

"And in fifteen minutes, too," the man near Lodge growled apprehensively.

"Ain't no sonofabitch in the Potomac army could or would do it."

"Not even with little Mac riding out ahead."

"You know . . . ," one of the men began.

"What does it matter?" Lodge cut in. "It's over, and we had no part in it."

"I can pass that up, too . . . but I keep thinking . . . "

Then there was nothing to think about. From a distance of perhaps one hundred and fifty yards, the mysterious bluecoats resolved all outstanding questions by letting go a volley of riflery into the New Yorkers and Pennsylvanians.

"Stop it," Lodge shouted, running toward the blue-clad men across the field. "Stop it. You're firing into your own men."

But a second volley sent him sprawling and sliced the wavering uncertain Federals around him to pieces. Men fell; men writhed. A handful fired kneeling and prone, and the rest began to run backward down the slope toward the bridge.

"Stop it," Lodge shouted again.

A hand struck his shoulder, pushing him flat. It was the New Yorker who had been beside him since the beginning of the assault.

"You goddamned dumb old sonofabitch, why don't you go back to your spuds and hard biscuit? Them's Johnnies. They got 'em a bunch of U.S. overcoats. But they're . . . "

Then the pressure on Lodge's shoulder eased as he heard something above and behind him that sounded like a sledgehammer hitting a ripe melon.

"You dumb old . . . ," the bald-headed New Yorker was saying as he sat down in the dirt and stared curiously at a spreading stain on his tunic that turned the fabric from blue to black, and a visible cavity in the middle of the stain. "You dumb . . . ," he said, shrugged, and lay back like a heap of clothes from which the living body has been suddenly, inexplicably withdrawn.

There was no court-martial for Lodge afterward. There was too much ferment in the Army of the Potomac just then, and anyhow, it seemed to the high command that Lodge might well stand to gain rather than lose by public trial.

So rather than reprimand him, they sent him west. He joined an ambitious task force commanded by a stubby cigar-chewing former regular army man names Grant. The object of the force was to clear the last bastions of Confederate resistance from the Mississippi so Union supplies could flow from Memphis to New Orleans without running under the guns of Port Hudson and Vicksburg.

It was a long siege. Cutoff from bases of supply for months on end, Lodge learned the craft of impressments from enemy civilians. He learned their hundred pitiful tricks of concealing food: hogs turned loose in the woods; smoked meat hung in trees; chickens tied leg-to-leg and stuffed into brier patches; cornmeal sewed into pallets.

It was mean work. But it was done on a large scale, and the cause for which it was done (according to the rare notes Lodge wrote back to his former campaign manager) shone as clear and pure through the smoke and horror of war as a great beacon shines through fog and heavy seas to stiffen the resolve of faltering mariners. "When this cruel war is over," Lodge said, "the millennium will burst upon us as a great new sun, and bathe the lives of all in the perfect waters of freedom and brotherhood."

But if he mixed his metaphors, his attitude toward his work was characteristically unmixed. A woman with five speechless tow-headed children and no man on the place would come asking that he spare her cow and two pigs.

"Because we ain't got nothin' else," she would say over and over again in a flat monotone. "We ain't got nothin' else."

"You'll have to *find* something else," Lodge would tell her. "My men need meat."

"Ain't nothin' else to find, and I got no man to go lookin' even if they was something'."

"Where *is* your man?" Lodge would pounce on her.

"Fightin'," she would say. "He's fightin'."

"With the rebels?"

"With Mr. Joel Thoomey's Long Gun Rangers," she said.

"Rebels."

"Mr. Joel Thoomey's . . . "

"You have no food because your man is a traitor to his country. He has betrayed his country. He has betrayed his own country, and so you and your brood will be hungry. The punishment is not mine; it comes from above. The wages of sin."

And the woman would leave as expressionless and dry-eyed as she had entered, cast perhaps a final look at her milch cow penned with the rest of the day's loot. Then she would walk the long miles back to her home, rustle in the ash at a cold fireplace until she found the loose stone, and from under it take a single gold piece – which she would give to her fourteen-year-old son.

"You go to Tennessee and they'll sign you up there," she would tell the skinny impassive replica of herself. "And when you see your paw, tell him what's happened here, and not to spare none of 'em, man nor beast, woman nor child. You tell him to get on with the killin' and then youall both get back soon as ever you can. Me and the children will make out. They's things in the woods, and your froggig . . . "

On to Vicksburg, and then the long miserable siege that dragged through late spring and into summer. The heat was almost too much for Lodge. When he was not actually occupied with duty, he retreated into his tent and sat in the humid darkness sipping from a diminishing supply of brandy held over from his Washington days. When, as a matter of fact, the Confederates surrendered on July 4th of 1863, the colonel was unable to attend the formal capitulation. Instead, having polished off a quart of his constant companion the night before, he was, at the very moment of the historic occasion, walking (he dared not even try to ride) with stiff measured strides in search of a division medical station. When he found it, he would ask for something to quiet a mild case of dyspepsia, and spend a few idle hours in the wrecked barn making clear the distinction between officers and contract surgeons – and between loyal men and rebels.

He turned the brandy snifter in his hands, cupped it and inhaled slowly. He closed his eyes tightly and then opened them to the moonlight and the shadowed lawn, the long tatters of cloud that moved across the moon's face and deepened for a moment the motionless darkness of the yard.

So long a journey, Lodge thought. So far in space and time. So much blood, so much agony, and still no end in sight. A people as intractable, as tough and unyielding as the tropic richness of their land. Chop away vine, cut down weeds, and in a day or so they have grown back as thick as before.

The roots, he thought. One must reach the roots and rip them from the soil of this country. Otherwise all the death will have been for nothing.

He sipped the brandy and watched the moon's pale light sift through the window and illuminate the rug near his feet. A feeling of exultation rose in him. Nothing had been accomplished really. Not yet. The serpent had been scotched. The killing of it remained.

Lodge's mouth curled. There was a humor in it. It was almost comic: after all – after the commissary, after the debacle at Sharpsburg, and the threadbare triumph of Vicksburg – after all, he would be instrumental in bringing down the South. When the serpent ceased its writing, his own heel would on its head. And from its ugly bones he would rear a monument.

Supper was done, and they were walking down the long, shadowed path that led to the main road. Amos had filled his pipe, and Rye, no smoker, walked beside him, hands clasped behind his back.

"You mean to keep that letter to yourself?" Amos asked him.

"Nothin' to it," Rye answered. "Nothin' dat makes any difference. He comin' home soon."

Amos turned, frowning. "Well, by God, it makes me some difference. The difference is that at least we've got one boy back out of this goddamned holocaust."

146

Rye did not look up. "He comin' home in a Yankee uniform. Wif an officer's rank."

For a moment Amos said nothing. "At least those thick-skulled bastards can see ability when it comes along. It's the wrong army, but at least he got ahead."

Rye stopped and met Amos' eyes. "You ain't makin' nothing easy fo' me," he said evenly. "I know you want me not to hurt, but dis ain't no help. You didn't send Morrison to the Confederacy fo' Phillipe to shoot at him. Dis wasn't all a joke."

"No," Amos said. "It wasn't funny. I don't know what sent Phillipe across the lines up in Maryland, and God knows I hope nothing we ever did to him sent him to a Yankee recruiting officer. But he chose to go and he chose to join, and now you say he's alive and coming home. So we have it to live with. Maybe, when he comes, I should beg his pardon."

"Pardon," Rye grated. "Jesus Christ, pardon. Mo' like shoot him down and ask God's pardon we didn't do it befo' he left here."

Amos shook his head. "Beg his pardon for not ignoring you with your hesitation, putting off what he had a right to know before he went to Virginia. It never occurred to you he might not want to fight with Morrison."

"It never occur to me any mahn don't want to fight fo' his own people. Yo' fight fo' de people who care about you."

Amos smiled and knocked his pipe against a tree. "It's easier for a free man to say that, don't you reckon?"

Rye squatted next to one of the tall pines that flanked the main road. "Ain't nobody in dis town know I'm free. Fo' all dey know, I'm yo' slave an' has been always."

"Because you never wanted anyone to know. You said it would be easier with nobody knowing. Because they'd resent a free colored man owning half a plantation with a white man. I told you they could resent and be damned. We could have seen to any of them that resented too hard. At the least, you could have told Phillipe there were no bonds on him. Knowing that, he might never have . . . "

"Let it lie," Rye cut him off. "We come too far to go over it all an' see where we done right and wrong. Ain't no goin' back now."

Rye stood up and started toward the house. "I have yo' room ready when you get done with yo' pipe."

"Don't stay up," Amos called after him. "You go on to sleep,"

Rye stopped and handed Amos the letter Raisor had brought. "You want to see what he says?"

Amos walked back up the path with him part of the way.

"I can't read it in the dark."

"It makes dark readin' wherever you be."

Just short of the front porch, Federal sentries had built a small fire. While one of their number shuffled around the several acres of the yard, the rest sat beside the fire talking – drinking, Amos suspected, whenever they were sure no officer was within seeing distance – and a sergeant, dark-bearded and broad-shouldered, played softly on a mouth organ. Amos tried to remember the tune. It was something drawn and mournful from the Appalachians: about a girl awaiting her lover who had already found his death.

They paused within the glow of the Federals' fire. Amos unfolded the letter. Rye paused, watching him, and then continued past the fire toward the house.

The fire's light, irregular and weak, barely reached the white wrought-iron bench. But Amos settled himself, relit his pipe and squinted at Phillipe's letter:

> *... you have been saddened maybe and shamed because of what I did after leaving you with a promise to be faithful to Morrison and to keep him safe as you did his father. I cannot tell or explain all of what has passed, but I must try to say some of these things before I come home to you and the town where I was raised up ...*

Amos' eyes watered from the effort of reading in the poor light. He let the letter fall to his lap and sucked on his pipe. Overhead, the moon rode among small clouds, looking like one of the paper lanterns that had been hung around the porch and yard at parties and fetes before the war, when both the boys were home.

... the town where I was raised up, Amos was thinking, remembering the peninsula of Virginia, deep woods, an infernal sun, the rich fields and the slow singular way of life he had known then.

The second son of a Revolutionary officer, who had served with Francis Marion in South Carolina and later moved north to command section of Washington's artillery before Yorktown, Amos Stevens had been born in Williamsburg in 1813.

His raising had been as simple and clearly directed as any raising could be. His father, whose loyalty to Washington faded as Hamilton's influence mounted, was an old Republican of such outspoken opinion that he had found himself in personal combat twice with Federalist planters nearby, who could not brook the name of "petty tyrant" which Marcus Antoninus Stevens publicly affixed to each of them. On the first occasion, he had stood to receive his angry challenger's first shot. It had been a clean miss, and laughing immoderately, Marcus Antoninus had carefully lowered the hammer on his own pistol, handed it to the gaping physician in attendance, and strode off the field with his hands in his pockets, whistling.

The second encounter was less fortunate: Marcus took a ball though his shoulder which so unsteadied him that he was able neither to give as good as he had gotten or afterward stroll laughing and whistling from the field.

"By God," he had said to his son later, "the damned monarchists are improving their aim. Next time, I'll shoot first. To hell with long-suffering."

Which last sentence might sum up the substance of the Stevens boys' education in worldly matters. "Suffer nothing obnoxious for long. Restraint," their father told them, "is the crown of a brave man, and the retreat of a coward. Never stand for injustice; never suffer it to be exercised upon you, and never stand idle while it is loosed upon your neighbor. Have a decent respect for all men's opinions – so long as the men in question are themselves respectable and decent."

"Anarchy," Amos' father had said, "something near anarchy . . . seasoned with *noblesse oblige* and enlightened self-interest: that is a *government*. The best government is a decent man in the company of decent men. Failing that . . . for want of decent men . . . the least government commensurate with good order. One law not subscribed to by the majority of those to whom it will apply . . . a single paltry regulation passed other than by the representatives of those to whom it relates: that is tyranny, sir. That is more than reason for revolution. Because a single evil statute begets its own kind and in the begetting bloats with pride and contempt the framers of such laws. And soon the phantom of fat George rises and stalks the legislative halls. No enormity seems dangerous to those who stand to gain by further outrage. Then, sir, then what might have been accomplished by a strip of horse-hide or at most a single bullet requires a whole generation offering its best blood to purge the result of having suffered that single wicked law.

"The people," Antoninus would go on, "the people are rarely wise, rarely right in their judgments taken singly. But wise or foolish, right or wrong, sir, the *people* are those who must obey the laws made in their name. If they elect a food or demand a foolish law, then let them learn by the suffering such foolishness must bring. Let them starve, let them suffer. *But let their will prevail.* For if they do not find out their best interest in a decade or even in a generation, sooner or later the hard school of their imprudence will bring them to wisdom, and they will right the wrong. So long as they have the power, justice and right can and must be discovered and made to rule – and they will have become wise in the process of their blundering search.

"But if a tyrant be allowed to set himself up, whatever good he may do is only a contingency and leaves the people as ignorant as before. Put your trust in the people, for the people are all we have: *we* are the people, and if there is greatness and beauty in a land, it must come from the people. If you speak of a just and honorable government, you are saying that a just and honorable people have raised up a government in their image. A government may surely be worse than the people it essays to govern, but it can never be better than they. The people first, the people last – the people always."

It was an education laced with horsemanship and Shakespeare, the pre-Socratic philosophers and the making of hard soap. Amos and Rye learned to survey land and to erect a cabin or a cotton-house single-handed. They swam and hunted, carried John Locke on their hunting trips and talked of Rousseau while they floated on their backs in the James River.

Then it was time for Amos to ride south. His father gave him the best horse on the place, a purse full of gold coins, a tiny miniature of his dead mother, and a leather-bound set of the writings of Thomas Jefferson.

"If there is something more that you will need," his father told him, "you had best look to yourself for it."

Amos and Rye (who had been given the second-best horse on the place, a purse of gold for himself – and a small reserve for Amos in case of emergency) mounted and started out, with Antoninus and Amos' elder brother standing on the bottom step of the porch, hands in pockets.

"Suffer nothing unjust," his father called after him, "least of all to be unjust yourself."

"Good-bye . . ."

"Trust the people," his father had shouted.

"Good-bye . . ."

"'Ware of whores who do not look it," he father grinned and roared before the road's turning had cut them off.

Amos shook his head. It was a long way and a long time from Virginia. He worked the muscles of his shoulders, stamped blood back into his legs and watched a Union soldier pass by the bench, his rifle trailing, his eyes glazed with fatigue. "Awright," the Federal called to the men around the fire, "you sonsabitches can draw straws for the next duty. I'm done with it."

Amos turned back to the letter, leaning forward again, trying to catch the fire's wavering glow. Even in good light Phillipe's small, carefully turned writing was hard to make out.

> . . . Morrison could not see the wrong, the sin in human bondage, and I had not words to tell him. The bondage had gone on too long. It had gotten a reason and a language of its own, and there was no way to argue against it because I had no words . . .

I knew it, Amos thought. That damned silliness of Rye's not telling Phillipe or Morrison that he was free. Morrison not knowing, and maybe a word, maybe a careless order when he was tired, or after a battle. And Phillipe went over.

> . . . While I write, I keep looking for good words. I know what I want to say. The other colored men I have been with have a language for this thing. It is talk of lashes and poor food. It is verbs of heartache and shame. Families divided and women taken against their will when a master's belly churned. Now there is a new language of pride and how a man should walk upright and ask no other's leave to come and go. I understand this talk, and I have bled to make it true . . .

Amos closed his eyes and leaned back against the trunk of the oak. He could feel the same cool evening breeze that had swept across his face on the place east of New Orleans, the first land he had owned coming south from Virginia. He remembered the girl, an Irish name and an Irish smile, but hands red with work as they built the place up year after year alongside Rye and his wife. And he remembered the day after he and Rye and had come back from Mexico.

They had taken the boys with them that afternoon after leaving the graveyard. It was almost dark when they reached the unfinished house, the replica of Thomas Jefferson's Monticello that they had begun half a dozen years before.

Caught, impacted in the light of a rising moon, awash in ground-fog, the house seemed to have the timeless impenetrable quality of polished stone, the inscrutable smoothness and singularity of a monolith. It looked as if, cold and perfect against a huddle of oak and cypress behind and on either side, it were some kind of monument to a vanished age, and neither hollow nor warm enough for human occupancy.

Amos had touched a piece of weathered lathe with his toe. It splintered with a dry snap. "What do you think?" he had asked Rye.

Rye had said almost nothing since leaving the cemetery, had said nothing at all since they picked up the boys and ridden out from New Orleans.

"I can't think," Rye whispered. "I don't wanna think."

Mo and Phillipe had walked to the house with them. They boys ran up and down the circular front steps, pushed open the unfastened door, stared back outside toward their fathers through glassless windows.

"Ya, Poppa," Mo screamed. "it's spooky!"

"It's mighty big," Phillipe had called. "Big as a barn, and all white inside."

The boys' voices faded as they ran deeper into the long corridors, the empty rooms.

"All I can think of," Rye went on, "all I can think of it dat raised crypt in de graveyard. All I can think of it dat cold stone over her. How she like to laugh and sing. How she talked about us buying' free one day fo' de chilrun."

Amos did not move his eyes from the cold white façade of the house. "She's free now," he said. "What about this place? By rights, a piece of it is yours."

Rye's voice was cold and distant. "I don't want none of it. Let me be shet of it. I got dat graveyard in my soul. I can't stand walkin' through dis place an' seein' her plannin' curtains or sizin' fo' rugs with Miss Kathy. I can't get ready fo' dat."

"All right," Amos said. "I reckon you've said it. I reckon the guts are pulled out of this dream. Maybe we . . . "

"I don't want no mo' dream," Rye went on. "What you ain't got, you can't miss. I don't want ever to want anythin' again."

"Call the boys," Amos said. "Let's go back to town. We've got a lot to do."

By then the moon was high, and if he had glanced over his shoulder as he walked, Amos would have seen, diminishing, becoming smaller and smaller, a fabulous house with two small boys, one black and one white, tumbling out its untended doors, and running as fast as they could to catch up with him.

III

7 JUNE 1865 — At noon the streets were still thick with mud, still deep in yesterday's rain. Up and down Texas Street, women shopped and coveys of children ran barefoot, splashing from one plank sidewalk to the other, into alleys, and into the vacant lots that stood rank with summer weeds between stores, offices and warehouses along the street.

Pony Mueller's tired horse was tied in front of Ramsey's saloon. Inside, Pony stood up to the bar with a brace of Union soldiers. He was buying. He had even offered to buy for some of the draggled townsmen who stood farther down the bar or sat in chairs across the bare gloomy room. But the Southerners had covered their glasses or turned them upside down when Ramsey brought the bottle. Pony shrugged. There was no need trying to understand men who turned down free whiskey.

"What you got to do is knock off the easy ones first," Pony told the Federals confidentially. "You got to leave the tough ones till last. You got the widows and the ones who come home early missing an arm or a leg. You go easy on the big planters till you get the small fry plucked clean."

"How far along are you?" one of the soldiers asked him.

Pony smiled broadly. He was feeling good. The bottle was his, and he had money enough – or cotton waiting to be turned into money – for all the whiskey he could drink.

"Well," he said with gentle modesty, like an entrepreneur in the midst of scoring a fabulous coup. "I can't complain. I confiscated thirty-five bales yesterday and sixty today. Then I sold 'em to myself for ten cents a pound, and shook hands on the deal. I got 'em warehoused and got a boat on the way up from Baton Rouge. When I get it to Memphis, I got it futured at a dollar and a quarter."

"Where'd you do your fighting?" one of the soldiers asked pointedly.

Pony blushed only a little. "I was at Fredericksburg," he said portentously. "I was at Chancellorsville."

What he did not say was that he had sprawled under a tree near his sutler's wagon above Fredericksburg with a spyglass watching Burnside's human sacrifices pound themselves by regiment, by division, into bloody stew at the base of Mary's Heights. Or that, at Chancellorsville, he had been the only pimp attached to the Potomac army to get his own stock of hookers back across the Rappahannock and set up in decent fashion to receive the shattered and demoralized victims of Stonewall Jackson's superlative final lesson in guts-as-tactics.

"Well," the questioner said, himself only a veteran of the comparatively easy last months at Petersburg, "I reckon a man who saw them two has got some profit coming."

"I only want a fair return," Pony said. "I wouldn't even be in this line of work but for the government asking loyal man to serve."

Down the bar, a farmer was telling some friends about his mules.

"Six of 'em. The most mules any man in the parish managed to keep. But one of them Treasury sonsabitches said they had to go on account of they was rebel supplies or somethin'. Shit, the Confederate army took 'em and used 'em for two weeks. I never got nothin' but a piece of paper promisin' Jeff Davis would pay."

"Maybe if you took their oath," another farmer said, glancing nervously around at his friends.

"Say I'm sorry I fought? They can take them goddamn mules."

"You got children to feed."

"Ain't bread alone," a third man said. "The way things are, a child needs to believe in his pappy more than he needs eats. What with the newspapers and the Yankees sayin' every man who took up arms was a traitor, my boy wants to know how come I traded."

"I hear that oath . . . "

"Bullshit. That oath don't help a man with mules branded CSA. You got to swear you love them stars and stripes, and promise you won't do it no more."

The first man sneered. "Then they let you kiss a picture of Lincoln's dead ass and hold onto your mules or land – till the tax man comes."

"Tax man?"

"Sure. What they don't take outright, they're gonna make you sell for back taxes you owed the rightful Louisiana government."

"What the hell government was that?"

"The one Ben Butler kept goin' with bayonets down in New Orleans."

"They gonna get a man goin' or comin'. This is worse than the goddamn war."

"What's you expect? Peace?"

"It ain't gonna be peace for long if they steal my mules and my cotton, take my tools and tax my land out from under me. They gonna have 'em another war."

"I'm too tired. I ain't got but one leg left."

"That's so. We all of us tired. But I ain't gonna starve without goin' for the man who's starvin' me."

Pony poured the soldiers another drink. "If you happen to see some Confederate supplies around," he said, "there's a good bonus for information."

"Confederate supplies? You mean mules?"

"Or horses. Or cotton or corn or any damn thing an army could of used."

"I saw some pretty good-lookin' horses yesterday. But they didn't have no rebel brand."

Pony shook his head. "That don't matter. You just find out where they keep those horses. I can take care of it."

"Ain't that kinda dangerous?" one of the soldiers asked Pony. "How long do you figure these folks are gonna sit still for it?"

Pony stared at him in surprise, his pale lumpy face flushed with the whiskey. "Why, they got to stand for it. It's the law. It's the United States government."

The Union shook his head. "Yeah, I heard they had to sit still for Lincoln back in '60. And I spent four years trying to hold 'em still, and

155

by the time me and a million or so other fellers had 'em quiet, Lincoln was stretched out cold with a Southern bullet through his head."

"They learned," Pony said. "They knew better now."

"Shit," the second soldier blurted. "I reckon Mr. Lincoln learned somethin' too. I reckon a couple hundred thousand loyal Northern men learned some Southern soil cultivation by bein' buried under it. These people ain't worth a damn for doin' as they're told."

"We got the right on our side," Pony said portentously. "And right makes might. His truth is marching on."

The first soldier shook his head. "Sure," he said. "I guess you're right."

Down the bar, one of the farmers was almost crying in his anger.

"Niggers," he said. "I seen 'em registerin' niggers to vote. Some little squatty-assed sonofabitch clerk from Minneapolis sittin' in front of a curtain. So I elbowed in amongst the niggers and said, 'Here now, I been a voter all my life. I want to sign up.'"

"Did he sign you?"

"Sign hell. He kinda looked at me and looked down at the table he had all his papers on. Then he kinda twisted his head around toward the back. Then he told me he couldn't sign me up. Not till I get me one of them pardons."

"You got to get on down there and nuzzle ole Andy Johnson's behind. You got to tell that Tennessee turncoat it was you that sold your own folks out and him that was a patriot."

"So they told me to move on and went back to signin' up the niggers. They was puttin' some of Jess Spence's niggers on the role, and you know goddamned well Jess would kill any nigger he owned who turned up readin' or writin'."

"Signin' niggers to vote all day and stealin' mules and cotton all night," an old smallholder said slowly, loud enough to be heard down the length of the bar. "If this here is U.S. government, I reckon we was right to have that war no matter how it went."

"It might be we'll need a little more," someone said.

But Ramsey poured glasses full up and down the bar, and the hot afternoon wore on like the rim of an iron wheel.

Inside Don Juan Cleburne's store, it was always twilight. The high shelves were filled with jars and cartons. Harness and implements, new and used, hung from pegs and nails driven into the walls, the frames of the shelves, and the dark rafters overhead. Barrels and hogsheads littered the floor space, and old furniture, dust-covered books, used clothing and sacks of grain and flour were stuffed into corners. There were no windows, and one huge oil lamp swung dismally down into the center of the cramped room. It did not illuminate, but simply made the bulk, the outline of crates and cases visible enough to keep Cleburne's custom from doing themselves injury before they could trade.

Cleburne lived in the rear of the store. Back there, in a room almost as large as that in which he kept his stock, he had stacked more possessions. There were mirrors in gilt frames, crockery and silver from France and England – by way of destitute planters' tables and cupboards – a set of dueling pistols with ebony handles and delicate engraving on the dark burnished barrels, a pile of Mexican lace scarves and shawls, and more jewelry than he had ever bothered to tote up – some of it solid gold fine enough to be scored with a thumbnail.

There, amid five years' plunder and a dozen years' hoarding before that, Don Juan Cleburne was lowering himself into an overstuffed library chair with cracking leather upholstery and wads of cotton padding leaking from its underside. He paid no attention to the fine mahogany table inlaid with walnut in front of him, or to the cheese and bread lying on the table (not on a plate, but on the table itself, tough and crusted and each marked not with a knife but with teeth). He turned up the wick of a dented chimneyless lamp and tried to do some figuring while he waited.

So far, so good, he thought. He already had a Union commissary officer in his pocket. Not a sergeant or even a lieutenant, but a captain. One of Lodge's staff. Show me a commissary officer, Cleburne thought, grinning to himself, and I'll show you the crookedest sonofabitch in any man's army. Put a man out in the skirmish line and he'll fight for home and the old flag – whatever flag it happens to be. But you put him in amongst canned goods and barrels and hundred-pound sacks and he'll sell Lincoln or Lee out before you can spit a snuff tin full.

Before the Union supply train had even been unloaded, the captain, so anxious was he to go on the take, had sent a corporal to Cleburne's back door. The corporal, a businessman on his own (and who, before getting on with the business proposition of his superior, had sold Cleburne two sides of bacon and fifty pounds of white cornmeal stolen from the wagon in which the captain kept the odds and ends he had managed to salvage from the outrage of regular inventory that Lodge demanded), had put it to Cleburne this way:

"He's like a virgin sixty years old. Jesus, it's enough to make a stone statue laugh. He's got maybe six months or a year left before they retire him, and now with it so close he sees how little that pension is, and he wants a store of his own back in Pittsburg, and he can smell all the money that's gonna be movin' from one set of pockets to the other around here. It's about to kill him on account of these Treasury agents and all."

The corporal had grinned wolfishly. "You got to lend him a hand," he snickered, "even out of charity."

"Sure," Cleburne told him. "I'll see what I can do to help out."

So if Cleburne needed food – good flour or beef or canned goods – he could get it quickly and cheaply. He could get blankets. He could get drugs. He expected that sooner or later he could get power and guns.

It's like you fool with a young girl, Cleburne thought. If you can get hold of her hand and hold it for a while, you can go on up her arm and catch hold of a titty. After that, it's just the when and the where. If I was to say "guns" to that slabfaced Yankee sonofabitch, his mustache would run up his nose. But he'll come along. He's got to come along. The ones like him all come along.

Cleburne heard the back door rattle as someone hit it softly with the flat of a hand.

"All right, it's open," Cleburne called out.

He watched the man slouch into the room. No matter how many times he saw him, he was still taken with curiosity by the long skull grizzled over in colorless hair, the lips paper-thin and yet protuberant as a Negro's. Cleburne liked to watch him move, especially across an open space, a street or a room, his shoulders hunched as if in anticipation of a blow about to fall out of the guileless air.

He was like a ferret, Cleburne thought. Lean and snaky, quick and edgy. Ready to rip out a throat or lick a shoe with equal facility. And there was no pose, no stance to it. He planned nothing and worked by and toward no design at all except a regula of avarice etched into his nervous system alongside brutality and obsequiousness. Cleburne had wondered for fifteen years what he did with his money.

Cleburne watched him cross the room slowly, his eyes squinted against the weak lamplight and roaming over the jumbled heaps of furniture, packing cases and nameless objects that filled its far end almost to the ceiling.

"Murray, sit down and get your eyes off them trunks and boxes."

Murray Taggert rubbed his unshaven chin and went on sizing up the piled crates and cases that formed an almost solid barricade across one side of the room. He had been in this room dozens of times, but the rite of entry was always the same; he would try hopelessly to guess what the trunks and cupboards and cases contained, what they might be worth even empty. And each time, Cleburne would call him down.

Finally Murray found an empty hogshead and pulled it close to the table. It sat far lower than a chair, and Murray bestrode it with his chin just above the table's surface, his pinched squinting eyes turned up toward Cleburne as if in solemn and determined mockery of Cleburne's own defect.

"Well, Murray, what have you got?" Cleburne broke the silence.

"Nevermind," Murray droned. "I got me a piece of things."

Cleburne smiled. "You got yourself a piece of open ground and a wood cross if you mess with me," he said pleasantly. "I know about the registrar's office."

"You don't *know* nothing'."

"O yes," Cleburne laughed out loud. "Lodge or one of his dog robbers has you bought and paid for, but I bought me one of Lodge's things. He told me about how they had you behind that curtain shakin' your head and noddin' when a man tried to register. My mouthpiece told me you'd disenfranchised damn near every white man in the parish."

"They're rebels," Murray said righteously. "I didn't make 'em do it."

"O sure," Cleburne went on. "That makes it all right. They wouldn't soak you with kerosene and set you off just on account of tellin' God's own sweet truth, would they?"

"Nevermind," Murray snarled.

"All right. I won't mind. If it slips out, I'll let it go. But you rest easy about that: you got enough on your mind with the other thing. The big thing."

"What thing?" Murray asked uneasily, his face twisted and working unpleasantly, poised just above the table top like that of a hideous child.

"I had in mind Pony Mueller's quick-developed nose for spottin' mules and cotton hid out in the woods."

"Listen," Murray gasped, "that ain't none of my doin'. Honest to God. I ain't been tellin' . . . "

Don Juan Cleburne came out of his slouch and leaned forward. The banter was gone from his voice.

"Don't shit me, Murray," he rasped. "Don't go swearin' off what I *know* what you've been doin'. You set up old Lady Marshall last evenin'. You set up Mike and Sam Reynolds today, and ain't any of 'em got cotton enough left to stuff a pillow. The Reynolds boys lost five mules."

"You can't prove nothin'," Murray mumbled. "You can't prove a thing."

Cleburne's expression was placid again. "Use your head, Murray. I don't *have* to prove anything. There ain't a man in this town who wouldn't just as soon slit your throat as slaughter a pig. They know what you are. They know what you did before the war. They know what you didn't do while the war was on – and they got a good idea of what you're up to now: not just that you're sellin' 'em out, but maybe even how. You messed yourself up out on the porch yesterday. When that water-witted little lieutenant offered some gold for pullin' that gun, you was up and ready before he could finish talkin'. There wasn't a man on the porch who missed it. You were ready to go out and help the Yankees for a couple of dollars. Now what do you figure they'd do if I was to say the Federals had offered you a hundred dollars for duty behind that curtain – or Mueller had slipped you nearly twice that much to kinda talk in your sleep about cotton and mules and such?"

"They seen it was Sentell went to that cannon," Murray choked. "They seen him do it."

"Don't be a fool all your life," Cleburne cut him off. "They ain't studyin' Sentell, except maybe one or two of 'em would like to shake his hand for savin' their hides if they had guts and brains enough to stop him on the street with people watchin'."

"They better watch him," Murray said darkly.

Cleburne shook his head slowly.

"You couldn't sell it in a million years, Murray. Sentell came back out of the war bound and determined not to get close to anything again. They know what he is. They know what he ain't, too. They know goddamned well he didn't stand against the whole town and hold to his parole for two years just to turn around and throw away the very thing he'd bought at such a price when the Federals came in."

"He helped the Yankees . . . ," Murray started in doggedly again.

"Tell it to the town," Cleburne said shortly. "Maybe there's enough damn fools in the town to believe even that of him even with you sayin' it. I wouldn't want to overestimate 'em."

"He ain't no different from anybody else," Murray said, as if to himself. "He'd sell for the right price."

Cleburne's bad eye trembled furiously. "You go right on figurin' that way," he barked, "and you'll end up as dead as Lincoln. There's men you buy and men you can't. And even of the ones you can, there's those with a crazy price tag. I knew a man, a sheriff, who wouldn't let a killer go for money, not even for a hundred in gold. But who opened the cell door in return for nothin' but hearin' the truth about a story that didn't' concern him at all."

Cleburne wiped his face with an outsized red handkerchief. "Anyhow, forget Sentell. Even if they were to take it into their heads to shoot him or stretch him, that wouldn't take you off the target. You're right in the center ring, and I'm callin' the shots."

Murray's chin almost touched the table. His eyes, always drawn tight and narrow, looking always swollen and impassive, were pressed now lid to lid. He looked as if he were about to cry. The angry truculence he had roared at Cleburne's charges was gone.

"What do you want?" he asked Cleburne. "How much do you want?"

Cleburne eased himself back to the overstuffed chair. He smiled broadly and crossed his hands, fingers twined, across his belly. "That's what I wanted to hear," he said. "Now we can do business."

"How much?" Murray asked numbly.

Cleburne raised his eyebrows. "O no," he said, "You got it wrong. I don't want none of that money you milked out of Lodge or Mueller. That's all yours. All I want is to know."

"What the hell do you want to know?" Murray asked, weak with relief.

"Whatever happens," Cleburne told him. "I want to know ahead of time when Lodge means to have a horse shod or a letter mailed. Whatever they got on the stove, I want a spoonful to see what it tastes like."

Murray stared at Cleburne in amazement. "That's all you want? You ain't lyin'?"

"That's all for now," Cleburne said. "We'll wait and see how things come along."

Murray wiped his mouth with the back of his hand. "About that vote registerin'," he began. "A man's got to make out. I got a daughter."

"Vera?"

"Sure," Murray said. "That little girl ain't got nobody to look out for her, and I . . ."

"Stop it," Cleburne said. "You ain't given that girl nothin' but a bad time since your wife turned coward and died on you fifteen years ago."

"Naw," Murray told him, still anxious. "I . . ."

"What you got," Cleburne cut him off, "is a chance to stay alive and maybe turn a few dollars if you stay limber, sprout eyes in the back of your head and remember God is a long way off, but I'm a minute's walk from City Hall and Ramsey's saloon."

Outside, the sun was gone. Another bank of clouds had shrouded the sky above the town, and the spring temperature was dropping rapidly. Cleburne turned up his lamp and settled deeper into his dilapidated chair. He liked the darkness. It blunted the edge of things, took away the distinction between fantasy and reality, between beauty and ugliness.

Like that other spring, he thought. The one at Vicksburg. Like all the springs when he was young and had nothing but breath and a pair of fists and the goddamned eye. Always cold, or at best squatting next to another man's fire, and him giving space and maybe a crust and a strip of fatback because Cleburne seemed good for a laugh, or lacking the laugh, damned well strong enough to chop wood for that fire he was using up so freely.

His heavy face was impassive and he had forgotten the talk with Murray. He had even forgotten the gold and china and bric-a-brac piled around him, and for the first time in years he thought of his own beginnings and the long road stretched out behind in space and time that had brought him here and now.

Son of a Kentucky tinker with wandering feet and hands to match, got on a dim-witted girl who, had she lived in England half a century earlier, would have been called simply and accurately a slavey, in the Tennessee wilderness between Knoxville and the North Carolina line, Don Juan Cleburne was born to be a dupe. He was born wall-eyed, and his mother's poor lean milk did him no good. Before he could find a beverage more to his liking, his father (who had failed to do his ugly little son's mother even the courtesy of providing the 50-cent fake brass wedding ring usually given when marriage was disagreeable) had left eastern Tennessee behind and found himself a berth on a wagon train moving westward into the Trans-Mississippi country, which at that time (1810) was not even wilderness properly speaking, but rather a realm as mysterious as Africa's middle or the upper Amazon, and as well known to French explorers of two centuries earlier as to the Americans who pushed due west from Tennessee rather than make the hazardous but at least sane jaunt downward into what would one day be the Southwest. Miles Cleburne, hitching his mule to the back of a wagon and, dumping his few tools into a leather sack, had mentioned opportunity and fortune to his son's mother. Had even suggested vaguely that he might send for him if the pickings seemed good and the air healthy.

The girl had watched him ride off, her thick lips moving (not in prayer: her lips always moved soundlessly, her mouth was always open and voiceless, and Miles Cleburne had blacked her eye once in an attempt to cure the idiosyncrasy, but Lula was incurable: excepting only Miles Cleburne himself, whatever she had, she kept), her eyes glazed and unfocused, and her hands twisting in young Don Juan's swaddling rags till the baby bowled out in pain, and even for a moment or two after that.

Don Juan: a misnomer of such proportion as to almost give the name itself new connotation rather than merely make its cockeyed fleshy young bearer a laughingstock, a dupe. The name he had of his father:

"Jesus," Miles Cleburne had said when a deaf midwife had handed him his son, "sweet crawlin' Jesus. I seen better-lookin' kids amongst the victims of a Indian massacre. He's too goddamned ugly to live."

And the midwife, ancient and hearing none of it, smiled and smiled and smoothed the baby's damp hair. She pointed to his tiny squinted unaligned eyes.

"Won't miss a bet," his father laughed. "He'll be able to see a dollar comin' from both ways at once."

So of course, Don Juan. From a small store of knowledge, and a bottomless supply of humor, a name to give the boy a solid start. Born to be a dupe, and no mistake.

And raised at first to be the same: until, her lips moving and eyes still glazed like cakes of ice frozen and melted and frozen again, his mother had left him (three years old then) in the back of a bakery in Cincinnati, where she had been working eighteen hours a day for two dollars

163

a week and found, to keep some long-standing date with disaster only a little more final than what had gone before. When they fished her out of the Ohio River, her baker-employer identified her early the same afternoon, and by six o'clock that evening, young Don Juan was in the Cincinnati waifs' home and, it seemed, one step closer to the uncontested inheritance of dupedom.

But a higher determination was at work. By the time Donny Cleburne was fourteen, the docks of Memphis took shape before his eyes, and the orphan asylum was no more than the shabby homespun on his back and the unforgettable memory of oatmeal gruel (unsugared) in his mouth. A week's work at a slave-pen took the homespun off his back, and a week's consorting with his new friends (butcher boys, bank runners trusted only with unendorsed checks and mortgage papers, livery stable turd-wranglers, fledging pimps) scratched the flat flavor of oatmeal out of his mouth and replaced it with the brassy tang of cornsuds carefully aged for six weeks.

He fed the slaves awaiting sale or transfer. He washed down the incoming human cattle and doctored minor cuts and bruises (and frequently covered insignificant blemishes with a daub of stove polish properly cut to match octoroon or mulatto, applied full-strength to genuine Africans unblessed by a dilution of white blood). He learned to price and to choose; he learned how to make a questionable specimen run back and forth across the yard until it either fell or demonstrated good wind. He learned to put aside the occasionally beautiful Negress for which Memphis bloods (who would not dare bid for attractive wenches at public auction) were likely to pay a tidy sum.

He learned more: he found that good wind and beauty, placid disposition, and loyalty were priceless attributes in a slave – and conversely almost worthless in a free man. A cockeyed slave was doomed to scrub pots during the day, to play Cuffy-the-jester all evening. But a cockeyed white man, given the slightest measure of dignity and a pinch of determination, could stand as tall and go as far as an Apollo (and the truth of this would be proved soon enough on a gallows in Virginia where walleyed John Brown, laved in blood, would chant the mystique of more blood till a Southern noose snapped him into myth; proved in the streets of New Orleans where cross-eyed Ben Butler, once a supporter of Jefferson Davis for the Presidency, would hang and bully and outrage until the Confederate Congress offered a bounty on his head and pronounced him a common enemy of mankind).

164

But finally Cleburne learned that bad eye or no, a man had to make his own way or make no way at all. Not merely that he had to work and look out for himself, but that he had to guard each inch of position he managed to attain, stand ready to fend off any challenge to his dignity, his worth. And what he learned, he remembered – for a time at least.

By the time he was thirty, he was in Alabama with a string of his own Negroes, buying, selling (and occasionally renting to the Alabama sports whose amusements and tastes differed not at all from their Tennessee cousins') and keeping his eyes open for whatever shift might offer itself. A little speculation in land, a little cotton futuring, even some penny-ante railroad stockjobbing in northern Mississippi. Then, just a few days short of what he supposed was his thirty-second birthday, he sold out a parcel of land in western Alabama and bought the girl.

It was in Vicksburg, and he was only an hour from the boat for New Orleans when he stopped at the open auction. Flush with Alabama profit and with the best part of a quart of upcountry store-bought bourbon in him, he was feeling wise and lucky and expansive, and when they brought her out of the women's pen (not much of a pen as he would discover; hardly pen enough to keep the women in, and built flush up against the men's enclosure with only a span of chicken wire between them), the look of her almost snapped him sober. But not quite.

Sober enough to realize that she was the most beautiful woman he had ever seen, black, white, or mixed. Sober enough to touch the up-tilted breasts beneath her tight shift with his poor eccentric eyes; enough to feel his sprawling belly quake and dip as she mounted the block slowly, modestly, and stared over the collection of possible buyers, loafers, and levee loungers that had suddenly changed from a cluster of disinterested random characters into a solid and almost harmonious male body, and which (like a single mindless hot-loined animal) was poised breathless, waiting the auctioneer's hard pitch in order to breathe again.

But not sober enough to catch her name. She did not need nor did he require a name. He watched her belly, her arms, her thighs. Without realizing it, he was looking for some flaw, some grotesque imperfection that would break the stasis, permit him laughter, and a casual walk on down to the New Orleans boat. But there was nothing to help him. Her feet were small and perfect. Her legs was full at the calf, small at the ankle – not the long unbroken line of shank, from knee to heel that most Negresses made do for legs. Her thighs, like her breasts, spread the thin shapeless shift tight in front, and her hair fell, rich and untangled, almost to her waist.

And the auctioneer kept gilding the lily. She was sound and healthy, had a good disposition, was a willing worker. And more: the white blood she bore was of the first quality – of a family which must remain nameless, but which name would be familiar to every gentleman present. Cleburne missed most of it. He licked his lips and wondered why in God's name she was offered for public sale. He thought of what she would bring at a quiet sale in Memphis (or so he thought he was thinking), how selling her at all was folly: how a renting proposition would make her pay for herself over and over again (and later, when he was squirming in the upshot of it, teetering as perilously near the edge of total dupedom as he would ever get, he would remember thinking of her commercial possibilities and draw from that memory just enough wry dignity to survive the evil time).

Then: "What am I bid, gentlemen?"

It opened at a thousand dollars. No astounding price, to be sure, but no ordinary opening bid either. At two thousand, Cleburne managed to drag his blurred eyes from her long enough to sing out twenty-two hundred. But his bid was over sloughed in a flurry of one- and two-hundred-dollar raises, and before he could compose himself to name another figure, the price stood at forty-one hundred.

"Four thousand five hundred," he cried hoarsely.

"Five thousand," another voice put in.

And from all over the docks, from hovels and taverns and harness and tackle shops, men were drifting toward the auction platform. Negroes, solemn and less than solemn, stood at the back of the crowd whispering and nudging one another as the price rose. Even some common white women, packed together in small groups, catcalled and laughed raucously but without conviction as the bidding advanced.

The men paid them no mind. Paid them not even the courtesy of a glance or a frown but continued to stare, not so much at the drama peaking on the auction block, but rather at the subject of that drama, who still stood motionless and more than graceful with sunlight soothing the planes of her high cheekbones, slanting along the ruler-straight thrust of her nose, lighting the hollows of her dark eyes.

166

"Five hundred more," Cleburne incredulously heard himself saying. It was time for the New Orleans steamer to deport. It was last call. There would be no other boat until the next day, and a man in New Orleans sat with a suitcase full of land options on river tracts south of Baton Rouge: valuable options to be had cheap for cash, the same cash Cleburne was bidding for a spectacular Negress while the New Orleans boat blew a final whistle, shrugged off its gangway, and began the twisted passage of the river below Vicksburg.

With some men gambling is a mania, but even the most startling manifestation of such unreason is based in comedy: because all the common gambler stands to win is more of what he is wagering. He risks the whole of what he possesses, a sufficiency usually, in hope of getting more of what he is willing – no, anxious – to lose. But what had hold of Cleburne was another species of malady, one more reasonable, more lethal, more intoxicating. Because all he could possibly lose was money, and unless he were to win, he would not even lose that; what he stood to win was beyond measure or description, labelless and inscrutable. Not a prize, because prize suggests unalloyed good, something useful and desirable without qualification. But if he won her, there was no telling what he might be getting. Beauty beyond comprehension or comment. Grace. Possibly warmth. Possibly even love. Possibly agony.

Say all of these (ignore the alternate possibility that nothing beyond beauty was present, and that even the degree of beauty was overstating itself in these first frenzied improbable minutes). Then what could he do with them? Where enjoy them? A Negro woman taken to wife (or to bed or to heart: certainly not to a minister or priest or justice of the peace in any town south of the Ohio River) would have to produce a surplus of value never dreamed in economic philosophy, because what she produced would be all the pleasure her dauntless white mate was likely to get out of life.

"And five more than that," his competitor shouted.

By then there were only the two of them: Cleburne and the other, and even as he held all the elements of his situation in suspension (the departing steamer, the lost options, the preposterous amount of money being bid, the future he would be shaping for himself if his money prevailed), he paid her the final compliment of keeping his eyes fixed on her. He did not turn to see who opposed him, to weigh his competition as he had done so often before, to calculate how far the other might go. And as he watched her, her eyes found his, picked his face out of the anonymous flesh-hungry rabble stretched out before her like wolves in the pit. She did not smile or shudder or give any sign of notice or recognition, but rather seemed to study him as seriously as he had studied her. No heat, no passion: only a kind of fine detached concern. Not haughty or withdrawn; almost clinical, as if she were a kind and sensitive doctor staring into the poor mis-made eyes of a patient who craved understanding (the better counterfeit of love) as much as – or more than – cure.

And even as he bid again, he blushed.

"Sixty-five hundred dollars," he said without force or bravado.

Because there was almost no sound now around the auction block, only a faint and uncertain whispering, an occasional muffled and self-conscious squawk from the white whores, who had by now seen their own best price so terribly overmatched for a Negro wench that even their anger had stuttered into silence and rendered any remark they might make self-condemnatory. And because now he was under inspection, too. Now she could make out the two men who were matching purses to determine who would have her, and she was not so much examining them as her own future at their hands.

"Sixty-five hundred one time," the auctioneer said reverently.

"Seventy-five hundred," Cleburne's rival yelled.

"Eight thousand five hundred," Cleburne almost whispered.

And after a quick outburst of exclamation, the crowd was quiet again, watching both the girl and the auctioneer.

"Eight thousand and five hundred once," the auctioneer whispered back at Cleburne. He licked his lips and paused, his eyes fixed on the ancient unsteady pine podium before him. "Eight thousand and five hundred twice and fair warning . . . "

Now it was in the fire. Now, unless his rival was more substantial than he seemed to be, it would be over in another instant. At least this part of it would be over. Even if the other bidder had money enough to keep it going, it would end in seconds. Because Cleburne had nine thousand in gold, and a few hundred over. It represented cold mornings at the slave-pens long before the owner had even risen; it represented long hours and hard-scrabble and luck. It was all he had, and for certain the biggest accumulation he was likely ever to get. Now, even as the New Orleans operator would soon be closing the case on his watch with a frown and shrugging as he sent a messenger to offer the options to another and more dependable customer, Cleburne felt the cold exhilaration of total risk scattering and pulsing in his veins. What difference did the money make? This was what money was for. This . . . she . . .

"Third time for eighty-five hundred dollars . . . and sold to the feller in the hard hat right down there. . . . "

And the flare of excitement boomed and peaked within him. He tried to get hold of it all: the crowd, not yet breaking up, not yet beginning to eddy and spread out to pass the word of a new myth for the town and the territory, but holding together and silent only until he showed his money and took the girl in his custody, until the reality and certainty of it was beyond alteration or dispute. The auctioneer, who still stood humbly confused in the posture of his biggest single sale. The girl, enigmatic, neither smiling nor frowning – nowhere near tears – serene, almost somnolent except for her eyes, and moving her hands easily up and down her thighs as if she were wiping away the stains of one task and readying herself for the next. Himself, flushed and twisted with the sweet-sour impulse of costly and imponderable triumph, his bad eye completely out of control, slanting one way and then another like a drunken beacon and the weight of gold in his leather sack pushing the intoxication almost past bearing.

He counted out the money while the auctioneer wrote a bill of sale. The first rank of the crowd pressed close, and once, when nervousness made him drop a twenty-dollar gold piece, a sloven in burlap shirt and cord trousers, a copse of colorless beard hiding his lower face, squatted to retrieve the coin and handed it back to Cleburne almost reverently. Cleburne stopped his counting for just a moment and looked at the tramp. There was something sinister, familiar, about him. Then he felt the shock of recognition: the featureless rummy without past, without future, who was meekly offering him the tribute of his own gold was pathetically, laughably cockeyed.

Then it was over. The crowd had broken up, dissolved and scattered into a thousand chattering components in saloons and stores, stables and smithies, repeating the unlikely but immediately provable story of the man who had paid eighty-five hundred dollars for a nigger woman.

And there would be no end to it, Cleburne knew. It would not go the rounds of Vicksburg for a week and die, or even struggle outward as far as Delhi and Jackson and Hard Times and Natchez and fade into the general folk currency of that shadow-treasury that had already claimed Crockett and Bowie, Boone and Luther Pratt. Rather it would burgeon:

it would reach as far as Memphis in recognizable shape, possibly with his name still attached. It would arrive in New Orleans as quickly as he – no, he and she – would, and by the time it had moved back and forth a few weeks, the sum would be at least ten thousand (and still mounting), and his own infirmities might include a hunchback, a hook-hand, a cleft palate, a terrible scar, the very mark of Cain, on his forehead. And the girl: God only knew. Another Cleopatra, a mother of Caliban – probably the former, so that the story could draw its convention, its form, from beauty and the beast.

More than all that: he would be interdict. Not only from "decent" society, with which he had no experience and for which he had nothing but the firm healthy suspicion and dislike that every woods creature must have for its counterpart bred in a zoological garden, but as well from the short-crop, hard-handed people with whom he had lived and come to manhood, and who, divided from the planters and bankers and factors by all else, were at one with them in the matters of states' rights, individual freedom, and the question of the Negro.

It had to be New Orleans, that much was certain. Free Negroes, Creoles, half-breeds, and a myriad of mixtures lived there, and there were even Negro slave-owners there. Not that it would be right. Not that, because even the free Negroes would sneer at a walleyed white man with a loud uncultivated voice and callused hands, who could do no better than buy a Negro wife.

But he could make do there. He could use the little money he had to hire a building and erect a slave-pen, a place for new transient owners and traders to store their merchandise for a night or a week.

Now he had the bill of sale in hand, and the leather sack tied to his belt felt empty. He glanced at the girl out of the corner of his good eye. Now she was looking at him. She folded her arms and smiled. Not at him or at the auctioneer, least of all at the bill of sale that represented her life as surely as did her own blood, but perhaps at the last tatters of the diminished crowd, a handful of white whores who were last to leave.

"You gone take her with you, sir?" the auctioneer asked, some of the burlap-clad rummy's reverence in his voice (not because of what Cleburne had done: by tomorrow the auctioneer would be laughing and making gamy guesses as to what the girl was doing for Cleburne; rather reverence for any man who could afford to drop eight and a half thousand dollars on a scarred pine lectern top and casually accept in return the bill of sale for a Negro woman).

"Could I leave her here for a little?" Cleburne asked out of a dry throat.

"I only sell here," the auctioneer told him. "I can ask the owner."

He pointed past the slave yard toward a long, uncovered porch. A man in white: white hair, white suit – even white shoes. He sat with a long slender cigar in his hand and watched Cleburne and the auctioneer without apparent interest.

"Never mind," Cleburne said. "It don't matter. I can take her with me. You, girl, you ready to travel?" he called to her roughly.

"My clothes," she answered.

Answered and struck. The voice alone was worth a thousand dollars, he thought stupidly, desperately.

"Get 'em and bring 'em here," he told her.

While she was inside, he tried to let some of the afternoon's excitement ease, find its level. But it was no good: too much had happened too quickly. This morning he had been ready to buy land; this afternoon he had bought a woman – and a woman whose use would cost him still more than the outrageous price he had already paid. His nerves (he had nerves: beneath his bluff weather-beaten impenetrable surface were nerves enough for a platoon of deserters. Nerves enough to have been duped – no, trapped – into the auction, and more than enough nerves to feel, now that it was over, as if he might lose the remnants of his stingy lunch if he did not soon begin walking off some of the tension) still quivered; and added to the hard unromantic afterflow, the anticlimax of the auction was mounting, desperation at the problem of what to do with what he had bought.

She came back out. The shift still stretched tight across her breasts and seemed about to split at the single badly sewn side seam as she walked. But her long, uncommon hair was done up in a kerchief, and she carried a carpetbag that would not fasten, out of which more kerchiefs and unrecognizable cloth things protruded.

They walked. Not toward town, because the myth – the story in transition – would have already gone that way. It would be moving more leisurely than in the levee saloons, but moving nonetheless with house Negroes and lackeys amusing their masters; maids titillating their mistresses with this fable gotten almost out of the air by black wireless that required not even the formality of drums as it had in Africa. They walked out of town southward.

"We can't get no hotel," he told her. "Not even a hotel down on the docks. Because one kind of hotel won't take your kind, no matter how clean or well-vouched-for, and the other won't sell my kind space no matter how drunk or worthless or ugly. And either kind might call the marshal if I asked for one room between us."

"I could stay back in the . . . "

"No," he said sharply. "I know you were there, and I know you were God knows where else before there. But that was before I come across you, and whatever you were worth before, you're worth the best part of ten thousand dollars now, and that goddamned pen don't look like no bank to me."

So they walked into the hills and bluffs and woods alongside the Mississippi. The day was failing. The heat had broken, and the sun moving from their right shoulders downward was gilding the long, undramatic waves of the river. They sat at the base of a huge oak and watched cargo boats and barges move soundlessly up and down the wide highway of dark water that seemed so placid and harmless.

"Here," she said, touching his arm lightly, touching him for the first time.

He turned his eyes from the river. It was cold cornbread and a sliver of fish.

"It ain't pheasant on a gold service," he grinned.

"I never had nothin' on a gold service. Once I saw some gold plate."

He ate some of the bread and fish. "That auctioneer could hammer him out service for eight."

"It ain't his. The man will get it."

She ate a smaller piece of bread, no fish, and stretched luxuriously. "It will be cool tonight. "

Cleburne laughed (the nerves were showing: he had laughed more in the past half hour than in the last two years). "But not too cool."

"No, not too cool." She searched in the carpetbag and came out with a soiled width of silk comforter. "We need to find a stand of pine. Pine straw will keep the damp off."

They moved up the bluff and found a patch of pine, magnolia, and sweet gum still overlooking the river so that they could see up and down its length for several miles and watch the spring sunset that was more like a gentle implosion, a bright nova shattering not simply the western sky but the woods, the boats – whatever else might lie on the far side of the river, and the river itself, and then, with the clouds all fired, falling in upon itself, fading slowly, then more rapidly.

Then the sun was gone. Behind it was left only scattered swatches of flamingo and gray – almost purple near the bottoms of the clouds – and the suddenly noticeable odor of wood smoke filtering from some near cabin where a family of poor whites put together an evening meal – probably of greens and bread and fish – not supposing that within range of their cook-fire smoke a crudely made cockeyed small-time white man was spending his last few untroubled minutes this side of irredeemable heresy with a Negress whose beauty was as far from their imagining as was the act of her new owner.

But the sun was gone, and there was the beginning of dew, a long almost imperceptible draught of chill river breeze that moved them back from the top of the bluff. Cleburne was not thinking of heresy now. Nor of troubles, nor of money gone beyond retrieve. Only of the woman with him there, and not even of what future might be ahead of them, but only of how to get through the next few hours without mishandling her in such a way that she would withdraw from him that part of herself which was not, could not be, included in any bill of sale devised by law.

She's been looking at me for three hours, he thought. And she ain't laughed or even grinned that special way they do, or turned away from me. But I could ruin it. I could and I might, and once it's ruined you can't fix it, and then not only the ten thousand's gone, but the thing I was trying to get with the ten thousand, even knowing that the money wouldn't buy it but only give me a chance at it.

The dark was as solid and impenetrable now as the woods around them. Only once in a while could they see, faint against feathery low clouds, the reflection of a passing steamer's bright running lights.

"It could rain," he said, lumbering slowly to his feet.

"It rains somewhere every minute," she said softly out of the darkness. "Some of the rain goes to everybody, my momma used to say."

"Your momma..."

"Far off, and dead now, I expect."

"Any people? A husband..."

"Nobody."

"I never asked you your name..."

173

"At that place, they called me Sally. My momma called me Lira," she said.

He could tell she was slipping out of the thin cotton shift. He felt it land, carelessly thrown, at his feet. He began unbuttoning his shirt. The raw ends of his nerves twitched and hummed in the river breeze.

"It could rain tonight, Lira," he said again.

He heard her stir and pull the fragment of stained silk over her.

"Hurry," she said.

They had been in New Orleans three or four months when she told him she was pregnant. Not exultantly, not sadly or shamefacedly, but in the soft inarguable way she always used to express herself.

It had been a good time, and Cleburne walked and ate and worked – even cursed the intractable free Negroes he had hired to help him at the new pen – from within an aura not merely of happiness, but of worthiness and self-respect. Sometimes at first he would grin to himself wryly and think what kind of white man owed his moral salvation and future growth to a Negro woman bought and sold across the counter like a sack of rice or a bushel of potatoes. But he was seldom wry now, and the aura seemed even to move those he did business with. By the time she told him about the baby, his pen was about to become two pens, and he had already outdistanced some old New Orleans hands, taken customers from them.

"I reckon I know why he's so good at it, why he inspires confidence in nigger-traders," one of his competitors would say. But the talk seemed to do him no harm. There was a charm: there had to be. She was even proof against the very myth of which she was a part.

But the baby: it was strange that he had never thought of the possibility before. He had no reason to think that he was sterile or she barren, but the idea of children had not even scratched the surface of his mind in the months they had been together.

Because maybe I didn't want to think about it. Maybe everything was too good for us and I didn't want to think about the one thing that could make it all not only not good but almost a nightmare.

So when she told him, he nodded and went on working, changing his habits only to the extent of leaving the pens at noon on Tuesdays and Thursdays, going by the French market for salad stuffs and olive oil in tiny wooden cruets, and having a brief lunch with her in the common patio of their pension (which catered to mixed bloods only in that tight circumscription of New Orleans society, and the dubious landlord of which had permitted them room only when Cleburne had claimed that he himself was the product of a union of the kind he and Lira had formed).

Not that he forgot the child. He merely placed the idea of it in abeyance since there was no way he could handle that idea as potential fathers usually do. He could not build imaginary careers or fortunate marriages, political advancement or plantation grandeur for the child – could not in fact dream anything at all beyond the simple hope that it would be physically whole and responsive to hard rearing.

And the months passed quickly. It was winter, and the work at the pens eased up enough for him to spend Saturday afternoons with her. Then spring. It was March of 1842. Before dawn one morning, less than ten minutes after he had risen, she called.

"Now," she said. "You'd better get the woman."

He pushed aside the bright cotton curtain she had hung to divide the kitchen-sitting room from the bedroom. She was lying beneath the same shard of silk that she had refused to throw away even when he had bought her two good Chickasaw blankets. Her face was tight, the mouth's corners pulled down, her complexion blanched from warm light brown to a pale jaundiced yellow, and her hands gripped the rungs of the secondhand iron bedstead above her head. "Are you sure?" he asked, feeling as soon as he had said it the idiocy of his words.

"Why do men always ask that? Yes, I'm sure," she said. Then with as near a smile as she could raise: "Hurry."

That day the pens were tended by a one-armed broken-headed relic of Andrew Jackson's cotton-bale stand against the British. He told customers that Mr. Cleburne would be down when he had taken care of some personal business. The veteran did not give anyone Cleburne's home address.

The old woman hummed something in a foreign tongue and pushed the towels back down into the black iron pot.

"She said 'now'," Cleburne was telling her.

"She right. It just goin' slow."

"Is anything wrong?"

The old woman fixed him with eyes as bright and green as jade pieces. "I dunno. So far no troubles. But it hurtin' her unnatural. *Dios.* Should be no pain yet – not pain like this."

"A doctor . . . "

"If señor wish."

By the time he had found his doctor and returned, the worst (what should have been the worst) was past. The child was coming, and after a look, the doctor stepped back into the kitchen with him. Cleburne offered him whiskey.

"Mississippi whiskey," the doctor observed politely.

"Yes," Cleburne said distractedly.

"No fear, monsieur. She has good hips. She appears well nourished."

"Yes."

"She is perfect," the doctor went on. "Beautiful beyond beauty. Tell me, is she kind also?"

"Yes," Cleburne said. "Sure. She's a good woman."

"Then you are blessed. A toast to her and to your young one."

And before they had drained their glasses, a mixed cry rent the cotton curtain between the rooms. First hers, and then louder than hers, the baby's.

"They . . . "

"It is nothing," the doctor said over the top of his glass. "The parting is usually attended by mutual shouts."

The woman came in after a minute or so. Her seamy emotionless face, like the visage of a tortoise, turned from him to the doctor, from the doctor back to him. "*Señor*, come."

The doctor started toward the curtain. "No, the old woman snapped, her eyes bright and slashing. "The *señor*. Not you."

Later the doctor was gone, and the old woman, for an extra fifty cents, had agreed to go out and get something to cook for him. He sat in front of the fireplace staring into the low flames, the crisp crumbling heaps of log ash. I never counted on this, he was thinking. The hard looks and maybe shame and some troubles making our way. Even her deciding that what I bought couldn't possibly include love. But not this.

She was sleeping now, while the flames eroded a piece of dry oak into ash and a flush of heat. While Negroes cried vegetables and oysters outside in the streets and the old woman shopped from one stall to the next with the tortoise face composed and unravaged further by the outrage of what she knew.

What she knew, without thanks to Mendel or science, was that no offspring of a pure white and a part Negro parent can be darker than the darker parent. And as she shopped and sorted out her knowledge, she accepted without even having heard it, the story Cleburne had told to a dubious landlord when he rented the pension. Because the child, a

176

boy and healthy, was as black as the deepest recess of the fireplace into which Cleburne was staring now. As black as the glossy skin of an eggplant the old woman fondled absently.

"You want it, Momma?" a mustached clerk asked her roughly. "You gonna buy it or not?"

And Cleburne was at the edge of his tether. What he knew for certain was as bad as what he could only guess.

It ain't mine, he thought. No way it can be mine. My old lady wasn't nothin' but river-bait, but she was white all the way back to Abraham. Because her people never had no chance to do what I've done. No eight thousand dollars and not eyes enough to look for anything past the color of a hide anyhow. And the old man: not spine enough to even stay around till his not-wife decided she'd had enough. And him probably born the same way. Nothin' there. Jesus, this is how far it's come: I'd give another eight-thousand to know that my grandpappy was the king and imperial blackness of all the niggers that ever lived.

Then he heard her call. Not weakly the way a woman fresh out of first sleep after childbirth calls, only softly as she always called to him.

"So I prayed," she was telling him, "I prayed asking the good God to do me this one more thing. He brought you to the levee, and I prayed this one more thing for us both. But he didn't answer. I asked too much."

And she told him what had happened the night before the auction. How the buck, who had been chained within sight of her all the way down from Memphis, had broken through the cheap wire that separated the men from the women, and how, with his big field-hardened hands at her throat, he had taken her again and again until just short of morning. The pen-owner had found them, taken one look at her (who, of course, he had been planning not to auction publicly but by a quiet private sale at which she would surely have brought at least three-thousand dollars – or possibly he would not have sold her at all, but built her a small place near the pen and contracted her to interested young connoisseurs) and ordered the fractious buck beaten from eight o'clock until ten. Then he told the auctioneer, who had just shown up, to sell the girl for the best price he could get.

"But the whipping couldn't take his stain off of me. They had to let me go, thinking that putting me out on the block was fair warning to anybody that something wasn't the way it seemed. But they didn't even think about anybody like you. Neither did I."

"No," he said, kneading her hand between his two. "They never figured for me till I got there. But then they figured quick. I was slow that day, or maybe it never occurred to me that anybody would ring in a shill when they were trying to move you. But that other fella, that other bidder . . . "

"Yes," she said. "Yes, but you never looked at him."

"But I heard him pushin', and I pushed. And later I saw him."

"When I went inside for . . . "

"On the porch in a white suit. I saw him but then I didn't even know I was seein' him. Didn't know that I was lookin' at the opposition who had just been biddin' on his own property, and was smart and cold enough to slide out just a few hundred short of all I had. But if he had overbid . . . "

"He would have sent a boy to you before the next New Orleans steamer, and the boy would have said the big bidder had backed out and that the owner was willing to let me go for maybe four thousand – or even less if you had felt like dealing."

"And all the time knowin' . . . "

"No," she said. "Not knowin'. Maybe it would have been all right. It had a good chance to be all right. He knew why you wanted me, and that with any kind of luck at all the baby would be yours and not his, not that big black man's, who couldn't even swallow after he saw me on the steamer down from Memphis."

"But there wasn't any luck," Cleburne choked.

She stopped the compulsive moving of his hands. "I can't say that. We had a lot of luck. I did anyway."

"I only meant about the baby. That black sonofabitch's hardgotten baby."

"My baby," she cut in. "Not the way I wanted or when I wanted, but still mine."

"I guess it's mine, too."

"Yes," she smiled. "You own the baby. Whether you want it or not, it's your baby."

"Go to sleep," he said, leaning over and kissing her. "Don't worry. I love you. And I got a stake in that little bugger."

While the old woman cooked, Cleburne tried thinking again. But there was too much working inside him for his brain to sort. There was the Negro to hate, the pen-owner to butcher in his imagination over and over again. There was Lira still to love, and this squalling mindless black baby to cope with. Too much.

He walked down to the pens after supper and checked in with his straw boss. Then he walked along the levee to see the steamers, docked or moving in and out of the port area like so many bulky fireflies. He could hear fiddle music and laughter.

He had played himself into a corner, and in this particular corner there was a stool and a dunce cap. No, he thought. It ain't that way yet. And it don't have to be. It won't ever be that way till I decide to let go. If I stop loving her then I'm face up against the wall with a point on my hat. But if we go on loving, this ain't any worse than what we started out with. We walked out of ordinary living the minute I opened my mouth at that rigged auction, and for all anybody could ever tell, I knew, or at least had a good idea why they were putting her on the block and this black baby is part of the risk. I don't have to look like a spayed bitch unless I want to. Only if I snap now, only if I let go now, then I'm wiped out for sure.

But Cleburne had forgotten something. The old woman brought it to mind when he came back from the walking.

"You want to get the doctor again," she told him without excitement.

"What's the matter?"

"If I knew what the matter is, I take care myself and don't call no doctor for two dollar. I think fever. Both got fever. I don't know."

So the French doctor came back. He spent an hour behind the cotton curtain, and came out finally chewing on the scrap of mustache that divided his long, pleasant face.

"Fever, yes," he said. "Some fever."

"Will they be . . . ?" Cleburne asked numbly.

"The beautiful woman, your wife, is not good. The child I cannot say. All over New Orleans they have this. Something in the water or an insect. People die. Some people survive it."

"Nevermind some people. What about her?"

The doctor shrugged sadly. "I don't know. I think she will die."

"It was wrong praying," she told him when he went in to sit with her. "I asked for something. I asked for love and to be free. Now He's answering. I've had the love. I'm fixing to get the freedom, ain't I?"

179

Cleburne shook his head, closed his eyes savagely to clear them. Nothing could look sillier than a cockeyed man crying. "It's only a fever, he said. "You're gonna be fine."

"It's the fever," she said without apprehension. "Typhoid or yellow jack. And the baby?"

"He's a little sick too," Cleburne told her, "but he's gonna be all right. When youall are well, maybe we could go to the Indies. It's different there."

She smiled. "It's not different, and neither of us is going far. I started something with that prayer. What I didn't think of was you. But I prayed before you came along, big man. I never reckoned there would be you. You were the love, all the love."

It was almost noon then, and she slipped off into unconsciousness, coming out of it only a few times. Toward sundown, when she opened her eyes, he would call her name, but she would look at him without recognition and pull the scrap of dirty silk close around her against the chills which came closer together now, and racked her until her teeth clattered like minstrel bones shaken in an empty room.

The old woman sat on a hassock near the foot of the bed with her rosary moving quickly between her fingers. *"Santa Maria . . . "*

There was only the silence, the heat and the long ponderous drone of the old woman's endless petitions. "Now and at the hour . . . "

I'm losing it, he thought. I'm losing every way I can lose. All the way back down to the docks, back to that orphan home – except I don't even have the youth I started out with. I had money and I set it on the table and rolled for something bigger than money.

" . . . and at the hour . . . "

And I won that first throw. I got what most men with money ain't got the spine to try for. I got it, but life is made so you can't stop rolling. Your dice or the house dice. You got to roll and sooner or later they all go bad. There's snake-eyes on all dice, and some crap out the first roll and lose everything, or they hold back and lose it a little at a time. But they got to go on rolling, and sooner or later what you think is luck – but which is nothing but the houseman pausing to take a deep breath – gives out . . .

" . . . of our death . . . "

And your pockets and your guts are empty, and you sit like this, and wait for the night.

" . . . of our death . . . "

She waited for the sun to set. When the low clouds were going from gold to pink to purple-gray, she roused a moment and reached for Cleburne's hand.

"My baby . . . "

"Don't you worry about your baby. It's got my name. It's my baby."

She smiled and seemed to sink back into the pillow. Her hands fumbled with the worn silk comforter.

". . . all the love," she whispered. "All the love and now free."

She frowned as if she had forgotten something.

"Kiss me," she said breathlessly. "Hurry."

The old woman, who had moved toward the clothes hamper in which the baby lay, still fingered her rosary. Then, in the silence, she moaned.

"*Señor*," she choked. "*Señor* . . . "

Cleburne did not raise his head from the shabby piece of comforter. "All right," he said tonelessly. "All right, I know."

When the Vicksburg sheriff carried him in for trial, Cleburne sat staring in silence off the back of the wagon toward the bluffs and the woods beside the river.

"It was bad enough to do what you did with that money," the sheriff told him without anger or even accusation – as if he were lecturing a recalcitrant schoolboy. "But it was pure sore headed to come back and shoot down a man who didn't do you no more wrong than to afford you the chance to be a fool."

Cleburne moved his shackled arms to get blood back into his wrists, and went on staring. He was thinking of the white hair, the white suit and white shoes. Without pleasure or remorse he called to mind what the double-shotted scattergun had done to all that whiteness.

"He kept a sloppy place," Cleburne mused half to himself, half to the sheriff. "He ought to have kept them slave-pens in better shape."

The sun was nearly down, and the clouds were thickening again. There might be more rain, and if it went on for too long, the levees, almost untended for the past four years, could overflow. Cleburne thought of what the dusty room contained. It always came back to money. He had not counted or made the slightest display of it because it was not that kind of money – not the kind he wanted and needed. It was only ordinary money to buy ordinary things if he should need or want them. Not the kind of gold to fill a weather-beaten patched leather saddlebag which lay folded and rotting next to a worthless carpetbag without a clasp.

They'll be busy over on Fannin Street tonight, Cleburne thought, smiling again. They'll run Bessie's girls ragged and have 'em limping for a month. And on the cheap. This first night, before the girls catch on, it'll go for a whack and a holler. Then they'll find out there's money around again, and it'll cost the price of a fair mule to get a smile and a quick handshake. He wondered if maybe he should try to buy some of the houses on Fannin. Not to run, not to operate. Too much trouble, too much action. But a landlord don't have to risk a shiv or a case, and he can still siphon off the cream. Or maybe cotton land. Or railroad stock.

Cleburne heaved himself out of his chair and walked unsteadily through the store and out onto the porch. The usual collection of malcontents, former Confederate soldiers and farmers with time on their hands, had cleared out, and the street was empty except for a pair of Negroes leading a cow, and a few Union soldiers laughing and chaffing in front of Ramsey's saloon across the street and down a few doors.

It was moonrise, and Cleburne, seeing the clouded disk of the moon stark and lusterless in the undarkened sky, breathed deeply, rubbed his hands across his bulky shirt and turned back into the gloom of his shadow-filled store.

IV

7 JUNE 1865 — Down in front of Maxy's Hotel, it was the same moon, but Vera Taggert was paying no attention. Rather she sat in a rocking chair on the hotel porch, staring out into the lengthening shadows.

She had wanted to wait for him at the hotel. Even with a shabby foyer, shredding wallpaper, a collapsing staircase, it would have been better than the shack. The hotel looked, in these latter days, about as good as any of the fine houses out from town now that everything had fallen apart. But now there was no way, and she would have to go back to her father's cabin and wait for him there – wait to see if Morrison Stevens would be coming home at all.

She had saved her pay from the hospital (they had begun paying her there when some of the Confederate army doctors found that she was

182

as competent as most of them, and in no position to do volunteer work with her father gone and giving her no money even when he turned up from time to tome) for almost three years with no plan in mind except perhaps to buy a dress for his return. But now, sitting on the hotel porch, she realized that the one thing she should never have tried was saving.

Because now her money was valueless. It had been next to valueless for months, but the word of General's Lee surrender had dissolved what little virtue it retained. For weeks before the Federals arrived, Confederate currency had been worthless.

Ed Norton Senior, who had taken over the bank in addition to his own grocery and dry goods store when the bank president had enlisted in the Southern army, handed out what currency was left to whoever wanted it among his depositors, and finally to anyone who asked for the bills as keepsakes of a murdered nation (and Murray Taggert, Vera's father, disbanded from the army by the simple expedient of walking away from camp even before the surrender, had carted away as much of the currency as he could get and carry in a single trip: because, he told Cleburne, it might be worthless and again it might not be, but if they were giving it away any man with sense ought to take as much as he could lay hands on out of principle, and on the slim chance that the Confederacy was only moribund, not dead, and might yet manage to redeem its paper) and burned the rest on a sad heap behind the office of the *News*, with a score or more of the townspeople looking numbly on.

So after all there had been no savings, and no dress to buy even if there had been good money for it. There was only the memory of almost four years of death and pain and loss, a tired body and a cheap suitcase filled with old dresses and shifts. And the waiting.

And now, with Union officers and noncommissioned officers and the Treasury agent camp-followers moving into town, the hotel owner, Horace Maxy, pleading necessity, hard times, the need of his family – pleading, indeed, far more than the situation called for – asked Vera to move out.

She was waiting for her father to finish whatever it was he did in town that passed with him for business. There was no place else to go but back to the shack. No: she could have gone to the Sentells'. Mrs. Sentell, who had nursed with her from the war's start, who had listened to her letters from Morrison and in turn read her what the major had to say from Vicksburg, had asked her half a dozen times to leave the hotel and come share the empty house. Even after the major had come home, Mrs. Sentell had wanted Vera to come. But that was no good. She had come this far owing nothing outside her family, and she could go the rest of the way. Mrs. Sentell was kind and good, but that only made obligation deeper, and Vera, beholden to her father for twenty years' indifferent keep, knew the taste of indebtedness. She wanted no more of it, and if there had to be more, better it be increase of an old (and profoundly despised) account rather than inception of a new.

A tail end of river breeze ruffled her hair, and Vera leaned back in the rocker. The old man might be in Ramsey's. He might be in that dark cavern that Cleburne ran. Or he could be stealing Yankee grub out of the warehouses and stables at the head of Texas Street where the Unions had bedded down. He might come for her in ten minutes, or it might be dawn. Maxy, shamefaced (possibly because Vera had laid out his only son after sitting up with him the night of his death in the Shreveport Military Hospital two days after the battle down at Mansfield) and obsequious, had offered to let her have the room for one more night, but Vera had ignored him and carried her own single bag and small handful of parcels out to the porch to wait. It seemed that life was compounded of two elements: waiting and fighting – which, taken together, make a good definition of war.

Vera Taggert understood war. Not only because of the slim packet of letters on cheap paper folded to make their own envelopes – bitter awkward letters full of death and hate and the tedious detail of dying and hating and at first postmarked Luray or Winchester, later Spotsylvania Courthouse, and finally Petersburg. Not only because of the endless coming and going of troops through Shreveport, and the periodic threat that the Union general Banks might try his luck again against the upper Red River, but mostly because this war, the one they had all been part of, was for her only the most recent campaign in a struggle that had lasted her whole life.

The fighting had begun before she was old enough to understand that violence in one form or another is the concomitant of every human life. It had begun with her father, Murray, drunk and vicious at home as he was sodden and obsequious outside it, beating her mother who was perpetually drunk too, but never vicious – only defeated and fuddled even without the drink, and who drank only in order to better stand what defeat and fuddlement alone could not help her bear.

It had gone on for a long time, and when Vera remembered her mother alive it was without rancor or anger. It was also without pity. When her mother's swollen insensate face rose in memory, Vera remembered the woman as if she had been some regrettable but foreseeable battle casualty. Not a warm friend or even an especially close acquaintance, but closer and warmer and more to be kindly considered than the common enemy that had destroyed her.

With her mother's death, the first phase of her war had come to an end. A buffer state had fallen. New aggression would be leveled directly at her, and even then – a little over seven years old – she had begun to construct her strategy. Not tactics: these were to be born out of the moment, out of the quick heat of the situations as they arose. It was the overall plan, an end to be determined and kept in view, that she had to set for herself.

She ignored her father as much as that was possible, and spiked her coolness with an occasional burst of fury that set the old man back on his bottle or even out of the house. It may have been her size, the demonic set of her pale tiny face, or the grim contrast with her mother (that poor worn casualty who, had she lived, would have neither supported nor deprecated her daughter's conduct, but would likely have followed her husband to the bottle or the barn in the face of Vera's outbursts) that put him off so handily, but whatever it was, it kept his hands in his ragged pockets and off of her until, by the time he decided it was past time to teach her proper respect, it was indeed. She had grown enough to substitute a stick of firewood for mere fury, and the matter of filial respect rested pretty much where it had before: no respect was forthcoming from Vera, and no offense was taken by the old man. After all, she cooked and washed and sewed for him. Respect is a fine thing but it never plucked a stolen hen or scrubbed filth out of a crusty shirt.

So that phase was a draw. There was no affection between the contestants, but the world had lumped them into grudging symbiosis, and it would have to stay that way until one or the other saw clear advantage in a change, or the myriad small currents of resentment and discontent built to a lethal charge.

And while her father went through his paces at Cleburne's or did a desultory day's work (Negro work always, or possibly even work that no master would set a house-Negro to) to supplement what he cadged and flattered out of rubes and planters' drunken sons in the saloon or the hotel lobby, Vera washed clothes not her own, raised a few chickens, cooked grits and sweet potatoes – and planned. Too young at first for marriage to mean more than emancipation, she would dream that one of the town boys, Ed Norton or Clayton Silsbee – or even slovenly Dowd Silsbee – might fall in love with her at day school and carry her off. So that for the rest of her life she would live in the plush oblivion of nice china and plentiful coffee. There would be dresses – not a great many, but of good stuff – and the underwear would not chafe, and what talk there was would be soft and careless and polite. She would be a merchant's wife, or the wife of a livery-stable owner, or at least of a journeyman carpenter. No more breaking a skim of ice on water before she could wash her face in the morning. There would be a quiet chocolate maid to warm the water. Breakfast would be eggs she could eat instead of sell; bacon instead of gummy fatback. All of it would happen not because it was romantically inevitable (neither word meant much to her then, and only the latter word would ever come to mean anything to her in all the years – and campaigns – ahead), but because she would learn how to *make* it happen.

When school got underway, the fall of her fourteenth year (1859: in Virginia, so her father babbled between curses, they had hanged a goddamned lunatic atheist bastard who had come with guns to rape and murder and turn the niggers against their masters), with the old man stymied, held at bay, she found herself under assault by the very boys who had for so long composed the fragile distant elements of her dream. Ed asked her to the dance they had at Rickter's Dancing Saloon. And Vera, whose social life up to that time had consisted of trips into town two or three times a year, found herself besieged not only by Ed and Clayton (who were only town boys after all and modest enough elements considering that it is as easy to dream oneself consort of a king as the missus of a merchant) but by young men with names like Benoit, Larkin, Flournoy, Madison, Leseure, Mason – and Stevens. All of them plantation bred, the sons of men who were either wealthy in money or in slaves and land. Now she was caught in a new kind of problem: her strategy had been too meager, too undemanding. Now she would have to study a whole series of possibilities that dwarfed the best hopes she had cherished before. Now, instead of peopling her imaginary future with counters like Ed Norton and Clayton Silsbee, she could use (and it was always the same name: never Benoit or Flournoy,

Leseure or Larkin) Linus Morrison Stevens as a peg not only for the old dream of comfort and leisure – but for new visions as well.

Because Linus Morrison Stevens filled Vera Taggert's bill so fully that she found herself almost unable to assimilate him seriously into the old often-used fabric of her dream. The dream was overawed by the simple possibilities of the reality. He was the son of Amos Stevens, owner of 9,000 acres in Caddo and Bossier parishes, 50 slaves, interests in New Orleans real estate and New York stock companies (legend had it that, on an early trip to New York, Amos Stevens met a hard-nosed loud young man whose store of table conversation had chiefly to do with barges and boats and canals, and the future of cheap water transport west into Ohio, invested some money in the young man's venture more in order to purchase a measure of dinnertime silence than in hope of any return. Later, years later, he had received a check from a Northern bank, and a bill of sale from that same stock. The bill of sale required his signature, an enclosed note said, and the check, which no bank in Louisiana could redeem with cash on hand, was signed by that same man, no longer young, but supplied now with something more than talk. The signature read: C. Vanderbilt.), and he could ride and shoot, swim and fight with the best in the parish, and it was generally conceded that the best in Caddo parish could hold their own with the best in the South, that is, in the world. And the really wonderful part, so far as Vera could tell, was that Mo's pure exuberance and animalism was untainted with the slightest tincture of self-denial, thought, judgment or restraint. He might not live long, she calculated, but the time he lived would be as full and as rewarding as life can be. She had learned a long time ago that length of life (her mother had managed, with the help of corn liquor, to hold on for forty-seven years, and to officiate as chief – and sometimes only – mourner at the burial of five children) is not measure of its worth, and that twenty minutes of Mo's kind of living would be worth, conservatively, forty-seven years of any other kind.

So now defensive strategy could go by the board. Now, instead of holding out indefinitely in hopes that some reason for resistance would sooner or later materialize, she could begin to plan for a push on somebody else's stronghold, for a fight in the enemy's country.

The dance, as it turned out, was no battle won. Ed, still young and uncertain of how young ladies were to be treated, spent the whole evening beside her, fetching her little glasses of punch, asking if it were cool enough, dancing her nearly into exhaustion, and making it clear that Vera was his partner and no relief was sought. Once, for a moment, Mo Stevens stopped and passed the time. He smiled at Vera, complimented her frock (which represented eleven months of hidden washing-money), and the sale of half the chickens she had hatched that past summer: money she had planned to save for a trip to Vicksburg, which, she had heard, was bigger and prettier than New York, and a lot nicer), and continued to stare at her while he made as if to talk to Ed Norton Junior.

Later, when all the older people had begun to gather their wraps and raise their eyebrows at their young, Mo came by again. He asked if Vera would like to dance, and she was almost to her feet, already speaking, already weighing and considering subjects and tones of voice and expressions and volume of laughter proper to Mo's remarks when Ed Norton rose with her and announced that they had best leave. Mo shrugged, smiled one final time at Vera and moved on. Vera wilted, but she was used to setbacks. The only setback that is final, she remembered, is the one that gets you buried.

All this was still strumming through her mind in fiddle-time as Ed Norton drove her home, as she brushed aside his clumsy hands and kisses at the door of the cabin, as she lay down unsleeping on her pallet and watched with bright eyes until dawn began breaking across the cool sky, and she heard her father grunt toward wakefulness as his only rooster coughed and clattered hesitantly somewhere in the yard.

It was later, after Ed Norton had come by to tell her how sorry he was that he couldn't take her to the Thanksgiving dance at the Sentells', that she began to realize how, ironically enough, Mo Stevens might be, for all his wealth and capacities, an easier mark than any one of the town boys. Because, Ed Norton said, his mother (Ed's) forbade him taking the daughter of Murray Taggert to a dance or a picnic or a social of any kind at all. Not because Vera was, so far as Mrs. Norton knew, one whit less than she should be, but simply because whether she was hovering at the borne of decency or a certified virgin-saint, she could not overcome what the old man was. Less than Vera Taggert, she was Murray Taggert's daughter, and right or wrong, charitable or cruel, that relationship made her, in Mrs. Norton's estimation, anathema to any son's mother in north Louisiana.

As for Ed, Vera let him off with a smile almost whimsical, with a light word of forgiveness for the broken arrangement. He left her smiling and considering in the armless rocker that so often lurched her father into drunken sleep. He left her, and wondered all the way back to town, to his father's store, whether he had said too much, had made of the truth a bludgeon that had shaken her very sanity. But the cruelty had been his mother's anyhow, he thought (though something ugly and just less than thought kept winking and shining in the crevices of his dialogue with himself), and Vera would be safer, happier, better off finding someone more nearly her own kind.

And as he rode out of the yard, Vera was thinking almost identically the same thing. She was thanking God or Jehovah or the force of gravity or whatever rules earth and sea, men and their destinies, that Amos Stevens' good wife (no less nor more virtuous, Vera guessed, than Mrs. Norton) was buried deep and lying long in the graveyard of St. George's Protestant Episcopal Church downtown. She smiled quietly and recalled hearing somewhere that St. George had been a slayer of dragons, a famous protector of maidens.

It was spring before the next skirmish of Vera Taggert's war began. It was the spring of 1860, and the fresh start of her fifteenth year. There was something dark and portentous in the air. The porch of Cleburne's store was filled afternoon and evening with unsmiling men, and on weekends Captain Flourney drilled his Caddo Rifles. Up in Benton, Bossier parish people had started a unit of dragoons and Caddo boys had flooded across the Red River to join it. In case of trouble, everyone said. In case of trouble, the cavalry beats walking every time. But infantry, Captain Flourney would say, infantry is absolutely essential, and a fine rifleman can always give a good account of himself. And everyone at Cleburne's or at Ramsey's saloon would nod and agree.

But none of this slowed sap, stunted spring grass or obscured a certain tang in the cool air. As far as Vera was concerned, political trouble was no kind of trouble at all. In fact, it kept the old man in town jawing instead of underfoot. Now her only problem was to find a way of picking up the thread that had been strung between her and Mo the preceding fall. She needed reasonable entrée. Better it be something under the character of what Mrs. Norton might call "genteel." Best it be done quickly, whether genteel or downright coarse. The only advantage in gentility, as far as Vega could tell, was that in case of a misstep, genteel tactics made possible another go at it. If the gambit she chose was too obvious, it had better be a damned good one, because nothing on earth scares as easily as a seventeen-year-old boy with money in his pocket and no idea of what else he has in his pants – and, Vera thought, nothing stays scared longer.

But good commanders have a way of making their own luck. The second-rater worries and frets, consults maps, rechecks his logistics and sends for support no matter how heavily he may outnumber the enemy. The first-rater checks everything once, and then puts his plan and his weapons to the test.

Vera's test came soon enough.

She had walked into town to buy a few supplies. Most often the old man did the buying, but Vera knew that you cannot meet the enemy where he is not, and so, dressed in the single pretty frock she owned (the same one she had worn to the dance six months before), hair washed and tied behind, brown flawless face and arms and legs scrubbed to a sheen, she made the trip.

On the way back, the luck she had prepared for came to pass. It began to cloud up, then to sprinkle lightly, and finally to pour. As she ran off the road toward a copse of pines, she heard hoof beats pounding through the dirt-become-mud of the road.

"Hey, pretty," Morrison Stevens yelled from behind her as if he had raised a fox. "Hey, girl, hey."

Vera didn't stop. She acted as if she had heard nothing. Under the pines, quickly, she tossed back her soaked hair, combing it with her fingers, and sank demurely down upon the still dry pine straw to await his coming.

She could thank the rain for this first contact with the enemy. Before it was over and the sun came out to strike sparks off the wet leaves, she had taken the first skirmish clearly and gotten a ride home besides.

And for the rest of the spring and summer, she saw him every day. He would come riding across the length of unplowed pasture between her house and the unpaved road, pushing his blaze-faced stallion, standing in his stirrups, waving to her.

"Hey, Vera . . . hey, honey . . . "

He would come in the morning just after the sun had risen behind the woods, and the first hard beams of it would strike across the pasture and fix him, illuminate him there as if he were some amazing bas-relief depicting youth and strength and the overflowing vigor of those who have no stake or purpose in life except the living of it. And Vera, finishing her early chores, with her father's breakfast cornbread and pork and single egg cooked and going cold at the back of the stove, with the handful of laundry done and hung on a piece of rope between the cabin and the hen house, would step outside wiping her hands and untying her apron, smiling quietly to see him come.

He leaned from the saddle and pulled her up behind, and they rode east and south, past the outskirts of the town toward the Red River. On the way, there were fields of tiny cotton plants that stretched as far as they could see, divided only by lines of trees for windbreak, or narrow paths barely wide enough for a wagon. Negroes leaned among the plants, chopping meticulously with short stylized swings at the weeds which already were as high as the cotton.

"They ought to have been cleanin' out this field three weeks ago," Mo shouted over his shoulder as they rode past. "But it would shine and then it would rain, and the ground-water was so high that the rain would stand for a week, and by the time the sun drawed it up, she'd be rainin' again, and you can't get a nigger to chop in mud."

They rode on into the sandy uncultivated flats where the spring grass was already high, and tall cottonwoods turned their leaves from green to white as morning breezes touched them. Down at the river on the Caddo parish side, they stopped. Mo hobbled the stallion, and they walked down to the edge of the brown, swift-flowing water.

"It'll be down by the end of June," he told her. "It always goes down then, and here, all along here, there's usually a big wide sandbar that pokes out into the river. Because the way the channel's been runnin' the last few years, it always eats off the Bossier parish side and puts it down over here. My father says if it keeps up, we'll have us six hundred new acres in another four or five years."

"Somebody's losing' it, ain't they?"

Mo grinned maliciously. "Sure, I reckon. But some lose and some win. It ain't like we were taking anything. It's the river. It's how the river acts."

"Sooner or later, it'll turn on you," Vera said as she looked out across the sunlit water toward the raw slashed bluffs upstream on the far side.

"I reckon," Mo smiled again. "I reckon one day the channel's goin' to change. The river will get sick of the same old way down and frisk itself around. Then we'll get some of the eating-away and some sucker down toward Coushatta will go to bed with a farm and wake up with a plantation. Boy, Poppa will howl then."

"Nothing stays the same," Vera sighed.

"Not much. It comes and goes." Mo looked at her out of the corner of his eye and put an arm around her shoulders. "That's why you got to make good use of what you got while you've got it."

Vera smiled without looking at him. "We're talkin' about land."

"Sure," Mo said. "I reckon."

Maybe he knows more than I thought, Vera mused. Maybe those damned nigger girls at his father's place could tell me just how much he *does* know.

Mo was pulling long stalks of Johnson grass and chewing the juice out of them. "*Tempus fugit,*" he intoned glumly.

"What?"

"Latin," he told her carelessly. "They learn you Latin down at the school in Alexandria. It means if you don't take it, you ain't gonna get it."

"Is that what it means?"

"Free translation," Mo admitted. "That's the sense of it."

"I guess it all depends on whose mule's getting shod," Vera said. "Some things you can't take all at once. You have to go at it slow and easy. Like fishin'. You never dove in after a trout, did you?"

"Not lately," Mo said. "Did once when I was a kid and that damn fool Phillipe dared me."

"Did you catch him?"

"Yeah," Mo grinned. "Yeah, I sure enough did."

"Fool's luck," Vera blushed. "You couldn't do it again."

Mo passed her a slip of grass and began spreading a horse blanket under a tall sweet gun near the water. "Well," he said judiciously, "all I can do is get wet tryin'."

For the rest of the summer, Vera alternated offense with defense. She was within spitting distance of her objective, but the threat of being disarmed even at the gates of the enemy's citadel was always there. A few times Mo's counterattacks forced her to epic measures – if epic is properly defined as defense of a close place against odds.

But it can't go on forever, she thought as the summer burned on. Sooner or later either he's going to ask me to marry him or I'll stop worrying whether he asks or not. Or he'll decide the nigger wenches are more his style and let me get home out of the next rain the best way I can.

So day after day, with him in the bright sun, in the woods, at the river, riding into Bossier parish or west the few miles into Texas in Amos

Stevens' black open carriage, she found herself not only caught in another draw as closely balanced as the one she had established with her father, but found moreover that her own will to resist was becoming pitted and corroded by Mo's constant undemanding presence. Whether he knew or didn't know what summer and woods and moonlight before darkness were for, she knew or at least considered she did, and the balance, the finely wrought mechanism of her hopes, was beginning to crumble and give way under the combined force of Mo's daily attention and her own craving.

I can lick him, Vera thought. I can either wake him up if he's really still asleep in them games and hunts and rompings with Ed Norton and the rest of them, or I can make him bleed every time he thinks of me if he's already fired and just trying to play me. Or I can even play him until he's old enough to see that I got something he can't get on a possum hunt – at least not on any kind of decent possum hunt. I can do any one and whip him flat till we walk out of that damned Episcopal Church right in front of Ed Norton's mother and the rest of them fancy planters. But I *got* to hold on. I got to.

And in the meanwhile, Mo's father had finally asked someone what his son was doing with the long summer days and half the nights.

"Don' ask me Morison's business," Rye shrugged. "What he do, dat his study."

"I didn't ask you to spy on him," Stevens bristled. "I just thought you might know. Or at least I expected Phillipe would know."

Rye shrugged again. "I don' know but what dem boys tell. Phillipe don' know *nothing*. He jus' like me when I was young: what you say to me in Richmon' town so long ago, was I to bruit yo' business to yo' fatha?" God's steamy eyes, you sold me de day after, huh?"

Amos Stevens poured himself some brandy and went back to his newspaper. "It's the time," he growled irrelevantly. "You can't get a straight answer out of a nigger any more. You ask one a question, and he'll ask you a question back."

Rye grinned and stoppered the brandy. He licked his fingers and studied Stevens' frowning face over the top of the Richmond *Enquirer*. "Safe to suppose Morrison gone say somethin' about dese days. He wait de time."

Stevens looked up. "By the time he says, I'll have heard it from the blacksmith, the stablemen, three field-niggers, and some irate father with his hand stretched out palm up."

"He never befo'," Rye pointed out.

"That's just why," Amos said. "It's coming time. He hasn't had his shotgun out in two months. When they stop running rabbits and bucks, you can bet they're after does."

The summer was done, finally. It was winter, and he was gone back to Louisiana Seminary (where he would do indifferent work in engineering under the superintendent of the school, one W. T. Sherman, a Northerner, red-headed and irascible, who some of the students judged to be an out-and-out lunatic. Mo's view was less harsh: Cump Sherman was just not much good for anything. So he taught). He wrote Vera that he would be home by Christmas despite all the hoorahing and political uproar Lincoln's recent election had caused. The hell with politics, Mo wrote. We got too much to talk about. We got a lot to talk about.

This time she would be ready for him. She had enough money for another dress. There would be a dance during the holidays, maybe more than one. It was only an interrupted campaign, not a lost one or even a drawn one. The sun was still high, and her lines were in perfect array.

But during the late afternoon of December 21st, her new dress in a paper package under her arm, she was walking down Texas Street toward Market Street. She heard the cheering and yelling begin near the newspaper office and spread up and down the street. The roadway was filling with men: merchants in shirtsleeves, workmen, Negroes in livery or tatters, laughing, roaring as if suddenly and universally, for freeman and slave alike, bonanza had arrived. Women looked down out of windows, and a few of them waved blue flags with hand-sewn Louisiana pelicans on them. Someone in Martin's bakery began playing a cornet, and all up and down the street, mixing, mingling, the men and even the women who had cast aside their reticence just this once, were singing:

Look away, look away,
Look away, Dixie land . . .

Out of Cleburne's store a handful of young men ran double time down the stairs in their gray and black Caddo Militia Company uniforms. Someone was riding a horse on the boardwalk in front of Mrs. Terry's Ladies' Shop. And then, up on the top step of Cleburne's store, she saw her father with a huge dragoon pistol (not his own), and the sound of its report made her squeeze both hands tight over her ears. Her father was drunk, and he fired the pistol into the air over and over again, while the Negroes laughed and jigged in the dirt street before him, while Cleburne himself, who almost never came out of the store, leaned against his doorjamb smiling darkly, and a woman thrust a tiny flag into Vera's hand.

In Dixieland
I'll take my stand
To live and die in Dixie...

And finally, with more men galloping up and down the street, raising clouds of dust, obscuring the Christmas wreaths in the store windows, she came abreast of the *Shreveport News* office and there, stuck to the glass, was a fresh page of newsprint, and in enormous uncompromising letters it said:

SOUTH CAROLINE SECEDS
The Union is Dissolved

She did not move of her own volition, but the crowd jostling to see for themselves, shunted her away from the window. She could hear the cornet again, and someone else had added a flute and drum, only now, instead of "Dixie" the cornet was playing something wild, something full of fire and agony, something to bring up the blood boiling like molten lead, to make a man run and run onward until his lungs gave out and his heart burst: *da   da   da-da   da-da   da-da   da-da   da da   da-da   da-da   daaaa*

The charge, like something she had once seen in a history book Mo studied: the Tartars who rode in a straight line and killed and killed until they fell from their ponies exhausted or killed themselves. And later, when she would sit with the thin packet of letters written on cheap paper from places in Maryland or Virginia – and one from Pennsylvania – she would remember this day and try to recall what thoughts she had had as the crowds pushed her on down the street and the bugle crashed over and over, and dust from behind galloping horses' hoofs rose in the cold winter air like blue smoke. But she could remember nothing except a cold finger of fear that touched and probed within her, and the tall words chiseled grimly into flimsy newsprint: *the union is dissolved.*

And up on Cleburne's porch two loafers, drunk themselves, lifted her father on their shoulders while he finished reloading the pistol and started firing it into the air again over the heads of the crowd.

On the 22nd, Mo came home. Not first to his home as custom and manners would have had it – as even Vera would have understood and had it – but to her cabin. Her father was still in town, still drunk, and absent since the morning before, and she sat alone in the kitchen-sitting room near the fireplace with a scrap of woolen bedspread wrapped around her shoulders. She heard the stallion pound into the yard, heard it rear and snort, and heard him curse it back to all fours and tie it to one of the porch posts which served in place of the hitching rail her father had almost put up at the insistence of her mother a dozen years before. Then his footsteps on the porch, fast and heavy and certain. And the door open into darkness, and him moving out of shadow toward the fire, into her arms.

And later, if she could never quite remember her thoughts that afternoon outside the *Shreveport News* office, she would never forget the feeling that swept over her when she felt the solid mass of his body close to hers, the fresh chill of his lips against her neck, her mouth, her eyes.

Why, she thought, strength leaving her again, weakening her legs, making her arms numb around him, her fingers dance out of control, why, I love him. I *love* him. Not for a house, not for maids or late-sleeping, and even for that other. I just love him. I really do.

"I love you," he told her, and there was no coltish hesitation in his voice. Whatever had been imprisoned in that damp newsprint was working strange things. "I love you, Vera, as much as I can love. I love you," he was saying.

And Vera, hardly standing now, more nearly lying erect in his arms, pressed her hands to either side of his face and turned his head so that the firelight caught and illuminated his eyes as he eased her down upon the thick fur rug in front of the fire.

The union is dissolved, she thought dreamily. That's what they think. Before January was over, Louisiana followed South Carolina out of the Union. Young men forgot school, planting, store-keeping and hostling. Now they were wearing colorful uniforms, hand-sewn like the little flags. They spent their time drilling or drinking on Cleburne's front porch or standing in front of the *Shreveport News* where the telegraph office rented space.

The air was still electric, and what had looked at first like a mad festival that would flare and then fade back into the regula of day-by-day went on without sign of lessening. Mo had her working on a tunic of dark blue serge with gold facing up both sleeves, and a tight round collar with red and gold tabs of captain's rank.

"I didn't go lookin' for it," he told her. "They would have me captain them. I never wanted it."

"Jesus," her father guffawed on one of his increasingly rare trips home, "that little sonofabitch thinks he's a admiral. What's he givin' you to sew up that slipcover?"

"Nothin'," Vera snapped. "Shut up and eat them eggs."

"Nothin', I'll bet," her father snickered. "Nothin'? You can do better than that stitchin' up croker sacks for Miz Rising to sell up to Silsbee's stable. They put just as good a grade of shit in 'em, too."

"I told you to shut up," Vera yelled, dropping the tunic and standing up. "If there's a fight, I know damned well where they'll find you."

Her father hunched over his cold eggs. "If they find me at all they'll need 'em a better set of needlenoses than that Stevens monkey you got. Anyhow, I ain't seceded from nothin'."

"You ain't got spine for fightin' anything bigger nor less brittle than a jug."

"No reason, you mean, Cleburne said it last night. If it comes to shootin', it'll be a rich man's war and poor man's fight. That six-bit dandy of yours'll find hisself a jug and let the river boys and the piney-hill scrabblers take all the slugs. Then he'll get him a medal and trot home and buy up their places."

Taggert dodged the firedog, but the old kettle caught his half-finished plate of eggs and spattered them all over his shirt and plants.

"Get out," Vera was yelling, "or this is gonna be the first place up for sale."

Mo left for northern Mississippi in late January. Over the blue tunic he wore a short gray cape that the town ladies had made for all the company officers. He wore the cape over one shoulder, and his red and gold collar tabs glistened in the pale sunlight.

All around them, young men and their families stood talking quietly. Body-servants were stowing trunks and satchels aboard the train, and behind the passenger cars thoroughbred horses were being loaded to follow their masters. There was no shouting, no cheers or flag-waving.

"They were tryin' to hook on the horse cars up ahead of the passenger cars," Mo was telling her, trying to pass the short time left, trying to make her laugh. "And Major Sentell, he told the engineer that the horses could stand our downwind better than we . . . "

"Your father," Vera put in without smiling. "Why ain't . . . ?"

Mo looked toward the train longingly. "He said he'd rather make his good-byes at the place. He's got work. They wanted him for the convention, and now they want him in Baton Rouge."

"Have you told him . . . ?"

"Honey," Mo said, stretching his neck in the confines of the bright collar, "I never got a chance. Listen . . . "

"Never mind," she said without expression. "Never mind. I see."

"No, you *don't* see. How could I tell him I was going to fight, and then tell him I was studyin' gettin' married without even drawing a breath between? When I get home . . . "

The locomotive groaned and blew a dense cloud of steam from under its wheels. "It's all right," she said. "It couldn't have come to anything now with the excitement and all anyhow. We'll have to wait."

"Vera . . . "

"Yes?"

He picked up his carpetbag and began walking toward the nearest passenger coach. All the windows were up and men and boys were leaning out talking and holding hands with their women. Mo took her arm.

"You got to wait for me, hear? I want this for us. I want it more than anything. I'd stay now but . . . "

"I know," she said mechanically, "you got to go."

"No, listen. At first, right after I asked you to marry me that night at your place, I didn't even know how come I asked you. I was scared about what my paw would say, and scared of havin' a wife . . . "

Vera turned from him. Punishment, she thought. Punishment for wanting him the wrong way. Pray or wish for lace curtains and fancy china, and when love comes, you lose it. "All right," she said. "You don't have to go on. Just forget we ever said anything."

"No," Mo almost shouted. "Why don't you listen to me? That was right after. But with all the war talk and everything, I got to thinkin' about us, and it seemed right. It is right. I'm grown enough for some

Yankee to shoot at me, so I reckon I'm grown enough to get married even without my paw's say-so if it came to that. I want it for us."

She turned back into his arms. They stood on the chill platform isolated from the milling crowds of people who moved back and forth from the tiny station house to the train. Mo kissed her over and over again.

"And when I came home to you that night," he whispered. "When I came home with the whole country comin' down around my ears, and we . . . "

"Hush," she said, touching his lips with her finger. "You don't want to shame your wife before you marry her, do you?"

He blushed and grinned. "No, I ain't goin' to shame you no way. Not here, or up there either."

Then Phillipe touched his sleeve and picked up the carpetbag from where Mo had dropped it. He motioned toward the train.

"Tuck it up, Morrison," he said quietly. "Time to be travelin'."

Another kiss and Phillipe, on board the coach, had to reach out to catch Mo's hand and heft him onto the moving train. All around her the mothers and fathers, wives, children, lovers were waving good-bye, begging for letters, wishing God's protection while the train inched past the station platform, out past the roundhouse and a huddle of maintenance buildings, getting smaller and smaller as it crept down the tracks toward the east. She went on waving long after he was only a smear of darker hue against the train's dark side, after the train itself had disappeared into a stand of pine that flanked the track and the sun fell behind a bank of low heavy cloud that promised early rain.

For four years there were only the letters. At first they came from Corinth in Mississippi. Then, by the early summer of 1861, the letters began to be postmarked from North Carolina, and finally from Richmond itself. After that, the letters were few – not more than one every several months – and the places at which they were written read like a history of the Army of Northern Virginia. He wrote from near Chantilly; from Mechanicsville; from a camp near Luray; and then from Sharpsburg, Maryland.

Vera read the letters more as an astrologer reads the stars than as simple communications. She tried to reach through the paper to feel him beyond it; tried to sense whether he was sick or disheartened, whether he was afraid.

He wrote her in a letter from Fredericksburg in December of 1862:

199

I can say now that I am not afraid of anything on earth. At first I was frightened that I would show badly when it came to fighting. Then that passed and I had time to think about regular ordinary fear: I thought of all the dead men and men torn all to pieces I had seen, and how death here is like air or water. You don't waste time worrying if the air or water will give out, and you can't worry about death or wounding because after you have been here a while you know that the chances of not being killed or bad hurt are thin as the seat of a parson's pants.

I am now as you know a lieutenant in the regular army. They took my militia rank when we got up here after Manassas. But the way things are going I should end up a major because out of the 47 regimental officers I know, only 21 are still in the field. Anyhow, after what I have seen at this town, rank is nothing and life not much more. On the 13ᵗʰ inst. Burnside tried us here, and while the newspapers say he was repulsed with great slaughter, that is mere words. What happened there at the wall below Mary's Hill made men in my company cry like children, and an artillery officer refused to fire on the enemy any more.

They attacked us for several hours, wave after wave of them, and it was hopeless from the start. I do not know how many of them died, but in front of our works there was a wide field of perhaps 20 acres and it was covered solid with dead and wounded, covered in some places three or four deep. It was enough to break the heart of a stone statue to see them attack bravely when they knew we would not give way and could not be got out. I understand one officer said to Genl. Jackson, O general, it is sorry work to kill such brave men, and Stonewall replied, No, kill them all. If the brave men are killed, the cowards will not threaten our independence. Genl. Jackson is right, but it is a hard thing to look on the face of a dead man who has nobly given up his life and not be sorry that humanity lets quarrels come to this. But there is duty and there is right, and sympathy is not the part of a soldier. I will write again soon if God spares me. If God spares anyone.

Between letters, there was work. By the end of 1861, the town had grown from five or six thousand people to almost twenty thousand, and a military hospital had been set up to take care of men wounded or taken sick in Texas, Arkansas, central Mississippi, and north Louisiana. She worked alongside the town girls, and within a few weeks of starting, had shown that she could work twice as long as the strongest and most willing of the socially prominent young ladies. And as the wounded men continued to flow in, Vera's ability began to override birth and breeding. When the girls were asked to nominate a supervisor for themselves, Vera was the uncontested choice. Even Ed Norton's mother came to help as the number of patients increased – and she took orders from Vera.

Murray Taggert came and went on his own, and stayed away from his daughter. At the start of secession, he bought feed-grain and vegetables and poultry for Cleburne. The storekeeper supplied him with a rig and some money, and he traveled in northwest Louisiana and east Texas buying, speculating, and doing nothing whatever to improve his name in the town. Toward the end of 1862, he disappeared: simply rode out of town with Cleburne's rig, a few dollars, and as many chickens as he could load on the wagon.

"It ain't like I was surprised," Cleburne told Vera one day at the store, "because it had to happen one day or the other. I was just gamblin' that I could make the cost of the rig and a piece of profit out of him before he decided to scratch the itch."

"If you're lookin for sympathy, you better talk to somebody else," Vera told him. "Anybody who'd hand that old fool a horse pistol and let him go to shootin' it off his porch, and then set him up in business had got to get stung. Did you get the worth of what he stole before he stole it?"

Cleburne grinned. "It was close. I reckon he paid for the mule in April, the wagon in July. I got four months' profit before he decided to go on his own. I guess I did just a little better than break even."

Vera shook his head. "Well, you're the first human being that ever come out better than even with him. My mother lost everything you can lose, and I spent eighteen years holdin' steady."

Later there was word that Murray had been seen in Memphis and in Iuka, Mississippi, before Van Dorn was shot by a husband whose eyes lost their scales at an inopportune moment for the Confederacy. Not only seen, so the word came back, but seen in a Confederate uniform with corporal's stripes and a roving commissary's impressment commission.

"Jesus," Cleburne said when Vera passed the word on, "you done underestimated the old chickensnatcher. All your life you thought he was worthless, when the truth is that he was just a specialist without no practice. He might come back and buy Caddo parish when this thing is over."

"If he does, that's me leavin'," Vera said.

It was Cleburne's turn to shake his head. His walleye roamed the shelves behind her. "Listen, that old man ain't stealin' a chicken here and there now," he said. "He can steal wholesale and show 'em his permit to do it."

Then they heard nothing more until late July of 1863. Vera had just left the hospital where the wounded and sick men lay silent in the gloom of Vicksberg's fall just a few weeks earlier. She saw Ed Norton's mother standing on the bottom step of Cleburne's store talking to the proprietor.

"Miss Taggert," Mrs. Norton nodded politely.

"Miz Norton," Vera answered just as politely.

"I was telling Mr. Cleburne about the card from Edward."

"I thought he was in . . . "

"He was," Cleburne said, "but some of 'em broke out the night before Pemberton sewed up his Judas-deal."

"He wrote from central Tennessee," Mrs. Norton said. "He mentioned Major Sentell . . . and your father."

"My father," Vera replied, setting herself for whatever revelation they might have.

"The Yanks finally put salt on his tail," Cleburne said. "I beg youall's pardon. A figure of speech."

"They must have got the drop on him with a cannon and him in a well. Or did he surrender to their paymaster?"

Cleburne roared, his bad eye bouncing hilariously from one woman to the other. "Maybe he offered to buy Grant's army, guns, mules, traps, and all."

Mrs. Norton bristled. "I see no humor in any of this. We are beset by our enemies on every side. I should think levity . . . "

"Aw, Miz Norton," Cleburne said disgustedly, "you ain't gonna win no war by puttin' on a long face. We might as well squeeze a laugh out of it."

"... with your father, whatever he may have been in the past, having sacrificed himself for the Southern Confederacy..."

"O Lord," Vera breathed, and thanked God again that Ed Norton obeyed his mother, "the old man sacrificin' himself. Lord God."

"... donned our uniform, marched beneath our flag... which is more than *some* have done," Mrs. Norton went on angrily.

Cleburne looked at her unsmiling. He managed to bring the bad eye close to focus alongside the good one. "Are you standin' there takin' up for Murray Taggert?" he asked solemnly.

"Why...," Mrs. Norton faltered, "why..."

"That's something," Vera said wryly. "That's really something."

"And him not here to listen to it," Cleburne clucked with mock sadness. "I wish I could have gone along with him. I could of died happy to think that I was enshrined in Miz Norton's heart."

"No," Mrs. Norton flared. "No... I ..."

"But I got me a vital occupation," Cleburne apologized. "Somebody's got to buy food and make sure the good folks are supplied."

"Sure," Vera smiled grimly. "With maybe the price of a mule and a wagon slippin' into his pocket while he's being vital."

"If a man don't look out for himself...," Cleburne began.

"I know," Vera said. "The old man used to say it all the time." Taggert got home in October. He was draggled and shoeless, and told a story that made even the thin-haired, deaf old loafers cackle and nudge one another. It had been a near thing, capture despite heroic resistance, escape at mortal peril, journey home through the four suburbs of hell with rest-stops in the purlieus of purgatory. Like that.

And then, without more than a casual visit to Vera at the hotel where she had stayed since the hospital work began, he went back to Cleburne, made some sort of peace with him, and started his purchasing and peddling again almost as if nothing had intervened between his riding away with Cleburne's mule and wagon and his return without hat or shoes.

But Vera had other things to concern her. The hospital overflowed after Vicksburg, and by the summer of 1864, General Nathaniel Banks (the perennial dupe of Lee's army, the man called "Commissary" Banks by Jackson's troops after his disastrous and costly retreats in the Valley of Virginia) began his push up the Red River. At Mansfield, Banks met Richard Taylor (whose father had known how to deal with brigands from the saddle and from the White House) and found his luck no better along the Red than along the Shenandoah. On his way back toward the safety of the Mississippi and Federal gunboats, Banks fired the city of Alexandria and allowed his disgruntled heroes to pillage and devastate in accepted Yankee fashion. But he did not break up Taylor's army or seriously threaten the Louisiana capital, now at Shreveport.

Still he sent enough wounded Confederates into Shreveport to flood the hospital facilities completely; the women of the town had to work now – not simply in the graceful fashion of Lady Volunteers but desperately and for long hours. The grace and fashion of noble war for high emprise had faded into the terrible monotony of a blood-letting without discernible end, without recollectable beginning. The wounded filled stylish homes now – even the improvised Governor's Mansion had its quota of tortured flesh – and every day was amputated from the one before by moans and shrieks out of which no glory or patriotism could possibly be distilled.

Some of the women broke. Mrs. Pearson, the Episcopal minister's wife, fell into a reverie and dreamed of the rolling adorable hills of Maryland. Mrs. Norton, too much beset by blood and bone and bodyless limbs, too long without a letter from Ed, who still rode and ravaged with Forrest's mythical legion in western Tennessee, Mississippi and Alabama, began to cry one afternoon as the wounded from Mount Pleasant were being brought into the hospital, and could not or would not – at least did not stop it for a week and a half.

Of them all, only Vera (and Ellen Sentell, who did not count as one of the local ladies because she had small traffic with any of them, and for all her natural and social leverage in the town, handled herself as well as Vera, as well as any of the surgeons, keeping her own counsel while her son, paroled from Vicksburg by then, nursed his own unhealing wound and fought a sub-rosa battle against unspecified furies of the kind that Vera understood well enough) kept up the pace without faltering. She was moving between the beds when the first doctor staggered off his cot in the darkness before sunrise, and still at it when the same doctor called for an orderly to help him find his cot again late that night.

Between calls, she read the letters that came more and more infrequently. Now they were from towns and hamlets in Virginia again. No more from Maryland or Pennsylvania. No more filled with the hope that all the death and misery might justify itself. Now the letters were markers on the way down from near Chancellorsville, from Spotsylvania Courthouse, from a tent near a bend in the North Anna, from a place called variously Cool Arbor, Cole's Crossing – or Cold Harbor, and finally from a small railhead south and east of Richmond called Petersburg.

Mo wrote toward the end of March in 1863:

This time we are in for it for sure, no food worth talking about, ammunition either made on the spot of raw lead and charcoal and niter and paper flimsy, or damp from the trip behind broken-down mules in this goddamned rain. The trenches are hell-holes, and they ought to issue blue jackets to the rats. The town is a shell without any women or children, and I have not been out of the works since Christmas anyhow. I say this. I say if Genl. Lee can take us out of this dead end and in shape to deal the Yanks more misery, then he is no general at all but the Holy Ghost and Messiah rolled in one.

What I say is not to scare you or to sound high-flown, but I expect to die in this place, and I want to say it to someone I love. I can't write it to Poppa because he has got agony enough I know. But I have to say this and say that dying here is sour and no good and only done because we cannot shame our people by quitting. But, Vera, it is all right and if I never see your face again, you show this letter to Poppa after it is over, and he will take care of you knowing that I have done my whole duty, asked nor taken quarter, and that my last wish was to make you my wife.

What will be left of our country when this war ends only God knows. It may be as a preacher here said to me in private, that perhaps we have reached the late evening of our day with nothing but a long night ahead, and that the survivors will have to bear worse than anything we have suffered . . .

After that there were no more letters. There was only the daily communiqué on brown paper tacked up on the window of the *News*: the Union breakthrough at Five Forks; the brief bitter encounter at Saylor's

Creek; the cutting of the railroad toward Lynchburg; and the closing of the ring near a quiet village called Appomattox Courthouse. Then even the telegraph broke off, and rumor did for news.

But working in the silent wards alone at night, or walking down Milam Street through the starved spring sunlight, she knew what all of them knew: that the Union killing machine was coming closer, and that even as the Southern soldiers slowed it, fouled its workings, stalled it and pressed it backward for a moment here and there, the juggernaut was pressing on, the grinding promise of a hateful metallic future.

Now she sat on the porch of Maxy's Hotel, her hands folded, her face composed in some remarkable counterfeit of self-control. The weather had turned again, and the rain was gone, at least for a while. There was almost no traffic now, and the shadows had disappeared, melding into unbroken darkness.

Now she had time to think. The moon, throttled and subdued by thick wedges of cloud, turned the street a pale white for a moment and then faded once more. Vera rocked slowly, her eyes closed, the fresh breeze carrying a scrap of dark hair across her cheek.

She thought of the patronizing efficiency of the Union doctors who had taken over operation of the hospital, of how one of them nudged another when they saw the scanty supply of drugs and medicine the Southern doctors had been using, how they frowned at the hospital's facilities and how, finally, they had dismissed the women volunteers, preferring their own male orderlies for the work.

And Vera frowned, thinking of the wounded Confederate soldiers who were still in the hospital. Who were now simply victims, as if they had been injured in a mine cave-in or a train wreck. The army of which they had been part was dissolved; the nation for which they suffered no longer existed, and in the Yankee Congress, that dead nation was already referred to as "the so-called Confederate States," as if the country for which so many had sacrificed life and property and family had never been more than an illusion, a bad dream of unusual duration in the mass mind of The Indivisible Republic.

She could think of herself again. She could think of the thin, sharp-featured little girl who, ages before, had launched a campaign of her own, and who had nearly won her objective before a larger, more portentous war intervened.

But what was the use of thinking now? He might be dead in the ruins of Petersburg, or lying in the shallows of Saylor's Creek. He might have been cut down in the merciless cavalry charges along the railroad, or strangled in the muddy road on the way to Appomattox.

Even if he's alive, she thought, what good will he be? He was proud and he always won, and if he comes back what good will he be to himself or anybody else?

The moon broke through the clouds again, and Vera watched as it illuminated an open field down at the end of the block. Confederate troops had been camped there before Kirby Smith announced the surrender, and what grass spring had provided was churned into the mud beneath and littered with ruptured barrels, empty crates, broken wheels, with piles of rubbish and bits of paper too small to salvage. From where Vera sat, it looked like a battlefield.

She heard the wagon before she saw it. That'll be Poppa, she thought. You don't even see him at first. He always gets there before you know it.

Murray was fairly steady on the wagon seat, and when he reined in the single slack-shanked mule, it was with less than his common viciousness.

"All right," Murray said without offering to help her with her things. "Come on. This ain't no fifteen-minute coach stop."

"You can hold on," Vera said evenly. "If you ain't gonna help me lug his stuff, you can at least hold that mule steady."

"This mule is tired. It's been a long day."

Vera climbed up on the unpadded seat, and Murray slashed the mule across his rump carelessly. "How many people did you sell today?" Vera asked him.

Murray ignored her and reached under the seat for a bottle. He fumbled with the cork and finally jerked it free with his teeth. As a lonerider, slumped in his saddle, rode past them. Murray spit the cork into the street, stared at the horseman, and leaned back to drink. Vera had turned away, staring at the passing storefronts without seeing them.

"'Bout time you was considerin' your paw instead of them scarecrows up to the hospital," Murray coughed from the liquor's bite.

"I ain't comin' back to look after you. You do all right."

Murray pouted. "There ain't a drop of good blood in you. I reckon it's the old lady in you. She wasn't . . . "

"Leave her out of it. I don't want you talkin' about her. I don't want you talkin' to me any more than you got to. I got nothin' more to say to you now than when I left."

"Listen, if you mean to stay out to my house . . . "

"That garbage dump," she slashed out. "That damned pesthole. You bet I mean to stay there till I see somethin' else. I reckon I earned that right."

"Well, you better get a civil tongue. I ain't gonna . . . "

"Old man," Vera said quietly. "Don't give me any of your airs. You save that for them bums at Cleburne's and the saloon. When I can get shut of that place, I mean to do it. Till then, you keep clear of me, and I'll stay out of your way."

"What if I don't stay clear?" Murray sneered.

"Then you're even a bigger fool than I took you for."

"Still waitin' for that short-peckered boy of Amos Stevens, ain't you?"

Vera paid to attention to him. They had reached the edge of town, and she kept her eyes on the scattered houses they were passing.

"I remember when them Stevens came into town," Murray snorted. "I was out in front of Ramsey's with Kemp Clayton, and this fella with one arm comes ridin' in. Big tall Indian-lookin' sonofabitch with a snotty-nosed kid on behind, and a nigger ridin' just as good a horse right beside him, and that nigger with a little nigger perched behind like a parrot on a elephant's ass. And a whole flock of high-toned niggers on two wagons and a pair of coffins settin' in the wagons. And that cold-eyed sonofabitch sees me and looks down off his blooded stallion like he had just bought Shreveport and says, 'What way to the churchyard?' And I says, 'There's four churches. Maybe you want the Hebrew church.' And he says, 'I want the Protestant Episcopal Church.'

"So I told him where it was, and Kemp kinda laughs, and says, 'You got a lot of fancy niggers there, fella. How about sellin' us one?' And that big-time bastard turns up his nose like he smelled shit fresh on the ground and says, 'That's funny, I was just thinkin' of buyin' *you* for *them.*'"

Vera stared at him, her mouth twisted into something like a smile. "He would have been throwin' money away. Wasn't either one of you worth the price of a good nigger."

Murray paid her no mind. "Sure now, he took hold of this town and run it without even tryin' to run it. Run it without a word except when some of these cheap bastards come out to his place with their hats in their hands and asked him about everything but when to crap. And that nigger Rye walked down the street like whatever belonged to Stevens was part his. Many a time I started to shoot that nigger just on account of how he looked. I don't know what kept me from it."

"Maybe on account of you knowin' that Amos Stevens and those two boys would've hunted you down like a mad dog and shot you in church or jail or in the Governor's Mansion or the President's outhouse. Maybe it was that."

Murray stared at her over his empty bottle. "I wasn't never afraid of that one-arm sonofabitch. Nor that skinny-assed boy and his pet nigger."

"Sure," Vera said, "it was pure Christianity kept you off Rye."

I'm going to pound her head in one of these days, Murray thought. No warning; no hard words. I'm just going to up and break her goddamned neck with a stick of firewood or a poker. I feel it coming on. She ain't a thing but her old lady with more meanness and smarter.

"Anyhow," he said as he wiped his mouth on his sleeve, "anyhow, that young one is nothin' but mold and weed and roots now. He's one Stevens who ain't gonna trouble anybody. Whatever else, the Yanks did for him."

"Shut up," Vera said flatly.

"You watch what I . . . "

Vera turned to him. "You're doin' pretty well," she said quietly. "You don't want to get killed in your sleep while there's money makin', do you?"

Murray's shoulders slumped and he dropped his empty bottle off the side of the wagon. It ain't worth it, he thought. It wasn't never worth it. You'd just as well shack up with a wildcat as try to get one up on her. Bad blood tells.

The clouds closed in for good then, and the rest of the way to the cabin was dark.

V

7 JUNE 1865 — It had been a long ride down, more than seven hundred miles of riding at night and stealing food and dodging Union patrols.

It was late afternoon now, and he was thinking of blood and its cheapness. His reflexes were tuned so high that the squeak of his own saddle under him, the sloppy mud-encrusted gait of his horse in the lowering twilight, made him twist his head from side to side like a trapped ferret that hears or imagines it hears the trapper a dozen miles away.

As he rode southward into the town, not meaning to stop or even pause to see how it had changed, a Union private without rank or responsibility (not even on duty at the moment, but torn between the saloon or the whorehouse or a muddy stroll up one of the residential streets before going back to his cot in the old rebel warehouse) happened to be loafing in front of Ripinski's dry-goods store when Mo turned off Market Street and started west.

The sun was down by then, but the spring moonlight was bright enough for the Union private to see his uniform, to see his cap and the gray trousers with a wide gold stripe. It was bright enough for the private, cold sober and not even nursing some formidable grudge against a superior, to see the tarnished brass buckle that was stamped CSA, and to respond by ordering its wearer to rein up.

His voice alone might have been enough. A voice with the sharp nasal twang of the Northern plains states in it, and surcharged with a note of certain and incontrovertible authority that would have sounded insulting in an officer, let alone in a blond stringy boy whose nearest approach to war had been the day before when he had stood with the rest of the squad before a porch full of silent men in sullen unbroken downpour and almost sat down in the mud when he realized that he would not have to be the instrument of authority after all.

But Linus Morrison Stevens paid no attention to the voice. Not because he had not heard it: he had seen the loitering soldier as he turned off Market Street into Texas. He had kept the bluecoat in sight as he rode toward him, his eyes squinted to see if the boy was armed. Seeing no weapon, he turned his eyes back to the rutted street and, when the Union private called out for him to stop, he paid no attention. An armed Yankee might or might not be dangerous, depending on the man. One without a gun was no worry to man or beast. If the harsh voice and the tone of pretended authority made his jaw tighten, it was not enough for a run-in. It had been almost three years since he would have been willing to risk his life for a discourteous word. He was not sure any longer what he would risk his life for.

But the Union private, almost as if his lieutenant's malady of the day before were contagious, could not let it go. He called out again as Mo passed abreast of him, and getting no more response than before, ran alongside Mo's horse and reached for his leg.

Mo touched his horse lightly with his heels. The Union private broke into a full run, slipping and staggering in the mud, grabbing for Mo's stirrup.

"You rebel sonofabitch, you better stop . . . pull up you stinking traitor."

Mo could feel the flesh grow rigid along his jaws, and his teeth clench. It crossed his mind to simply use his pistol on the Federal: to shoot or pistol-whip the idiot into the muddy street. It would be extermination, he thought almost detachedly, but they'd call it murder sure as hell. I didn't come this far to decorate a Yankee gallows.

" . . . pull up, you rebel bastard . . . "

All right, Mo thought, if I can't do what I want with him, I reckon I better do what he wants.

He jerked his reins tight, and the tired staggering mare reared up almost throwing Mo despite his preparation, and neatly stopping dead in the spot where the reins pulled short.

The blond private, building up speed, determined to drag Mo off his horse, kept his forward motion, tried desperately to hold his balance as he lurched past the rearing bay mare. He ran on a few steps more with long drunken strides, trying to cut his speed more quickly than he had gained it. But the mud offered him no purchase and he lost his footing.

Mo brought the mare down and ran his hand along her trembling neck. There was not much left in her. Then he looked over her head at the Union private. He was trying to turn over, to sit up, but the mud was almost a foot deep in that part of the street, and he could gain no traction. Finally, wallowing like a hog, or like a wagon being rocked out of soft sand, he managed to roll onto his back and sit up.

Mo leaned forward, his reins held loosely, his face relaxing almost to the point of a grin. The mare snorted and lifted her hoofs delicately as she passed around the dark heap fuming and struggling in the roadway.

Looks like one of them snowmen we built the winter after Fredericksburg, Mo thought. Only made of mud. And he ain't got those fine side-whispers like our snowman had, those fine Burnside whiskers.

"You yellow rebel bastard," the mudman howled in frenzy. "You don't have the guts to face a man equal."

Mo rode on a few yards with the grin still as nearly potential as one had been for a long time. He would enjoy telling his father about this. A small safe victory, amidst a large and final defeat. You came, sooner or later, he thought, to be thankful for a victory of any size. If some power above threw them away, you still had the memory of them. The memory, he thought, trying to recall the words: *of duty faithfully performed.*

" . . . yellow like every stinking traitor to come out of the South. Hill, Jackson, fat-man Longstreet, goat-beard Lee . . . "

Mo pulled the reins tight again. If the mare had had any strength, she would have reared once more. But this time she merely stopped, and her head dipped down toward the cold slime around her withers.

I reckon that's enough, Mo thought, his face hot, his hand moving toward his holster. I reckon either that's enough, or nothing will ever be enough again.

He steered the mare toward a hitching post in front of Martin's bakery. As he swung out of the saddle, his hand moved from the butt of his pistol to the belt buckle. No call to kill him, he thought, wondering at the coolness of his mind, the hot and jerky response of his body. Whatever needs doing won't call for a gun. Shame him more without. He turned and walked toward the Union soldier, who had finally gotten his legs under him again and was trying vainly to paw some of the viscous mud from his face and hair.

"You goddamn well better come back here, rebel," he blustered. "You already assaulted me. You're going to have six months of stockade if you're lucky. Colonel Lodge . . . "

"I was riding past," Mo said mildly.

" . . . said we don't have to take any smart business from . . . "

"And you made some remarks."

"No man who sold his country and flag and honor . . . "

"What did you say?" Mo asked, his voice still soft and incredibly even.

"Huh?" The Union soldier stopped his harangue long enough to realize Mo was speaking to him.

"I asked you what you said to me as I rode past just now."

The Union soldier frowned. None of them acted the way a man should. They never crawled, and they hardly ever burst out yelling or cursing. This one looked tired and beaten flat. Harmless and dirty and anxious to get home.

"I said I'll just clip those rebel buttons off your coat and take that pistol and carbine and those epaulets. Then maybe I'll just put a little of this damned mud on your braid."

The soldier wiped his hands pointlessly on his filthy tunic and fumbled in his pockets for a penknife. He watched Mo's face as he tried first one pocket, then the other. He saw nothing, and after a long moment, he found the knife.

"You know when you're whipped, don't you, rebel?" he said grinning under the hardening mud.

Then with the knife open, he reached for Mo's jacket.

Long afterward, when Mo was lying under cottonwoods in a circle of shade watching the Neches River squirm beneath an August sun, he remembered the Union soldier's crusted face, the certainty in it as he reached to saw at Mo's buttons. Mo remembered, too, how easy, how unpredictably easy it had been to order himself and wait for the perfect moment. He remembered thinking: not yet. He ain't close enough, and if he gets loose I don't have enough left to run him down. Wait. Wait till he honest-to-God believes he's got a tame one.

Then he felt the boy's hands on his clothes, and the control drained out of him like liquid from a smashed keg. He lifted his knee in a short piston-like motion, and the Union soldier bent double with a surprised muffled grunt. Before he could fall, Mo caught him by the front of his tunic. He set the Union soldier upright with his left hand and hit him in the face with his right. There was the brief satisfactory collapse of flesh and bone under his fist, but he took no pleasure in it. He had never enjoyed inflicting pain, had only taken some kind of measured satisfaction from sensing himself an administrator of justice. He hit the boy again with his right fist, then caught hold of the muddy tunic with his right and began hitting the soldier with his left. He did not count the blows. He stopped thinking about what he was doing because there was no resistance at all after he lifted his knee, and the rest of it was as mechanical and automatic as plucking a chicken.

It seemed to go on for a long time there at the edge of the slippery street with the plank sidewalk only a step or two to Mo's left, and a large sign hanging out from the wooden building front that said:

MILTON KLINE
Cotton – Beef

He remembered later, lying just out of the sun, with a narrow river channel running slow as syrup below, how he had felt like part of an incredibly old and ramshackle machine with rods and pulleys in his mind as well as his arms and hands: a machine which had no other function than to smash this boy-almost-a-man into pulp that would merge into the muck beneath his feet. He remembered that some hallucinated word or phrase had risen and fallen in his mind like the round mallet of the Roman coxswain who had established rhythm for the galley slaves. There was no way to tell how long it had gone on. All he could remember of duration was the lingering lengthy sadness he had felt at finding no satisfaction in it, and not even the vaguest hint of a justice in the making.

Then suddenly he had felt a pain in his fist so sharp and overpowering that he had almost cried out. Something had broken in his left hand. The lever was tripped: the machine shuddered to a halt.

He let the Union soldier's tunic go, and saw the boy fall away from his hand like a sack of flour emptied of its contents. The soldier fell rigid in a pose of comic pratfall like a minstrel clown. He lay utterly still on his back in the cold mud, and his face was a dark blur coated with drying mud and richer liquid that flowed slowly into his empty eyes and had not begun to dry at all.

Mo raised his eyes from the street and saw in the light of a flickering streetlamp men gathered on the porch of Cleburne's store across the street. There were more leaning against the doorpost of Ramsey's saloon or half-seated in the window recess or squatting on the boardwalk in heavy mud-crusted boots and shoes. None of them moved, and there had not been a sound since the fight began. He could not tell how long they had been watching or how much of it they had seen.

Then fatigue came suddenly, presenting its bill without warning or preamble, and if it had not been for the silent men across the way, he would have sat down in the muck next to the crumpled soldier and waited till the vertigo and the profound weariness passed. But they were there, and some of them, at least, recognized him: it was Amos Stevens' boy, and he was home from Virginia. He had come this far on his feet or in his saddle. He had two miles or so left to go. He meant to make it the rest of the way with mud nowhere except on his boots. With careful precision he walked the few steps to where his mare still stood, head down, reins hanging loose, not quite touching the ooze. All he asked for, the last request he would make that stemmed out of the war, was that he mange to gain the saddle.

He took a deep breath and held it for a second as he placed his foot in the stirrup, gathered up the reins and grasped the saddle horn. Then he heaved himself upward, feeling a new rush of giddiness pass hot and cold at once through his arms and legs. But by the time it had disoriented him, he could feel the saddle under him and he held fast to the pommel until it passed.

I could use some brandy, he thought as he turned the horse toward Crockett Street. I could have used a dozen bottles on the way down, but I never needed it like now.

He was riding past the clumps of silent men then. As he drew abreast of the streetlamp, he tried to recognize the faces. There were faces he knew, but they seemed to melt and run as he stared at them. Their features blurred, and one of the men looked for a moment like the Confederate major at Saylor's Creek; then like the mangled Union officer whom he and the sergeant had shot. He saw a gray-headed man who smiled wanly at him out of the shadows, but before Mo could place him, the hair went yellow and the smile twisted into a contorted glare of final agony, and it was the blood trooper in the smoking grass who had called for the Mother of God – or was it the Union soldier who lay crumpled in the mud a few yards behind him?

The drumming inside his head would not stop, and the heat and cold still flushed through him like molten lead chased by spring water. He twisted the reins around his wrist and jammed his feet as far into the stirrups as they would go. There was no moisture left in his mouth and he could feel the dryness of his forehead. It was as if a noonday sun stood overhead rather than a cloud-marred moon. He rolled his head sideways one last time, and saw the dark enigmatic door of Cleburne's place, with a thin unsteady pattern of light wavering far back inside the store. Then he lowered his head and paid no attention to anything but the road and the enormous delicacy of his balance in the swaying saddle.

For two days Amos Stevens had done his best to avoid Colonel Lodge. In the morning he had stayed in his room (not the room in which he had slept for almost twenty years: Lodge had taken that. Rather the room Morrison had left four years before), later going down the back-stairs to join Rye for lunch in the kitchen. In fact, there was little reason for his precautions. The endless string of petty Federal officials, legiti-mized thieves and aspirants to both categories had kept Lodge fairly occupied – so occupied that he had hardly time to set the garrison quarters in order and establish the new local government to his satis-faction. He had no time at all during the first few days to think about the man whose hospitality he had preempted.

In the afternoon Rye and Amos still sat on the porch. They had pulled their chairs and the wicker table away from the steps to stay clear of the loafers and place-seekers who gathered in the yard before down and lounged there, talking and guffawing, under the eyes of two Union sentries standing at some approximation of attention on either side of the door. Some of them would be called in to see Lodge and then come out to swap stories again. Some would go in, come out and ride away. Some never went into the house at all.

"I don't know where they came from, Amos said. "There's not a local man in the bunch, but you can tell they're not all Northerners."

"Po' whites from Arkansas and some up from New Orleans," Rye grunted. "Trash befo' de Yankees come, an' trash now. Been followin' de army and stealin' everything de army overlook. Girl work fo' Mr. Norton tole me dey gettin' hold of most all cotton in the parish. Some-body tellin' 'em who got cotton laid up, who got mules. Dat big one name Pony got him a running' iron."

"What does he need with a running iron? He's got a Yankee license to steal."

"Sho, but it only cover Confederate property. What he been doin' is sneakin' into a barn or pasture nighttime an' puttin' CSA on de stock. Next mornin' he come along whenever he wake and say, 'You got rebel mules dere. I see de brand. Dey belongs to de United States, and I'm de United States.'"

Amos frowned and chuckled at the same time.

"My God," he said, "at that rate, I expect I'd better keep you in at night, and you'd better keep your belt cinched up tight."

Rye pursed his lips. "Whuffo' you' want to fool at a time like dis? You ain't never learn what yo' poppa say about a time fo' levity an' a time fo' serious?"

"What else can you do?" Amos grinned. "We may be whipped but we're not dead. We may have a pack of locusts on us, but the road they came in on goes both ways. Maybe the sooner they break all the china and steal all the pigs, the sooner they'll get the hell out of here. I don't reckon my laughing will make them stay any longer."

But Rye knew better. He knew the waiting was beginning to tell on Amos. He knew that laughter was an alternative to short temper and depression, but an alternative that would work for only a while longer. If Mo was coming home, he would be home soon. If he was not home by the end of June, he would likely not be home at all. Rye saw Amos' face in repose. There was no humor in it. He knew what Amos was thinking.

"What about de letter?" Rye said shortly.

"Letter?"

"Phillipe Crowninshield's bill of particular fo' sellin' hisself to de Unions."

Amos shook his head. "Whatever else, Phillipe had you leaned like a schoolbook."

"What you mean?"

"I mean he said you wouldn't understand what he was trying to tell you. He was right."

"Dat boy ain't growd so smaht I can't follow what he say," Rye snapped. "Even wid a Union coat an' bars on the shoulder, he ain't nothin' beyon' me."

"He's beyond both of us. He's walking a new way in a new age, and he's sorry about what the parting did to us but he's too much like us to be sorry for the parting "

"Talkin' how dey made him free," Rye snorted. "He been free since twenty years ago."

"You should have told him," Amos said softly. "I told you when we sold out down south and came up here he ought to have beeen told and Morrison ought to be told before they grew out of just being a pair of boys and got to understanding what they were, what they would have to be to one another.

"So if I tol' him," Rye shot back. "I say maybe, 'You free as any mahn, an' you can do or not do as you see fit.' Den what you reckon we got? We got us a nigger boy too proud to do de work he got to do, an' too black to step higher."

"It won't always be that way. Anyhow, you took your freedom like a man. Why couldn't you trust Phillipe to do as well as you?"

"I was a growed mahn wif a wife an' child, an' only one frien' in de world an' not full of ideas beyon' me. An' de way it *will* be ain't de way it *is*."

"I reckon he might not have gotten the idea if he'd known he was free, that there was nothing to fight for."

"I dunno," Rye subsided. "It too late to amen' de past. He be here soon, an' we see what de Yankee made of him."

"I liked the letter," Amos mused. "I was so glad to hear he was alive, I would have liked almost any kind of letter. But it was a good letter. There wasn't anything to be ashamed of in it. He had a hard choice. I reckon he made it as well as any man. I reckon his reasons were better than those of half the Union army."

"Judgin' from de Union army I seen so far, dat wouldn't take much doin'. Robber in de parish jail can give as good reason fo' he action."

"It's a new world," Amos went on as if he had not heard. "Made of abstractions and ideas instead of family and land. Maybe when the agony is done, it will be a better world. Christ was three hours on the cross and three days in hell to buy us a new world. . . . "

"It ain't my worl'," Ray said with finality.

"It's all the world there is left," Amos said.

It was almost dark, and the chill had begun to settle in their bones when Lieutenant Raisor stepped out onto the porch.

"The colonel's compliments," he said with forced cordiality. "He wishes Mr. Stevens to take supper with him."

Amos glanced at Rye. "I think not," he said casually. "Mr. Crown-inshield and I have plans for the evening."

The lieutenant stiffened. "The colonel's request was not an invitation. He directed me to say he had business with you."

"Maybe he wants to make arrangements about the rent," Amos said, winking at Rye.

"Supper is at seven," the lieutenant said with controlled indignation.

" . . . as soon as he can clear the money changers out of the temple," Amos finished as the lieutenant stalked back inside. "I don't know about that boy," Amos added. "I wonder if he did any fighting."

"What I wonder," Rye said gloomily, "is if dat no-good son of mine is comin' home like dat. Lord God."

"Well," Amos comforted him, "there's still a few sticks of firewood behind the stove. I expect you could crack him once or twice if he sasses you."

"I gonna break his head if he start in about how his blood bought me free."

"On second thought, I reckon maybe you better not fool with him," Amos drawled.

"Huh?"

"Assaulting a Federal officer could get you hung.

This time it was Rye who grinned. "Not if you is a good ole honest darkie," he snickered.

There were four of them at the table. Colonel Lodge, Lieutenant Raisor, a white-haired captain of quartermasters, and Amos. When Amos reached the table, he nodded briefly to the others and took a seat. Before he was settled, a Negro began serving his plate.

"No," Amos stopped him. The colonel is presiding here. See him served, and I'll take care of myself."

Lodge stared at Amos for what seemed a long time. He was thinking that the man personified what he hated as well as any could: proud, a slave-owner, used to command and obedience far beyond anything an army officer could require. Gifted with a set of manners and customs preserved intact from the eighteenth century and utterly contemptuous of any social order but his own. A man intelligent enough to understand the nature of defeat, but too self-centered to let that knowledge show through either by ill temper or by forced good will.

Probably full to overflowing with hatred and hope for revenge, Lodge thought. With his property up for confiscation at my whim, his Negroes freed and their value lost to him, his son gone with the damned rebellion. And still he comports himself as if he were eating at the table of a friend. These people will be difficult to change. The more absurd the belief to which a man clings, the more stubbornly he holds to it.

"I hope you are not overly inconvenienced," the colonel said with sincerity.

"Not at all," Amos said urbanely, meeting the colonel's eyes. "I usually sup with Mr. Crowninshield. I'm sure he finds the change diverting."

Lodge continued staring, his gray expressionless eyes fixed on Amos as if he were an exotic specimen.

"I was not aware that Southern gentlemen took supper with their slaves."

"I was never aware that Southern gentlemen had any particular usage touching upon that matter," Amos answered smoothly.

"It is common knowledge . . . ," Lieutenant Raisor began.

"It is Northern speculation," Amos cut him off. "Whatever you were going to say."

They started to eat. The captain of quartermasters, a shabby uncertain man with a tiny speckled brush of mustache and pudgy white hands, the fingers spotted with ink, seemed uncomfortable sitting between Amos and Lodge. Lieutenant Raisor sat straight on the foremost quarter of his chair like a sleek, eager – and untried – hound waiting for his first point.

"I think you are aware of our position, Mr. Stevens," the colonel said finally, breaking the brittle silence.

Amos placed his fork on his plate and raised his eyebrows politely. "I beg your pardon?"

"You served as a member of the so-called Confederate legislature in this state. You hold property in excess of one hundred twenty-five thousand dollars. On either count you are subject to confiscation and loss of civil rights."

"O that," Amos said deprecatingly.

Lodge frowned. "It is hardly a matter to be brushed aside. Treason is not simply a gentlemanly failing."

"In the last unpleasantness," Amos said coolly, "it was the clear duty of a gentleman."

Lieutenant Raisor sputtered in his water. "If that is gentility . . . "

" . . . you want no part of it?" Amos smiled at him politely. "I think you have nothing to fear on that point."

Lodge's face began to flush, his nose a little ahead of his cheeks. "There is no purpose in our trying to settle by debate what has been decided by arms."

Amos inclined his head. "That is what I would say in your position, Colonel. I wonder you didn't say it sooner."

Lodge ignored the thrust. "I asked you here this evening to make you an offer."

Amos said nothing.

"If you will lend your authority and knowledge of these local people to the United States in the months to come, I believe it may be possible to save your property and set aside any proceedings against your person. It may be President Johnson would consider a pardon . . . "

Amos listened politely.

"Do you understand me?" Lodge said irritably.

Amos shrugged. "I don't know," he said. "If you want me to cooperate in helping you keep order in Shreveport so you won't have to turn your guns on the people, there's no need to bribe me. I don't want them massacred. If you expect some other sort of help . . . "

"The United States does not bribe its citizens," Lieutenant Raisor grated.

"I'm not a citizen of the United States," Amos answered easily. "Do you bribe foreigners? Or what do you call bribes?"

Lodge was struggling to control himself. This man, this one-armed rebel, was playing with him like . . . He did not consciously call Robert Toombes name to mind, but the image was there, and it brought the blood into his face so powerfully that he seemed to feel pressure in his ears, behind his eyes. On his right, the mousy captain of quartermasters, who had said nothing since the meal began, was playing with his food nervously and looking toward the hall door as if some treasure lay beyond it.

"I am not asking you to be an informant," Lodge said hoarsely, "and I am offering you no more than consideration for your assistance. There are other men in town who may view the preservation of their freedom and property more seriously."

Amos met the colonel's frown with a tight-eyed expression of his own. The bantering tone of his voice was gone.

"The kind of men you can buy in Shreveport will be useless to you. The kind you need will not be for sale."

Lodge smiled without humor. "After a few weeks with the Treasury agents, I suspect there will be a surplus of reasonable men in this city."

Amos looked at him wonderingly. "Do you really believe that? You really believe a few cotton thieves and chicken-snatchers will break these people down to a size you can use? You would, I suppose."

"I would?"

"I expect you've not had much experience with men who value their good names and the opinion of their associates over property and advancement. I reckon you're going to get an education here."

"If anyone is educated," Lodge shot back, his voice rising, "it will be you. It will be the people of this parish. I have the authority, the force . . ."

"You do," Amos agreed. "All you have to do is decide how to use them without firing off a local war all over again. That could happen, you know."

"Don't you people know when you're beaten?" Lieutenant Raisor put in. "Can't you see all your airs are no good now?"

Amos smiled at him kindly. "We know exactly to what degree we're whipped. And we can live with defeat – to that degree. But if you press us beyond that degree, attempt to reduce us to peonage, shame us and break us into a peasant class to supplement the niggers, then we would have nothing whatever to lose by starting guerrilla warfare."

"Nothing but your lives," the lieutenant sneered. "We'd eradicate you."

"Our lives, if you have bare existence in mind, mean a good deal less to us than you seem to think. The only life that matters to most of us is the kind of life we choose to lead. If you effectively deny us this, you'll have to go all the way."

"If I'd already sacrificed an arm to a dead rebellion . . . ," the lieutenant began.

Amos' smile widened. "You're a little confused, Lieutenant," he said. "Your people didn't take my arm. I gave it to them."

Even the captain of quartermasters looked up. He stopped cutting his meat into smaller and smaller pieces. "Gave it?" he said in a surprisingly deep voice. "Gave it?"

"Outside the City of Mexico under the walls of Chapultepec," Amos said dreamily. "On a hot ugly day in 1847 when I still believed the Union was worth defending."

"I'm . . . ," Lieutenant Raisor began.

"Never mind," the colonel cut in. "You're excused, Lieutenant. I'll see you after this."

The lieutenant upset his water glass in rising, but he paid it no mind. He caught his pistol and belt from the sideboard as he passed, and left the room as quickly as he could, leaving the hall door swinging behind him. Colonel Lodge turned his eyes toward the captain of quartermasters, whose mouth was pulled down so far that it made him look as if he were making faces to amuse children.

"If you're done with your meal, I believe we can excuse you, Captain," Lodge said without inflection.

The captain had long been through. In fact, he had hardly touched his meal to begin with and had lost his appetite progressively as the conversation developed. He was too old for all this, he had been thinking, and it had been some monstrous joke that had dragged him from behind a War Department desk just months from retirement and decked him out in field blue to purvey merchandise for a host of paid killers. He glanced at Lodge with relief, and as he rose from the table, smirked uncontrollably at Amos as if they had been, for thirty minutes past at least, co-conspirators in the discomfiture of Lieutenant Raisor and Colonel Lodge. Amos smiled back at him pleasantly as he passed out of the room, walking nearly backward and closing the door so quietly that they could not hear the latch engage.

"I think you had better consider my arrangement," Lodge said, his flat depthless eyes on Amos again.

Amos reached for a cigar, fumbling slightly as he pulled it out of an inner coat pocket. He bit off the end, sighted along its length, and put it between his teeth without lighting it.

"As of the present time, Colonel, I have only two assets left to me in the world."

"You have no assets left at all except by sufferance of the United States," the colonel remarked dryly.

"The assets I have in mind are non-negotiable and not subject to confiscation, but I mean to keep them both. One is the good opinion of Shreveport. The other is the good opinion of myself."

"You can retain both," Colonel Lodge said. "Neither will be lost if you serve openly and honestly as a spokesman, a kind of witness to reality. You can speak to the various classes of people here and caution them, explain where their plain interest lies."

Amos laughed shortly. "These people, of whatever class, determine their own interest. They don't solicit my views, and they don't expect me to volunteer them. Anyhow, if I spoke for you – no matter how sane or obvious what I said – I would have no currency with them at all."

Lodge struck his fist into his palm. "I need someone to establish contact with these people."

"It seems to me a battalion of troops is enough to contact a civilian population pretty forcefully."

Lodge got up from the table and paced back and forth in front of the French windows that opened upon the lawn. He saw riders coming up the graveled way but paid them no mind. He turned back to face Stevens, his eyes narrowed and glittering. "I would like nothing better than to make myself clear through force. I have no personal objection whatever to making this city another Carthage. But my orders are to pacify, not to immolate. I will have to give evidence of a constructive attempt to control here through normal civil procedures before I will be permitted free use of the cavalry – and of the infantry."

Amos' eyebrows raised. "You have more troops coming?"

Lodge's face warped into an approximation of a smile. It was unpleasant. "Yes," he said. "There will be three hundred infantry here within the week. United States Colored Troops from Arkansas."

Amos' expression did not change. "I expect you may need someone to contact the people, all right."

Before there could be more, Lieutenant Raisor came into the room. "Sir . . ."

"I told you . . ."

"One of the men, sir," Raisor broke in, "they've found one of the troopers all broken to pieces in town."

Lodge caught the young officer by his arm. "What happened? Was it accidental?"

A red-faced sergeant stood just beyond the door behind Raisor. "Hell no," he called out. "It was the goddamndest beating I ever did see. I believe they used a twelve-pound sledge on him."

"Where is he?" Lodge asked Raisor, paying no attention to the sergeant.

"We took him to the hospital," the sergeant bawled across Raisor's shoulder.

"How serious is it?" Raisor asked the sergeant, who took his question to be an invitation into the room.

"Bad," he said familiarly. "Broken nose, fractured cheekbones, eight or nine teeth gone – some of 'em down his throat, the doctor said. And all cut up. His forehead looked like a road map. He ain't got any eyebrows left. Jesus, Colonel, he's a worse mess than if a shell had gone off in his face."

"Do you have the men responsible?" Lodge asked him sharply.

"Men?" the sergeant asked.

"The men responsible."

"Aw, no, Colonel. We just found him lying out in the street while we was patrolling. There wasn't a soul in sight."

"Did you look for witnesses? Did you go to that saloon and put the fear of God into those loafers?" Lieutenant Raisor asked.

The sergeant looked at him glumly. "I asked around," he said. "But I figure you ought to know how much use it is to try to scare those fellers."

The lieutenant blushed. Lodge cut in angrily, "What are you doing then?"

"We're looking," the sergeant said sullenly. "We're doing all we can. Unless you want us to round up every able-bodied man in the parish."

"Better not overlook the women," Amos said softly, flicking ask from his cigar.

"What?" Lodge said turning. "What did you say?"

"I said, you'd better not overlook the women."

"No woman whipped that trooper," the sergeant said. "I ain't even sure it was one man. It looked more like a dozen men held him down and let a horse tromp on his face."

"I want witnesses," Lodge grated. "I want witnesses. I want the men responsible, but I have to have witnesses. If you find the men and bring me one witness, I'll hang the lot within two weeks."

"He ain't dead yet," the sergeant said. "You can't go hanging people for . . . "

"Yes," Lodge said shortly, "I can do exactly that. Bring me the men and some witnesses."

The sergeant saluted and walked out with Lieutenant Raisor behind him. Lodge strode across the dining room to the wine cabinet. He poured himself a glass of brandy and drained it in a single draught. He faced Amos Stevens and turned the empty glass between his palms. "Now," he said with exaggerated courtesy, "I believe you were saying I would need a contact with the people."

Within a few minutes it was over, and Amos left the dining room, walking slowly toward the front door. He needed air. He needed darkness broken only by the winking end of his cigar. Now Lodge had high cards in his hand. With a Union soldier beaten, the whole town was under indictment, and Lodge had no further need of kid gloves. With three hundred Negro troops on the way, what had happened to the trooper might be no more than a gentle introduction to a theme of over whelming violence. Let the Negroes conduct themselves flawlessly and still there might be trouble. Let one of three hundred make a thoughtless or drunken mistake, and there could be a holocaust.

As Amos opened the door, Rye almost ran into him coming from the yard.

"Come on," Rye said. "Get a good hold on yo'self an' come on."

"Did they find where you buried the brandy?" Amos asked him.

Rye looked at him strangely, lovingly. "Naw, when I buries somethin', ain't nobody gonna find it. I just found somethin' out here on the groun' dat you was thinkin' might be under it."

It was not what Rye said or even the way he said it that impelled Amos through the door and into the yard. It was something else: a feeling, a pressure that he denied even as he went down the steps, that he rejected even when he saw the blurred shape of a horse standing head down under a near oak.

No, he thought as he moved through the night with Rye beside him, I won't think it until I know it. I won't even ask Rye because he could have meant any one of a hundred things. I don't want to hope or believe it until I have him in my arms where nothing can take him without taking me too.

But as he neared the spent trembling mare, he saw something propped against the foot of the tree, a white motionless alien face swimming in darkness with eyes closed and a tangle of untrimmed beard below. And before he could reach the tree, before he could hope to make even the most summary recognition, he felt strength drain from his legs as some long stored reserve of love rushed to replace it for the last dozen stumbling yard, and he believed.

Rye had turned down the lamp and shut the door silently behind him. On the wide bed, Mo lay unmoving, a tumbler of brandy half empty in his hand, his eyes open to the moonlight that slanted down through the tall windows and fell across the pale counterpane.

He could not seem to close his eyes. The muscles in his neck and shoulders were twisted tight. His hands twitched without volition and he could no longer even feel his legs.

The brandy glass felt heavy in his bruised hand. He held it up to the moonlight and studied its silhouette. I could have used this up in Tennessee, he thought. Coming home through that goddamned Yankee-loving country where they back-shoot, side-shoot and top shoot. With the rain following me from Appomattox through to Knoxville and then starting again outside of Little Rock. Jesus, that ride. That bad ass-breaking, soul-killing ride.

Mo sat up enough to sip the liquor without pouring it onto his shirt. The second swallow began unwinding his neck and shoulders and he could feel its healing power pulsing in his chest and belly. Before he had finished swallowing, the ride was forgotten. Inexplicably, he felt randy.

That's what comes of no eats. I should have stayed up long enough to eat something. Without some potatoes or greens under it, this damned French stuff puts you up to things. You can't help getting ideas.

The ideas were there, and the memories with them. Remembrance of summer evenings dancing on a flower-trimmed barge at Caddo Lake, the long, fragrant spring beginning with wisteria, ending with magnolia and gardenias. And that last brief winter of 1860 when he was old enough to court but still too young to enlist without his father's consent. And the courting itself.

I expect Poppa would have let me join up that fall if he'd known I was trying to get a little moonlight on my tail with Murray Taggert's girl. He would have taken me over to Captain Flournoy and had me signed with them Greenwood Guards before I could get my stuff packed. If the damned war had held off another year, he'd have been on to Vera and me. Telling me to think about it a long while because blood shows. O sweet Jesus, that's one thing I found out for sure the last four years. Nothing shows like blood.

And maybe Poppa and Mr. Sentell talking about how a man should pick himself a bride. Poppa talking about family and position, and Sentell knowing Poppa well enough to see that he was only saying it because he thought he should since I didn't have any momma to say it. And Sentell asking, "Is that the way you matched yourself, Amos?" And Poppa rubbing his chin and looking like he'd been caught talking dirty in school. "Well, no, Edward. But that was a long time ago and that was New Orleans and this is Shreveport, and this is now." And Sentell saying how it seemed to him a lot better for everybody and a lot less wear and tear on the hide and innards if a man married himself a woman he wanted to bed down every night and would be willing to pay for instead of getting paid to marry a woman he couldn't face without at least a breakfast table between them.

But before they even got a chance to start all that, I had beat a path over that ten-acre patch of collards and cornstalks of Murray's, lifting Vera up behind me and heading for the pine woods or up toward the lake.

Mo put down his empty glass and stood up. For a moment the vertigo was back, but it passed and he walked slowly to the open window. Below, the lawn was dark under wide oaks even where the mottled and uneven moonlight spread.

I probably got home just in time. After Saylor's Creek and that goddamned major, I couldn't hardly hold down any food.

He wondered how it could be that less than three months before he had walked – not run, but walked – directly and unswervingly up to a Yankee fieldpiece with a dozen Alabama boys and shot the crew to death between salvos. He wondered why the fear had been nothing then. And why now, home and far safer, even the music of insects out in the yard, out in the fields, tightened the cords in his neck and brought his shoulders up.

Too much of a bad thing, he decided. Too much of that blood showing and too many of them Alabama boys who walked up with me got carried back in a sack or buried right where they fell. I reckon you can take that crap for a month or a season or maybe even a year or so. Then you get into this mood. You get to probing in yourself and you find the soft place, the place that shudders and covers its eyes like a little child. You find a breaking-place you never knew you had. Then I guess you say, Well, I got to forget I found that place, or maybe make a joke out of it. Or maybe you could fence it around with home and General Lee and states' rights and our way of life. Till the fence gave way.

He fumbled on the bureau for the brandy bottle Rye had left behind. That's a smart old nigger, he thought. Smart and good as gold, and a better man than half the white men I ever saw.

Mo poured the tumbler full to the brim and sat down in a stiff uncomfortable chair beside the window. This was not his room. His father had moved into it. This was the guest room, and it had the flat damp smell of a room long unused.

We used to come up here and hide out, Phillipe and me. When they wanted us to go into town and we had some fishing or hell-raising planned. It smelled the same way then. Like my life. Like nothing living had ever slept here.

He threw down half the brandy. I got to get hold of myself. I got to get steady and clear-headed again. Because if they didn't kill that black sonofabitch Phillipe somewhere in the war, he's gonna show up here sooner or later. He won't be able to stay away. And when he shows up, I got to have one more good fight left in me. If I ever want to have peace again, I got to kill that nigger. I've killed too many men who never did me a personal hurt to let that bastard live after what he did at Sharpsburg. Sooner or later.

By then the room was cold. He wrapped a thin blanket around his shoulders and stared at the unfamiliar ceiling. He put the empty glass down and tried to get his mind at rest. But sleep came slowly and even when it came, when the brandy's peace began to close his eyes, there was little rest or renewal in it because somewhere between sleep and waking, he found himself standing again on the bank of a narrow creek south and west of Richmond in early morning. He was alone watching an endless line of thin mules and runty horses being hustled toward a flimsy bridge ahead of the infantry columns. The mules and horses were dragging wagons loaded with supplies and ammunition and wounded men and even a few women and children who had begged to be taken beyond the widening range of Union skirmishers and cavalry patrols as the Southern army began flooding westward out of Petersburg's trenches. Behind the wagons, barely staying in column despite the hoarse shouted commands of hatless and sometimes coatless officers riding up and down the long unwieldy line, were hundreds of men without rifles or canteens, without packs, without organization. Some marched head down and seemed to have their eyes fixed either on the drying mud of the road or on their own feet wrapped in rags or in shoes held together with string and rawhide, while others looked straight ahead as if their eyes were frozen on the sunny fields and the next uncluttered line of the horizon that seemed so far beyond killing and suffering.

They were two or three thousand men in the leaderless demoralized army of derelicts: remnants of broken regiments from Alabama, from Louisiana, from Virginia and the Carolinas. Pickett's men, Ewell's men, Rooney Lee's men. Grizzled shirtless old men of thirty-five with filthy hair stringing down their backs or tucked into tattered shirt collars, faces burned and weathered by four years in the sun of their own country and the wind and rain of Maryland and Pennsylvania. Youngsters fifteen and sixteen – some no more than thirteen – stumbling along holding the fragments of homespun and butternut around them, stepping mechanically onward shod in outsize Union boots and covered with blue coats gathered on a dozen battlefields or taken from fallen friends. Men and boys from Manassas and Chancellorsville, from Seven Pines, from Cold Harbor. Mean and boys – all of them men now – who had nearly fulfilled their boast that a Southerner was worth two Yankees any day and who, despite that, were staggering across the width of Virginia in the sun of an April morning with Federal cavalry prancing along in the quiet fields, watching, feinting, slashing into the long broken-hearted column almost at will to burn wagons, to shoot horses, to kill with impunity and then, laughing and catcalling, to ride back out of range before those who still had rifles could form up to drive them off.

Mo, standing on a rise of ground near the bridge across Saylor's Creek, could see a Union cavalry patrol as it knifed across the road through the broken and crumbling rear of the exhausted column. He saw troopers firing their pistols into a tiny knot of unarmed stragglers who had dropped beside the road to rest a moment, who had thrown up their hands in surrender when they saw the Federals galloping toward them. One of the mounted men, young and incredibly natty in his fresh blues, fired a final shot into a shoeless gray-haired old man who was kneeling in the weeds beside the road with his hands over his face as if he could not bear to see the coming of that inexorable bullet launched toward him so lightheartedly. Above the rumble of the wagons and the rustle and clatter of the groping column, Mo could hear the young trooper's shrill laughter, sounding like a miniature bugle call, warping the morning air.

If we win, if we lose, he thought, I'll hate and hate until they run me into the earth or the last one of 'em is rotting in a Southern ditch. Jesus, if I forget to hate, if a morning dawns on me that I remember good luck or day's duty before I remember hating, drag me down to hell and make me straw boss over the Yankee army.

The Federals galloped back into the fields on Mo's side of the road, made a wide circle to put ground between them and the dusty hopeless mob on the road, and then stopped beside the creek, dismounted, and began to water their horses. They had stopped less than half a mile from where Mo stood.

In the bright sunlight, he could see the flint of their insignia, and the sun's flare reflected off the barrels of their new repeating rifles. Their uniforms were clean and even their saddles and bridles were bright and unstained. They weren't at Yellow Tavern, Mo thought with the anger still hot and moving within him. They weren't at Bucktown, either. O Jesus, if you'd've just left us Stuart. You take Jackson and Hill, you take regiments and divisions, you take bandages and forage and you leave us with nothing but our own hands and guts and it ain't enough to stop 'em when there's a thousand new ones every day and a thousand less of us. Jesus, have they got bigger churches in Pittsburg and New York? Have they got preachers who know how to reach you? Maybe you're an abolitionist yourself. Maybe you and King Abraham made yourselves a deal.

The Federals had picketed their horses now and had built tiny fires to warm coffee and cook pork. They lounged casually in their un-patched clothes and watched their sleek mounts crop the tender spring grass and lap the creek's slow waters. Some of them smoked and others stood watching the Confederate column lurching across the bridge and turning south – still helpless, still unled, still ripe for their vulture-tactics. They could smell the degeneration there, the stench of desertion and straggling, the odor of impending collapse. Mo heard that same high gleeful laugh again as one of the troopers pointed toward the road, toward the battered carcass of an army that lumbered toward its final hours without food or ammunition, emptied of spirit and hope.

And Morrison Stevens knew. He knew, and the knowledge filled his mind and burned behind his eyes and almost pressed him to his knees. The sound of the tortured column behind him, shuffling across the timbers of the narrow bridge grew and swelled in volume until it sounded as if a dark sea were washing across the tawny fields before him, wiping out the countryside, leveling the towns, covering the South with a scum of unbroken sickening blue.

Now we'll never be shut of 'em, he thought despairingly. Now they're going to send a proclamation around saying how we can live and what we can make and where we can sell it. Now we're just a bunch of ragtail helots ankling home with our butts hanging out, and they'll come to us and say, "King Abraham says to do this. The king says for youall to stop this here." It won't be worth living.

Then, as he was about to move in and join the helpless press at the bridge, try to bring some order into it, he saw a small bunch of Confed-erate cavalry riding tightly massed and dragging a few light field-pieces behind. Some of the riders dismounted and cleared a way through the human log jam on the road so that the horses and guns could pass through. As they rode up the gentle slope toward Mo, one of the officers hailed him.

"What are you watching, Lieutenant?" a tanned major with one arm called to him. He rode to where Mo stood and eased himself out of his saddle carefully.

"I'm watching a stand of buzzards, Major," Mo answered, grinning faintly. "Look over there."

The Federals were sprawled under trees and taking their ease in the stubble of the unplowed field where it dipped to meet the creek. Four or five tiny fires were going, and the odor of coffee and bacon traveled downwind to them. A sergeant came up to join the major. Short and grizzled, his face a hairy chunk of red slate, he breathed once deeply and caught the aroma from Federal fires.

"Goddamn," he said. "I'd murder the bunch of 'em and stomp their carcasses to jelly for a mouthful of that coffee."

He seemed to see the major for the first time. "I'd save that bacon for you, sir," he finished.

The three of them turned back, and even as they turned, they heard an impossible sound. Above the endless monotony of the moving column behind and the occasional shout or laughter from down the creek where the Federals camped, came the sound of a cornet. The sound was light and quavering, unsure. But it was unmistakable.

"How 'bout a waltz!" someone shouted. "How 'bout a dance an' a little bit a' ass-pinchin', Sarge?" another one of the cavalry boys cried out.

The sergeant smiled apologetically at Mo and the major, his mouth still set as if the smell of coffee kept it in shape, and half turned half toward his men. "I'll pinch your asses in a powder chest," he growled loudly. "Keep yer mouths shut and them guns handy to drop."

"Just a Sunday picnic," the major said to Mo in a tired voice. "Just a walkover. They skirmish a while and rest an hour. If they don't hack the poor bastards to pieces here, they'll catch them down the road a way."

"Major," Mo said as if he had not heard, "when they mount, they're coming up this way. They'll ride down the creekside here and try to come up onto the road where it turns into the bridge. Right through this high grass, up that long slope there."

The major squinted against the bright sun and followed Mo's pointing finger. He looked past the rank shoulder-high weeds that had survived the winter, that obscured the knot of men at the top of the slope from the Federals who lay with coffee and hardtack listening to their bugler with his other horn.

"I guess that makes sense, Lieutenant," the major said. "What have you got in mind?"

"It's been so easy for 'em," Mo said without taking his eyes from the distant Federals. "So damned easy. We haven't been able to organize any resistance worth talking about since yesterday afternoon when Gordon hit 'em. I saw 'em shooting men who were trying to surrender to 'em this morning. They just laugh and shoot anything in front of 'em."

"I guess that's their orders."

"Well, by God, I'd like to make their orders harder to carry out."

The major shrugged. His face was expressionless, and, like Mo, he was still looking toward the Federals who had begun to pour the remaining coffee on the little fires and pack their gear back into their saddlebags. "What have you got in mind?" the major said again.

"Sir," Mo asked almost pleading, "would you be willing to stop here a little and do a job of work that needs doing?"

The major looked at Mo calculatingly and pushed aside a sheaf of yellowed grass to get a clearer view. The Federals were pulling their mounts away from the stream now and beginning to mount up. Mo heard that loud high laugh again, and gritted his teeth waiting for the major's answer.

As they watched, the Federals formed squads. The officer in front motioned up the slope toward the high grass, and Mo and the major could hear a whoop of laughter well up from the troopers as they began to advance.

"Jenkins," the major called back to the sergeant, "pull those two Parrotts up here and bed them down in this grass. Put the small piece in between. Load with canister or grape or whatever you have. Pebbles, horseshoes. Break up your canteens if you have to, but fill those guns to the muzzle. Then fan out the rest of the men through all those patches of brush and weeds. Make sure they've got twenty rounds apiece. And keep all the shooting low – just off the ground. We're fixing to have company."

"You heard him," the sergeant bawled. "Let's see what you can do with them repeaters now. The more you kill, the more coffee they'll be."

The major turned back to Mo smiling tightly. "Is that what you wanted, boy?"

"Just exactly, sir," Mo said, pushing forward in the grass and checking his own Spencer as the Federals began to ride slowly forward. Ahead of the main body, four or five troopers, carbines at the ready, road in a crisscrossing pattern through the fringes of the grass five hundred yards from where Mo and the major stood.

"Well," the major whispered, "they haven't thrown away all restraint yet."

Mo whispered in answer even though he knew the leading Federals were still too far away to hear. "Not quite all, but they've got their eyes so full of them poor bastards on the road that a little patch of dried-out grass don't mean a thing to 'em."

The Federal outriders moved smoothly through the far edge of the grass. As they rode, it became deeper, rose above their horses' bellies, then became high enough to obscure them from the massed troopers behind.

"All them blue bellies in the rear can see is hats and saber waving," Mo whispered tensely. "I think . . . "

"Never mind," the major said, not whispering this time. "The boys have done this before."

From their raised position, they watched the last of the outriders enter the tall grass, loping smoothly, looking from side to side without particular care or interest.

The major frowned and looked down at his single hand. There were little half-moons of filth under the fingernails, and the back of it was tanned deeply and covered with tiny scratches in various stages of healing. Dirt had caked up in the lines of the palm, and the frieze of hair on the back was singed to its roots by powder flashes. "Mighty hard to keep a hand clean when you don't have another one to help it out," the major said irrelevantly.

Mo said nothing, still looking at the grass into which the Federal troopers had by now disappeared. When he saw them next, they would be almost on top of him. The major talked on.

"You know, this is all a damned waste."

"Sir?" Mo said politely. It was a question, but he went on squinting, trying to detect movement in the thick twist of weeds and grass in front, trying to spot the first telltale sign of the outriders.

"All the way from Petersburg," the major was saying. "All a damned waste. General Lee knows we're used up. He knows Sherman is south of us. Why go on killing and being killed when ten thousand more deaths won't change anything except the degree of hatred between us?"

Mo's face hardened. Still looking ahead, he spoke through clenched teeth. "I don't know why. I ain't had a chance to ask General Lee. I just mean to do what I've been told to do."

The major ignored the sarcasm. "In a few minutes, we'll cut fifteen men to ribbons. Maybe twenty if none of those scouts yell soon enough. And after we shoot and bayonet the ones left, we'll limber up and ride on and around the next bend over the bridge, or the bend after that one or by another creek, they'll be laying for us. And none of it will count. This army hasn't got another week's fighting in it."

"I don't know anything about all that," Mo said coldly. "I've never asked if any of this would count. They told me to kill Yankees, and I've been doing it for four years. I've killed a lot of 'em, and they've killed my friends and nobody apologized on either side, and I mean to go on killing 'em till they stop me or I hear not to, right out of General Lee's mouth."

The major shrugged and motioned to the sergeant, who lay outstretched just behind them. "You hold up those damn bunnies with the fast lanyards," he said out of the side of his mouth. "If we're going to do this, we want to do it right. I don't want a pack of survivors going out and finding more cavalry to hound us with. Wait till the main body is right up in your muzzles."

The sergeant nodded and squirmed backward toward the guns.

"I guessed you never asked what the killing was all about," the major said to Mo with careful politeness.

"I never found anybody who cared," Mo snapped back. "If invasion of a man's country ain't reason enough to fight, I don't reckon any reason's going to be good enough. I come up here from Louisiana to keep a bunch of white trash from ruining my home. They've got New Orleans and that no-account sonofabitch of a Butler fixed it so a white woman can't walk down the street without a Union pawing her.

They're got Baton Rouge and they told the niggers to push white men into the gutters when they felt like it, and if one of 'em objected, he'd eat a Union bayonet. If they get to Shreveport they'll turn it into a shooting gallery and whorehouse combination. I got all the killing reasons I need. I mean to stop all that."

"Well, you can't put a stop to it," the major said aloud. "We're whipped, boy. They've whipped us to pieces, and now they're eating the pieces. Even a damned snotty-nosed kid lieutenant ought to be able to see that."

Mo turned to the major without expression. His eyes had something like amusement behind them. "Piss on you, you one-armed wreck," he said without heat. "They may have you whipped, but they got some more work to do on me."

The major's face went from red to purple, and he reached to free his pistol. Mo swung his carbine around until its barrel almost touched the major's chest. "Just shoot at Yankees," he rasped. "It you want to call me out, it'll have to be later."

The major didn't answer because now the first of the Union outriders had pressed through the grass and into the Confederate positions, and as he rode almost over one of the guns, a soldier in gray dragged him from the saddle and jammed a knife into his throat before he could cry out. And then, as quickly as he had stabbed, the Confederate pulled jacket and cap off the dead trooper, twisted into them, and leaped onto the trooper's rearing mount. Down the width of the grassy slope, three more Confederates had done the same. Only one trooper had managed to scream, and his scream was buried in the hoots and yells of the Confederate who had already killed and taken their victim's places, and who were beckoning back to the main body of riders to move up, to hurry, to make it double time to cut the rebel sonsofbitches to pieces at the bridge.

And the Federal officer, seeing the signal from his advance guard, spurred his black stallion and waved his saber in a wide circle overhead. The troopers closed behind him, beating their horses' sides with knee and heel, their yellow neckerchiefs trailing in the soft morning breeze, their voices raised in exultant laughter, their gold and scarlet standard whipping stiffly at the top of a slender lance.

"My God, that's pretty," Mo whispered reverently. "Look at 'em stay tight. There ain't three feet between 'em. O Jesus, let those fuses be all right."

And the major beside him lifted his single grimy hand high above his head so that the sergeant kneeling behind could see it fall. The swaying pounding line of troopers, shouting like unchained furies, tensed and ready to send more of the rebellious scum to hell, crashed through the last insubstantial screen of weeds and grass at the top of the long slope and saw for a single instant the huddled figures in gray and the shiny little fieldpieces that lay between them and the already scattering remnants of brigades and regiments on the road ahead. And then the major dropped his hand.

The grass was an inferno, filling instantly with dense gray smoke and a volume of sound that glued Mo to the earth. Before the cannon's thunder had receded, screams of men and horses joined it. The grass had been cut almost completely away by the flail of metal, and when the smoke began to drift off with the light morning breeze, he could see the shattered remnants of Union cavalry wheeling and pitching, horses rearing and throwing off blue-coated riders as if they were outsized flies that stuck and pestered. As he watched, the sharp-shooters opened fire, and of the dozen or so Federals who had survived the canister, only four or five, bent low across their saddles, managed to gallop beyond the rifles' range.

"You mounted men, go get 'em. Don't bother bringing 'em back," Mo heard the major shout. The Confederates who had killed the Union outriders trotted past them and broke into a gallop on the open ground, pounding hard after the few troopers who were fleeing back down the slope.

And close to the cannon, hardly a dozen paces from where he stood, Mo saw the cannon's work: an almost unmoving huddle of shapeless bodies, horses and riders chopped into gruel, crushed into the soft damp soil of the Virginia field. Almost motionless, but not quite. Because here and there in the midst of the choked jumble an arm or a leg moved, a horse shuddered and twitched. A hand slanted upward apparently sprouting from the plowed dark soil itself, its fingers spread or clenched and pointing upward toward the climbing spring sun that was already turning the dampness in the grassy stubble into steam. He heard voices, tiny and indistinct, sounding somehow like no more than shrill penny whistles or church chimes after the deadening roar of the cannon. For a moment he could not hear the ubiquitous rumble of the wagons or the shambling uneven tramp of soldiers on the road behind. Only the doll-like crystal voices shimmering and keening strangely in the vast silence that stood over the evil stew in front of him.

The major was prodding his shoulder. "You didn't even fire, boy. I thought you were a stone-tailed killer."

"It was the cannon," Mo whispered dreamily, still listening for the tiny silver voices that seemed to fade and then return to this hearing. "I guess it was the cannon. I've never been right up next to an artillery section when it was firing on infantry or cavalry. I guess I just forgot."

"That's all right," the major said casually. "There's still work to do. You can help clean up."

"Clean up?" Mo said absently, still looking out over the quiet field, still hearing the tiny voices, something almost like fairy laughter clear and silvery, still seeing hands, red and caked with dirt, pawing skyward, legs kicking in awful regular spasm, spurring the torn earth. A horse neighed terribly. The major pushed Mo toward the open portion of the grass firmly but not unkindly. "Just move out with my boys and shoot whatever's still twisting around when you get there. Don't miss any of the horses."

"That's not my kind of work," Mo flared indignantly, stopping and turning to face the major. "That's not officer's work. You've got plenty of men to do it."

The artillerymen had slung their guns again, and the sharpshooters had moved up behind the major, waiting for orders. The sergeant had stepped up next to the major, and Mo stood a half-dozen feet beyond them all – almost at the beginning of the parched and grooved and ruined ground where heaped flesh and smoldering cloth lay thick and ugly.

"It's your kind of work, all right," the major said. His face was hard and set now, and there was nothing casual or friendly in his voice. "You wanted killing, figured out this little slaughter, and I'm going to see you get your own piece of it. I'm giving you an order."

"You can't give me an order," Mo said. His face was as set, as stubborn as the major's, but his voice wavered the least bit. "You can't do a damned thing but ask me. And I say no."

"And I say yes," the major came back quickly. He drew his revolver and pointed it at Mo's belly. "This is your party and I mean for you to have some of the cake."

The cannoneers and sharpshooters stood at ease behind the major and watched the exchange without expression. One or two were lighting pipes, and one was squatting a few yard to one side with his pants down and his arms thrust out in front of him for balance. Like the rest, he watched without concern, only faint lines of personal strain about his eyes. Killing, pushed past a certain point, destroys distinctions. They were – had been for months – killers, not soldiers. And they killed whomever they were told to kill.

"Sergeant," the major was saying conversationally, "you escort the lieutenant around and see he does his duty by those troopers. If he balks, shoot him in the face. You don't want to shoot him in the back, now."

"Yessir," the sergeant said placidly. He stepped toward Mo with his carbine at port. His face was as bland as if he was pacing off the distance between two hammock posts in his own backyard.

"You're crazy," Mo shouted at the major. "Just as crazy as hell."

"Why, sonny," the major grinned widely, "I'm as crazy as Jeff Davis. Maybe I am Jeff Davis. Go on out there now. For Dixie, boy. For Dixie."

And then as quickly as it had come, the major's smile was gone. Mo came awake suddenly, and his shirt, stiff with sweat, was like a ponderous drift of ice or snow across his chest and belly, oozing around his neck and settling under his arms. Clawing his way back to consciousness, pushing the livid colors of the dream behind him did no good. The difference between dreaming and thinking was not a worthwhile difference. At least in the dream there had been sun and a blue sky ribbed with high delicate china clouds. At least there had been that sky standing over the muddy pudding of blood and flesh and leather beneath, and the sky had seemed to mean that no matter how bad it might be, all of it was transitory, and that what they were doing could be buried and what remained to do could be forgotten if only he could break free of these crazy men who wanted him to butcher unarmed Yankees, to do the very thing the Federals themselves had been doing since Five Forks.

What I'll do is get my mind on Vera, he thought. I'll work up her breasts, and the way her arms tapered white and soft like they were carved out of cloud. I'll see her mouth and the way it moved when she was leaning over me and how it was wet and how it caught the slivers of moonlight or turned sun and candle into my eyes.

He frowned and closed his eyes, and for a moment she was there. She was there and naked to the waist, her breasts small and the pink and white of them enough to blind him, and his love large and tumbling through his mind and soul and belly all at the same time until her arms, white like drifting clouds, soft as the down of an egret, closed him in.

But the vision splintered and the clouds were puffs of quick vengeful smoke from those tiny brass guns, and thin darts of light were musket fire. Pink went red, and what he saw beneath his frown of concentration was himself following the unblinking sergeant out into the wasted channel of the little guns out to the first squirming body in the swatch of destruction.

It had been a boy lying on his back next to the shattered carcass of a roan mare. The boy had had light, almost colorless hair, and a soft boy's face, pale and terrified, as white and wrinkled as a kid glove. His right arm had been laid open from shoulder to wrist as if a careless medical student had dissected, and then been called away for drink, a smoke, a walk outside the operating room. The boy's mouth moved slowly, swallowing air, closing and opening in ghastly parody of some outsize fish, and his lips were trying to make words. But a rill of pinkish blood had begun to trickle out of the corner of his mouth and course down his chin and puddle on the ground beneath his head, and no words, no sound, came.

Mo remembered thinking, If he makes a sound, if he only groans or coughs, I'll put one in him. I'll do it for sure. Because that goddamned major would hole me without looking back and this here poor broken-up sonofabitch would have sliced my guts out if he could of gotten to me. Come on, you towheaded bastard, just cluck to make it easy for me.

But the boy had made no sound, had gone on making his great gulping motions while the blood came faster and spread in a large pale medallion on the ground beneath and beside him. And finally, after what seemed a long time, the sergeant had prodded Mo. "Somebody's got to get shot," the sergeant said noncommittally.

"And you don't give a damn who, do you?"

"I didn't say that, Lieutenant," the sergeant said with wide disinterested eyes. "You said it."

Then the problem resolved itself. The boy's face flooded with color and he raised himself on his uninjured arm, the bleeding remnant of the other casting a circlet of drops out into the bright morning air. He shouted so loudly that even the soldiers trudging along the road must have heard him over the commotion and the noise of the creaking wagons, so loudly that Mo and even the sergeant fell back a step.

"Blessed Mary ever virgin," he cried as if his lungs were bursting, as if he were addressing a present person.

Mo's bullet punctuated his shout, caught him in the throat, and the sullen stream of blood burst out with incredible new speed and cascaded down his chin and onto the unfaded front of his dark blue tunic.

Further along, there had been the Union commander, a captain who had ridden at the head of the attacking column and who had been so near the cannon when they had fired that his horse and his legs had disappeared together in a spew of scarlet atoms. He lay facing the sky, unblinking, with his hands pressed tightly over his belly, pierced by shrapnel, which had begun to swell so that his entrails were showing white and pale yellow between his fingers.

Mo cocked his pistol and aimed it at the calm bearded face. Then the captain's eyes found his, and something like a smile warped the wounded officer's lips.

"Why, you'd be the mercy patrol, I suppose," the captain said evenly, no hint of pain in his voice.

Mo's hand dropped to his side, and even the sergeant stared unbelieving. The officer fumbled inside his tight-fitting tunic and drew out a leather wallet bound around with several pieces of rawhide.

"This is my special events packet," he said, his breath beginning to whistle in his throat now. "You'll find my wife's address inside. I'd appreciate it."

The captain closed his eyes for a moment, pressing the lids tightly together, but under his dark beard the mouth remained firm. Finally he looked up at them again. "I'd appreciate it," he said in that tiny crystalline far-off voice that Mo had heard before. "Maybe I'll be able to do something for you in return."

Mo stood motionless, his pistol hanging forgotten in his hand. The sergeant swallowed loudly and reached for the wallet. "It'll go where it's supposed to, sir."

Then the sergeant, stepping back a pace or two, snapped to attention and saluted the captain, who smiled one more time and said:

"All right, son, get on with it. If you don't hurry, you won't be able to catch me. I'm getting away from you."

Mo raised the pistol, thinking, Don't close your eyes. If you close your eyes you might only hurt him worse, and if you hurt him and don't kill him you won't sleep till hell's a half inch deep in ice. Do it like Poppa would. Clean and straight out.

But something was wrong, something was playing tricks with his eyes, misting them and making it hard to sight properly. He looked at the sergeant who was chewing a wad of tobacco rapidly, compulsively, and the sergeant was having the same trouble.

"By the way," the captain was saying from what sounded like a long way off, "you boys make up a nice ambuscade, but we were careless. Careless as hell. If Phil Sheridan ever heard . . . "

Mo and the sergeant fired together. Both shots were clean, and they turned toward each other with relief beyond the need of words, and then moved toward a tangle of mangled horses and bloody harness and blue uniforms a few gards farther on.

Then he broke it off, found himself sitting erect with that cold distant sky and the delicate clouds fading before present darkness. The moon was nearly down by then, and the brandy bottle was drained. Outside, the dumb thunder of insects held its pitch, and a single owl moaned on the edge of the fields.

I wonder how long you dream about that business. You got to get shut of it sometime, or nobody who ever fought could have stayed out of the asylum.

He shook his head as if he had tasted something bitter. *I don't want to sleep with Vera in my arms and go to dreaming of Saylor's Creek every night. I'd just as soon go back to doing it as dreaming about it.*

He slid between the sheets again and closed his eyes. This time he dreamed of high sandy banks along the Red River and the sweep of sweet gum and cottonwood that stood tall and deep along parts of the river, and of the cypress-covered bayous, dark and wonderful with slow water and invisible birds clattering and diving for silvery small fish. He dreamed he was home.

VI

8 JUNE 1865 — The morning after they found the beaten trooper, everything was changed. For the first two days it had looked easy to them. Except for the brush in front of Cleburne's store, it had been as smooth as militia drill. Which was just as well, since not more than fifty of Lodge's men had ever fired a shot in anger, and of that fifty, so far as anyone could tell, only Lodge's first sergeant had the kind of experience one attributes to a veteran. So the apparent ease of it had been like the

rain's breaking the afternoon they marched in: it was an omen, but not the kind they had taken it to be.

The morning after they found the trooper, there were half a dozen patrols – all mounted with carbines at the ready – riding not only through the center of town but out into the country for a mile or two as if to discover and counter a fresh rebellion brewing.

On street corners and in stores, the off-duty Federals walled their eyes and glanced behind them whenever a woman's footfall sounded on the sidewalk or floor. The children had a field day.

"Boo, Yankee," out of an alley as a pair of Federals passed.

"Kid, you don't want to do that. You could get hurt."

"Yah, Yankee. Like youall hurt that fella last night?"

"Get on, bluebelly. Here's your mule."

"Yankee Doodle come to town ridin' on a pony."

"Rode back out, his head a mess, his brains all macaroni."

Their unchallenged control of the town was no good to them at all. They could do any number of things to any number of people – if they could lay hands on them. Cleburne told Sentell what had happened when the trooper finally came around enough for Lodge to question him.

"It was shameful," Cleburne said, his grin spiced by that roving independent eye. "He told 'em he was down past Ripinski's place and thinking about a walk or maybe the saloon when all of a sudden six or seven come out of an alley, and all of 'em had clubs and they kept it up for ten or fifteen minutes. Said one of 'em was a great big man smellin' of rye whiskey. Said he thinks they let the horses tromp him when they was makin' their getaway. Told the feisty little lieutenant the big man had him a hammer."

Sentell didn't smile. "A regular pack of assassins," he said. "Do they have any idea about who was in on it?"

Cleburne shrugged, still grinning, his random eye wrecking the morning. "They brought Joe Hobbs in because he seemed big enough and likes his whiskey. Anyhow, he's a blacksmith."

"Well?"

"The boy said sure enough, Joe was the big one and take him away quick before he got out of that bed to even things up."

"I expect it'll go hard for Joe."

"Not a bit," Cleburne grinned on. "Seems Joe Hobbs was with that sergeant shoeing his black stallion when word come about that boy.

And the sergeant was the first one there. They turned Joe loose, and the colonel was talkin' about hangin' the boy if he come up with any more stories out of his head."

"So it's still a mystery," Sentell said.

"To the Yankees."

"Meaning what?"

"I ain't gonna fart around with you, Major Sentell. I admired what you did the other afternoon when the Unions rode in. I never held with all the talk about you and that that parole. A man does what he thinks he has to . . ."

"Thanks," Sentell said. "What about that trooper?"

"You're the man to tell me," Cleburne said without smiling. "You're Amos Stevens' good friend. I don't have to tell you."

"Amos? You've lost our mind counting money in that back room of yours."

"Naw, not Stevens," Cleburne said irritably. "You tryin' to play with me? It was that damned boy of his and you know it. He come ridin' in about dark. I was inside the store and he come in all hunched over on a mare. This Union kid yelled something' to him, and he straightened up and come off the horse. By the time he was through, you could say he'd done the work of six or seven men with eight-pound sledges. I've seen healthier lookin' men than that Federal in their coffin."

"So Morrison made it after all."

"You couldn't kill him with blastin' powder," Cleburne said glumly. "But if he keeps up whippin' every Union that gives him a little lip, he's likely to get a lot of people killed. It ain't smart."

"We haven't been what you call smart for a long time," Sentell told him.

Cleburne stared at him with his good eye, the other fixed on something behind Sentell.

"It's about time to be smart, ain't it?"

Sentell shrugged. "Smart men die just the same."

"That's so," Cleburne said good-naturedly. "But not of a bullet aimed for somebody else. I'd hate to go down as an innocent by-stander."

"You ought to tell those used-to-be soldier to stay away from your store, then. If it had gone all the way the other afternoon, you might have caught a bullet meant for Ed Norton Junior clear back in the store."

"That's so," he said again. "But you got to balance one risk against another. If I was to invite a Confederate soldier off my porch, I'd just as well close up. The way it is, there ain't a good side. There's just the middle and trouble."

"I hope it's not cutting into your profits."

Cleburne was grinning again. "Naw, it ain't got to pinchin' yet. But you tell Mo Stevens he ain't at Petersburg anymore. Tell him it's all over, and that these blue bellies ain't fair game anymore."

Sentell started across Texas Street to his horse. "You tell him," he called back to Cleburne. "You tell him how it is when you see him."

That afternoon Sentell rode out to Amos Stevens' place. There were a few Union soldiers in the yard, and four guarding the door with fixed bayonets. They looked him over carefully and then sent him on to the kitchen where Amos and Rye were sitting over coffee.

"It's their coffee," Amos said, "but I bought it from Cleburne. It seems he's already made a contact."

"He would," Sentell said, shaking hands and sitting down. "I understand you had a visitor show up last night."

Amos and Rye both smiled. Barring the known color of the new arrival, either one could have been the father.

"Not, it was a permanent dweller come back," Amos laughed. "He figures he'll stay on a while."

"I'm glad he made it. I was thinking if he didn't get here soon, he probably wouldn't get here at all. Any word on the other traveler?"

Rye's face clouded over, but he poured coffee for all of them and said nothing.

"All right," Amos said to him. "Go on. I could tell him politely, but that's not enough. You've got to show how damned loyal you are."

"Got a letter," Rye said sullenly. "He comin' from Washington City."

"So they're both whole," Sentell said. "I guess you know what the odds were."

"You can say whole," Rye went on. "He comin' home a Yankee officer."

Sentell looked at Amos. "That can't be. A Negro could serve, but not with a commission."

"This particular nigger did," Amos said. Then he told Sentell what the letter had contained, how Rye felt about it.

"He thinks Phillip is a mercenary," Amos said with disgust. "It's a waste of time talking to him. To listen to him, you'd swear he was a planter himself."

Rye smiled. "You know better," he said. "I ain't no planter. I still got me a little money left."

Sentell laughed. "I expect you heard about last night," he said.

"Last night?"

"The Union soldier."

"O," Amos said indefinitely, "I heard there was trouble. I understand there was a disagreement between one of them and a townsman."

Sentell leaned across the table. "It was Morrison. Cleburne and some of the others saw him. If Lodge doesn't know, he should be able to guess when he sees Morrison turned up all of a sudden. If he can't guess, I expect he can buy something better than a guess."

"Who would be selling?" Amos asked. His Tartar's face had not changed expression as Sentell spoke. For all it reveals, Sentell thought, I might as well be confessing the beating myself. "Even if someone sets up as a salesman, he'll have to testify in a court-martial to make his product do the job. Anything less would be just teasing the customer," Amos said.

Sentell leaned back and pushed his coffee cup toward Rye. "If you're right . . . "

"Striking a Federal soldier is a hanging offense," Amos said with mock piety. "They can't get a conviction – much less Sheridan's approval – without a witness and a corroborating witness. What they have now is a child who played at arms with a man – never mind who the man was, but he was that – and if you're right, a shadowy peddler who has the information they want, but no way of delivering it in open court with even an outside chance of living twenty-four hours afterward – much less able to find another of his kind to take that same nonexistent chance with him."

"You sound as if you enjoy this," Sentell chided him.

"No, you know better," he said quietly. "I have no taste for violence, and no pleasure in conniving. I'm only stating the way it is."

"Like Machiavelli," Sentell said. "Not the way men should be, but the way they are."

"That," Amos said, "is about it. There are no principles involved here at all. So far as I can make out, the Unions have never had them, and I think I'd better spend some time with Morrison before I say anything about our people's principles."

They talked for a while longer, but Union sentries passing through the kitchen seemed to be curious, and the conversation turned to taxation, confiscation and the like.

"Have they come to you yet?" Amos asked Sentell.

"Not yet. I expect they want to take care of people with movable property and such. They know where to find me."

"They'll take the place on the river," Amos said.

"I expect so. They won't be getting a whole lot."

"Two thousand acres on both sides of the river? I expect they'll be satisfied for the amount of trouble it will be to fill out a tax lien against you in their City Hall."

"It hasn't been worked in three years," Sentell said. "I haven't grown anything but corn and beans and such. A few cattle, if they haven't wandered away or been stolen in the last two weeks."

"What will you do?"

Sentell almost smiled because it seemed that he had been faced with the same question more often in the past five years than any one unmarried and nonpolitical man should be. This time it was the land. What would he do? He wondered if Amos meant how would he live or what course would he take to save the land. He expected it was the first. But Amos knew there was money from land Sentell's father had once owned and finally sold in southwest Louisiana and Texas. Some of the money – a large part of it – was still on deposit in St. Louis. If Amos was asking what he would do to save the land, he should have known the answer to that, too.

"Nothing. If they take it, I'll bring my guns and books into town. Most of my things are already in my mother's house."

"No struggle?" Amos asked gently.

"None. I have nothing to fight with. More important, nothing to fight for. It would be silly to spend money and time to save land without a son to hold whatever I might win. The stakes are different with you. You have to fight."

"I'm tired of fighting," Amos said. "The boy's back. He can do the fighting."

"I expect he's a good deal more tired than either of us."

Amos shrugged. "I reckon. But how can I fight? I haven't had more than enough cash for food and fodder in two years. I have the land. Or it has me. I haven't got any money to defend it with."

"You'll think of something."

Amos stared a Sentell. "Has he talked to you, too?"

"Who?"

"Lodge. You sounded as if . . . No, you'd be no good to him at all. You're only good for yourself, good for me."

"What are you talking about?"

"He wants me to cooperate with him," Amos said. "He says he can save this place. He said he could save all the land."

"What does he want you to do?"

"I think he wants me to talk to the right people Norton, MacKenzie, Flournoy – the men who have position or money or friends enough to hold things down while the Unions nail the lid on."

"He has trooper for that," Sentell said.

Amos smiled and shook his head. "You know better. Lodge is no soldier, but even he knows better. After last night he knows for certain his soldiers can't hold this town – not even the center of it – much less Caddo parish unless he can get either positive assistance or at least the tacit help of no action at all from the men who can get a hearing around here. He can't even put a coffin around the man who broke his boy-soldier all to pieces. How can he hold things together?"

"He has martial law if he needs it."

"Not worth a damn. Maybe if they let him take hostages. Maybe not even then. And he knows last night wasn't even a start. In Shreveport there are a hundred or two hundred able-bodied men back from the war. There may be four or five hundred in the parish. If they decide to farm days and wait for the night to cut Yankee throats, he'd have to call for a division to hold things together."

"What did you tell him?" Sentell asked.

Amos shrugged. "I told him no. I can't rent to him what doesn't belong to me. And if I were to rent it, it wouldn't be there anymore. I can tell the people to be patient and wait for things to get better because there's nothing else they can do. But I can't tell them that for Lodge's sake or for his pay, either. My way and my time. Not his."

Sentell wondered how many people would have turned the offer down. Then he wondered how long Amos would be able to hold out. Whether he knew it or not, Lodge had either found out who whipped his flunky or would find out soon. Then, witness or not, proof or not, trial or not, Morrison would be in the center of whatever happened. If the witless Union soldier had drawn that much violence from him with a word, Sentell thought, what could Lodge do if he set his mind to it? He could prod Mo into a noose before the week was out.

"You'd better talk to Lodge again," Sentell told Amos.

"Why? Have you seen him?"

"Not lately," Sentell said. "I think I saw him once a few years ago."

"Stay clear of him," Amos said, pushing his cup away. "He makes you feel unclean. I had to act as if I were in a play so I could keep my hands off his throat."

"That sounds like the man," Sentell said. "I wanted to kill him that afternoon, but there was no time for it and not much chance I could get it done before they shot me."

"You may get another chance," Amos said dryly, "if you can get to him before Morrison or one of those hotheads on Cleburne's porch."

"No," Sentell told him. "If Lodge wants me to kill him, he'll have to press his hand pretty far."

"I think he may," Amos said. "I think he may go further even than he thinks he will now."

The kitchen door opened, and Amos cut himself short. It was Morrison. He was much taller than Sentell remembered him, but it could have been that he had lost weight in the months before Appomattox and on the long trip home. He was shaven and dressed in fresh linen so new and unworn that it looked strange, since none of them had had a new shirt or pair of pants since the outbreak of war. His face was pale and lined, and even shaved, with his hair combed back, his eyes and the hard, nearly invisible line of his lips destroyed whatever illusion of gentlemanly unconcern the clothes might have fostered. He offered Sentell his hand.

"Major," he said. "It's good to see you again."

Sentell stood up and shook hands, watching his face for some sign, some familiar mark or curve of bone that would match him with the nineteen-year-old boy who had left Shreveport with his body-servant four years before. There was nothing. His face was narrow and drawn, and as Sentell shook his hand, he could see that the darkness around Mo's eyes was not simply the lasting shadow of fatigue, but the result of a hundred tiny broken veins in the flesh of his cheeks, and of his skin's being pulled tight along the bones of his face. It could have been the face of a fifty-year-old man or of a worn and patient fifteen-year-old boy who had suffered incredibly.

"Sit down and take coffee," Rye said protectively. "You got to stay off yo' feet fo' a few days."

Mo looked at Rye and smiled. "Poppa says you worried more than he did."

Rye smiled. "I knows you. I thought you might fin' some place you like better den here."

Mo shook his head and sat down. Sentell noticed that he had kept his left hand near his body, his thumb hooked in his belt casually. But Sentell could see the knuckles bruised and swollen, and a long cut running across the back like a piece of dark thread.

Amos followed Sentell's eyes. "They had a little trouble in town last night," he said.

Mo was sipping coffee, but they could see the corners of his mouth curl upward. He wiped his mouth on a frayed napkin. "I wonder if there might be some bread and butter," he asked Rye kindly. As Rye rose, Mo turned back to Sentell and his father with measured courtesy.

"What would youall like to know?" he drawled. "I can't say whether I killed him or not, but he won't ever look the way he did before. Would you like to know what he said to me?"

"You know the Union commander is staying here in the house?" Amos asked.

"Rye said so."

"They almost saw you last night. The guards on the porch had walked back to saddle Lieutenant Raisor's horse. They'll want to know about you, about where you were last night. They'll want to know about your hand."

Mo looked at his father calmly. "If they want to know, I expect I'll have to tell 'em."

"What do you mean to tell them?" Amos asked of him.

Mo shrugged. "Something. Anything. Whatever they've got a hunger for."

"They've got a hanging appetite," Sentell said.

Mo came close to smiling, but only close. "They'll have to wait for that," he said.

"How long?" Amos asked, his heavy brows knotted with concern.

Mo looked at his father with that expression of kindly detached concern. The way a doctor might look at a patient with whom he was not emotionally involved, but for whom he wished great good nonetheless. "I don't know, Poppa. I got no way of knowing. I got to see what's here. I got to see how bad it is and how good we can make it. They might have the rest of their lives to wait. The might get a chance next week." In front of City Hall, there was a path of grass. Once the marshal (not the current marshal – not the Memphis Federal clerk who demanded that a Union trooper not only guard his door but escort him home as well – but an earlier marshal who had been able to remember the great log raft that blocked the Red River to navigation until Henry Miller Shreve scattered it in the 1830s) and the mayor had wanted to establish a five-acre park across the street from City Hall, but the cost of land – especially in the middle of town – was already too high to allow for such use. So they cut a few yards off the front of City Hall itself, and planted it green and set a flagpole in the center with a bench in the shade of the building and some fine gravel laid on a path from the street to the door.

In summer, most of the old men spent some time on the bench. Some would come in the morning and stay until noon, then they would consult their watches, shake hands with one another solemnly and start home as others began arriving to take their places. There was no purpose, no premeditation to it. It was simply the way most of the old men had done for years – since the square of grass and the public bench had been put there in front of City Hall. Now some of the morning loungers moved down to Cleburne's after lunch, but not many. Because most of the men on Cleburne's porch were young and lean and sometimes short-tempered and cruel. They had been hurt too much, most of them, to realize or care when they were causing pain. Most of them cared nothing for the old men, and the few who went to spend an hour on Cleburne's porch in the afternoon were old men who could not help enjoying the loose violent talk that crackled like captive lightning between the empty hogsheads upturned for seats, and the high steps that could accommodate ten or fifteen and still leave room for customers to pass up and down.

"There don't seem to be any end to it," Ed Norton Junior was telling Don Juan Cleburne. "They steal the chickens, and then come back later and charge you a tax on the hen house."

Cleburne shrugged sadly. "Price of losing," he said almost wistfully. "I reckon we got to bear up under it."

Norton frowned. "That's so, but it comes out finally that bearing up won't see it. If they aim to starve us outright, I may end getting some more Yankee blood on my hands."

"Suicide," Cleburne said, wagging his head. "This too shall pass. I reckon they'll go away sooner or later."

"Sure," Ed Norton muttered. "They'll go away after they've stolen everything portable. I understand they're trying to figure a way to carry the whole damn parish away with them."

"They do seem prone to stealing," Cleburne said piously.

"Prone? These sonsofbitches would steal a fart if they could get it in a sack."

"How long do they figure we'll put up with all this?" one of the old-timers, who spent most of his time on Cleburne's steps, said.

"I don't expect they give much thought to us that way. They done whipped us all. They don't expect we'll try single-handed what we couldn't do together."

"They *better* give it some thought," Ed Norton Junior snarled. "Because I got figured in my mind just exactly how much I'm gonna take before I bust loose and shoot me a few of them blue bellies."

"That kind of talk don't help," an old man said.

"What kind of talk do you reckon *will* help," Ed Norton sneered. "Maybe you ought to go talk to that purple-nosed Yankee colonel and give him a little Jesus-and-justice talk."

The rest of the young men laughed, but the laughter faded quickly.

"We'll wait and see," Ed Norton said. "We'll wait and see."

As they waited in the shadow of Cleburne's gallery, just out of the blistering sun, they saw a Union private with a hammer and an armful of bills swagger up to the door of Ramsey's saloon. He hammered away while two or three other soldiers stood watching, rifles slung over their shoulders. Then, finished with his work, the private cocked his head to one side and squinted at the sunbright paper. Behind him, one or two of the old men wandered up from across the street.

"Well, god Almighty," one of them said.

"You like that, Granddad?" the Union simpered. "Here's a few spare copies for your old buddies over on the porch."

The old man walked slowly back to Cleburne's while the Federal soldiers moved down to nail more of their posters at Silsbee's, on the doorpost of Martin's bakery, on the door of Nathan Ripinski's dry-goods, notions and sundries store.

Ed Norton Junior took a copy, handed the rest to the others, and read:

PROCLAMATION

In order to maintain order and civil tranquility in Shreveport and Caddo parish, the following shall apply to all adult citizens within the jurisdiction of the undersigned:

1. Any violence or disrespect shown the flag, military personnel, or civil authorities of the United States as authorized by the military commandant undersigned will be punished immediately and with vigor. In the case of male offenders, the punishment may run from a jail term or corporal punishment to death. In the case of female offenders, any such will be treated as a woman of the town plying her trade, and may expect no assistance should she receive the kind of salutation commonly given one of her calling. In severe cases, such female may, at the commandant's discretion, be punished a male offender.

2. Any display of flags, photographs, currency, or other equipment (including uniforms) connected with the so-called Confederate government will be punished as stated in (1) above.

3. Any attempt to bribe, coerce or mistreat a freedman for any cause whatsoever will be punished as stated in (1) above.

4. Any attempt to avoid the payment of lawful taxes, current or past, or confiscation of property according to the provisions of United States law, or to hinder or impede a lawful representative of the United States Government in the act of tax collection, confiscation or registration of freedmen for voting will be punished as stated in (1) above.

Signed by me this 8ᵗʰ day of June, 1865.

Jonathan Lodge
LT.-COL., U.S.V.

"This is his answer to last night," one of the old men said. "That's what whuppin' that Yankee soldier stirred up."

"Shut your mouth," one of the younger men, a beefy unsmiling landless farmer from out in the parish named Hornsby, grated. "Nobody needs to apologize for beatin' the ass off a Yankee, old man. Best you keep that in mind."

"If he pushes that paper of his very hard," another of the young men drawled, "he's gonna have him another war."

Ed Norton Junior scuffed the toe of his shoe against a porch rail. "I'd just as soon kill as sit still here," he said quietly. "Truth is, I don't know much but killin'."

Hornsby's eyebrows rose in surprise. He moved over closer to Ed Junior. "Tell me somethin'," he said. "Did you get to likin' it? Did you ever get to where you kinda looked forward to it?"

Ed shrugged. "I got to where it was like pickin' my nose. I could take it or leave it."

"Till you got a snootful. Then you had to, huh?"

Ed turned to Hornsby, a slow smile growing. "Yeah," he said. "When you get a snootful, you got to."

Down on the steps one of the old men was telling about bears he had seen within the parish limits back at the turn of the century, a few years after the purchase. Bears taller than a man. "You had to kill 'em out to live in peace," he was saying earnestly, and overhead, the sun had started down into the west. But it was taking its time.

She sat on the stepless porch in the lengthening shadows, in the growing darkness until the ground-mist began to rise and drift across the face of the moon like thin smoke. Then she went inside and cleared the table. There were no scraps – her father ate everything put on his plate – and she let the tin plates slide into a tub of water.

Usually she washed as soon as a meal was done, but tonight she had no strength for it. It had been her first day back in the cabin in a couple of years, and she had not remembered how completely without grace or even dignity the place was. It had been hot, blistering hot, all day, and she had tried to hem up some of the cloth she had brought from the hospital to make a dress. But as the day wore on, as her eyes lifted from the sewing from one cobwebbed wall to another, from the dirt floor to the greasy table stained and stolid in the middle of the small room, to the dark iron stove jammed against a wall, its broken flue pointing not up, but out through a hole chopped in the solid logs of the cabin wall, she had put down the needle and lain back in the armless broken-back chair. There was no hurry, really.

Not because she believed less that he would come back. That was a proposition she did not question. Too much depended on it. If she went on believing – for months, even for years – and he did not come, at least something else might happen, someone else. But if she stopped believing (no matter what she thought, no matter what the old man said), that would be the end of it. Not just the end of love and hope and purpose, but the end of her. Because then she would have to look at the cabin and see it not as an ugly way station between anonymity and realization, but as a permanent and unchanging fixture of her life. She would have to look at Murray and see him not simply as a warden who kept her penned in filth and misery, but (changing none of the filth and misery – only its meaning) as her father. And one day, no longer believing anything, she could imagine herself driven to defending him. Not merely to others, but even to herself.

It must have been like that for Momma, Vera thought. She married him believing there would be a nice little farm or maybe a decent cabin somewhere, or even less, fail the farm or the cabin, at least love and good treatment and the amount of respect any town will give to a woman no matter how poor her family is, so long as her man acts like a man and makes some kind of gesture in the direction of work and thrift and honesty. But she got none of it – not even the respect – and finally believing got to be more effort than admitting, and she let it go and went for his whiskey, thinking maybe that what you can't beat or even stand to a draw you have got to join so you stop being yourself and become someone or something else that won't or maybe even can't hurt like a onetime believer hurts.

The lassitude still held Vera. She touched an open seam and smoothed the heavy cotton homespun of the skirt. Those seams could be pulled tighter now, she thought. She had lost weight, over the last six months, and there was no reason to think she would be getting it back. Then she rose slowly and stepped onto the porch again. Or started to.

But before she moved past the doorsill, there was the muffled unmistakable sound of a single horse turning in from the road to town. Not her father. It was too early, and no mule, even pressed to his limit, make that kind of steady rhythmic staccato when he galloped.

Hold on, she thought, gripping the unpainted splintered wood of the doorposts. Either a stranger, one of those cotton-grabbing scum look-

255

ing for the old man, or Ed Norton wanting someone to look to his mother. Or a soldier, or a nigger or any one of a hundred likely or unlikely . . .

Then she could see the single rider passing through the thirty or forty yards down the path to the main road. And she knew, not knowing, trying to deny at least as strongly as she was affirming, and thinking suddenly and eccentrically that if it was, the dress was undone and she had thrown away her time, and, chilled without reason, as if the unfinished dress cold somehow keep it from being, she turned back into the house, but even turning heard him call out across the vague and edgeless space still dividing them. Not in a familiar voice (because, she thought as she head him call, she could not remember his voice as it had sounded four years before – much less project what those four years might have done to his voice as well as to him) or even in a familiar tone, but only the two syllables of her name as if he were beginning a petition or ending a chant.

But she did not turn back toward the door, rather went on looking across the desolate cabin so bare of love or purpose or future that even in its filth it seemed sterile, and remembered afterward how, bathed in the soft buttery light of a single lamp perched on the end of the table, everything in the long single room had leaped into dramatic, almost unbearable relief; the handmade sideboard without cupboard doors or even level shelves. The racked and patternless white crockery cups, the long sheet of zinc on which she washed dishes and light laundry. The rusty shotgun leaning barrel-down and loaded and cocked beside the low shelves on which her clothes and possessions were stacked. All of it seemed animate and determined to imprint itself upon her mind as if to say: This is real. This is all there is. You hear nothing but the night and what you see is no more than accommodating mist shaping itself around a dead dream like a cloud moving from figure to figure, form to form and always only a cloud no matter what.

But the horse moved up to the cabin, and as the hoof beats dissolved into snorts and pawings, another sound detached itself, and she heard the solid assertion of boots across the thin planking of the porch and she knew it was no cotton thief or mule brander, no straggler or Negro, and she knew. And she knew.

They stood with half the room between them because as he had called her name for the second time, she had moved from the sound of that alien voice as if it were a flail. At the third calling he had been inside the room, and Vera had been facing the squat iron stove, her shoulders hunched against whatever, whoever it might be – afraid not of who it was, but of who it was not.

Mo moved toward the table and rested his hands on the back of a poorly made chair. When he spoke, his voice was soft and uninflected, and he looked at her across the dim flare of the oil lamp which made shadows on his face that looked like scars in motion.

"I would have come here first . . . last night . . . but there was no way. I was lurchin' in and out of my saddle and my horse was ruined and I couldn't have gotten here. All I could have done was fall out in the road and have somebody find me and not know what to do with me, or maybe have the Yankees find me and know exactly what to do with me after they saw my hands . . . and all day today I was getting' my legs back and . . ."

He stopped and breathed deeply, watching her back. His shoulders slumped as if he were still riding against the rain that had followed him down through Tennessee and Arkansas.

By then Vera was trying to turn, to say something. But she could not trust her voice. She could not step quickly past the table, past the four years that stood between them, because it would have been like embracing a stranger, like being suddenly and perversely false to the memory of the very man her arms would be around.

Then she turned and saw how much of a stranger he was. A thin haggard man with large eyes and a mouth neither large nor small but thin and sharply defined as the edge of a wound. He was no boy at all; most especially not the boy-man-wraith who had played squatter in her dreams for so long. He was dressed in fresh dark clothes and a shirt whose collar was too large. His hands on the back of the chair were burned dark with weather, and the left one was bruised and deeply cut around the knuckles. He didn't look like a soldier – not even a beaten one – but like one of the wounded anonymous men in the hospital who needed not so much to be loved but to be bathed and possibly prayed for.

"I prayed . . . ," she began. Then she stopped, abased by the loud artificial sound of her own voice.

"I reckon I did too, in a way," he said. "Almost all the time I wasn't cursin'. At first I prayed it would end quick so there wouldn't be a lot of dead and maimed, and so we could come home independent and get to livin' again. Then it started goin' sour and I prayed we'd win even if there wasn't anybody left to enjoy the winnin'. But by Petersburg that was no good either, so all I prayed for was to kill as many of them as came near me, and then to get home to you and Poppa in one piece or even two or three so long as I was alive. Maybe the last prayer was modest enough for Him."

"Third time . . . ," Vera head herself say incredulously.

" . . . is a charm. That's so," Mo finished. "I wonder if I might sit down."

As he moved from behind the chair, Vera dropped the apron she had been twisting in her hands. Time dissolved as quickly as space, and she came into his arms so suddenly that it surprised them both. Mo staggered back a step, and then pulled her to him. As he kissed her – not softly, not even lovingly, but as fiercely as a castaway presses his mouth to water, his hands moved over her body heavily, frankly – not guided by affection or even lust so much as by wonder.

Sweet Jesus, he was thinking, I had forgot. I had forgot so completely that I couldn't have imagined this to save my life. I could see pictures. I could remember sounds and smells. I could remember how she made me feel. But not the touch of her. Not the softness and the give of a woman's flesh under my hand.

Vera's eyes were closed, and with them shut she could merge the substance of him in her arms, pressed against her cheek, with the dream that had held her steady for so long.

It will be all right, she thought. It will be all right if we can just go on from here without waiting. I don't want to wait for anything. They've already got four years from us. They can't take any more. Whatever happens, we've got to go on from here together.

"One night in Tennessee . . . ," he started, his voice thick and unsteady.

"Almost every night," she echoed. "Except when I was workin' all night like after Mansfield."

They stopped and moved apart, his hand still on her shoulders, hers still on his arms.

"A wide circle," he smiled. "It looked like it might not go all the way for a while."

"I thought after that place above Richmond, near the river . . . "

"The North Anna," he said slowly, tranced by the name. "And Spotsylvania."

"They said almost everybody . . . "

"They made it worse than it was. Almost all the Unions. Two to one, for every man we buried."

"You're all right?"

Mo sat down and stretched his legs beneath the table. "Sure," he said. "I'm fine. I need a little sleep and some food."

He smiled again, this time with something more than the appearance of politeness. "And maybe a little of your time."

Vera did not sit down. She could not stop moving even long enough to collect her thoughts.

"You were surprised to see me?"

"Yes. No. I knew you'd come. I knew it for sure because there was nothin' else to be sure of, nothin' worth knowin'. But not tonight."

"I figured your father would tell you."

Vera felt the chill again. It burst at the base of her neck and ran down her spine like a spill of river waters. "How? Why did you think . . . "

"He saw me. He saw me ride in last night. There were some men in the street, and he was on a wagon."

She shivered as a gust of night breeze brought shards of mist through the door. "Sure," she said. "That would be right. I should have thought of that ahead of time. That's one more I owe him."

Mo looked at her quizzically. "What is it? What did I say?"

"Nothin'," Vera smiled thinly. "Not anything. The war's over. There can't anything much be wrong."

They walked along the main road in the darkness and turned down a twisting wagon track toward the river. High up, above the trees, beyond the low-lying mist, the moon rode clear and cold past long tatters of cloud. Patches of mist shook and eddied around them as if it were alive, and as they topped a grassy rise that turned suddenly to weed-strewn sand, the river lay coiled before them, wide and slow moving, dotted with sandbars and sparkling dully under the moon.

"Right over there," Mo said softly, "close to that next bar, Phillipe pulled me out of the channel one summer. I tried to swim the river three times running, and on the way back that last time, I gave out. Just gave out and began to lose headway and knew all of a sudden that this was the end of it, and nothing I could do was gonna get me out."

"And he went in after you?"

Mo shook his head. His face was turned from her and she could not tell if he was smiling or frowning. "Hell no. He didn't have to. He

259

didn't have to even get his feet wet. What he did was lean over and grab hold of my hair and pull me onto the sandbar like a beached whale. Then he saw me spittin' water and being sick and he looked worried, and then I managed to stop that after a little and he got to laughin' about it."

"I reckon he was relieved."

"So did I, for a while," Mo said. Now she could see his face, and if he had been smiling before, he was not now. "Then with one thing and another I saw I was wrong. What he was laughin' about was the idea that his master could get himself into a corner where he had to count on his nigger to bail him out. It was funny that one man had the say-so of life and death over another man, and yet that first man didn't have such say-so over himself."

Vera frowned. "I don't see it's funny. I don't see it's anything at all."

"I didn't . . . don't . . . see why it was funny, but I got a laugh on that black sonofabitch, and I may just let him in on it before I kill him."

Vera felt the night wind at her shoulders. "Don't talk about killin'. Forget killin'."

Mo paid no attention. "I'll tell him he was free that day and free after it, and that he could have turned away that day and left me goin' under, just as free, just as unresponsive as any man in the parish. He could have done it that day just the way he did it ten years later at Sharps-burg."

"What are you talkin' about?" Vera said. "If he . . . "

"Not a thing," Mo cut in. "They wouldn't have done a thing because he was a freedman's son and a free man himself. Since 1847 in that other war when Rye and Poppa went out together. Poppa told me today when I got goin' on Phillipe. Said he was free, had been free, and if he wanted to cross Antietam to the Yankees, it was his business."

"You mean youall didn't own him?"

"Hadn't owned him since Mexico. We don't own Rye. Poppa said Rye owns a piece of the place."

"My God," Vera said. "You mean they're partners?"

"I reckon you could say that. And they meant for Phillipe and me to carry it on. Poppa still wants it."

"Carry what on?"

"The place. He says he'll get the taxes paid, and when the Yankees leave, Phillipe and I can take over and run the place together."

"Partners?"

Mo laughed harshly. He made a gesture as if to sweep the idea away. "Yes, that's it. The Gray and the Blue brought together. A broken-down worn-out Confederate and a fresh cocky nigger Yankee. Don't that sound like a fairy tale?"

"He'll never come back," Vera said certainly. "He won't come back."

"Maybe. Maybe not. But if he comes back and finds out and goes smellin' after the land, all he'll get is enough of it to cover his face."

They found a tall tree bent toward the water, part of its roots exposed by the crumbling bank, and sat in its shelter as the wind skipped past, ruffling Mo's hair, bringing goose bumps to Vera's arms. They sat without talking for a long while. Then Mo turned to her.

"I want us to get married. I want – no, I need – you with me. Any way it goes, there's not gonna be easy times for any of us. There may not be anything ever but what we can find with each other."

Vera moved closer to him, placing her chilled arms between his coat and the warmth of his body.

"It's like drought or flood," she whispered. "It can't go on forever. We can wait."

"We may not have to wait," Mo said ominously. "We may be able to hurry it. We built a levee, and the water flooded over. Maybe we can find something to push the water back."

Vera laughed into the mist. "You can't push water away. You got to ride on top of it till it goes back on its own."

"That's water," Mo said. "That's how it is with water." He looked down at his bruised knuckles, and then his bruised hands were upon her again, and the mist closed around them like the wall of a phantom house.

VII

2 JULY 1865 — It was the beginning of July, and the rain came now only in late afternoon and evening cloudbursts that left the earth dry as before by the next day, but which kept the trees and even some of the grass in shaded places unnaturally green long after it should have been drained of color and beginning to turn the same strengthless tan of the desiccated soil.

Ed Norton Junior scratched himself through his buckskin shirt and kicked a broken crate into position beneath his feet. If he stared from the long, shadowed gallery and across the top of the building opposite, he could see the air and the green branches behind shudder as heat radiated up from the metal roofing. It gave him the sensation of being in an imaginary world. As the air and the solid reality of distant trees shook in July heat, so the situation he found himself in seemed to be a quaking construct of disordered reason. Not real, not important. And whatever is wrought in an imaginary landscape is as much dream as the landscape itself.

Lately, saying nothing to his friends who passed the sweating directionless afternoons on Cleburne's porch with him, Ed Norton Junior had taken to making believe. He was almost twenty-two, and he knew better, but the afternoons seemed to go on forever, and sprawl one into the next, so that imagining seemed no more a waste of time than talking. Less of a waste. He had been home only two months, and already he was tired of the endless recitals of how it had been at Chantilly; how they had stopped Grant cold on his way to Petersburg; how the war was lost at Sharpsburg or at Gettysburg – or at Vicksburg or New Orleans, in 1863 or '62 or '64. He was even tired of remembering the marches and battles he had taken part in through middle Tennessee and northern Alabama. He was too close not to remember the blood and the blisters, fatigue that touched the bone and seemed to slice the nerves into tatters. It would be years yet before any of them could make those night rides and broken afternoons, those assaults and the thick ubiquitous mud into the constituents of myth. One day it would be the stuff of a thousand gray-bearded Xenophones, but not now. Not just yet. Because they could still feel, if not physically at least in the tranced fiber of the spirit, pain that had been permanent resident in back and neck and shoulders even before the ride to Fort Pillow – the decision at Brice's Crossroads and afterward.

So it was better to dream. To sit on Cleburne's porch and imagine that there had been no war (because even imagination has its limits, and he could not imagine that the South had won), that all the remembered agony of Vicksburg and afterward had been simply other and earlier products of this same imagination, and that now it was the way it had been before, with nothing changed. He would dream of his father's home freshly painted and the parlor cleared for a soiree. He would remember the stiff starched cuffs of his father's Philadelphia shirts, and the new stylish wide cravat he had been given for his eighteenth birthday. He could remember his sister's tenth birthday. There had been a party for Cissie and her friends. There had been candlelight and the cool pearly afterglow of evening while the family ate before time for the guests to arrive. He had eaten lightly, remembering the piles of refreshments standing in the pantry for the party. Why eat chicken or beef and vegetables with tarts and cookies waiting?

Sometimes he even recalled the work: hot dusty work in the yards or fields with sons of his father's friends, or the dull ciphering of figures behind the counter in his father' store. Handling crisp currency and shiny gold coins fresh from New Orleans or Philadelphia. Studying a man's credit, trying to guess what merchandise would move and pay for the space it occupied. Over and over he dreamed quiet scenes and plenty. He dreamed of cleanliness and peace. Then one of the Union would stroll past, chewing on a cigar. Or Pony Mueller, who kept clear of Cleburne's – by daylight at least – might inch by on his way to City Hall with a handful of tax liens or altered deeds, or, glancing from side to side like a cornered ferret in a hen house, push through Ramsey's spring-doors for a furtive companionless drink. And that would be the end of imagining. Ed Norton Junior would come back to reality with a jolt as powerful as if he had fallen from the roof past which he had been staring.

It was now. There *had* been a war. He had lost it. Not just the dead Confederacy or even the crippled South, but him: he had fought and at the end of fighting, though he had not been able to tell it (since even in the victorious days at the start he had been no less famished, no less dog-tired) they had said it was over and it was lost.

And now there were bluecoats walking the streets as if they owned them. Because they *did* own them: held them by force of arms and collected taxes from those who used them, and paid the Negroes (and a few whites whose meager acres were falling under the hammer of Pony and his rivals) who repaired them. Now there were laws and proclamations made by no man native to the parish – unless the ignorant suffrage of new Negro voters who had yet to cast their first ballot was considered. There was confiscation and disenfranchisement, the daily report of local dead – boys he knew coming home to tell of the deaths of boys he had known. Silsbee's son, dull and friendly, given to all-night rides into east Texas, exhausting horses every twenty miles going and coming: blown to pieces at Five Forks with no horse under him and only the cold April mud for a place to rest his shattered parts. Allen's two sons at New Market: one an officer shot even as he commanded his brother, a Virginia Military Institute Cadet, to charge Federal artillery point-blank at the cost of his life. And even those who had come back were maimed or robbed of their manhood by too many foodless forced marches, too many small costly victories that had turned at last into a single priceless defeat.

He forgot the tarts and the dances and the newly minted gold coins, and the tall undemanding corridors of green beyond the bakery roof went gray as a passing curl of high cloud obscured the sun and turned a lounging Federal uniform from blue to black. He heard the monotonous drone of voices on the porch around him: it was always first Manassas or Fredericksburg – or the Brice's Crossroads he himself had seen. Never Petersburg or Franklin, never Atlanta or Missionary Ridge – and never never Appomattox Court House.

"Why don't youall shut up that goddamned bilge?" Ed Norton said. "Why don't you just shut up or talk about crops?"

There was a moment of silence. Then one of the others, almost apologetically said: "I don't hardly never talk about crops since they took up my land for taxes."

Ed Norton Junior flushed and felt the rising morning heat drive sweat out of him even under the shade of the gallery. "I'm sorry," he said. "I reckon this heat . . . "

"Enough to push a man past carin'," someone else put in.

"It was hot before," another man added, his voice as measured and precise as one in a tragic chorus.

In the street, a handful of jobless Negroes shuffled toward City Hall, passing under the newly painted flagpole. The patch of grass over which they passed was still green, but Ed Norton Junior thought idly that it could not possibly survive July.

Even before Ed Norton rose and walked the few blocks from his home to Cleburne's porch, Barney Wilkes was on the street. He would leave his room at the back of Nathan Ripinski's store as the sky began to lighten and roam about the downtown streets, poking at trash cans, peering into alleys, pressing his nose against the glass of store windows, carrying the reddish stub of his left hand defensively buried in the tattered and patched wilderness of his worn shirtfront.

Barney Wilkes was qualified for both the City Hall bench and a place on Cleburne's porch. He was past sixty and jobless – living on handouts and make-work local people fabricated for him. Beyond his age and indigence, he had something more to recommend him to the people: he was a veteran of John Bell Hood's Texas Brigade, and in the forenoon of September 17, 1862, next to the wall of a square white church outside Sharpsburg, Maryland, Barney Wilkes, far too old to have been drafted, too poor to have felt the pressure of *noblesse oblige*, and too proud to let younger and wealthier men do his fighting for him, had had his left hand, his right eye, and right ear shot away, and his brains hopelessly scrambled by a Union shell. He had been sent home with a letter from his regimental commander which commended him to the generosity and affections of his fellow townsmen.

The town had replied as well as it could. Barney was rarely a problem, except when the fear came over him and he imagined himself back near the Dunkard Church with McClellan's artillery darkening the sky with its endless supply of shells. Most of the time Barney was quiet, almost dreamy, and anxious to do his best for whomever he happened to be working. The worst part of his injuries seemed to be what the shell had done to his sense of humor. Before the war, Barney had had no particular fun about him. He had worked hard, spent little time in saloons – none at all in the brothels – hence out of the way of boisterous and ill-measured humor.

But the Yankee shell seemed to do for Barney what a long life spent in dissolution rarely managed to do for even the most accomplished sports. It had made a lethal practical joker out of him.

Most of the time, the jokes were both pointless and harmless. Barney would, for example, paint white circles around a mule's eyes, put a hat on the animals' head and lead it around at night from one Negro cabin to another. He would force the mule's head in a window and give a low stifled moan. The results generally left little to be desired as far as Barney was concerned, and since the Negroes almost always managed to find their way back to work by the next morning, nobody cared much if it kept Barney occupied.

But sometimes the pranks had more substance to them. Like the time Barney set fire to a wagonful of hay (drawn by the same mule who had just managed to rub away the latest application of white-wash from around its eyes), terrifying the driver and mule, and watched the burning wagon crash into a vacant building at the corner of Milam and Spring streets across from the Confederate Departmental Headquarters. It had taken most of the headquarters company to douse the fire, and three hard-eyed troopers to keep the owner of the building (which, by worst luck – or by Barney's idiot strategy – also owned the wagon, the hay, *and* the long suffering mule) from shooting Barney on the spot.

Thirty days in a makeshift army stockade near the Red River had done no good. On the day he was released, Barney had picked a double handful of cockleburs from the autumn fields on his way back to town, and reaching Texas Street, had carefully and impartially distributed them under the saddle of every horse along the way to Cleburne's porch. Then, for the next hour or so, he had sat dreamily nursing the poorly healed stump of his left arm and watching the action in the street.

When the Union army entered town, Barney had a bad time. The blue uniforms and the fieldpieces, the rapid movement of the horses and the endless yelling and blustering sent him into one of those transports in which he believed himself at Sharpsburg again, facing Hooker's corps and retreating inexorably backward toward that tiny white-walled church. It was almost a week before he came out of the huddle of dirty blankets he occupied in the shed behind Ripinski's dry-goods store and began cautiously and quietly moving around the streets again.

"Looks like the Yankees done killed ole Barney's fun streak," someone told Ripinski. The dark sympathetic Jew shrugged and turned his hands palms up.

"I dunno. He don't even eat for a week. He drink a little water, he take maybe a soda cracker, a slice of bread. Now he's up again and I worry more than when he's laying back there sobbing into a dirty quilt. What if he make a mistake? These men, these Union, they don't know. They don't care."

"Nothin' to worry about," the customer laughed. "Looks like the Union put out the spark. No more scared niggers. No more people throwed all over downtown. No more big fires."

But things didn't work out that way. Because on the morning of July 2nd, while Ed Norton Junior was climbing out of his bed and staring into the colorless predawn light of another meaningless day, pulling on his boots to walk down to Cleburne's, Barney Wilkes was already up and nosing around the streets and alleys like a pointer raising quail.

A few minutes after an ill-tempered and disheveled squad of Federal soldiers had gathered, yawning and rubbing their eyes, to run up the United States flag in front of City Hall, and then dismissed, still grumbling and cursing the early duty, Barney came humming into Texas

Street from the alley beside Cleburne's store. He was supposed to sweep and wash windows for Ramsey at the saloon that morning. But he stopped in front of City Hall and let his eyes travel slowly up the length of the flagpole. He studied the stars and stripes for a long moment, and then giggling to himself and glancing around to see if anyone was watching, he began to fumble with the rope and lower the flag.

It was only a few minutes past dawn then, and the streets were deserted. The sun was still caught in the lower branches of trees over on Milam Street, and the flagpole was in shadow. Barney worked patiently with his one good hand and the raw useless stump of the other. It took him almost five minutes, but no one interrupted, and at last he had it down. It was good, he thought dazedly through the milky haze of damage that skimmed over his brain like rank alkali on water. It was real good, and now what to do with it.

Then, down the street in front of Silsbee's stable, he saw the mule. Vera was coming out of Martin's bakery with a tiny sack of expensive rolls. She was still exhilarated, still more drunk with happiness than she had ever been before. They had been together every day, every evening. He was no gallant by anyone's measure (but then, he had not been that even before. He had been arch and clumsy and frightened and loveable. Now he was none of those things, but something immeasurably better – or worse) but he was gentle and quiet, and when he touched her it seemed he could not yet believe they were together. That day he was going to take her down by the river. She was supposed to meet him in front of City Hall. On the way, she had stopped to find a little food cheap enough to buy and special enough to break the monotony of greens and rabbit and grits. As she came out of the bakery, she saw Barney Wilkes coming down the street from Silsbee's stable toward City Hall. He was riding that selfsame mule he had twice made accessory to his mummery before, and he was wearing a ragged gray jacket and kepi he had not worn since the fall of 1861. As he passed, seated firm and upright, Vera could hear him singing "Dixie" under his breath, struggling with the words, losing and regaining the tune:

Wisht I was . . .

Now a few women doing early shopping and a handful of men passing to work or starting their loafing early were on the street. As Barney passed beyond each of them, there was a burst of shocked laughter, each passerby adding his hilarity to that of the last. In Ramsey's saloon (which had taken to opening at six-thirty since the end of the war), a few early customers heard the commotion and stepped outside to see. They stayed to roar in their turn, some of them laughing for the first time since coming home.

The volume of sound mounted until it brought Cleburne and Ripinski out of their stores and began to fill the street with everyone awake and able to hear. By the time Barney had wound his slow progress to the patch of green in front of City Hall, Texas Street was as crowded as Saturday at noon.

> *. . . in Dixie,*
> *Away . . . away . . .*

Barney paid no attention to his audience (neither did the mule. The mule was paying little attention to anything, and when Barney pulled it up short before the ravished flagpole, it lowered its head to the grass and began nuzzling it like a cow). Rather he raised his voice, tuneless and shot through with a fine tremolo of idiocy, and began roaring his song at top volume while he nudged the mule, still mouthing fresh grass as if it were embarrassed, in a slow circle until its draped and star-spangled behind faced City Hall directly and revealed to collected puppet officials and minor military the cause of general and chaotic laughter.

> *. . . I'll take my stand,*
> *To live and die in Dixie.*
> *Away . . .away . . .*

If Barney had chosen any morning of the past month, he might have managed to finish his performance and be led away at the end of it by Ripinski or Ed Norton Senior or whoever might have stopped laughing first. There probably would have been no trouble, because the few Union soldiers assigned to guard City Hall had no orders concerning madmen or mules and, even if the dear old flag was being shamed, a whole streetful of local people would have held the troopers' initiative to a minimum. There would have been no trouble at all, because even the mule's owner, inured to his beast's being regularly purloined, standing then at the end of the crowd, his arms strapped around his quaking middle, had no intention of arming Lodge's marshal with a complaint against Barney.

"O my God," he groaned. "I've had that iron-headed sonofabitch for eleven years and he ain't never showed up so good."

"You never give that mule a fair chance. I bet if Barney was to stuff them stars and stripes up a little further, he'd plow a furrow clear up to Fort Smith without stoppin'."

But Barney had no luck. He had had none at Sharpsburg (there had been little there for anyone, and Hood's Texans got none of it) and he had none that day. Because even as he started his song for a second time, gathered his wind and began squalling again, Colonel Jonathan Lodge turned the corner of Spring Street into Texas with half a dozen men, and seeing the gathering crowd, cantered through the dust toward City Hall.

> *. . . down South in the*
> *Land of Cotton*
> *Good times there . . .*
> *Not forgotten . . .*

"What is that?" Lodge called over to Lieutenant Raisor, who rode beside him. "What are they doing? If they are demonstrating . . . "

Raisor and the sergeant rode ahead and drew up behind Barney Wilkes. The sergeant saw the flag even as the lieutenant noticed the empty pole.

"How about that, Yanks?" someone at the front of the crowd yelled, and the rest chorused laughter.

"There's youall's mule," a boy shrilled.

"Hell no," the owner roared. "That's my mule."

By that time the lieutenant saw the flag too. "Sergeant," he shouted, as if by reflex.

"Yessir," the sergeant answered stoically, clambering down from his horse.

> *. . . Look away,*
> *Look away . . .*

The sergeant pulled Barney Wilkes from his borrowed mule, and as the old man landed in grass not yet dry of dew, Lodge's escort piled off their mounts and jerked him to his feet.

"Bring that man here," Lodge rasped. "And what is that tied to the mule's rear? Is it . . . ?"

The sergeant drew his shoulders up as if he felt the rain of that first day in Shreveport again. "Yessir," he said. "It's the flag. I'll get it loose."

"Yes," Lodge said distractedly, his face filling with blood, his hands knotting into fists on the reins. "Yes. Bring me the flag. And bring that man here."

The crowd was quiet now. Even the children had stopped laughing and running about. Now Lodge was the only one left on horseback. He sat stiff and straight above the soldiers and the people, his mouth working, his nose and cheeks suffused and purple. Below Lodge, Barney sitting on the grass, was singing on in monotone.

> *. . . Dixiland where*
> *I was born . . .*

Raisor cuffed him lightly but Barney went on with it while the rest of the soldiers milled around uneasily and the sergeant stood with the rescued flag held clumsily in his hands,

"I'll turn him over to the marshal," Lieutenant Raisor said.

"No," Lodge thundered. "Stand him up. Stand him up and bring him here."

Two of the soldiers pulled Barney toward Lodge. He made no resistance, but went on leading an invisible chorus while Lodge and the rest stared at him.

"Run that flag back up the pole," Lodge said quietly, precisely.

There was no sound as the flag lurched skyward in short, even spurts.

"Present arms," Lodge called out into the silence. "These people will uncover, Lieutenant. If one of them stands under a hat, see to him."

But Lodge was more concerned with the flagpole and Barney Wilkes than with the crowd along either side of the street. As the flag reached its zenith, Lodge saluted, then snapped his gloved hand back to the reins.

"Now," he said, his voice carefully controlled, too casual for the circumstances, "tie that man to the flagpole."

"Sir," Lieutenant Raisor began, "I think . . ."

"You think nothing," Lodge cut him off, speaking no louder than in conversation.

The two soldiers who had hold of Barney moved to the pole, but neither of them tried to tie him. They stood, each one holding his by an arm, waiting for something more positive.

"You heard," Lieutenant Raisor said through his teeth. "You heard the colonel . . ."

"We ain't got no . . ."

"Get me a coil of rope," the sergeant yelled at the soldier standing in the doorway of City Hall. "You didn't break up this goddamned silly mess when it started, now get me some rope or I'll have every sonofabitch of you digging this town a sewer system on your own time."

"Sergeant," Lodge said as the men scuttled out of the doorway, "see that the flag is secured, and then get a whip from one of the teamsters."

The sergeant looked upward at Lodge as if he had not heard. He had done a good many things in the past month that seemed to have nothing to do with soldiering. But he had never garrisoned a hostile town, had never wondered whether a bullet would crash into his head as he walked at evening down a quiet street. And he had never laid a whip on a man's back – much less on that of an old man missing half his eyes and hands and all his wits.

"Sir," he said. "I fought for that flag, too. I was . . ."

"Sergeant," Lodge said, his voice beginning to rise, "you have an order, not a license to preach. Do your duty or hand your command over to the next rank below you."

"Get me on of Tony's whips," the sergeant called to one of the lingering soldiers.

Then, as the crowd began to murmur like an ill-tempered animal awakened suddenly, the sergeant stood by while someone brought a coil of fresh rope and the two troopers holding Barney erect cut off enough to tie him to the pole.

If it keeps up like this the sergeant was thinking, some of us ain't gonna ever see home again. Some of us are gonna get plots right here. Because this hard-assed Boston man and this silly-assed lieutenant have got to push and push, and these folks ain't near ready to see an old man in a rebel cap get whipped like a dog.

Some of the folks felt just that way. By the time Mo Stevens rode up, dismounted, and joined the crowd, Barney's show was over. But the latecomers were hearing of it by whispers from those who had seen it happen. A dozen young men off Cleburne's porch pushed forward to the edge of the crowd where the rest of Lodge's escort stood with drawn pistols or carbines at the ready. Mo saw Ed Norton Junior and a man he knew only as Hornsby.

"Well," Ed Norton said, his face drawn and determined, "it's good you got here."

"I just came in to meet Vera," Mo told him. "What's goin' on?"

"They got that poor old man," Hornsby blustered. He was a heavy red-faced man without intelligence or patience but brave to a degree and in a way that only stupid sentimental men can be. "They got him fixin' to whip him."

"That's too bad," Mo said evenly, looking past the young men to where Barney stood, his face blank and unmarred by apprehension, still singing in a low innocuous monotone.

"Too bad, hell," Ed Norton burst out. "They ain't gonna do it. We're..."

"You're gonna get a dozen men killed," Mo said casually, "for one old man?"

"*That* old man was at *Sharpsburg*," Hornsby blubbered, nearly in tears. "Those goddamned..."

"I was at Sharpsburg," Mo said.

"You didn't get all shot to hell there."

Mo smiled. "I didn't know you were a better man for having bad luck with a shell."

Ed stared at him coldly. "All this sounds kinda funny after what you did to that Yankee sonofabitch the night you come home."

Mo shrugged and went on looking at Barney as one of the soldiers arrived with a muleskinner's whip. The trooper offered it to the sergeant whose hands stayed by his sides as if the whip were a lethal serpent.

Upon the boardwalk fifty or sixty feet from the patch of grass in front of City Hall, Vera was still watching. From Barney's ride to the arrival of the whip, not fifteen minutes had passed. She had seen Mo walk into the crowd, and now she could see him standing only a few feet from one of the white-faced Union troopers whose carbine was pointed just above the heads of the crowd. Mo was looking at the tableaux on the little spread of lawn while Ed Norton and another man talked animatedly to him. He was frowning, not so much in anger or even in disgust as in concentration. It was as if he were trying to handicap a quarter horse by eye alone, or deciding whether he could leap across an abyss without a running start.

He's got to know more than that, she was thinking. He's got to have learned better or he wouldn't even be here. He wouldn't try anything with that many of them pointing rifles down his throat.

But she was not sure at all that he knew, or if he would pay any heed to the knowledge if he had it. She remembered him on horseback before the war; she remembered what he had said that first night after he returned. As she watched him, it seemed she had not drawn a breath since Barney began his ride.

"It was a mistake that night," Mo was telling Ed Norton Junior. "I let that boy get next to me."

"Mistake?" Hornsby echoed.

"Sure. You don't fight an enemy because he gives you some sass. You fight him because he threatens your existence. Then you try to fight him on your own terms. That boy was no threat to me, and I took him on his own ground. He might have had a dozen other Unions waiting down the alley for some fool just like me to ride in. If he hadn't been a child and a stupid child at that, they'd have me out there where the old man is – only with a firing squad instead of a whip. I was lucky. The more I think about it the more I see I was lucky."

"But what are we gonna do about Barney Wilkes?" Hornsby wanted to know.

"Nothing," Mo said flatly. "Not a thing."

"You goddamned . . . "

Mo caught the other man by his shirtfront and pulled him close. "Watch your mouth," he said evenly. "There ain't any law that keeps me from givin' you what the Federal got. And I'm in better shape to give it now,"

Ed Norton grabbed his arm. "I don't care what you say. We can't let 'em whip that poor old fool. We got to risk it. We got pistols, we . . . "

"There's no risk at all," Mo said. "It's a sure thing. And their game all the way. For one old man's hide, you'll pay with ten or fifteen lives and maybe kill a couple of them. Then, if that colonel is what he looks like he is, after they bury you, they'll whip Barney anyhow."

"Jesus," Ed said. Hornsby slipped from Mo's loosening grip and stood helplessly as they turned back toward the flagpole.

"Are you ready, Sergeant?" Lodge asked, as if the sergeant were about to blow assembly or give orders to troop the line.

"Sir...," the sergeant began, his misery showing through.

"The proper answer is "Ready, sir," Lodge told him impatiently.

But the troopers, still fumbling with Barney, did not yet have him secured to the pole.

"What's holding you up?" Lieutenant Raisor asked nervously, more than conscious of Lodge's growing anger and the restless ugly crowd beyond.

"We...," one of the troopers started to say.

"It's this arm," the other one apologized. "It's his left arm, Colonel. I mean he ain't got no hand, and every time we get him tied, that stump slips out and we..."

"Tie his legs and neck, then," Lodge told them without expression.

"His neck?" the first soldier asked.

"Lieutenant, are these men hard of hearing? We've wasted too much time at this as it is. I want it done, and done quickly."

"Sir," the sergeant blurted out, "that old man is crazy. He ain't in his right mind. We ought not..."

"Obviously," Lodge smiled. "Any man who insults and degrades the flag of his country is mad. But it is a kind of madness that can be laid with enough force. All of us have learned that lately. Do your duty, Sergeant."

By then the troopers had Barney secured. One tore off his matted, patched gray jacket and faded shirt with a single motion. The sergeant raised his whip and then paused as he saw Barney's back. It was already trenched and laced and crosshatched by dozens of scars, some thin and indented, a few broader and rising from the flesh like reefs in a sluggish bay.

"Shrapnel," the sergeant said. "The poor old..."

"Sergeant," Lodge snapped, and the whip descended.

Later, some of them would claim that Barney had made no sound at all, that he had taken the beating as Prometheus suffered his vulture. But that was wrong and did Barney no more credit than the truth. Because as the whip ravaged his shoulders and stripped away bits of old scar tissue (even with the sergeant trying desperately to strike as easily as possible without giving Lodge reason to turn the job over to another man, and trying not to land the flail twice in the same place), Baney was not silent at all. It was not easy to hear him then because the crowd had, with the first blow, begun to yell, and a few of the young boys had thrown rocks at the distracted Unions holding carbines and pistols on the pulsing angry mass of people, but Barney was still singing even as the whip's fury sent his poor battered wits tumbling back to a white-washed church west of Sharpsburg and that proud hour when Hood's men had chilled the forward surge of Hooker's corps' advance. He felt the fragments, large and small, enveloping him again, and the same thunderous music scattered like confetti through his vacant mind.

Look away . . .
Look away . . .

Ed Norton Junior pushed forward from the crowd, reaching for the nearest of the Union troopers, but Mo grabbed his arm.

"No," he said harshly. "Not now, and not this way."

"When?" Ed asked him angrily, his eyes filled with tears. "If we don't do it now, when?"

Mo turned toward the rest of them. "I don't know yet. But when we hit 'em, we'll make 'em bleed for the old man and for every man they ever butchered. On our terms, our time."

"We can't let 'em . . . ," Hornsby started.

"Yes," Mo said. "We can. We have to."

The sun was high by then, and from the steeple of the Methodist Church a watcher could have seen it sparkling and reflecting from the slow current of the Red River, dissolving in the endless sweep of pine, oak, cypress, and sweet gum to the east and south. He could have seen, too, the flag of the United States running easily before a west wind over a silent town.

VIII

2 JULY 1865 — It was over by the time Sentell arrived at City Hall. The soldiers had cleared a path for Lodge and his escorts, and a few of the younger men had been put into the two-cell jail for cursing troopers in performance of their duty. Morrison Stevens and Vera Taggert had Barney Wilkes on the porch of the bakery, and a circle of men, most of them former soldiers, stood silent and hard-eyed around Mo and Vera. Barney was conscious and smiled up at Sentell as he knelt beside him.

"Hot, Major," he said smiling weakly. "Jesus, hot."

"It is, Barney. What have you been up to?"

"That cornfield," he croaked, his eyes widening. "Jesus, did you see it out there? Lord God, you couldn't walk but you'd be stepping on some poor soul. We was by the church. You know the church, that little Dunker church?"

Sentell looked at Mo. He was holding a damp cloth to Barney's back while Vera swabbed beneath it.

"We know the church," Mo said gently.

"I was beneath some kindlin' they had piled up and chocked," Barney began rambling again. "They got range of us," he moaned. "They . . . Major? Major?"

"All right, Barney."

He held the stump of his left arm up. It was scored with rope burns. His eyes were red-rimmed and perspiration poured down his cheeks. "Will it have to come off, Major? Will I lose it?"

Vera bit her lip and went on working. Sentell took a corner of Mo's rag and wiped Barney's face. "I reckon you may, Barney. But they have good doctors. It will be all right."

"Youall wouldn't leave me up here, would you?

"No," Sentell told him. "When we shake the dust of Maryland off our feet, you'll be right with us."

"Because I got to get home. I'm savin' my money to buy me a mule. Maybe a pair of mules. Even with a hand gone, if a man was to own a pair of good mules . . . "

"He'd be in high cotton," Mo said. "He'd be all right."

"All right," Barney whispered and fell back.

"Goddamn them sons . . . ," one of the men behind them began.

"No," Vera said. "He's just passed out. He's an old man."

"But hard," Mo said.

"Yes, hard," Vera said.

"Bring Barney along to my place," Sentell told Mo.

"Wait a minute," one of the men behind cut in, "how come you're so damned interested in Barney? You wasn't interested in none of us enough to fight the Yankees after you come home in '63."

"Keep your mouth out of it," Mo said. "It's none of your business."

"O yes it is," the red-faced man stuttered. "Old Barney's one of our folks. He fought like the rest of us. He didn't' come draggin' home from Vicksburg and spend the rest of the war in his parlor."

Sentell stood up and faced the man talking. "If you want to carry this on, you'd better get a pistol. The only way I answer white trash is to blast it out of my way."

The red-faced man backed off, and one of the other handed him a pistol he pulled from under his shirt. "All right, big boss. I got a pistol. Where's yours?"

"Ease off of this," Mo said, frowning at the red-faced man. "Hornsby, you're not doin' us any good. If you don't like the major, stay to hell away from him. If you've got to shoot, shoot a Federal and do it by yourself so they can hang you that way. Right now you can help us carry Barney over to the major's house. After you hand back that pistol."

When they reached Sentell's house, one of the Negroes helped Mo carry Barney into the house. Hornsby and the others headed back toward Texas Street, while Vera and Sentell sat on the veranda.

"It's hard to believe he's the same boy – man," Sentell corrected himself. "There's no fun or horse-racing left in him."

Vera smiled, but the fatigue showed through. Sentell wondered if it was the aftermath of her long months working in the hospital, or the tension that played around Mo like invisible lightning.

"No," she said, "there's not much of anything left in him. Except maybe hate, and even the hate isn't something alive, something he wants. It's like a man brushin' flies away. He don't think about it or want it: he does it like he breathes."

"That Union soldier . . ."

"That's right," Vera went on. "He told me about it. He can't even remember anything except that boy yellin' something and makin' like he wanted his buttons. When he started remembering again, he'd smashed that trooper all to pieces and broke a knuckle on his left hand."

"You fixed it?"

"I fixed it," he nodded. "It wasn't much, and the only doctors left around here are wearin' blue coats. Even a Yankee could put that two and two together."

"He'll be all right after a while," Sentell told her.

Vera shook her head silently. "I thought so. I thought, If he's in one piece, there's nothin' it could have done to him that I can't fix. I can ease him. I can wake him out of bad dreams. I can give him rest and love. I can give him sons."

She glanced up at Sentell quickly, as if she were expecting disapproval. "I love him. I've loved him since before it all started."

"I know. You'll be able to bring him around."

"No. Because there's nothing in him for me to get hold of, Major. No need in him."

"There's nothing but need in him," Sentell said.

She shook her head again. "You're talkin' for yourself or the rest of the men. I don't know about that. But he's cold without you even being able to tell it. Even when he kisses me . . . "

"Yes?"

"It's as if he was somewhere else doing something else, and lettin' his body have its way. I can't tell you about it, I can only feel it."

"Give him time," Sentell was saying.

"Give who time?" Mo said easily as he came back onto the veranda.

"We were talking about Barney," Sentell lied.

Mo shook his head. His expression seemed constantly on the verge of breaking into a loveless humorless smile. "I reckon he's about out of time. Between the Yankee shell at Sharpsburg and the Yankee lash today, I figure they'd about done him in."

"They had no call . . . ," Vera began.

"Honey," Mo interrupted, "they don't need any cause. They didn't have a cause four years ago."

He paused, and the odd crooked smile burst through. "I've got to thinkin' they're just downright mean. Like a bad horse or a dog when the heat's gotten to him. Major, do you remember what they did to March Tomlinson's bay when it kicked down the stable and killed him?"

"They shot it."

"But they didn't draw up a battle line or lay in supplies, did they?"

Sentell said nothing. He saw where Mo was headed. Vera looked tense. She was biting her lip again, and her dark complexion seemed flushed.

"No," Mo mused. "We just spotted that damned mean horse down near the sandbanks on March's place, and we bushwhacked him from fifty or sixty yards away. Must have been fifteen or twenty of us, and that horse weighed another ten pounds when we finished puttin' lead into him. Then we pushed him into the river and went on home. We weren't soldiers. We just had a crazy mean killer horse to get rid of, and that's how we did it. Then there was that little old sandy-haired dog Nathan Ripinski's boy had. It went mad one August and got to slavering and walking kinda twisted and humped, bitin' grass and so on. And a couple of us rode out and we bushwhacked that dog. It only took one shot, and that dog never hurt anybody. That was before we were soldiers, too."

"What are you getting at, Morrison?" Sentell asked him finally, knowing as well as he did.

"Why, nothing," he said softly, almost humbly. "I was just thinkin' about Yankees."

"Why don't you *stop* thinkin' about 'em," Vera burst out. "And start thinkin' about yourself?"

Mo grinned again, his smile smooth and engaging. "Why, honey, those two are the same thing. If there's a bad horse or a mad dog around, a man owes it to himself to . . . "

"They're not mad dogs," Vera cut in. "They just soldiers doing what they have to."

Mo's smile vanished, and Sentell could see just how old he was, despite the few years he had. "Now, honey," he said icily, "why don't you just trot back and tell old Barney all about that? Maybe you can catch him when he's not somewhere between here and that Dunker church."

Vera's eyes sparkled with tears. "I expect we'd better go now," she said. "Major, I'll be by to see Barney tomorrow, if it's all right."

"I'll be here," Sentell said. "My mother will be glad to see you again. She remembers the help you gave her at the hospital."

Vera tried to smile. "She gave me more than I could give her then. She was mighty kind. Not all of the women were that kind."

Sentell smiled. "She's seen too much to be any other way."

"We saw a lot together," Vera said, rising and walking toward the steps with Mo. "I expect we may see some more."

"Come on,," Mo said. Major, I'll see you soon."

For a long while that afternoon, Sentell sat in his study staring into the side yard. Gardenias were blooming and with the French doors ajar, their thick passionate odor made him think of the past. He remembered suppers on a veranda screened with gardenias tied painstakingly to the lattice work, and ballrooms swirling with white – white of costly gowns, white of cape jasmine blossoms – and the light careless music of a string orchestra. It had meant next to nothing then because he was past looking into pretty faces for a sign of recognition – already too old to give up his comforts, his reading or the long unaccompanied ride in early morning up toward Caddo Lake or alongside the river. But now that the suppers and the dancing were gone for good, there seemed to be an empty place, a vacuum in the texture of life filled only by the memorable odor of gardenias – and the brittle inexorable voice of a young man made for dancing and late suppers lecturing Sentell on the disposal of mad dogs and vicious horses.

"Has the past got hold of you?" his mother asked from the study doorway.

He turned from the yard and smiled. "Invasion of privacy," Sentell said.

She dropped her shawl on a dictionary stand and sat down in his father's overstuffed leather chair. "Pick another word beside invasion," she said. "Anyhow, it was only a guess. I've been thinking about the old days more and more."

"Because they were better?"

"Lord no," she smiled. "They weren't better. I guess they were harder in most ways. But it wasn't like now: all the whispering and sneaking. All the land up for sale and the Yankees handling parish business. And soldiers in the streets. I can remember when your father's uniform was the only regular army uniform in this town."

"I can remember him on Independence Day," Sentell said, "standing straight and saluting the flag or offering a toast to the Union. I wonder if he would salute or raise a toast now."

His mother drew off a pair of string gloves and set them on the edge of Sentell's desk – his father's desk, before.

"I don't know. No one dared predict your father. Captain Sentell was his own man. He might have defended Atlanta – or he might have laid siege to Richmond. Either way, you can be sure he would have been troublesome."

She leaned back and rang for one of the two colored girls who were still with them.

"I understand there was some unpleasantness downtown today. A man was whipped."

"Yes," Sentell said. "Barney Wilkes. The old man missing a hand and an eye."

Her face clouded with concern. "He whitewashed the house just a month or so before you came home. He got lime from Cleburne and did the house. He wouldn't take but fifty dollars. Where is he? I want to fix him something. Do you think he'd like some chicken soup?"

"I thought you might want to do something. He's back in the third bedroom."

"Why didn't you say so?" she said, picking up her shawl and gloves and starting for the back of the house. She left Sentell wondering where she would find a chicken expendable for soup.

One of the girls came in. "Didja ring just now, Major?"

"It was Mrs. Sentell, Sarah. She'll be back with the old man I brought in."

"Dat ole man on his way, Major."

"I'm afraid so. Do whatever you can to make him comfortable."

"Sho."

Just then there was a knock at the front door, and Sentell rose to his feet.

"You want me to git it, Major?" Sarah asked.

"No. Go on back with Mrs. Sentell. I'll take care of the door."

By then the day was gone, and after it came a soft yellowing twilight that made the trees and shrubs look like the heavy pigmented creations in an antique French painting. As he passed the doors open onto the lawn, that trick of light froze each tree, each bush, and the long sweep of grass into a single uninhabited landscape that seemed all the better, all the more perfect for the absence of a shepherd and his love. Then he had reached the foyer, the front door. When he opened it, the sky had already darkened a shade or two with that incredible and geometric instantaneousness of evening, and there was barely light enough to make out the features of the dark slender man who smiled and extended his hand.

"Major Edward Malcolm Sentell, I think."

His teeth made a flicker of light in the deepening shadows of the porch as Sentell took his hand.

"Come in, Charles," Sentell said. Bouvier stepped past him into the hall.

He was thinner than Sentell remembered – or perhaps he had been just as thin at Vicksburg, but they had all been thin there, and Sentell had not noticed then. His black hair was threaded with silver in a wide streak through the middle, but his olive complexion seemed as youthful and smooth as before – until he passed near the library lamp. Then Sentell could see the minute pattern of countless lines and corrugations that spread from the corners of his eyes like the rays of a complex creek system. There were tiny scars, too, no larger than smallpox marks, along his left cheek. His eye on that side seemed dull, glazed – yet so little different from the other that Sentell wondered whether it had always been that way, and he had forgotten. Then he glanced down and noticed Bouvier's left arm.

It hung by his side, encased from fingertips to sleeve in black, and somehow, without asking or even considering an alternative, Sentell knew the black covering extended upward under his coat sleeve, and that the arm was useless.

"I see you're surveying the establishment," he smiled. "Ravaged. Dented and cracked. Shat at and missed, shot at and hit. The arm's not good. The eye's not good. Even the smile is damaged."

As he spoke, he smiled. Sentell could see that only one side of his face moved. His smile was a twisted sneer worse than none at all.

"Nerves," he said lightly, as if mentioning a trivial indisposition. "Shattered nerves everywhere. And all for a damned railroad trestle over a river whose name I've forgotten in a campaign that changed nothing in a war that was lost when I last saw you. That's the story. What have you spent you time at?"

Sentell sat down and said nothing.

"You're staring," Bouvier said, still lightly, but with an edge of tension showing through. "It's not good form to ogle cripples."

Then Sentell found his voice. "I'm staring at a friend I had no expectation of seeing again. Most didn't come home."

Bouvier shrugged, his shoulders moving in that effortless Gallic gesture of complete dissociation and repudiation that had been the scourge of staff meetings and councils at Vicksburg. "They were the lucky ones. Died free, died quickly for the most part. Almost all of them died well. A lot of them died carrying less metal than the surgeons dug out of me. When I got home I told my father I could never have replaced Ney. Do you remember what Napoleon asked when someone suggested that a most punctilious officer be promoted to high command?"

"Yes," Sentell answered. "He asked, 'But is he lucky?'"

"You see? Even you couldn't have lied that flagrantly to the emperor. Sometimes I think I lost the war single-handed."

"No," Sentell said, starting to smile. "Nobody had any luck. The day Pemberton was planning to surrender, General Lee lost his luck in Pennsylvania."

"He would have lost it at Fredericksburg if I'd ever gotten up there with my own unit. He would have been lucky to get away from Burnside alive."

They drank brandy – from a bottle Amos Stevens had given Sentell. Bouvier mentioned Masterson.

"It took me most of two more years to understand him, and even now I can't feel him, but I know what went on . . . what must have gone on . . . inside him. I see the ground red as far as eyes can reach out beyond the Alamo, and the buildings on fire. I can see men scattered around like scrap paper or broken dolls, hanging over guns, off parapets. Christ, I can hear the howling and the flat unechoing sound of the rifles. And I can see myself in the middle of it with an empty pistol and a broken saber, and a dozen Mexicans coming for me, and me thinking, My God, is that what I dreaded? Is that what made me feel as if someone were pouring ice water down my back? Is this what I wanted to avoid? Then they're on me, and I throw the pistol at a head and jam the pointless end of the sabre into a belly, and in that instant, with the rest of them tearing me to pieces, and me knowing no one else is left, I think, My god, this what I was born for. This is what it was all about."

Bouvier was flushed, and the glaze of his useless eye caught the lamplight and diffused it until his whole face seemed distant, like a face seen through water. He picked up his paralyzed hand and dropped it into his lap irritably, like a sash weight, a piece of unwanted scrap.

"I think that was it," he said, his voice calming, lowering gain. "I think that's what it meant to him."

"I don't know," Sentell said. "We only talked about the war with Mexico. He didn't like it. He was sorry for Mexico."

"It's no good to be sorry," Bouvier said, his voice quiet and controlled again. "I want to go back to that hill where you buried him. I want to stand there with the river breeze shaking my hair and ruffling my clothes, and say, I'm not sorry, Sam. I'm not sorry about the earth tight around you, covering your eyes, filling your mouth. You picked the place and the time, and you said remember. So now I remember everything, and I have too much sorrow for myself, sorrow for the bad luck that put me in losing battles in a lost war and then brought me out of them with one eye, one arm, and life hanging around my neck like a rotten scapular."

"What are you going to do?" Sentell asked him. "Luck or not luck, you've got thirty years . . . "

"Call it thirty years to kill," he cut in, that half-smile warping his face.

There was nowhere to go in that direction. "How was it in Tennessee?" Sentell asked him.

He pointed at the gray streak that cut through is hair. "Not age," he said. "Not one strand of it is due to age. It was terror. Simple belly-robbing terror. There were times I wished I'd gone with you after the siege."

"It was bad?"

Bouvier shrugged and took more brandy. "Worse than Vicksburg and better. We were just as hungry most of the time, and a lot more tired. Most of us died or got killed or shot up. But we hit back. We saw Federals dead and hurt and running as if St. Michael was behind them with a comet tail. It made the hunger and the lack of sleep easier. But the fear worked on you. Not fear of death or injury or even fear of defeat, but that mile-by-mile, minute-by-minute fear that you were riding into ambush and wouldn't even see the man who shot you – much less have a chance to shoot back. That's where the gray hair came from."

"It doesn't sound any worse than the shelling at Vicksburg," Sentell said.

Bouvier shook his head stubbornly. "It was worse. All the shell could do was kill you or cripple you, and even at that there was no man behind to follow up what it had done. There was no way for them to surprise us. Remember the mine? Remember what it cost them just to try to surprise us? This was worse, because no shelter could guarantee you five minutes of peace without wondering where they were – the same way they wondered where we were."

Bouvier stopped and stared into his glass, the right corner of his mouth curling upward.

"It was like animals in the dark. You wouldn't have liked it. There was nothing for you or Masterson in it."

"I was busy enough," Sentell told him. "I might have been as well off with you."

"That's right," he said, his face lightening. "I was at the hotel. I heard the clerk and another man talking after I asked the way to your house."

"They've been talking for a long time. But none of them seems to want to put his theory to the test."

Bouvier laughed. "I expect I took the easy way after all. All I had to face was Yankees, and not even the best they could put in the field. You had to face the men coming home, the women who were waiting. How was it?"

How was it? Sentell thought. It was like the siege continued, except you were in your own town, your own house, and the besiegers were your own people. And you were weaponless, defenseless because no one dared – or cared – to push it to the point where you would be justified in shooting him down in the street. You sat and starved with a bellyful of food, and every time word would come of a Southern defeat, you would get your gear together and oil your pistol and get ready to ride out. But you would think against your will: Your name on that flimsy piece of paper in some Union file or crated in a Memphis or New Orleans warehouse. Or possibly even lost so that the physical evidence of that promise could never be brought to bear against you. So that all remaining between those last battles and yourself was the slender filament of a promise made to the enemy.

But it had been enough. By the spring of 1865, when the end was beyond doubt, he had no more feeling for any of it. He would stop in front of the *Shreveport News* office to read the crabbed script of news dispatches on a piece of discolored paper, and the words might have been from Gibbon or Tacitus for all they meant to him. It had mattered once. It had mattered enough to make Sentell forget Mexico, to drive the bloody children in that upper room out of his mind. But after Vicksburg, he had remembered again – had remembered, and had wondered whether the promise was made to the Federals, or to himself – and whether it was honor or simply disgust that kept him in Shreveport while his country was perishing in the woods east of Chancellorsville, and in the pastures near Spotsylvania Courthouse.

"It was like yours," Sentell told Bouvier. "All fear, all rottenness. Except there were not even little victories. Nothing but the last stand every day."

Bouvier stretched is legs in front of him and fumbled a slender cigar out of his pocket with his good hand. "I can't imagine you afraid of this rabble," he said slowly. "There couldn't have been anything left in town dangerous enough to make you catch your breath."

"No," Sentell said. "You don't understand. Not these people. Not even the army people who kept coming by politely asking if I was ready for a command, and saying with all the gentility the war had left them that I had a duty, a clear duty."

He told Bouvier about the ride from Vicksburg on a charity horse. He told him about the homecoming.

It was the second day after Sentell had finished the ride. His legs still felt no stronger than broom straws, and he could eat little at a time. But he wanted to walk, to see what two years of war and the news of Vicksburg had done to the town.

The streets were crowded with men in uniforms and parts of uniforms. There were scores of Negroes loading and unloading wagons. All the main streets were packed with moving men and horses. It looked like gold had been found nearby. He saw a warehouse near the riverfront. Across it in large block letters was printed:

NORTON & SON

"Sure it's bad, Edward," Ed Norton Senior told him. "It's terrible. I wish to God I could have been with youall. But these folks have got to eat. The army needs supplies. And now I've got the bank to look after. Jesus, I'll be lucky if I get out of this war alive. I haven't seen my wife in . . . She works over at the hospital. You wouldn't know her. Hands rough, eyes red. Never sees a bed from one day to the next."

Norton's bland anxious face worked as he talked. He glanced at his watch and shouted to an overseer who kept the freight moving into the warehouse. Then he turned back to Sentell.

"Ed Junior was there," he said, his voice lowering, the tone of forced purpose fading from it. "I didn't ask you because I know there were thousands . . . "

"I saw him. He rode out before it was over. I expect he'll be in Tennessee by now. He wanted to find Forrest."

Norton's face was frozen between relief and confusion. "Rode out? How was it he . . . ?"

"The word got out that Pemberton meant to surrender. Ed Junior decided against it."

"Well," Norton said doubtfully, "I mean he didn't do anything wrong . . . "

"No," Sentell told him. "There was nothing wrong with it. He had no responsibility when Pemberton decided to quit."

" . . . because I wouldn't want it around that he run out when . . . "

"He didn't run out," Sentell cut him off. "He rode out."

" . . . because we've got a business to run. When the war's over, a good reputation . . . "

"Ed Junior has a good name," Sentell said shortly, angrily. "If he lives to bring it home with him."

Norton frowned. "Well, sure. He'll come home. He's got to come home. We need him. He's got to come home."

The rest of the town was the same. Full of business and foreboding, but letting the loading and unloading, the making and selling of things, screen out the fear. There was no use thinking what the fall of Vicksburg might mean. Thinking about it made it no better. Ignoring made it no worse.

"Sure they ignore it," Cleburne told Sentell. "What did you expect? You can't ask more of people than what they are."

"They're not much, then."

"That's it," Cleburne smiled, his eyes roving, moving separately along the crowded street. "Not much. None of us are much. You take the strong and the weak and the difference between is nothin'. Listen," he went on, "you ain't no child. You knew what people are. They hate and love and sell things and cry at night partly on account of the darkness and partly on account of knowin' what daylight will show 'em. Except the young ones. They hate and love and kill. Night and day don't mean anything to 'em. It's all one and it won't stop ever. And it don't. It don't stop till it does, and then they're past knowin'."

"I expect you picked up your philosophy in New Orleans."

Cleburne stopped smiling. He stared at Sentell for a moment as if he expected him to say more. "No," he said finally. "No, I reckon I got it in Mississippi. I got most everything worth havin' in Mississippi. I kept losing' stuff in New Orleans. I reckon it was the climate."

"Maybe the Yankees have cooled it off," Sentell said.

Cleburne studied the street without answering. Inside the store, one of his clerks, hired like the rest by the week and rarely working longer, was casually cursing a Negro who claimed to have bought moldy corn.

"Massa say . . . "

"You tell Massa to kiss my ass. We got a war on. If he don't like the corn, you tell him to . . . "

"When will you be goin' back?" Cleburne asked suddenly.

"I don't know," Sentell told him. "Whenever the Federals exchange for me."

"You mean they got you paroled?"

"That's right."

"Jesus," he whistled. "You could be around a long time. I hear they ain't exchangin' any to speak of. 'Course, nobody pays much mind to them papers."

"I signed my name to a promise."

"Sure. Ain't no man in his senses goin' up to one of them hellholes to stay till it's over. But . . . you mean you're goin' to honor that parole?"

"I signed it freely. What else can I do?"

"Jesus," Cleburne breathed. "What else . . . Listen, if it goes bad, and you get short of money, how would you like to work my counter some? I wouldn't even have to run inventory twice a week just to stay in business."

"It might come to that. We can't run the river place any more. Most of the people have been impressed for work-gangs."

"A one-man business always had the edge," Cleburne said. "If you don't depend on nobody else, they can't let you down. I ain't depended on anybody in twenty years."

"Somebody let you down?" Sentell asked.

"No. Yes," he said, his face losing that constant expression of amused withdrawal. "You can't depend on nothin'. Soon as you start dependin', you start losin'. What you do is dedicate all you got to the simple proposition of takin' care of yourself. The rest of it is a hundred different kinds of suicide."

"I've heard that view," Sentell told him." "But it works out the same. You end dead that way as sure as any other."

"But only dead," Cleburne came back. "Just dead. Not made a fool of, not killed a couple of times before one killin' finally takes."

"You have to pick a piece of ground and stand on it," Sentell said.

"No," he barked, "that's what you don't *never* do. What you do is find a piece with six or eight good hidin' places and a dozen or so ways out. You travel so light, so empty, that nobody with anything much in the way of baggage can even see your dust. That way you never lose."

"And you never win."

"All right," Cleburne said, the ubiquitous smile rekindling. "All right, you don't. But you just said there wasn't a way to keep from losin'. You said we all end with a mouthful of mud. My way, you run a long race and you see lots of other casualties before they bring you down."

"What should I do?" Sentell asked him.

"If it was me, I'd go on back to duty with maybe a speech or two about how my blood was still at the service of my country. Then, first chance I got, I'd put a bullet through my leg. Not bad enough to cripple me, but plenty bad enough to put me out of the war business."

Sentell knew Cleburne too well to doubt him. Just to hear more, he asked, "How would you square that with your conscience?"

Cleburne's eyes widened, and he fumbled in a barrel beside him for a cracker. "If I had a conscience – which I ain't because that was in the luggage I shucked a long time ago – I'd look around this goddamned town till my eyes lit on Ed Norton Senior or Ramsey or that thin knock-kneed bastard Maxy who runs the hotel now that Sam Platten went and got killed for glory. I'd look around and say, This country was built on the idea of enlightened self-interest. There ain't no such thing as an enlightened war, and the best self-interest around seems to be sellin' goods to the savages.

"Look," Cleburne finished, "the only ones you'd ever have to makes excuses to are the very ones who won't be back to hear 'em. If you was to come back with a phony hole in your leg, there wouldn't be a man in this town dare to call you on it. Because most of 'em ain't got no kind of hole at all, and a big number ain't never been anywhere that holes was bein's passed out."

"Suppose I just stay, leave it the way it is?"

"No," Cleburne said positively. "It won't work. You ain't hurt. And worse than not bein' hurt, you're gonna tell these folks you can't go back on your word. So half of 'em will want your neck stretched for ever givin' your word to the Yankees, no matter what the reason. And the other half ain't gonna like hearin' talk about promise and honor and sworn word, because they all sold out the first time a Confederate purchasin' agent with a heavy wallet and light mind come along, and they been sellin' ever since even though they was mostly raised to believe . . . or at least give lip service to that honor and promise and sworn word of yours. What do you expect? They sure as hell ain't gonna build you a marble pedestal to stand on."

"What group would you be in?" Sentell asked him.

He smiled and tossed fragments of crackers into his mouth. Then he wiped his hand on the soiled front of his shirt. "Hell," he said, "I'm in a special category. I sold out so long ago, I can't even remember. Only I sold out to myself. I wouldn't never hate you because you can't do me no harm. On the other hand, I wouldn't help you neither."

Sentell said nothing, still watching the street where a cluster of young men, freshly recruited – more likely drafted – followed a sergeant dressed in a neat, well-tailored gray uniform, the like of which none of them would ever see.

"'Course you wouldn't ask for no help," Cleburne mused.

"If you ride a fast horse and stay clear of ditches, you don't generally have to ask. Anyhow, people being what you think they are, only a fool would count on help, and only a man counting on it would be fool enough to ask."

"Goddamn," Cleburne said, his grin looking almost genuine. "I could of said that."

"Sure you could," Sentell told him. "So could I."

"So you were looking right at it from the beginning," Bouvier said.

"I was looking all around it," Sentell told him. "But the looking was only to chart the ground, to see where I would be walking. Because I didn't want to step on a torpedo without even knowing it was there."

"How did you tell them?" Bouvier asked. "Or did you tell them? Or did you let them find out by simply staying until the question asked itself?"

It had been neither way. The torpedo had been there simply waiting to explode. Sentell had talked to Amos Stevens.

"When it comes out, there'll be a lot of hard talk," Amos told him. "They've forgotten the idea of honor. I don't even like to think about what they'd be willing to pay for a clear-cut victory over the Union."

"What do you think?" Sentell asked him.

Amos poured some brandy and rubbed his fingers over a volume of Calhoun's speeches.

"I think it's over for us. I think Mr. Darwin's idea may have social applications as well as biological ones. I think your generation is divided against itself over the price to be paid for survival, and my generation is waiting for permission to retire. I wonder sometimes what Lee would do if he knew a single lie, one bald-faced self-perjury, would give us our independence. I wonder the same about Davis and

Johnston. Then I consider the younger men – and there seems to be less room for speculation."

"Would you foreswear yourself to save the Confederacy?" Sentell asked.

He leaned forward and pounded his glass down upon the desk. "Hell no," he cried. "Hell no. Because my word has been worth more than gold in this parish for fifteen years, and in Orleans parish before that, and all through eastern Virginia before that. Because there's not a while man or a nigger walking this earth who can say I lied or dealt sharply or used any influence but what was rightfully mine to use. I want the South free and independent, but if it has to wait for that freedom until I break my word, then it had better prepare for a long war."

"Selfishness?"

"Certainly. Every goddamned mother's son of us is selfish. What a man won't do for money, he'll do for a woman; failing either of those, he'll act out of spite or hatred or for the simple purpose of gouging a place for himself in the clay of history. And if that's his concern, Attila the Hun is as well lodged as St. Louis of France. Every man is singular: a species of soul unto himself. I was raised when it was possible to hold honor as the chief singularity any man should aspire to. I never asked my father whether he had lied or stolen. Not because I assumed he hadn't, but because I preferred not to investigate that possibility. I don't intend to ask Morrison – if he comes home – because he wouldn't even understand the question."

"So honor is an eccentricity, a quirk or a fashion like knee-britches?" Sentell asked.

"Look around you," Amos said, his face ashen and empty. "Look around and tell me integrity is the natural state of man."

"Suppose you were my age," Sentell said. "Young enough to reconsider – young enough for it to matter."

Amos shook his head. His hand was unsteady as he poured both of them a drink. "I spend too much time being glad I'm not that young. Being thankful that I've met most of my tigers already."

"What would you do?"

"I'd do what you're going to do. Be selfish my own way and hang on to what I believed in with my teeth and fingernails and tell the rest of them to go to hell. Knowing what selfishness I was guilty of, but knowing too that it was no worse than the selfishness of conscripts who won't fight or men who pay substitutes or take advantage of the twenty-slave provision or sneak their cotton down-country to sell it to the Unions. That's what I'd do, and dare any man in the parish to call my hand on it."

Amos was breathing hard, his face full of color again. "It's not likely we'll win this war," he said more calmly. "You know that. And your going or staying would change nothing. You know that, too. And when it's over, when the killing is done, there won't be a hundred thousand dollars gold left in Caddo parish. On top of that, there won't be enough able-bodied white men to see to a thousand acres. So if you can come out of this bloodletting with anything – anything of value at all – then you'd better study to do it."

"What did you have in mind?" Sentell asked him.

"Your good name," he said. "The integrity of your word among a pack of jackals who will hate you for still having anything – even though it's something they have no use for, something they can't understand any longer – and hate you for the way you preserved it. But knowing that, they'll have to trust you, put faith in you, simply because by the very way in which you incurred their hate, you proved worthy of trust. And there'll be no one else to trust."

He sank back in his chair, his face red, his hand trembling on the base of his glass.

"I wish I could go through it for you," Amos said. "I wish I could trade skins with you for a while. Not because you'll falter or slip up, but because you'll get no pleasure out of it and I would. You can't enjoy it. You're still too young to take pleasure in personal dogma even when you know you're right. You'll worry it like a dog mouths a bone in a feed sack. You'll stay with it, but there'll be no comfort in it – no excitement. If I could do it, it would put ten years on my life."

"If no one decided to take that ten and whatever else you might have left."

"No," Amos said. "They won't back-shoot you. It hasn't come to that. If we lose, then I'd watch my back a little more closely. I'd stay from between lamps and windows. But while Lee is in the field it won't come to that. The price they exact will be high enough, but it won't include blood."

Amos was right. For the first few weeks, nothing was said. But finally casual questions began. Someone asked where Sentell's next assignment might be. One of the women at the hospital wondered openly in front of his mother how long his leave would extend.

"With things going so badly," she added apologetically.

Sentell's mother told him at supper, as if it were an anecdote – something to break the day's monotony.

"I told her I expected you'd be home for quite a spell."

She smiled and passed him chicken and dumplings. He put more on his plant than he could eat. "No use in surprising them" she said.

"Do you think he would have signed the parole?"

She placed her hands on the table as if they had suddenly become too heavy to support.

"Possibly," she said. "Possibly. If the only alternative were a prison camp. Your father never could have borne that. Torture or starvation would have been fine. But filth and vermin, abusive guards and always the chance that illness or injury might have bent his knees . . . No, I think he would have signed."

"It wasn't prison," Sentell told her. "I wasn't afraid of prison, it was only that . . . "

She smiled and reached across the table to touch his hand. "I know," she said. "You're too much afraid of fear to worry about bedbugs or chains. He left you that."

"I don't think he was afraid of fear."

"No," she agreed. "Not of fear itself so much as the appearance of fear. He once told me his injury from the 1812 war was God's culminating and ultimate blessing, and that it took a great weight from his mind. He said that with his spine frozen straight, he could not bend even if fear should overwhelm him. It was the idea that someone should think him afraid that plagued him."

She paused a moment, and the firm line of her jaw slackened as if from sudden inexplicable fatigue. "Of course, he never was afraid. Not even on the borderline this side of fear. Nothing outside him meant enough for him to fear its loss, and nothing within was soft enough to tremble."

"I'm not afraid of appearances," Sentell said. "I only fear making a mistake that might be irretrievable."

"No," she said, smiling again. "You wouldn't be afraid of appearances, I suppose. Not fearful and caring nothing for what you seem to be. And not like your father after all. You get that from me."

"I'm going to stand by the parole," Sentell told her. "I'll stay here until they exchange me."

"Of course," she said, as if there had been no question of any other possibility. She stood up and walked toward the window, glancing quickly at his father's portrait above the fireplace. But it was only a glance, and then she moved on to the window and stood gazing at the riot of summer flowers flaring and moving softly in the garden.

"So in order not to compromise yourself you will have to compromise us – your father and me – compromise the part of you that is me and cares nothing but for the feeling of being truly right no matter what the appearance of it, and the part of you that is him and still demands at least a chance of not only feeling right but appearing right, too."

"No," he said. "Not him. Not the appearance. I told you . . . "

"You told me you would stand on the parole. The parole is a form, a gesture."

"But the gesture . . . ," Sentell began. "This time the gesture is . . . "

" . . . what is right," she finished for him. "I expect you've seen Amos Stevens."

"Yes," he told her. "Yesterday. He said . . . "

"He said wild horses couldn't make him break the gesture of that lost forgotten piece of Yankee paper. Despite it being only Yankee paper, and not a contract between gentlemen or even between a gentleman and his inferior, but between a gentleman and his own executioners."

"Yes, he said that. Except the last. It wouldn't matter who owned the paper. No, yes – it would – does matter. It matters more because if it were a contract between two gentlemen, it would require no paper at all, and even with an inferior on the other side, there would be the town and the whole undifferentiated class of inferiors looking on to see that contract kept, and so there would be nothing in holding to it but evidence that any man turns like a weathercock in the presence of opinion. But co-signed with them, with the butchers, it becomes completely my own with nothing to hold me to it but my own will, my own sense of what has to be. It cuts through and makes me decide whether honor is for the parlor and the ballroom and even the racetrack and here – those places – only. Or whether it goes into the dressing room and the chapel – and even to the gallows or the coffin with you."

"And so would you . . . ?"

"No," Sentell stopped her. "Don't even ask. I'll tell you – answer what you were going to ask or what you should have asked. If I signed a pact with the devil, would I stand by it? Yes. Of course. If I signed it sober and took his coin – took Helen or whatever the contract called for – I'd stand by it into hell and tell the rescuers to go find a fool or a weakling to redeem."

"It wasn't that," she said. "I was going to ask if you would visit your father's grave with me. I knew the rest of it except the words. Because it sounds like what he might have said."

"Would he have broken his parole?" Sentell asked her in surprise. "Do you think he would have broken it?"

"Without a doubt," she smiled gently. "Broken it before a voice could have been raised to ask whether he would or not, and then gone back to the war sitting like a wooden soldier on some poor miserable horse with a fancy pace. And been tormented by conscience not at all while he looked for the dying-place."

"Then it started, I suppose," Bouvier said, a quizzical detached expression on his maimed face.

"That's right, then it started. It started with a question on the walk in front of Ramsey's saloon."

"A fine place for a debate on abstractions."

"And it went on to some of the local women cutting me and my mother on the street. And, finally, as you would expect, it come to the attention of the Confederate authorities."

"Who said nothing about what they had heard," Bouvier smiled, "But sent someone with an assignment for you so that you could turn it down before their attention became official. The most punctilious dead army in history."

Sentell shrugged. He had no feeling for any of it now. It was like reciting the lineage of Henry VII or repeating the Apostle's Creed. He told Bouvier the rest of it without feeling resentment or interest beyond its worth as a story. It seemed to have happened to someone else.

"That much is right," he said. "But it went higher. It stopped with the commander of the department."

"Kirby Smith? The grand mogul? That must have been quite an interview."

It had been almost no interview at all. Sentell had gone to the white frame headquarters building at the corner of Milam and Spring streets and waited until an orderly called him into the commanding general's office with a soft voice, as if he were an acolyte in front of the altar or a coffin peddler sizing up a heartbroken client.

Kirby Smith sat behind a broad oak table covered with neat piles of documents, pencils, ink, small maps, government stationery, a book or two, and some cracked and decaying letter files. His face was lined and sunken above a luxurious beard, but his eyes, large and beautiful as a woman's, still held some of that strange endearing naiveté Sentell remembered.

"Edmund," Sentell said. "It's good to see you."

Kirby Smith stood up with the stiff formal manner of a martinet or an elderly rich man.

"Edward, sit down."

They looked at one another for what seemed a long time. It had been the better part of twenty years since Sentell had seen him, but what was between them was Mexico, the old Army, and the mutual astonishment they shared – that all former United States officers shared – that they should be meeting again as rebels against the government they had fought for so shamelessly.

"Major Tyler tells me that you are on parole from Vicksburg."

"That's right," Sentell said. "It was a bad place to be cornered, no way out, and no way in even if there had been someone willing and able to come in for us. A doomed fortress. Like Chapultepec."

Kirby Smith studied his hands. His eyes were turned down to the desk top, the balding front of his head shining with perspiration.

"You've never forgotten the little cadets, then," he said so softly Sentell could hardly hear him.

"No," Sentell said. "Have you?"

Kirby Smith looked up, his dark honest eyes even with Sentell's "God gives forgetfulness to those he despises. I suppose he still loves us."

"He tortures his children," Sentell said, "to purify them."

"And what of the instruments he uses?"

Sentell shook his head. "Instruments," he repeated. "Are you talking about us or the Yankees now?"

Kirby Smith pulled his chair closer to the desk. From the papers and pencil stubs he plucked a pair of fragile gold-rimmed spectacles and hung them around his ears. "I expect we'd better talk about both," he said. "There's no cure for that other. The only difference between us is that I have never been sure that there was a remedy even before it happened."

"Life is a disease of matter?" Sentell asked wryly.

He stared across the cluttered desk at Sentell again, his eyes hardened and concentrated by the spectacle lenses. His voice was unruffled, resigned.

"Life is a compulsion," he said. "There is no alternative to life."

"Except the practice of our profession."

"You should never have resigned," Kirby Smith said. "There was no reason to. Killing goes on. It goes on in your name whether you take part in it or not. There is no honor in handing over a bad job to someone else."

"Which would be as relevant to the present as the past?" Sentell asked.

"Yes," Kirby Smith said. "The killing is still going on. It will go on for a long time no matter what happens. The killing stopped mattering after the first man fell on either side. All that matters now is which side gets sick of it first or cannot keep it going any longer. There are no metaphysics or ethics to it. It's like gears grinding."

"I think Tyler misrepresented me," Sentell told him. "As I must have misrepresented myself if you think I resigned after Mexico because of a little blood. Killing or the lack of it has nothing to do with this. I gave my word to the Union officials. I regard myself bound by that promise."

Kirby Smith's eyebrows raised behind the glasses, but he said nothing. Then, after a moment:

"The paroles are being freely violated on both sides," he said mildly, without emphasis.

"Is that a recommendation?" Sentell asked.

"No. It is an observation."

"Noted. Which leaves me to say only that such violation is against my concept of honor."

"All right. And your country?"

"The last time I dedicated myself to fighting for nothing more than a country, my dedication put me in a roomful of maimed children. That was blindness, and at least as much my fault as the country's. But this time my eyes are open, and I don't mean to do for the Confederacy what made me lose all respect for the Union. I was used, degraded once, before I even knew that nations or governments demand you run the risk of degradation as a patriot's hazard. The damned United States sent me to lynch Mexico; you're not going to send me out to butcher my own integrity."

"No," Kirby Smith said wearily. "Of course I'm not. I would never even have sent for you except that qualified officers are being killed as quickly as we can find them. We need . . . "

"I'm sorry," Sentell said shortly, more brutally than he had intended.

"All right," Kirby Smith said.

And then as Sentell rose, not offering his hand but moving toward the door and turning one last time as he reached it, Kirby Smith took off his spectacles and began rummaging through the piles of documents on his desk, his shoulders hunched forward, bent into the curved and permanent crescent of a clerk searching diligently for some letter or manifest that, found, might clear away the immense confusion of an unbalanced account.

"And that was the end of it," Bouvier breathed.

"That was the beginning," Sentell told him. "It got worse. Then the war began to go so badly that the town forgot about me. No: not forgot. Simply went into shock. There was A. P. Hill's trouble at Mine Run, and the west was coming apart. It was all too much for them to keep me in mind. It was so bad that they had either to kill me or ignore me. And it never got better."

"No," Bouvier mused. "It never did get better. How did you feel at the end of it? How do you feel now? Was it worth it?"

Sentell looked at his scarred frozen face, and fumbled for words. Not for a set speech to defend himself, not for an apology. He looked for the right words, knowing that there were none.

"I don't know," Sentell said. "I'll never know. You went on to join Forrest. Was it worth it?"

Bouvier tried to smile again, but the paralysis made him look as if he were in pain. Or possibly it was not even meant to be a smile.

"I have to say yes. Because if I say I don't know, I disarm myself."

"Disarm? You've been disarmed. It's over. The guns are all on their side now."

Bouvier shook his head. "O no," he said. "You're ahead of yourself. Nothing is over. Nothing is settled."

"What do you mean?"

"You haven't forgotten our conversation in front of the tent have you?"

"You mean the talk about guerrilla warfare and rest of it?"

"That's right," Bouvier said. "And the rest of it. As much more of it as the situation calls for."

"You haven't had enough of killing?"

Bouvier paused and studied the carbon-darkened lamp chimney, his eyes glowing in its muted light. The he found another cigar and waited for Sentell to strike a match.

"I never started into this for the sake of killing. The killing was incidental. It's still incidental. I began killing when they invaded my country. I'll stop when they leave."

"They're here to stay," Sentell said.

"Yes," he laughed loudly. "Some of them are."

"Did you come here to . . . ?"

"Not to kill," he said. "I came here for a little relaxation, the society of a brother-in-arms, and to meet a friend."

"A friend?"

"That's right. Another old comrade from a different campaign. He lives in Memphis, and we decided to meet halfway between there and New Orleans. Shreveport seemed like a good place. Anyhow, I wanted to see you and meet your friend Amos Stevens. He's well remembered in Orleans parish."

"And your friend," Sentell asked again, with some dark and inchoate premonition, a feeling almost of dread, as if Bouvier had brought with him – besides his ruined face and useless arm – some kind of wild and unpredictable order, and that he, Sentell, was becoming a part, a function of that regimen without even realizing it.

"O," Bouvier said brightly, "my friend is a surprise. Day after tomorrow is Independence Day, the Fourth of July – you remember the Fourth of July – and my friend will be your surprise. I think everyone should have a surprise for the Fourth of July."

IX

3 JULY 1865 — The road south from El Dorado had no surface except that which a thousand teams and single riders had pounded through the pine woods and across the red soil of stump-filled pastureland. With good fortune and strong animals, the trip required a day and a half for a single man riding. For a column of men marching, it was

three days at least, and with the season alternating between dust-boiling heat and sudden torrential bursts of rain, it could take as long as five days.

Phillipe Crowninshield was heading them, and they were two companies of United States Colored Troops from the permanent garrison at Little Rock. He had not wanted the assignment, had offered his resignation at Washington to an embarrassed War Department undersecretary who shivered and grew nearly inarticulate when faced with the realization that, despite clear regulations to the contrary, there was a Negro commissioned officer in the army.

But the wave of postwar resignations had almost swamped the Department, and there were not enough career officers to handle both the western frontier and the sullen semi-provinces of the South.

So he had taken the job. Not of commanding the colored troops, but simply of overseeing their movement from Little Rock to Shreveport where he would hand them over to Colonel Jonathan Lodge, and then become a civilian automatically.

Now it was almost done. They had left El Dorado almost four days before, and they were beginning to move into country he recognized. He would see a turning in the dusty swing of the road, and remember the configuration of land beyond it. He remembered a long, gradual slope of land still covered with original trees where they had hunted. He remembered a tiny crossroads village where the store owner had kept a bear chained behind a lean-to. Once Mo had gone for water there and had run full-tilt into the bear. Phillipe smiled, remembering the store owner and the mutual surprise of Mo and the bear.

But that had been a long time before, and now there was nothing to smile about. The land was deserted: empty cabins and fields going back to grass and saplings. Some broken stalks of last year's corn turned gray and swamped with weeds. But almost no people.

They couldn't stay, Phillipe thought as he rode at the head of the column. With the cotton embargoed and most of the able-bodied men gone to warring, there was no way for a family to stay on the land. Into town, Shreveport or maybe over to Minden. Or into Texas. But into town, and the land gone back to what it was before they put us to currying it. Full circle. Only now instead of whites marching us into woods and fields, we're marching ourselves, and this time we'll get the fruit as well as the tillage.

300

Phillipe had received no answer to his letter home. He had expected none. His father was no fool, he thought, except where Amos Stevens was concerned. That was where the smartness stopped; that was where all the hard lessons Rye Crowninshield had learned in fifty years of being a Negro in a white man's country collapsed into irrelevance. Amos Stevens was something else. Morrison Stevens was something else. White men were white men, but the Stevenses were in a class by themselves.

In a class by themselves, Phillipe thought bitterly. Because they kept us in hell with kind words instead of a piece of chain. Because they were both smart enough to know and hollow enough to use the simple truth that even an animal, a black gorilla, is easier to handle with kindness and trust than with a chunk of kindling and a rope. In a class by themselves because they were head and shoulders above the rest of the fools in Caddo parish, held the name of good men – and still owned and profited out of slaves as much as any of the rest.

That's it, he thought, turning to glance back at the sweating column of dark-faced men behind. The name of good men. So long as a man who owned a Negro can stand tall and be called a leader, there can't be any safety for us. Because it will depend on Stevens. If he wants peace he can get it. If he wants our blood, only the army can keep a black man alive in the parish. And I don't trust him to want peace. I wouldn't trust him any more than I'd trust any other man who trafficked in human agony. If he owned me, used me – held me like he holds a parcel of land – how can I trust him to take the loss of me kindly?

His father would still be there, he thought. Would still be brewing tea and pouring brandy. Still spending his afternoons either on the porch or in the saddle beside Stevens. Or in the indeterminate green haze of the backyard beneath the dogwood and mimosa trees with a volume Stevens had suggested he might like. He would be there even with the full knowledge of his new freedom, paying no more attention to it than he had to his slavery. Paying no attention to anything outside the scattered acres of Amos Stevens' land, and the bounds of his own narrow world.

Did he ever once think of what slavery means? Phillipe wondered. Did he ever think that it might be Amos Stevens' shrewdness instead of his love or his honor that kept the lash from playing arbiter in disputes? Did he ever consider that, even if his own bondage was as easy a physical burden as life is likely to set on any man, there were others who were born into hell, sojourned there, and died hating enough at last to reap another hell?

One of the noncommissioned officers rode up beside Phillipe.

"How about a break, Lieutenant?" he asked. "These boys are wearing down. You keep speeding up the pace."

Phillipe drew in his rein. "I didn't mean to," he told Sergeant Samuels. "I didn't know I was goin' any faster."

Samuels held up his hand. "Ten minutes?" he asked Phillipe.

"How long we been movin'?"

"Hour. Maybe hour and a half."

Phillipe shook his head. "I mean to break it up every hour. Let 'em have twenty minutes."

He dismounted and turned his horse loose in the summer grass. The rain clouds had moved off for a while at least, and the ground beneath was dry and thick with springy weeds and vines. Samuels checked the line for stragglers and then came back and joined Phillipe. "They found some blackberry bushes back there. Even the stragglers are closing up."

Phillipe lay on his back, staring at the sky through slitted lids. "They'll come down with boils. You don't find blackberries without they got poison vines and such around."

"City boys," Samuels smiled easily. "None of us know this country. It's getting close to your home, huh?"

Phillipe shrugged. "Yes, if you call it home."

Samuels' eye widened. "Home is the place you're from. Where you grew up. I thought somebody said you had a father down here at this Shreveport."

"That's so," Phillipe said. "A father who don't know he's free yet."

"Be good that you can tell him."

"He's been told. It ain't for lack of tellin'. He just don't care. I knew when I got started in all this that he wouldn't care."

Samuels nodded frowning. "Seems strange. I was born free, so it doesn't mean so much to me. But it seems a man would reach out and take hold of freedom. Unless there was something he cared more for."

"That's it. A gray-haired one-armed old white man who got my poppa given to him for a present when Poppa was five or six years old."

"Your poppa cares for this white man?"

"Cares? Jesus Christ, he can't see the open road of his own gain for lovin' Amos Stevens."

Samuels was loosening his shoelaces. "Don't you suppose he's got a right to do that?"

"I didn't fight for him to stay the same as when he was a slave."

Samuels move his bare feet in the grass. Then he leaned against a tree. "Free means a man can do what he wants. You want to make your father do what he don't want to do?"

"I want him with me. I want to get us some good land and set up for ourselves. Like a man and his son ought to."

"You planning to send a couple of us out to Stevens' to prod your poppa with a bayonet?"

But Phillipe was paying him no mind. He was remembering how he and Mo had argued about slavery.

"I don't see where slavery rubs you," Mo had said. "Do you want to go away?"

"No," Phillipe told him, "I don't know any place but this. I don't know anything else."

Mo shrugged. "Then how does it matter whether you can go or not? I can't go to the moon, but I don't lose no sleep over it."

"Nobody can keep you from going to the moon. Nobody owns you."

Mo shrugged again. "I don't know about that. I guess everybody is owned. A woman can own a man. She can make it so he can't do what he wants because of her. A child is owned by his parents. Parents sure enough are owned by children. They can't go and come when they want."

"But look at those niggers in the fields."

"Look at old Lubbock down the road. Ain't no overseer with a big bad eye standing over him. But he's in the field before a nigger on our place climbs out of bed, and when every field hand in Caddo parish is back in his cabin, old Lubbock is still at it."

"Because he wants to."

Mo shook his head. "No, he don't want to. He don't like calluses and a burned neck any more than the next man. But that forty acres has got hold of him. It's a lot harder master than my poppa."

"But it belongs to him. It feeds him and takes care of him for the work he does."

"Don't this place belong to you? Don't you feel like this place is as much your poppa's and yours as it is ours? When they come here, didn't neither one have much except the other. Lost both their wives in New Orleans with the fever. Your poppa and mine set this place up.

Because my old man holds the paper on it don't mean much. The land belongs to all the people who sweat for it. It feeds you and me alike, don't it?"

Samuels called him back. "It's twenty minutes," he said apologetically. "I would let you lay for a while, but . . . "

"No," Phillipe said. "You did right. We got to get movin' again. We can make the river by later afternoon. I want these men under a roof tonight."

They rode through a grove of pecan trees and past a motionless bayou. At the sound of the horses' hoofs, turtles dropped from sodden logs into the water. Samuels saw a moccasin ooze from a low branch onto the dark humus at the water's edge. It was cooler moving under the trees.

"You never told me how you came over," Sergeant Samuels said. "Did you walk all the way North from down here?"

Phillipe slackened his mare's pace. "Lord no," he said. "I guess I'd just gone on frettin' if Morrison Stevens hadn't carried me up to Virginia. Then on into Maryland."

It was good to talk. Phillipe's eyes stayed on the decrepit road ahead, but he went on talking, as much to himself as to Samuels. About their leaving Shreveport.

"Boy," Rye had told him, "you see many a year an' no one ask you should earn yo' keep. You most a grown man an' never pay de patient grocer. Now we askin' token on yo' account."

His father pointed at Mo, who was dressed in his uniform and cape, taking leave of Amos.

"See him," Rye said. "He got to go fo' to carry dis good name where de enemy stand. He do what fightin' there be. You see to him, you care fo' him. In all case you bring him home. If he be drunk wif triumph, put him on a mule an' see he don't fall. If de conflic' go against us, you bring him home. If he die, you bring him home. He belong here. As you do."

"So I promised him. I promised to bring Morrison home."

"It wasn't in your mind to go over?" Samuels asked.

"No. Not to leave Morrison. Because he meant some to me. He was all the friend I knew. And my poppa and his poppa. It was all thick and tangled, and there was love in it. You got to feel something for people you been raised up with. Love or hate. And they never gave me reason to hate. I hated what I knew about us bein' slave. But I didn't' know anything to say about it, anything to do about it. So I promised."

"Seems you had it good. Lots of folks in Pennsylvania might have swapped places. Where I grew up, you worked from can't-see to can't-see digging coal or laying track. And if you didn't work you didn't eat."

"But you were free. A free man."

Samuels smiled. "I know how you must feel. Free is like a new toy, I guess."

Phillipe was thinking back again. "It was like a sword laid across my soul," he said dreamily. "I got to thinkin' about it. I couldn't leave off thinkin' that a hundred miles north of where we were, a man could be black and free at the same time. But I didn't think of runnin'. That tangle, that web of feelings runnin' across one another: what I felt, what my poppa wanted, what Morrison was to me as a man on the one hand, as a slaveholder on the other. Those Southern men fightin', bleedin'. Not one in fifty of 'em ever owned a slave. One big tall man from Arkansas told me he never seen a colored man in his life till he joined up. I don't know, it was like a swamp with the word 'freedom' bitin', makin' me itch like a skeeter."

"So sooner or later you just naturally had to scratch," Samuels said.

"If it hadn't been for goin' up into Maryland, I don't know I ever would have. But we went up with A. P. Hill's division of Jackson's corps. We took Harper's Ferry. It was the fall of 1862. And word came we had to go across the river and on up to a place called Sharpsburg. That was on a mornin' in September, and we marched all day without more than two or three stops.

"There were clouds, but it didn't save us from the heat. Half the men started marchin' never made it up to Sharpsburg. Morrison had a little mare he found runnin' loose after the second Manassas, and he rode up and down the line tryin' to push the men harder. Faster, he would say, for the love of God faster. General Lee needs us up the road."

"He had that right," Samuels said. "It was Hill's division kept the war from being over that day."

Phillipe went on, mechanically, as if he were delivering an oral report to a superior.

"Then I fainted along the way. We had come across all kinds of rich food at the Ferry. It was a Union supply dump, and we ate like a pack of wolves. We hadn't had much for a month or so, and we ate smoked turkey and ham. We had pickles and anchovies. There was candied

fruit and a bakery full of fresh bread. I ate till it was a sin. When I
stopped bein' hungry, I kept right on eatin' in case we went another
couple months without. While they had the Union soldiers signin'
paroles, we finished stuffin', and formed up. Morrison had been usin'
his rank to save food for the colored people, the body-servants and
wagoneers."

"Have they got their fill?" Mo asked Phillipe.

"Sho', they've crammed their bellies so full the next time they hear
war, they'll think picnic."

Mo smiled. He had put a Union tunic on over the shredded rags of
the uniform he had brought from Shreveport. He had new Yankee
shoes, and a broad-brimmed black hat with the United States insignia
ripped off. "Here's a tinned lobster," he told Phillipe. "You get it
packed in your croker sack so we'll have it when we hit the road."

"O no, man," Phillipe groaned. "Not the road so soon. Ain't this
damn army got another division . . . "

"No division like the Light Division," Mo grinned. "Take on the
Yankees and the Prussians along with 'em. We got to go farther north.
They say McClellan's finally settled on a place where he'll fight. We got
to go before he thinks about it and changes his base out to Nevada
territory or something'."

Phillipe did not smile. "On and on. They won't quit. Youall ain't
gonna quit."

Mo shrugged. "Who the hell started it? Anytime they get hold of
themselves and decide to turn us loose and go on back North . . . "

"Maybe youall should turn us loose," Phillipe said dully.

Mo put his hands on his hips. His eyes narrowed. "That's the second
time you've said somethin' like that while we've been fightin'. What's
wrong with you? Have you turned into an abolitionist or something'?
Ain't you eatin' as good as I am? Have I shamed you?"

Phillipe shook his head. "Aw, no, you know not. Food's all right, no
shame. Except all the time you've got a collar on me."

Mo's eyes widened. "Collar?"

"You got a piece of legal paper with my name on it back home."

"I ain't never seen it."

"It's there. You know it. I know it."

Mo rubbed his finger around the sweatband of the captured hat. He
looked angry and embarrassed.

"I don't know nothin' of the kind. I just know you're a crazy nigger and your poppa would kick your ass if he heard you bellyachin' like a Boston schoolmarm. Hell, we may not even get home to see that paper."

"Aw . . ."

"Anyhow, what did I tell you before? Didn't I say I'd get Poppa to free you just as soon as we won this war and got on home? If you don't want to be my nigger, you can go anywhere you want. I can see you get free, but I can't make the eats be free after that. I can't give you no seven-league boots and a way with women. You ain't never gonna be satisfied. Free or bond, you got somethin' chewin' on you. Maybe it's 'cause you never had no mother since you were just a little thing."

Phillipe put the lobster in the sack along with some wine and tinned oysters. "I had as much mother as you ever had."

"That's so," Mo answered thoughtfully. "I reckon it's somethin' else."

Samuels fell back a few yards to check the stragglers. But the column was well up, and the rest of the noncommissioned officers were keeping it in motion.

Phillip had stopped talking by then. He was hunched over in his saddle and had not even noticed how the clouds were closing in again.

Samuels was pulling his waterproof free from his bedroll. "If it comes on hard, I reckon we could pull over and eat," he said. "If we march in the rain and then the sun comes back, we'll boil some of them. They haven't worn down enough leather or covered enough country to get used to marching this far."

"All right," Phillipe said. "Tell 'em to hold up in that patch of sweet gun up the road. No use waitin' till they're wet. If it's just a shower, we can march 'em on dry."

Samuels smiled. "There ain't a Sharpsburg up ahead."

Phillipe looked up from his saddle horn. "O no? You better wait till you get to Shreveport before you tell me what it ain't."

They ate with the rain scattering in light bursts overhead. But the trees were heavy with summer leaves, and only the runoff reached them.

"No worse than that damned leaky-roofed place in Pittsburg where Daddy raised us," Sergeant Samuels told Phillipe. "No more water on you, and a hell of a sight cleaner."

"Tell me how it was to grow up free," Phillipe asked suddenly. "How was it to wake up knowin' you could do any damn thing that crossed your mind?"

"No," Samuels said, expressionless. "You've already got steam up. You finish with yourself. You go on telling me how you got here. When we hit Shreveport, I'll buy you some beer and tell you all about being free. One beer ought to cover it."

Phillipe finished his hard biscuit and washed out his mouth with tepid water. The biscuit seemed dry and stale enough to use for a sponge.

"We marched four hours without but ten minutes' stop," Phillipe told Samuels. "Then I fell out. Just fell down in the road like a common drunk. I don't know, maybe it was the smoked turkey or the two loaves of raisin bread. Maybe it was the dust and heat on the road up out of Shepherdstown. But when I came to myself, Morrison was leanin' over me, and behind him on the road, common soldiers marchin' past sneered and pointed. 'Look at 'em,' one man said. 'That kid officer takes better care of his nigger than his horse.' 'Maybe he means to ride that darkie if his horse goes lame,' another one called out.

"Morrison looked over his shoulder at them, his face dark and angry. But he didn't say nothin'. He helped me up and held on to me. 'Let 'em talk,' he said. 'Let 'em talk. They know there's more of us goin' up this road than comin' back. It makes 'em say things.'

"Then, no matter how I tried to argue him out of it, he made me mount his horse and ride while he caught up with the men and marched with 'em."

Samuels pulled a slab of preserved beef apart slowly.

"Man treat you that good," he said, "seems like it would be hard not to care about him."

Phillipe looked up. "I loved him. I loved him that mornin', but that was the start anyhow. 'Cause as I rode, some of his men kept remarkin' about a nigger who rode while his master was on foot. 'I thought we was fightin' to keep that from comin' to pass,' one of 'em yelled out. 'Hell no,' one answered him. 'I'm fightin' to get 'em all on a horse just like him – and keep 'em ridin' North.'

"Maybe it was too many such things said all at the same time. Or maybe the ridin' North itself, knowin' that freedom was only a few score miles away in Pennsylvania. I don't know what it was, but I felt my heart grow cold against those men, and I felt it harden even against

Morrison. At first I thought, O God, I am sinnin' and you have got to turn my head from these thoughts. Let my mind not turn to evil ways and pay back love and kindness with deceit.

"But the nearer we came to Sharpsburg, the more I felt my heart goin' to stone. I couldn't look at Morrison marchin' in the dust beneath me. I could only hear the guns far off, like strange thunder where no clouds stood overhead, and I thought a mighty army was buyin' my freedom with its blood while the men marchin' below me there were hurryin' to raise the price higher and higher.

"So soon we could see smoke risin' over the fields and trees. We could even see the little toy cannon of the Union troops far off across the stream, droppin' shells into the Confederate lines.

"Before that, when I heard the sound of battle, it had been a terrible thing. It pressed on my spirit and drove me to pray. But this time it was different. The roar of cannon and rifle was the sound of a great bell booming out freedom and plenty for all this sad land's children. I began to think that in the dark of night I could cross over the little creek to the Union."

Then they arrived. Morrison took a handful of food from the saddle-bags. He smiled up at Phillipe.

"You stay back here out of trouble," he said. "Keep a close eye on this pony in case we have to get out of here in a hurry. If the Yankees bust through, maybe you could stop one and talk abolition with him. If you do, you better keep up your guard. I hear they ain't too serious about it."

He looked at his pistol and then, turning to join the regiment, he reached up and touched Phillipe's hand resting on the saddle horn. "You take care," he said. "I got to go kill Yankees."

For the rest of the long afternoon, Phillipe had rested in the shade of a tree beyond the battle area. He heard the Southerners cheer as Hill's division moved into place and pushed Burnside's corps to a halt. He heard the endless racket of musketry, the shrieks, the low boom of artillery. The wounded, walking and carried – some crawling – move past him to the medical tent to lie untended under wagons, to tear the grass in agony at the base of a shattered fence post

Then it was night. The sound of cannon had ceased, and only a rifle shot now and then broke the new silence. The distant sobbing of the wounded on either side of the Antietam creek banks, at the stone bridge, seemed as much part of the night sounds as the hum of insects, the brittle scratching of crickets. Phillipe, his stomach settled at last, raised his head to hear. It sounded to him as if both maimed armies were keening into the raw wind under a starless sky, as if the earth itself were crying for her children.

By then Phillipe was on his feet and moving. Not with a plan, not even with clear intention. But moving because he had to move, and heading north toward the battered stone bridge where Burnside had committed his corps that afternoon.

He walked quietly over the field and down a little ravine toward the creek. He passed clumps of bodies sprawled in the darkness like children's toys thrown aside. He came to the bridge.

On the other side of the creek, in a curve of land with a patch of oak clustered thick and dark around it, he could see a tiny campfire with a few men lying close by. He began to crawl across the bridge on all fours so he could be sure the men at the fire were Unions, and not an advance post of the Confederates. The bridge was strewn with bodies from artillery and rifle fire earlier, and he couldn't keep from retching as his hands slipped under him in pools of blood heavy and viscous as jelly. As Phillipe reached the far end of the bridge, he heard the solid metallic snap of a musket hammer. Before he could move forward or backward, a figure had moved from behind the stone rail at the bridge's end. Phillipe saw the gleam of a barrel pushed close to his face.

"All right, hand-and-knees, what are you?"

"I'm . . . "

"Talk up 'fore I pull this trigger and then look over what's left for myself. Are you a loyal man?"

"I . . . "

"All right, get on your feet and come on over to the fire. Don't walk too fast, and keep your hands out where I can see 'em."

They walked slowly toward the fire. Phillipe felt the sweat cold and clammy on his back. He was not afraid they would shoot him. It was another kind of fear, and there was no name for it.

Union soldiers lay around the fire like sacks of corn meal. The exhaustion on their faces was permanent – as if it were part of their flesh. Only when one or another of them turned under his waterproof blanket or, still sleeping, cried out at what he saw in dreams, could Phillipe distinguish them from the corpses scattered on either side of the creek and across the bridge.

"All right," the sentry said to him, "what did you come over for? Is the food all gone? Was your company commander a sonofabitch?"

A few of the men around the fire stirred and sat up at the sound of the sentry's voice. Their complexions matched the puffs of gray ash at the fire's edge.

"Come on over into the light, mister, and tell us why you sold out your rebel stock," one of the seated men called out. Phillipe stepped into the circle of the fire's light and tried to tell them about freedom, what he had been thinking about for so long.

"Hell," the man with the musket groaned. "More contraband. It's just another nigger."

"Yes," Samuels said softly. "That's the way it would have been. I worked around army posts, fed horses, slopped hogs, patched harness from the time I was a little boy trying to help feed the younger ones at home. If I had gone in and said, I want to be a soldier, they would have kicked me out into the yard. Then the war came and they needed bodies. To fill the ranks. Or to fill the graves."

"But I was over there," Phillipe said. "and there wasn't any turnin' back. So I moved on North with the army, and a colonel with red eyes and smellin' of brandy showed me how to enlist in a regiment of the United States."

Samuels was running a stem of grass between his teeth, staring out at the fading rain. "They signed me up one afternoon and gave me the rest of the day off and five dollars. The next morning I started my military duties. Currying cavalry mounts and shoveling out the stalls."

Phillip stood up and brushed off his trousers. "I know," he said. "It wasn't like I thought. There wasn't a thing in the men I joined that hadn't been in the men I left. Except none of the Unions wanted to own me, to work me. They didn't give a damn if I lived or died or just went up in smoke like a powder charge. They just looked through me. Bur they didn't think I was livestock."

Samuels shrugged. "Given the choice of being a horse or a vacant place in the air, I don't know you can choose."

"But we got to choose. We did choose."

"Just taking up space, being in one place at one time, is a kind of choice," Samuels said. "That doesn't mean you had any chance to do different. You did what seemed the least bad of a rotten lot."

Phillipe wiped perspiration from his forehead. The rain had not cooled the air, and it would still be a long, hot march. "I don't know," he said. "I don't even know if I started out to cross that bridge. I just got to walkin' when Morrison didn't show up by dark. I kept hearin' 'freedom, freedom' in my ears and walkin' on. And then I was over. I guess I started out lookin' for that freedom. I wanted something' better than love, knowin' there's nothin' better than love."

"Well," Samuels said, with finality, "you got it. You're free as a great big bird. You even got men under you, and the power of life and death over them."

"That's right," Phillip said, walking toward his mare. "I got it. Come on. Get the men on their feet. We got to move."

It was still cool under the tall trees that surrounded Amos Stevens' house, and the Union sentries (two again now that the town seemed to have gotten over Barney Wilkes' punishment) dozed on the porch like field hands and, like field hands, kept a corner of their napping minds ready for the sound of authority issuing from the house.

Amos Stevens and Sentell sat in the side yard with a pitcher of ice water between them on that same table dragged off the porch when it became evident that the sentries were there to stay.

"This is North Carolina tobacco," Amos said, pointing his pipe stem at Sentell. "Not well cured, but cut better than that damned hemp we used to get from Arkansas."

"The old ways," Sentell smiled. "Just get you a twist of good tobacco, and nothing has changed. I'm surprised you don't need at least the bourbon, too."

Amos made a depreciating gesture and chewed on his pipe stem again. "Virginia, Edward. It put smoke in my lungs, but it never set whiskey in my heart. The old gentleman, my father, was not much of a drinker. He believed that, as a great deal of liquor dulls the mind discernibly, even a little of it was likely to do damage you couldn't see."

"He loved his reason," Sentell said.

"He did that. I guess it's well he never lived to see Jefferson's country debauch that reason and seethe itself in blood."

"I expect the signs were clear enough."

Amos' expression turned serious. "And getting ready to be more so. Lodge's niggers will be here by the Fourth of July. The cavalry is sched-uled to move out within a week, and the niggers will be garrison. They and Lodge's staff people, and a few armorers and hostlers."

"He seems to want trouble worse than his government wanted peace. I'm afraid he's going to get it."

"Not yet," Amos said. "Not just yet. I mean to do some talking before anybody starts shooting. If I can keep all of them talking, maybe there won't be any shooting."

Sentell frowned. "I wish I could help you."

Amos touched his arm lightly. "I know. You should be doing the talking anyhow."

"I don't have a permit," Sentell said. "I didn't kill long enough. I didn't enjoy it enough."

Amos pulled his empty sleeve from behind him and leaned back in his chair. "Morrison enjoyed it. So help me God, I think the only thing in the war not to his liking was the outcome."

"Maybe he thinks he ought to feel that way. Most of them talk that way at Ramsey's and on Cleburne's porch. The more farms the Unions confiscate for taxes, the looser the talk gets. Every time a mule turns up lost, strayed, or stolen, they start cursing a little louder."

Amos shook his head. "We were at table last night. Morrison decided to accept Lodge's invitation to eat with him. I expect he felt ready. I think he wanted Lodge to try him."

"Well?"

"Not five minutes passed before Lodge was discussing the condition of that Union trooper so mysteriously beaten," Amos said. "Then it was the crime of Barney Wilkes. He couldn't turn loose of it. He kept watching Morrison the way a moccasin eyes a sparrow. He wanted something – anything. And that damned sottish tongueless captain of quartermasters, mouthing his food and staring at us through the tines of his fork. And that boy, what's his name? The lieutenant Lodge uses for an executive."

"That would be Raisor," Sentell smiled.

"Raisor?" Amos affirmed. "He looked as if someone had jammed a ramrod up his fanny. Turning his head from Lodge to Morrison, frowning, shaking his head. He looked like a puppet being handled by a lunatic. I think old Barney – what happened to Barney – disturbed him, but I'm not sure he knows it, or even knowing it, if he can imagine what to do before something worse happens. He's too soon out of West Point and too edgy about having missed the big circus. Everything makes him nervous. He liked to have driven me crazy, and me trying to follow what Morrison and that cold-eyed lantern-jawed Boston son-ofabitch were saying so I could head it off short of treason before witnesses."

Sentell crossed one booted leg over the other. "Lodge," he said dryly. "Lodge. When I saw him last across the Mississippi, he wasn't fighting."

"That would be right," Amos said. "He was tending supplies for Ord or one of the others."

"Best Morrison stay clear of him. I think he wants trouble. I think he really wants more killing."

Amos' eyebrows raised. "He can get it," he said. "Lodge knows something about Morrison and that trooper he whipped. And Morrison is almost ready to tease him about it. Almost but not quite. As if he were waiting for something. What do you think?"

Sentell's face darkened. "I don't know. I only think I know. When I know anything, I'll tell you."

"All right,' Amos said easily. "By the way, when are you bringing your friend out?"

"That's strange," Sentell said, still unsmiling. "He asked last night when he might have the pleasure."

"Anytime," Amos said. "I do all I have to do in the morning. Rye sees to the people who are staying on till next planting. I have a lot of time."

"I'll bring Bouvier tomorrow," Sentell told him. "I expect he'll charm away some of that time."

Then they turned, hearing a sound from the direction of the house. It was Morrison walking with that long stride and careful step that seemed an odd and unpredictable outcropping of the same blood that had shaped his father's features.

"You've gotten to creeping up on people like an Indian scout," Amos told him.

Mo did not smile, only acknowledging his father's remark and Sentell's nod with a brief movement of his own head so curt as to suggest he was in no mood for good humor – possibly not even for good manners.

"How's Barney Wilkes, Major?" he asked abruptly as he sat down.

"His fever is down but he's weak," Sentell told him. "He can't raise himself up for so much as a drink of water."

"Maybe I was wrong," Mo said slowly, his face still grim and set. "Maybe we should have taken the old man away from 'em."

"You wouldn't have made the corner," his father said. "There'd have shot youall into dog food."

314

"That's the way I figured it," Mo said. "But what else is there? Everybody dies."

"Most of them live first," Sentell said gently. "You've got a lot of life ahead of you."

"I'm afraid you may be right," Mo said. "I can see myself fifty whipped pointless years from now. Tellin' my kids how I fought the good fight. Then one of 'em will ask, If you fought so well, how come you're here? The good ones died. Some of the bad one too, but almost all the good ones."

"There's no virtue in being killed," Sentell told him.

Mo stared at Sentell. "I'm surprised to hear you say that, Major."

"What the hell is that remark supposed to mean?" Amos asked him.

"I hear the major fought well from Shiloh down to Vicksburg. Then I hear that he came home."

"You hear right," Sentell said. He returned Mo's stare coolly, his own eyes level and unblinking.

"Well," Mo said, "there was still fighting – and dying – after Vicksburg."

Amos was irritated. "Major Sentell had signed a parole."

"I heard that."

"Do you need an explanation of why he held to his word?"

"I don't know," Mo said. "I was raised to say things straight out. But I don't know what to say. There's a man's word, and that's worth something – used to be worth something. Then there's his country, his people. It seems like a man shouldn't put himself – even his honor – ahead of his own country."

"If a man can't think well of himself, hold himself and honor of supreme value, why in hell should he care about his country?" Amos asked angrily.

Mo shrugged unhappily. "I don't know. I guess all I can say is that I fought till there weren't any more bullets or food or even other men to fight beside. And if General Lee had said, We're gonna ride into the hills and keep on fightin', I'd have rode into the hills. I'd have lied or stole or shot women – whatever it took – to win that war."

Sentell spoke softly, no trace of irritation in his voice. "If you'd done all that, what would you have won?"

"My freedom," Mo shot back. "I'd be a free man maybe. Not a prisoner of war with a pack of Yankee gutter-sweepings marchin' down my streets."

"You'd be a slave to what you had done. You'd have kept the Yankees out of your streets by becoming a Yankee yourself."

Mo's eyes narrowed. "I don't like bein' a loser. I don't give a shit about philosophy, but I sure hate like hell to be a loser."

"You lost like a decent man," Amos put in.

"That may console you, Poppa. It don't take any edge off the Yankee bayonets out there on the porch."

"In time bayonets rust," Sentell said. "They rust and fall apart."

"So do men," Mo said. "Some men fall apart even before the deluge came."

Sentell rose to his feet easily. He stood as tall as Mo and heavier. His ruddy complexion was the least bit brighter than usual. "I think I'd best get back into down."

"Sit down, Edward," Amos said. "Morrison don't . . . "

"The major said he has to go, Poppa," Mo put in quietly.

"I'll see you tomorrow," Sentell told Amos.

"See you do," Amos called after him as Sentell walked up toward the house. "And don't forget to bring your friend."

Mo stretched his legs out in front of him and slumped in his chair. "You mean he's still got a friend around here?"

"You're goddamned right he does," Amos snapped. "I'd say every man in town who doesn't honor liars and practitioners of expediency is his friend."

"From what I hear, there must not be too many fellers like that left," Mo answered sardonically.

Amos paused a moment. "That's so," he said. "It's like you told us. Most of the good men are dead."

It was almost dark by then, and Amos and Mo sat a long while in silence. It was Mo who spoke finally.

"I expect I'll get married," he said matter-of-factly.

"All right," his father said from the shadows beside him.

"Is that all you have to say about it?"

"Did you want a blessing or an argument? You can have the blessing. Because saying you figure to marry is the first normal thing you've come up with since you got home."

"I'd rather have the argument than a sermon."

"What you'll get is a clout upside your head if you don't mend your manners. Or maybe more than that."

Mo shook his head irritably. "Don't talk like that, Poppa. It don't mean anything now"

"You're too old for dressing down?" Amos asked.

"That's right," Mo said. "That's right. I decide my own manners now."

"All right," Amos said, his voice soft and precise. "But not here. Not in my house. If you had spoken to me the way you addressed Sentell . . ."

" . . . you'd have called a Yankee guard off the porch."

"Goddamnit," Amos shouted, shattering the quiet of the darkened yard, "who's been feeding you that pap?"

"I hear what there is to hear. I didn't think much of it at first, but . . ."

"Then you lost your frail wits and took to believing that gin-mill yarn that Sentell went yellow?"

"He stopped fightin'," Mo burst out defensively. "He came home from that goddamned sellout at Vicksburg and never showed his ass outside town again."

"He was on parole," Amos said, as if that were all that needed saying.

"Parole," Mo spat. "Hell, half the Unions at Petersburg had been paroled and broken it one time or another. A parole wasn't worth the paper they printed it on."

"So you expected Sentell to act like a Yankee?"

"I expect an officer to find himself a command and go on fighting," Mo said, still angry, feeling his certainty diminishing.

"He gave his word" Amos said. "He gave his word because the alternative was a prison camp and at least back here he could see to planting and picking and try to get a little cotton into the market."

"So he kept his word to the Yankees and broke faith with his people."

"A man can't break faith with anyone by being true to himself."

"Jesus," Mo groaned, "right out of Shakespeare. Next you'll be quotin' Thomas Malory or Walter Scott. That's dead. It's all dead. A man's word is just like a hammer or an awl. If it's in a man's interest to keep his word, he keeps it. If he has to lie, he does it. For his people. If a man will die for his people, he'll sure tell a lie for 'em. That honor you talk about is as dead as the Southern Confederacy."

Amos squinted, but the darkness was complete now and he could only see the outline of his son's head above the black shrubs, against the lighter sky. "But Sentell had no part in killing either one of them," he said.

Then they were silent again, each still shaken by the exchange, not only because of what had been said, but because of what had almost been said, and because nothing like it had ever passed between them before. After what seemed a long while, they heard Rye's voice from the house calling supper, and still wordless, rose and walked toward the faint kitchen light side by side, but not together.

X

3 JULY 1865 — Lieutenant Stanton Raisor was sweating. The moisture crept downward through his hair and soaked his high collar (purposely tight: it had been the style at The Point to have one's uniform tailored closely, so closely that the faintest departure from military posture caused the uniform itself to correct, by pinch and bind, the failing human material it contained). When he moved too quickly, the trees and even the streets themselves seemed to waver and shake under the late afternoon sun.

At a bare desk in City Hall the lieutenant studied a sheaf of papers covered with a precise crabbed hand. The lieutenant was planning a parade.

Passing by him, going into one or another of the musty, poorly lit offices on either side of the main hall, were soldiers doing the work of clerks (there had not yet arrived from Memphis or New Orleans enough civilian paper-fumblers to handle the sudden and overwhelming crush of warrants and attachments, evictions and processes that Pony Mueller and his colleagues had kicked into the air like dust behind a terrified horse. In and out of the offices moved Negroes, laughing or open-mouthed, frequently on no business at all except to see City Hall for the first time as possessors – even possible future tenants – of this piece of public property that their sweat had helped to build. Then there was the marshal – Andrew Tocsin, a thin sallow-faced man with skin trouble and a plug hat that would have seemed comic property even on the pomaded head of a Louisville sport. The marshal, possessed of title and office and even a pair of purposeless flunkies to copy orders and smile when smiles seemed called for, hovered around Raisor's desk – not because he expected the lieutenant to give him orders to be copied or even because he felt called upon to ingratiate himself with Raisor, who for all his status of executive officer remained a flunky himself not so much by choice or tendency as by nature of the chain of command. The marshal walked past Raisor's desk because, fresh from a citadel of Union strength, a town long ago reduced to order by some other Lodge, he could not escape the kind of apprehension a man always feels when he is pulled from just outside a lion's cage into the cage itself. It is not that he is necessarily closer to the lion: it is simply that the relationship has been changed, and new relationships of such kind always merit study – no matter how adept the lion tamer who has dragged you into the cage; no matter how toothless the lion may seem.

"Is there . . . ?" the marshal asked Raisor.

"No," the lieutenant told him. "No and no. If I need a runner, I've got one. If I need advice, I'll ride out and see the colonel."

"You don't need to . . . ," the marshal began sadly, his nameless uncertainties and his newfound dignity warring with one another.

"What I need is quiet," Raisor answered shortly.

The marshal turned away with what an uncritical mind might have called dignity – or possibly the stiff-legged apparent hauteur of a man trying to find out which side of the bars the lion is on – and began his chief occupation: walking into each office once or twice an hour to see if things were going smoothly. Raisor went back to work.

But the work went badly. He was trying to determine a route which would permit the new Negro troops a maximum of exposure to Shreveport's citizens, and yet (and this his private concern: not part of Lodge's order, which had simply provided for the colored soldiers to be revealed at length and in detail to those whom the troops would be handling) at the same time be the shortest and least tiring on men who had been marching off and on for over three weeks. But he could not concentrate on the street plan before him. He thought of the Negroes marching down from Arkansas. He thought of Lodge's cold single-minded determination to use them as a kind of personal military arm.

"Let the Negroes do their duty," he had told the lieutenant. "There is still rebel sentiment here, mark you. There are a hundred – no, a thousand like that filthy old man we whipped, who would insult the flag, or like that other human offal who beat young Grubbs and is still smiling about it somewhere – possibly somewhere nearby. But the Negroes will solve the problem for us. Sooner or later, now or a month from now, a Negro soldier will do something, commit an act or only say the wrong word, and the rebels – those with rebel hearts – will try to treat that Negro as they used to. Then we snap off the weed close to the ground. Not the root, mind you. The root will be a long time dying, and to kill it in short of that time we would have to exterminate the whole citizenry. But that Negro, whatever he says or does, will rouse a few of them, and we can take their measure. Then another Negro at another time, and a few more will try their hand. By the time we have been here a year all the brave traitors – the few left from battle – will be taken care of, and this place will be as tranquil as Boston Common. Since men like Stevens will not help us, we must find out our own best shifts."

A consummation devoutly to be hopes, Lieutenant Raisor thought. But he had no faith in Lodge's notion, no hope at all that it would work – and charity only for the colored troops who, without knowing, were to come into town not only as guards, wardens – whatever occupation troops generally are – but as ignorant *agents provacateurs* as well with their commander's stated anticipation that they would do something certain to bring the already critical temperature of the town to a full boil.

But Lodge had answered Raisor's question before the lieutenant had even asked it.

"Soldiers are meant to be used. We are used. McClellan was used until he was unfit for further use. Pope and Burnside and Hooker were used, and each one turned out to be a blunt hatchet. The soldier's duty, the soldier's glory, is to be used. And this town, this stifling pestilential town, is full of enemies. To use a soldier – or a dozen soldiers – in order to smoke out incipient treason is clearly within the bounds of my duty and theirs. And above that, what greater tribute can we offer these Negroes than a chance to trap the very men who have done them harm in the past and would damage them again, given the chance?"

Raisor had not answered. Lately, since Barney Wilkes' whipping, he had said as little as he could to Lodge. Not because of the intrinsic cruelty of method that Lodge seemed to admire. The lieutenant, in theory at least, was used to violence and its uses. But not to Lodge's sort: you did not beat imbeciles or children or women, because it was uncivilized to do so. And, more to the point, it was certain to enrage the enemy and make him resist even more bitterly.

There was more to Raisor's gradual disenchantment. It had started in front of Cleburne's porch the first week of June, the day he himself had come so near to renewing the war locally by a single act of bad judgment.

But that Sentell had stopped it, the lieutenant mused, staring at the street plan before him without seeing it. He stopped it even knowing that some of them would call it collaboration. Not for me or the men I was supposed to be leading – but not just for those men on the porch, who pass him on the street without a word either. For decency. Because they've tried killing and he helped, and they had already tried arguing and he probably helped, and none of it was any good, and he wants it stopped, so when I was ready to start it up by accident – all right, by stupidity – again, he walked over and pulled the fuse and stepped on it.

"You say somethin', Lieutenant?" one of the passing soldier-clerks asked him. Raisor's head jerked up. His eyes narrowed, and he shook his head, not even glancing at the man.

"But not the colonel," he whispered. "Not him."

"Sir?" the clerk asked.

"Nothing. Go on," Raisor told him.

Certainly, he thought, onto an idea now, feeling the tug of it like channel water on a swimmer nearing the middle of a river. Certainly. He wants it to go on. Wants there to be killing. Wants the confiscation and the rest to go on until these people decide they might as well die fighting as starving. He didn't get enough of it at Vicksburg. He wants more of it, and he'll . . .

But one of the troopers was at his elbow. "Column from the north coming up on the far side of the river, sir."

"Is it the garrison relief?"

"Well," the trooper grinned, "it's a pack of niggers in blue suits toting rifles."

"Raisor stiffened. "Those are United States troops," he grated. "Which side did you fight on?"

The trooper blushed sullenly. "I *thought* I was fighting to preserve a white man's union," he growled.

"Keep your thoughts to yourself. Mount up and go over there. Tell the officer in charge we'll ferry them over in the morning. Tell him the colonel says he can come over himself tonight and leave a dependable noncommissioned officer in charge."

The trooper turned away, his hand grazing his cap in something like a salute. Raisor let it go and tried to go back to work.

He had been staring at the street map for what seemed a long time when a shadow fell across the desk. He paid no attention until the shadow cleared its throat.

"I need me a couple of troopers," Pony Mueller said.

"Troopers?" Raisor said, his mind still on the Negroes and what Lodge meant to do with them.

"Yeah, I need me a couple."

"What are into that the army will have to get you out of?"

"I ain't *into* nothing," Pony answered, saddened by Raisor's innuendo. "I got to go take over a big piece of land outside town tomorrow, and the marshal says he won't even saddle up by himself."

"What's wrong with the marshal?"

"He says it's too much land. He says if we set foot on it, all the planters in the parish will come after us. He says he didn't come here to commit suicide. He says he wants troopers."

"Where are you going?" Raisor asked him.

"Sentell's place. I got him on the list. He owes and he ain't paid. He ain't even come by since that delinquent tax list was posted. I'm going out to put a seal on the place. It belongs to the government at midnight tomorrow night."

"He has a day yet."

"He's had two weeks," Pony said. "And he ain't even come by the tax office to say he ain't got the money and could he please have some time. So I want a couple of troopers."

"Take a couple from the stable," Raisor told him. "Take any who'll go."

"I'll need an order," Pony said dubiously.

"Show them your battle wounds," Raisor said, turning back to his papers, and leaving Pony simply a shadow on the bare desk again.

Almost before Pony Mueller had left City Hall, the lieutenant hurried through his parade plan, paying little attention to the easiest or the quickest route. Then, buckling on his pistol belt, he strode out past the patch of green lawn with its lonely flag pole, past the empty bench, and down Texas toward Travis street, named decades before for a hero of the Alamo.

"How long, O Lord," Samuels groaned. "My butt hasn't got any feeling left in it. I can't remember when this damned horse wasn't part of me."

"No far," Phillipe said wearily. "See that line of trees up there? On what looks like a ridge?"

"Sure," Samuels answered. "I've seen nothing but trees for two weeks. Are you sure there are any towns down here? God, this South."

"That ain't a ridge," Phillipe went on. "It's the start of the bluffs. On the other side is the river."

As they rode on, the trees became cottonwood and magnolia and even a few cypress rather than scrub pine and oak, the soil seemed lighter, and the earth was heavy in Johnson grass and waist-high in a variety of weeds.

"It thickens up as you get near the water," Phillipe was saying. "Look. That's sand mixed with clay underfoot now."

They topped the low ridge suddenly, precipitately, and they were at the river.

The water level had begun to recede, leaving exposed long flats of white sand covered with brush and pieces of log and driftwood. A gum tree had fallen when spring's high water undercut the bank beneath, and now its roots stood tilted wildly skyward, its stripped leafless branches resting like a bridge between the bluffs and the water's edge. The river itself was dark, a reddish-brown color, and from where they watched, its current was so slow that only by following a piece of floating log or the low-lying carcass of a tree bobbing up and down could they tell that the river was moving at all.

A Negro corporal had broken ranks and pulled off his boots. "Whut river dat?" he asked Samuels. "It ain't de Mississip. It ain't Old Man."

"It goes to the Mississippi," Phillipe said. "It's the Red. Comes down to make the border between Texas and the Indian Territory. Goes down to join the Mississippi above Baton Rouge."

"Never seed it. Don' know it. How much mo' we got to walk?"

Samuels dismounted. "Get back with the rest. We're stopping here."

"How much mo' . . . ?"

Phillipe drew a deep breath. "Not much," he said, his eyes still on the flat deceptive plane of the water's surface. "It's already down some. Every spring it comes up to make a commotion and push folks around. But after Independence Day it mostly loses water from upstream and falls. By August a man can wade across."

The corporal wagged his head. "Ain' gone try wadin' dat river, suh. Where de ferry?"

"Down south and west some," Phillipe said. "There's still a piece of trail along here. Not road, but where weeds are broke down and the wagons will pull."

The column began moving down the solid ground above the riverbank. They rounded one final sweeping curve in the river, and saw on the opposite side a huddle of buildings and a long wharf. Farther down, on a rising bluff, Phillipe could see the remains of earthworks built to guard the city from Union gunboats.

"All right," he called back to the sweating, staggering men, who had begun to drop rifles and knapsacks and fall beside them on the sandy ground. "That's Shreveport. That's where youall are goin'. Take a look, 'cause it's a hard town and it won't look fine and amiable once you cross over. On the other side, it's hard."

"Won't stay hard long," somebody bawled out. "Reckon we got some softenin' here."

The rest laughed while Phillipe climbed down from his saddle and gathered the noncommissioned officers together."

"Just settle down," Phillipe told them. "We wait till somebody comes. Youall let your men rest. Let 'em cook if they want, let 'em bathe in one of those pools where the river left some water when it fell. But keep 'em together. We could move this afternoon. Or maybe tonight."

Samuels was already stretched out. "Man," he said, "I don't care how bad they are over there. I'd rather fight Forrest's whole cavalry than march another half a mile."

"If I could walk instead of fight, I reckon I'd walk," Phillipe said. "I want to settle down here and raise things. Corn, beans, field peas. Maybe some hogs. And cotton to sell."

"Could you use a hand?"

"What?"

Samuels shrugged. "My time is up. If I don't sign on for another time around, I'll be a free man tomorrow."

Phillipe reached across and caught Samuels' arm. "You mean you'd like to get some land down here with me? You want to work a farm?"

"There's nothing up in Pennsylvania but mines and more horse stalls to sweep out. If I have to shovel horse turds, I'd like for it to be my own horse."

Phillipe sat back. "If I had a partner, my poppa wouldn't have to work hard. He could just watch the crops growin'."

"If he comes."

But Phillipe was staring across the river at the miniature houses behind which the sun was falling slowly, setting the distant trees afire, coloring the whole skyline a deepening red.

"It's been a long trip," he said abstractedly. "I remember how we used to sit like this and look west toward Vicksburg. There wasn't a river between us – just a line of those graybacks who could hit a pie pan at two hundred yards. But the sun would set behind the town, and every evenin' somebody would say, 'It's on fire. Rebels all burnin'. Johnnhy-Reb, Johnnhy-Reb, fly away home. Your house is on fire.'"

"Your children will burn?"

Phillipe turned back to Samuels. "I never heard anybody say that. I forgot that part of the song."

"I don't reckon the rebs have."

"No," Phillipe said slowly. "They don't forget. They may not ever forget. You're from the North. You don't know what kind of men these are. I lived with 'em, and I fought 'em. I know what they can do."

"Vicksburg," Samuels said. "We all heard about it. About the fever, and that damned silly canal Grant tried. About the massacre when Sherman tried to get in from north of the town. How bad was it?"

"They sent a regiment of us," Phillipe said. "Not to fight. Not then. Then white men fought and niggers dug holes in the ground. Then set up to diggin' mines. They had us burrowin' like moles toward the rebel lines to plant powder charges. I remember thinkin' how different that was from the way Southerners fought. I thought of how Morrison wouldn't eat at the same table with a rebel officer who had planted armed shells along a road on the retreat up the Virginia peninsula before Seven Pines. He told that officer there was a difference between war and assassination, and that a man who didn't know the difference wasn't fit company at table for a man who did. Shootin' from ambush, mistreating' prisoners of war, makin' things harder than need be on women and children and old folks – Morrison called all that poor work not worthy of a gentleman."

Samuels smiled. "That was early in war," he said softly. "I wonder if he finished thinking the same way."

Phillipe's mouth twisted. "No," he said. "I don't reckon. After Sherman, after all of it, I reckon he wishes he'd helped plant those shells and shot some prisoners, too."

"I guess you end up doing what you have to do."

"Anyhow," Phillipe went on, "we planted their powder for 'em, got a couple of men killed with cave-ins, but got it done, so far as anybody could tell, without the rebels knowin'. So they promoted me to sergeant for what I'd got done, and then they told us as a reward for good diggin', they were going to let us lead the assault when the mine went off. Most of the colored men were proud to be fightin' because it was a freeman's work. But some of 'em thought another way."

"You can count on it. They gone send us where it's hot. They gone get they money's worth outta every black skin they roust out an' put a uniform on," one of the Negro soldier had said.

"Shut up," Phillip told him. "Suppose you die tomorrow? If you're gonna die, you're gonna die. Tomorrow they're gonna give you a chance to die for yourself, for your people. If you live, you'll get cut down in a whorehouse with a belly full of cheap whiskey and your pants still wet from some no-good woman. What have you got to do so important you can't die tomorrow?"

"Leave off him, Croneyshiel'," another said. "What he say, it's a fact. When it lookin' good, they get 'em a white regiment to march on in like a parade. But when it dirty and ugly and killin', they lets us take the honor. I don't need no honor. I don't need much more army neither. Least over in Georgia they wasn't nobody achin' and prayin' in his bed for to get your head in his gunsights."

"Yeah," the first soldier said, "and what if all your mine stuff don't put them Johnny Rebs into the coffin business? What if it don't even slow 'em up none? What youall think happens to a black man captured over there?"

The third soldier lit his pipe and spiraled the match into a puddle between his shoes. He went on looking at the dirty water. "I hear you don't have to worry none about that. I hear it's kill the niggers, spare the whites."

"Shame," Phillip snorted. "It's a goddamn shame youall got losin' and surrender on your minds. What's the matter if they don't take prisoners? Men chargin' a fort or a works ain't goin' over to surrender. Youall are goin' to fight, to take the rebs' surrender. Think like men." Phillipe watched the corporal making a small fire for him. "We got us a rabbit for youall," the corporal told Samuels. "Dey catchin' rabbits all over here. Like shootin' fish in a barrel."

As the corporal moved back to the fire, Phillipe began talking again.

"So we waited. Waited till the generals thought fit to blow the mine. But they waited too long. Because between the time we finished up and the time they gave the word, the Southerners had found us out. One way or another, they had found us out. And they were ready."

"Traitor?" Samuels asked.

"I don't know. It could have been. We had a few go over at night. But they probably heard us. It didn't make any difference how they knew. But a lot of men ate an early breakfast that day and laid out dead before nightfall.

"The blast went like we planned, and a whole section of the rebel works disappeared in smoke and dust with pieces of rubble flyin' high in the air and fallin' back as far away as where we lay waitin' to go forward. It was a terrible sight."

And for a moment he was glad that Morrison was in Virginia instead of Mississippi (or was he in Maryland, heading for Pennsylvania that day?) and sorry for the mine and the men who would die from it. Afterward it seemed to him that he had prayed for the first time since he rode north with Morrison toward Sharpsburg, saying, Lord God, make me treasure this freedom and do no shame in this freedom, remembering the blood it has cost on both sides.

Then he raised his head to see a tall column of dark smoke and dust, to hear in the echo of its roar the order to advance beside some Indiana men. A young officer near Phillipe, a white man commanding his company, shook his head and muttered as they strode forward through the smoke.

"If the mine did them so much damage, where are the bodies? I see all kind of rubbish, but where are the dead and injured?"

"Maybe the blast blew them all to pieces," Phillipe coughed, trying to keep up, his rifle heavy and cold in his hands.

The white captain shook his head and fingered his beard thoughtfully. "No," he said as they passed through the grassless wasteland between the Union and Confederate lines. "No, there are always bodies. Even a light artillery duel catches some of them. Look ahead. Nothing but dirt and junk. Do you hear anyone moaning or screaming? We're in for it."

The captain was right. Ten minutes later he was dead right. They crossed the parched ground toward the dissolving pillar of smoke that guided them into the breach in the Southern lines. They climbed over the freshly turned earth and some of them managed to skirt the edge of the deep pit hollowed out by their powder. On the far side of the crater they found another wall of dirt built up in a long semi-circle. Phillipe wondered about it, but there were men behind him pushing, and he shouted to his own troops to get past the hole and on to the next line of works.

"You want some of this coffee?" Samuels asked Phillipe again.

"Huh?"

"I'm not going to hold it all day."

"Thanks," Phillipe said. "My mind was somewhere else."

"I know where your mind was. You said how terrible that blast in the rebel lines was. Then you just went on staring out over the water with your mouth open. It must have been bad."

The corporal carried two long sticks over to them. On each a half rabbit was cooked and dripping hot juice. "You gone like dis," he grinned at Phillipe. "Beats dat tacky-bread an' bully beef. Lookie dat gravy runnin' off."

"Thanks," Phillipe said. "See everybody has some."

Samuels ate slowly, chewing each bite of meat for a long time. "He's right. It tastes like chicken."

"You never had rabbit before?"

"Not that I remember. Not many in Philadelphia."

"Lord," Phillipe said, finishing his own meat and wiping his hands on the grass.

"Go on about Vicksburg," Samuels said. "Looks like we've got plenty of time."

Phillipe took a pipe from his saddlebags and filled it with chopped leaf. He walked over to the fire, tamping the tobacco down. The corporal handed him a burning splinter and he walked back over to Samuels.

"I remember an officer of the Indiana troops had gone down into that pit and got himself mired on horseback. At the bottom it was soft and damp, and that horse was kickin' and tryin' to get a foothold, but it kept goin' in worse, and the officer didn't seem to have sense enough to get off and pull or call a couple of his men to help. There was a bunch of Indiana men down in the hole and comin' up the inside of it. Because there wasn't room enough for all of us to get into the rebel works so some people had to go into the pit and back out.

"So finally that Indiana officer got smart and left his horse and got to formin' us up to go over the second line of works before the rebels could get ready. There was already some rifle fire, and men were fallin' where they had climbed up on top of the old works to either side of the crater. Somebody near me pointed up there and said, 'Thank God for them white men. They got to carry Old Glory out ahead.'

"I turned to that lowlife and was sayin', 'Shut up, it should be one of us with the flag,' when everything stopped. I mean it was like at home in the evenin' when Morrison was whittlin' a Colt's pistol out of a piece of pine and I was readin' a book and Poppa or Mr. Stevens had said, 'Time for bed,' and we paid no attention and one of 'em came in without us even seein' and pinched out the candle or covered the lamp. It was morning, and I was standin' one minute in that dawn light, and then it was dark. I was fallin' a long way with my own voice in my ears sayin' *flag flag flag* over and over, and the fallin' was floatin' and my voice echoed as if I was speakin' low in a cavern somewhere, and slow circles of light turned and turned before my eyes though I don't know if my eyes were open or closed and the colors were changin' in the circles while they went faster and faster. And the echo went faster: *flag flag flag flag flag flag.*

"Until the circles all came together and made one circle that was the sun far off and hazy with smoky blue clouds moving swiftly across it, and the echo was one long roar from somewhere above me. I heard a lot of smaller sounds under the big one, and I tried to get to my feet or at least my knees, but I was pinned down, and while I shook my head to clear it I recognized the little sounds were screams, and the screams were coming from a man whose body was twisted and trapped under mine. He was screamin' in my ear. I turned to see him and help him if I could, but there wasn't nothin' to do because his face was gone, and all that you could see was a wet red plaster image of a head with pink and yellow where the mouth and teeth should have been, and no eyes or hair. And blood bubblin' up with the screams like water boilin' up in a teakettle. It got dark again for a moment or two, and when I came to myself the man had stopped, and I remember thinkin', before I managed to get free from the other dead men on top of me, that I had fainted like at Sharpsburg and was ashamed, and thinkin' that the dead man beneath me was so torn to pieces by shot that I couldn't tell if he was colored or a white man. Or even whether he was a rebel or a Yankee.

"After I was free of the bodies, I tried to get my bearings. I had been knocked into the crater by a blast, and now I was climbing the inside of the crater nearest the rebel line. I thought they must have counter-mined against us. But when I got to the edge and looked out, I could see the muzzles of cannon. All along the rim of that strange inner line was cannon and riflemen, and what had knocked me into the pit was an artillery salvo.

"By then it was over. I don't know how long it had lasted, but it had torn our assault to pieces, and left hundreds of men dead or dying between our lines and the crater. And for the handful still alive, there was no way out. Only the side of the crater nearest the rebels was sheltered, and when the artillery stopped, there was still rifle fire and nobody could pass through it and live."

There were other men from his regiment down in the crater with Phillipe. The officers were dead or missing, and he could see no white soldiers alive except for a few twisting and writhing in agony who would not live to reach a dressing station.

Then the Confederates were there. Phillipe was feeling his head care-fully and trying to tie a handkerchief over a long cut above his eyes, when he saw the dirty unshaven figures looming at the edge of the crater. They looked even more disreputable, more wolf-like, than those rebels he had seen a year before at Sharpsburg.

"Jesus, Son of God," one of the Negroes cried out. "Comes de sword of vengeance."

"Shut up," Phillipe said loudly enough for all of them to hear. "Youall are soldiers."

But the man who had called out was squirming down into the hash of mud and corpses at the bottom of the crater, and some of the others, eyes rolling, mouths open as if there were no air, looked ready to bolt.

"If you move, youall are done for. Stay where you are."

"Praise Jesus Christ," one of them sobbed.

The Southerners were all around the pit. One or two of them stood immobile in amazement when they saw the Negroes. A few cursed and raised their rifles, and Phillipe could feel the chill of fresh perspiration on his neck, down his back. One tall redheaded scarecrow called out for an officer, and the hatred in his face, coupled with his beard and his heavy breathing, made him look like a demon from hell.

"Lord," Phillipe whispered under his breath, "take my soul and for-give my lies and transgressions. Let my poppa know I love . . ."

Then some officer arrived. One of them, a tall man with dark hair touched by gray, deep-set eyes, beardless and erect, seemed familiar, but the cut above his eye, the heat, the confusion, made Phillipe's head spin, and the Southern soldiers' way of fingering their triggers as they stared down into the crater kept him from studying the officer carefully.

The redheaded man argued to shoot them there. But the officer shook his head and talked to another huge Confederate major with a saber. Finally the second officer ordered them out of the crater. Phillipe climbed slowly to his feet, his legs trembling, wondering if he would ever reach solid ground alive.

"I started up," Phillipe told Samuels. "Then I heard that man who had tried to dig him a hideout. The one who was shot bad and prayin' while the rebels gathered around. He was beggin' for help. But the rest of them just kept their eyes on those rebel white men and went on climbin' like they hadn't heard anything. I called out and told 'em to help me with the man down at the bottom. One of 'em sneered and said, 'Big Sarge, you just a nigger again like the rest of us, an' I hear the real boss callin'.'"

"Goddamn," Samuels said.

"I was ashamed for all of us. Because the freedom had come, and it hadn't done anything for those men, and when a rebel yelled at 'em, they left their own and went back to slave ways right off."

"That's hard," Samuels said, shaking his head.

"So I called out to that redheaded rebel soldier up on the edge of the hole. I said, 'Johnny Reb, if any man comes out of this pit before the wounded are helped, I wish you'd shoot him.'"

"That's it," Samuels laughed. "That's right. One of those rebels was worth ten like that trash you had in the crater with you."

"Lord," Phillipe went on. "When I said it, I like to have fallen backwards myself. That rebel stared down at me, and his rifle came up, and I thought sure to God he was goin' to shoot me right there, never mind what his officer wanted. But he just cleared his throat and told the other colored men to get back down and help with that man, that they were still in the army.

"Then, as I climbed out of that damned hole and got to my feet, I recognized the officer who told the soldier to make us prisoners. It was Mister Sentell of Shreveport, an old friend of Amos Stevens, a man I had known since I was a little boy and came up to Shreveport. But as I passed by him, he had just finished talkin' to the other officer, and he was starin' off across the gap in the rebel works, at the piles of dead men and dying sprawled far out into the open ground between the crater and our lines, and he paid no attention to me. And that was the end of it."

"End?" Samuels said quizzically. "Seems like that would've just been the start. How did they treat you?"

Phillipe laughed without humor. "Hell," he said, "they treated us just like Unions had done most of the time. They set us to diggin' and had white men overseein' us. They worked us and fed us and chained us up at night. Except for the chain, and for knowin' I was a piece of meat with a price again, it wasn't much different. Anyhow, we didn't stay long. When Vicksburg surrendered, they put us on a transport right off and sent us up to Memphis. After that it was better."

By then the sun was gone, but the sky was still light and the clouds, golden, gray and purple, lay spread over the distant town beyond the river like a patchwork quilt.

"I guess you know . . . ," Samuels began. But then they heard voices down by the water, and Phillipe rose to his feet and saw a small boat tied to some brush, and a white Union trooper climbing out of it. Phillipe and Samuels walked down the slope toward the river.

The trooper was lighting a cigar as Phillipe reached him. He made no sign of seeing Phillipe's epaulets, recognizing his rank. He looked at the colored soldiers who had begun gathering around with tolerant amusement in his eyes.

"Colonel Lodge's compliments," he drawled. "You're supposed to camp right along here till tomorrow morning. About seven or seven-thirty, they'll start ferrying you over."

"Camp here?" Phillipe frowned.

"Yeah," the Union trooper grinned. "Colonel wants you fresh for tomorrow. It's Independence Day and the colonel means to have a parade."

"Why can't we go on over and . . . "

"No," the trooper cut Phillipe off, his grin wide and clearly insulting. "No, because he wants to make the parade a big thing, don't you see? It's gonna be his Fourth of July present for the rebs. You're going to be the surprise. Any messages for the colonel . . . sir?"

"No, nothing," Phillipe barked. "Get back over there. Tell him orders received."

Down below, the river inched by, its channel obscured and uncertain, its waters spreading darkly, darkly spreading to join the long shadows and the unalloyed night that fell from above, rose from the river itself. It struck Phillipe with sudden clarity how much wider the Red River was than Antietam Creek. It seemed much wider than he remembered.

It had been less than an hour after Sentell had returned from Amos Stevens'. He had looked in on Barney Wilkes and found his mother covering the old man with a worn blanket.

"He hasn't any fever," she said. "I think we can let him go back to Mr. Ripinski tomorrow. He wants to go back. He says young Isaac misses him. They fish when Barney has no work, when he's all right. Do you think he'll be safe on the street?"

"I think so," Sentell told her. "Lodge has used him up. There wouldn't be any point in going after him again – unless he misuses another flag."

He mother frowned. "I think Colonel Lodge must be a wholly bad man. Why do you suppose he hates us so? Enough to injure a crazy old man."

"I expect he hates rebels, disorder, treason. More than that, I expect he hates us for what we are, for what we believe and admire. He really shouldn't trouble himself."

"What do you mean?" his mother asked.

"I don't think we'll be these things he hates for long. I expect we'll change. I think if he gives us time, we'll become something he can understand."

Before they could speak further, they heard three short, clear knocks at the door, then silence. After a brief moment, three more.

When he opened the door, Sentell saw the glint of gold epaulets catching the foyer's light and throwing it back in his eyes, and he thought Lodge had decided to round them all up: Amos, Morrison, the Nortons. Or perhaps, still smarting from the beating of his trooper and the shaming of his flag, Lodge had kept them all under surveillance and had seen Bouvier. But the voice quelled his imagination.

"Major . . . Major . . . Sentell, I wonder if I might speak to you?"

"Of course," Sentell said without even wondering what Lodge's Lieutenant Raisor might want. "Come in."

So he was sitting, ill at ease, on the edge of the same chair that Bouvier had used the evening before. He was so obviously young. Not young simply in the meaningless chronology of years, but young beyond any correlation of age. It was still important to him that all the details and amenities of his profession be carried out scrupulously. And he was troubled concerning the propriety of this visit.

"What can I do for you, Lieutenant?" Sentell asked him.

"Do for me?" he repeated, licking his lips, trying to find something to do with his hands. "Nothing for me. I came to . . . I mean I heard about your parole. I heard about your refusing to fight against your country even when they . . . It required courage to stand for the right, and honest men shouldn't have to suffer. Because now the country needs honest men. Especially here in this place. So I can about your land."

"I think someone had misled you," Sentell told him quietly. "I didn't fight after Vicksburg because I had given my word not to fight until I was exchanged. I was never exchanged."

"Yes," the lieutenant said eagerly, shifting still further on the edge of his chair. "I understand. You gave your word to the United States, so you . . . "

Sentell shook his head. "I must be saying it badly. If I had not made that promise, I would have been armed and waiting for you on the outskirts of town. At the very best, I would have stepped off Cleburne's porch that day just to get out of the line of fire while Norton and Hornsby and the rest cut you to pieces."

"But even so, you signed that parole to the United States, your country."

"*Your* country," Sentell said, suddenly angry. "*Your* country; not mine. The only thing on that sheet of paper that held the slightest significance for me was my signature. I was bound by it. I would have been no less nor more bound had the paper been a promise to take Wilkes Booth's part in doing away with Lincoln."

Raisor eyes widened. "I thought," he said loudly, accusingly, "I thought out of this nest of rebels that you . . . "

"Were an honest and upright man," Sentell finished.

"Yes," he said, still angry, still off-balance and substituting Lodge's dicta for his own thought. "I thought you had some sort of principles." His face was still open, still that of a boy whose spiritual credentials had been offered and rejected. Crude vicious rebels he understood. Ignorant slave-killers and venal small-goods peddlers he grasped with ease. But a well-mannered, more or less respectable traitor was still outside his ken. It would be a while before he could sneer at soft-spoken rebels as easily as the disreputable kind one found in prison camps or in the blasted streets of defeated towns.

"I came here to do you a favor," he said with exaggerated dignity. "I thought you deserved . . . "

"What do you think I deserve now?" Sentell asked sharply. "I'm exactly as I was that day at Cleburne's. Or was it to your illusion, to your misinterpretation you wanted to do a service?"

Raisor ignored Sentell's remark. "I would have been here sooner, but they stopped me at the stables. Mueller and the marshal wanted troopers to go out to your farm . . . plantation. They mean to confiscate it. I think you should have a chance to pay . . . "

"I won't be paying the taxes," Sentell told him. "I paid the taxes for 1865 to the Confederate government."

"You owe taxes to the legitimate government. For four years back."

Sentell shrugged. "There's nothing to debate. I owe your government nothing. And if I did, I have none of your paper to pay it with."

Raisor seemed to relax, almost as if, having discharged some esoteric concept of duty to himself, it was a relief to know that this was the end of it. "You mean to let them take it? I thought Southerners . . . their land . . . "

"We're past land," Sentell told him. "Those who can pay the taxes can't pay Negroes to work it or buy seed to plant it. The men holding onto their land are deceiving themselves. I expect the next men to profit off this country will be Northern men."

"No," Raisor said. "We have land of our own. In Indiana my father has . . . "

"Then why did you invade us? Why take what you don't want, what you can't use?"

"Because this is one country. Because it had to be all free or all slave."

"All right," Sentell said, weariness creeping into his voice. "All right. It's one country now with half a million fresh corpses under it. And I expect you could call it free – if you aren't a Confederate with your civil rights gone and property confiscated."

"I could ask the marshal to . . . "

"No," Sentell cut him off. "Forget the land. I've forgotten it."

Raisor stood up. "One more thing," he said. "If you could tell your friends . . . "

"What friends?"

"All right, these people. Your neighbors. Tell them not to cause trouble. Tell them to do as the colonel directs."

"What are you talking about?" Sentell asked. "You have proclamations and troops. These people don't need me to point up the moral for them."

"Because," Raisor went on earnestly, "if there should be an insurrection, any real trouble, Lodge would turn the Negroes loose."

"What?"

Raisor looked past Sentell, his mouth tight, his voice stiff and formal as if he were speaking at attention.

"He wants a chance to clean out treason in this town. He'll let the Negroes nudge you people, and if you respond, he'll let it go to a bloodbath and have no one to justify himself to but Sheridan."

"Who considers mass retaliation against civilians a normal procedure."

"I'm not discussing General Sheridan's methods. I'm not even breaching a confidence. Colonel Lodge told me what he had in mind. He didn't ask me to keep it secret."

"Because he didn't know what kind of associates you were about to cultivate."

"I received no order to avoid you," Raisor shot back. "The colonel expects me to use my own discretion."

"All right, you've used it. But why not Amos Stevens?"

"Because I don't know what Mr. Stevens might do with the information. I believe you're a man of honor, no matter what motive you might claim. You kept to you parole. I know Union officers who broke theirs."

"So you expect me to use what you've told me honorably?"

"Yes," Raisor said, the boyishness showing in his face again. "You were in the old army. You kept your word. You wouldn't act without honor now."

"No," Sentell admitted. "Not now. I'll use what you've told me with honor. If I can figure out a way."

Raisor left Sentell sitting in the library staring at the empty seat which he and Bouvier had occupied. Sentell knew what Bouvier had in mind. Now he knew what Lodge would do, how the Union commandant might counter an uprising. It was as if Sentell were standing high above a field of battle, able to see what each side was about to do, about to see the lethal flaws in each idea. But able to warn neither side. He could tell Bouvier so that he could call off his campaign or he might tell Lodge so that Bouvier could be forestalled without bringing on a holocaust. But Bouvier would not call it off, and Lodge might ignore him in order to have an excuse to turn Shreveport into another Carthage. Sentell wondered if there was any use in talking. And yet he wondered if he could add current silence to past inaction and still survive in his archaic pavilion of personal integrity while foundations crumbled and birds of prey thundered in the barren land outside. There was Job, and there was Samson. One was beggared, childless, and alone. The other betrayed and blind.

Across the street from Cleburne's store, in the lobby of Maxy's Hotel, a tall man in a black suit stared past the water-stained curtain, out the window at Ed Norton Junior. It was nearly dark, and Ed still sat on Cleburne's porch, his face set and expressionless, against the failing sun. The man's eyes, deep-set under heavy brows, seemed fixed on Ed as if he were some priceless object.

His face was bony, with high ridges beneath his eyes, a receding hairline, and a dark, gray-streaked mustache that ran over the tight corners of his mouth into a trim beard. But it was his eyes that had stopped the clerk cold when the latter started to question the name *John Smith, Memphis, Tenn.*, still damp on the latest space on his register.

"We got a lot of 'em named Smith nowadays," the clerk simpered. "Maybe you'd just as soon made it John Brown for variety."

"Not likely," the tall man said, his opaque eyes drilling into the clerk's, his large hands knotted into fists on the counter's edge.

The clerk subsided, thinking, beyond a shudder of irrational, almost animal fear that spurted through him like a double-shotted charge, how the cold-eyes man looked like someone whose picture he had seen and how terrible it must be to die.

BOOK THREE
. . . And Wait for the Night . . .

. . . they staked all and lost all, their lives remain, their property and their children do not. War, emancipation, and grinding taxation have consumed them. Their struggle now is against complete confiscation. They endure, and wait for the night.

—James Shepherd Pike

I

SHREVEPORT, LA: 4 JULY 1865 — "Well?" Colonel Lodge asked testily. "Any minute now, sir," Lieutenant told him.

They stood before a window on the second floor of City Hall. Directly in front of them and only a few yards above their heads, the flag of the United States hung limply on its pole. Around the window, red, white and blue bunting was tied in place. Below, on the little plot of green (still green, but beginning to bleach in the unremitting heat of midsummer) and to either side of it, white troopers were drawn up. A few farmers and a handful of children stood along the street near hitching rails or sat on the edge of watering troughs, their eyes fixed on the eight or ten troopers who were doubling as bandsmen, playing Northern marching songs and patriotic airs. At the foot of Texas Street, barges had brought Phillipe Crowninshield's men across the river, and they were assembling to begin the parade.

"Tell the band to play louder," Lodge said shortly. "I want the townspeople out on the street. I want them to see this."

"I think they already know about it," Raisor said. "I don't think they'll come out. They'll stay in just to make it clear that we have no effect on them."

"No effect," Lodge muttered. "No effect. Before we leave this town, we will have shattered its foundations and given it new ones. It will be a different place."

"I wanted to talk . . . ," Raisor began, but Tocsin's wheedling voice cut in.

"Colonel," the marshal whined, "I got papers on the Sentell land down on the river."

"All right," Lodge said, paying no attention.

"They might... I thought some soldiers, maybe some of these nig... I mean colored troops... "

"When the parade is over, get what you need. It's only a confiscation. Don't act as if it were a battle," Lodge said, still staring down Texas street where the first ranks of colored troops were formed and beginning to march.

"Colonel," Tocsin was saying, "I wonder if these colored troops are such a good idea. I mean, there's bound to be trouble. We don't need trouble. General Sheridan doesn't want trouble."

Lodge turned from the window, thumbs hooked in his pistol belt. "Trouble? If there should be trouble, only the townspeople will begin it. And they will be the only ones to feel it. The United States does not have trouble with its citizens."

"Look," the captain said nervously. "Some of the people... "

Now the street was beginning to fill. Men and even a few women had collected along the walks, and others tethered their mounts, watching the Negroes gathering by the river. The tiny band, one cornet and a baritone horn carrying the melody, struck up "Hail Columbia." At the front of the colored troops, a Negro corporal carried another United States flag.

"I guess they just got more curiosity than meanness," the marshal said.

Colonel Lodge's quasi-smile warped the corners of his mouth, and he turned back to the window, placing a hand on either side of the sill and leaning forward to stare into the street.

"I thought I told you to get on home," Ed Norton Junior said to his sister.

"Ain't goin'," Cissie answered sullenly. "You ain't my daddy."

They were standing in front of Martin's bakery across the street and a little west of City Hall. Down at the foot of Texas Street they could see dark blue figures rushing back and forth, preparing to march up the long, gentle slope from the river. Across the way, a tiny band blared out a song – something about how girls loved the cavalry. A yellow dog sidled up and down the ranks of troopers standing at attention around the flagpole, and a small Negro boy darted after him with a piece of rope while two white boys tried to catch him at the end of each rank.

Ed Norton Junior reached for his sister, but she stepped back, avoiding his hand easily.

"Let her be," Hornsby told him. "She just wants to get a look at the trained apes in blue suits."

"She'll see enough of 'em," Ed barked. "She oughtn't be on this streets. There ain't no tellin' what could happen."

"Mightn't anything happen," Hornsby mused.

"And it might be somebody'll take a shot at 'em before they even get dressed up to march," Ed said. He spoke to his sister again. "I've told you the last time. Either get for home, or I'm gonna chase you all the way. Then I'm gonna thrash you when we get there."

"Aw, Ed Junior," she began, but started walking anyhow, her blond hair flouncing as she headed toward Market Street."

"Reckon it's hard to take advice from losers," Don Juan Cleburne said behind him. "I heard a little old boy say, 'If they can't even whip the Yankees, what's the use of payin' 'em any mind?'"

"I'd tear some of his hide loose, if he was to lip me like that and I was his paw," Hornsby said.

Cleburne shrugged, one eye on each of them. "He ain't got no paw. Allbee West's boy. Paw got killed in the Valley."

Then the troops by the river began to march. There were not many of them, but they filled the center of the street and raised dust behind them until they seemed, in mass, to be more numerous than the scattering of townspeople who watched them marching westward out of the morning sun.

"Man over at the store wants to see you," Cleburne told Ed Norton Junior.

"I'll be here a while," Ed answered without turning from the street. "You can tell him where I am."

"Says he wants you over there," Cleburne grinned impudently. "Says that's an order."

"Tell him to kiss my ass," Ed said. "I ain't takin' no orders. If some Yankee sonofabitch wants to see me, you tell him where I'm at. Tell him to bring a warrant while he's at it."

"It ain't no Yankee," Cleburne said, his grin fading. "He said you were a good soldier, that you'd know a proper order when you heard it."

Ed felt hair on the back of his neck stiffen. He kept his eyes on the street, listened to the tuneless music with its gait of false hilarity, and tried to account for the odd sensation that seemed to make the street before him unreal, like a part of his afternoon imagining.

"He said if you weren't in the saddle and over to him directly, he'd break your goddamned arms and legs and he wouldn't send no executive to do it neither."

"What else did he say?"

"Nothin'," Cleburne answered. "That's all."

It was enough. Ed Norton Junior went on watching the approaching Union, but his mind was back in Tennessee. The Negro troops, small boys running back and forth across the dusty street, the tiny figure of his sister disappearing around the corner of Market street – all of it was illusion, and the reality was a battle line in central Tennessee.

The Unions, outnumbering them three to one, were closing quickly, and Ed could hear a panicked voice down the narrow road, beside which they lay, shouting that a company or maybe even a regiment of Yankees was behind them.

"Shut your mouth," Ed had yelled. "Shut your goddamned mouth. Youall keep firin', hear?"

But the very clarity of the sunlight, the sudden slackening of Union fire, had set off some kind of inexplicable reaction among them. Men who had fought for three years with no more thought of running than of surrendering began to grow restive. A few moved from the road's edge back to thickets and fallen tree trunks. One or two kept moving toward a patch of dark woods perhaps a quarter-mile from the road.

It was all up, Ed Norton Junior remembered, standing in front of the bakery. They could have just walked over and taken the guns out of our hands. It was finished. Except for him. Except for him.

Because even as the best of them had been ready to spook like a high-strung horse, a single horseman had thundered toward them. Not across the wide stubble field to their left, but down the road itself, paying no more attention to the renewed crackle of Union musketry than to the stone kicked skyward by his horse's hoofs. He rode among the retreating riflemen and drew his mount up short.

"Sonsofbitches," he shouted, "what in hell's goin' on here? I done told youall to stick to the road. When I say stick, I mean goddamnit stick."

A few of the men kept walking rapidly – not quite running – toward the edge of the woods where their horses were being held.

"Hey," the officer on horseback yelled, "where in hell youall goin'? Stop tryin' to slip out of line. Git on back here."

The men paid no attention, and one youngster, who had dropped his rifle, jumped to his feet and started after the others.

"I ain't gonna tell youall to come back again," the officer called no louder than before.

But none of the men stopped, and the officer, his flat gray eyes glinting in anger, drew his pistol, cocked it, and took aim at the boy who, turning at the last moment, met not only the basilisk glare of the officer on horseback, but a bullet as well, which plucked him from the ground and tossed him into a clump of low bushes, his face up-turned to the sun, its light fading from his eyes.

The rest of them stopped. "Git back to the road," the officer told them. "And drag that one with you."

Ed Norton Junior, still frozen by the velocity of the action around him, watched the men pick up the boy's body by the arms and pull it behind them as they came back to the side of the road.

"You can stay here and take a chance on them Yankees sonsabitches killin' you, or try fer them woods and have me kill you for sure," the officer said, his eyes still angry, moving from one man to the next. He looked at Ed Norton Junior as Ed studied the three stars encircled by a wreath on his high collar, almost obscured by his gray-streaked beard.

"What are you lookin' at, boy?" he asked roughly, jamming his pistol back in its holster.

Ed stammered for a moment, trying to find an answer not only satisfactory to the man on horseback but to himself as well. "A soldier, sir," he said finally.

"You best believe that, boy," the officer said, riding back onto the road, stirring the quiescent Union pickets to renewed firing.

"Come on," Ed told Cleburne, "we'll go on over to your place."

"You know this fella?" Cleburne asked him.

"Don't you? Don't you recognize him?"

Cleburne shrugged. "Naw," he said. "I never seen him before. If I'd seen him, I'd sure recollect. Looks like a damned Indian or somethin'. Looks mean."

"You best believe that," Ed said under his breath. Then aloud to Hornsby: "You comin' over to Cleburne's?"

Hornsby hesitated. "Uh . . . You go on ahead. I just thought of somethin' I got to do. I'll see you over there."

"Don't get spooked by them niggers," Ed told him.

"Haw. More likely the other way around."

"All right," Ed said. "Give 'em a real bad look."

He and Cleburne pushed their way through the crowd on the edge of the street, and crossed over as the first of the colored troops came even with City Hall.

"Surprised Lodge ain't got some of his soldier boys along the street here," Cleburne said as they reached the far side. "He must think he's got this town flat cowed."

"Well?"

Cleburne rubbed his chin and studied the crowd carefully. "Naw," he said. "It'll take more than a handful of troopers and Pony Mueller to hone the edge off things around here. It's just like a tiger asleep. I hear one of 'em asleep looks like a big pussycat. Only fools go out when the first of a hurricane's past."

Ed and Cleburne elbowed their way onto the porch, then turned and looked back at the marching troops.

They were dusty from the long march, and indifferently in step. But they were not too tired to show pride. They were winners. They, who had been so long not simply losers but non-contestants, were now part of a victorious army, and their expressions, the tilt of their tired shoulders, showed it. Most of them were young, and most of them had been born in slave states. Now they stared curiously at the shabby undistinguished collection of men and women in homespun and cast-offs and wondered, the freeborn and the former slaves, how such a collection of mendicants had managed to hold them or those like them so long in bondage. But there was no hatred in their faces because they saw nothing worth hating.

Ed watched them pass, his mind still full of blood and anguish and Tennessee. This was what it had come to. Hundreds of thousands of corpses. Men without arms or legs or eyes. Some hopelessly mad like Barney Wilkes. Land confiscated, voting and citizens' rights gone, and the whole country, without gold enough even to fill a sleeping tiger's tooth. All of that so former slaves could march down the town's main street and proclaim, with the shuffle of their boots and the clatter of their rifles, a new order, a fresh beginning. America is dead. Long live America, he thought. Then from behind he heard a deep voice.

"Git your eyes full, boy. Don't look back here. Keep your eyes on the street until you can't stand to look no longer. Then come on inside this man's store and tell me what you aim to do about it."

345

Ed stared ahead of him, but now he saw no Negro troops, no street. It was a hillside in northern Mississippi, and he had just been picked for the general's bodyguard. It was no medal of honor like the Yankees had, and there was no reward to it unless a chance to get killed quicker was reward. But it put him close to the cold-eyed relentless Spartan that Sherman, himself something other than human, had called a devil incarnate.

"I don't need to see any more," he choked. "I don't need to see any more."

"You comin', boy?"

"Right behind you," Ed Junior said, turning and starting into the cool darkness of Cleburne's store. "All the way down the line, General Forrest."

On the east side of Ramsey's saloon, five or six women dressed in ragged silk with brightly colored shawls and shiny patent leather shoes stood apart from the rest of the crowd. Not far apart – hardly even far enough for anyone to notice – but the farmers and shopkeepers and especially their wives left a few feet clear on either side of the women. A tall brunette with pockmarked face and large liver-spotted hands sneered at the townswomen who gave her and her draggled girls occasional covert glances of disdain.

Miss Bessie Gruber ran a house on Fannin street. It had been a source of high income and high times while Kirby Smith's boys held the town. But unfortunately they were no longer in her pocket, and it had become necessary to slap a few of her patriotic boarders into disloyalty in order to stay solvent.

"I ain't gonna hustle no Yankee for no kinda money, Bessie," a tow-headed mean-eyed girl from Mississippi had said the afternoon Lodge's troops had limped into town.

"You'll fuck who I tell you to fuck," Miss Bessie had told her with cheerful asperity. "If youall want food in your bellies you got to take the other in the other."

"Other your ass," Silvie spat viciously. "My pappy'd hitch up his team – if he's still got one – and ride over and kill the whole damned bunch of us. He didn't raise me to be no whore in the first place, and even a self-respectin' whore has got to draw a line somewhere. Next thing you'll ask us to . . . "

"No," Miss Bessie had said quickly. "No, I wouldn't ask youall to do that. You just take care of these horse-soldiers and I'll take care of the rest."

Now Miss Bessie watched the colored troops marching past. The time had come, and as they lurched past in broken step, she watched them casually and considered. She had plenty of considering to do.

Phillipe Crowninshield was disgusted before the parade ever began. Some of the men were lurching about, still only half-sober from their night across the river. Someone had found a skiff, and in a way too involved to sort out, had managed not only to find whiskey but to buy it, transport it across the river, and resell it to half the company. Before the more dependable noncommissioned officers could stop them, most of the men were stone-blind with the liquor.

"Lucky we got any able to stand up," Sergeant Samuels said, as they docked at the head of Texas Street.

"What they goin' to look like?" Phillipe asked hollowly. 'You know what, Samuels? Like a pack of runaway niggers comin' back from spreein' in east Texas. You know what these white people goin' to do? They all come to see colored soldiers march in. But they're goin' to see somethin' else. Then they're all goin' to start laughin' and say, 'Hell, it ain't nothing but niggers in blue suits.'"

"Listen," the sergeant told him, "we can get them mostly sober. I'll get some cold water and some . . . "

Phillipe shook his head. "No good. We gotta parade right now. We ought to be marchin' now. You get 'em in ranks, and I'll see if I can get 'em straightened up."

The sergeant saluted and began collecting the other noncommissioned officers while Phillipe pushed his saber to one side and looked up the long incline of Texas Street. He could see the flagstaff and the top floor of City Hall, and closer to him, there were knots of civilians, most of them staring at him. A few Negroes had walked down to stand near an empty warehouse a dozen yards away.

"Big shots," one Negro man said enviously.

"Big enough," a raucous soldier called back. "Big enough and den some."

A colored child, his eyes big with worship, walked over to Phillipe. "Youall really soldiers?" he asked.

"That's right," Phillipe smiled.

"Lemme see yo' gun."

347

Phillipe drew his revolver and let the boy put one dirty finger on it. "Who youall gone shoot?"

"Nobody," Phillipe said. "I hope."

"Shit," the little boy said disgustedly. "Soldiers got guns to shoot folks wif. If you ain't gone shoot nobody, you ain't no soldier."

Phillipe shook his head, and the little boy watched him unblinkingly. "Soldiers only shoot people when they got to shoot 'em," he told the child.

"Soldiers *always* got to shoot folks," the boy said, backing away slowly, his dark eyes opaque and certain. "'Cause my poppa say dat all soldiers ever do."

"Your poppa's wrong, boy," Phillipe called after him, surprised at the volume and vehemence of his own voice.

"Naw," the child said, walking faster, shaking his head. "My poppa knows. Soldiers always shoot folks. Dat's what soldiers is fo'."

Now always, Phillipe thought. Not on and on. Not unless they have to, unless they can't do anything else.

Then the sergeant touched his sleeve. "I got them all standing," he told Phillipe. "It may be we can pull them through it."

"All right," Phillipe said, rising and hitching up his belt. "However it turns out, we might as well get on the other side of it."

"Listen," Sergeant Samuels whispered, his flat earnest face working with emotion, "you just get out front and keep moving. If any of them falls down, I'll stick a bayonet in his ass. Don't even look back. Just you keep looking at the flag and thinking how good it is to be a free man. You hear?"

"I hear," Phillipe smiled thinly. "You just keep watchin' 'em and be careful with that bayonet."

"All right," Phillipe called to the troops, "this is where youall goin' to show what you got. These people never saw twenty free colored men in one place at one time. All they ever saw was niggers that one or another of 'em owned. You goin' to show 'em the difference?"

"We gone show 'em plenty," someone bawled. "They gone see a whole lot.

Phillipe eyes narrowed. "So march straight and look like youall are proud of them uniforms. They know youall fought free. They know that better than they know anything. What you got to show is you know what freedom is for. Ain't no use bleedin' for a prize and then droppin' it in the mud. Let's get movin'."

Then they were marching: a line of black and blue between two ranks of white and butternut. Marching into a new world, Phillipe thought. No longer laboring-engines or amateur clowns. No more property to be used or even sheep to be kindly herded, but men to be reckoned with as men. Even if they hate us, he thought, it won't be the same. They can't hate us like that anymore. Not like mosquitoes or wolves or a rainless summer. They'll have to look at us and know our faces and find ways of coping with us just as they handle one another. And that's enough. That's plenty. Just to know that they're watching us and thinking, What can we do about those men?

Out in front of them, a corporal carried the flag of the United States, holding its staff far out in front of him, swinging smartly in step with the distant music of the troopers' tiny band. On either side of them, as they advanced down Texas Street, the townspeople stood, two or three deep in some places, each one of them tight-lipped and inscrutable. Some of them, ragged and thin, farmers in from the parish, a few from east Texas, held towheaded children. A handful of young men stood in front of Cleburne's store, and ranked along his steps sat the elderly crowd – long since displaced from their City Hall bench by Lodge's troopers and by their own remembrance of Barney Wilkes at the flagpole.

You can feel it, Phillipe thought. It's in the air like smoke. You can smell the hate. But it's real hate. They hate us for the uniforms, for the guns. They hate us just like they hate the white troopers. So they're already giving us that much without even knowing it's a gift.

I wonder if they recognize me. I wonder if any of them know me. They see a black man in a Yankee uniform out in front of a column of others. They see an enemy. They see everything they were ever afraid of, everything they dreamed on a bad night. They even see black men armed for the purpose of making them obey. But they don't see me. No more than that day in the station when Morrison and I headed east. There was Mo and that girl Vera, and then a dark blank hole in space carrying some luggage, and maybe – only maybe – later somebody was passing the time of day with Rye Crowninshield, that good loyal darkie who you could always trust, and they said kindly, 'Where's that boy of yours, Rye?' And he told them, and they whistled and said, 'You better hope he stays low and looks smart and don't get no crotch-rot from one of them upcountry wenches.' And him lookin' at the man and maybe – no, not maybe – nodding, courteously enough not to seem uppity, but not broad enough to look like truckling. And hating the man. And hating the dirty narrow world that spawned the man, but still, without even thinking, weighing every word and look and gesture to the last incalculable jot so as to keep that man dosed with his own superiority, so as to keep that stinking narrow world from falling in on him.

They were abreast of Cleburne's porch when Phillipe saw him. He was sitting on the top step beside an old white man in a broken-crowned hat that had no color or clear shape left, but which looked like the wreckage of a sombrero. He seemed shrunken, and his crisp curly hair was no longer grizzled in the splashy salt-and-pepper pattern Phillipe remembered. Now it was solid white, bright and bleached the color of old bone. Rye was staring out at them: not at Phillipe who marched just behind the flag-bearer, nor even at the whole company, but at the picture they presented. There was no sadness in his face, no tightness: none of the signs of control, of hopeless surrender that marked the people around him. His face was composed, almost relaxed – except, as Phillipe could see from fifteen yards away, that his nostrils were flared as if he had sniffed something offensive, and his mouth was pursed, curled into an expression of rejection and disdain.

A man seeing salvation in front of him and looking like it was dam-nation, Phillipe thought. And he don't even see me.

But even as he thought, Rye's glance closed with his. Phillipe saw his father's eyes widen, his lips tighten.

I could hand 'em over to Samuels. I got 'em here. That was all I had to do. I could turn 'em over and go see him, talk to him. He's my father. No matter what he thinks, he'll listen. He's got to give me that . . . "

Before he heard the report, the flat innocuous clap of the rifle, Phil-lipe saw the color-bearer lurch forward, lose his balance and tumble to his hands and knees, the flagstaff clattering to the ground, raising dry acrid dust as it fell. Then the sound, and even as the sound ratified what he saw, Phillipe was drawing his pistol and whirling around in the middle of the street, seeking a target: an armed man, a man running.

"Halt," he called out to the colored troops who had, some of them, already halted and brought their rifles from their shoulders into posi-tions of readiness. One man – more nearly a boy – his eyes huge and white, had dropped his weapon and was looking vainly for an escape route.

"No," Phillipe yelled at him. "Stand fast. Don't nobody cock a gun. See where it come from. See if you can . . . "

And still turning, still watching the shuffling whites who moved back from the street, pulling their children with them, stepping into stores, melting into alleys, turning down side streets, he walked toward the sprawling color-bearer who, even as Phillipe reached him, clambered to his feet and began running down Texas Street toward the stables where a few white Federals stood casually on guard."

"No," Phillipe cried. "Don't ruin it."

But the color-bearer ran on, a short slash of red angling downward across his right buttock, his fists clenched, arms pumping as he found his pace.

Phillipe stepped back in front of his men, and one of the townsmen still in front of Cleburne's pointed at the flag lying untended in the street.

"Somebody git a mule," he chortled.

"Where's Barney's mule?" another joined in. "I see a rag to keep his butt warm."

"Did youall see how it got there?"

"Lord God," the first man choked, "I reckon."

"Maybe that nigger general I saw movin' off so smart was goin' for a mule."

And as Phillipe blushed, his mind full of hatred and shame, he saw his father on Cleburne's steps, above the laughing whites. Rye was sitting alone now, and his eyes, fixed on the street and those who filled it, were no longer marked so much with disdain and with disgust.

Phillipe pulled his attention from the porch and leaned down to pick up the flag at his feet. Sergeant Samuels stepped over to him. "Let me have it," he said, his face clouded, determined. "It won't fall anymore."

Phillipe nodded. "Forward," he called. "Forward march."

"Lissen," Murray Taggert was saying, "You done milked me dry. There ain't a bale of cotton nor a goddamned mule in this parish you ain't had a look at. I even showed you that damned widow's hogs. Now you done sold and drunk up all the movables there was, and you're getting' land on your mind. Jesus, next thing you're gonna want me to git you a set of tongs and a fireproof sack so you can steal the sun."

"Naw," Pony said earnestly. "I just got a little business in mind. There ain't nothing to it. I'll be giving you the money. All you have to do to make five hundred dollars is open your mouth."

"Some business," Murray frowned. "All I got to do is open my mouth the way you got in mind and that five hundred would be buyin' me the biggest funeral they ever had in Caddo parish. What's wrong with you? Ain't you got no sense? Don't you know what they'll do if I go in there and tell that marshal, 'I bid three thousand for Sentell's place which is for sure worth forty or fifty thousand, and which you and that Ohio squarehead have done stole with a bunch of Yankee soldiers standin' by for strong-arms?' Shit, you got to be crazy."

They were sitting under some pines about three miles outside of town. The road to Texas was just out of sight, and in a weed-covered field there were the remains of an abandoned cabin. The land belonged to Pony Mueller. It was the first piece he had bought as a kind of experiment. The owner had disappeared during the last year of the war, and the Confederate government, harried beyond any hope of normal civil function, had managed to confiscate it before the end, but had had no chance to resell it. Pony had bought it to see if anyone was likely to cause him trouble on the general principle of a Northern man buying Southern land. The twenty arid acres had gone for a song, and no one had paid any attention. Pony believed the very lack of hurrah proved something.

"Naw, look," Pony told Murray. "They might go for me. Even with the troopers, some of 'em might go for me. But not you. They don't love Sentell. They hate him. You know they hate him. I ain't heard nothing since I got to town except how some good Southern man ought to put a bullet in that turncoat."

"You seen anybody try it?" Murray wanted to know. "You heard anybody volunteerin' to take the job?"

"Naw, but they ain't likely to take up for . . . "

"Not likely?" Murray said with measured disgust. "Not likely?" Sure to. Sure as hell sooner or later to decide that a yellow-dog half-hearted rebel is better than a church-of-God Yankee because with that particular rebel, even if they can't be sure what he will do, they know for goddamned sure what he won't do. Anyhow, people got to stick by their own. Don't you think we got no loyalty to each other?"

Pony Mueller studied the other man with his wide unwary eyes. He saw Murray's neck was dirty. As far down the front of Murray's collarless shirt as he could see, the skin was dry and crusted and red. Murray's fingernails were long and unkempt, packed with the same reddish soil that discolored his face and neck.

"I'll give you seven-fifty," Pony said grandly. "I'll give you two-fifty now and the rest of it when you hand me the deed."

That was it. That was what Murray had been angling for. Not a thousand or even eight-hundred and fifty, because he had calculated that Pony Mueller could be moved to seven-fifty and not a cent beyond. Had calculated it, and was as certain of his judgment as another man might be concerning a horse's value or the right price for a cord of wood. Anyhow, Murray was thinking, the seven-fifty is only a piece of it. Clear profit for nothing.

Because he did not much fear bidding on the property. Not that there was no danger in it; simply that seven-hundred and fifty dollars had been seventy-five months' wages for Confederate soldiers, and a price like that was worth a risk. Especially a risk that was nebulous, that might or might not eventuate into something uneasy and close. It was enough money to justify a chance because it was enough to stay ahead and beyond any instrumentality that chance could likely bring to bear on him. And there was something else, too.

"Not another goddamned cent," Pony broke into his thoughts. "I mean it. I'd rather get my ass shot off than hand out all my profit to a middleman."

"I know," Murray said before he could stop. "I mean I know how you feel about them profits. All right, you got a deal. Lemme have the cash."

"I wouldn't want there to be any slip-ups," Pony said with casual menace. "I mean I can hire all kinds of talent around here."

Murray squinted at the trunk of the tree and ran his hands through the pine needles around him. "You know me," he said. "I deal straight with them that's straight dealers."

"Sure," Pony said. "I know you. And you know me. I'm a straight-shooter."

"That's my kinda feller," Murray smirked, rising to his knees, spitting against a tree, and pocketing the gold pieces Pony held out. "You got to know what kind you're dealin' with."

"I know just exactly what kind of feller I'm dealin' with," Cleburne grinned. "And the feller I'm dealin' with knows just how far he can push without his arm getting' bit off."

Murray sat on a packing box outside the counter. Behind him the front door was a square of yellow light strung around with moldy harness, handmade brooms, lanterns, coal scuttles. On the far side of the counter Cleburne sat, his hands folded across his belly, his heavy features relaxed in enigmatic composure. There were no clerks in the place (the last had turned up missing that morning), and Ed Norton and his friend had vacated Cleburne's back room. Outside, the street was almost empty. There were no customers.

"I ain't never give you no reason . . . ," Murray began. But Cleburne shook his head slowly.

"Just that mule and wagon," he said without accusation. "That and the thing over at the registrar's office. And one other thing."

"What thing?" Murray asked, his eyes squinted, his mouth working slowly behind draggled whiskers. "What thing you talkin' about?"

"Only a somethin' about Vicksburg," Cleburne chuckled. "Only what one of them commissary boys told me before he moved on. About a little skinny dirty sonofabitch that come through the line one night toward the end, starved to hell and ready to sell all the women in the Confederacy into whoredom for a corn pone and the drippin's out of a dollar bottle of Yankee whiskey."

Cleburne paused for a moment. His hands unwound and began to scratch slowly, rhythmically along his ribs. "Am I reachin' you?" he asked Murray.

"You're just talkin'," Murray said uneasily. "I got nothin' better to do than listen."

"This hungry broken-down little bastard I'm tellin' you about didn't have nothin' better to do than buy himself a meal and a head start out of town west before the surrender by tellin' the Unions that some Confederate cavalry was goin' to try to break out later that same night."

"Jesus," Murray breathed, looking behind him toward the door.

"Yeah," Cleburne grinned lazily. "Ain't it the worst you ever heard? What do you reckon that skinny little feller's chances would be in a Southern town? I mean even if there wasn't no proof – just a strong suspicion."

"God Almighty," Murray choked. "It was just somethin' to say, just a meal ticket and a pass out of that hell-hole. There wasn't no breakout. I made it up."

"Shut your goddamned mouth," Cleburne rasped, suddenly hard, the torpor fallen away. "This commissary boy was infantry then, and he heard all this outside regimental headquarters just before they sent him and a bunch out to patrol where that little bastard said they'd try to come through. And sure enough, they tried. Except they run smack into an ambush and most of 'em are rottin' in a swamp south of Vicksburg so a skinny little feller in a hurry could get him a meal and a little edge on the crowd."

"You ain't no better than . . . "

Cleburne's eyes were grim, and for a moment both of them worked together, met Murray's and held them.

"It ain't no question of better. It's a question of smart and useful. I just thought you'd like to know about how smart I am and how useful you'd better be."

As Cleburne talked, Murray's hand closed about the neck of a bottle on a crate beside him. It was below Cleburne's line of vision, the counter cutting him off from sight of it, and with a desperate lunge Murray crossed the space between them and clambered half-way up the counter, the heavy bottle descending through the air as his knees slipped and skittered up the front and onto the scarred wooden top. Halfway, but no farther. Because even as the bottle began to arc downward toward Cleburne's head, even as the instant's excitement filled Murray's veins to quell his terror, a short barrel materialized within two inches of his forehead, and he heard Cleburne speaking softly – again almost as if to an unruly and recalcitrant child.

"Just lower it," Cleburne was saying. "Just let it down so as not to break it and maybe I'll be able to let this hammer down easy. Go on now. You put it on back over there and get down off that counter."

It was then that Murray realized his right arm was caught: impacted in the air above Cleburne's head as if a blast of unutterably cold air had frozen him just as he was in the act of smashing, cancelling out the only person in town who could chill him without even a word, simply a glance.

He dropped back off the counter trying to figure whether his arm had stopped involuntarily before or after he saw the derringer. Was it the gun or did Cleburne have the sign on him? Then, as if he had spoken aloud, Cleburne began to answer him.

"Like I was sayin', I'm smart and this little hideout pistol is useful. Now you done made me wonder whether you got even the minimum amount of brains it takes to be useful. There's rock bottom even to throat-cuttin' in bed and back-shootin' down in the swamps."

"Lissen," Murray breathed heavily, putting the bottle down and turning back toward Cleburne, "lissen, you ought not push a feller. You ought not goad a man like you done me. I never done nobody harm, but you . . . "

"Why don't you shut up before you convince me?" Cleburne said. "You know what went wrong as well as I do. It wasn't that derringer put you off, and it sure to God wasn't no last-minute twinge of Christian conscience. You know what it was."

"Naw," Murray answered, fascinated now, no longer even concerned with pretense or repair of the situation. Interested for the first time in pure knowledge. "Naw, I don't know what."

Cleburne's eyes narrowed to sleepy crevices again. He smiled as if at that same troublesome child.

"It took you by surprise. It was something new. You never looked a man in the face before when you was killin' him."

Cleburne went on grinning. Murray slumped on the dirty burlap of a cornmeal sack, his shoulders sagging, his face drained.

"All right," Cleburne said after a moment. "I got a little piece of land I want you to buy for me."

He paused again, studying Murray's haggard face and twitching unclean hands. "That is if you want to," he said deferentially.

They had walked out in the coolness of morning along a flat grassy stretch of pastureland studded with cottonwood and sweet gum, and down shallow crumbling bluffs to a narrow ledge of sand that ran along the Red River for miles on the western bank opposite the main channel.

Even when the sun rose above the scattered trees, it was still cool near the water. A strong wind blew along the river's length whipping gusts of dry sand into tiny spirals that rose, skittered across the slow-running water, and dissipated like mist under the mounting sun.

Out in the current there were white sandbars lying perpendicular to the shore, and an uprooted tree, branchless and weathered, lay like the colossal wreck of an ancient bridge between the disintegrating bluffs and the smooth unflawed surface of a sandbar.

Vera raised her arms over her head. "It's good here. I wish I never had to see that town again. When I think of Shreveport, it's always a ward full of bloody people moanin' and dyin'."

Across the river on the Bossier side, a Negro fisherman was drawing in trout lines, tossing catfish into a bucket. "It don't make much difference where I go," Mo told her. "I see those bloody people in streets, down in the woods. I see 'em floatin' in the river right now, and sprawled out for a half-mile along the shore. Dead mules, broken wagons. At night it's like a picture gallery or a wax museum."

"That passes," Vera said. "If it didn't pass, nobody who ever came back out of a war would be able to go on with it. Look at Major Sentell. He fought in two, and I don't reckon he misses his sleep."

Mo's face tightened. "He ought to. He ought not sleep a night while he's on earth. I'd rather have dreams of the men I had to kill than dreams of men I ought to of killed and didn't."

"I'd as soon not have either one," Vera said shortly.

They climbed back up the bluffs and walked slowly through the short grass under a stand of cottonwoods. The cottonwood leaves, light green on one side, silvery-white on the other, flickered and moved under a probe of river breeze. The sun stood almost overhead now, and Vera looked for a place to lay the quilt and food hamper Mo had brought. She could not see the wagon or the single angular razor-ribbed horse that had brought them from the cabin.

"Here," Vera said. "Right here. Look at those gum trees."

"Almost solid shade," Mo agreed. "Won't be any sun under here till late afternoon. In case we fall asleep."

Vera smiled softly. "You think we might fall asleep?"

"Naw," Mo said, his face relaxing, his arm circling her waist. "It ain't that hot yet."

After lunch, Mo leaned back against the trunk of a gum tree with Vera in his arms. Far out across the river they could see children running along the shore, stopping to look into the water, tossing pebbles or bits of wood at one another. Their voices, shrill and faint as insects murmuring, came across the water, scratching the silent humid surface of the afternoon.

"They don't even know how things are," Mo said, his voice touched with envy. "All they know is the river's cool, and if you get the right place, you might hook onto a twenty-five pound catfish."

"They'll find out how things are soon enough," Vera said lazily, her eyes fixed on the chaotic geometry of leaves above. "Let 'em be children while they can. We were nicer before. When we were children."

"Nice ain't enough," Mo said. "It never was enough. Nice don't put clothes on your back or a gold piece in your pocket. It don't stop bullets or make 'em hurt less. All you can do with nice is giggle while some bastard punches your face in."

Mo felt Vera stiffen in his arms. "It always comes back to that," she said. "It don't matter where we start, we always come back. That's where you itch, ain't it? Four years scratchin' just gave you a taste for it. It didn't cure the itch."

Mo looked down at her, his face expressionless, his eyes flat. "The bug that got us to itchin' is still here. You can't stop itchin' while the blowfly buzzes. You got to swat him first."

"Even a mule learns to live with 'em."

"But that skin of his goes right on twitchin' and trying' to get shut of 'em even after his head has figured there's no way to do it."

"You ain't a mule," she said, reaching up to touch his cheek. "Are you?"

"I don't know," Mo said, feeling the strain of rhetoric easing, the nodes of tension dissolving in his back and shoulders. "Maybe there's mule back in the family line. You never saw anybody more hardheaded than Poppa."

"What did he do now?"

"If he ain't takin' up for that two-timin' nigger Phillipe, he's lookin' out for Sentell. Seems like you got to be some kind of goddamned outcast to get a good word from him."

"Maybe he thinks you're too hard. Maybe he thinks all the hardness and meanness didn't do any good so you might as well try forgiveness and love."

"Jesus," Mo mused. "Your insides have turned into peach preserves. It's nice and it's love and forgiveness. Seems like them bloody people you saw washed all the grit out of you."

Vera's eyes narrowed. She let her fingernails arch on the skin of his cheek. "I got plenty of grit left," she said. "The way I got mine, I ain't likely to lose it. But grit's a poor meal. 'Specially at every sittin'."

"You eat whatever you got to eat."

"Is hate the only thing on your menu? I don't mean to stay around to do the servin' if that's the best you can drum up. I've seen too much hate. I got raised on hate. Every time the old man set foot in the cabin I get another mess of hate. If hate was food, I'd of weighed a ton before I was fourteen."

"No," Mo told her softly. "That ain't all. I want to have a good table with all that love and forgiveness you want on it. I want everything a man can rightly have. Only I been makin' do with this hate for a long time. You got to let me taper off."

358

"You sound like a drinkin' man."

"It's like that."

"You know what they tell a drunkard?"

"What?"

"Let it alone. Just stop. Just don't take any more at all, and that's that."

"That's not easy," Mo said.

"Nothin' is easy," Vera said quietly, seriously. "Not anything. I gave up on easy things when I was too little to reach the top of the stove. He told me to cook or he'd break my back, and so I pulled a chair up to the stove and cooked."

"What did you serve him? Mo asked wryly.

"That's right," she said. "Hate."

They lay together for a long time. Vera, nearly asleep, put her arms around Mo's neck and pulled him down to her. Her eyes were almost closed. She breathed softly. "What is it?" she asked. "What is it you want? What can I give you?"

"I don't . . . ," he began, but he did know, and his hands began to move automatically. Her clothes gave way to his touch and oddly, as if somehow he were a distant observer of himself, he noted that his hands were trembling, that the muscles in his legs and stomach were tight, constricted, as if he were in physical peril. Her eyes were open now, and her hands caught in his hair, behind his head. He leaned over to kiss her while he fumbled with his shirt, while the observer within him, feeling no love – not even lust – watched, passionless and detached, what was at best one more subjection of his body to something outside himself. Like riding a weary horse. Like shooting an injured man. Like pounding a boy into pulp with his bare hands. As he kissed, as he touched, as he moved into love, or its simulacrum, he tried to feel. Not simply the chill exquisite sensation of excited membranes too long unnaturally dormant, but to feel in the deep unexposed fiber even below the cold observer's platform. But there was no response there. No sunlight, no shadow. Only the ruddy inalterable shape of hatred filling the battle-blasted niches and corners of his soul like banked fire, eternal and regular.

Beneath him, she moaned, her eyes closed again, the strained cords of her neck standing out in tortured relief through her flesh. Her fingernails raked his back, but the pain was as distant as the pleasure. He looked down the length of his thin belly as it rose and descended, an inane rhythm, meat seeking meat, realizing itself in giddy friction. Inside, the observer shrugged. None of it mattered.

Pretty bad, he was thinking. Last time I had a hard on was seven miles from that goddamned hole in the wall of hell called Five Forks with their cavalry pourin' in like Tartars and us too hungry and broken to even fall back in order, reorganize. And that time it was from bein' scared and not from thinkin' of women. Every time I think of askin' her for this or not even askin' but just goin' for it, I think of her body. Not white and soft and movin' under me; I think of it dead or full of pain and fever. Shot. Crushed. I can't think of a human body without gettin' sick over what they came to. A lovin' body turned into pulp with musket balls or slivers of shrapnel the size of your thumbnail.

He wanted more than this. More than this grunting and straining. He wanted to love her, but there was no way. Not yet. Maybe later he could forget what he had done to human bodies. Maybe he could forget what bodies came to, what he had seen in the wilderness, in the crater, along scores of roads across the length and breadth of Virginia that were always the same muddy dusty road with its cargo of ruined flesh in ditches on either side.

Vera's mouth moved. Her eyes were open now, and she saw him staring past her toward the river, his eyes wide and passionless, his face remote an uninvolved.

"Don't you . . . ?" she gasped. "Don't it make any . . . ?"

"Hush," he said tonelessly. "Hush and come to me. You've got to come to me."

It was late afternoon and the sun was ebbing from torrid gold into an edgeless ruddy mass swaddled in low-lying clouds. Above them, tall pillars of cloud stood like the parapets of a fairy castle, shifting, changing as they watched. Mo touched the horse's rump, and they moved westward, back to Shreveport.

"I want you to come eat with us," Mo said. "You've got to meet Poppa."

"I know your father," she said, her eyes downcast. "While you were gone, we'd pass the time of day in town. He was always kind."

"Did he ever talk about me, about us?"

"No," Vera shook her head. "I reckon he thought he should wait for you to bring it up, to say what you mean to do. A gentleman don't get caught in other folks' business."

"Gentleman," Mo said slowly. "All the right ways, the proper manners. A gentleman never willingly causes pain."

Vera turned toward him. "Don't make fun of him," she said. "I wish to God I had a father like him."

"It gets old," Mo shot back. "It gets old and tired when you've studied causin' pain for four years. You think life itself is one long scream of pain, and a man like Poppa who talks about not causin' his share is talkin' rubbish. He's tryin' to turn his back on life the way it is. It catches up with you. It's caught up with him. There ain't nothin' but pain all around him, and he still wants to hold to those gentlemanly ways. If he's not careful, those ways are gonna get him killed."

"What do you mean by that?" Vera asked him quickly. "What's that supposed to mean?"

"It means times will be worse before they're better."

"Too bad for a good man to live through?"

"It could be that bad. Too bad for even a normal non-gentleman with mean ways and no care for kindness at all."

Vera shivered. "Sounds like the kind of time my father could do real good in."

"He might," Mo said evenly. "There's worse than your father in that town."

"No," Vera shouted at him. "No. There's somethin' I know all about. There ain't nothin' worse than him. Not here or anywhere."

"All right," Mo said soothingly. "I believe you."

They had come a mile or so back from the river when the horseman, riding out from town, drew alongside them. He was one of the ragged anonymous young men who spent their afternoons on Cleburne's porch. Not one of the locals, but from Greenwood, from out in the parish or from Bossier or east Texas. Mo didn't know his name.

"I come to tell you there's a meetin' tonight," the boy stuttered, smiling at Vera. He was tall and rawboned and probably not twenty yet. "It's over to the Nortons' about eight o'clock and Ed Junior said to tell you not to miss on account of there's somebody you want to meet gonna be there."

"Who would that be?" Mo asked.

"Dunno. Only Ed Junior said he was big. About as big as a man gets. The biggest."

"Reckon there'll be room for anybody else in the house?" Mo drawled.

"Huh?" the boy asked blankly.

"What kind of a meetin'?" Vera asked him. "What do they need a meetin' for?"

"Huh?"

"The meetin'? How come?"

"O," the boy answered brightly. "It's about them goddamned carpet-baggers. About all the thievin' and stuff. About votin'. But mainly I reckon it'll be about them niggers."

"You mean those new troops?" Mo asked. "Are they here?"

"Yeah," the boy said. "They come in and didn't get down Texas Street before somebody took a shot at 'em and scattered all of them U.S. soldiers just like they was plain ordinary niggers."

"What's the hurry about this meetin'?" Mo asked.

"Ain't no special hurry," the boy said broadly, blinking his colorless eyes. "Ed Junior just figures we might as well get to figurin'. Ain't no use waitin' a month or so before we go after 'em."

They rode the rest of the way to Murray's shack in silence, the useless love of early afternoon, the meeting and its purpose standing between them like invisible earthworks.

II

4 JULY 1865 — One of the Negro guards kept peering around the edge of the house at them. He wore iron-rimmed spectacles, and his kepi stood an inch above his head, buoyed up by his knotted hair. It was his first afternoon on duty, and he meant to do it right.

Sentell and Bouvier paid him no mind, but when Rye brought fresh glasses and lemonade out to them, his face was taut, and he leaned down to whisper harshly in Amos' ear.

"Sar, if you' company reprehend dat one 'round de house, please lemme know. If he got shot or stab . . . or suppose boilin' water should fall from out a high window . . . "

"Listen," Amos told him in the same stage whisper, "that nigger isn't causing any trouble. If you see him throw down on us with his rifle, you might yell or drop a plate. Short of that, let him have some fun. He doesn't even know what he's doing here. He probably thinks we're plotting to get chains on him again."

"A good thing," Rye snapped. "Dat sorry bastard look better in a cage den a uniform."

"Haven't you even got any sympathy for your own people?" Amos grinned.

"My people," Rye groaned, eyes shut, hands wringing one another. "God Almighty. My people. Dat snake-eater never come from de islands. Dey ain't got no such on de islands."

Rye gave the glasses and pitcher a final professional glance, and then turned back toward the house. Sentell noticed that he had begun to stoop forward a little.

"Your man doesn't seem to take his freedom very well," Bouvier observed.

Amos' eyebrows raised. "It's not his freedom that troubles him. He just doesn't like the idea of being inundated by his inferiors."

"Maybe he found it easier in slavery," Bouvier persisted.

"He never found it easy," Amos retorted, the least edge in his voice. "Not in thirty-five years of bondage or eighteen years of freedom. Neither of us found it easy."

"Eighteen . . . ," Bouvier's immobile face showed surprise. "You freed him before . . . "

"At the end of the other war," Sentell said. "Before Amos or Rye came here."

"Then he has money of his own?"

"A share of this place," Amos said. "If there is a place when these goddamned locusts leave."

"The sooner the better, is that right?" Bouvier asked casually.

Amos Stevens looked at him narrowly. "I'd say that. Generally."

"You have reservations?"

"And old man has reservations on everything," Amos told him. "I have reservations about paradise. As for getting rid of Yankees, I'd reserve judgment until I heard the method proposed and what would happen afterward."

"Does it seem to you there are numerous methods available?" Bouvier asked.

"It seems to me there aren't any at all right now," Amos said.

"Some people think there is a way."

"Some people," Amos snorted, "have a taste for speculating with human lives. Most usually lives other than their own."

"North of here," Bouvier went on, "the people have begun organizing. They've set up secret societies. They stand together on everything. They ride at night to hold the Negroes down, to terrorize the carpetbaggers and Federals."

Amos glanced at Sentell. "I never knew it was our purpose to keep niggers down. While they were property, there was no such problem. Now that they're free, they have the rights of citizens."

"That sound uncommonly like Mr. Lincoln," Bouvier said, a twisted smile spreading across the right side of his face.

"It sound like common sense to me," Sentell put in. "Short of deportation, there can't be another permanent solution."

"This is a white man's country," Bouvier answered shortly. "It will stay a white man's country."

"O," Amos said easily. "A white man's country. Broken by white men, plowed by white men, harvested by white men. Is that what you claim?"

"You know what I mean. It has always been controlled by white men since the Indians were pushed back. It always will be."

"A white man's country – for the niggers to work," Amos said softly. "It seems to me a country belongs to the men who built it, who work it. It belongs to the men whose sweat and blood have made it fertile and livable. That would mean blacks and whites."

Bouvier's dark skin flushed darker. "It belongs to those who can hold it."

"In that case," Sentell laughed, "I expect you'd call it a Yankee's country."

Amos joined in the laughter, but Bouvier, struggling to hold his temper, remained silent.

"I'm sorry, Major Bouvier," Amos said, his laughter past. "I don't mean to be a rude host. It's only that our conception of the South differs. I've always judged it to be a country for men willing to work hard for the right to be completely free. Only a man who owns land is really free, and whether that man is white or black, on his own land he'll be a good bet to stay free."

"We have to think of ourselves," Bouvier said. "We have to protect ourselves. We need you to help us."

"Me?" Amos said, surprised. "What do you need with me? What can I do? You know my views, and you know I live under Lodge's guns."

"We need you because people trust you. They know you. They know what you stand for."

Amos placed his glass back on the table. "But I can't make out what you stand for."

"Freedom," Bouvier told him. "I want freedom."

"What about the niggers?" Amos Stevens asked him directly.

Bouvier paused, placing the fingers of his right hand on the table top. "We mean them no harm. We only mean to keep them from taking over under the shadow of Yankee bayonets."

"Back to method," Sentell said. "What methods do you have in mind?"

"That would depend on what we need. We don't want any trouble if we can avoid it."

"I wouldn't push Lodge," Sentell said.

"It if requires pushing Lodge to keep him and his scum in line, then we'll push, and push hard."

Sentell looked at Amos without expression. "Lodge can exterminate you," he said to Bouvier.

"He won't because trouble is one thing he can't use. They want this town orderly and quiet. He'll take some losses, see what he has to do, and play along. In six months we can have things almost the way they were."

"No," Amos said. "Noting will be like it was."

"We don't mean to let Lodge have his way," Bouvier said sharply. "We aren't going to let him impoverish every decent white man and raise up the human trash. We aren't going to let him destroy our society and hand over the ruins to a pack of black savages."

"And violence?" Amos asked quietly. "To stop him, violence is as good as any other method?"

"I wouldn't rule out terrorism on principle," Bouvier said slowly.

"No," Sentell said. "I don't expect you would."

"I don't need lessons in decency from you. Clean hands are a luxury we can't afford. You paid too much for yours."

"In surgery, clean hands are a necessity," Amos observed mildly.

"But not in the butcher's trade," Sentell cut in.

Bouvier looked from one of them to the other. He held his left arm, still swathed in black, close to his body. The fingers of his right hand drummed silently on the arm of his chair. "Mr. Stevens, will you come to the Nortons' this evening? We differ on method, but I know we both want the South to be healthy again."

"Yes," Amos said, staring out into the stand of pine that bordered the side yard. "We need health. We need to take a deep breath."

"And put aside the past," Bouvier offered.

"Including the recent past," Sentell added.

Bouvier's mouth stiffened. He started to answer, then thought better of it. He turned back to Amos. "Then you'll come tonight?"

Amos' eyes snapped back to Bouvier. "I'll come," he said. "But don't count on me for a testimony. I'll hear what you say, but I won't lead this town into more agony. There aren't ten families in the parish that haven't lost a son or a husband or a brother. They've had enough agony."

"That's right," Bouvier answered quickly. "We want to give them peace. And freedom."

"Tell him to wait," Colonel Jonathan Lodge told Lieutenant Raisor.

"Sir, he's been here over an hour."

Lodge's dead eyes widened. "Never mind how long," he said precisely. "He'll wait until I decide to see him."

Lieutenant Raisor bowed with exaggerated care and stepped out of the library. Across the hall, in the front parlor, Phillipe Crowninshield was sitting in a chair he had helped to upholster years before. His eyes were fixed on a painting of Aurelius Stevens that had been sent south when the old man's estate was settled. Phillipe remembered the day it had been uncrated. He remembered how Amos Stevens had propped it in a chair, and wordless, moist-eyes, turned to Rye.

"Well," Amos Stevens had said softly.

"Yep," Rye had answered. Then they had sat down across from the painting for a long time, both silent and caught up in shared memories while Mo and Phillipe fidgeted, yearning for the outside.

"I'm sorry," Raisor said. "Maybe it won't be much longer."

"What? I beg your pardon," Phillipe said. "Not yet?"

"No," Raisor said blushing. "He has a lot of work. It seems they want more reports in New Orleans all the time."

"Yes," Phillipe said soberly. "They would want to know everything. They need to know everything."

"We have men looking for that rifleman," Raisor said awkwardly. "They're going through the business places and houses up in town. Maybe they'll find . . ."

"They won't find anything," Phillipe said. "Not a piece of wadding or a spent shell. These men can melt into solid stone. You never find any man of 'em if he don't want to be found."

"But your men . . . "

"They won't find a thing but a lot of grinnin' people. People watchin' black men tryin' to soldier."

Raisor said nothing. Outside, the sounds of summer afternoon droned monotonously. A white soldier standing guard sneezed, and a lounging Treasury agent with his face hidden under a black slouch hat slapped at a mosquito. Back in the kitchen, someone dropped a pan and cursed in a low full-throated tone, the words blurred beyond understanding.

"Your man was lucky," Raisor said finally, the silence adding to his embarrassment. "If that shot had . . . "

Phillipe cut him off without anger or intended discourtesy. "My man got hit right where the bullet was aimed. If the man shootin' had wanted his head off, he'd be coolin' in a shed somewhere now. But they didn't want to kill one of us. Not yet. They only wanted to shame us. If they'd been out to kill, they'd have shot me first and then holed a dozen of us. They could do it. All these men shot for meat in time past. They shot at your folks for four years. They scarcely ever miss. You don't want to count on 'em shootin' wide."

"We should have disarmed them," Raisor fumed. "We should have made the whole gang of them march by and drop all their guns in front of City Hall. We could . . . "

"Not in a hundred years," Phillipe said wearily. "You don't understand, man. These people, they feel and think different from you. Maybe, if they felt like playin' with you, some of 'em would have brought old rusty shotguns and flintlocks and a dragoon pistol or two, and grinned as they threw 'em down in front of you. But not guns. Not real guns. Not Henrys or long Springfields. They wouldn't have brought in a Remington pistol or one of those English rifles with a telescope sight on it. Even with martial law. Even if they never meant to shoot at another livin' thing. Because a man down here without a gun is no kind of man. A gun is their own personal guarantee of rights. It makes 'em secure – or at least dangerous even if there ain't any security. It means food to a poor man. He can add a rabbit or a piece of venison to his hominy and greens and cornbread. If he owns land, that gun is his deed. You can't get their guns without you want another little war in every town south. You can't keep the peace goin' for their guns."

Raisor shrugged. Without knowing why, he felt his ears redden. He didn't like a lecture on tactics from a . . . lieutenant. "I'll see if the colonel is free yet," he said brusquely.

The same thing, Phillip thought, sinking back into the familiar chair. The same thing. Doors closed, and men not listening because after all what can you hear from a black boy? Even a trained black boy with a blue suit and gold bars. And them thinking if he was a soldier, even a piss-poor soldier, he could have held those damned savages in line this morning. He could have kept that one from dropping his flag and bolting like a stuck pig. And thinking, What good is a lot of niggers to hold mean white men down when those same white men used to carve up a nigger on a Saturday night and save him for Sunday dinner? What good is a pack of clowns to keep tigers penned?

"All right," Lieutenant Raisor said from the hallway, "the colonel is ready for you now."

Colonel Jonathan Lodge was wiping a penpoint carefully with a fragment of a cambric handkerchief. Despite the heat, his tunic was buttoned to the collar, and the cuffs that showed beyond the end of his sleeves were crisp and white. As Phillipe came to attention and saluted in front of Amos' desk, Lodge remained absorbed with his little task, his eyes fixed on the pen.

"Lieutenant Phillipe Crowninshield . . . "

"All right," Lodge cut him off. "Find a seat."

Phillipe felt anger rising in a hot tide. He sat on the edge of a chair commandeered from the dining room.

At last Lodge was satisfied with the sheen of his penpoint. Turning it over once more, he tossed it aside and raised his eyes to meet Phillipe's.

"You mean to turn those Negroes over to me?"

Phillipe's mouth tightened. "I brought a detachment of Union States troops to this place. My service is done when I leave this room."

Lodge shrugged. "Your service," he said without inflection. "What I want to know is whether the men you brought will be of any use to me."

"They'll fight," Phillipe answered sullenly. "Some of 'em have seen fire."

Lodge smiled coldly. "A very little fire seemed to discomfit them this morning. Those who were in a condition to hear it."

"They were tired. The march broke them down, and this town . . . "

"If the town disturbs them, perhaps you had best march them back to Arkansas before you end your . . . service."

"They're all right," Phillip answered, more loudly than he intended. "Tomorrow they'll be fine. The march had 'em on edge, and that shot . . . "

"You mean if I can find ways to keep them sober, I may be able to get some use out of them?"

"If you need them, they'll fight as well as . . . "

" . . . white troops," Lodge finished blandly. "Of course. Given rest, a drink, a little warning, and a handful of troopers to stiffen them, we should be able to hold any number of rebel civilians at bay."

Phillipe stayed silent.

Finally Lodge spoke again. "Do you plan to remain here?"

Phillipe eyed him levelly. "I mean to stay. I mean to buy land here as soon as I can. I want some land."

Lodge studied Phillipe for a long moment. His expression relaxed, and his hands met before him, fingers interlacing, thumbs pressed together.

"You mean to buy some of the land our people have confiscated?"

"I have a few hundred dollars," Phillipe said stiffly. "I don't need a lot. Just enough to keep my father and me."

Lodge's mouth curled.

"Even our special agents haven't knocked down land cheap enough for you. You'll need money. And your father. Doesn't he work here? Isn't he Stevens' man?"

"He's his own man," Phillipe flared. "Amos Stevens don't own flesh anymore. Nobody owns anybody."

Lodge pursed his lips. His eyebrows arched. "No one owns another in legal bondage," he said slowly, precisely. "But it seems Stevens has as strong a hold on your father as if he was chained to him. He won't go with you."

Phillipe rose to his feet. His voice carried through the closed door into the hall. "He *will* go with me. Maybe not today, but he'll come. He'll come along with me. It's freedom now, and all these people will come around."

Lodge detached one hand from the other and pointed at the seat from which Phillipe had risen. "Perhaps if you had a piece of good land. If you were able to buy some land and put it in your father's name

369

as well as your own. Freedom means the right to hold property. Perhaps then he would . . . "

They talked on for a while longer before Lodge turned to the small safe he had brought into town on one of the commissary wagons. Turned away from Phillipe, his smile was fixed and lifeless, and the light in his colorless eyes was as chill and impersonal as an aurora. When he faced Phillipe again, he tried to appear interested, but his smile, his eyes, were the same, and his voice, harsh as a ratchet, concealed nothing. His mind was on something else, and quick disconnected images of Paul, of Boston Common, of darkness and violence almost made him dizzy. He wondered that Phillipe didn't notice it. But Phillipe, watching Lodge's burdened hands as he turned back from the safe, was thinking of something else himself.

Instead of turning toward the front door as he came out of the library, Phillipe paused and then headed down the long hallway for the kitchen.

His father was slicing thin pieces of bread from a large thickly crusted load. Rye squinted at the size of the slices, moving his knife with slow careful strokes. Behind him, on the huge wood stove, a pot of vegetable soup simmered. Across the kitchen sat the silent young Negro who prepared food for Lodge and his officers. When Rye finished, the young man would begin. On alternate evenings, Lodge's man cooked first.

"Poppa," Phillipe said softly.

Rye finished with the bread and fanned the slices out over a chipped plate. Then he began pulling a head of wilted lettuce apart. He seemed not to hear.

"Poppa," Phillipe repeated.

Rye did not raise his eyes to the doorway. Across the kitchen, Lodge's cook watched Phillipe with mounting curiosity.

"Ain't nobody on dis earth to call me Poppa," Rye said without emphasis. "You better go on down in town, young mahn. You find lots of shiftless niggers follerin' Yankee soldiers around. Maybe one of dem is yo' poppa."

"Poppa, don't do this to me," Phillipe said, moving closer to his father.

Rye straightened behind the scarred old kitchen table, his hands pressed against it knuckles down, the knife still in his right hand. There was no anger in his face – no hatred. Only an unconcealed shadow of contempt. "Boy, you done sold out whatever poppa you had. If you wants people, you best stay close to dese Yankees 'cause dey's all you like to have."

"Listen, Poppa," Phillipe cut in excitedly. "I got money. We can have a place. You and me and a man I met in Virginia. Sergeant Samuels, a colored man from Philadelphia. He was born free, Poppa, and he wants to stay down here to help the colored people."

"Best you stick wif him," Rye said. "You stay wif yo' kind, I'll stay wif mine."

Phillipe flushed. The Union cook across the room, still sitting with his chair unbalanced, its front legs up in the air, its back against the kitchen wall, was watching and grinning.

"Goddamn it, Poppa, you're a free man. I won that for you. All of us won it for you. You don't have to stay here. You're free."

Rye's eyes narrowed. He pointed at Phillipe with the knife. "All you and de rest of 'em bought wif yo' guns was blood. Youall never bought me free. I been a free mahn since 1847. Amos Stevens set me free in de City of Mexico. He give me a paper sayin' I was free. It said yo' momma was free. An' it made you free, too. Now tell me what you bought me. Tell me who my people is. Go on, start tellin' me."

Phillipe reached for the edge of the table. The late afternoon heat crested over him suddenly. He saw the knife, the face of the Union cook split into a wide and uncomprehending grin. Out the rear window of the kitchen, floating in the brazen golden sunlight, he saw Amos and Sentell, heads bent together over a flimsy table. Turning toward the door, he heard the harsh edgeless flow of his father's voice.

"Keep walkin'," Rye said from an immense distance. "Keep on goin' and think how you turned on yo' own folks. You was a free mahn when we sent you off wif Morrison, and you was a free mahn when you sold out to the blue bellies. Stay wif 'em now, 'cause dey's all you got."

The hall was swirling ahead of him as he walked toward the front door. It was the long march, he thought, and the unrelieved heat of Shreveport from which he had been so long removed. But chairs on either side of him and the wide mahogany-framed mirror near the door seemed to eddy like thin waves of river water breaking on dark sand. Outside, the porch was no better, and the two guards, one white, one black, watched him curiously as he moved across the yard toward a grassless place in front of the hitching post where his horse was tied.

371

He mounted slowly with Rye's voice still clear and ineradicable in his ears. Out beyond the yard, the land was empty. Where he remembered waist-high cotton as far as he could see, there was only an acre or so of corn, a patch of pole beans, and some tomato plants, greens and cabbage in small weedless rows just beyond the trees. The rest was grass, long stems of Johnson grass and light brush valueless and unharvestable. As he snapped his reins automatically, he noticed in his left hand a wad of fresh greenbacks, pledges of gold issued by the United States.

After Bouvier left, Amos and Sentell stayed in the yard for a while. Rye joined them toward evening, and the three of them sat watching the sun fall down the sky like a crippled bird. They tried to talk about old times, but it was no good. Rye was quiet – polite and warm as ever, but filled with the realization that his son was in town, and that all required of him was to put off his own conception of honor, of loyalty, in order to hold Phillipe in is arms. What made it worse for him was that no man – least of all Amos or Sentell – was holding him to that honor and loyalty of his. No one in the town, not even Morrison, would have held his going to Phillipe against him. There are any number of worthy conceptions, but that of a son binds as nearly as all the rest. Or so Sentell and Amos would have thought.

"A little supper?" Amos asked, breaking the silence.

"I think not," Sentell said. "Even if we can avoid Lodge, I'd prefer not to cross with Morrison again."

"I don't think you have to concern yourself on that score," Amos said slowly. "Morrison seems to be detained in town a good deal. He even sleeps there sometimes."

"Reckon he gamblin'?" Rye asked listlessly.

"I wish he was," Amos said. "Hell, I'd settle to know he was spending his nights with that Taggert girl. At least that would be normal and no harm in it."

"You think it's this business Bouvier came for?"

"I know it. None of them can leave it alone. It's not the carpetbaggers or the confiscations. Not one of those boys in fifty owns a mule or an acre of land. It's not even the nigger troops or Lodge's having Barney whipped. I think it's because all they know that the only thing they really know how to do, is killing. So now they're spoiling for a reason – any reason – to do what they'll do even without a reason because it's all they've done for four years, and all they can do without money or land. They can still exercise that skill."

"They can be exterminated, too," Sentell said, thinking of Raisor's warning.

"You know what Bouvier would say to that."

"I think Bouvier was killed somewhere in middle Tennessee sometime between Vicksburg and Appomattox," Sentell said. "Now he's searching for someone to administer the *coup de grâce*."

"That could be," Amos mused, "but he'll get a lot of boys killed whose lives still have some wear left in them."

Rye stood up. "Reckon I fix somethin' to eat," he said, "if youall goin' to de Norton place."

"I won't be going," Sentell said.

"Yes, you will," Amos said quickly. "O yes, you will. I'm not going over there alone. I'm not as fast or even as solid as I used to be. They'll mostly be young, and I don't want anything slipped by me. I want you with me."

"They won't trust me," Sentell told him. "I don't want any trouble with them."

"You mean you don't want to have to kill one of them," Amos smiled.

"All right, I don't want to have the choice between killing one and seeming to be cowed."

"It won't come to that yet," Amos said. "Maybe later, if things go wrong for them. Somebody might take a shot at your back as he rode out of town with those Federal niggers after him. But not now. Not just yet."

"Are you going to join with them?" Sentell asked.

Amos shook his head slowly. "I don't know. I reckon not. If I could keep on top of them, if I could be sure of holding them in, I might give it a try. I don't have anything to lose. But I can't be sure of myself anymore. Sometimes I forget things."

He rubbed his hand across the lower part of his face. Sentell had not noticed how tired he looked. His eyes were drained of color, and his single hand moved erratically from his chin to his chest. "I can't take chances," he said apologetically. "Too many people keep their eyes on me. I don't want to make any mistakes that other folks will suffer for."

"With Bouvier and the rest of them on one side and Lodge on the other, anything you do will be a mistake by somebody's reckoning."

"That's so," Amos smiled without force. "Action is wrong and inaction is wrong. You see why I want you with me?"

"I see," Sentell said. "For whatever good I'll be."

They ate on the back porch. Rye served them without words. When he had served his own plate and sat down, even Amos, his mind on the meeting ahead, noticed his silence.

"All right," Amos started lightly. "What have I done now? It's not late enough for me to wear that damned shawl around my neck. What's wrong?"

Rye stared at Amos, his dark eyes full of pain. "De boy was here," he said slowly. "he come to the de kitchen talkin' about land and me comin' wif him. He lookin' large and well. He taller den Morrison, I believe."

Amos reached for his hand. "Did you sit down with him? Did youall talk?"

Rye shook his head. "Naw," he said roughly. "What I got to say to him? Say, How come you give all yo' folks into de enemy hand? Say, You done ruin de land dat nurture you and all yo' people, so welcome home? I tole him to go on wif his land and all the Yankees he come to be so close wif."

"Goddamn," Amos ground out. "It's not bad enough that mine has taken leave of his senses. You had to match him. Now between the four of us there's two fools: one young white and an old black one."

"I do what seem right to me," Rye said defensively. "How come you want me to turn on you?"

"God Almighty," Amos said helplessly. "I don't want you to turn on me. But I don't want you to turn on your own boy, either. He's come home in one piece, which is more than he or you either one had a right to expect. I don't want you to throw that away. Not because he came home in the wrong color uniform."

"Amos is right," Sentell said. "The sooner you reach out to him, the sooner all of us can start putting the past where it ought to be. Behind us."

Rye shook his head again. "Dey's too much behind us to forget. We been too many places to stop here."

Amos looked from one to the other. "That's the way a lot of people feel," he said, "who wore both colors of uniform."

Ed Norton Senior's place was out Texas Avenue beyond the Episcopal Church. It was two stories with a front almost as awesome as the

Parthenon. Barney Wilkes, who helped with the carpentry, had once told Sentell that a strong breeze could blow down the columns supporting the porch.

"Ain't nothin' to 'em," he had said. "That feller cut every corner he come to, and maybe cut a few that wasn't corners at all. He may sit down to a Christmas dinner one day and wind up with somebody's shoe from upstairs in his plate, garnished with a servin' of cheap plaster. I wouldn't walk across the floor of one of them upper rooms, and I would talk no louder than a whisper anywhere in the damned house."

That had been a few years before the war when Ed Norton Senior, sometimes merchant, broker and investor, had acquired his first money. If he had waited until the war, until he had the bank and began handling cotton for the Confederate government, he might have been able to make his house what it appeared to be. Or perhaps that was unfair. How much of his money he had been able to convert into gold or U.S. greenbacks no one knew then. Or later, for that matter.

Ed Norton Senior was a short, whey-faced man with pale hands that seemed deceptively soft. Only a few people knew he had worked cattle in the 1840s – too young to be embarrassed by his failure to go to Mexico. He had made enough on the range to move back eastward and set up his store. By the time of secession, he was making as much lending on land as by storekeeping. (Somehow Cleburne had always managed to hold the country people, a number of the planters, and the small Negro trade there was in those days. The polite town trade had gone mostly to Norton – as the townsmen in need of money had come to him, while Cleburne, on his own, or following Norton's example, had held his custom with loans as well as dry goods.) And by that time, too, Norton had carved himself the singular kind of niche in town from which no one expected him to descend into anything as unbusinesslike as war. Had Barney or Morrison or Sentell failed at least to volunteer, the talk might have been worse than ugly. But Norton had made no move to serve, and his lack of motion had caused no talk at all. Patricians and able-bodied plebs were dedicated from antiquity to the slaughter. But antiquity had never experienced, so had not taken into account, the petty merchant with his eyes open and his nose pointed skyward.

They were in Amos' carriage, and from half a block away he and Sentell could see horses and wagons, a fly and a carriage or two tied up and down in front of houses on either side and across the street from Norton's.

"My God," Amos snorted, "do you see how careful they're being? Scattering their nags up and down the street like that? Just draw an x in the middle of the concentration and the Unions can march in for coffee."

"Maybe they're not even trying to be unobtrusive."

"Maybe they'd better," Amos said, "no matter what they decide to do. I wouldn't put much past Lodge even without any cause. If they give him reason, I wouldn't put anything past him."

"Neither would I," Sentell said as they tied up half a block from the house and walked toward it in the failing summer light.

It was too cool for a July night, and Murray Taggert wished he had stayed home.

"How much further?" Andrew Tocsin asked nervously. His voice quavered. Murray figured it was chill mixed with fear.

"Maybe a mile. We come to a rise and there it is. You just top that rise and there's the house with the river down behind it."

The two Union soldiers rode clumsily. The Negro had no knowledge or experience with horses. The white trooper was drunk. Both of them wished they were back in town.

"It's clouding up," the marshal ventured. "We ain't going to be able ... "

"You ain't goin' to steal the place and pack it into town on horseback," Murray said shortly. "All you got to do is put up that sign. I could feel my way to do that."

"What if they got some men ... "

"Shit," Murray whispered.

"They could lay for us in amongst those trees," the marshal went on. "There could be a dozen of 'em."

"Why don't you shut up before you get that nigger skittish."

"He's under orders. He's got to do what I say."

"Shit," Murray said again.

They moved from a twist of second-growth pine and saw a dark ridgeline ahead.

"There it is," Murray said. "Right on the other side."

"Hadn't we better get off the road?" the marshal asked, drawing up his horse.

"You mean go up through the brush?"

376

"Yeah. Then if they were trying to ambush us . . . "

"Goddamnit to hell," Murray burst out. "You act like it was still a war on. No. Because they wouldn't of let you out on board a horse in war if they ever wanted to see their horse again. Can't you make believe you're a man just long enough to attach this piece of property? Anyhow, everybody who might take a shot at you is in town at Ed Norton Senior's house. Makin' like they won the war."

"They wouldn't shoot you," the marshal said accusingly. "They . . . "

"They'd only cut my nuts out and make me a necklace out of 'em," Murray said serenely. "Just keep goin'."

From the top of the ridge they could see most of Sentell's place. The house and outbuildings were set against a ribbon of glistening river. Above, the moon struggled behind massed clouds.

"There you are," Murray said. "Maybe two thousand acres of river land and a good solid house."

"You could live pretty good on that," the marshal said.

"Sure," Murray answered. "Why don't you bid in on it tomorrow? Reckon it's legal, ain't it?"

The marshal shivered. "Jesus," he said. "You couldn't give it to me. Right now there might be a hundred of 'em waiting for us to . . . "

"Shit," Murray said, and rode down toward the house.

There was no way to tell how many men were at Ed Norton Senior's. The handful of poor horses and swaybacked ancient mules in front and along the street (most of both horses and mules having been bought back from Pony Mueller or one of his colleagues by those who had managed to hold back the price from the general collapse) meant nothing, because the majority of those who most wanted to attend the meeting had come on foot. They had come back to Shreveport from Tennessee or Alabama or Mississippi, or all the way from Virginia, on foot, and they were still that way. They would have walked a long way for what they expected the meeting to be.

Ed Norton Senior's parlor and dining room were jammed with men. Some were in homespun britches and patched shirts, but many of them wore collars and cravats. Every element in town was represented. Even gentle Nathan Ripinski sat uncomfortably between Hornsby and a light-eyed soft-voiced boy from out in the parish who had not yet shaved but who had, in sight of half his regiment, pulled five Union cavalrymen from their saddles and killed them with their own weapons in the summer of 1864 near Mansfield, Louisiana.

More men, coming in through the back door, were piling up in the kitchen and moving slowly through the long hallway toward the front of the house. Ed Norton Senior went from one group to the next, greeting each man (most of them either his creditors or Cleburne's) as if it were a Christmas party instead of a clandestine political meeting that verged on – or more probably passed over – the boundary of treason.

There were only two lamps burning in the front of the house. Candles burned in the hall and the dining room. "No use to advertise," Ed Norton Senior whispered below the quiet din of conversation around him. "We don't want a nice social evening messed up with uninvited guests," he winked broadly.

In the parlor some of the old country men were questioning Ed Norton Junior.

"That boy didn't even tell me nothin' except about the niggers and that you was havin' this meetin'. What're youall aimin' at?" a farmer asked.

"We need to get ourselves organized," Ed Junior said, loudly enough for those around to hear. "We've lost land and mules. We've had cotton stolen and people whipped, and now they've sent in niggers to see to us. How much farther do they have to push to get a rise out of us?"

"Shit," someone said. "They can push pretty hard for my part. I still got lead in me from tryin' to keep 'em out of Baton Rouge. We done lost the big one. You want to start up another little one?"

Ed flushed. "We don't want to start anything, but we figure to get set up before it's too late. First it's stealing, then it's Barney Wilkes beat all to hell. Now it's niggers. What do you figure is next? You reckon they'll give us back the vote and pay off on Confederate bonds?"

"I reckon we pretty much got to do as we're told," the man said.

"The hell you say," Hornsby put in loudly.

Others in the room raised their voices in agreement. Most of the older men – especially those who lived in town – remained silent.

"Any yellow sonofabitch who'll knuckle under to the Yankee deserves just what they'll give him," Hornsby stated, rising from beside Ripinski and walking toward the tall farmer who had spoken first.

"Gents, gents," Ed Norton Senior said accusingly as he came back into the room. "We got plenty of trouble without scratchin' up more between ourselves."

"That sonofa . . . ," Hornsby started.

"Let it drop," Ed Norton Junior said. "Poppa's right. We got to stay together."

Near the front door, some of the gesticulating, arguing men fell silent. Amos Stevens and Edward Sentell pushed past them. Amos' empty coat sleeve was folded inside itself as Rye always arranged it, and his shirtfront shone brilliantly white in the faint candlelight. Sentell, dressed in black too, looked around the hallway at familiar faces that offered him no sign of recognition.

"Good to see you, Mr. Stevens," someone finally said. "Ain't seen you since the legislature shut down."

"Good to see all of you," Amos answered quietly, without warmth. Then he made a remark to Sentell, who nodded. They stood without saying anything else until Ed Norton and his son pushed through to them.

"Gents, gents," Ed Norton smiled through his sweat. "It's good of you, Mr. Stevens. And Major Sentell." Norton frowned slightly. "I didn't reckon a meeting of this kind would much interest you, Major."

"It doesn't . . . much," Sentell said, bowing. "Mr. Stevens insisted I accompany him."

"Sure," Ed Norton Senior said, the slight frown giving way to a confused smile. "Surely. Well . . . won't youall come into the dining room? We've got a few chairs up close to where the speakers will be. For folks whose opinions count a lot around town here."

"I thank you," Amos said, his eyes alight, his mouth carefully controlled.

"Thank you," Sentell echoed, his own mouth curling slightly at the corners, his eyes meeting those of Ed Norton Junior and moving past as Ed struggled for words that did not come.

By then it had begun to quiet down. Those who could squatted in the dining room or parlor or stood at one of the two doors, craning their necks inward from the hallway. Bouvier came down the narrow stairway and pushed into the rear of the dining room where a table was set up with water pitcher, glass, lamp, and a single chair. Facing the tightly packed assembly, he raised his good arm, his eyes on Amos Stevens and Sentell.

"Gentlemen," he said in a voice just loud enough to carry, "I will not have to introduce the man who has come to speak to you tonight. What I will have to do is caution you to make no demonstration, no outburst, when he comes in. Some of you have seen him today or yesterday, but have not recognized him because he did not fight here. But his name is already engraved in the mind and heart of every Southern man, and among those of us who fought with him it has been said – with no offense intended – that he was the greatest of our leaders, not excepting Generals Lee and Jackson and Stuart.

"But he comes now not as a military leader. Rather as an interested Southern man who, like all of us, is appalled by the nature of Yankee rule. He comes to tell us that we are not alone or helpless in our hatred of this occupation. He comes to give us the same kind of hope and guidance he gave his troopers throughout the hard times we all knew in Tennessee and northern Mississippi. Gentlemen, I give you Lieutenant General Nathan Bedford Forrest of the Confederate States Army."

"My God," Amos said under his breath.

"They went all the way to the top," Sentell said as softly. "All the way."

Amos turned to Sentell. "Maybe you'd like to debate Forrest on the question of violence or nonviolence?"

"No," Sentell said slowly. "I'd as soon debate Alexander Stevens on the Constitution. If Forrest tells them to fight, nothing on earth will hold this town in line."

"Not even reason or principle?" Amos asked slyly.

"Not even Lodge," Sentell answered.

Ed Norton Junior and Morrison Stevens were at the front of the dining room on one side of the wide double doors that led into the parlor. Forrest at the rear of the room stood behind the little table, towering over it, his Asiatic features alternately illuminated and shadowed by the feeble coal-oil lamp on the corner of it. Out in front of him the men seemed quiet, but behind hands, out of the corners of mouth, they whispered.

"You hear about what he tole Joe Wheeler?"

"At Brice's Crossroads he . . . "

" . . . right through Memphis in the middle of the night, an' he come back with a Yankee general's britches on his saddle."

" . . . three of 'em. He stabbed one, shot the next un and clubbed the last one to death with the barrel of his pistol. By hisself on account of his escort was over murderin' Federals somewhere else, an' . . . "

Ed Norton Junior prodded Mo excitedly. "Is he big enough? Is General Forrest big enough for you?"

Mo shook his head slowly. "I reckon," he said. "I never thought to see him. I thought seein' Stonewall and General Lee was all one man was likely to do. Now I've seen 'em all. All the tall ones."

"You better believe that," Ed said reverently.

"I didn't come to this town to argue the pretties of constitutional redress," General Forrest began. "I ain't here to question the outcome of the war. We got whipped. But not so bad whipped that we're ready to lie down and hand this country over to Yankee Republicans and niggers. If they don't let us vote, there ain't but one way to counter 'em: scare them sonsofbitches that *can* vote so's they won't even think about it. So's the sight of a ballot box will make 'em sick to their stomachs. If we can't hold property, or if they tax it away from us, put the cold hollow fear of God in them who might think of buyin' it. If we can't bear arms in broad daylight to look after ourselves and our womenfolk, wait for the night to take up our guns. And then right in the dark what wrong they do us by day."

"Well," Amos whispered to Sentell.

"Yes," Sentell replied. "He just snapped the chain. Now the tiger's loose."

Forrest paused and looked around the room slowly. His eyes, dark and brilliant under heavy brows, seemed to focus for an instant on each man. He stared at Amos for a long moment.

Then the general was speaking again.

"This ain't vengeance. It ain't even, in my mind, politics. It's survival. We already done it in Tennessee and Mississippi; they gone to doin' it in Georgia and Alabama. Youall can do it here, or you can go under. Today you get a herd of Yankee flunkies for federal marshal and Treasury agents and vote registrars. Tomorrow, when they've sucked all the cream off the town, you'll have niggers in them jobs. And the worst class of nigger they can find. Because the good nigger is mindin' his business and tryin' to stay from between us and the Yankees till he can see how it's gonna go.

"I didn't come here to preach the sword," he went on. "Right now we need plowshares worse. But even a whipped folk has got pride and dignity, and lackin' both, they still got sense enough to see how far you can go before they're on the way to bein' wiped out.

"I leave it with you," General Forrest said slowly. "It's your state and your town. It's your lives. I leave it with you."

General Forrest sat down. Bouvier moved from the hall doorway where he had been standing. Next to the table he waited while the room filled with murmurs of restrained conversation. His face, immobile and frozen into perpetual stasis on one side, turned, sweeping the room as Forrest's had. He watched the men, heads leaning together in excited, almost soundless debate. Sentell saw the corner of his mouth twitch upward on the unparalyzed side.

"I wish I knew what he's thinking," Sentell said softly.

"What?" Amos Stevens said, turning to Sentell, his eyes vague and confused. "I'm sorry. I reckon I was thinking of something else."

Sentell looked at Amos gently. "It's nothing," he said. "We'd better listen to Bouvier."

"All right, men," Bouvier was saying. "I guess there's nothing any of us can add. We know of our own experience what the general says is true. Now we should get on with . . . "

"Hold on," someone called out. "Ain't we gonna get a chance to ask General Forrest questions?"

Bouvier turned. Forrest nodded. "All right," Bouvier said. "if you want to ask questions, let's get on with it."

"Uh, General," the voice asked, "these Federals. Do you reckon we can run 'em off?"

"Not a chance," Forrest said easily. "You got to get used to havin' them bastards around. We don't aim to run 'em off. We aim to keep 'em tame. Keep 'em off balance by showin' 'em just what we'll put up with and what we won't. If they pass a law sayin' a man has got to not spit on the City Hall floor, why I expect I'd go along with it. If they keep on stealin' horses and runnin' niggers into office, I believe I'd let 'em know I was against it."

"How would you do it, General?" another voice asked.

Forrest almost smiled. "I'd shoot the horse-thief out of his stolen saddle the first time I saw him by himself. I'd go by and see that nigger some evenin' after chores."

The laughter following came as much from tension's release as from the general's humor. Mo and Ed Norton Junior found themselves laughing helplessly, leaning back against the wall, tears in their eyes. Ed rubbed his sleeve across his face. "It ain't that funny," he said to Mo accusingly.

"Listen," Mo told him, no longer even smiling. "You better get all the laughs you can right now. There ain't goin' to be too many once we get this started."

"General," Ripinski raised his hand shyly. "General Forrest." "Sir?"

"How long do you think all this go on?"

"I don't follow you."

Ripinski tried again. "How long before they let us live like people are suppose to live? Without soldier in the street. Without taxing. Without thieving the animals, the property."

Forrest shook his head slowly. "You want to ask me somethin' I can answer. I can't tell you nothin' about that. So far as I can see, they won't be a man in this room who lives long enough to draw a breath free of 'em. They look like they mean to stay until they make Yankees out of every man in the South."

"They'll be a while at that," someone bawled.

Then Amos Stevens was on his feet. "General, all of us respect and appreciate you and what you have to say here tonight. But most of these folks are tired of killing. They're tired of living with cocked pistols and one eye open all night. For the sake of winning a war, a man will do pretty near anything. But that's past. It seems there ought to be a way to make terms with these Federals, something short of more killing."

Forrest stood listening with arms folded. "I got to go along with you, sir," he told Amos. "There ought to be a ground where men who talk the same language and live on the same land and fought the same Englishmen for their independence could meet and do business. But it ain't so. It wasn't so four years ago when they went to keepin' our niggers and sendin' John Brown into Virginia. It wasn't so when they told us it was do things their way or fight. And now it's a good deal less likely to be that way. They've done whipped us in the field and you don't give much ear to a man you've just knocked on his ass. I wish there was a good way, sir, but I don't see one. I don't even see the chance of one."

"What if they decide to annihilate us?" Amos asked. "We can't hold off the Union now any better than we could three or four months ago."

"Well," Forrest said, "they may try to finish us off. They may even do it. But I don't reckon so. Because we ain't gonna meet 'em in the field with an army. We're just gonna do a little shootin' at their backs. A little barn-burning and such. It would cost 'em a lot of time and trouble and money . . . "

"They'd do the time an' trouble," someone called out, "but they sure don't mean to spend no more money on us."

Out of the laughter, Forrest went on, " . . . to wipe us out, and it would be a whole lot easier to settle things quiet. Not up in Washington. Up there the Black Republicans are goin' to make you think a Southern white man is shit in a dirty jar. But down here, in the towns where the troops have got to go on with their solderin', I think we can make it hot enough to force a deal."

"And what if you're wrong?" Amos pressed him.

"If I'm wrong," Forrest said lazily, "I reckon we'll find it out. Anyhow, the worst thing goin' around is death, and most of us here seen too much of that to pay it a lot of mind."

Amos sat down. The rest of the men were quiet, waiting. Then Forrest moved from behind the table to sit in the row of chairs along the front. Ed Norton Senior seized his hand and pumped it, whispering loud compliments as he did.

"Looks like your poppa's goin' to be strong for us," Ed Norton Junior whispered to Mo, his voice heavy with irony.

Mo shrugged and kept his eyes toward the front. "Looks like your paw's in love with General Forrest."

Ed Junior flushed. "At least I know what side my paw's on."

"Do you?" Mo drawled. "I don't recall he fought for either one."

Ed Norton Junior moved from the wall to face Mo. "Maybe you'd like . . . "

"Don't act like a fool," Mo snapped. "Get back over here. Your poppa's a real grade-A patriot. If he'd been at Vicksburg we'd all be free. Is that okay?"

Ed Junior's flush grew deeper. "I never meant that," he said shamefacedly.

"Just shut up and see what Charlie Bouvier's got up his sleeve," Mo said. "Whatever it is, you know we're goin' to be doin' it. It won't be your paw or mine."

"I guess they're too old," Ed Junior said.

"I reckon so," Mo said after a moment.

"If the questions are done," Bouvier started, "I expect we might discuss just what kind of organization we're going to set up. The general has told a few of us what his people around Memphis and southwest Tennessee have done, and most of us like it pretty well."

"Sounds like your Major Bouvier is a lifelong resident of Shreveport," Amos said softly.

"It sounds like he means to peddle patent medicine to the whole lot of us," Sentell answered.

"A hell of a dose," Amos murmured.

Bouvier went on. "They started a society in Tennessee, a circle of friends. Men bound together by ties of kinship and neighborhood. And most of them by membership in the army of the Confederacy. Today it's only a scattering of men determined to hold out against Northern thievery and political ambitions. Men ready to die before they let the Yankees reduce them to peonage in their own land. But tomorrow and the day after that – when all of us join together in secrecy – it will be a force as strong as the armies we served with. It will be an invisible empire, and no carpetbagger or Negro or local traitor will be able to draw an easy breath while he stands on Southern soil. I want those here who will take our oath to remain. I want those men to know that the discipline will be as strict as Stonewall called for, and the pay will be only what General Lee was able to give you: 'the consciousness of duty faithfully performed.'"

Bouvier paused and turned his eyes to Sentell.

"Of those who decide against staying, all we ask is silence and secrecy. We ask them not to betray what they will not assist. Wisdom dictates that they do what we ask. All right, now talk together, and when you've finishsed, General Forrest will initiate those ready into the circle."

The room dissolved into motion and sound. The voices were not loud, but intense, and Sentell could hear the give-and-take behind him.

" . . . git your ass shot off . . . "

" . . . hungry anyhow. What can you lose?"

" . . . rather move out than go through . . . "

" . . . ready and willin'. Shoulda started the day them sonsabitches marched in."

"Coulda started afore that. With some who lives hereabouts . . . "

"What are you going to do? Sentell asked Amos.

Amos yawned. "Well, I guess I'll go home. I get tired early nowadays."

"You won't join?"

"Can you see me out there with them? Backshooting niggers?" Sentell shook his head.

"And there's no way I can slow 'em down. If my word is worth a dime to 'em, Forrest's is worth a ten-dollar bill."

"Maybe we could talk to him."

Amos frowned. "Edward, the talking time is past. You can join 'em or sit back and watch. Anyhow, I'm leaving."

As they stepped into the foyer, Cleburne passed by, headed back into the dining room.

"You staying?" Sentell asked him.

"Aw," Cleburne answered without a smile, "what else would you have me do? I can't very well hang back. You know Ed Norton Senior has got over his fear of broken windows and spoiled goods enough to hold a meetin' like this. Well, the rest of us ain't got no choice. I mean, it's right." Cleburne's serious expression began giving way. "It's the only way, Major. What with all these folks, and all the young fellows for it . . ."

"A man has to stay with the competition," Sentell said.

"He does," Cleburne said softly, his eye ranging over Amos' shoulder. "It's a cutthroat stomp-and-gouge game."

"Heavy baggage," Sentell said wryly.

"Yes," Cleburne said. "But it all depends on how you balance it up. A piece on one side . . . and a piece on the other."

He stepped past him as Mo and Ed Norton Junior came into the hall from the living room.

"I don't expect you're goin' home yet, Poppa," Mo said coolly.

"That's just what I'm doing."

"Somebody her been talkin' to you, Poppa? Somebody sayin' General Forrest's all wrong."

Sentell blushed.

"I had my mind made up before I came," Amos said. "I just wanted to hear for myself what youall had planned. I wanted to see how far you'd press these other folks."

"Maybe somebody was talkin' to you before tonight," Ed Norton Junior put in, staring at Sentell.

"Keep your mouth out of this, boy," Amos cut him off.

"We're all in it together," Mo told him. "We're all part of it."

"Maybe they'll bury you all together," Amos said.

Mo studied his father for a moment. "You've turned all the way around, ain't you? All the way. You were as much secessionist four years ago as any man in town. You stood up in the legislature and at the convention."

"Don't read me past history, What I was, I'd be again. We tried it and lost. There's nothing to try for now. Except to put it behind us."

"Right straight out of Sentell," Ed Junior snickered.

"Boy," Amos said softly, "don't make me shut your mouth for you. Go on in there and see if you can nudge your father over far enough so you can kiss the general's ass a little too."

Ed Junior cocked a fist and threw it, but Sentell had his wrist before he could move a foot toward Amos. Mo did nothing, only watching his father as if he were some rare breed of beast. Ed, flushed and grim, turned and stalked into the dining room.

"That was your place," Sentell told Mo, his eyes even, his mouth drawn and white.

"Don't tell me my place," Mo said ominously. "I don't need you to tell me my place. You forgot your own place two years ago."

Amos turned to Sentell. "I expect we'll go now," he said, his voice worn and cracked. "There's nothing here."

"That's right," Mo said to their backs as they started for the door. "Not a goddamned thing but your own folks fixin' to put their lives in each other's hands. Nothin' for you."

Sentell opened the door for Amos. Mo followed them, only a step or two behind, his voice rising angrily. "You just as well go the whole way with him, Poppa. You just as well walk on into Lodge's office and fill in whatever Sentell forgets when he spills his guts like a paid-off gentleman."

Sentell's open hand caught Mo solidly across the mouth, tumbling him back into a coatrack, knocking a mirror into shambles as he fell heavily at the door of the parlor.

Sentell's hands trembled, but his voice was as smooth as that of a teacher explaining a concept in geometry.

"If I hear my name in your mouth again – for any reason at all – I'll kill you wherever you are. Not dueling or with ceremony, but the way a man kills a mad dog: any way at all."

Mo struggled onto his haunches, brushing broken glass off his threadbare coat. "We'll settle this," he snarled. "You ain't done with me."

"You heard what I said," Sentell said. "You've used up all your youth and all your free mistakes. You heard what I said."

From the dining room, the living room, men had surged into the hall, and Ed Norton Junior moved toward Mo.

"Leave him alone," Sentell rasped. "Let him get up by himself."

Then Sentell turned from the rest of them. He and Amos walked down the porch steps. Ed Norton Senior, bustling from the back of the house, pushed through the knot of men gathered around the door.

Listen, youall," Ed called. "You don't want to go like this. Amos, you ought to come back . . . "

Neither Amos nor Sentell paid any attention. Above them, the bright moon was high, riding cold and passionless through scattered shards of clouds. The street was empty, and moonlight filled it with a chill pulsing glow as if time and its processes had stopped or reversed themselves. Their carriage stood covered with dew, its horse still and motionless, crystals of moisture catching and reflecting moonlight along its back.

"Why don't youall come on back?" Ed Norton Senior called a little louder, but his voice beginning to fade in the distance. "Youall want to watch what you say. You want to watch what . . . "

They were walking rapidly by then, and Norton's porch had constricted into a smear of yellow light surrounded by darkness. Beneath their feet even the dust was gilded silver, and Amos felt Sentell's arm around his shoulders. But the clouds were beginning to bunch up and thicken, and the night was chill beyond his remembering.

III

5 JULY 1865 — That morning low clouds obscured the sun and dissolved in short torrential bursts of rain that swept across the town over and over again, laying summer dust and breaking tall brittle weedstems that forked up between buildings and along fences.

Texas Street was almost deserted. A few horses and a wagon or two stood in front of Ramsey's saloon. Through the grimy window of the saloon Ramsey's smoky lanterns hung over the bar shone out dimly into a soft continuing drizzle that fell on the iron roofs between cloudbursts.

From his porch, Don Juan Cleburne watched the rain and the empty street. A few minutes before, the Federal morning patrol had ridden past. This time there had been a single pair of white troopers. The other six had been Negro infantry mounted.

High horses, Cleburne thought. Them tall Kentucky breeds. Higher the horse, the farther you got to fall. Man on a pony don't get far fast, but the way down is a lot easier. If them niggers know what's stirrin', they'd be hustlin' up donkeys. I guess niggers just naturally fall heir to bad luck, he thought, smiling without humor. Jonah must have been a nigger. Or a poor white. Or at least a Confederate major come down with a case of principles.

Down in front of City Hall the handful of horsemen dismounted and walked inside, shoulders hunched against the rain.

Changin' the guard. It must be seven o'clock. They're always on time. Maybe Lodge can even keep the niggers on time. Until they settle down and figure out they can get whiskey whenever they want it. Then the timetable's in for some trouble.

I should of bought that gdamned saloon when I could, Cleburne thought casually. That sonofabitch Ramsey's got business all around the clock. When they can't buy harness and won't buy flour and don't need fodder, they can always find a dime somewhere. But you can't cover all the doors. If I had me that saloon, there'd be some Baptist preacher come in and drag all my trade into a revival tent. The least thing you can say for a store is no preacher ever come into town askin' people to swear off food and hardware.

The rain became heavy again. Cleburne shivered and pulled his coat closer about him. It was not cold, but the air was thick and filled with dampness. In the street, ruts full of water caught the slim gray light, winking it upward into Cleburne's eyes.

Mud, Cleburne thought. Mud. They must of imported it with 'em.

Down Texas Street, a pair of Federals, one Negro, one white, came out of City Hall. Shoulders curved beneath the rain, they walked slowly down toward Ramsey's, pausing beneath the overhang of stores and shops as the rain's volume rose and fell.

There's two or three dollars easin' right in on Ramsey, Cleburne mused. All he has to do is pour it in a glass and pick up the money. No weighing or lifting. No dickering, no cut rates. Maybe four dollars if they're tired and wet enough. I ought to of bought that place.

They were tired and wet enough. The white trooper stood in front of Ramsey's and stared down at his hands. The backs were white and bloated from exposure, but the palms were stained dark brown. "Look," he said to the colored soldier. "Those goddamned reins are still shedding. I get the saddle sloughing all over my butt, and the reins turning my hands dark. You can't get a good saddle . . . "

"Nemmine de saddle," the other said. "What I need dey got in dere."

The trooper glanced across at Cleburne, who still sat on his porch. "Maybe we could buy us a bottle over there and carry it back to the . . . "

The colored solider, squat and heavy, stared at his companion. "You 'fraid of dese farmers?"

The white trooper flushed. He took off his kepi, slapped it against his leg and watched a spray of water droplet dissolve in the damp air. "Hell no," he said. "They haven't got anything south I'm afraid of. You don't worry about a bunch you've whipped, unless you're yellow."

"I ain't yella," the colored soldier grinned.

"I just thought we could drink down at the stable and not . . . "

"Dat lootenant show up and put us bofs on report. An' take de whiskey. Anyhow, I ain't nevah got a look at none of dese people since dey stopped working' me fo' nothing. I got a mood to see 'em drinkin' bitter whiskey."

"Sure," the trooper said without conviction, "but . . . "

"Come on," the colored soldier urged. "I know dese parts. You jus' stick wif me."

Inside Ramsey's the walls were the color of unhealthy flesh, sallow and peeling. No two tables matched and some of the chairs, scarred remnants of empty parlors and dining rooms, had come from Cleburne's back room. Part of the bar was rebuilt out of packing cases salvaged from a Confederate supply dump. The mirror behind the bar reflected multiple images like a fly's eye, each one fractured and broken again along cracks radiating outward from bullet holes left behind by a Texas regiment later wiped out in the long agony of Jubal Early's retreat down the Shenandoah Valley in those dying days of late 1864.

Ramsey was bald, and his head, under the shaky lurid lantern above the bar, looked as if it were rubbed with oil. His hands and eyes moved continuously as if motion alone implied some sort of accomplishment.

Along the bar and scattered among the mismatched and dilapidated tables, a few customers sat: farmers without land, without mules or seed, labor or money. Small operators who had hauled lumber and vegetables from east Texas until the Confederates commandeered their wagons and the Federals confiscated their mules.

Ramsey was pouring liquor the color of water out of a bottle so old and often used that even soap and water could not clean it.

'"Texas?" one of the men at the bar asked.

"Hell no," Ramsey said. "This here is Mississippi whiskey. This whiskey come up from . . . "

Ramsey's mouth stayed open, but he did not finish the lie. He was staring toward the doors which had just flapped inward, and at the two bluecoats who stood in the scuttling noisy wake of the swinging doors.

Following Ramsey's eyes, men along the bar and at the battered tables turned to stare at the soldiers. Not so much because of the Negro as because of the combination of his color and that of his uniform. Union soldiers had used the bar, and local Negroes, too. But there had been no Negro soldiers. It was something Ramsey had never thought of before.

"Ramsey," someone growled.

Ramsey shrugged his shoulders. "You want to call out the militia?" he shot back.

"I've stood here drinkin' next to Yankees and next to niggers. But I stick on a Yankee nigger."

Ramsey paid him no heed. Walking down the length of the bar, he met the two soldiers at the end. "Youall want a bottle to carry out?"

"We . . . ," the white trooper said.

"Naw," the Negro said. "Jus' put a bottle on de bar. We won' trouble you to wrap it up."

"Listen . . . ," Ramsey began in a confidential tone.

"Nemmine," the Negro cut him off. "We don' want to lissen. We come to drink."

Ramsey flushed and placed his hands on the bar. Up and down it, among the tables, the townsmen listened without watching.

"Don't youall reckon you ought . . . "

"We reckons fo' some whiskey," the Negro said. The white soldier grinned foolishly.

Outside, the storm was building again, and through the dirty front window, beyond a sheet of gray rain so singularly unbroken that it looked like fog, Don Juan Cleburne rose heavily and shuffled inside his store as a stooped figure in a worn Union poncho climbed out of the muddy street, up onto the porch, and into the store after him.

It was in greenbacks, and Murray could see that the bank seal was still on the paper around them, and even the stamp of the Union Commissary Corps in dark smudged superimposition across the flimsy packet.

"Don't get too fond of it," Cleburne was saying. "You won't have hold of it long enough."

"Listen," Murray said, his eyes twisted nearly closed even in the darkness of the unlighted store, "listen, the more I been thinking about this . . ."

Cleburne winked at him. "We been to the edge of that before. Just flap your mouth when your friend the sheriff or marshal or whatever you call him puts Sentell's place under the hammer."

"I don't . . ."

"Naw," Cleburne went on smoothly, "you don't want to make a mistake. This is a bad time for mistakes. Too many people worked up. A man makin' a slip now might never get a chance for any more."

"Mistake . . ."

"Like throwin' that property to a Yankee carpetbagger."

Murray's expression did not change, but even without being able to see him clearly, Cleburne knew he paled. Cleburne slapped the packet of money down on the counter. "Ain't no sense in a mistake. A man from around here can hold that land without more than losin' friends – which you got none of to lose. But if a man from around here was to hand it over to a Yankee, God only knows what they'd do."

"They'd kill . . . ?

"I mean God knows how they'd kill him."

"All right," Murray said. "When I come back, you got to . . . I mean I don't even know none of them Yankees except to see."

"Sure," Cleburne said, nudging the money. "Just don't change your good ways."

Outside the rain tapered off. The constant tattoo on the metal roof eased. Murray picked up the money and walked onto the porch. Through the drizzle, he could see horses reining in at City Hall. One of the riders stood for a moment at the foot of the empty flagpole. Murray squinted into the dirty pearl of morning light trying to make out the rider's face. But it was a long way, the rain and mist stood between, and the rider's face was dark.

The white trooper struck the bar with his glass.

"I ain't dry yet," he coughed loudly, self-consciously.

"Dat's right," the colored soldier laughed. "Dat's the way. Hey, barkeep."

Ramsey looked out at the silent tables helplessly. The men there gave him no help, no sign of support. His hands moved across the soiled front of his apron in short uncontrolled pivots from left to right.

"Barman," the Negro solider called irritably. "is you got any more whiskey? Or do you mean to go out to the horse after it?"

"That's okay," the white trooper laughed into the soundlessness. "That's funny."

Out in the room, one of the men smiled cruelly. He half turned in his chair to watch the soldiers. "That nigger has half bought him a coffin," he drawled.

"I'm about ready to cover the balance," someone answered.

Ramsey brought another bottle. The white trooper poured two drinks and pushed one over to his companion. "They're pretty tame," he said. "They've come along since Petersburg."

"Don't look no cleaner," the colored soldier observed.

The trooper stared at his glass, suddenly morose. "Get me a clean glass," he called down the bar to Ramsey. "I want a clean glass."

The rain was falling heavily again. It fell out of the dense clouds in long shuddering skeins, lashing the trees, cascading down roofs into overflowing barrels. The streets shimmered like canals, as if there were no mud beneath the water. A few men were on the streets now, walking slowly, carefully along the slick planks of the walkway, pulling ragged coats around their shoulders and tramping doggedly into the street, the rain an unchanging and inalterable condition beyond escape.

A solitary tousled Union horseman rode down Texas Street, his mount mincing through the water. Two Negroes in front of Norton's store, their clothes the color of the drenched earth, loaded sacks into a broken-sided wagon. They worked slowly, giving neither attention nor care to the drizzle that splashed and streamed over the sodden bags and down their arms.

The flagpole in front of City Hall was still bare, its brass knob dark and reflectionless under the dingy sky. In windows, lamps glowed weakly. Clerks copying manifests, orders, receipts, moved close to what light there was.

Downstairs in the parish clerk's office, the United States marshal, his composure regained from the night before, was handling the business of his government.

"Thirty acres, ten pasture, five timbered . . . pine and scrub . . . the rest in tillage up to the time of confiscation for nonpayment of taxes to the legitimate government of Louisiana in New Orleans."

"Any mules with it?" one of the Yankees drawled.

"No mules. They been took up separate," Andrew Tocsin said piously. "We sell off the mules in the late afternoon."

"Any niggers?" another asked.

"That ain't funny," the marshal said.

"It sure ain't," the first man said, nudging his partner. "The government bought 'em up at prime prices and slapped blue coats on every damned one."

"Do I hear a bid?" Tocsin droned.

"Hundred," someone said.

"Hundred-ten," from another.

"Any more?" the marshal paused. "Sold for one-ten to Whitey Blacock. Come set down your money and pick up your deed, Whitey."

"Whatcha gonna do with that little place?" one of the men asked Whitey.

"Well, I'd dig it up and carry it back to Indiana, but you can't do it. I may make the fella on it a tenant. Or maybe I'll secede it from the Union."

The laughter stopped when Phillipe Crowninshield walked in and took a seat at the back of the room.

"What are you looking for, boy?" Andrew Tocsin said loudly.

"I've found it," Phillipe said shortly. He was still dressed in Union blue, but he had taken off his shoulder tabs, and in place of the gold insignia two patches of darker unweathered blue slowed clearly.

"All right, sit down and be quiet," the marshal blustered.

Tocsin fumbled with a sheaf of papers, looking back and forth across the room. Pony Mueller sat like a sack of stones in the front row of chairs, his eyes fixed on a soiled faded United States flag tacked to the wall behind the marshal's table. His pale ill-defined face was set in total repose. Only his eyes moved a fraction as Murray Taggert sidled into a corner seat at the end of the row.

"All right," the marshal said finally, clearing his throat. "Now we got a tidbit for you fellers who've been savin' your butter-and-egg money."

394

There was a scattering of laughter again as the marshal sifted his papers, searching for the proper document.

Murray Taggart sat dripping and motionless, his head cocked like an anxious hound's, his hands raveled in the flimsy material of a slouch hat, his eyes intense as if the marshal's face, amidst some transfiguration invisible to the rest, emitted a preternatural radiance.

"This here place," the marshal began ponderously, "belonged to one Edward Malcolm Sentell of this parish, formerly an officer in the Army of the United States who give service and good-will to the so-called Confederate States of America. On top of that, he didn't pay no taxes and made no attempt to pay taxes though notified.

"This place," the marshal told them, "is seventeen hundred and fifty acres located six or eight miles north and east of the city on the Red River. Twenty-five acres pasture, two hundred and fifty timbered pine, oak and trash trees. No second growth. The rest is grade-A cotton land, most of it two years fallow. On top of that, there's a good house ... "

"Southern gentleman house?" somebody asked.

Out of the laughter, Andrew Tocsin went on. " . . . good house, barns stables and outbuildings, furnishings, and . . . "

"Nigger houses out back," one of the Northerners added pointedly.

"Do I hear a figure?" the marshal asked, his eyes meeting Murray's squint.

"One thousand," one of the Yankees said. "Lemme have that deed so I can get on over to Ramsey's."

"Hold your mule," the marshal said, still looking at Murray.

"Thousand and five hundred," Murray croaked.

"Make his show money," someone bawled.

"You got money?" the marshal asked Murray.

"Shit," Murray said. 'I ain't biddin' my breath." He held up a thick wad of greenbacks. Pony Mueller's absent eyes narrowed as he noticed that the packet was still sealed.

"All right," the marshal said. "Fifteen hundred."

"Two," the first bidder ground out.

"Two and two-fifty," Murray said mechanically, glancing down at Pony.

"Three, goddamnit," the first bidder shouted. "I said three thousand, you little dried-up fucker."

"Three and five . . . ," Murray began doggedly, but another voice oversloughed him.

395

"Five thousand," Phillipe Crowninshield interrupted.

The marshal flushed and his shoulders sagged. He was tired, he was ready to pick up his slice of the deal from Pony, and he was not up to playing games with recent slaves who had come across a cache of worthless Confederate money.

"Boy," he said wearily, "we're conducting business up here. Either shut up, or I'll have a soldier throw you on back out in the weather."

Phillipe stood up and walked to the table. He dropped a double handful of bills in front of the staring marshal. "That's the five. If it goes higher, I got this. He pulled another wad of money from his pocket and riffled through it slowly.

"Goddamn," one of the Northerners wheezed. "Massa must of retired him on full pay."

Phillipe paid no attention. His eyes followed those of Andrew Tocsin.

"Where'd you get this?" the man asked Phillipe hollowly.

"Did you ask that little squint-eyed man?" Phillipe answered without malice. "Or the first man who bid?"

"I'm askin' you."

"When you get their answers, I'll give you mine."

"Is that nigger of Stevens getting' smart about me?" Murray asked.

Phillipe turned toward him, anger breaking to the surface. "What your mouth, old man."

"Listen," the marshal interrupted.

"Are you turnin' down my bid?" Phillipe asked him bluntly.

The marshal looked at the money, at the dark empty patches of cloth on Phillipe's shoulders. "Naw," he said grudgingly. "I'll take the bid."

"Six," Murray croaked. "Six thousand."

Phillipe took a step or two back from the table. "Seven," he said.

"Seventy-one hundred," the first bidder quavered.

"Seventy-five," Phillip said, his voice still low and level.

"Seventy-seven-fifty," Murray cried, coming to his feet, his shapeless hat twisted in his hands.

"Eight," Phillipe said with clipped finality. "Eight thousand dollars."

Murray stood trembling, rainwater mixed with perspiration running out of his thin hair and down the seams of his face. His eyes seemed screwed tight against potential tears now, and he cleared his throat loudly.

"Are you gonna let that nigger take land away from white men?" he breathed. "Are you?"

"There ain't any telling whose throat he cut for that money," the first bidder put in. "Anyhow, it seems like a man who fought for the Union ought to have first call over some . . . "

"Boys," the marshal said, "all I can do is what I can do."

"They've got to have lunch, rain or no," Cissy Norton was telling her mother.

"This summer rain is enough to ruin your lungs even inside the house," her mother snapped. "If they'd gotten to bed at a decent hour – or even at four o'clock sober – they'd have remembered to take their lunches along. They can come home if they're hungry."

"No," Cissy shot back. "They're working for us. And Daddy's finally got Ed Junior off Cleburne's porch and down to the place. If Ed comes home for lunch, he won't go back. He'll sleep the rest of the day. It was only the whiskey and all those men telling what they were going to do that got him down there today."

"I wash my hands of it," Mrs. Norton shrugged. "If you want to die up there in your bed and be buried alongside all those soldiers from the hospital, that's your affair. You're old enough to have sense, and I'm too tired, too worn out to fight any longer."

"There are worse places to be buried," Cissie said slowly, starting toward the coatrack with a parcel of food under her arm.

Out in the street, the Negroes had loaded their wagon. One of them turned the mules down toward City Hall while the other, seeming to notice the rain for the first time, wiped his face with a sleeve just as wet. He stared into the clouds and shook his head. Then he climbed up beside his partner and they began the trip past Cleburne's, past the cotton-factor's office, past Ramsey's As they drew abreast of the saloon, they could hear loud angry talk, and the sound of breaking glass. One of the Negroes on the wagon shook his head again and looked uneasily toward the other. Then he clucked to the mules, and the wagon lurched ahead faster, throwing a spray of dirty water behind it.

In Ramsey's saloon the talk had been loud for some time. Out in the room there was no talk at all, but that silence was filled from the bar.

"You know," the trooper sneered, his voice reckless with whiskey poured in on top of fatigue, "you know, I was scared when I joined up. They told how rebels was seven feet tall among the short ones, and half alligator among the tame ones. I thought they were plenty bad."

"They ain't bad," the colored soldier drawled, his head sinking toward the bar, then jerking back upright again. "They jus' smells bad."

Ramsey was back in his corner, his hands working with the edge of his apron, eyes searching the roomful of silent men. He licked his lips and began inching down the bar.

"Well," Ramsey said to the room, "I been open all night. I reckon I'll close up and get a couple hours' sleep before the noon trade comes."

The Union soldier paid no attention to him.

"All right, everybody, drink up," Ramsey said. "I got to get some rest," he finished lamely.

"Lemme tell you about dese Southern white men," the Negro soldier said in a confidential tone. "They don' like work. Dey likes a pallet and some whiskey and maybe a houn' and a gun. An' a woman to cook up what they catches, an' to lay quiet in the de nighttime. Fo' de res', dey lef' it to de colored persons. Ain't a man in dis room but had him slaves or wanted 'em so he could lay out on de porch. What kind of man you call dat?"

"A piss-poor kind," the white soldier said piously. "A low-down kind."

"Ain't no good in a man who live off de sweat of another man," the colored soldier said, his eyes red and angry.

The white soldier finished his drink and pounded the glass on the bar. "More whiskey," he stuttered. "Goddamnit, more whiskey."

"You better fin' some mo' whiskey," the Negro soldier growled without looking at Ramsey.

"This is my place," Ramsey said, his voice low and unsteady. "I ain't gonna be told in my own place . . . "

The white trooper fumbled with his holster. He pulled out a Colt pistol with both hands and clumsily set it on the bar. "Whiskey," he mumbled. "Gimme that whiskey."

"This is my place . . . ," Ramsey started again. But before he could finish, the Negro soldier had raised the pistol and aimed it unsteadily at his head.

"You gonna have dis place all to yo'self if you don't come up wif some whiskey – now."

Ramsey's hands tattooed across his sagging belly. His eyes moved sporadically from one man to another. "I ain't gonna have no black . . . "

Half the mirror shattered into rubble as the ball struck it. Ramsey cringed at the sound, turned toward the Negro, still talking, his voice rising in pitch. "No, it don't matter," Ramsey howled. "I ain't . . . "

The Negro fired once more, his shot tumbling a pyramid of old bottles, spraying Ramsey with bits and shards of broken glass. Out among the tables, some of the men began to shift their chairs. One of them half stood at the second shot, his chair tipping over backward and clattering on the floor.

The Negro soldier twisted around at the noise. "Don' nobody move. Don' none of you white sonsabitches move an inch. I'd as soon shoot every one of you as look at you."

"You better . . . ," the white trooper said, started out of his stupor, but the colored soldier waved him silent with the pistol.

"Naw," the Negro shouted, his voice high and brittle. "I don' need no advice from you. Lemme alone."

He half turned back toward Ramsey. "I ain't gonna waste no mo' lead on yo' bottles. Where's de whiskey?"

Ramsey moved down the bar. "Fellas," he said to the room, "fellas, are youall gonna sit there and . . . "

"They gone sit dere or die on dey feet," the colored soldier cut him off.

Ramsey reached below the bar and came up with a bottle. He placed it on the bar and huddled in his corner again. The Negro uncorked it and drank.

"Now everybody calm down," the white trooper said, his confidence coming back, the liquor taking hold again. "Just sit on down quiet and be tame. You're gonna be all right."

The trooper cocked his head toward the door, but there was only the sound of rain. "Gimme that bottle," he drawled to his partner. "It's still cold in here."

"And what I can do is give this here land to the highest bidder," the marshal was saying unhappily. "Anybody ready to beat eight thousand? The place is worth five times that. You know it is. Just the acreage would be worth . . . "

"We didn't come to buy on no seller's market," the first bidder snorted. "I could buy Illinois land if I wanted to pay good money for it."

"Ain't nobody come to see that nigger walk away with a white man's property," Murray shrilled.

Phillipe stepped over to Murray's chair. He locked his hand in the other's soggy collar. "If you call me a nigger again, I'll bust that window with you," he said quietly. "Then I'll walk out in the street and finish what I start."

Murray's eyes widened. For the first time Phillipe could see the edgeless irises as they flowed outward, ill defined, into minute veins and cloudy balls. The pupils were large, like those of a cave dweller or a nocturnal animal. "Jesus Christ," Murray howled, "he's gonna kill me."

Pony Mueller was beside them, his bread-dough face mottled and angry. "That's enough," he said through his teeth. "Get your hands off him."

Phillipe relaxed his grip and turned toward Mueller. "I reckon that window's big enough for you," he said.

"Boys," Andrew Tocsin shrilled. "No trouble. It's only land. Just a piece of dirt. Do I hear eighty-five hundred?" he said quickly. "Eighty-five hundred?"

"Let it go," Pony said slowly. "Nobody wants it that high. Nobody but him."

Phillipe placed more bills on the table. "I'll take that deed now," he said. "The name is Phillipe Crowninshield."

"Just hold on," the marshal said sullenly. "No more bids?"

But the room was beginning to empty. Some of the Northern agents gathered at the door or in the corridor outside. They talked angrily, looking back at the table where the marshal was signing a piece of paper while Phillipe, hands locked behind his back, strode back and forth in front of a window that looked out on Texas Street and a patch of brown grass around an empty flagpole.

"Hold on," Pony called after Murray as the other began scrambling down the corridor toward the stairs. "Listen, you owe me . . . "

But Murray was gone, and Pony Mueller, no runner, a patient man who knew how to wait and what to wait for, walked down the stairs without hurry. As he opened the door, a fine spray of rain drifted across his face. It was warmer now, and the rain had diminished almost to mist. By evening, Pony thought, it would probably have cleared off. There would be a moon, and it would be easy to ride.

She could have walked down Milam Street to her father's store (where the remains of the warehouse were piled; where the little bank business remaining was handled), but halfway down, there was no walkway and when it rained, fifty yards of the street turned into thick viscous gruel.

Or she could have paid no attention to her mother (by then she paid little enough attention to anyone, least of all her mother) and walked down Fannin Street past a shabby huddle of unpainted brick houses that purveyed one form or another of pleasure and diversion to off-duty troops, past Miss Bessie Gruber's place. But Fannin Street was gray and unpleasant even on sunny days, and no one but jobless Negroes and workmen moving from one small job to another usually made use of it.

On Texas Street she could see Mr. Martin at the bakery. She could wave to her brother's friends loafing on Cleburne's porch. Best of all, she would get a chance to see the Negro troops up close, see how they handled themselves doing a white man's job.

So it was Texas Street. And, as if in consideration of her, the rain diminished and the clouds thinned for a while. Trees stood in sharp relief against the sky beyond the drab fronts and dark roofs of stores and buildings. Cissie watched the sudden light break into innumerable ripples on wide sheets of water in the street. It was warming again, and she shifted the heavy feed sack from one hand to the other. There was fried chicken in it, and cornbread, and the end of a run of pickles that had lasted them through most of 1864, through the winter and on into the spring. Altogether, it was a good meal. Better than most people were getting – unless they had friends among the Unions.

It had started gray and hopeless, Cissie thought, but the day might come to something after all.

"So it come to nothin'," Murray Taggert was saying glumly. "I didn't have that much money because you didn't give it to me, and you didn't give it to me on account of you not wantin' the place that bad."

Cleburne sat behind the counter staring at Murray without expression. "You didn't have it because I didn't think you'd need it. And because I wouldn't trust you with that much even if I had a gun on you. But you still could have got it. You could have roused 'em to throw that nigger out."

"No," Murray told him earnestly. "No, listen. I tried that. I got 'em goin', but that nigger is mean. He laid hands on me right in front of 'em. Nobody did nothin'. They all stood there and watched and didn't do nothin'."

"So you let a nigger – one of Amos Stevens' niggers at that – bluff you out of a piece of good land, and rough you up while he was doin' it."

"I didn't invent that nigger," Murray snapped. "He's got him some land, but he ain't put a plow into it. You wait for that. You wait and see if he ever makes a crop on it."

Cleburne leaned back, resting himself against the shelf behind. 'He won't make anything out of it," he said. "You can't hold on to anything you buy like that. You always lose out."

Murray paid no attention, his face twisted in hatred, and turned toward the slot of gray light pouring through the door. "You wait and see if he ever gets a crop out of it."

"Sure," Cleburne yawned. "I'll wait, and while I'm waitin' I'll figure out what to do with you."

Then, as Murray started to speak again, they heard a sudden burst of noise in the street.

The rain was stopped completely as Lieutenant Raisor rode into town. Water dripped from the eaves of houses. The sun, breaking through the clouds, caught beads of it and shattered into fragments of light. The lieutenant squinted against the glittering roofs and jeweled leaves.

As he passed Ripinski's on the way to City Hall, he saw Barney Wilkes sitting cross-legged on the porch with the Ripinski boy. In his lap, Barney had a skinny breedless puppy. With his good hand he was feeding it scraps of stale cornbread while Isaac Ripinski ran his hand across the dog's wavering flanks. Barney Wilkes was grinning foolishly at the boy, whose eyes were fixed on the bobbing head of the hungry puppy.

Raisor smiled briefly, not recognizing Barney Wilkes – possibly recognizing himself as the boy's dark eyes followed every movement of the worthless half-starved little dog.

Inside Ramsey's it was almost over. The white trooper had roused himself. He was staring raw-eyed out into the brightening street. Across the room, men still sat on the edge of their chairs, each one following the Negro soldier's lethargic gestures, the slackening quickness of his movements.

"Trash," the Negro sneered, the word falling off his tongue slowly like a drop of thick unpalatable molasses. "Po' trash. No money, no lan', no colored folks to do yo' work. An' no guts lef' to do yo' own. Ain't nothin' in dis room but common trash."

"You gonna get it, nigger," someone snarled from the bunched tables.

The colored soldier turned quickly. "Which one of 'em?" he asked the white trooper. "You seen. Which one?"

The trooper stared at him, trying to collect himself. "What?" he asked. "What?"

"Fo'get it," the Negro said angrily, still keeping hold of the pistol. "I'm tired of this place. Come on. Maybe dey's somethin' down at the de stables. Maybe some cards."

"Git back there and roll in the horseshit, you black bastard," a taunting voice called out of the shadows of the room.

The colored soldier stepped toward the tables. "I'm gonna kill de nex' one," he screamed. "I'm gonna kill de ..."

"Come on," the trooper said. "Come on before you quit talking and get around to doing it. They never told us we could kill 'em."

"Nemmine dat," the Negro rasped. "I ain't goin' wif no ..."

"Sure you are," the trooper said. "The rain is gone. We got to get back."

The Negro shook his head, not in negation but to clear it. "Lissen," he began, moving after the white trooper. "You doin ..."

"Come on," the trooper said. As he reached the door, he looked backward at the darkness of the saloon. The Negro soldier stepped past him uncertainly, still mumbling. But the trooper still stared at the silent tables, at the men inside, who themselves had not turned toward the door but remained motionless, faces stolid, revealing nothing.

"Goddamn," the trooper said, his voice almost sober for a moment. "I don't like their looks."

"Shit," the Negro said. "Dey ugly, but you ain't got no worry so long as you don't turn yo' back on 'em."

"I don't know," the trooper said. "I hear they were bad in Mississippi."

"Dat was a long time ago," the colored soldier grinned. "Things change. A while ago dey had me in chains. If I didn't work, I didn't eat. Look at me now."

The trooper leaned against a post, training his legs to obedience again. He looked at the Negro soldier, trying to focus, trying to understand what he was saying. "All right," he said finally. "That's real fine. They're down and you're up. You think they'll let it stay that way?"

The colored soldier rubbed his face. The whiskey's anger was fading. Something else less definable but no more tender was beginning to replace it. "Lissen," he said. "What we got, we gone keep. An' what dey still got, we jus' might git. Come on," he said. "I'm tired of dis place."

The trooper heaved himself away from the supporting post. "Sure," he said, but then he glanced up Texas Street and saw her walking toward the river, her back toward them as if there were no Union soldiers in the parish.

Cissie Norton was not paying attention to the stores she passed. The rain had cleared off, but it might begin again and she wanted to make the best of the interim to get the food, still warm, to her father and brother. Anyhow, there was nothing worth seeing anymore. Once in a while it was possible to find a bolt of cloth, some ribbon, even a tiny vial of foreign perfume at Cleburne's. But the rest of the town was a wasteland. Even decent food was scarce – except again, at Cleburne's.

"If I could be sure of which commissary man he was buying," her father had said, wiping his forehead with a bandana handkerchief, "I'd see if I could get me a piece of him."

But she was not thinking so much of that, of the lack of ribbons and sashes and skirts. Still walking, the brown sack brushing against her leg with its weight of chicken and cornbread, she was thinking of what things had come to, what there was to look forward to. She was thinking that there was no beauty left: only mud and men with guns, hatred and discontent. She had taken no part in the war, but the aftermath was hers as much as her father's or Ed Junior's.

She glanced across at Cleburne's front porch. It was empty. The rain, she thought. It kept 'em home. But they'll be along when it stops. To sit and talk and torture each other. Every afternoon the same. Down in front of Ripinski's, on her side of the street, she saw Barney Wilkes and Isaac Ripinski.

But the worst part, she was thinking, is that none of it belongs to me. I wasn't at the hospital helping. No one who went to fight belonged to me. The only part of it that's mine is losing.

Isaac waved to her and held his puppy up.

Cissie waved. "Where'd you get it?" she called down the walkway.

"It just come along," Isaac said. "I reckon it belonged to some soldiers. Not Yankees, some of General Smith's soldiers. He's pretty skinny."

"He'll likely stay that way," she called back. "What you been feedin' him?"

"Whatever there is," Isaac said. "Mostly cornbread and grits with fatback drippin's."

"Maybe I could get a hold of some bones," Cissie said.

She crossed the street, stepping carefully from one hummock to another, from one water-soaked ridge to the next. As she reached the far side, the rain began again. She stopped under the porch of an empty wooden building with dark glassless windows and an open door swinging free in the light breeze. Half a block farther down, she could see the faded sign that hung above her father's store. The chicken would be cold; the butter in the corn bread would be thick and unpalatable. She would have to get wet if the lunch was to be any good at all.

The street had darkened again and the rain mounted quickly. More heavy clouds from the southwest piled up over the town. Within a few moments from the time Cissie had first seen Isaac and Barney, she could barely see across the street.

Squinting, Cissie glanced again toward her father's store. She could no longer see the sign. She felt isolated: as if more than the crashing rain was cutting her off from the rest of the street. Behind her, a gust of moist wind made the door of the empty building shudder open. Cissie turned at the sound, her sack falling from fingers suddenly cold and insentient. She stared into the darkness beyond the door, eyes wide and frightened. But she did not see the two figures that ran through the rain from across the street in front of Ramsey's saloon, and who were walking slowly, purposely if unsteadily, up the walkway past Cleburne's, past the cotton-factor's empty office, toward the gallery under which she stood.

"Listen," the trooper said again, almost pleadingly. "We got to go on back."

The colored soldier weaved onward, his eyes following Cissie as she turned to look at the deserted building behind her. "Lemme alone," he said. "I don' have to go back. I wanna talk to dat girl. I wanna see what it's like talkin' to dat girl."

"What the hell do you think it's like?" the trooper mumbled. "A goddamned little reb kid. What do you think it's like?"

"Maybe more den dat," the negro said, increasing his stride.

"More than what?" the trooper asked.

"More den talk," the colored soldier said, his eyes still on Cissie Norton who was beginning to walk again, who had not yet looked back in their direction

"Why don't you let go of that puppy dog?" Barney was asking Isaac Ripinski. "You gonna pet the fur off him."

"What do you do with a dog?" Isaac asked. "You pet him," he answered himself.

"Sure," Barney said. "But you got to go easy. Too much of a good thing."

Isaac smiled. "Tell me about the time youall got into the Yankee supplies at Winchester. I want to hear about the turtle soup and the anchovies. Tell me about them clothes you got."

"The boots," Barney began automatically, his one hand moving out to stroke the wiggling puppy. "I had me a pair just like what Major Sentell wears. Long and black and made out of soft hide. But tough. They was good for . . . "

Isaac watched the dog while Barney talked. He raised his eyes when Barney's voice trailed off.

"It's just the rain again, Barney," he said gently. "It's not guns or anything. Tell me how to keep the ticks off this dog. Barney . . . ?"

Then he followed Barney's gaze across the street. Through a dirty curtain of thickening rain, he saw the two Union soldiers stopped beside Cissie Norton. The colored soldier was talking to her, but Cissie, turned half away, was paying him no mind, was edging toward the end of the walkway. Her father's store was only a short run farther on.

"What do you reckon . . . ?" Isaac began, still watching the soldiers.

"I don't know," Barney answered. "Who's inside?"

"Nobody," Isaac said. "I mean Poppa. And Momma in back. There ain't been a customer in all morning."

"You don't reckon your paw would have any kind of gun at all?"

Isaac shook his head, but he did not turn his eyes from across the street. He was beginning to feel cold. Not frightened or even apprehensive. Simply cold, despite the staggering lukewarm humidity.

"You know not. He don't believe in 'em. He saw too much in Germany and Poland. He never let me put my hand on a gun. He never owned one."

"I reckon . . . ," Barney started.

But Isaac was on his feet. Across the hazy distance, he saw the Negro soldier reach out for Cissie Norton. She dodged and tried to run – first toward her father store, then toward Isaac and Barney. Isaac could hear her voice above the rain's growl. She was screaming with fear or anger or both, but her voice seemed blocks away, and he could not tell what she was shouting.

"Cissie," Isaac called. "Cissie . . . "

"Lissen," Barney said, turning pale, the stump of his missing hand burying itself in the tatters of his shirt. "You . . . I got to call your poppa. Maybe them fellas in the saloon."

Barney started into the store, then turned and began running toward Ramsey's, his stump pressed close to his chest. But Isaac had paid him no mind. As Barney ran, Isaac was already in the street, in the rain. "Cissie," he called again, "what . . . ?"

But the Unions had pulled her back through the open door of the empty building. The rain almost blinded him, but he could see the trooper's back filling the dark doorway. Isaac wiped the water out of his eyes and slipped forward in the greasy mud. He teetered, caught his balance, and climbed up onto the boardwalk.

"What are youall doin' to her?" Isaac yelled at the back of the Union trooper.

The trooper did not turn. "Get out of here, boy," he snarled. "Nothing's happening. Go mind your business."

But Isaac stepped closer. Cissie was not screaming now, but he could hear her struggling and crying beyond the door. Out of the darkness, he could hear the colored soldier talking softly, laughing softly, coaxing, questioning.

"What's that nigger . . . ?" Isaac shouted. "Why don't you make him turn loose of her? Ain't you even . . . "

"Boy," the trooper said, half turning in the doorway, still blocking it with his body, "I won't tell you to move on another time."

But Isaac, still wiping the rain from his eyes, tried to push past the trooper. "Even a Yankee . . . ," he shouted. "That nigger . . . "

The colored soldier turned to the door, his face contorted. "You gonna shut his mouf," he gritted. "You gonna do it, or you want me to?"

The trooper held Isaac back with one hand. "Listen," he said, "don't give me any more shit. The kid is going to have every broken-down rebel in that tavern out here. You had your fun, now let's get . . . "

"That nigger," Isaac yelled. "He . . . "

The colored soldier shoved Cissie back into the darkness. "Awright," he snarled, reaching under the arm of the trooper, snatching his pistol from the holster. He raised the pistol and aimed. Then, fast as raising it, he clubbed it and hit the boy across the head. Isaac fell to his knees, hands plastered across his face. The Negro soldier hit him again. And once more. "Awright," he breathed heavily, pistol hanging from his fingers by the barrel, its butt darker than walnut, damp and gleaming in the faint light through the aimlessly swinging door.

The trooper stood in darkness. Only his face showed, pale and bright with sweat. "Jesus," he said. "You dumb sonofabitch. You . . ."

The Negro soldier straightened, his mouth open, the whites of his eyes turning in the darkness. "Leave it go," he said. "Don't say nothin' else."

He righted the pistol slowly, his dark hand closing over the moist butt. "I ain't got a thing to lose," he said, his voice rising above the sound of the rain.

Outside the square of light cut cleanly by the door's edges, Cissie lay still sobbing, her dress torn, her arms smudged by dirt on the unswept floor.

The trooper was cold sober now. His mind was churning out past the last feathery grasp of whiskey. "We got about five minute," he said slowly. "To get out of here and get under cover. If we get out of here. If there is any cover."

The Negro aimed the pistol casually, not at the trooper – not even in his direction. Simply leveled it at an imaginary point somewhere in the darkness. "Yeah," he said finally. "Maybe five minutes. You know anybody?"

Cissie moved tentatively. Neither of the men paid any attention to the sound.

"This girl," the trooper said. "I know this girl over on Fannin Street. She wants out of that house. I told her when we pulled out . . ."

The Negro grinned. "Sho," he said, glancing toward where Cissie was trying to crawl farther into the darkness. "Sho. She might."

The trooper squatted and turned Isaac's bleeding face into the faint light. He put a hand on the boy's chest. "I didn't figure it to go this far," he said. "Even the army . . ."

"Nemmine de army," the colored soldier spat. "Day's a back way out. Come on."

As he rose, the trooper dimly saw Ripinski coming out of his store. From Ramsey's, men were walking rapidly along the street. He backed into the shadows at the sound of voices and heavy shoes on the board-walk drowned out the splash of the rain.

IV

5 JULY 1865 — The rain lashed the window of Sentell's room, wetting the curtain, dampening one side of his bed. As he awoke in darkness, Sentell felt that he had forgotten something, left something undone, and from the dereliction evil would be sure to follow. The chill that bound his shoulders and sluiced across his belly was not from the windblown rain alone, but from within as well. He sensed disaster. It was a pressure, an intangible stirring behind his thoughts. Sentell recognized the feeling. He had had it at Vicksburg.

As he dressed, Sentell wondered what good his seeing Phillipe might do. Perhaps unite him with Amos and Rye, gather together at least that much of a shattered town. But it was not Phillipe who held the power of destruction or peace in his hands. And neither Bouvier nor Lodge was likely to see an example in Phillipe's being reconciled with Amos and Rye.

The night was done, though, and the bed was unfit for sleeping. Sentell needed the ride, and in God's certain economy, perhaps he could expand a head-clearing canter into some kind of human currency for Phillipe and the old men.

So he rode down to the river and beside it to the northwest, toward where, miles away, it formed the boundary between Texas and the Indian territory. His coat grew heavy with rain, but Sentell's horse was steady beneath him, and riding was better than sitting in a library caught between the butchered past and a future that roiled ahead like the maelstrom. He remembered the words of Marcus Aurelius, written in a soldier's tent somewhere in Germany: *In my father, I observed mildness of temper, and unchangeable resolution in the things which he had determined after due deliberation, and no vain glory in those things which men call honors.* He thought of the common grave of Leonidas and his Spartans at Thermopylae, and that of Bonham, Travis, Bowie, and Crockett at San Antonio de Bexar, and of a phrase Masterson had once used when Bouvier had chaffed him about his Texas nationalism: *Thermopylae had its messenger of defeat. The Alamo had none.* And somehow, without wanting to, Sentell thought again of the Helvetians high in their mountains gazing downward at the Roman legions bearing progress and modernity toward them as Captain Cook's venereal sailors carried it to the South Sea Islanders. Sentell remembered Masterson – remembered him so clearly and so well that tears started up in his eyes and ran down his cheeks with the rain. It was not simply the unutterable sadness of a friend lost, but more nearly that profound emptiness felt when a man tops the crest of a hill to look down on his own land and sees nothing but a blackened ruin no longer even smoking, where his house, the house of his fathers, has stood. Masterson, Sentell thought, after all, the luck was yours. You became part of the land while it still belonged to us. And now merged with it forever, no one of them can take you from it – or it from you. And even that kind of possession must be better than none at all. By then Sentell had turned and started back into town.

He rode through tumbling mist toward the stables where the Federal troops were still bivouacked. He had no way of knowing whether Phillipe would be with his men or not, whether Lodge had found him some quarters fit for an officer – not for Phillipe's sake but because of the uniform he wore – so Sentell rode up to the old Confederate cavalry stables from behind. A Negro sat in an open doorway, packing clothes into shabby saddlebags. He wore a colorless canvas coat over his blue uniform, and his kepi was bare, the insignia removed.

"I'm looking for Phillipe Crowninshield," Sentell said, still mounted.

"What for?" the Negro asked. His dark eyes met Sentell's evenly. His voice was neither obsequious nor discourteous.

"I want to talk to him," Sentell said. "It has to do with his father."

The Negro stood up, his eyes still steady. "Anything wrong with his father? Did somebody . . . ?"

"Nothing is wrong. Nothing that Phillipe can't take care of."

"Phillipe," he mused. "You know him?"

"I knew him. I saw him ride into this town."

"He was walking when he came in," the Negro said matter-of-factly.

"Not the first time," Sentell said. "The first time he was riding behind his father along with Amos and Morrison Stevens. And their mothers."

"Uh huh," the Negro said, dropping the saddlebags and the bunched clothes. "He told me about that time. You're Edward Sentell, the major. The one at Vicksburg."

"I was there."

"Listen," the Negro said. "I'm Samuels. Crowninshield is a friend of mine. I talked to him about his father. I said he can't let some idea part him from his blood. I told him we have freedom now. I told him freedom is nothing unless you do something with it. I told him. . . ."

"You must have told him everything I had in mind."

"It wasn't any good," he shrugged. "He used to know it. He used to tell the men. He used to say a free man stood tall, and that you could measure what his freedom was worth by the way he carried himself. Until he came back to this town. Then it started going to pieces on him. He's afraid of this town. Not of getting shot at or run off. Afraid to go near his father and that man Amos Stevens. Afraid he might say 'yessir' by accident."

"That's not much of a way to carry himself, is it?"

Samuels slammed his hand against the scarred unpainted side of the barn and turned away. "You said it. It looks bad. It makes me afraid. It makes me feel like a field hand in a hundred-dollar suit. I don't want to feel that way."

Samuels looked up at Sentell quickly, his expression on the edge of mistrust and antagonism. "You know what I mean," he said hoarsely.

"I know," Sentell said. "I expect victory is about as hard to carry as defeat."

Samuels' face eased. He reached up and rubbed Sentell's horse's flank absently. "Yeah," he said slowly. 'I guess you know what I mean." Samuels told him where Phillipe was. And as Sentell rode into the center of town, up Marshall Street, past Milam to Texas Street toward City Hall, he wondered if Lodge might have given Phillipe a job. Making a federal marshal of Phillipe would be as certain a way to generate catastrophe as any Sentell could imagine. Phillipe serving summonses, eviction notices, making arrests, dispossessing small holders. A former local slave who had served in the Union army. Lodge would have his insurrection before the first leaf fell to an autumn wind.

Sentell started to go into Cleburne's to hear about the outcome of the meeting, but there was no need. He would hear soon enough without asking. As he passed City Hall, he saw a few of the carpetbaggers loitering inside the door. They stared into the rain like animals peeking out of a log. Phillipe stood apart from them.

In front of him, some of the Yankee agents walked down the steps raising collars against the rain, glancing back at Phillipe resentfully as they slogged through the mud toward their horses, toward Ramsey's, toward the hotel.

Phillipe was just out of the rain, pulling a Union poncho over his head. His dark face was composed, emotionless, and his eyes seemed fixed on the banks of gray cloud that passed by overhead.

"Phillipe," Sentell called to him from the street.

411

He looked up. Sentell could not recognize the quick-moving partner and co-conspirator who had moved as a boy alongside Morrison Stevens like another finger on the same hand. He did not smile. Sentell wondered if Phillipe recognized him.

"Major," Phillipe said. "A long time."

"Can we talk?" Sentell asked him.

Phillipe shrugged. "Do we have something to talk about?"

"On Cleburne's porch."

"I'll meet you there," Phillipe said, stepping into the rain and loosening the reins of his mount from the post.

Sentell looked into the store. At the back, Cleburne squatted behind his counter. On the other side Murray Taggert, shoulders hunched, back toward the door, listened to Cleburne, whose hand moved before Murray's face in a slow arc, pausing to punctuate his remarks. Sentell could hear Cleburne's voice, smooth and even, but his words were lost in the rainfall.

Then Phillipe stood beside him. Sentell, turning, offered Phillipe his hand.

"You never shook my hand before," Phillipe said. There was no accusation in his voice; he was stating a fact.

"You weren't a man before," Sentell told him, his hand still between them. "I've never shaken Morrison's hand either."

"A man," Phillipe repeated. "No, I wasn't a man then. Now I'm a free man."

"You haven't been anything but a free man since the first time I laid eyes on you."

He took Sentell's hand, shook it and let it go as if it were an unpleasant duty.

"You knew about that? About what my poppa claims?"

"I know you father told you the truth. He's been free for twenty years. I expect he was free before that. Amos would never have sent after him if he'd decided to go."

Phillipe struck one fist into an open palm.

"So Stevens ends up making me look like a black clown after all. I kill and get shot at and break my heart to earn what somebody already gave me."

"You did what you felt called to do. Would you have done differently if you'd known?"

"No," Phillipe almost shouted. "I didn't want that man's gift. Who is he to give my poppa or me what every man's got comin' naturally? Like at Vicksburg in that crater, you handed me my life when those red-eyed bastards were fixin' to shoot us down because we were colored. What do I owe you? They had no business even thinkin' of shootin' prisoners. You didn't give me anything. It wasn't any man's to take from us."

Sentell stared at Phillipe. "What are you talking about? I didn't even know you were at Vicksburg. You were . . . the sergeant with the bandaged head. After the mine, after the assault."

"Sure," Phillipe said. "It was me. And those men you had, they wanted to kill all of us."

"You had no business there," Sentell told him. "They hated you because you were an invader. Anyhow, my men shot no one. I gave them orders and they obeyed. It was my place to do so. What passed between your father and Amos Sentell was something else again."

"What do you mean, something else?"

"Your father was a slave. Somehow his natural rights had played out on him. Like the rights of the men who built the pyramids or the people Caesar's legions dragged in chains to Rome. If all of nature groaned at Rye's predicament, neither nature nor your Yankee friends did much more than wring their hands and ignore the law in order to help him. Whether you like it or not, those rights you claim your father had naturally were so much wind until Amos Stevens handed him that piece of paper. And then, with all his natural rights strung on him like tinsel on a Christmas tree, and Amos' paper to prove those rights were legally his, your father decided that he couldn't use those rights to get anything he wanted more than what he had. And that's the way it stands with twenty years for Rye to reconsider."

Phillipe had half turned toward the street as Sentell talked. He was leaning against a pillar of the porch, one hand on his chin. When Sentell finished, Phillipe turned back to him.

"Did you ever figure Amos Stevens knew what Poppa would do? Did you ever stop admirin' his honor long enough to see that that piece of paper might turn a restless nigger into a nice quiet dependable slave? One so nice and dependable that even the Union army and his own son comin' to him on his knees couldn't break him free?"

"You don't have much respect for your father, do you?"

413

"What respect do you have for a man who turns from freedom and his own blood to serve a master?"

"If I had the choice of serving Amos Stevens . . . with or without that paper . . . or being free on your terms, I'd be pouring coffee and polishing spoons right now."

Phillipe shrugged. "I didn't think we had anything to talk about. I was right."

"I thought you might have something else to say to your father. His staying with Amos doesn't stand between you. Any more than your Federal uniform does."

Phillipe shrugged rain from his waterproof and walked toward the porch's edge. Then he turned back toward Sentell. "I said what I had to say. I reckon the blue coat was too loud for him to hear over."

Sentell started to follow him off the porch. Then, at the steps, Phillipe paused. "Your land . . . ," he said slowly.

"My land is gone," Sentell told him. "The Yankees own it."

"No," Phillipe said. "I do."

Sentell stared at him, not understanding.

"I bought it," Phillipe said. "I just bought it."

"All right. Then it's yours."

"You ought to have paid those taxes," Phillipe said shortly. "Standin' on those Confederate tax receipts cost you a lot. You ought to have paid."

"I couldn't pay," Sentell told him. "And I wouldn't have paid if I could. I had no way to work that land."

"I'll work it," Phillipe said. "Samuels and me. We'll work it and bring in a food crop before frost this year. And next year we'll have some hogs. And cotton."

"Good luck. I hope you can make it pay off."

"Why shouldn't we make it pay off?" Phillipe said irritably. "Don't you reckon a colored man . . . "

But Sentell was paying no attention by then, because from down the street, over the steady tattoo of rain on the gallery, he could hear shouting. Not the sound of a man's voice, but a high treble cry like that of a girl with inordinately strong lungs. He squinted toward the river, past Ramsey's saloon, past the cotton-factor's. It came from near Ripinski's store, but the rain was too thick, the overcast too dark, to make out anything that far off.

"It sounded like some woman," Phillipe said. "Those soldiers . . . "

"Come on," Sentell said, pushing Phillipe down the steps ahead of him. "It better not be a woman. It better not be those soldiers."

There were already a dozen men around the door of the vacant building across from Ripinski's when Phillipe and Sentell got there. They could see Nathan Ripinski standing inside, his face obscured by shadow, his back bent as if he were speaking to someone on the floor. They could hear sobs behind him, and a long hysterical moan as Ed Norton Junior came out the door past Ripinski with his sister, scratched and covered with dirt, leaning on his arm. Ed Norton Senior put his coat around her and spoke to her quietly. Behind them, Nathan Ripinski had not moved. A few of the other men pressed into the building and stood near him, all their eyes bent to the floor a foot or so inside. Barney Wilkes, his hair plastered around his ears, leaned against the unpainted wall. He pressed his stump against his soaked shirtfront and shivered.

"That nigger and that trooper," Ramsey was telling the silent men. "What the Norton girl was sayin'. They left my place drunk after I told 'em to move on. And what she said . . . "

"What is it?" Phillipe asked Sentell.

"I can't tell," he said. "But maybe you'd better go down and meet Samuels at the barn."

"Don't tell me what I better do," Phillipe snarled. "I'll stand here till I'm ready to go."

"Suit yourself," Sentell told him. "I thought you had a farm to see to."

Cleburne moved in among the men, pushing and passing the time of day as he came. For all his high prices and low deals, most of them took him with grudging good humor. They could only guess at his sources and connections, but, wherever his flour came from, it made decent bread. They parted to let him through.

"What kind of trouble youall got?" he asked Ed Norton Junior, who had come back from taking his sister over to their store.

"Hangin' trouble," Ed said. His face was composed, his voice low and level. He was past anger. "I got a sister a couple of Union fumbled around with. Why don't you ask Mr. Ripinski what he's got?"

But Nathan Ripinski was not answering questions. He came through the doorway with his son in his arms.

"You want me to fetch one of them Yankee doctors?" someone asked.

Ripinski shook his head. "Is no need,. What can a doctor do for a dead boy?"

"No," Cleburne said, almost banteringly. "He ain't dead. Young Isaac . . ."

Ed Norton Junior cut him off. "He's dead, Cleburne."

They stood full in the gray light by then, and the boy's head bobbed on his father's arm like the carved invertebrate head of an ill-used puppet. His open eyes, filled with stiffening bright blood, stared into the continuing rain, and his jaw moved in strengthless rhythm with Ripinski's uncertain steps.

"Jesus," Murray Taggert said behind Cleburne. "Who done it?"

"A couple of Yankees," somebody said.

"Just up and killed a boy?" Murray asked, his face screwed up in elaborate horror. "Just killed him like that?"

Ripinski stopped at the edge of the wooden walk. He staggered one step more, and then sat down heavily, his feet in the mud, rain beginning immediately to dissolve the blood on his son's face and wash it into the street.

"No," Ed Norton Junior said, still calm. "No, not just like that. They were trying to rape my sister and little Isaac saw 'em pull her in there. He came over. The nigger was at her and the white man was standin' guard for him. Little Isaac started yellin' and fightin' the trooper. Then they did it."

Cleburne looked around him. "Who saw it? How come, if you know what happened, whoever saw it didn't step in?"

"My sister saw it," Ed answered, his voice sounding almost disinterested. "She saw it. And Barney saw it."

Barney, still leaning against the rough plank wall like a punished child, turned to stare at Ed Junior when he heard his name. His mouth worked as if he were talking, but there were no words.

"You mean old Barney didn't . . . ?" someone began.

"Lissen," Barney shrieked suddenly, his voice drowning out the rain's monotonous staccato. "We tried 'em. We come up past that church and let 'em kill us till hell wouldn't have no more. Hood never said we let him down. He never said it. We done all flesh could do. We wasn't gods. You ain't got no right to call me down now. I left a piece of me up there. Youall don't need to stare at me like that. We done what we . . ."

"All right, Barney," Ed Junior said. "It's all right. Youall did fine."

"We did fine," Barney repeated mechanically, his voice lowered, the sound of the falling rain rising above it again. "We did fine."

As Barney's voice faded, Ripinski began to talk. Not to Barney or to any of them. But to the mud. To the dark sky.

"In Poland, when the weather come bad they drink and then in dark night they would come. Would burn the temple and houses, kill the men and carry the goods away. They would laugh and vomit and kill more and force the women into the square and they would rape and slash with knives and toast the Tsar before they killed the women. But never did they butcher the children. When my father fell to them, they push me back into the shop. 'No, little boy,' they say. 'Later. We come again when you are man.'"

"I've got to go," Phillips said, his face gray, his mouth trembling. "Samuels . . . "

"Even those Cossack . . . "

"You talk to Major Bouvier," Sentell heard Ed Norton Junior tell Cleburne. "Tell him."

Sentell moved to Ripinski's side. "I'll carry the boy if you want," he said.

But Ripinski paid no attention. His face, streaming with rain, was set not in the hard lines of resistance but in an inalterable expression of hopelessness.

"Why don't you leave him alone?" Ed Norton Junior said to Sentell. "He don't need you."

"But is no difference here," Ripinski said. "Is all the same. Is a victor, the rest meat for his table."

"Where were you when it happened?" Ed Norton asked Sentell.

Sentell ignored him. Ripinski had risen to his feet, swaying under the weight of his son's body. "Momma," he was saying. "I forgot Momma. She must . . . "

"She don't know," Cleburne breathed behind Sentell. "They . . . their women stay out of things till somebody calls 'em. She'll be in the kitchen. Or in the sittin' room and he'll take her boy to her and she'll cover her face and they'll do whatever Jews do after the butchers have cut out what they wanted and gone on."

"Are you thinking about coming off dead center?" Sentell said to him without turning, watching Ripinski as he disappeared through the doorway of his shop.

Cleburne laughed or snorted. Sentell could not see his face to tell which. "One way or the other," Cleburne said. "One way or the other."

Then one of the men standing back in the shadows noticed Phillipe, who had mounted his horse in front of Cleburne's and started riding slowly up Texas toward Market Street.

"Is that the nigger?" he shouted. "There he goes."

"Sure that's the nigger," someone else yelled in answer.

The men began moving down the walkway, Ed Norton cutting in front. "Hold up," he shouted. "Just hold up. You know what we got to do. The general . . . "

But they began to press past him, one yelling, "That's the black son-ofabitch braced us in Ramsey's, too."

Cleburne was still behind Sentell as he turned and moved to catch up with them. "Well?" Cleburne asked.

"It's Rye's boy. He was with me on your porch when the noise started."

"Sure enough," Sentell heard Murray Taggert call out. "That's the nigger tried to kill me in City Hall an hour ago. Come on . . . "

But before they could move on Phillipe, the street was full of horses. It was Lodge and his escort.

"Hold up, goddamnit," Ed Norton shouted once more. "Youall hear?"

Lodge's escort watched the crowd nervously. More than two or three of the Southerners gathered together in one place made them nervous. Some of them wondered why Colonel Lodge had not declared martial law. Only Lieutenant Raisor knew why.

Lodge stared at the jostling shabby men. "What are you doing here?" he asked. "What has happened?"

Cleburne faded back into the shadowy doorway where they had found young Ripinski.

"I come to carry my sister out of the empty buildin' where one of your nigger sonsabitches left her lyin'," Ed said conversationally. "And on the way out, we picked up a dead boy your nigger and a trooper beat to death before they got boxed and moved on."

Lodge's eyes narrowed. "Someone was killed?"

"Someone sure was," Murray chattered. "Little ole boy nine or ten got his brains beat out and . . . "

"Shut up, Murray," someone said.

"You saw the men responsible?" Lodge asked Ed Norton Junior.

"No, my sister saw 'em."

"I seen 'em at the saloon," another put in. "It was the same ones. They was bad drunk in there and come on down this way."

Lodge ignored him. He was still looking at Ed Junior. "Your sister. Can she identify them?"

"My sister is yellin' and cryin'," Ed told him coldly. "When she gets to where she can identify her own poppa, we'll feel better."

"Then all you know for certain is that a hysterical girl claimed to have been attacked by two soldiers."

"Barney saw 'em," someone put in.

Lodge looked at Barney, who still cringed against the damp wall. "The idiot," Lodge said shortly. "You want the idiot to bear witness against two of my men. What will he swear? That they ambushed him on the Hagerstown Pike? Or that he remembers them from South Mountain?"

As he finished, Lieutenant Raisor rode up beside him. Raisor wore no cap and his tunic was unbuttoned. His voice, not yet low and settled, was raised in excitement. "Colonel," he began, "I heard about it. It had to be Jefferies and a colored soldier named Curfew. I checked the duty roster. They . . . "

"Shut up," Lodge cut him off. "When I require information, I'll ask for it. There is no proof any of our people was involved in this. It might have been one of these worthless rebels standing in front of you. Rape and child-murder go well enough with treason."

"Goddamn," someone shrieked, and the tight knot of men closed around Lodge's horse. His escort, three troopers and three mounted Negro infantry, drew their pistols. One of the Negroes, his eyes white and terrified in the gloom, cocked his piece and pointed it at Murray Taggert – who fell down in the mud and was nearly trampled by a rearing horse as he clambered back onto the boardwalk.

"Stand where you are," Raisor shrieked, still pawing his own pistol from its covered holster. "I'll shoot."

"What the hell you mean to do about this, Lodge?" Ed Norton Junior cried.

Lodge held tight reins on his horse and backed it off a pace or two from the men. He had not reached for his own pistol, had shown no sign of fear. Only his complexion, dark and flushed with blood, showed that he felt anything. "Do?" he almost shouted. "Do? Not a damned thing. I have nothing to do here but keep treason down and order in these streets. If you think a crime has been committed, take your complaint and your hysterical girl and your corpse – if you have one – to the marshal."

"That won't get it," someone shouted in rage. "You ain't gonna get past this like you got past whippin' Barney. Goddamn you for a Yankee . . . "

"Take that man into custody," Lodge cried. "You, Raisor. Take that man."

Raisor and a pair of the troopers cut a farmer out of the pack of men. The man, hatless and bundled in a loose skin jacket, tried to run, but was bracketed between their horses.

"Disturbing the peace," Lodge said calmly. "And vilifying an officer of the United States. Tell the marshal I shall fill out charges when I reach City Hall."

The men began pressing forward again. One of them had a short length of pipe. Another's hand was under his coat. Before Lodge could give another order, Ed Norton Junior was between him and the men, calling out, "I done said twice to hold up. That's an order," he shouted, his voice rising. "Now do it."

"An order," Lodge muttered.

Then, as if nothing had happened, Lodge began speaking again. "Of course, if you wish me to take notice of this alleged crime, I might find it within the range of my duty." He paused as the men turned back to face him. "Whenever I receive information as to who was responsible for the beating of Private Griggs here in the street."

"A deal," someone sneered.

Lodge smiled. Not in triumph, but out of some cold ugly knowledge that seemed to be his own special preserve. Not generated by war or victory, but out of the man himself.

"An exchange of information," he said serenely. "Something you want for something I want."

"Sit in hell till somebody comes to tell you," a voice cried. "Sit in hell and . . . "

"All right," Ed said. "Youall break it up and go on home. Ain't nothin' to do now. We heard what kind of law we can expect."

Lodge turned and rode toward City Hall, his escort trailing, the Negroes glancing back over their shoulders at the dissolving crowd of men behind. Finally there were only Ed Norton Junior and Sentell.

Ed leaned against a hitching rail, the rainwater running through his hair and down his face.

"Major," he said, his voice brittle and tired. "We've had words, but I'm past words. You're a Southern man and you soldiered as good as any at Vicksburg. Are you ready to come in with us after what you seen today?"

Sentell watched the fatigue creeping into his eyes, the lines of tension groove his forehead.

"I'll let you know," Sentell told him. "You'll hear from me by tonight."

"Yep," Ed said. "Blood opens up new paths. It happens that way every time. You had to put your hand into the wound, didn't you? No, I'm not blamin' you. I don't know how to blame you. Before, before today, it was pride and shame of losin' and anger on account of you carryin' yourself like you didn't even know what losin' was, much less had done it as much as the rest of us. And you keepin' your word like a treasure they couldn't get when we didn't' even have a silver teaspoon left to keep. But now it's just fear. Deep down dog-rotten fear. They put hands on my little sister and they killed that boy for tryin' to stop 'em, and Christ Jesus with a crystal ball can't see where they'll draw up. Lodge won't rein 'em, and they sure ain't gonna hold themselves in. And that leaves us right where we was four years ago. Nothin' but our guns and out guts between us and the basement of hell. We got to try it all over again just like we hadn't even thought of doin' it before."

"Did you ever think that Lodge might be goading you to that?" Sentell asked him.

Ed looked back quickly. "Ridin' us for a big fall? Maybe he is. But if he wants a fight, he's gonna get it. It's a fight or one at a time like Barney and Ripinski's boy. Either his way or ours. There ain't any help for it."

Sentell shrugged. He assumed none of them would listen – Ed Norton least of all, next to Morrison. But faced with Ed's reasoning, a paraphrase of Forrest's, but still with the ring of some terrible truth in it, the balance Sentell had held for so long, at least in his own mind, began to shift. There was still honor and the exquisite satisfaction of his word preserved intact. But honor, once a constituent of any life he wanted to live, began, even while Ed Junior talked earnestly, as he had talked in the trenches at Vicksburg, to lose its bouquet, and the pledge

Sentell had made to the Union began to feel not like an uncomfortable necktie but like a hangman's noose.

Ed faced Sentell, his hands open and hanging at his sides. "Jesus, Major, how long can you hold out? I know – every sonofabitchin' one of us knows – you ain't yellow and you ain't a Yankee man. What we say, what everybody does, it's all they know to do. You can't ask 'em to be a part of whatever it is you've been doin'. Even if they figured you was right, you can't expect 'em to stand by and cheer while you show what your given word is worth. Not when the promise was given to their enemy. Not when the promise cost 'em a major while the war was still on and a leader after it was over. Ain't no people on earth can give you that. Nobody can give you that."

"Tonight," Sentell told Ed Junior.

"He who is not with me is against me," Ed said without sententiousness, fatigue drawing down the corners of his mouth. "Tonight Major Bouvier will be up to my poppa's house. They'll be meetin' about Cissie and Ripinski's boy. If you was to come and stand with Major Bouvier . . ."

"All right," Sentell said again. "Tonight."

But that afternoon, while Sentell was reading what Tacitus had to say about the Germans, a towheaded country boy knocked at the door. Sentell's mother showed him into the library.

"Major," he grinned as if they shared a secret, "I come from Major Bouvier. About that meetin' tonight."

"I told Ed Norton Junior I'd be there," Sentell said.

"Naw," the towheaded boy went on grinning, his pale eyes moving curiously around the room. "They done changed it. Major Bouvier says you ought to come on out to Al Offut's old place around midnight or half after. They don't want to try Norton's no more. What they mean to do is meet out beyond town. With the killin' and all, that Union colonel is gonna have his ear to the ground. Major Bouvier says he's got to take care of outstandin' business and then he'll be out to Offut's after midnight with the rest of 'em. For a plannin' meetin'."

Sentell watched him for a moment, but the boy did not look at him. His eyes, pale with colorless lashes, were moving from one bank of books to the next. "All right," Sentell said finally. "Is there anything else?"

The boy rubbed his stubbleless chin. "You got a lot of books," he said.

"That's true."

"What do they say?" he asked, his eyes turned on Sentell suddenly. "I mean, a man don't waste good time without he gets somethin' for it. What do them books learn you?"

"It's hard to say," Sentell told him. "What did the war teach you?"

He grinned as if Sentell had asked him the one question for which he was prepared.

"Shit," he said, 'that's easy. It learnt me how to kill."

Then his grin, crafty and fugitive, widened. "Sure," he laughed, "them books is about killin', ain't they? That's how come you got to be an officer. All my officers were big readers and it took me till now to figure out how come."

V

5 JULY 1865 — At eleven that evening, Sentell was ready to start riding. The Offut place, empty since its bachelor owner had fallen near Mansfield in 1864, was perhaps twelve or thirteen miles outside town on the Texas road. It was six or seven miles past Murray Taggert's dozen acres, and for all its owner having been dead a year, was in at least as good repair. No one had purchased it yet, and it would be as good a meeting-place as any.

Sentell and his mother had finished a late supper, and, as he pulled his coat from the library closet, she sat in front of his desk, talking of the incident in town.

"So this afternoon, Mrs. Logan asked if you were ready at last to take your proper place alongside your neighbors. I told her I couldn't say, that you made your decisions privately."

"I wonder if Mrs. Logan realizes that the place she has in mind for me will probably be stretched out alongside my neighbors when the Federals get done."

Mrs. Sentell smiles briefly. "I don't believe Mrs. Logan thinks at all. Her son died in a Yankee boxcar on his way to a prison camp in Maryland. Dead sons tend to cloud the mind. Especially when the killers are still on the premises."

"Did she talk about what happened?"

"She called it a rape and a murder," his mother said. "She was a quarter right."

Sentell frowned and dropped his coat on a table. "A quarter right?"

"Yes. There was no rape. I'm not certain there was a murder."

"I don't know about the rape," he said, "but the Ripinskis are laying out their son. The undertaker seems to be acting on the assumption he's dealing with a corpse."

His mother shrugged. "I was at the Nortons' after I heard. I talked with Cissie."

"She said there was . . . "

" . . . no rape. The Negro held her, he talked to her. He didn't seem to have assault in mind. He only talked to her."

"Did he tell her Nathan Ripinski's boy fell and hit his head?"

"No. She saw it. She thinks the Negro lost his head, lost control of himself. She says he didn't seem rational."

"What do you mean?"

"Before Isaac came across the street, even while she was screaming and trying to get free, she heard what the Negro was saying. He asked her what she liked to eat, how it felt to go to a dance. She said he touched her as if she were a piece of china and he were a collector. There was no lust in it. Have you ever talked to Cissie? She's a very self-possessed little girl. Beyond the panic, she saw what was happening."

"Then the Negro dragged her into an empty building and posted the trooper for a guard so he could pass the time of day with her, and find out her taste in food and party dresses?"

"Yes," Mrs. Sentell said soberly. "Something like that. He wanted to know her name and if she loved anyone. He asked her how it felt to love someone."

Sentell said nothing, shaking his head.

"But all he got for an answer, of course, was more shrieks and more struggling, and then young Isaac came to the door and began yelling too. And the Negro, who had not done with her, who must have been building up to some other question in the only way he knew, turned and pushed her away and hit Isaac. Cissie said he hit Isaac two or three times. And afterward he talked to the trooper as if he had meant to rape her, as if that were what the whole thing was about."

"None of it makes any sense," Sentell said. "They were both drunk. She can probably thank the whiskey for being whole."

"I don't know," his mother said. "I wish I knew what the Negro was after."

"He probably wanted to quiet her before . . . "

His mother frowned. "Don't be dense. You can't quietly rape a woman. If it's quiet, it isn't rape."

"Well?"

"I don't know. There's no use going on about it. For your purposes, I expect it will be put down as a murder and attempted assault. There are limits to how fine the edge of judgment can be honed."

He nodded. "Anyhow, we have a dead boy to account for."

There was a ponding at the front door. Mrs. Sentell rose and turned toward the hall. "There are half a million dead boys to account for," she said.

It was Barney Wilkes. His thin hair was plastered across his face, and he held the stump of his maimed arm close against his chest. His eyes moved from Sentell to Mrs. Sentell.

"Youall," he began, and then, swallowing hard, fell silent. He tried again. "Youall didn't see it. If you was to of seen . . ."

"What, Barney?" Sentell's mother asked him.

"No, ma'am," Barney shook his head fiercely. "No, ma'am. I'll tell the major here. I ain't gonna tell you."

Sentell's mother glanced at him and shrugged. "I'll see you later," she said. "When you come back from the meeting."

Then, almost before she had closed the library door, Barney started.

""I don't want to talk about Isaac," he said. "I should of run over there, but when he started yellin' at that trooper I got to runnin', and I went in Ramsey's and went to tellin' 'em about the Unions and then they finally come on out and went down there, and I don't even remember nothin' but the boy, little Isaac, lookin' like he was in an attack. I don't remember nothin' else. It was like I had been somewhere else.

"Until later that puppy come up and got to whimperin' at me, and I took him around back and got some scraps out of Mrs. Ripinski's kitchen while she was down to the undertaker's. And when I come out there was this girl in the alleyway."

"Girl?" Sentell asked.

"I seen her before," Barney said. His talk was almost compulsive. Sentell had never heard him go on so long in one connected speech. "I seen her over to Fannin Street goin' and comin' around Mrs. Gruber's place. She lives in Mrs. Gruber's place. So she was in the alleyway. And she says to me – while I'm feedin' the puppy – she says: 'I want you to find that Confederate major. I got somethin' for you to tell him.' An' I said: 'What major? You mean Major Sentell?' An' she said: 'I don't know no Major Sentell. I mean that dark Frenchie named Bodier or whatever. The one with the face all froze. The one who bosses the men.' I said: 'What do you want with him? Why don't you go talk to him yourself?' 'Naw,' she said. 'If old lady Gruber found out, they'd fish me out of the river. You got to get word to him.'"

"What word?" Sentell asked impatiently.

"Jesus," Barney said, wiping his face with a piece of empty sleeve. "I'm fixin' to say. She told me to say them two Yankee soldiers was hid out in Mrs. Gruber's place. They was stayin' in a room like it was a hotel instead of a whorehouse, and Mrs. Gruber didn't know which way to go. She was afraid to tell the Unions for fear of them two in case they didn't even get no punishment, and she was afraid to tell the folks around here for fear of the Unions."

"Why did the girl . . . ?"

"Lissen, I'm gonna tell you," Barney cut Sentell off. "God, Almighty, what ain't I gonna tell you. She said Mrs. Gruber sent her up there to keep them two quiet. Said Mrs. Gruber tole her to do whatever they wanted. So she went up for a while, and then first chance she got she snuck out and come across to me."

"Why . . . ?"

"On account of the nigger. On account of havin' that hangin' over her all the time she was up there."

"Did he . . . ?"

"Naw," Barney went on in a puzzled tone. "That's the funny thing. That nigger done killed a little boy and dragged a girl into a empty buildin' for some, and when it's right there, he just tole her to go on out and leave him alone. She said he had hold of the foot of the bedstead with both hands. That he was shakin' and goin' on about blood and mischief so she couldn't even tell if he was drunk or crazy. Then the trooper took her over to her own room and they . . . "

"Then if the Negro didn't . . . "

"Because that was what he said then. She didn't know what he might say if she went in again or if she was even around when he come to hisself. She tole me she didn't mean to push her good luck till it had to give way to bad. He didn't pay her no mind then. But suppose he sobered up."

"But the trooper. Was he drunk?"

"Naw. She said the trooper was cold sober and plenty able. It was just the nigger who carried on."

Sentell tried to digest what Barney was telling him. He needed to understand it before he rode out to meet Bouvier, the Nortons, and the others. Not that anything he could squeeze out of it would make a difference to them.

"So anyhow, I went for that Major Bouvier," Barney went on. "I went to the hotel and around to the Nortons', and then I went on by Cleburne's on account of the men still campin' out on his porch, but that major wasn't nowhere. So I didn't see nothin' but to tell Cleburne and ask him to pass it on."

"Why Cleburne?"

Barney's eyes widened. "Why, on account of what he is."

Sentell frowned, not understanding. "What is he? A kind of parish bulletin board?"

"Why," Barney said, "he's the second man. They voted him second man. Some kinda grand gargoyle or somethin'."

"Second man?"

"He commands under the major. If that major was to get killed or somethin', Cleburne would be commander."

"My God," Sentell said before he could cut it off. Then he thought, This has to be a joke. Not just Cleburne – all of it. I'm worried over nothing. If I ride down Texas Street tonight, Ripinski's boy will be sitting on the walk with his dog. Maybe even the war was an hallucination. But he said: "Why Cleburne? Why not Ed Norton Junior? Or as long as they were in a mood to put a man like Cleburne in, why not Ed Norton Senior?"

"Well," Barney scratched his head as if the question had never occurred to him, "he's a pretty big man. And he's about the only man can get supplies easy. He even got some lead and powder last week. Just on account he didn't fight in the war ain't no sign he . . . "

"All right," Sentell broke in. "What did Cleburne tell you?"

"Nothin'. Not anything. He said I done right and to send that girl around to him if I was to see her again."

"Well," Sentell asked, "is that it?"

Barney pursed his lips and shook his head as if he were disgusted with Sentell. "Jesus, Major," he said, "naw, it ain't it. It ain't even the top half of it. All that was what went before. What I come to tell you was tonight. It was what I seen tonight, maybe an hour ago."

Sentell looked at his watch. If he didn't start riding now, he would be late to the meeting. "I have to go out to the Offut's place. Do you want to ride with me?"

"Naw," Barney said. "I don't want to go nowhere. I done my part. I don't care what they do. Anyhow, they ain't gonna be out there yet. They wouldn't go right out after what they done tonight."

Sentell closed his watch and leaned back in his chair. "Go on," he told Barney. "What happened tonight?"

Barney said: "I was in the hotel lobby when the rain stopped. I've been cleanin' out spittoons and layin' out towels since them Yankee agents come in and put a rush on rooms. I was lookin' out at the mud and thinkin' about how that boy wouldn't never grow up, how that nigger cut him off like he was the top of a turnip. It was close on to ten-thirty then, and the lantern glow caught on the water in the street and come back at me like light across the river. And I got to needin' a walk. I got to needin' some kind of air without cigar smoke and the smell of sweat in it. So I walked over to Marshall Street and down as far as Fannin and took that puppy with me. I don't know why I turned there to where it drops off and goes down toward the houses. I mean, it's slick and you can break yer goddamned neck if you ain't but ten and fast as a cat. But I went that way. Maybe I wanted to see Mrs. Gruber's on account of knowin' they was in there. I don't know.

"But I come even with Mrs. Gruber's and the lights was out. Not even the porch light on. It was like she was closed down. There was lights on either side of her house, but she was blacked out. And by then it must have been close on eleven. Most all the Unions was on back to barracks, because Lodge gives 'em two weeks in purgatory if they don't make that eleven-o'clock deadline of his. So I stopped down from Mrs. Gruber's a way, under that big oak that juts out in the street in front of Hobbs's Forge. I just kinda squatted down under that tree thinkin' of them two Yankee sonsabitches all comfortable and maybe pumpin' away in there while Ripinski's boy was cold and headed for a hole in the ground tomorrow mornin'. I wondered if I could get me a pistol and sneak in there. But that wasn't no good and I knew it, and knowin' it I just squatted down hatin' that house and everything in it. And Isaac's little puppy pissed up against the tree and shivered with his wet fur.

"Then the door opened. Down the hall behind, you could see a low light like a candle or maybe a lamp back of a curtain, and against that little light I saw 'em come out. The trooper was ahead. You could see his shoulders fill up the door, and when he stepped out onto the porch that handkerchief they wear around their necks stood out against the dark. There was a woman with the trooper and they stood on the edge of the porch laughin' real soft and pushin', kinda nudgin' one another. After then the nigger came out. He stood over to one side by himself with his cap jammed down around his ears. He leaned up against a post with wisteria vine growin' up against it and looked out into the street. I thought, Lord, he's seen me, and I caught hold of that puppy and put my hand over his muzzle. But the nigger was just starin' out at the mud, watchin' moonlight break through the clouds and scatter all over the puddles.

"Then the nigger said something to the trooper, and the trooper laughed again and slapped the girl on her butt and run her on into the house. When she shut the door, they come down off the porch, the trooper walkin' like it was his house he was comin' out of. The nigger was different. Kind of hunched over like it was still rainin', and the cold of it getting' through his jacket. And they started across the street right toward me.

"But before they got their boots wet good, I heard this sound. Right off, I thought it was thunder, that the rain wasn't out after all. But even as I thought thunder, I looked up and the clouds was broke up and the moon ridin' clear and bright. So I looked down Fannin and there they come.

"Major, you never seen nothin' like it. They musts of been thirty or thirty-five of 'em, and they filled up the whole street from one side to the other. They was dressed in sheets or somethin' white with pillow-cases over their heads, and some of 'em with red things like dunce caps and masks and one with horns and eyes that shined like they was in a jackalantern."

Barney stopped. "How do you reckon they managed that?"

"Managed what?" Sentell asked.

"Them eyes shinin' like that," he mused.

"For God's sake, Barney."

"All right," Barney said. "They come on up Fannin Street till you couldn't hear nothin' else. They come on till you couldn't see nothin' but them sheets and whatever they wore on their heads. Except the Unions. Except that trooper and that nigger. They was talkin' and the trooper kept pointin' over toward me – except he must have been pointin' over to the stable up on Texas behind me. And the nigger was shakin' his head. Once he put his hands over his ears. They was so wrapped up they didn't even hear it. They never looked up until the whole street was flooded with them riders, until they was almost under the hoofs. Then the trooper looked around and he pointed and reached for his pistol, and the nigger turned and saw 'em and covered his face, and then the riders reached 'em and went over 'em. But then, just then, as the first horses reared up and come down, I heard – over the horses – that nigger yell out: 'Jesus Christ!' And the horses come down splashin' the mud and water, diggin' up the street, and movin' on so the next rider came over the same place. And they come past me. One of them horses hit me with his shoulder, and I fell back against that big oak and the puppy broke free and run off somewhere. And they rode on up Fannin toward Market Street. And they was gone.

"But the trooper and the nigger was still there. And the muddy water in the street was beginning to settle so that you could see the moon shiverin' off it like it was cold, and then stop and stand still with pieces of cloud racin' across it like little kids racin' for home.

"And the whole time, the whole time it took, there wasn't a sound except for them horses. Not a word, not a yell if you don't count that nigger yellin' out for Jesus. And then I got up and shook the water off that them horses splashed all over me and come on over here to tell you."

Sentell slumped in his chair. It was as if a spring inside his backbone had snapped. Barney, whose eyes had been fixed on the window behind Sentell as he finished, stared squarely into the lamp at Sentell's elbow. A wispy smile formed on his lips, and he brushed his face again with his empty sleeve.

"Ain't that the damndest thing you ever heard?" he asked in a sprightly tone.

VI

5 JULY 1865 — This time all of them could be sure: Bouvier really meant to smile. He stood behind a scarred handmade table at one end of dead Offut's single room, and a lamp's rays firing upward across his maimed face infused it with a singular aspect of ruddy health one moment, doused it the next in a pattern of mottled darkness and streaked light

that brought to mind not the fact but the fancied appearance of leprosy. Still he was smiling, and the smile caused some of the men in the front to snicker nervously and stare at one another in feigned uncertain good-humor.

Bouvier had arrived late. He breathed heavily and drew a mud-stained glove from his paralyzed hand (under the gray glove was the black covering he never removed, and one of the men, a drummer in small notions who worked the northern part of Caddo parish near a tiny community called, with blunt misdirection, Plain Dealing, thought of the Chinese boxes and what one invariably found in the final tiny box as he remembered hearing that the major's useless hand and arm were always wrapped in that same black covering).

"Gentlemen," Bouvier said as men continued to press into the cabin, "we would have met at our original time, but a matter of special importance arose. You have all heard of the death of little Isaac Ripinski this morning. But death's horse has a way of running wild once the stable doors are thrown open. I have to tell you that this evening, only an hour ago, that same steed brought two soldiers of the Union army down even as they left an establishment of high-class entertainment."

The room was silent. Even the men in back who still pressed inside made no sound as Bouvier paused. Then he began again. "I speak figuratively, of course. About the steed."

Laughter began with those who were still coming in, who had ridden up with Bouvier. It spread through those who had been waiting until even the imaginative drummer from Plain Dealing, staring at an ugly thick-lipped man next to him whom he had never seen, began laughing as if Bouvier's remark had somehow triggered a long forgotten but hilarious private joke.

Bouvier lifted his good arm and motioned for quiet. "Please, gentlemen, don't hold the wake before the inquest. Mr. Ed Norton Junior would like to give a brief report on our first operation."

As Ed Junior stepped into the lamplight, he saw Mo Stevens come in and move forward to stand against the wall near Bouvier. Ed grinned self-consciously as if he were about to deliver a grammar school graduation speech.

"Well, first of all, the major and them who was with him are sorry youall missed tonight's doin's. But there wasn't no time for a full meetin', and anyhow youall know an action like this ain't regimental business. It was a patrol, a reconnaissance in force with a double execution along the way. What was done to Ripinski's boy and my sister today ain't wiped out, but the scale don't hang quite so heavy against us tonight."

"You mean youall bushwhacked them two Yankee sonsabitches right in town?" someone asked in an awed voice.

"Just that," Bouvier said with precision.

"Just that," Ed Junior echoed. "We got word from Cleburne, who heard it from one of them girls in Miss Bessie's place about where they was holed up. The rest was just waitin' with a man staked out to make sure they didn't make their move till night, till our time come around."

"The rest was silence," Bouvier laughed.

"I'll be goddamned," someone said.

"Jesus, what'll Lodge . . . ?" another started to ask. Then his voice died out.

"Lodge ain't exactly in our calculations," Ed Junior sneered. "He'll do what he does. But he ain't got a witness, and he ain't got a suspect – no more than when that towheaded Yankee bastard got whipped a month back. Lodge has got two of what we got one of: corpses."

"He ain't gonna let it lay," a short swarthy farmer from the north of Bossier parish across the river said slowly. "He ain't gonna sit and swap killin's with us just whenever we got a mind to stir things up."

"Well, he was goddamned sure not goin' after them two blue bellies himself. Most of youall heard his terms this mornin'. We hand him a man to put that Yankee soldier's whippin' on and he'd *see* about Isaac's killin' and my sister. You want to play them rules?"

"Hell no," Hornsby blustered. He was standing among those who had ridden in with Bouvier. The butt of a Remington pistol protruded with careful ostentation from his belt. He elbowed the drummer from Plain Dealing. "You want that kind of thing?"

"Me?" the drummer squeaked. "Aw no. Hell no."

"Anyhow," Ed Junior went on, "it's done and over. You can't fix a pair of trampled Federals."

"All the kings' horses couldn't do that," Bouvier put in bitingly.

"Not even ole Barney's mule," someone shrilled.

"That's *my* mule," a deep voice cut in.

And the laughter broke again in raucous uncontrollable waves as if it were part of a necessary and inescapable ritual. Ed Junior's raised arms did no good. Hornsby howled, trying to outdo his neighbors. The drummer gasped and choked, his eyes not simply moist but actually running with tears so copiously that his cheeks were covered as if he had been suddenly and overwhelmingly bereaved.

"All right," Bouvier said finally, moving back to the table, displacing Ed Junior. "All right. We've got planning to . . . "

Then he saw Sentell enter. "I told you," Ed Junior said triumphantly. "He *said* he was comin'."

Bouvier's mouth twisted. "His word is good with you?"

"Sure," Ed Junior said frowning. "Major Sentell's word is worth . . . "

"All right," Bouvier said quietly. Then aloud: "Gentlemen, give Major Sentell some room."

The crowd turned to stare at him. There was neither surprise nor expectation in most of the faces. They had no opinion of Sentell, or possibly had two opinions, each working against the other. They had learned to leave him alone. At least most of them had.

"What the hell is he doin' . . . ?" Hornsby started, his voice loud and blustering in the silence.

"Let it drop, Hornsby," Bouvier said. "Major Sentell is welcome. Every organization has its regular members and its special cases. The major is a special case."

"Special my ass," Hornsby answered. "He don't want to fight. Who says he's special?"

The question hung unanswered for the least part of a second. "I do," Bouvier said softly.

"Don't let me interrupt," Sentell said. "I'll just listen if I may."

"Perhaps we can have a word together afterward," Bouvier said, his voice still smooth and courteous.

Sentell nodded.

"It's well the major is here," Bouvier went on, raising his voice again, ignoring Hornsby, who continued to stare at Sentell after the rest had turned back toward Bouvier again. "Since our next step has to do with him in a manner of . . . "

As Bouvier paused again, Sentell turned with the rest. It was Amos Stevens pushing the door shut behind him, shuffling over to the un-painted wall where a farmer rose and offered him a chair. Amos shook his head and squeezed the man's hand. Then he took a frayed muffler from his neck and faced Bouvier.

"It seems all our separated brethren are coming back tonight," Bouvier observed pleasantly.

"They can go . . . ," Hornsby began. Then he saw Bouvier's face and let it drop.

"Won't you have a seat up here, Mr. Stevens? Your neighbors always like to have you with them," Bouvier went on.

"You're kind," Amos said without warmth. "This will do. I don't reckon to be here long."

Bouvier shrugged. "Then we'd best talk about our next work."

"Will it take all of us?" someone asked cautiously.

"It will take every man we can mount," Bouvier said firmly. "If it gets done right, there may not be any more night-riding for a while."

"Whatcha got cookin'?" one of the men asked.

"More disciplinary work of the sort we handled out tonight," Bouvier told them. "Two Unions outraged the town and paid the price. There is one more Union – no, two more, I understand – who need strong persuasion. One of them is a Negro who served as an officer in the Union army. The other is his man, a sergeant.

"The Negro came from Shreveport," Bouvier went on. "He was the property of a Shreveport man who treated him more than kindly. He rode north with that man's son and at Sharpsburg, while his young master slept, he went over to the Federals and began shooting and killing the very people who had raised him, trained him, and given him a respectable place to fill. When he came back to this town, it was with Union epaulets on his shoulders, a Union commission in his pocket, and a hatred for us large enough to engulf the whole parish. Today he made it clear what he wants, what he intends here. He purchased the land of a man who fought for the Confederate States, who lost that land because he refused to pay Yankee taxes."

"That nigger's gone too far," someone shouted.

"Wait," Bouvier said, holding up his hand for quiet. "As an isolated act by a white man, what Crowninshield has done would be cause for a whipping, maybe tar and a few feathers to send him back North again to stay with his keepers."

"He'll get more than . . . ," Hornsby started.

"But what he has done is not an isolated act. And he is black as the ace of spades."

Amos stared at Bouvier – or past him – rubbing his long muffler between his thumb and curled fingers. Sentell kept his eye on Amos, and moved through the dense gesticulating crowd toward him. Mo, still standing against the wall, paid no attention to his father. His eyes were quick with excitement, and he did not look away from Bouvier's dark frozen face.

Bouvier's hand was raised again and his eyes, bright as Mo's, flicked across the mass of swaying men, searching out the faces of Sentell and Amos Stevens as he began again.

"This Negro will put himself at the head of every ignorant former slave in Caddo parish – perhaps in all of north Louisiana. He has every credential: slave birth and rearing, a Union uniform and land taken from a leading white man. And he has one advantage that even Lincoln lacked: a black skin. Given success, allowed to hold that land, there will be no stopping him. There are two of them now, but there will be more. He must have strong backs to work that place, and every Negro who goes there to work will stay to worship: 'This man is our leader,' the ignorant bucks will say. 'Not the Union white man army or the white man government: this man who sweated like us, who threw off his own yoke and fought to cast off ours; who walked into the very city of his bondage and took up the land of a whipped rebel.'"

Bouvier paused, his voice ragged, his twisted face shining with sweat. "Do you see?" he cried with evangelical fervor. "Do you see what Crowninshield really means to you?"

"Yes, goddamnit," Hornsby roared, and the room answered in one deafening blast of sound. Now the men were answering for themselves. What had begun with fear and confusion and uncertainly was beginning to sort itself out and take form around Bouvier's personality. If he lacked two good arms of his own, he was bending a hundred arms to his purpose. The shaping was almost done now: only the tempering would remain.

Over the uproar, Sentell was trying to talk to Amos Stevens. "Don't make any mistakes," Sentell almost shouted. "He has them past fear. He had them past reason with Forrest, and now they've tasted blood and even the fear is gone. Don't say anything. Let me talk to him afterward."

Amos shook his head. "That boy is nothing to you," he said, his voice almost drowned in the tumult. "I've not old enough to let this pass. I'm not that old."

Sentell caught his empty sleeve and turned Amos about roughly. "Yes, you are," he said, his voice edged and brusque even over the howling that continued all around them.

435

Amos stared at him. "You . . . ," he started, beginning to flush with anger.

Sentell shook his head. "We can thrash it out later. I want you to let me talk . . . "

"You can talk if you want, goddamnit," Amos choked out finally. "But you can listen to what I tell him first."

He pulled away from Sentell and shoved the men in front of him aside. Sentell moved forward behind him, but made no effort to stop him. Bouvier was gesturing for silence. Ed Norton Junior and Mo Stevens stood near him now, talking, pointing at an imaginary map. Mo grinned and drew his finger across his throat. Ed Norton laughed and put his arm around Mo's shoulders.

"You, Major," Amos boomed, waving his single arm at Bouvier. "You, Bouvier."

Bouvier beat the table with his good hand. Ed Junior and Mo both raised their arms for quiet.

"Mr. Stevens," Bouvier smiled courteously. "Quiet there. Mr. Stevens wishes to speak."

"I have a question," Amos rasped.

"Certainly, sir."

"Do I understand you to be provoking these men into an attack on Phillipe Crowninshield?"

Bouvier's smile widened. He turned his frozen face toward the rest of the men. "Yes, you could say that."

"Then stop it," Amos barked. "There will be no night-riding against one of my people. The men who make that ride will deal with me."

For a moment, Bouvier stared at Amos as if he had not heard him. Mo's eyes slitted and he leaned forward toward his father.

"One of your people," Bouvier repeated. "That Negro is one of your people?"

"He is precisely that," Amos said. Around him, the rest mumbled. Hornsby started to say something, but Bouvier waved him silent.

"I had thought these were your people," Bouvier said, covering the close-packed mob with a gesture.

"So they are," Amos answered. "But Crowninshield is the son of my man. He has been part of my family since his birth. His mother is buried in our ground – next to my wife. He belongs to me."

"Not since the Yanks come," someone snickered.

"He belongs to me as his father belongs to me. In the same way I belong to them. There is love and warm feelings between us. I will not have him killed."

Bouvier nodded patiently. "It may be you belong to him, Mr. Stevens," he said. "It seems all of us are about to have black or Yankee owners. But as for love and warmth, Crowninshield and his partners get their love in Madam Gruber's establishment and their warmth from the blood of children."

"That's a lie," Amos snarled. "Save your rhetoric for the bumpkins. Phillipe has no more in common with that Northern filth than I have."

"Which seems to be a good amount," Mo inserted loudly, bitterly.

"Shut your mouth, boy," Amos answered. "I'm talking to the major."

"I'm sorry, Mr. Stevens," Bouvier said. "I can't call operations off because they result in lacerated feelings. You must understand . . . "

"You better understand this," Amos shouted. "If a sonofabitch in this room hurts that nigger boy, I give my word as an honorable man I'll lacerate his ass for him. He'll wish to Christ he'd never seen the inner edge of Caddo parish."

"Say, honorable man," Mo sneered, "does that go for me?"

His father stared at him. Not as a son or even as an acquaintance. As a man to be reckoned with. "It does," he said slowly. "If you, or if any one of your gang, kills Rye's boy, I'll have your life before the Yankees can get a saddle on a mount."

"Mr. Stevens," Bouvier tried to cut in.

"You talk pretty big for an old one-armed man," Ed Norton Junior blustered. "I wonder can you back it up."

"If Mr. Stevens finds himself lacking chips," Sentell said almost casually, "I believe I can find a few."

"Edward," Bouvier said quickly, "this isn't your quarrel."

Sentell moved up to the table. The lamplight showed thin streaks of gray beginning to spread in his hair. His eyes were cold, distant. There was no passion in them.

"You just finished a civil war," he told Bouvier. "You want another one? Is that your specialty now?"

"The Yankees . . . ," Ed Junior began.

"Damn the Yankees," Sentell said shortly. "I mean between us. Between you and me, Charles, after what we went through together at Vicksburg. Between Phillipe Crowninshield and the people he grew up with. Between Amos Stevens and his son."

"Don't you worry about me," Mo shouted. "I don't need . . . "

"Boy, there isn't hardly a thing you don't need," Amos said, the anger gone from his voice.

"We mean to survive," Bouvier said doggedly.

"By killing your neighbors?" Sentell asked.

"That black Yankee bastard ain't no neighbor of mine," someone bawled.

"Amos Stevens is. And you heard what he said. You heard what I said. Phillipe's quarrel is his. And his is mine. That's how it is. So the killing stops here, or there just isn't much telling where it will stop. If you kill Amos Stevens, there isn't a moderate man in the parish whose hand won't be raised against you."

"And if you try for Sentell, you'll have to kill me or I'll kill you," Amos said, almost smiling.

"So it's a circle. Break it and you're finished," Sentell said.

"We could get 'em both right here, now," Hornsby said. He reached for his pistol with exaggerated menace.

"Stop it," Bouvier shouted. "We want no trouble."

"We got trouble," Mo said. "You can't get rid of trouble by whistlin' it away. You got to bury it."

Bouvier paid no attention to him. "If Mr. Stevens feels that strongly about it, I expect we'll have to change our plans. A house divided against itself," Bouvier said ironically. "You know the phrase, Mr. Stevens."

Amos ignored the thrust. "Then I have your word that Phillipe will be let alone?"

Bouvier inclined his head, his static twisted features unreadable. Then he looked up. "You have my word," he told Amos Stevens. "You have my word on that."

Amos studied him for a moment. Then he turned toward the door. Around him, the men gave way, muttering to one another.

"You can't give him your . . . ," Mo began furiously.

Bouvier caught his arm. "Of course I can," he said. "Of course I can give him my word."

He turned to the rest of the men. "We'll meet again. You'll get word. Keep your mouths shut about tonight. If you are arrested by the Unions, remember your oath."

They began filing out, quietly at first, then beginning to talk. Hornsby was angry. He held the Plain Dealing drummer's arm and pointed repeatedly back toward Bouvier. The drummer nodded without pause, and the men around him listened intently. At the table Ed Norton Junior and Mo were still arguing with Bouvier. Mo struck the table with his fist and gestured toward the door. But he saw Sentell still standing in the middle of the room and kept his voice down. Ed Junior turned away and stared at the ceiling abstractedly. "Goddamnit," Ed Junior said without heat.

Bouvier pushed Mo out of the way. Before Ed Junior could turn, Bouvier had him pinioned to the wall, only the toes of his boots still on the floor. "You remember the price they set on disobedience at Vicksburg?" Bouvier rasped, his voice louder, more overpowering than Sentell had ever heard it before. "On disobedience to orders before the enemy?"

"We shot 'em at Black River," Ed Junior said, his answer muted by a twisted collar tight at his throat.

"We still do," Bouvier finished, pushing him halfway across the room. "This is no private war for your amusement. This is the same war fought another way. The same men, the same cause, the same enemy – and the same discipline. Do both of you understand me?"

"Sure," Ed Junior said placatingly.

"What?"

"Yes sir," Ed said, and headed for the door.

Mo followed, pausing by Sentell for a moment. "You put the old man up to this," he said carefully. "That makes one more I owe you."

Sentell ignored him. And as Mo reached the door, Sentell did not turn to see how he and Ed Junior stopped with Hornsby and some of the others just beyond the door. Nor did he see any change in Bouvier's expression as Ed Junior silently grinned from the doorway and waved. Sentell's eyes were on Bouvier's face, and there was nothing to read there but pain.

Sentell was outflanked from the start. As the room cleared and he heard horses riding into the fog, he faced Bouvier across a scarred width of shoddy pine table. It seemed to him that the last traces of that precociously young major of artillery had vanished. Not physically: except for the face, except for the motionless arm, his body was the same. He had gained no bulk, and as he moved around the table, his ruined face bearing a terrible parody of a smile, Sentell saw the same grace, the same effortless flow of weight from one leg to the other that had made Bouvier easy to recognize by stride alone at Vicksburg.

But there was something more to him now: an unstudied nonchalance, a kind of total self-control so absolute that nothing could penetrate it, nothing stall it or turn its purpose. The old tension, the piano-wire nerves and emotional reflexes were gone. The boy was boiled away. Only the hard angles and the unstrained mettle of the man were left. Sentell had no hole-card of age or experience to play now. Chronology meant less than nothing. There is a point at which additional experience registers itself as mere attrition, adding no wisdom, no tincture of authority – only wearing out and breaking down the very substance of man upon which wisdom and authority depend for articulation. So they were matched. Except that Bouvier was in motion, acting and pressing others into action while Sentell, knowing the momentum that action – any kind of action – breeds, was trying to apply brakes on a downhill run.

Bouvier wasted no time fencing. "All right," he said before Sentell could ask, "I lied to your old man. I'm calling off nothing. You knew that. You don't even have to ask."

"That's right," Sentell answered, his face dark and angry. "I knew what you said and how you said it was too plausible. I didn't think you'd turn away from something you'd begun."

Bouvier shook his head. His voice was strangely light . . . almost cheerful. "Never turn away from a job till it's done. Didn't your father teach you that?"

"Yes," Sentell said. "My father was a zealot too. He said that with no qualification. If I had been the same kind of madman, I suppose I would have accepted it about a bad job as well as a good one."

"One man's meat," Bouvier said. "Anyhow, your old man is safe. Stevens will be home by the fire when we settle with his renegade Negro."

Bouvier paused. His eyebrows knotted into a frown. "Did you see how he accepted my word? No questions, no suspicions. After I harangued these sheep to the point of making them men for a few hours, old Stevens simply took my word when I said I'd call it off. Can you imagine that?"

Sentell turned from him. "Yes," he said, staring out the door into the midst. "I can imagine it."

"You'd think a man that old, a man who had lost an arm in battle, would be smarter. You never know."

Sentell turned back. He moved past Bouvier and sat on the edge of the table, slapping his palm with his gloves. "You never known," he repeated. "What I want to know is when. When are you going after Phillipe?"

Bouvier's frown gave way to something like a smile again. "You don't expect me to tell you?"

"There's nothing wrong with my word," he said.

"No," Bouvier pondered. "The Yankees will vouch for that."

"When?"

"Why?"

"Because I want to make certain Amos is in that house of his tomorrow or the day after or whenever you do it. I don't want him to do by accident what he means to do on purpose. He could ride out there anytime – probably just the time you choose."

Bouvier walked slowly around the table. "He is given to night-riding? With that taste for evening air, we could have used him."

"No one uses him."

"All right," Bouvier said abruptly. "I'm tired. I need rest. Will you give me your word to tell no one what I say to you?"

Sentell paused, his gloves poised near his open hand. Then he met Bouvier's eyes. "You have it," he said.

"That's good," Bouvier said, as if he were musing to himself. "I have your word. I feel as secure as a Yankee parole officer."

Sentell reddened. His gloves clapped against his palm. "You've got what you asked for. Now return the favor."

Bouvier relaxed. "It's all gone, isn't it?" he said.

"Gone?"

"What we had before. What you and Masterson and I carried through that damned rat-trap across the river."

Sentell shook his head. "We change."

"Or we don't change."

"Let's get on with it," Sentell said. "We're not historians. Leave the dead to bury the dead."

"We're dead," Bouvier said flatly. "We're extinct. There's no future for either of us."

"Not yet. Save the requiem until you've roused Lodge enough to oblige you. Then let the children sing it. They can all gather in front of City Hall and weep for their fathers. Dead burning out a Negro's farm."

Bouvier started to answer, but Sentell struck his gloves against the table. "You said you were tired. So am I. When?"

"Two nights from now," Bouvier said softly. "After midnight. We'll invest the place except for the river side. That will leave Stevens' nigger the choice of shooting it out or trying to swim."

"You can almost walk across the Red now."

"It gets harder with men on horseback shooting at you."

"You know the end of all this, don't you?" Sentell said, just short of anger.

"Surely," Bouvier answered. "Surely. What can we do but terrify a few niggers and kill a few others and whip or hang or ride down Yankee carpetbaggers and soldiers who are not themselves the root of the trouble? We treat symptoms, you say?"

Sentell nodded.

"But mightn't that be enough?" Bouvier went on. "Terrorize a few and the bulk will mind its manners. Did we have to kill every man in an attack to turn back the Unions? Did we have to get to the root of things and assassinate their officers to break them at Fredericksburg or Chancellorsville? Sooner or later, the Negroes and the Yankee buzzards who are buying this land and dispossessing us will realize that Federal soldiery can no more protect them from us than it can ward off snakebite. Then they turn. Then they play along or move on. Then we belong to ourselves again."

Bouvier's voice had risen. He paced back and forth in front of Sentell as if the cabin were once more full of his supporters. He gesticulated with his good arm, pointing, driving home his arguments. The lamplight caught only the healthy side of his face as he stalked across the room in one direction. As he returned, only the stiff immovable portion with its numberless tiny scars was visible.

"Or suppose not? Suppose night after tomorrow is our last night out? Suppose all of us here and in Marshall, Texas, in Colfax, in Mansfield – suppose we are all ambushed? Then we're no worse off than now, and we can leave a charge to those mourning children you put in front of City Hall. With every drop of blood we would say to them, 'Remember. Remember and grow strong and avenge us.' A lot of little Alamos," Bouvier smiled suddenly.

"You mean it," Sentell said in bewilderment. "You really mean it. You'd as soon lead those men to be butchered as to doing butchery themselves."

Bouvier shook his head. "Leave the meat market out of it. Not as soon, not voluntarily. Only knowing it could come to that and knowing – not planning or even anticipating – that dying well beats living badly all to hell."

He paused to draw a breath, and tried to smile once more. "I thought you admired the Alamo."

Sentell frowned. "I admire it because it made San Jacinto possible. Without that, it was meaningless."

"And San Jacinto made your trip to Chapultepec necessary, didn't it?" Bouvier said sadly.

Sentell said nothing.

"A man who uses knives should know that they cut two ways," Bouvier said. "And he finds out they go deeper than he plans."

"Can't you put away your knives?" Sentell asked.

"Not with their bayonets at my throat."

"A wagonload of corpses," Sentell said, "and nothing changed."

Bouvier stopped pacing. He stood in front of Sentell, waiting for him to raise his eyes. "I should think a wagonload of corpses would change a good deal just by rolling into town."

The lamp guttered as Sentell rose. Bouvier stared after him as he walked out into the ground-fog. Finally, he snuffed out the lamp and stood in darkness, his single hand moving slowly across his scarred face like the hand of a blind man searching the features of a stranger.

VII

6 JULY 1865 — Somehow the night was good to them. Vera was on the porch when Mo came. They did not go inside or even pause there to talk. She handed up a comforter and some cornbread wrapped in paper and then let him lift her onto the saddle behind him.

There was still moonlight and the sky, broken only by the tops of pine and oak and cottonwood, stretched out above them flecked with stars like a dark pond of tiny unmoving silvery fish. Beneath, the tall grass was still heavy with yesterday's rain and fog stood like currentless water around the horse's uncertain hoofs.

Mo prodded him on toward the river. He kept the reins in his left hand, pressed the horse's head down with his right. "Hold tight," Mo told Vera. "If he spooks, he'll throw us all over the parish. Branches scare him. In a mist, almost anything scars him."

Vera was paying no attention. Her arms were tight around his body, and she stared past his head upward toward the moon. She let the uneven rhythm of the ride lull her almost to sleep. It was so bright, so clear high above. But from the ground up to the height of the horse's shoulder, the mist stood like smoke around them. So instead of watching trees and brush materialize and disappear, she kept her eyes on the moon.

It rode like a cold chariot, smashing through fragments of cloud, chasing other bits as if it consumed them in order to fuel its brightness. She wondered if there had ever been people on its chill pitted face. She had seen that enigmatic surface once through a telescope. A wounded Confederate major had passed his evenings, hour upon hour, staring into the heavens and muttering about the folly of humankind. Once he had invited her to look at the moon.

"You love the moon?" he had asked.

"Yes," she had told him. "I do. It's so clean, so beautiful. It ain't like things we live with. It's something else."

The major had laughed shortly. "There are always illusions and always an instrument to destroy them. Here," he had said, "come and see your beauty up close."

She had leaned smiling to the tiny eyepiece. As she focused and found the moon's blinding disk, her smile had died. "Medusa," the major had snarled. "The face of a dead world. Pits and mountains. Cold – my God, as cold as a grave in the shadows of the craters. Dust and broken rock on the plains and the sun's hot rays forever standing overhead. There is no sound, no laughter, no call from one human being to another. Not even tears or screams. No air, no seas, no life. Do you know what it looks like? Do you want to know exactly what it look like?"

"No, it's not . . . "

But the major, his voice a hoarse whisper, was not talking to her any longer.

"It looks like a battlefield," he had said. "Like Gettysburg. Or Cold Harbor afterward. If the lens were strong enough, we could see the corpses, thousands of stony corpses sprawled across her face, left over from a war that ended before our world even began."

444

He had stopped and swallowed. "It looks like a battlefield," he said again.

And Vera, pushing aside the flimsy metal tube and holding down her tears, had run from the window, from the dark ward smelling always of carbolic and corrupt flesh, onto the street. But above her, in the shrill and inescapable perspective, was the moon, and she had turned her eyes to the sky again, shaken by the new, the unspeakable, but still looking upward and understanding perhaps, something about beauty.

"It's low," Mo was saying.

"What?"

"The river. You could get over to Bossier parish without wettin' your hair."

Vera laughed. "They got a ferry for that. You don't even get your feet wet."

"I hear the Federals are checkin' every man who crosses the ferry."

Vera shrugged. "They act like old maids. They can't quit lookin' under the bed."

Mo reined in his horse. "They won't be easin' off any time soon. Two of 'em got killed tonight."

Vera's eyes snapped downward from the moon. "Did you . . . ?" she asked, trying to see the side of his face.

"I was there. I guess maybe twenty or thirty fellas had a hand in it. It was kind of a funeral party for Nathan Ripinski's boy. He won't go under alone."

Vera dropped from the saddle and walked across sandy ground, down a long incline toward the river. Mo tied his horse to a thin sapling and followed her.

"You couldn't stay away, could you?"

Mo shrugged and kept walking. "We been over this ground before. I don't want us to argue about it. We can have a good thing. We can have any kind of life we want."

Vera tore a blade of grass lengthwise. She put the stem between her teeth. "You've got to be alive to have any kind of life. The Unions ain't goin' to let this pass like they did that boy you whipped."

"We've got 'em goin'," Mo said, paying no attention. "All we got to do is show 'em that they can't break us, that they'll lose two for every one of us they get. When we're done, they'll either pull out or let us run our own country – so long as we salute that stars and stripes rag of their and don't make too much fuss about their stinkin' Union."

"It won't be that way. They won a war. They ain't goin' to let a few ratty horsemen tell 'em what and how and where. You know that. You see it as plain as I do, plain as your poppa sees it."

"Never mind my poppa," Mo spat. "Act like I didn't have a poppa."

Vera shook her head. "I saw 'em come back to the hospital with holes and cuts and tears and snags all over, inside and out. But none of 'em lost their senses any worse than you. Your poppa hates the way the war went. He wanted us free. But failin' that, he don't want us all dead or livin' on dirt forever. He says the people have got to forget what's past and go on with what's here and to come. He's right."

Mo pulled her down roughly to the sand beside him. "Forget all that talk. I want to talk about us."

His hands moved down either side of her neck to her shoulders. He slipped her dress down across her upper arms. "You look good with it like that. With the moon on you, and that frock down like a ball-dress. Before the war . . . You remember the dance?"

"I remember," she smiled, her eyes on the slow wrinkled water below. "Mostly I remember how I didn't have nothin'. Just that shack and a father who hadn't never been worth a pot of pee."

"Your poppa has stood with us," Mo said accusingly.

"You don't want to talk about that," Vera said matter-of-factly. Then she turned back toward the river. "I remember every time I went into Norton's store. I almost got sick to my stomach lookin' at the bolts of silk and the ready-made dresses. They had hats from Memphis and lace up from New Orleans. And I'd buy twenty pounds of meal or maybe five jawbreakers and slice of salty. By the time I was done with school, all I could think of was getting' out of that shack and away from that mean sorry sonofabitch."

"You hadn't ought to talk about your poppa . . . "

"Leave off it," Vera snapped. Her face was bright with recollection: not the pleasure of it, but the anger. She was remembering herself as she had been, and the sharp edge of that old hunger bought tears to her eyes.

"I wanted a big house," she went on. "I wanted some of that silk and sheets so soft I couldn't feel 'em under me. And hats. Jesus, I wanted me a cupboardful of Memphis hats. I wanted music in the evening and a moon like this. There was always a moon like this. And I wanted you."

Mo stared at her. "Me? How come me? What did I have to do with it?"

"You *were* it," she said. "You were the key to open the big treasure chest. If I got you, the rest of it just came along."

"Goddamn," Mo said. "It sounds like you was buyin' a pig. If you pay for the tail, you get the hams and shoulders."

Vera laughed and tossed her head backward. Her hair tumbled around her shoulders. "When you don't have nothin', romance don't come into it. Like in a war," she said archly. "It's not that you like to kill other folks. You just do what you have to. That's how it is when all you got is hunger."

But Mo was stiff and withdrawn. "All the way through it, I kept thinkin', You don't want to let those bastards put you underground because you've got love waitin' for you. No matter what else, even losin', I had that. No: I thought I had that. What I had really was somebody waitin' for her Memphis hat money to come back and be spent. Somebody hopin' her New Orleans lace and warm parlor wouldn't take a bullet in the head somewhere up in Virginia. Christ Jesus," he finished, and slumped over on one elbow.

Vera did not bother to comfort him.

"All right," she said, "as far as it goes, that's so. But then . . . "

"Then I came back, and you figured lace or no lace it was better to have a man than not?"

Vera's shoulders, white and luminous in the moonlight, shook. At first Mo thought she was crying. "No use in that," he said roughly. "You just said more than you should have."

But Vera hid her face in her hands, turning away from him.

"Come on," he said. "You just as well cut it out. You can't change . . . "

Then he realized she was laughing. Her hands fell away from her face and fell backward on the sparse damp grass. Mo reddened with anger. "If you think it's so goddamned funny," he blustered.

"It is funny," she said. "Funny that I used more silk and lace to tie bandages for four years than I could of used up in a lifetime of dresses. It's funny that I wanted you to lift me up and now I'm tryin' the best I know to bring you one rung at a time out of hell."

Mo's anger dwindled. "All the same though," he said, "I guess I hadn't even thought of it before. I've been so much taken up with fightin' the Unions I'd forgot myself. I'd forgotten what I'd lost. My country, most of my friends buried between the Mississippi and the Potomac, even what my poppa and I had together. And I expect the land will go before Lodge and his bullyboys move on"

"It'll go for sure if Lodge catches you."

"I ain't goin' to wait for Lodge to drop his other boot. He dropped the first one on Ripinski today. Whether you sit still like a good dog or chew off his leg, you might get hit with the second one. Whether the land goes or not, I ain't gonna be housebroken by that thin-blooded sonofabitch. What good would land be if there wasn't a man to tend it? A dog can't do nothin' with land – except fertilize it."

Vera's laughter was gone. "A dead man can fertilize a field."

"You really worry, don't you?" Mo asked gently.

"I won't humble myself," Vera told him distantly. "I said I love you before you ever went off killin' people. It didn't mean so much then, but it came to mean everything. When the lace and hats turned into bandages and gun-waddin', and the houses burned or empty, I thought about you. I wanted you back. But I'm not goin' on any more. You can . . . "

"I will," Mo said and pushed her back onto the grass.

That night it was chilly and damp, and a constant wind blew down the river. As they lay under the shabby comforter with Mo's horse blanket under them, they could hear the slow rhythm of water washing up onto the sand, the insects and night birds. The moon reeled down the sky's long road and disappeared, leaving behind a double handful of stars scattered like seed corn in dark earth. They were not cold, and until the sky began to lighten, neither of them spoke again.

He was still silent, and standing on shaking legs among the human fragments of an infantry company he had commanded for the past three days. Commanded not by order but by the happenstance of meeting thirty or forty men still more or less under arms, still believing that they constituted a portion of the Army of Northern Virginia. They were past hunger and on the far side of fatigue when he had come across them on the road beyond Saylor's Creek. If any of them, Mo included, had been subject to physical collapse, it would have happened the first – certainly the second – day out of Petersburg. Now they hardly thought of food or rest. They operated on nervous energy alone, and it seemed to Mo that he had never before been sharper, faster in response.

He had joined them beside a muddy crossroads while they buried their lieutenant (they had had no captain for two months, and even the lieutenant, dead now and past caring, would never appear as such on an official roster because, failing to receive a replacement for their captain, the company had elected the hardest, most graceless sergeant left among them to a lieutenancy and had paid for the choice by losing twenty-two men in as many hours – including one whom the lieutenant himself had shot for refusing to carry ammunition like a pack-mule). They had come across Mo and placed him in command as the Praetorian Guard had appointed emperors in the hopeless late afternoon of the Roman Empire.

Now they stood about or lay on the wet ground waiting. None of them knew where he was. Someone, the sole survivor of another company, had said they were within a howitzer shot of a dingy village called Appomattox Court House, but they had seen neither courthouse nor village and they had been ordered by a major on horseback to hold where they were, and to resist any attempt by Union troops to move on them. They had obeyed not only from soldier's habit, but as much from the awesome feeling attendant upon seeing a field-grade officer for the first time in almost three months.

"I thought all of them had give it up and gone home," someone said, only half joking.

"Where should we expect 'em to come from?" Mo had asked the major. "We don't even know where the front is."

The major had stared at him with an odd expression. "They could come from anywhere. The front is all around you."

"Sir? Not to the west. The west is clear."

"General Gordon says otherwise. Sheridan is there."

"Then . . ."

"That's right," the major said quietly, hurriedly. "You'll get orders. Don't shoot if you see Unions moving to the south or east."

"Don't shoot?"

"Goddamnit," the major barked. "I said it plain. There's a truce. If they don't move on you, don't fire."

"A truce," Mo repeated dumbly.

The major had not answered, had spurred on his bony mount and disappeared into a grove of trees to the north. Then they had waited.

Mo had almost fallen asleep, but as he drifted between sleep and waking, he had heard a peculiar sound from the direction in which the officer had disappeared. It seemed at first to be a cheering – as if hundreds of men were whispering in unison. Then it became a moan.

"What do you reckon?" one of the men asked.

"Can't say. Sounds like a whole regiment got the bellyache."

"Shit, ain't nobody in this army had feelin' in his belly for a week. Mebbe they all stubbed their toes at the same time."

"Lissen," someone else said, "whyn't a couple of us walk up through them woods and see what's stirrin'?"

Mo stood up. "I'll walk over. I want to see what's over there. We might have to move that way."

"Or they might come at us thataway," one of the men said softly.

As he reached the far side of the trees, Mo walked carefully. There was no front, no established lines. One side of the trees might be Confederate; the other under direct Union fire.

But there were no Unions. There was only a long stock-path of a road, rutted and muddy, and lined thinly on either side by dirty scarecrows, some with guns, more without, who stood now soundlessly waiting and watching down the road where a few horsemen were riding toward them from the direction of the noise Mo and others had heard.

"What's goin' on?" Mo asked one of them.

"I ain't sure," the man told him, swallowing hard. "But General Lee had truce called. He was up the road talkin' to Whiskers."

"Grant? The general was talkin' to Grant?"

"I dunno what it is, but . . . "

Then the horsemen came abreast of them. The rider in front sat his gray mount as if he were on parade. Not with the studied poise of a martinet, but with the unconscious erectness that comes with a final effort to conquer fatigue by pure act of will. Mo studied him – not to identify him, but to make sure that he was not himself hallucinating, was not reshaping a staff officer's unfamiliar features into the image of a face he knew better than that of his father or himself.

Some of the men on either side of him stepped into the road. They touched the flanks of the gray horse, reached upward and stroked the officer's boots which were mud-streaked to the ankles and polished mirror-bright above. Other men from father down the road followed behind trying to close around the gray-haired, bearded man who nodded from side to side automatically and lifted his gloved hand from time to time in recognition of the ragged affectionate cheers that followed him. But his eyes, deep-set and circled with blue, did not lower themselves to the road. They were fixed straight ahead as if a triumph or a martyrdom lay at the end of his ride.

Mo had not moved except to pull off his ragged cap. His mouth, surrounded with a scruff of soft dirty whiskers, was partly open. Then he heard what the men following the riders were saying.

"It's over. They done cornered us and the general . . . "

Some of them were crying. One bald-headed sergeant sat in the cold mud of the roadside with his head, hatless and shiny, hanging between his knees. "O Lord," he was choking. "O Lord, You coulda had me at Sharpsburg or up in Pennsylvania. You coulda had me twice at Manassas and You come close to takin' me off at Gaines' Mill. How come You spared a man for this? How come . . . ?"

Near Mo, a dark-haired private soldier, his clothes covered with mud, rags wrapped around his feet, was carefully smashing a spotlessly clean Enfield rifle to pieces against a stump. "Blow it, Gabriel," he was shouting. "Blow your goddamned bugle and be done with it. There ain't a thing left to . . . "

As the riders moved out of sight, two of the scarecrows across the water-filled road squared off. "I don't give a pinch of mule shit what you say," one of them shrieked hoarsely at the other, "if he give us up to them Yankee bastards, he's a treasonous old sonofabitch. If he's lost his grit, he ought to of turned over his command and . . . "

But the second man was on him, punching, gouging, screaming. "You call General Lee a name, you . . . "

And others, tears still cutting through the grime on their faces, gathered around.

"Kick his nuts for him," one of them bawled. "Lemme have a piece of him," another yelled.

Next to Mo, a soldier – or a boy – with a Sharps rifle and two bandoleers of cartridge ammunition and the hard features of a middle-aged man pulled on his sleeve.

"Sir, is that right? Is it so that we've quit?"

"I don't know," Mo said, the image of the gray-haired rider still before his eyes. "I can't tell you anything."

He felt suddenly sick. As if the strain, the lack of sleep and food, was all about to collect its due in one burst of overwhelming weakness.

"Wait for orders," Mo said, hearing the flat quack of his own voice. "Just wait for order and do your duty."

Then the weakness billowed upward like smoke or mist, paralyzing his legs, chilling his guts and bubbling into his throat and eyes as if he were drowning in it. It was like sleep coming on with the velocity of a rifle ball. He felt himself staggering backward into the brush and weedy stalks just off the road, and he gave way to it like a child who has staved off bedtime far beyond the usual hour only to find the effort useless and the postposed defeat not only inevitable but even pleasant, and darkness like a warm blanket pressed around him.

Then he was awake again, awake and flooded with a cold and unspecified fear as if there were something he had to do, or a place he should have gone but never reached. His eyes were wide open, and the night spread about him, breached only by starlight, seemed alive and filled with movement. He felt Vera beside him.

"What?" she asked drowsily. "Did you hear . . . ?"

"I don't know," Mo said, his voice hoarse, breaking like an adolescent's. "I was remembering, I mean dreaming. I thought I was . . . "

"A fox," Vera said, still half asleep, stretching, her body touching his beneath the ragged comforter. "If you come awake too quick," she said dreamily, "it gives you a headache all day. You better . . . "

He was listening to her voice, but the words meant nothing. He looked down at her face framed in dark coils of thick shiny hair. It was as if he had come from Virginia to Louisiana in a single instant. All the loneliness and fear, the frustration and the numberless kinds of hunger he remembered wrenched him again stronger than before. He pulled the comforter down and looked at the dark centers of her breasts, the unconscious grace of her arms, the abrupt narrowing of her waist. It was more than desire and less, and his hands reached for her with a will and direction of their own. At first the touch itself was a physical shock. She stirred and opened her eyes.

"What?" she asked. Then she looked up, narrowed her eyes and saw his expression. She smiled and raised her arms slowly.

"About that lace," she said, her smile widening, her body moving to meet his. "And the hats."

He was breathing as if he had marched from Petersburg to Shreveport without stopping. As if he had run across a measureless field under fire. He felt spasm after spasm break within him like summer lightning. "You're cold," Vera whispered. "You better pull up that cover. You . . . "

"No," he told her, kissing her shoulders, her breasts. "No, I'm not cold. Don't talk. Don't do anything but what you're doing."

The stars had begun to fade and dawn, gray and lifeless, was spreading, unfolding above them. The sky was the color of limbo, and they lay caught in each other's arms. From a distance they could hear a rooster and a single mockingbird. The wind freshened, carrying the smell of the river to them. By the time the sun rose, they were asleep again, and this time there were no dreams.

Lieutenant Raisor was sick of it. He was sick of the alternating dust and mud, of the suspicion and hatred that followed him as he passed among the townspeople. He was sick of Lodge's insane single-mindedness and the stubborn resistance of the parish. Most of all he was sick of bloodshed and the portent of more to come.

He had commanded a burial detail that morning. There had been a yawning and disinterested guard of honor, a perfunctory volley of musketry, and plain wooden coffins covered quickly with clods of soaked earth. While they were burying the soldiers, the other end of the churchyard was full of people in shabby clothes surrounding a smaller coffin. There were summer flowers scattered over the coffin and chairs for Nathan Ripinski and his wife. The rest of the people, heads bowed, eyes turned toward the Unions until the two undecorated graves had been filled and soldiers marched off, stood in silence until the rabbi finished.

Now Raisor was riding through almost deserted streets with a detachment of grim troopers and nervous colored infantry awkwardly riding extra mounts. Behind windows, at the edge of a half-open doorway, Raisor could see shadowed faces, a hand. The people watched him and his men as they rode past. They watched, and Raisor knew that some of them were ready to do more – had already begun to do more. His hands held the reins more tightly than usual; his back was rigid. He felt as if there were a dozen invisible rifles leveled at him.

Raisor's nerves were gone. In addition to the mounting pressure, he had had almost no sleep the night before. When he had finished his work for Lodge, as he was pulling off his boots, Rye Crowninshield, his face expressionless, eyes bright and inscrutable, had knocked on his door to tell him what a late patrol had found sprawled and crushed into the mud of Fannin Street. Lodge had been in the study. He was standing at the foot of the stairs as Raisor came down, buttoning his tunic.

"You heard? The Negro told you?"

"Yes sir."

For a moment, Lodge could not say any more. His face, dark as Rye's, filled to bursting with blood yet stiff and void of emotion, turned from Raisor to a pair of draggled troopers who stood dripping mud on Amos Stevens' rug.

"Bring them here. Drag them her behind your horses," he shouted.

"You mean them dead soldiers, Colonel?" one of the troopers asked, horrified.

Lodge clenched the rail of the banister as if to keep from falling. "The rebels," he choked. "The murderers. I want them here. I want them flayed until there is not an inch of unscarred flesh on their bodies. Do you hear? Do you hear me?"

"We hear you, Colonel."

"How many have you taken?" Lodge asked the shivering troopers.

"Sir," one of them answered, "when we got there, we found the two of 'em spread out in the mud and some of them girls lookin' out of the windows of one of them houses. There wasn't anybody else there. We didn't get anybody."

"The women, did you make them tell you what they saw?"

The other trooper scuffled his boot across the rug. "Sir," he said uneasily, "we asked 'em, and one of 'em told me she couldn't see anything on account of she was on her back with . . . "

"Shut up, Patterson," Raisor said automatically. "How many times were they shot? Could you tell?"

"Hell, sir," the first trooper said, "there wasn't either one of 'em shot. They were rode down. They were trampled."

"We looked 'em over for hoof prints," the other trooper said, earnestly, "but you couldn't make out one from another, and we . . . "

"Shut up," Raisor said again. "Colonel, we'll have to wait till morning. They've scattered by now, and all we'll do is stir up more mud and grind the men down if we start now. If we . . . "

Lodge struck the banister rail. "I don't want your opinion. I want the rebels. Not in the morning, not later. I want them now."

Raisor shrugged and looked across at the troopers who in turn stared at the wet rug. Then a Negro soldier was at the kitchen door, walking down the hallway uncertainly. "Dey's a man," he began slowly, studiously, "an' he wants de cunnel. He say he kin . . . "

"Get out," Lodge said shortly. "Tell him . . . "

" . . . tell de cunnel who did . . . what was did tonight. He say . . . "

Lodge turned back to the Negro. "A small man, bad eyes, poor clothes?"

The Negro slowly shifted from one foot to the other. He seemed bored. "He look like dey poked him out from under a barrel a garbage wif a pointed stick."

"What?" Lodge frowned.

"White trash," the Negro shrugged laconically.

"All right. Tell him . . . never mind," Lodge paused. "I can see him. You," he jerked a thumb at Raisor. "Come along."

Murray Taggert was moving around the kitchen like a bobcat in swampland. He paced from the fireplace to the door, cocked his head over his shoulder to stare back at the fire. He rubbed his hands on his dirty trousers and spat into the hot ashes. In his pocket he carried a silver-trimmed wallet full of bills. It was more than he had been able to save in a lifetime of scratching and clawing. He had gotten it earlier that evening with a minimum of risk, as usual. Now he was angling for still more – or at least a chance to hold and use what he had.

When Lodge and Raisor came in, Murray wasted no time with prologue.

"They didn't say nothin' to me," he whined. "What happened was they all of a sudden got up and got whoever was to hand. I wasn't there. I was . . . workin' my place. You got to chop cotton this time of year. So when they come by I was in the field and they went on and laid low till dark and meantime somebody tipped 'em off where them two – yer two – was, and the next I know is out to Offut's place when that Major Bouvier started talkin' about horses and all, and then I had to go again. They put me out to guard in case some of youall was to . . . "

Lodge cut him off with a gesture. "Never mind. I don't pay for excuses. I want the names of all of them."

Murray squinted hesitantly. "I . . . "

"Well?" Lodge barked.

"I need a pencil and somebody to write them names down," Murray wheezed, collapsing into a kitchen chair.

Raisor leaned against the wall, fascinated. He had been with Lodge almost every moment, but he had never seen Murray before, had had no idea that Lodge knew anyone outside the garrison and Amos Stevens' house.

"When you finish the names, there will be something else," Lodge was saying to Murray.

"Somethin' else?"

But Lodge was talking to Raisor. "The names," he said. "When you have the names, begin to pick them . . . " Lodge paused, his hands resting lightly on the kitchen table. "No" he said loudly, hoarsely. "Let them be. Keep the list, but arrest no one."

"Sir," Raisor began. "You just got through telling me to . . . "

"Don't be a fool. You bring them in, I question them. And each one of them will have a dozen witnesses who swear he was at his fireside with a checkerboard or holding family prayers when those men were trampled. Let them alone."

"Not even the rebel major?"

Lodge's colorless eyes were bright with excitement. "Bouvier, the one from New Orleans? Him least of all. Take him and the rest would collapse. Leave him alone. Let him think we know nothing."

Murray had left the room. Through the door they could hear him pouring out names in a quiet raspy monotone while one of the troopers wrote them down with painful exaggerated care, scratching loudly, making the pen sputter and spurt ink across rough paper.

"An' Ed Norton Junior an' Paul Mitchell from over to Bossier parish an' Esdras Mitchell his brother, from up to Benton, an' C. W. Turner out on Milam Street, an' some little sawed-off peddler out of Plain Dealin' an' . . . "

Lodge listened, amused. "A bad intriguer," he said, his lips curling briefly. "Even Judas Iscariot had to possess intelligence."

"This one will never hang himself with a halter," Raisor said, not trying to hide his disgust.

"No," Lodge said softly. "Not by his own hand. It will never come to that. They will beat him to that."

"Sir?"

"One way or the other," Lodge finished.

Raisor shook his head. "This is sickening. It smells of the Borgias. There is nothing soldierly about it."

Lodge stared at him. "Chivalry, Lieutenant? Perhaps you are on the wrong side. There are only two kinds of soldiers: those who win and those who lose. The only attribute important in a soldier is victory. The rest is gilt and trimming. We will win. I will press this animal in the next room for a name, and when I have the name, you will get your orders."

"Name," Raisor burst out. "My God, he's given you the name of every man in the parish, including the bedridden and half the names in the Episcopal cemetery."

Lodge shook his head impatiently. "Not the right name. I want the right name. A man of importance among them: a man of intelligence – with Taggert's character."

Raisor shook his head. "You won't find him. Not those things in the proportions you need. Not in the same man."

Lodge tapped the table with his fingertips. "Don't be naïve. He is there, and Taggert will know him. Taggert will know him as blood knows blood."

So Raisor had left to look over the two closely written pages full of names while Murray went back into the kitchen with Lodge. Once in a while, Raisor could hear Murray's whine rising above Lodge's low determined voice.

"Lissen, I could get my ass . . . "

"Now lissen, you ain't got that kind of money . . . "

"I don't care. Even if you was to try me, it'd only be prison. If they get me, it . . . "

Raisor caught himself drifting off to sleep. He sat up quickly, snapping his eyes back to the paper. The two troopers, not yet dismissed, sprawled in a corner asleep, past even the pretense of military propriety. Raisor turned his head toward the stairs. At the top, Rye Crowninshield stood watching him. One of the troopers coughed in his sleep and turned over, the butt of his pistol clattering on the pine floor.

Then Lodge was at the kitchen door. "I have it," he told Raisor excitedly. "I have the name."

Behind Lodge, the kitchen was empty. The back door was ajar, and the room was full of chill air, the smell of the night. "He may have earned his money finally. This may be worth ten troopers."

Raisor's eyebrows lifted. "How do you mean to pay Taggert the difference?"

But Lodge paid no attention. He had stepped into the hall and kicked the muddy boot of one of the sleeping troopers. "You," he said irritably, "come with me."

Then, following the staggering trooper back into the kitchen, he glanced at Raisor. "That will be all, Lieutenant," he said. "Until morning."

"But . . . ," Raisor started, curious despite himself.

"There will be orders in the morning," Lodge said with finality.

Raisor shrugged as the kitchen door closed. He nudged the other trooper with his foot. "Tell the sergeant to set up a burial squad in the morning. Then go to bed. There's nothing else to do tonight."

Now he was riding down the slope of Fannin Street, his patrol spread out on either side, carbines at ready, each of the men scanning apparently empty windows, squinting down alleyways. As they neared Bessie Gruber's establishment, Raisor saw a handful of women and old men standing under the trees across the street. In the middle of the street, four or five little boys stood where the Unions had found their two men. One of the boys saw Raisor and his men coming. He pointed, yelling to his friends in high childish falsetto:

"Here comes a bunch of 'em. Lookee, here some of 'em comes."

When Raisor's men drew abreast of them, two of the boys fell kicking and writhing in the dirt, pantomiming agony. The others, neighing and prancing, trampled over them, back and forth, again and again.

"Help," one of the boys howled up out of the dirty street.

"Ain't no help," one of the others roared, stamping viciously close to his prone companion's head. "Ain't no help for you Yankees or niggers this side of judgment . . . an' nothing but hell on the other."

"You boys break it up," Raisor commanded.

"Whatcha fixin' to do, Yank?" the boy asked.

"Youall gonna do us like you done Isaac Ripinski?" another asked.

Raisor's face reddened. "Get off the street," he shouted, louder than he intended.

The boys scattered as a pair of troopers spurred toward them. They pushed past the few old people at the edge of the street and vanished, running and tripping, into an alley.

At the end of the street, where Fannin ran into an open field, Raisor reined in. "All right," he said. "Corporal Patterson, carry them back to City Hall, check with the marshal and turn them loose."

As the horsemen rode back the way they had come, Raisor followed them slowly, the distance becoming wider until the patrol disappeared at the head of the street. Raisor paused in front of Bessie Gruber's house where two Negro infantrymen stood at the bottom of the steps.

Their rifles were bayoneted, and both men held them at port, ready to use. Raisor wondered why Lodge had sent the Negroes alone, and why he had given the order direct to Sergeant Packard instead of passing it through him. The Raisor frowned. It was not hard to figure out.

As he spurred his horse onward, he saw a girl leaning out of an upper window. She gestured to him. "Hey, Yank," she called sweetly. "Whyn't you come on up? See how we go at it in Mississip'. Whyn't you come on up?"

Raisor lowered his eyes and rode on. He wondered how much the girl charged, and what she might find to buy worth more than what she sold.

VIII

6 JULY 1865 — Don Juan Cleburne was not at ease. He did not like to leave the store during the day. He did not like riding across open fields and through narrow trails off the main road where a stray farmer hunting rabbits to replace his lost corn and depleted pork might happen to see him and wonder, where a loose-tongued Negro on his way to fish the bayous along the river could notice him and mention it to another . Most of all he did not like the hard straight-backed unpadded chairs that Lodge supplied.

"You beat me to it by maybe an hour," Cleburne was saying. "When that nigger soldier wearin' old clothes came in with your letter, I thought, Where did he get this one? You over did it. There wasn't a field nigger in the parish ever wore nothin' that poor. He just as well of come in his uniform with a guard on white mares and a mulatto playin' 'Hail Columbia' on a cornet. If the white people didn't pay him no mind, you can be sure every nigger on Texas Street knew he was one of your soldiers before he ever pushed that broke-down mule into town. They probably even knew who youall had took that mule away from."

Lodge watched Cleburne carefully. "I wanted to save you embarrassment," he said, clearing his throat, angry at his own anxiety not to offend Cleburne.

Cleburne turned his good eye on Lodge. The other fixed trancelike on the large window behind and to Lodge's left as if it were watching for unexpected visitors.

459

"Embarrassment," Cleburne snorted good-humoredly. "Listen, you got to understand one thing right off: we ain't playin' with mean kids from across town, and the stakes ain't a bloody nose and goin' to bed without no supper. The only thing keepin' you alive right now is they know killin' a colonel will bring Sheridan and half the Yankee army down on 'em. They know too that you ain't gonna call for a regiment on account of one nigger soldier and a no-good trooper. Because it would look like you can't handle your own beat. So you can relax. But if they was to get the idea I had made free with what I know, they'd take a week to kill me. Did you ever see a man dragged through brush and burr-grass behind a fast horse?"

"You have my personal assurance . . . "

"I beg your pardon, Colonel," Cleburne cut in on him, "Your assurance ain't worth a good goddamn. You can't even put hands on the men that rode your boys down."

"I have names. Your name . . . "

"All right," Cleburne said patiently, as if he were instructing a child. "Murray spilled his guts and you got a list and he told you I could be reached. Suppose you bring in every man on the list. Do you reckon you could get 'em convicted even in a New York court? The dead trooper's own mother wouldn't pay Murray Taggert no mind. On top of that, I'll bet you them silver leaves of yours at least half the men on your list wasn't even in on it. Murray gave you the names of every man in the parish he figured was mean or gutty enough to night-ride. And probably the names of every feller he's got a grudge against."

Cleburne paused, grinning. "You got to learn just how to use fear," he said, a hint of patronage in his voice. "You overplayed it with Murray, so he just said anything he thought you wanted to hear. He knew you couldn't never be sure how much he was right, how much he was wrong – and how much plain lyin'."

Lodge's lips tightened. He was tired of the lecture. But self-control was part of his heritage. "I did get your name," he said.

Cleburne shrugged. "I hope you didn't pay much for it," he said. "Because I was plannin' to come see you this evenin' anyhow."

"You were . . . ?"

"Things are crestin'," Cleburne said, "and I can't use Murray anymore. He'll do for spadework, but when it comes to fine slicin', I'd rather do my own. If I make a mistake, dyin' for it won't seem quite so bad. I'd hate to die on account of that trashy sonofabitch."

"You can't *use* . . . "

Cleburne frowned with surprise. "You thought you owned Taggert? Lord, I figured you knew he was a rag doll on a stick. I even reckoned you knew who it was pullin' his strings. You Yankees really are kinda slow. You thought . . . " Cleburne began to laugh, and then stifled it, glancing around as if he might be overheard.

Lodge's face darkened. He was trying hard to hold on, but Cleburne was pressing him. He did not like to feel that his own plans had been second-guessed, that the initiative lay beyond him, and not only beyond him, but not even in Bouvier's hands; rather in the hands of a fat walleyed merchant who, so far as Lodge had known until now, had done nothing more significant than corrupt his commissary officer who, after all, had been pleading to be corrupted anyhow.

"All right," Lodge began, "you own Taggert. And this is play for large stakes. But you were coming before I sent the Negro. You weren't coming to inform me of a first mortgage on Taggert or that the rebels are using real ammunition. You had something else."

"Sure," Cleburne said. "Somethin' else. Since you been dealin' honest with Murray and keepin' it quiet, I figured it was time to get him out from between us. He costs you money and he pulls down my profit margin."

"He gave you the money . . . ?"

"Naw," Cleburne told him. "It wasn't enough to be worth hearin' him howl. He just kept me up on what you was doin', and told you what I said for him to tell. But I expect it's time to liquidate my holdin's. Things are comin' to a head, and when the pressure starts buildin' all around, ole Murray is fixin' to come apart and start makin' lists and givin' names to whoever happens to be closest to him with a pistol."

"So you came yourself. To deal for yourself."

"That's it. I figured you been payin' a little and getting' less for a long time. I figured you ought to be ready to pay a good price for a good product."

Lodge folded his hands. Things were moving too rapidly. Now it was under way, and one mistake could turn his clean-up operation into a new civil war. Not a full-scale conflict, but a long and vicious guerrilla war that might spread into the Arkansas mountains, the hills of east Texas, and go on for years. It was essential to judge quickly, and to judge right. He looked at Cleburne for a long moment. But there was nothing to see but a grotesque fat man with sallow freckled skin and heavy hands marked by labor, not recent but intense. There was no flaw in his commonness, no enigma, nothing surprising or mysterious about him. If what he had for sale seemed worth the price, Lodge would have to judge its value for himself. The gods were silent. Cleburne seemed no prophet.

"What is the product?" he asked finally.

Cleburne's face did not altar. He did not seem anxious. "The rag and tag, the leavin's and remnants of the Confederate army."

"The night-riders?"

"That's it," Cleburne said evenly. "You can buy 'em one by one, a dozen at a throw – or you can toss economy to the wind and pick up the whole goddamned bunch in a single lot."

Lodge stared at him. Not because of the offer, but because of the offhand way Cleburne made it. There was no hatred, no fear – not even venality in Cleburne's manner.

"You tryin' to guess how many you can afford?"

"No," Lodge tried to smile. "I was wondering what kind of man is glib in the act of betraying his people."

Cleburne's eyes widened. "Jesus," he wheezed. "You got hold of a new tune, ain't you? You killed every sonofabitch south of the Potomac River that tried to be loyal to his state and his family. There ain't a foot of clear ground in the South your bluecoats ain't let blood on or stole the goods from. Youall called us rebels – we had treasoned your flag and betrayed our sacred compact. Now I come in to make me a few loyal dollars and you start talkin' like Major Bouvier and his secesh squadron."

Lodge frowned, twining his fingers nervously. He had lost the initiative his rank and position had given him.

Cleburne was becoming uncomfortable. But it was in his back that the discomfort had settled. He heaved himself out of his chair and ambled over to one of the booklined walls. "What you want to know?" he said over his shoulder. "About how I feel when I sell? You ought not get in the habit of askin' that kind of question. It takes you away from business. You end up with philosophy. You end up askin' questions nobody can answer. And then you look back at what your life has been. And you go get yourself some wolf-bait and eat the only kind of meal that makes any sense. So you stay away from them questions. I started askin' 'em once. Then I saw – no, I felt where they had to end up. So I stopped. I stopped so long ago I can't even remember."

462

Now Lodge was up, out of his chair, and following Cleburne around the desk. "You want to sell them?" he asked.

"No," Cleburne said coolly. "You want to buy 'em. I put merchandise on the shelf. If I don't sell flour, I make it up sellin' harness. I sell things."

"You sell things," Lodge repeated, his flat colorless eyes bright with excitement. "You sell people."

Cleburne turned from the shelved books, his thumbs hooked into his belt. "People are things," he said with soft-spoken assurance. "Ideas, dishes, causes, furs, lumber, people. Those are things."

"How much, when?" Lodge asked breathlessly.

"Sure," Cleburne said. "You better get your own man on the telegraph to Alexandria. Or maybe you'll have to go to Washington. Because when you sent your nigger to me in them silly rags you stepped out of the small-change category. You can close the petty cash box and throw it away. From here on in, the price is folded and creased."

"When?"

"I ain't finished the first question. You better get authorized to draw ten thousand dollars out of the Treasury, because that's what you'll need."

"Ten thousand dollars? You want, you expect . . . ten thousand dollars?"

"Naw," Cleburne told him. "Not quite, but almost. The difference is what you'll have to spend for extra powder and ammunition and for coffins and grave markers and such. All of which you can buy from me."

"Powder?"

"You're gonna need a good deal of it, and I expect your commissary supply is way down."

"You bought . . . ?"

"Mostly. He may of sold to Bouvier. I never thought to ask. It don't matter. What matters is that ten thousand. The quicker you get it, the less trouble you'll have. As it is, you're gonna lose a couple more sympathizers before that money could possibly get here."

Lodge rubbed his chin roughly, staring back over his desk into the hot August noon. "Ten thousand."

"If you're got dickerin' in mind, you best forget it," Cleburne said. "There ain't gonna be any dealin'. My price is eighty-five hundred dollars. I want it in gold, but I'll take it in greenbacks on account of the extra time and trouble to get gold down here. Eighty-five hundred. No more, not less."

"Eighty-five hundred?"

"Are you gonna try to deal with me?"

"No," Lodge said. "No. I'll pay you for the product you say you can deliver. But why that sum? Why didn't you ask fo ten thousand? Or eight?"

Cleburne's face clouded. "You got to keep goin' back to that kind of question, don't you? Just say I got a loss on my books to balance. Leave it there."

"The money," Lodge said. "I can . . . "

"When I see the money, you'll get a delivery date on your merchandise."

"I have it here," Lodge went on. "My money. My own money. I don't have to send to Washington. My own funds . . . "

Cleburne stared at him in surprise. "You got it? You gonna lay out your own money? I never would have figured that."

Lodge's excitement almost overflowed. He wanted to reach Cleburne, to say something to him that he had never been able to phrase before. He wanted to tell this fat ugly expressionless man what moved him, what kept the springs and cogs of his being in operation. "You," he began almost inarticulately. "You know those questions? The questions you ignore, that you don't want to . . . "

Cleburne shook his head. "O no, not that again. Ain't you old enough to . . . "

"No, no," Lodge rushed on. "I asked. I asked all of them. I went on with it. All through the war, walking across those fields so thick with corpses that it seemed the whole world had been drained of life. And those months at Vicksburg, there was nothing to do but ask until the heat made thought stick inside the brain like candy. So . . . "

Cleburne squinted at Lodge. "So you came up with . . . "

"The pyramids, the Acropolis. Forests burned and civilizations crumbling, falling in upon one another. Nothing left but the earth, what we can torture into stone. The rest is ashes."

"You mean by ruinin' enough you can build . . . "

Lodge put his hand on Cleburne's arm, drawing him over toward the rough map of Caddo parish that hung near the large study window. "So I buy things," Lodge told him, almost whispering. "I buy things."

By then, Lieutenant Raisor had ridden the few miles between town and Amos Stevens' place. His eyes were rimmed with red and he could feel sweat and grime beneath his tunic collar. And his boots seemed as hot as if he had marched the distance instead of riding it.

There was more to it than that. As he rode past City Hall, a patrol had returned from out in the parish. Behind one trooper, a clumsily covered bundle was lashed down. Raisor had reined in.

"What have you got?" he asked one of the troopers.

"Sir, it's a fellow we found out the road north along the river. He was laid up under a tree with a bullet in the back of his head. I don't know him, but one of the men says he worked for the government or something. Maybe the marshal . . . "

"Let me have a look at him," Raisor said.

"Cut him down and pull that poncho off him," the trooper said.

When they had rolled the poncho off, Raisor looked at the swollen face of the dead man. For some reason, he was not surprised. He wondered how many corpses it would take to shake him, and whose they would have to be.

"Sure to God," one of the clerks said, looking out a second-story window. "That's Pony Mueller you got there. Who did it to him?"

"Nobody can tell," one of the troopers called up. "He was just layin' out there under a tree."

"Did he have a big thick leather wallet on him? With some silver corners on it?"

"Naw," the trooper said. "He didn't even have his pistol."

"You find that wallet," the clerk told him. "You find it and you'll have your man. He'll have him a pocketful of greenbacks too. Pony used to buy us drinks out of that wallet. He kept it stuffed."

"Thanks," the trooper had answered, dropping the poncho again. "Why don't you tell the marshal? This ain't any work for us."

Now Raisor was tying his mount in front of Amos Stevens' house. He pulled off his gauntlets and slapped them against his breeches. The sky above was a sheet of polished brass, and there was no relief from the heat. A Negro sentry on the porch called out to him.

"Cunnel say fo' you to git in quick as you come."

"I'm coming," Raisor said shortly.

"Cunnel say . . . "

"Shut your mouth and stand to attention."

465

The Negro froze beside the door again. As Raisor passed him, he saw the man's eyes move to follow him.

He wants in on things, Raisor thought. Never privy to anything, he wants to be part of decisions. If he knew what you have to be – what you have to become – to make decisions.

The long central hallway was dark and cool. Raisor loosened his collar and dropped his gloves on a table beside the door. If it had not been for the Negro's insistence, he would have stretched out in one of the chairs scattered along the hall. He needed rest. More than that, he needed to breathe deep and relax beyond the invisible bonds that were tightening around the town.

Then he heard Lodge's voice. "Lieutenant Raisor," he called. "Are you there?"

"I'm coming, sir," Raisor said wearily.

The study was almost dark. Lodge had pulled drapes across the large windows and lighted the desk lamp. He was studying the map of Caddo parish intently. Another smaller copy of the map lay on his desk. He motioned Raisor over to the large map. "We have them," he said. "Sooner than I expected – more perfectly than I had imagined." Lodge struck the desktop. "We can end it tonight."

Raisor stepped closer. "Tonight? You can end it? What kind of mistake have they . . . ?"

Lodge shook his head. "No mistake. None of them made a mistake. You could call it an act of God."

Raisor sat down without asking permission. The morning's tension drained out of him like stagnant water. He felt fresh chill sweat standing out under the wood of his tunic. He listened to Lodge mechanically while the colonel showed him the territory around Sentell's old place, the curve of the river, the extent of the fields, the position of woods and pasture, elevation.

"And when they close in, we will form another line to flank theirs at each end. When they commit themselves, when they move on the Negro's – on Crowninshield's house, we attack them from the rear. We can push them past the house . . . Here, this way. As they go past, Crowninshield will be able to punish them. And beyond the house is a long sandy slope, slippery and covered with weed. And then the river. Then the river."

"They'll have to go down to the river?"

"Look," Lodge said, his voice a hoarse whisper. "Look. They have to go down. We can cover the woods, this field. There will only be the river. And the sand is soft. It turns into mud. And then the water."

Raisor wiped his forehead with his neckerchief. "They won't . . . "

"No," Lodge said with finality. "They won't."

Raisor shook his head. He wanted to talk to Lodge. He tried to frame a sentence, some way of saying that this would be no end to it; that the end of it in Caddo parish would become the seed of a dozen new resistance movements all over the state, throughout the South. That the extinction of Bouvier's men would be like – Raisor struggled for the phrase – like the destruction of Travis and Crockett and Bowie, like the slaughter at the Alamo: a thing to remember, a thing to bless and draw strength from. And there were boys in Caddo parish who would re-member the rough touch of their father's beard as he kissed them and rode into the holocaust Lodge was planning. One day those boys would be men, and what had seemed an ending would prove only a new beginning.

Raisor stammered, "Those men this morning. Our men going into alien soil while those people buried their little boy across the church-yard in earth that belonged to him. And we, you and I, here now with this map. The river and this hill west of the house. We can't . . . "

"O," Lodge said, "we can. We will tonight."

"That boy yesterday," Raisor said, trying another tack.

"Kill the nits and you'll have no gnats," Lodge said abstractedly, his eyes on the map once more, not in answer to Raisor but as if in memo-randum to himself.

Raisor leaned over the cluttered desk. His hand almost knocked a heavy paperweight to the floor. "It's getting out of hand, sir," Raisor said. "This whole business is moving too fast. You can't tell where it will go. The informer, the man who told you about tonight. What if he's a double-agent? We could ride out expecting thirty of them and meet five hundred. They could have called for men from Arkansas and Texas."

Lodge waved him silent. He pressed his fingertips together, studied the ends of them, then let his hands fall to the desk. "No, he said. "Not too fast. Not fast enough. It is a century past time and a quarter-million lives spent and the task unfinished. Where will it go? To the sword again, and each time one of these barbarians draws a knife or lifts a rifle we can snuff out one more relic, destroy one more fragment of the

467

disease that flawed our past. We will end it. Not at once and everywhere. But here and now, we will wipe this parish clean of slavers and traitors as a ship's deck is cleaned – with powder and shot for holystone."

Lodge's eyes widened. He stood up. "We are building a new nation, a new birth of freedom. We cannot build on the human timber of rebels and slave-owners, spoiled plantation-sons and sullen peasants whose sole notion of protest is insurrection. We use what will fit. The rest has to be done away with."

"No," Raisor said uncertainly, "we need loyal men. But that boy was no . . ."

"He was the son of his father," Lodge went on relentlessly. "His dying makes no difference. We have lost men enough in this war to repopulate our largest city. We did not plan his killing or even countenance it, but if his dying – and the dying of those fools who butchered him – serve our purpose, then the boy will have done his country a service he would never had done voluntarily. We use what fortune sends us. We buy what is available and use it."

Raisor felt the sweat running chill and uncomfortable down his back. "This baiting them, forcing their hand. We're not at war now . . . we . . ."

"Then they have to fight on our terms, when and where we want them to fight. It *is* war. War for civilization. Don't you see," Lodge thundered, "the South has got to be destroyed? It must die. And out of the ashes we will build our monuments."

"The informer," Raisor said desperately, as if he were throwing down one final card, already aware that it would be trumped, and the game lost. "If he . . ."

Lodge's voice was a low monotone again. "Lieutenant," he said, "I would trust the informer farther than I can tell you. I know the man. He gives fair value for a fair price."

Raisor turned and started for the door.

"Your orders will be ready in half an hour," Lodge called after him. Then he stepped into the hall.

"Lieutenant, good faith between buyer and seller is the cornerstone of society."

Raisor shivered as the hall's cool air touched his shoulders. "Yes sir," he said, and closed the door.

He was stripped to the waist and his hands felt as if he were holding hot coals in them. He would have to stop soon, or it would be a week before he could work again. But he could not put down the ax without picking up a hammer. He had walked around the house, had stood in every room for long minutes. He had touched the walls and stood on the porch between the narrow columns looking out over the untended yard where there were cottonwoods and a few young oaks spearing upward out of the tall dun grass and dry weeds of midsummer. But then he would see a broken plank in the porch floor, or a loose piece of wainscoting under a window. Or there would be a single scrub pine that clearly had to go, that had to be chopped down and dragged away before the day was over.

Because no matter how long he might live, how many days might be ahead for him, there would never be another like this one. He breathed inward until the volume of air hurt his chest. He held his breath for a few seconds as if, after he exhaled, there would be no more air. He felt a feather of breeze play across his sweat-slick belly and chest. It was warm air, but it felt cool as it touched moisture. He closed his eyes and wished, as a child wishes, that the breeze would go on, that it would not die. Then he smiled and stepped off the porch, reaching again for the double-bladed ax.

But Samuels, in cut-off Union breeches, came from around the house.

"All right," he said. "Don't even touch that ax. You're done for to-day. We're both done. I didn't come in on this place to let it kill me."

"You see that scrawny pine there?" Phillipe said. "I can't stand it. It's got to go."

"Tomorrow," Samuels said. "When I finished that barn roof, I rigged some fishing poles. I've got an idea about that creek that runs into the river. It looks like . . . "

"You mean bayou," Phillipe laughed. "You Yankees got to learn how we talk here."

Samuels shook his head, smiling. "One day back on the land and you're a Southerner again. Maybe you ought to join up with those townfolk."

Phillipe turned serious. "You got to love the land. You can't but love it. It don't matter about those people in town. They just live on top of the land. It's a location to them. But we put too much sweat and blood into it. You can't get away from it. I never owned anything and now I got a piece of land just the size and shape I wanted all my life."

"Let's go see what kind of fish you got in your . . . bayou."

"Not now. We got too much work. We got to bring the lamps and blankets out of the wagon. We got that lumber. We could make us two bedsteads before night. Then we got that scythe to sharpen and that old plow to set straight so we can put in some late vegetables. We could go out with your rifle and see if any of Sentell's hogs stayed in the woods . . ."

Samuels threw up his hands. "I didn't spend most of the war on my belly just to work myself to death in one day afterwards."

"That's what freedom is for," Phillipe said without humor. "You work. Only it's for yourself."

"What do you know," Samuels chided him. "I hear you were a free man before you turned five years old."

"That's what my father says."

"All that fight and all those years of hate and you were free all along."

"I didn't know it."

Samuels shrugged. "A fact's a fact. Not knowing doesn't change it."

"Freedom is somethin' you know and feel. Or it's nothin'."

Samuels sat down on the steps. He studied his dirty army shoes. They were too large, and standing out from his ankles; the tops made his legs look thin as pipe stems. "That old man Stevens must be a good man."

"He owned slaves."

"He turned your poppa loose."

"And kept him all the better for it."

Samuels scuffed the tan sandy soil. "Your poppa made a free choice."

"No," Phillipe said angrily. "He felt beholden. He felt like he owed Amos Stevens."

"Fair exchange isn't robbery."

"What?"

"Like with us. If a man's your friend and does you a good turn, you want to stand by him."

"What if he owned you like a piece of land, like a mule?"

Samuels leaned back against a column. The white paint flaked off on his rough blue shirt. He shielded his eyes from the sun with one hand and squinted at Phillipe. "I don't know," he said slowly. "I wasn't ever owned. My daddy took Mother to Pennsylvania and I was born free. But the white man looked through me from the time I was a boy, and when it was me or a drunk white loafer to dig a ditch or paint a barn, you better bet they hired that drunk for two dollars and gave me ten cents to see he didn't cave in the ditch on himself or fall off the ladder. I was free to come and go. Except not in some towns where it was custom not to have niggers. And except some eating places and saloons where maybe you went to the back door or got served in the kitchen for the same price whites were paying out front. And except if you saw a white woman and she smiled, you had better hope she was laughing at you, because if she wasn't, you might not be able to move fast enough to get out of there."

"It wasn't like that everywhere."

Samuels lowered his hand and closed his eyes. "No, not everywhere. There were good men up there. Men who would do you good whenever they could. About like Amos Stevens. Except I never had that other thing from any of them."

"What other thing?" Phillipe asked.

"Love," Samuels said. "Like what keeps your daddy with Amos Stevens even when a piece of him wants to be out here with you."

"Choosin' against his own blood," Phillipe muttered.

"They say blood binds thicker than water. But they don't say how much the heart binds. They don't say how every year you spend with somebody ties you closer and deepens out the love. Even blood has a hard time wiping out forty years together. You ask an awful lot."

"I ask what I got a right to ask my own father."

Samuels stood up, still regarding his brogans. "I got to get some new shoes. These aren't fit for a proprietor." Then he looked at Phillipe. "Boy, all you can talk about is freedom and justice and rights and what you have coming. You may have fought like a tiger for Uncle Abe, but you've still got the better part of everything left to learn."

"I'm doin' all right."

"Well, you've got your land. But it won't fill you up. You've still got indigestion over rights and what they owe you. But what it comes to is that rights are what people let each other have. Like love. You got to be worthy of it most usually, and then wait and hope you get it. Sometime you do, sometime you don't. But rights are like love, and if they don't give 'em to you, you can't get a law passed. You got to do with what you get and keep trying to get the rest."

"I fought free . . . "

"You fought because you fought. You were a free man already – as free as you'll ever be – and when you finished fighting for what you already had, you spent that freedom buying a farm so you could slave on it all over again and likely not have as much as you did to start. Maybe less. Because even the colonel can't pass a law a to get your daddy out here – any more than he can make a law that says those white people in town have to like you."

"Come on," Phillipe said shortly. "That stuff in the wagon . . . "

But Samuels touched his arm. "Somebody's coming up our road. Off the main road."

Phillipe stepped to where he had left his shirt and pistol. He picked up the gun, hefted it, cocked it, and released the hammer carefully until it came to rest on a bright brass cap. His hand was tender from the day's work, and the wooden grip of the pistol felt almost like the ax handle. Both tools, he thought. Put down one and pick up the other. Depending on the job.

"It's that major," Samuels said. "He rides fine. I bet he looked good with a battalion back of him."

"Major?"

"Sentell. The one I talked to yesterday morning. The one whose land you got. The one you told me held those rebs back from cutting you down at Vicksburg."

Phillipe's eyes followed Sentell as his mount left the dirt road and cut across the thickly weeded lawn toward the house.

"He did what he was supposed to do. He was supposed to see prisoners taken care of. I don't owe him anything."

"Boy," Samuels drawled, "if you don't owe him anything, the world's debts must all be canceled. Did you ever think of how many officers on both sides didn't always do just what they were supposed to do? Who slipped once in a while?"

Phillipe did not meet his eyes. "I heard there was filthy things. I never saw any."

Samuels walked out to meet Sentell. "There was plenty to see. If you looked."

Sentell swung down out of the saddle. His black coat was almost luminous with dust. "You gotten started," he greeted Samuels. "There'll be a lot to do."

Samuels smiled and shook Sentell's outstretched hand. "I wish you'd kept this place up, Major. I can't get the owner there to turn loose for an hour."

Sentell walked up toward the house with him. Phillipe was sitting on the edge of the porch, oiling the trigger mechanism of his pistol. "Major," he said, courteously as before. But without warmth.

"Been here all day," Samuels said, "and not a fishing line damp yet."

"It may be longer than that you can fish. If I were youall, I'd stay together."

Samuels' eyes widened. "You think we might have trouble?"

"I know you're going to have trouble. Yesterday morning, a colored soldier and a trooper pulled a girl into a vacant building. When a boy tried to stop them, they beat him to death."

Samuels shook his head. "Phillipe told me. They ought to pay for that."

Sentell's expression did not alter. "They paid last night. They were ridden down by horsemen on Fannin Street."

Phillipe glanced up from his gun. "No time for law, Major?"

"If you mean this is the time for law, I'd tend to agree with you. Lodge did nothing. He made no effort to bring them in."

"I guess the colonel knows what he's doing," Phillipe said.

Sentell looked down at him. "That's right," he said. "I'm beginning to think he knows exactly what he's doing."

Phillipe stood up. "What can we do for you, Mr. Sentell?"

Sentell glanced at Samuels, who shrugged and picked up his pole to begin peeling it.

"I came to tell you that it would be wise to sleep one at a time. There could be trouble. The riders who cut those men down last night might figure youall easy game for the same kind of thing."

"We can take care of ourselves," Phillipe said coldly.

"Not sound asleep we can't," Samuels said. "Thank you, Major, for bothering. We'll keep an eye open."

Phillipe laughed shortly. "How come the warning?" he asked.

"Because of who you are," Sentell told him.

"You mean the man who owns your old place? The man you'd like to run off with a couple of words about night-riders?"

Sentell's mouth thinned, his jaw tightened. "Because you're Rye Crowninshield's son. Except for that, they could use you for target practice as far as I'm concerned. Better men than you'll ever be have died without warning. But there are not many men better than your father."

Phillipe stood close to Sentell, his eyes narrow and angry. "You like him because he behaves, don't you?"

"He behaves like a man," Sentell shot back, "not like a spoiled child."

"You wouldn't be puttin' those riders up to coming' after us, would you?"

But Sentell had control of himself again. "No," he said, "I wouldn't. I do my own work. Maybe three years in the Northern army have made you forget. Down here most of us do our own work."

Samuels voice came between them. "You don't know when, Major?"

"He ought to know," Phillip sided.

"Why don't you keep quiet," Samuels told him without anger. "You got to grow up."

"Listen . . . ," Phillipe began.

"No," Samuels cut him off. "I don't want to listen. I want to take up living again. I want to hear the wind across these fields. I want to hear the river moving beside me. I don't want to listen to you nursing old spite and hate without any reason behind it."

"I'll be going," Sentell said. "I wish you good luck here. This is good land. It needs hard work. I wish you both luck."

Samuels walked out to Sentell's horse with him. "Major, I wish I could ask you to stay for a cup of coffee. But we . . . "

"Another time," Sentell smiled. "A better time, perhaps."

Samuels matched his smile. "That's what I'm looking to," he said. "A good time for all of us."

"That's what we'll drink to then."

They shook hands once more, as if it were a ritual neither was quite accustomed to.

Back at the house, Phillipe watched them. He shivered as a stray tendril of wind played across his naked shoulders. No sun reached the porch now and it was cooler there than out in the open yard where Samuels and Sentell were standing.

IX

6 JULY 1865 — In the late afternoon, when he was not needed, Rye Crowninshield stayed mostly to himself. He would join Amos for

supper, perhaps for a glass of wine in the backyard afterward. But for the rest, he walked. Walked after the sun had passed its zenith over the hot fields, wading waist-deep in weeds, watching a handful of hired field hands working the vegetables planted beyond the rear yard.

There was little for him to do now. There were almost no house servants and nothing for them to do had they remained. There were no entertainments, no parties or dances for the young, no suppers or chamber concerts for the mature. The house was empty except for Amos, Rye – and the handful of Unions, including Lodge's small staff and a pair of quiet Negro orderlies who kept the house in order without asking instructions or advice from Rye. Outside, except for the garden which required no overseeing, no management worth the name, there was nothing that demanded his attention. And he had no skill in manufacturing tasks. He had spent too many years overmatched by jobs that never seemed properly finished to indulge in make-work. There was nothing to be done in the fields: no cotton had been planted. There would be no crop this year.

So he would walk. Thinking neither of the past nor the future – thinking in fact of nothing, but rather abstractions like freedom and slavery, justice and tyranny. He would walk under the oaks and pines that fronted and flanked the house and try to reconstruct Antoninus Stevens' voice in his memory. He wanted to find the flaw in it, the error that had destroyed all they had built.

He would walk through the house while Amos napped or read in his room, or in the evening after he was asleep. Rye would find himself moving almost compulsively long after the house was quiet. Down the long halls where Morrison and Phillipe had wrestled and whooped in another time. Past the silent library, disfigured by a conqueror's map of the parish hanging askew on one wall. Onto the porch where a Union sentry stood with his rifle grounded beside him, or cradled across his arm. It was usually two or three in the morning before he could sleep, and even then his legs moved involuntarily under the bedclothes as if they had purposes, intentions of their own.

He had come in that afternoon from the vegetable garden with a basket of pole beans when he heard Raisor's voice, almost a forced whisper, down the hall outside the library where Lodge worked. Rye put the beans down and moved as close to the kitchen door as he could without being seen. He could make out Raisor's words and Sergeant Packard's answers.

" . . . no question but this is correct. So the colonel thinks. They plan to begin gathering outside town about midnight. They know the last patrol will come in and disband about twelve-thirty. From then on, they expect the parish outside Shreveport itself to belong to them. They mean to hit the old Sentell place about one o'clock. They think it will be a shooting-match with Crowninshield and Samuels out there alone."

The sergeant cut in. "I could ride out with some men and we could hole up in the house . . . "

"No," Raisor said. "We don't know . . . he didn't know, the informer, I mean . . . whether they'd have someone watching the place. We can't take the chance. These people know the country anyhow. They could send a few scouts ahead to root us out. They colonel wants . . . "

"I know what he wants," the sergeant said shortly. "All right, sir. So you want us to go out in small groups and rendezvous near that old cattle pen north of town. What time should we . . . ?"

"By twelve-thirty. We need forty minutes or so to cut back east and south to Sentell's place."

"If they hit there on time . . . "

"Even if they do, we want them to have time to get involved in what they're doing."

"They may be done with it when we get there."

"The colonel wants to take that chance. If we try to go in ahead of time, a horse's snort, a rifle butt striking a belt buckle and it's blown up. We have to let them go in ahead of us."

"Then we push 'em into the Red River?"

Raisor said nothing. Rye felt suddenly and inexorably old.

"Those men . . . ," the sergeant began.

"We can't warn them," Raisor cut him off viciously. "The colonel wants these rebels. He wants them at any price. Crowninshield and Samuels will have to hold until we close in from behind."

"I was thinking of the Southerners," the sergeant went on quietly. "I was thinking if we got 'em really sewed into a corner, we could fire a volley over their heads, we could maybe bring 'em in. They'd get some prison time, but . . . "

"No," Raisor's voice was cracked and high as an adolescent's. "No warning to them either. The colonel doesn't want to bring them in. Do I have to explain it all to you word by word?"

"No," the sergeant answered. "No, Lieutenant. You don't have to explain a goddamned thing to me. Maybe you should explain it to yourself."

"Sergeant . . ."

"Sorry . . . sir."

"Afterward," Raisor said. "Afterward, if you were to put in for a transfer. I'm putting in. If you wanted to go with me . . ."

"What would we do, Lieutenant? Go out and butcher Indians? Or get sent to another Dixie town so we can go on binding up the nation's wounds?"

Rye heard Sergeant Packard's heels snap together. Then the sound of his footsteps faded down the hall toward the front door. As the door closed, Rye heard another sound. He stepped into the hall in time to see Raisor pounding his fist against the wall in slow measured strokes. Amos found him in the backyard sitting beside the wicker table. "You ought to at least bring a pitcher of cool water out here. Maybe a cigar if you haven't got eyes enough left to read. You look like a jockey without a horse."

"Leave off me," Rye said without anger. "I ain't got no fun left."

Amos stretched his legs before him as he sat down in one of the other chairs. "There's not much fun left anywhere around here," he said. "Maybe soon."

"Not soon," Rye said. "Lord God, not soon enough."

Amos frowned. "What's bothering you? You've been down in the mouth since the Unions rode in here. But not like this. What is it?"

"It's nothin'," Rye said quickly. "Maybe de heat. I don't know. It ain't nothin'."

Amos shook his head. "Put that boy out of your mind. Or else go on out there and help him build up that place. You've cut yourself in half with this business. Body here, and your heart skulking around Edward's old place like an unshriven ghost. A man ought to keep himself in one piece."

Rye turned away. "Let it lie. Pretty soon . . ."

"Pretty soon what?"

"Nothin'. It all got to end soon. It can't keep goin' . . ."

"One day we'll have both of them home," Amos said with feigned conviction. "The insanity will be over. It can't keep on, you're right."

Rye stood up. "I got to go in. If you wants dinner, call me. I could fix you a piece of chicken."

He started for the house slowly, his shoulders bent as if beneath a heavy rain. Amos watched him go, noticing with sudden clarity how tired and gray he was, how not only youth but even the strength of maturity had leeched out of him in the past few months. He's old, Amos thought. We're both old men.

As if at some tacit call, Amos' eyes turned toward the west. The sun, still standing above the distant trees beyond a weed-strewn field, was going red and tottering down the sky. In half an hour it would be evening, a brief twilight and then a long night. There would barely be time left for what one had to do. And no time left for oneself at all.

It is shameful for the spirit to give way first in this life, while the body yet endures, Marcus Aurelius said across the silence of seventeen centuries. And for a moment his words seemed somehow to cut a path of cool reason through the late afternoon's sharp importunate heat, the unbroken soundlessness of Sentell's library. The emperor was right, of course, Sentell thought. He was nearly always right. As if in his time, in the brief Indian summer of Rome's faltering virtue, Marcus had seen in compendium all the spiritual diseases that dissolve the will of man. The sadness of inner collapse was no less in his time than in ours. And no less shameful.

Outside, the grass had turned a sapless tan. A single spark could ignite it, and fire the whole block of houses and open fields between. There was nothing left of the summer but harvest, and that would be bitter, too. It is said that we reap what we sow, no more. But like most plausible remarks, there is no truth in it. What if, after the sowing, the field is stolen from you? And while half a hundred families scattered over the parish mourned lost sons, lost land, and lost hopes, Sentell wondered if there would be anything left to salvage. His own strength was failing. The burden of inaction he had taken up when he signed the Union parole was chafing not less but more as time passed. Now Sentell had added as moral supercargo a promise to Bouvier that permitted him to give Phillipe and Samuels no more than a warning.

It would be simple enough to break his oath. To Lodge, a word would be sufficient. But then all Sentell had done before would be not simply meaningless fustian, not just the cant of a mock-gentleman, but a vicious parody of honor which would have had, in retrospect, the final effect of saving his hide during the last bloody twilight days of the Confederacy.

Sentell had taken on too much. Finally, it seemed, he had believed like a schoolboy that unbending acceptance of specific personal debt, the punctilious discharge of stated obligation, would not only take the place of daily, hourly decision but even relieve him of any commitment to which he did not attach his sworn word. Sentell believed that a man chooses his ties, selects his responsibilities, accepting and rejecting as he will. And that, the task of such choosing once past, there would be no reason for him to regret or have second thoughts regarding his decision.

He poured sherry from a bottle Amos gave him when he returned from Vicksburg. The *Meditations* was still open in his lap. *Strive to be such as nature intended you to be. Reverence the gods, and help men. Life is short.*

And ugly, Sentell added silently. And unsatisfactory. Because a man cannot assert even the most modest claim against life and hold any hope that it will be honored. To live it cleanly and escape unsoiled was no easier than to bring down kings or sack a continent.

The day's heat was breaking then. Above, high clouds, remote and no part of the stewing earth below, were going gray and violet as the sun began its long plunge into the west. A mockingbird trilled somewhere beyond the house. Sentell put down his book and stared out at the wilted and moribund roses his mother had planted along the fence years before. The heat had blighted them. But then it did so every year. It made no difference. The following spring they would try it again and succeed for a month or two. Lacking consciousness, flowers did not count failures. Man had invented the keeping of accounts, the weighing of gain against loss. And the invention had broken his spirit with regularity ever since.

It seemed to Sentell that his life had become a desperate attempt to balance moral books against physical realities. But he had chosen a system more complex than anyone could handle. He had lent too freely of his capital, and too many debts he had left out of his tally were about to fall due. The result off this kind of thing, Sentell thought, is generally bankruptcy.

Aside from his word to Bouvier, there was the double-edged sword of looking out for Amos or helping Phillipe and Samuels. He could do either, but not both. Sentell could take a chance on Amos' hearing nothing, his staying home the night of the raid. Then he would be free

479

to go to his old place, tell Samuels and Phillipe nothing, and wait for the riders with them. But Amos would be on his own.

Or he could find some excuse to spend a long evening with Amos and wait afterward outside his house on into early morning until Bouvier's riders would have come and gone. Then Samuels and Phillipe would be on their own. Against thirty or forty men.

The third option cost everything. It was to break his word, tell Amos and ride with him to Phillipe's and meet the riders head-on when they arrived. The result, aside from Sentell's own dying, would be to perjure himself, to lead Amos to his death, and finally to save no one and nothing. Masterson's gambit, Sentell thought. An Alamo and to hell with whether or not a San Jacinto follows it.

"But Sam," he said aloud, "you kept no books." It was so simple. Transactions in the head. No buying or selling of futures. All debts contracted in the morning satisfied before sunset.

"You'll want some dinner soon?" Sentell's mother asked from the door behind him.

"Yes," he said, coming back from a long way off. "Surely. As soon as the sun is down."

"Look again," she said. "The sun has been down half an hour."

Sentell looked outside. The sun was gone, and that strange indescribable moment of early twilight had spread across the yard, across the street and houses beyond. But now there was a vivid yellow afterglow standing over the roses, over the dusty street, and each leaf and patch of grass stood out with an indelible singularity, as if suddenly freed from the burning unity they shared under the sun, they were conscious of their individuality – even as the darkness rose to plunge them into anonymity once more.

Almost every night Amos smoked a final cigar in the cool of the broad front lawn. Once he had spent that hour thinking of politics, of justice, of how best to guide a commonweal – or an infant confederacy. During the war years, he had considered speeches in the legislature, or measures to make Louisiana's participation in the war more effective. He had thought of Mo somewhere in northern Virginia, and it had seemed then that the antique pain of his severed arm returned sharper and more exquisite than when the wound had been fresh. But now there was no more politics to consider: no speeches or measures to create. And Mo had returned somehow from the maelstrom of war to drown slowly in the backwater of a vanquished province. Justice was in

Lodge's hands and the Confederacy was dead as a fever victim sleeping long and unattended beneath weathered stone in St. George's church-yard.

Maybe, he thought, we should have gone there together. Maybe even dead she could have mediated between us.

But he shook his head at the idea. Mo had no more clear memory of her than of his first pony, or of that crisp fall when he and Phillipe had huddled side by side in the wagon that carried them to Shreveport.

When honor fails to bind us, nothing else is likely to. He will not settle for honor. With four years of agony to learn in, he came home still ignorant of the fact that life without honor is a burden too great to bear. And he would ride at night like a wolf to avenge hurts that are past vengeance or adjustment. And turn from his father to a plausible Frenchman driven mad by suffering and defeat and determined to spread the burden of both as far and wide as possible.

Amos looked at the glowing tip of his cigar. And no honor in it anywhere. No equity, no hope. Except to suffer the Union like an ox bears the goad until they grow tired of the sport and leave – at least that way there will be men left to father a new generation. A generation that may retrieve what we have lost.

But not without honor. The very men who want to ride Phillipe and his man into the ground would swear their whole allegiance to Lee while they use methods that would sicken him and make him turn to the Unions in sheer revulsion from what his own have become. And no way out. Bouvier who gave his body to the Southern people and failing there bartered his soul to the devil . . .

Amos frowned and pulled on his cigar. It kept coming back to Bou-vier. He could not put out of mind that frozen and immobile face that seemed to have suffered so much that neither pity nor terror could move it. There was something . . .

"When I was younger . . . ," he said aloud, surprised by the sound of his own voice, glancing toward the porch to see if the Union guard had heard. But the guard was not there. Instead, Raisor stood on the edge of the porch with five or six noncommissioned officers fanned out in front of him on the lower steps. Raisor pointed eastward and made a wide circling motion with his hands. His voice was low, and Amos could hear nothing.

When I was younger, when the brain was flexible, Amos was think-ing as he watched them, I could find the connections, the correspondences. Now I wallow in fact and observations like a scow hauling shoats up the river. Bouvier . . .

Then Lodge stepped onto the porch. Raisor moved aside for him. Lodge's voice raised suddenly, and Amos heard:

" . . . there will be no way out for them. No way at all."

And the group of men dissolved, each heading for his horse already saddled by the Negro orderlies and held by them until their owners were dismissed. Lodge and Raisor mounted with the rest and rode down the long, shadowy path to the main road. As they passed Amos, Raisor was saying:

"Something good, something lasting for the price."

Lodge answered: "Speculation . . . destroy and clear a place to build . . . "

Amos ground out his cigar against a tree trunk. Rye's sadness like a man condemned. Or . . . one who had heard sentence passed on a loved one. But who could not act. Or who would not. And Bouvier's promise. Given as easily, as smoothly as the news that two men had been trampled to death without a hearing, without even the form of honorable law. Rye who finally was not his own man but riven by two loyalties: one to his son – but more strongly to his friend who might try to act if the sentence of execution . . .

It was not clear. He had no facts, only surmise and a collection of incongruities. But there was no waiting. What he did not know, he would not learn on his front lawn or snoring in his bed. What he needed to know, to find out for certain, lay six miles away at Sentell's old place. Amos dropped the cold husk of his cigar and started back for the stable. Then he paused and headed for the house. He kept no pistols in the stable, and if the surmise, the uncertainty that would not be laid, had substance to it, he would need them. As he mounted the steps two at a time, he thought irrelevantly how an hour's smoke before bedtime might yet have some value after all.

Rye had just begun the long process of clearing his mind so he could sleep for a few hours. Each night he would dismantle the present by remembering the past. He would remember the wild happy days at the New Orleans waterfront with the Mississippi spread out like an undulating carpet in front of Saranne and him. He remembered a gardenia twisted into her hair, the dancing, the Creole food. Night full of wine and laughter and love. Her tiny shack strung with paper lanterns at Mardi Gras, and the island songs.

But the present was not so easy to escape. He heard Amos' door slam, and footsteps moving down the hall, down the stairs. He rose heavily from his bed and stumbled to a window that overlooked the stables behind the house.

Down there, in darkness dissected by moonlight scattered through the trees, he saw Amos leading a saddled horse into the yard.

He ran past Amos' room, down the stairs, pausing only long enough to pick a woolen muffler off the coatrack beside the front door.

But as he reached the porch, he saw the bulky shadow of horse and rider fading down the dark path toward the main road.

The dinner had been as usual: one of the silver goblets worth more than all the food.

"I'm sorry about that chicken," Sentell's mother said afterward as they drank coffee in the library. "I was bargaining for some pork but that Yankee commissary officer outbid me."

"You tried a pinch of money instead of a bushel of charm."

"The farmer couldn't buy a bolt of cloth from Ed Norton or Cleburne with charm. And I expect I have at least as much money left as I do winning ways. I think graciousness comes from trusting that tomorrow will make up for today. I don't think I can do that anymore. Perhaps it's age. Perhaps even without the war and the rest of it, I would have become a pessimistic old woman."

"No," Sentell said. "You're not that way yet. You just think you might be if it keeps up. I don't think so. You had too many chances before."

"Your father? No, it was different then. He was what he was and I knew it, but I was young enough to say at first, He's not really so cold, so stiff, so out of love with all creation. And even later I could say, graciously and smiling, All right, he is then. But what we are on Friday is not what we'll be on Sunday. By the time I was too old to pretend, it didn't matter. And I had you. He never changed. But I did. And changing, I learned about all of you. About men."

"What about men?" Sentell was glad to put his mind off the afternoon's considering.

"You're all mad. Hopelessly, irretrievably mad. You parade and cavort and speak with the tongues of angels. And then climax the festivities by going out to butcher one another like beasts. Indispensable part of the pose. Men let conventions do them for morals, a flag for common sense, and a rifle for honest dealing. In the midst of damnation a man waves away the powder smoke and shouts above the groans that salvation is in his grasp. Win or lose, he learns nothing. Because madness cannot be taught away. Because a wild animal, no matter how pretty his pelt, is still a reasonless thing."

"Every man seeks the good, the right."

"There's no right in all this. There was never any right in it," she said hotly. "Any woman in town could tell you what it is: something inside a man's mind that looks and feels like right. Something that has the texture and the sound of right as surely as Mark's gospel. It runs alongside right and gestures and mimics as if it were right. But it stinks of death and the cheap liquor of a man's good opinion of himself. It reeks with selfishness and vanity, and not one of you is free of it. You can't be free of it. You're men."

"I thought you understood what I've done," Sentell said.

His mother's eyes were bright. "I do," she said. "I have all along. I understood more about it than you did – or do. The fierce part of it your father would have loved it if he had been gentle or thoughtful enough to pause in the first place because of mere blood and futility – and perverse enough to find that he could give over the killing and still be deadly proud and full of the merciless starch that stiffens men into madness."

"No," he said. "It wasn't like that."

"All of it," she said relentlessly, "was . . . is . . . And not only you but Amos Stevens, whose age does him no good at all. And Morrison, whose lack of age is killing him. And that poor fuddled Negro Rye, whose age means nothing. And Phillipe, who was born at Sharpsburg and is only as old as the graves along Antietam Creek. And that man Lodge, who must be older than Satan. None of you is sane."

"We do what we have to do."

His mother shrugged. "Which is an excellent description of compulsion: man's prime substitute for logic and love and decency."

"What brought you to that?" Sentell asked.

"Everything. All of it. Your father's frozen spine and the child inside you . . . my baby . . . who died at the horror of Chapultepec. I can't act as if it didn't matter or as if there was good in it. I can't do that anymore."

They sat for a while in silence. "What about Amos?" she asked. "He took Bouvier at his word, didn't he?"

"I expect so. But I can't be sure. He might decide to go out to the place any time."

"What would be wrong with that? Perhaps he could bring Phillipe to his senses."

"No," Sentell said. "He couldn't do that now. All he could do is get hurt. Or worse."

She raised her eyebrows and set her cup down. "You talked to Bouvier? He doesn't mean to keep his word?"

He paused. "No," he said. "I don't think so."

"You know. But you won't say. You know what he means to do, don't you?"

Sentell did not meet her eyes. "I can't say."

His mother poured more coffee for them and stirred hers slowly. "Now it comes full circle. One commitment to cancel another. You've obligated yourself to Bouvier."

"I needed to know. Because of Amos."

"What about Amos?"

"There was only one way to be sure. Only one way to make sure he wouldn't decide to ride out there despite what Bouvier promised. That was for me to know, and to keep Amos at home when . . . "

She stared at him in disbelief. "Then you know and you mean to keep silent?"

"It was a bad choice. But there aren't any good choices left, are there?"

"And Phillipe?"

"I told him there would be trouble. I don't owe him a detailed account. Except for Amos and Rye, I don't owe him anything. I handed him his life once."

Mrs. Sentell shook her head. "All right," she said. "Let that be. What about Amos? What are you going to do?"

"I'm going to ride out there and talk or play chess or declaim or stand on my head. Whatever it takes to keep him there while Bouvier and Phillipe debate the darker side of local politics."

She shook her head, her mouth tight, sudden lines across her forehead, at the corners of her eyes. "No," she said sharply. "You can't."

"What? What can't I?"

"You had no right to bind yourself to Bouvier. You have no right to do that, to take such a decision for Amos. He trusts you, depends on you. His own son has failed him and he called on you to sustain him."

"Sustain? Mother, for God's sake, I want to save his life."

His mother frowned. "I hadn't realized what an extraordinary valuation you place on life."

She paused, her head down, her lips drawn tight. "I'm afraid Amos doesn't consider his life worth quite so much."

"What could he do?" Sentell asked. "What could a dozen of us do? If Phillipe is lucky, he can slip past them."

"And if his luck fails and Amos is not there to share his luck, you will have failed anyhow."

"He'll be alive."

"No. He'll be as dead as the Confederacy. By keeping all this from him, you will have shorn him of self-respect. You will have said, 'Old man, you make rash statements to a mob, but you cannot make good on them so we will look out for you.' You will be saying, 'Old man, you have no strength left, and rather than let you spend the pittance that remains, we will hold you in a private asylum of secrecy and ignorance. What happens outside is nothing to you. Children and the senile must be protected. Even from keeping their solemn word. And an old man's word is like a child's or an idiot's: not binding.'"

"No," Sentell cut in roughly. "None of that is right."

His mother raised her head. Her eyes were bright and angry, and the candlelight blurred in the whiteness of her hair. "What I say is exactly right, sir. You mean to save Amos Stevens' body at a price no man of his breeding would pay. You have agonized over the inviolability of your own honor and found it more precious than your country and your people. And that was all right. It is all right. But now you deny Amos Stevens the same privilege. Do you think, when he hears of Phillipe's being killed, he will simply shrug it off and say, 'I would have kept my word but for circumstances'?"

"What can he do? They'll simply pile him on the top of the others. Bouvier isn't going to stop."

"Yes," she said, as if she were hearing an old and familiar name once more. "Yes, Bouvier. That's another part of it. You were so close in the siege. You and Bouvier and the Texas officer."

"That's over," Sentell said. "What we were is one thing. It's over. Now we're something else."

"Yes," his mother repeated abstractedly. "He is something else. Not an officer, not a gentleman. Not even a soldier. Hardly human. Something of a butcher, wouldn't you say?"

"I suppose . . . "

"And yet you believed him. He lied like a serpent to Amos Stevens, and yet five minutes later, when he casually admits his lie and then gives you a day and an hour for the attack, you accept his day and hour as if it . . . "

"My God," Sentell said, standing up so suddenly that his chair tilted over behind him. Before his mother could go on, he was struggling into his coat and heading into the study for his pistol."

She followed him. "It could be any time. Why now? Can't you . . . Why now?"

"Why not?" Sentell said, pulling her to him. He kissed her and held her at arm's length. "Listen, when I come back . . . "

She smiled, but the pain was as evident as if she were making no attempt to hide it. "Of course. When you come back. You'll want coffee. And the guest room for Amos, if he'll come. And tell the Negroes, tell Phillip and Samuels we have space here if they . . . "

"All right," Sentell said, stepping past her, almost running as he reached the door.

He saddled quickly and started toward the center of town to pick up the road that would carry him northwest along the river toward his old place.

You are all mad, his mother had said. Wild beasts behind masks of your own making, feigning the civilized – and all the while insane beyond help, senseless of values; purposes and meaning a morass.

The town seemed almost deserted. As he crossed Milam Street a Union trooper riding past glanced at Sentell curiously. But no one challenged him.

Sentell had almost reached the junction of Marshall and Texas streets when a detachment of Union passed riding toward the river. He reined in and let them pass. Any rider after dark was likely to be stopped and questioned.

As he waited for them to go by, Sentell realized how time had at last caught up with him. Honor was like Confederate currency: devalued – a museum piece. When no man's word is worth the breath spent to utter it, the fragile myth of honor is empty as that fabled tomb of Joseph's outside Jerusalem. The spirit of it had gone, and only form remained. And finally, he thought, honor is not as important as to be honorable – to serve the spirit and forget the tomb.

When Sentell turned into Texas Street, he understood what his mother had meant. He even remembered something Cleburne had said about excess baggage. And he realized that he would do whatever had to be done to bring Amos out of this not only alive, but unashamed. It was as if Sentell's blood had begun to flow again in veins dry since that long Vicksburg July.

Then, as he started down Texas in the wake of the Unions, spurring his mount, breathing deep of the night's cool air, Sentell saw Rye Crowninshield riding toward him, legs pumping the horse's sides, his bare gray head catching and reflecting light from the windows and lanterns he passed.

"Where is he?" Sentell called out as Rye drew even with him.

"He heard . . . ," Rye began, but his breath was gone. He sat atop his horse, shoulders heaving, his eyes on Sentell's and full of fear.

"Where is he?" Sentell asked again, reaching out for Rye's reins.

"He heard de Yankees," Rye choked. "Lodge an' de others talkin', fixin' to go to yo' ole place. De townsmen goin' fo my boy."

"And Amos . . . he went after Lodge?"

"He come upstairs an' got his gun. An' he rode out. So I start ridin' an' I don' know whether to go fo' you or go after him. So . . . "

"Come on," Sentell said. "If he gets ahead of the Unions, he'll be caught between them. We'll go the back way instead of following the road. We can get there as quickly as he can."

Behind them as they rode, clouds were building again. Summer lightning pulsed within the clouds and a cool wind rose, blowing on their backs.

"A ride in the evening," Cleburne called out pleasantly as Rye and Sentell passed his store. "Good for the constitution. If you care anything about the constitution."

"Why are you here?" Sentell asked him, reining in his horse.

"I own the place."

"Why aren't you riding with your friends?"

"I was with 'em earlier," he said, the end of his cigar glowing out of the darkness like a luminous eye. "But they said the supply corps ought not expose itself. They might need me worse later on, Bouvier said. Anyhow, the way they ride ain't healthy."

"It's worse than that," Sentell said. "Rye says Lodge and his men are on their way out to my old place. Do you want to ride out and . . . "

"Naw," Cleburne said lazily. "I reckon one ride is enough in a night."

"Listen," Sentell said, already moving. "You . . . "

"We been over that ground," Cleburne called. "Anyhow I been over it. You can't stop anything once it gets goin'. You can't even slow it down. You got to . . . ride with it . . . "

But they were already riding northwest out of town and Cleburne's voice, carried by the southerly wind, eddied and dissolved behind them.

Rye caught Sentell's arm as they neared the wooded rise of land that overlooked the old place – Phillipe's place. "We best walk now," he said. "Too many of 'em gunnin' aroun'. Dey mustn't catch us. We got to get Amos befo' dey gets set."

They tied the horses to a scrub pine, and moved through the darkness, weeds and brush and blackberry vine catching at their legs. Sentell almost stumbled as the ground began to slant upward.

Rye stopped close behind him. "Dey's somebody up ahead."

Sentell squinted into the darkness. The moon was high, and the clouds still lay behind them. But in the woods they could see nothing. Then Sentell heard metal against metal.

"Somebody's cockin' a rifle," Rye whispered. "Hear dem two clickin's, one of top of de other?"

They moved farther to the left and kept going. At the top of the rise, the trees gave out and the house was directly below, possibly fifty or seventy-five yards down a gentle slope. As they reached the top and edged toward the cleared space, Sentell saw the first one. A Union trooper lying prone at the foot of an oak, his rifle propped across his cartridge box and aimed down toward the house. Sentell waved Rye to the ground.

"There's one of them. They must be scattered all around here."

Rye stood up. "Amos gone down . . . "

"No," Sentell whispered. "You can't go down there. Not until we see him. Anything that moves will be a target. Anyhow, he couldn't have gotten far ahead. We took the back way. He would have stayed on the main road."

"Where you think . . . ?" Rye began.

But there was no need for Sentell to answer him. They had crept forward far enough to see the house and yard around it clearly in moonlight. The house was unlighted, but all around it men on horseback sat holding torches and guns. They were dressed in sheets or long colored robes, most of them. Only two did not wear masks. One of them was Morrison Stevens. He was closer to the house than the rest. And he was shouting.

"Come on out," he yelled, his voice shaking. "Come on. Ain't nobody gonna lay a hand on you except me. You can bring a pistol or a shotgun or whatever you want. I'll give you any edge, anything you want. Just come out."

One of the masked men, a strange pointed hat atop his head, took it up as Mo paused.

"You black sonsabitches, come out here like men or we'll burn you out like rats."

It was Hornsby's voice, and as he finished, he, Mo and the other unmasked rider came together to talk. Hornsby pointed at the house and waved his torch toward it. Morrison shook his head, appealing to the third rider, whose horse turned enough for Sentell to see his face. It was Bouvier.

"All the way down," Sentell said almost aloud. "All the way down."

"Look," Rye whispered hoarsely. "Dere."

Riding in from the main road, Amos was hunched forward in his saddle, digging his heels into the lathered horse. "Wait," he shouted. "Hold up."

Morrison saw him and rode out beyond the circle of hesitant men to meet him. "You couldn't keep out, could you? You couldn't stay home and read Jefferson or play chess with your old nigger, could you?"

"Now," Rye said, trying to rise.

"Wait," Sentell said. "Mo will see to him if it breaks right now. But maybe he can stop it. Maybe even now he can call them to heel."

"No," Rye said with certainty. "We can't put no trust in Mo. We got to go now or it ain't . . . "

"All right," Sentell told him. "Crawl. Crawl until we're near enough to do some good. You get hold of Amos. Pull him off that horse if you have to. If any of them try to stop you, I'll cut them down. Then the two of you head back for the horses. If you get past the Unions, you'll . . . "

"An' you?"

"I can lose myself out here. None of them will find me. Don't worry. We . . . "

But then, behind them, a Union soldier fired. The shot took Hornsby off his horse as if he had been a stringed doll suddenly jerked by the puppet-master. The rest of the hooded riders wheeled, and a voice behind Sentell called out:

"Who fired? Which of you fired? All right then, open fire."

The first reports shattered the night. Long fingers of orange laced inward toward the riders from every side. There was, almost simultaneous with the firing, a shattering of broken glass. Then they saw stabs of bright light coming from the house, from the windows. The combined firing dropped more of the riders from their saddles.

For one moment while the musketry broke around them, Amos and Morrison were face to face, only yards between them. The torchlight, lurid counterpoint to the moon, made them stand out like chiseled figures in an ancient frieze worn smooth and shadowed by whole ages. By then Sentell was up and running, his pistol forgotten and only Amos on his mind. He could hear Rye's breathing heavy and irregular behind him. But as Sentell ran, he could see Mo's face, twisted into a paradigm of hatred, frozen in that static and loveless expression so taunt and attenuated that, from a distance, it look almost like a tortured smile – or a grimace of agony.

"You brought 'em," Mo screamed above the confusion. "You sold your own blood."

But Amos had turned half away from Mo. He was staring up into the darkness, toward Lodge's troopers. "Wait," he called out. "Don't shoot anymore. Wait . . . they . . . "

By then Sentell was within a dozen yards of him. But even as Sentell tried to extend his stride, somehow cover that last insignificant stretch of earth more quickly, it was as if time had stopped or as if Sentell were trapped alone in a segment of it like a fly in amber. Amos' hand was lifted toward the rise where the Federals were. He did not see Sentell.

"Goddamn your soul," Mo shouted.

Then, even as he reached them, Sentell saw Mo's pistol level on his father. The report was buried in a second volley of Union rifles and the return fire of the riders, but Mo's hand jerked backward toward him, and a spout of flame reached out from it to touch his father's back.

"Don't," Amos cried one more, and fell from his saddle almost into Sentell's arms.

"Goddamn your soul," Mo screamed, firing again into the darkness, staring down at his father. "Your own people, your blood . . . "

But now the shooting was general. From the woods, the Federals had moved down toward the house, kneeling and firing, running closer to fire again. The riders returned the fire, some of them spurring directly into the Unions, bowling them over, using pistols and carbines like clubs. One of the riders threw his torch through a window of the house from which shots had come and another emptied his pistol into the same window. Sentell could hear Bouvier:

"Rally here. We can still take them. We're mounted against infantry. Gather and counterattack."

Rye was beside them then. He helped Sentell life Amos and together they moved, bent over and trying to skirt the battle, back up into the darkness of the woods. Amos was shot through his lower back. Sentell could feel the blood, warm and tacky, on his hands.

"He done it," Rye was crying. "I knew it. Like Phillipe, he do anything."

"Shut up," Sentell said. "Don't say anything."

Amos raised his head. He tried to put his arm around Sentell's neck. "Who . . . ?" he began.

Sentell glanced at Rye. "One of the Federals," he told Amos. "One of Lodge's men. He must have sneaked around the house."

"I thought . . . "

"No. He was too busy being loud and wrong. Anyhow, you're his father."

"Yes, I'm his . . . Phillipe? Where . . . "

"Still inside. I think he's all right. No one came out."

They had reached the top of the rise, and Rye trampled the brush and weeds down. They laid Amos on Sentell's coat. There was nothing to be done about the wound. Amos reached for Rye's hand. He was quiet for a moment, holding Rye's hand and staring upward into the darkness as if he were already a great distance from them.

"You knew about this?" he said to Sentell finally.

"Yes," Sentell told him. "I was coming to you. I was going to tell you and we were going to come out here together."

"We are together," Amos said softly. "You had to tell me."

"Yes."

"You can't protect anyone. We have to protect ourselves. You had to tell me because . . . "

Sentell began to cry then, but the moon was behind him and its cold indifferent disk floated above, obscuring his face from Amos.

"It's like the last time," Amos said, his voice reedy, soft as the sound of a flute far off playing an alien air. "There isn't any pain to it. Just deadness. No feeling but cold.

"It was a Yankee," Amos said dreamily. "That's good. It was Yankees the last time but then we were supposed to be one people. I wouldn't want my own to do this."

Sentell tried to keep him from hearing, but Amos could see Sentell's shoulders heaving. Amos fumbled for his hand. "It's all right," he said. "We're together. That's what you wanted."

"Yes," Sentell choked. "I wanted that more than anything else."

But Amos had lost much blood by then. What was happening – the shouting the firing, the chaos below – made no difference. He gestured Rye closer.

"Do you remember the mornings?" he asked. "Dear God, those Virginia mornings in the fall when we had to wash out of a frozen bucket. And the whole place dark with birds flying south overhead. Do you remember the place we built for the girls?"

"Don' talk," Ray said. "We remembers all of it de same."

"That place. Monticello. The long path up to . . . and the boys laughing. And the boys laughing."

"We'll move you in a few minutes or so," Sentell told him. "We have horses."

"No," Amos said. "Don't move me. This is fine. Except it's dark. And cold, Lord God, cold. I can't see your face. I can't see your faces."

Above, there was sudden thunder, and Sentell looked up to see the moon sliding behind those clouds that had been gathering as he and Rye rode out.

"I wish it was morning," Amos said. Then he was dead. The difference was instantaneous and there was no mistaking it. Sentell was holding him in his arms. Then he was holding what was left.

"That's all of it," he told Rye, his voice muffled and barely controlled.

"Lemme have him," Rye said. "Leave him to me now."

Sentell stood up and breathed deeply, the night air cold and alien in his lungs. Down at the house, the riders, those still in their saddles, had bunched up and smashed into the line of Federals barring them from the flat fields northwest of the house. More of Lodge's men rushed over to form a second line, but when the riders struck, the Union line collapsed like a paper lantern in sudden wind. The moon disappeared for good, and the scrambling confused Federals fired into darkness ineffectually. Inside the house, a glare of flames from the thrown torch slowly lessened and disappeared.

493

Against the dying light from the windows, Sentell saw someone moving up the rise toward them. But he did not crouch or even warn Rye. It seemed past time for that. And neither of them would be leaving Amos anyhow.

"Yankee, Rye," he said finally as the figure closed with them. Rye paid no attention.

But it was no Union. It was Bouvier. His scarred face, twisted still into the obscene parody of a smile, was covered with blood. Through the blood, two white rills cut down his cheeks. He was leading a limping horse.

"They shot you," Sentell said. He had no anger left even for Bouvier. There had been enough anger.

"Edward," he said across the gloom without surprise. "You, Edward. You know, I lied about . . . I'm sorry for that . . . I'm sorry . . ."

Sentell almost reached for his pistol. Not in anger, but with the same unutterable loathing one feels for an animal turned against nature. Risen from a slaughter pen of his own making, Bouvier was mumbling about a breach of his word.

"They shot you," Sentell said again, something close to judgment in his voice.

Bouvier shook his head and began to lead his mount again. He drew abreast of Sentell, still shaking his head. "It's not my blood," he said, looking past Sentell at Rye who still held Amos in his arms. "It's somebody else's."

Then Bouvier was in the woods, his boots crushing brush and limbs underneath, darkness closing around him like a shroud.

Rye had helped Sentell lift Amos and carry him down into the yard. The Federals had lit torches of their own, and Lodge was moving among the scattered bodies, walking back and forth, his hands clasped behind him. Lieutenant Raisor, pale and dirty, was getting an empty ammunition wagon filled with Union wounded. Raisor turned to Lodge.

"Some of those riders," Raisor said. "Some of them are still alive. Shouldn't we carry them . . . ?"

"Leave them," Lodge told him. "Until our wounded are back in town."

Raisor shrugged. He had nothing more to say to Lodge.

Sentell and Rye put Amos down in a clear place. Rye folded his arm over his chest and closed his eyes. Lodge saw them.

"Stevens," he said, scuffing the dust beside Amos' body. "So it came to this."

He looked at Sentell. "Somewhere," he squinted. "You were ..."

"At Vicksburg," Sentell said shortly. "In a barn after the surrender. I was asking help for a wounded friend."

"Yes," Lodge said. "No. Demanding it."

Sentell leaned closer to him. "This time we need nothing from you."

Lodge was still staring down at Amos. "One of my men ..."

"He was trying to stop it."

Lodge shook his head. "You can't stop this. Nothing can stop it. He should have known ..."

Sergeant Packard spoke to Lodge. "The troopers we left in reserve have picked up the trail of the rebs. They'll be heading west and our boys got fresh horses."

Lodge was still looking around the yard at the dark motionless clumps that broke the regularity of weedy lawn. "How many ...?" Lodge began.

"We lost eight men," Sergeant Packard said dully. "They lost four-teen killed. We should have done better. We had everything working for us. But we didn't move in quick enough. Then we didn't hold. It was like every other time. They got the sign on us. Some of the men backed up. Some of 'em broke when the firing got hot. Some of 'em never fired at all."

"Clean this up," Lodge said, paying no attention. His voice was un-certain and tired. "Clean it up and report to me at the house. I'll go back and wait for word from the troopers following them."

As the colonel turned to walk back into the woods where the Union horses were tied, it began to rain. At first it fell so softly that it was not rain at all, only a heavy mist standing in the air and drifting downward with immeasurable slowness into the half-dry dust of the yard.

Rye took off his coat and spread it over Amos' body. Sentell wiped tiny droplets from his face and started back up the rise toward where they had left the horses. Overhead, the lightning was muted and the thunder sounded like distant cannon. But the rainfall increased rapidly, and by the time Sentell moved into the shelter of the trees his face was covered with it, and water flowed down his cheeks like prodigious tears from a source that would never go dry.

X

7 JULY 1865 — Inside the house, the fire was out. The front room was still heavy with acrid smoke, and the faded hangings he had pulled down to smother the torch smoldered on the floor like fragments of wadding spewed from a fieldpiece.

But Phillipe had forgotten the flames. He was bending over Sergeant Samuels, picking him up. He tried to wipe a stream of blood from Samuels' mouth, but only succeeded in smearing it across his hand.

From outside, he heard a voice. It was a Northern accent.

"Crowninshield. Hey, Crowninshield, come on out. Did they get you? Anybody left in there?"

Phillipe walked slowly to the door and kicked it open. The yard was lit with pine knots and torches discarded by the fleeing raiders. It was light as a false dawn.

At the door, one of the colored troops met him, helped him lay Samuels down on the porch. Still dazed, Phillipe knelt beside him. Soldiers moved back and forth carrying bodies, placing them in two carefully separated rows: one for loyal men, the other for rebels.

"Dey got ole Sam," the colored soldier called out to others standing guard over a few wounded riders. "Dem sonsabitches kill ole Sam. Lookit him."

"Let that go," Sergeant Packard said. "Just tend to your duty. You can pay your respects later."

Phillipe looked at the captured raiders. Mo was not among them. Then he rose and walked down to an irregular rank of bodies stretched in the casual stasis of death.

"That 'un," one of the troopers was saying, "is old Norton's son. You go in his store for a sack of tobacco and he looked like he wanted to cut your throat. Reckon he tried."

"It cost him," another said. No one laughed.

They brought a towheaded young trooper into the light. His eyes, dull and unconcerned, were open and his hands still gripped into useless fists.

"He never was much in a fight," one of the trooper said. "Took him a week to get over coming into this town. Then he never did get over that whipping somebody gave him."

"If he'd stayed low and kept firing, he'd have come out all right. You can't stand up to cavalry. Not even irregulars."

The men set him down next to a colored soldier whose dun face was half shot away.

"They had scatterguns."

"Somebody in the house had a shotgun, too. Did you see this reb?"

The trooper nudged Ed Norton Junior's body over. His head was shattered, half of it scored and disintegrated. The other side was untouched. There was no pain, no anger left. His eyes were closed as if he had fallen asleep next to his rifle port in the works at Vicksburg.

"Buckshot," one of the troopers said. "Jesus, that buckshot. I'd rather they used a torpedo on me."

"I'd rather they give all this stuff up. Ain't this a hell of a place to die? Somebody's goddamned farmyard."

Phillipe walked from one end of the dead raiders to the others. Mo was not there. So it was not over, Phillipe thought. Not over. Maybe not even well started.

"Help me with this big bastard, will you?"

The Unions dragged Hornsby over to the line by his boots. "I saw him drop first. He was out there threshing around all the time we was closing in."

"Quiet him down?"

"Take a look. You won't find nobody quieter."

Across the yard, out of the torch's narrow spread, Phillipe saw Sentell leaning against a tree trunk. Nearby, his father knelt beside something covered by a coat. Sentell started walking back into the darkness, up toward the high ground that lay above the house.

For a moment Phillipe paused. He almost turned back to the porch where Samuels lay. But that was no good. There was something he had to say to his father.

"See?" he cried across the yard as he walked toward where his father knelt. "See? See what your white people tried to do to me?"

Rye did not lift his head. He held Amos' single hand tightly between his two dark one and his eyes were closed.

"See?" Phillipe shouted again in his excitement as he reached his father's side. "Do you see now?"

Rye looked upward toward Phillipe. His face looked as if it were hacked from ebony. There was no sign of paternity or even recognition in it. "Shut yo' mouf," he said slowly without raising his voice. "Dis is my white people here." He held Amos' hand to his chest. "Dis is my white people here."

497

The Union soldier began bundling the dead into canvas tent halves. Now that Lodge was gone, they paid no further attention to the strict segregation of Union from rebel. They lifted Hornsby's body onto a two-mule wagon. Others were hefting dead Unions over their shoulders and carrying them slowly through the rain to stack them next to Hornsby.

The rest of the Federals poked about in corners of the yard searching for dead or wounded who might have been overlooked, and a few had sprawled on the porch, appearing, in their fatigue, little different from the bodies lying in the rain.

Phillipe sat on the edge of the porch and looked out through the softly falling rain where his father had risen finally from beside Amos' body. Sentell was talking to Sergeant Packard while Rye stood near them, his head down, white crimped hair glistening in the fitful wisps of torchlight spread by rising wind.

He thought of the bridge at Antietam Creek, and the immeasurable trip across it from South to the North. He wondered for a moment if he could reach his father the same way: on his hands and knees. But a man has pride. Especially a man who has worn a bright blue uniform and fought to a great victory. His father would be heading back to Shreveport with Sentell and Amos Stevens. It was too long a way to crawl. And free men, Phillipe thought desperately, are never really lonely anyhow.

Just after sundown he came home drunk. He had gone behind the house with a small parcel and then come back to the porch with two quarts of whiskey. He stayed on the sagging porch while she cooked supper. Once in a while she would hear him curse aloud, hear a bottle strike the porch floor or the side of the tilted chair.

"Sonsabitches," Murray bellowed, squinting out into the shadows gathered around the cabin. "Stinkin' sonsabitches."

Finally he came into the house. "You got it ready? You done took half the night."

She put food in front of him and moved away from the table. He began to eat, setting the half-empty bottle of whiskey next to his plate.

"Ain't you gonna eat?"

"I don't want anything. I'm not hungry."

"You'll get hungry. You're gonna be glad to eat your daddy's provisions."

Vera paid him no mind. She was thinking of Mo riding in the night.

What if he comes back smiling and shows me his red hands and says, 'That nigger Phillipe paid it out, now I'm healed and now we can live. Now we can turn off the hate and make believe the scars come from a bad fall and maybe pick flowers alongside the Yankees. And all because finally I slaughtered one more man, a special nigger who had to go under before the war was over for me. Now let's have babies and invite some neighbors over and set out a side of pork.'

She wiped her hands on a piece of sacking. The room smelled of grease. There was the stench of stale oil and whiskey somehow dissolved into the planks of the floor and walls. She dropped the rag and walked to the door. There the evening breeze was fresh and untainted.

" . . . 'cause all the grub you're gonna get is what you get from me."

Vera breathed deep and looked upward to the moon. Its face was naked and bright, but a mass of dark thunderheads was gathering and beginning to drift toward the river.

" . . . 'cause that sour-mouthed young whelp of Amos Stevens ain't gonna be comin' back to hand you no more moonshine about love and get in your drawers for . . . "

Vera turned from the door. Her father had finished his food and pushed the plate away. Now he was done with the first quart of whiskey and fumbled under the table for the other.

"What are you talkin' about?" Vera asked him. "Come out from under there and tell me what you're talkin' about."

Murray sat up, already wringing the cork out of his new bottle. "It ain't nothin' to it," he smirked. "I just sold your smart-ass boy to the Yankees. I went up to that Yankee colonel and I said, 'How much for a broken-down reb?' And he says, 'Two quarts of whiskey and a twenty-dollar bill.' So I says, 'Tonight they're gonna get 'em a pair of niggers out on the river.'"

Vera sat down in a chair next to the door. She could hear him and the words were words she knew. But she could not believe what he was saying.

"An' so the colonel's gonna be out there when tight-ass and long-jaw shows up with his friends, and about the time he butchers that dangerous nigger, ole Lodge is gonna spread his eyes apart with about an inch of lead."

Vera spoke in a monotone. "You never did it. Because even if Lodge was to bushwhack 'em, some of 'em get out and they'd take a week killin' you. Not for a thousand dollars. You're mean enough, but you ain't nervy enough. You never did it."

Murray's eyes were squeezed almost shut, as if the weak lamplight were from a beacon or a torch. He was drinking the whiskey in long pulls as if he were afraid someone might take it from him, as if there were no time to finish it.

"That's all you know, girl. If you think I wasn't up to it, you get on into town in the mornin'. They like as not need somebody to identify what'll be left of him."

She said nothing. He talked on, ranted and cursed, stopping only long enough to pull on his bottle of Union army whiskey, to squint at her for some sign of anger, for a possible skillet or firedog coming at him across the cramped room. But she said nothing at all, and after a little more of it, he kept to the ranting and the whiskey and paid her no more mind.

"Sonsabitches treated their niggers better than me whilst the war was on, and then come home and went at it again. They wasn't one who'd of fed me as quick as feed one of them niggers. But it evens up. It always comes out on a balance. You just grin and let 'em kick your ass and you bear it and kiss whatever it is you got to kiss. Then the day comes. It comes and the tall shudders and falls, and the mighty feels dirt in their faces. Then you get to use your boot. You kick and kick till there ain't . . . "

But Vera had risen and packed her two nurse's frocks and a handful of underclothes into a feed sack. She stood at the door of the cabin watching her father as his talk thickened and slowed to a monotonous inarticulate gabble, and the raised whiskey bottle began marking commas as well as full stops. Then she turned and stepped into the night.

She was almost out of the grassless yard before it occurred to her: something that had been buried in the back of her mind for the better part of fifteen years. Something to do with her mother and herself. The kind of thing that slips in and out of the mind without catching in the loose and unrefined webbing of ordinary unheightened consciousness. Something, a kind of untidy end so long left unresolved as to have become a piece with the rest of the ordinary.

So she dropped the feed sack, walked into the house again past her mumbling drunken father to the back of the room and found what she needed.

Tranced still as she had been from the moment of his furious admission, and feeling nothing even now that could bear the name of hatred or despair, she raised the shotgun in one slow dreamy motion and pulled both triggers as it leveled with her father's hunched vindictive shoulders.

Even the unbelievable volume of its sound, the sharp recoil of the gun, and the last fractional vision of his face contorted and unsatisfied, his eyes squinting furiously past the buttery soft lamplight, did not stir her or break the rhythm of her movement. In the clamorous and instant darkness that flowed out of the blast, she set the shotgun down where she had found it and walked without pause past the first tiny flickering of ignited oil and raw whiskey running across the ruined table down onto the floor, and stepped into the yard again.

By the time she reached the road, the spewing flare of the cabin stood behind her like a dissolving sun, a star winking past nova into ash, and a curtain of thin uncertain rain had begun to fall.

I never came down this path at night before without running up against a tree or tripping in the grass of the path. Now I can see all the way to the road. Then, almost as incidentally as the shotgun and its possibilities had occurred to her, she thought: It's all right. It's still all right, only I should have done it ten years ago, or maybe even earlier, as soon as I could lift it and point it when I saw that she couldn't do it.

But the sound of the horse so near broke in on her, and she felt the wind stir as it passed in the road's darkness and then reared, pawing the air as its rider saw her.

"Sure," Mo said from above, "it would be you. Where's your poppa? Is he all right? He didn't show up. He didn't ride with us."

Vera stared up into the bulk of his shadow, darker than the sky beyond, make redly visible by the dying fire from behind her.

"No," she said. "He didn't' show up. But it's all right."

"All right?" Mo asked. "You mean he wasn't hurt? He wasn't caught? Then how come he didn't . . . "

"Because he was sellin' youall to the Unions. He told me he did it. Sold youall like you were sacks of feed or fresh pork."

"Jesus," Mo started down out of his saddle. "Him and my father. That snivelin' pinch-eyed sonofabitch was in it too. Instead of walkin' into his own library, instead of standin' there and spillin' it all to Lodge like a man – a stinkin' peopleless gutless wreck of man, but some kind of man anyhow – instead he must have put up the sure-enough long-confirmed bastard you been callin' a father to do it. Where is he now? I got to . . ."

"It's all . . . ," But she did not finish, silently pointing back at the shack, back at the last dark glow and the barely audible crackling of the burned-out ruin that looked now exactly like one of the deserted shambles Sherman had left in his path to immortality and the thanks of a grateful nation. And even pointing, she thought of Amos and how he must feel if he knew what Mo believed – wondering suddenly over that, merged with that, what had passed between them and how bad it had been. But Mo, his eyes large and bright, fixed on the decaying scarlet of the burned-out cabin, cut through her thoughts.

"You mean he's in there? You mean he's still in there?"

Vera looked up at him as if he had insulted her. "I told you it's all right. It was past due like a little bill you owe somewhere but always forget to pay up. Sooner or later you get around to it."

"All right," Mo stopped her again. "All right. You took care of your old bill, and I paid off a score that's been owin'. Come on up behind me. They can't be more than a mile or two back. They saw which way I was ridin' out."

She felt her arms raise through the rain toward him even as her mind fixed on what he had said. Her arms stopped in transit, and she moved back from his offered hand.

"You . . ."

"Come on," he said. "It's all right."

"You did something to your father . . . "

"He was there," Mo grated. "He was there at the front of half that garrison. He come ridin' in behind us, and then it was Lodge and his niggers, and they were shootin' from back there and from in the house, and he was there right in front of me with his hand out toward me with all the past in it and his face – his eyes askin' me to go back with him. I don't know, all I know is the Unions were behind him and I shot. I shot and he fell. I don't know if I was really aimin' for him, but he was there with Lodge and those nigger soldiers, and I cut loose, and I feel like it's all right now. Come on, get up behind me, honey. We got to ride."

All this breathless, like a small boy describing his first rabbit hunt, his first trip beyond the parish. While Vera moved step by step back from him, her own breath short and a sharp throb in her head like hoof beats on an oaken bridge, until she had moved off the road altogether and back a few yards toward the ashes of the cabin. And the drumming, the hoof beats in her head objectified themselves into something even Mo could hear.

"Honey," he called to her. "Vera, come on. They're on the road. Look..."

Far back toward town, but coming around the last curve, she could see miniature torches and hear above the hoof beats the sound of high harsh voices urging horses on.

"He must have come to tell you...," she began, her voice small and far away... so soft that she herself could hardly make it out because to speak any louder would risk not being able to speak at all. "He wanted to tell you they..."

"Never mind," Mo called, his hands groping where she had been, his shadow fully dark now that light from the burned cabin had gone out. "You got to come. I got to have you. I got to ride."

"No," she heard herself say, still in that bodiless voice that seemed too soft and distant to carry conviction. "No. All he wanted was..."

But now the miniature torches were growing larger and the pounding in her head was drowned by a fusillade of horses' hoofs. He reached into the rainy darkness for her one last time, like a blind man clawing for safety at the sound of an approaching tidal wave.

"No," she whispered, as his horse reared and lunged on down the road west, its rider still turning backward in his saddle – not toward the torches and the yammering onset of the troopers, but toward the shadowed and tenantless place beside the road from which she had retreated at his call, was still retreating even as the Federals clattered by, full of blood lust and vengeance, with all the night and half a continent to scour.

By that time, Cleburne was in the rear of his store with only an oil lamp to keep out the night.

He did not know what was happening at Sentell's old place; he was not thinking about it.

Instead he was seated in a huge dilapidated library chair purchased from some family that had sold it to him on their way to Texas to escape Union invaders during the war. In front of him, on a fine mahogany table inlaid with walnut carving, there was an unbelievably moldy leather bag so long empty that its new fullness had cracked and split the dry unpliable surface into a hundred tiny new crevices.

He was thinking of the tortuous round of the river at Vicksburg. He was thinking of the stiff continuous wind bred somewhere on the

Mississippi above Cairo before it plunged southward, and of how that wind broke and scattered among the trees that stood like archaic sentinels on the brush-strewn cliffs over the water. He was thinking of the surprising patches of warmth in pine straw, back from the edge of the bluffs.

On the table near the leather pouch there was something else: a worn carpetbag with a broken clasp, and a fragment of raveled silk comforter hanging out the corner.

Behind Cleburne a window was ajar, and a sweep of night breeze touched his back, shook the weak yellow light of the lamp. Above piles of books and rugs, furniture and old clothes, the lamp's faltering sent outsize shadows dipping and rising on the unpainted plans of the wall opposite.

"It could rain tonight," he whispered to the hurrying shadows.

They had started the first wagon back toward town almost as soon as the firing stopped. In it were six troopers and colored soldiers. One of the troopers had a ball lodged in his lower abdomen and each time the wagon lurched he screamed with mechanical regularity, as if the wagon's motion cued the sound and there was no necessary connection between it and pain. The rest were less seriously injured. One young Negro rode beside Raisor, holding a maimed hand wrapped in a trooper's neckerchief close to his chest, a pine-knot torch in his good hand.

"Dey can doctor dis hand," the boy told Raisor. "Day can piece it back together, Lootenant," he said with confidence.

"Sure," Raisor answered, flicking the reins and trying to screen out the continuous moans and occasional shrieks from the bed of the wagon.

The colored boy loosened the rag with his teeth and held his hand out for Raisor's inspection.

"See," he said. "It ain't so bad."

Raisor glanced at it and looked quickly away. A minie-ball, fifty or sixty caliber, had struck at the base of the fingers. The boy's middle and ring finger were joined to the rest by thin strands of bloody flesh. Bone and drying sinew caught torchlight dully. Even his thumb seemed warped, distorted, as if the bullet had thrown it out of opposition with the others. Raisor knew the hand would be amputated.

Even when they reached the main road, there seemed to be ruts every few feet.

"Jesus Christ," one of the troopers cried out, "can't you steer around them holes, Lieutenant?"

"I'm trying," Raisor said patiently as the wagon dipped steeply and righted itself.

It was still raining in short gusty bursts as heavy clouds passed over the moon's face.

One of the Negroes, shot through both thighs, tried to hold his legs on the side rails of the wagon to avoid the jolts. But between the slickness of the wood and the wagon's irregular lurching progress, he only managed to let them slide off and strike the wagon bed time after time. Each time he would scream, his voice phased with that of the gut-shot trooper.

"Keep yo' goddamn legs down," one of the other Negroes told him. "Ain't yo' got no goddamn sense? You makin' 'em bleed worse."

"Listen," Raisor called back over his shoulder. "I'm going to slow up. I can't keep out of the ruts. The whole road is ruts. I'm going to go slower."

"Slower hell," another trooper said. "My goddamned shoulder is pouring blood like a fountain. We got to get into town."

"Slow up," one of the Negroes said. "Dis man wif de hole in his belly can't take no more jouncin'. You slow up like you say, sir."

"Fuck that sonofabitch," the man with the wounded shoulder barked. "I don't mean to bleed to death out here while we take it slow."

"Shut your mouth," Raisor said flatly, a sound of authority in his voice.

"Lootenant," the young Negro beside him said, "you don't reckon goin' slow will do me no damage, do you? It won't make no difference about my hand, will it?"

"No," Raisor told him honestly, "it won't make a bit of difference." They were less than a mile from the edge of town when they reached the crossroads. The branch of road they were on ran roughly northwest-southeast and carried traffic that followed the Red River. Where the two roads intersected, the ground had been broken up, soaked, dried into dust and clods, harrowed by an endless succession of passing wagons and horses, and soaked again. In the angle where the two roads crossed, the mud was almost permanent and several feet deep.

"I don' know," the colored boy beside Raisor said. "It look like you could drown a hog in it."

"We can't go around," Raisor told him. "We've got to try it."

"Hol' on back dere," the colored soldier called brightly to those in the wagon bed. "Youall better hol' tight."

Raisor flicked the reins and the two mules raised their heads, speeding up their gait. The wagon plunged forward into heavy mud.

"Get up!" Raisor shouted. "Get up!"

The mules tried. Even when the wagon stalled in the center of the slough, even when Raisor and the rest could feel the wagon beginning to sink.

"Jesus," the trooper with the shoulder wound moaned. "You never missed a bump and now you've gonna drown us in mud."

"Keep 'em goin', Lootenant," one of the Negroes shouted. "You keep 'em movin'."

"Get up, come on," Raisor cried. "Come on."

But it was no use. The mules heaved in their harness, jerking the wagon forward. Then as they paused to pull again, the wagon returned to the new ruts its weight had carved. Each time, the gut-shot trooper screamed.

"Ain't gonna go," the young colored soldier said. "Mebbe if we was to get down and try to . . . "

"All right," Raisor said, dropping the reins and stepping gingerly off the wagon into the mud. "Those of you who can push, come on. The quicker you move, the quicker we'll get to town."

Two of the men climbed down from the back. The young Negro with the injured hand moved beside Raisor.

"We got to get on," he said. "We don't want dis hand to go bad."

As Raisor pushed against the wagon, the mules heaved forward. His hands slipped on the smooth wet wood and he fell, full-length, into the churned dark gruel beneath.

"Lootenant, lemme help you."

"It's all right," Raisor said, wiping his hands on the back of his breeches, trying to scrape the mud from his eyes. "I'm all right."

But he was not all right. Wave after wave of nausea swept over him. The slaughter, the rain, the long road riddled with pits and holes – and the screams of a man with an ounce of flattened lead riding in his belly.

"Sir," one of the Negroes said softly. "De trooper . . . "

"What?"

"De fella wif the minie in him. He dead."

"All right," Raisor said wearily, leaning into the wagon's bulk, seeking a grip, a place to hold so that he could move it from the mire of crossroad mud.

Colonel Jonathan Lodge stretched his booted feet under the desk and pushed away a handful of papers on top of it. There was barely enough for as much night as might be left. It was good brandy, although it might have been very bad indeed and still served.

For some reason, sitting in darkness behind the desk of a man not two hours dead, he thought of comedy. He wondered how brother Paul's death would play on the stage. He thought of laughter, not as from an audience or from a crowd of witnesses, but stark disembodied laughter spilling like blood over all of it: the riot, the war, and this travesty of peace.

He set his glass in the cleared space on the desk and tried to pull his legs under him. He felt a sharp pain behind his knees, in his calves. The muscles of his neck and shoulders seemed tight, almost atrophied. From the riding, from the tension, from the night wind. And the brandy was doing no good.

There had been a novel, some English novel he had read when he was a boy. Not the kind of novel his father would have approved – not even a very good novel. But he remembered one part of it. Something about a statue that bled. A piece of cold stone which drained blood like a living body. An absurdity. A monument does not cry or suffer or turn its head backward toward what is past. It stares out of blind marble eyes into a future without end or purpose or definition. A future passing forever like dark water, wearing imperceptibly at the adamantine roots of the universe.

He poured his glass full once more, and touched the sculptured gold insignia on his collar. He was thinking of laughter again: sharp tarnished laughter with no humor, no note of sympathy in it; he could hear it as if it were bubbling up from the bottle, flowing out of the walls. Then he realized that it was not abstract at all, that it was the sound of his own voice drenched with pain and certain knowledge, clanging and echoing in the corners of the darkened library.

Sentell and the sergeant arranged the canvas. When they had finished, the presence of Amos Stevens' body was blurred into a mound of indeterminate shape almost the color of the damp earth beneath. Rye still stood beside Amos, his head bowed, hands clasped together in a posture between prayerfulness and desperation.

The sergeant's men had gathered up Hornsby and Ed Norton Junior. Their bodies lay uncovered, sprawled like outsize broken toys in the bed of Phillipe's wagon. Next to them, the bodies of Samuels and the towheaded Union trooper lay swathed in tent-halves, their identical army shoes projecting outward over the edge of the wagon.

Hornsby lay face up, his eyes still open, red-rimmed with static inconsolable anger and staring into the darkness as if it were a comrade who had betrayed him. Ed Norton Junior, his buckskin shirt soaked and darkened with rain and blood, was turned on his side so that the shotgun damage to his head was not visible. His arm was casually draped over the canvas-wrapped body of Sergeant Samuels.

Sergeant Packard patted the canvas around Amos' body aimlessly. "That'll be all right," he said. "It'll do till you can get him home."

"Yes," Sentell was saying, his voice low and barely under control. "We can take him home this way."

"Listen," the sergeant said a little too loudly. "We could carry him on the wagon. We could . . . "

"No," Rye rasped out. It was the first he had said since Phillipe had gone back into the house.

"No," Sentell said at the same time. "No. We'll lash him to his horse. I'd rather take him home that way."

"It stank," the sergeant said, his voice still loud, not intimate or sensibly lowered below the hearing of his enlisted men. "There wasn't any sense in it. We could of taken the whole bunch with a volley over their heads. It didn't need to be this way."

"I don't know," Sentell said wearily. He didn't want to talk about it. But there was no sense in cutting the sergeant short. "They knew you were all around them. No one tried to surrender."

"You got to give men a chance," the sergeant went on doggedly. "You got to give them a second or two to see it's no good so they know they ain't being bluffed. So they can give it up still proud. You can't expect good men to throw up their hands like a pack of slaves. They won't do it. They never do it."

"You're right," Sentell said, reaching for the hanging reins of Amos Stevens' horse. "They never do. They never will."

Rye helped with the tying, and before the moon had set, they had Amos bent over his saddle and secured by ropes. Not the way Sentell had seen it done – had done it himself – with hands and feet bound together under the horse's belly. But with great care, and with no rope touching anything but canvas. It was not as secure as the other way, but if the trip were made slowly it would be all right. The rain was finished now and it was not a long ride.

"My house," Sentell said, wiping his forehead on his sleeve. "Not your place."

"Sho'," Rye nodded numbly. "He want yo' place now. Not where de Yankees are."

"Where will you stay?" Sentell asked. "Will you stay with us until Amos is . . . "

"I thank you," Rye said dully, in an almost unrecognizable monotone. "I reckon I could come to yo' place till I can think again. I can't seem to . . . "

"Your boy . . . ," Sentell began. "He'll want . . . "

Rye turned to him, his hand still on the last rope holding Amos' body in place on the motionless horse. "I ain't got no boy," he said flatly, finally. "We didn't neither of us have no son."

They rode carefully along the grassy shoulder of the road to avoid jostling their burden. Amos' horse followed Sentell docilely even in the semidarkness, as if he were choosing his own careful way.

As they reached the edge of town where small houses, unpainted shed and broken fences started, the sky began to lighten. It was not quite dawn when they turned off Market onto Texas Street, but the gray metallic color of early morning made the street's unrelieved shabbiness stand out in ugly contrast to the richness of the trees that stood above rooftops on either side. Even the dust beneath them had the soiled moldy shade not of earth but of a sheet or pillowslip long abandoned to the weather. Through the unwashed windows of Ramsey's saloon, a small oil lantern burned dully above the bar like a votive lamp in memory of a dead god. Ripinski's store was shuttered, the front door padlocked from outside, and the lock and hasp covered with a dark wreath ribboned in black.

As they rode past Cleburne's, Sentell saw that the familiar shadowy gap at the top of the steps was covered by a door. He had never seen the door closed before. By five o'clock Cleburne was always up and ready for business. Perhaps, Sentell thought, there won't be any more business.

Then, as they passed City Hall, the sun, so long impending, rose behind them from across the river. It caught the shards and tatters of red, white and blue bunting that still flapped aimlessly in the morning breeze. It gilded the copper roofing, shattered the regular reflectionless gray of City Hall's second story windows. It set fire to a bronze ball atop the empty flagpole. The sun was in the treetops, turning then suddenly from deep olive to brilliant green. It shivered in garish ripples along the eaves of houses and building, but it did not reach the dark and shadowed street below.

Down there a riderless horse bearing a clumsy burden had paused to drink from a trough filled by the evening's rain. A graying white man and stooped Negro bestrode their own tired mounts, patiently waiting for it to get its fill so they could go on through the half-light to a place where all of them could rest.

Houston, 1960
Baton Rouge, 1963

ABOUT THE AUTHOR

John William Corrington was born in 1932 and raised in Shreveport, Louisiana where he attended Jesuit High School (from which he was expelled in 1950 for having "the wrong attitude"). He received a B.A. from Centenary College (1956), an M.A. from Rice University (1959), and a D.Phil. from the University of Sussex (1965). He served on the English faculty at Louisiana State University and, at the time The Upper Hand was first published (1967), was Chairman of the English Department at Loyola University in New Orleans.

For the next two decades, Corrington lived in New Orleans with his wife Joyce and four children: Shelley Elaine, John Wesley, Robert Edward Lee, and Thomas Jonathan Jackson. During that time he left academia and took a J.D. at Tulane University School of Law. In 1978 he left the practice of law, formed a writing team with his wife, and scripted six feature movies and numerous television episodes. This writing career led the Corringtons to move to the West Coast in 1986. In 1988, John William Corrington suffered a heart attack at his home in Malibu and died at the age of 56.

This book is my deeply felt tribute to the fathers. I can remember my grandfather talking about General Forrest as if he were an honored and beloved neighbor who had not lately come by to visit. So when it came time to try a novel, I decided to write about the time the Federals occupied my country and tore it up so badly that, when things more or less settled down, no one in my family managed to get to college between 1866 and 1951.
                                          —John William Corrington

Made in the USA
Middletown, DE
27 August 2022

72407737R10285